MICHAEL CRICHTON

A NEW COLLECTION OF
THREE COMPLETE NOVELS

Feb 2002

MICHAEL CRICHTON

A NEW COLLECTION OF THREE COMPLETE NOVELS

CONGO

SPHERE

EATERS OF THE DEAD

WINGS BOOKS
New York • Avenel, New Jersey

This 1994 edition is published by Wings Books,
distributed by Outlet Book Company, Inc., a Random House Company,
40 Engelhard Avenue, Avenel, New Jersey 07001,
by arrangement with Alfred A. Knopf, Inc.

Random House
New York • Toronto • London • Sydney • Auckland

Printed and bound in the United States of America

Library of Congress Cataloging-in-Publication Data
Crichton, Michael, 1942–
[Novels. Selections]
A new collection / Michael Crichton
p. cm.
Contents: Sphere — Congo — Eaters of the dead.
ISBN 0-517-10135-1
I. Title.
PS3553.R48A6 1994
813′.54—dc20   93-40887
                              CIP

8 7 6 5 4 3 2

CONTENTS

CONGO

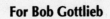

For Bob Gottlieb

*The more experience and insight I obtain into human na-
ture, the more convinced do I become that the greater portion of a man is purely animal.*
                    —HENRY MORTON STANLEY, 1887

*The large male [gorilla] held my attention. . . . He gave an
impression of dignity and restrained power, of absolute
certainty in his majestic appearance. I felt a desire to communicate with him. . . . Never before had I had this feeling
on meeting an animal. As we watched each other across
the valley, I wondered if he recognized the kinship that
bound us.*
                    —GEORGE B. SCHALLER, 1964

Contents

Introduction

Only prejudice, and a trick of the Mercator projection, prevents us from recognizing the enormity of the African continent. Covering nearly twelve million square miles, Africa is almost as large as North America and Europe combined. It is nearly twice the size of South America. As we mistake its dimensions, we also mistake its essential nature: the Dark Continent is mostly hot desert and open grassy plains.

In fact, Africa is called the Dark Continent for one reason only: the vast equatorial rain forests of its central region. This is the drainage basin of the Congo River, and one-tenth of the continent is given over to it—a million and a half square miles of silent, damp, dark forest, a single uniform geographical feature nearly half the size of the continental United States. This primeval forest has stood, unchanged and unchallenged, for more than sixty million years.

Even today, only half a million people inhabit the Congo Basin, and they are mostly clustered in villages along the banks of the slow muddy rivers that flow through the jungle. The great expanse of the forest remains inviolate, and to this day thousands of square miles are still unexplored.

This is true particularly of the northeastern corner of the Congo Basin, where the rain forest meets the Virunga volcanoes, at the edge of the Great Rift Valley. Lacking established trade routes or compelling features of interest, Virunga was never seen by Western eyes until less than a hundred years ago.

The race to make "the most important discovery of the 1980s" in the Congo took place during six weeks of 1979. This book recounts the thirteen days of the last American expedition to the Congo, in June, 1979—barely a hundred years after Henry Morton Stanley first explored the Congo in 1874–77. A comparison of the two expeditions reveals much about the changing—and unchanging—nature of African exploration in the intervening century.

Stanley is usually remembered as the newsman who found Livingstone in 1871, but his real importance lay in later exploits. Moorehead calls him "a new kind of man in Africa . . . a businessman-explorer. . . . Stanley was not in Africa to reform the people nor to build an empire, and he was not impelled by any real interest in such matters as anthropology, botany or geology. To put it bluntly, he was out to make a name for himself."

When Stanley set out again from Zanzibar in 1874, he was again handsomely financed by newspapers. And when he emerged from the jungle at the

Atlantic Ocean 999 days later, having suffered incredible hardships and the loss of more than two-thirds of his original party, both he and his newspapers had one of the great stories of the century: Stanley had traveled the entire length of the Congo River.

But two years later, Stanley was back in Africa under very different circumstances. He traveled under an assumed name; he made diversionary excursions to throw spies off his trail; the few people who knew he was in Africa could only guess that he had in mind "some grand commercial scheme."

In fact, Stanley was financed by Leopold II of Belgium, who intended to acquire *personally* a large piece of Africa. "It is not a question of Belgian colonies," Leopold wrote Stanley. "It is a question of creating a new State, as big as possible. . . . The King, as a private person, wishes to possess properties in Africa. Belgium wants neither a colony nor territories. Mr. Stanley must therefore buy lands or get them conceded to him. . . ."

This incredible plan was carried out. By 1885, one American said that Leopold "possesses the Congo just as Rockefeller possesses Standard Oil." The comparison was apt in more ways than one, for African exploration had become dominated by business.

It has remained so to this day. Stanley would have approved the 1979 American expedition, which was conducted in secrecy, with an emphasis on speed. But the differences would have astonished him. When Stanley passed near Virunga in 1875, it had taken him almost a year to get there; the Americans got their expedition on-site in just over a week. And Stanley, who traveled with a small army of four hundred, would have been amazed at an expedition of only twelve—and one of them an ape. The territories through which the Americans moved a century later were autonomous political states; the Congo was now Zaire, and the Congo River the Zaire River. In fact, by 1979 the word "Congo" technically referred only to the drainage basin of the Zaire River, although Congo was still used in geological circles as a matter of familiarity, and for its romantic connotations.

Despite these differences, the expeditions had remarkably similar outcomes. Like Stanley, the Americans lost two-thirds of their party, and emerged from the jungle as desperately as Stanley's men a century before. And like Stanley, they returned with incredible tales of cannibals and pygmies, ruined jungle civilizations, and fabulous lost treasures.

I would like to thank R. B. Travis, of Earth Resources Technology Services in Houston, for permission to use videotaped debriefings; Dr. Karen Ross, of ERTS, for further background on the expedition; Dr. Peter Elliot, of the Department of Zoology, University of California at Berkeley, and the Project Amy staff, including Amy herself; Dr. William Wens, of Kasai Mining & Manufacturing, Zaire; Dr. Smith Jefferson, of the Department of Medical Pathology, University of Nairobi, Kenya; and Captain Charles Munro, of Tangier, Morocco.

I am further indebted to Mark Warwick, of Nairobi, for his initial interest in this project; Alan Binks, of Nairobi, for graciously offering to take me into the Virunga region of Zaire; Joyce Small for arranging my transport, usually at short notice, to obscure parts of the world; and finally my special thanks to my assistant, Judith Lovejoy, whose untiring efforts through very difficult times were crucial to the completion of this book.

M.C.

Prologue: The Place of Bones

Dawn came to the Congo rain forest.

The pale sun burned away the morning chill and the clinging damp mist, revealing a gigantic silent world. Enormous trees with trunks forty feet in diameter rose two hundred feet overhead, where they spread their dense leafy canopy, blotting out the sky and perpetually dripping water to the ground below. Curtains of gray moss, and creepers and lianas, hung down in a tangle from the trees; parasitic orchids sprouted from the trunks. At ground level, huge ferns, gleaming with moisture, grew higher than a man's chest and held the low ground fog. Here and there was a spot of color: the red acanthema blossoms, which were deadly poison, and the blue dicindra vine, which only opened in early morning. But the basic impression was of a vast, oversized, gray-green world—an alien place, inhospitable to man.

Jan Kruger put aside his rifle and stretched his stiff muscles. Dawn came quickly at the equator; soon it was quite light, although the mist remained. He glanced at the expedition campsite he had been guarding: eight bright orange nylon tents, a blue mess tent, a supply tarp lashed over boxed equipment in a vain attempt to keep them dry. He saw the other guard, Misulu, sitting on a rock; Misulu waved sleepily. Nearby was the transmitting equipment: a silver dish antenna, the black transmitter box, the snaking coaxial cables running to the portable video camera mounted on the collapsible tripod. The Americans used this equipment to transmit daily reports by satellite to their home office in Houston.

Kruger was the *bwana mukubwa*, hired to take the expedition into the Congo. He had led expeditions before: oil companies, map-survey parties, timber-mining teams, and geological parties like this one. Companies sending teams into the field wanted someone who knew local customs and local dialects well enough to handle the porters and arrange the travel. Kruger was well suited for this job; he spoke Kiswahili as well as Bantu and a little Bagindi, and he had been to the Congo many times, although never to Virunga.

Kruger could not imagine why American geologists would want to go to the Virunga region of Zaire, in the northeast corner of the Congo rain forest. Zaire was the richest country in black Africa, in minerals—the world's largest producer of cobalt and industrial diamonds, the seventh largest producer of copper. In addition there were major deposits of gold, tin, zinc, tungsten and

13

uranium. But most of the minerals were found in Shaba and Kasai, not in Virunga.

Kruger knew better than to ask why the Americans wanted to go to Virunga, and in any case he had his answer soon enough. Once the expedition passed Lake Kivu and entered the rain forest, the geologists began scouring rivers and streambeds. Searching placer deposits meant that they were looking for gold, or diamonds. It turned out to be diamonds.

But not just any diamonds. The geologists were after what they called Type IIb diamonds. Each new sample was immediately submitted to an electrical test. The resulting conversations were beyond Kruger—talk of dielectric gaps, lattice ions, resistivity. But he gathered that it was the electrical properties of the diamonds that mattered. Certainly the samples were useless as gemstones. Kruger had examined several, and they were all blue from impurities.

For ten days, the expedition had been tracing back placer deposits. This was standard procedure: if you found gold or diamonds in streambeds, you moved upstream toward the presumed erosive source of the minerals. The expedition had moved to higher ground along the western slopes of the Virgunga volcanic chain. It was all going routinely until one day around noon when the porters flatly refused to proceed further.

This part of Virunga, they said, was called *kanyamagufa,* which meant "the place of bones." The porters insisted that any men foolish enough to go further would have their bones broken, particularly their skulls. They kept touching their cheekbones, and repeating that their skulls would be crushed.

The porters were Bantu-speaking Arawanis from the nearest large town, Kisangani. Like most town-dwelling natives, they had all sorts of superstitions about the Congo jungle. Kruger called for the headman.

"What tribes are here?" Kruger asked, pointing to the jungle ahead.

"No tribes," the headman said.

"No tribes at all? Not even Bambuti?" he asked, referring to the nearest group of pygmies.

"No men come here," the headman said. "This is *kanyamagufa.*"

"Then what crushes the skulls?"

"*Dawa,*" the headman said ominously, using the Bantu term for magical forces. "Strong *dawa* here. Men stay away."

Kruger sighed. Like many white men, he was thoroughly sick of hearing about *dawa. Dawa* was everywhere, in plants and rocks and storms and enemies of all kinds. But the belief in *dawa* was prevalent throughout much of Africa and strongly held in the Congo.

Kruger had been obliged to waste the rest of the day in tedious negotiation. In the end, he doubled their wages and promised them firearms when they returned to Kisangani, and they agreed to continue on. Kruger considered the incident an irritating native ploy. Porters could generally be counted on to invoke some local superstition to increase their wages, once an expedition was deep enough into the field to be dependent on them. He had budgeted for this eventuality and, having agreed to their demands, he thought no more about it.

Even when they came upon several areas littered with shattered fragments of bone—which the porters found frightening—Kruger was not concerned. Upon examination, he found the bones were not human but rather the small delicate bones of colobus monkeys, the beautiful shaggy black-and-white creatures that lived in the trees overhead. It was true that there were a lot of bones, and Kruger had no idea why they should be shattered, but he had been in Africa a long time, and he had seen many inexplicable things.

Nor was he any more impressed with the overgrown fragments of stone that suggested a city had once stood in this area. Kruger had come upon unexplored ruins before, too. In Zimbabwe, in Broken Hill, in Maniliwi, there were the remains of cities and temples that no twentieth-century scientist had ever seen and studied.

He camped the first night near the ruins.

The porters were panic-stricken, insisting that the evil forces would attack them during the night. Their fear was caught by the American geologists; to pacify them, Kruger had posted two guards that night, himself and the most trustworthy porter, Misulu. Kruger thought it was all a lot of rot, but it had seemed the politic thing to do.

And just as he expected, the night had passed quietly. Around midnight there had been some movement in the bush, and some low wheezing sounds, which he took to be a leopard. Big cats often had respiratory trouble, particularly in the jungle. Otherwise it was quiet, and now it was dawn: the night was over.

A soft beeping sound drew his attention. Misulu heard it too, and glanced questioningly at Kruger. On the transmitting equipment, a red light blinked. Kruger got up and crossed the campsite to the equipment. He knew how to operate it; the Americans had insisted that he learn, as an "emergency procedure." He crouched over the black transmitter box with its rectangular green LED.

He pressed buttons, and the screen printed TX HX, meaning a transmission from Houston. He pressed the response code, and the screen printed CAMLOK. That meant that Houston was asking for video camera transmission. He glanced over at the camera on its tripod and saw that the red light on the case had blinked on. He pressed the carrier button and the screen printed SATLOK, which meant that a satellite transmission was being locked in. There would now be a six-minute delay, the time required to lock the satellite-bounced signal.

He'd better go wake Driscoll, the head geologist, he thought. Driscoll would need a few minutes before the transmission came through. Kruger found it amusing the way the Americans always put on a fresh shirt and combed their hair before stepping in front of the camera. Just like television reporters.

Overhead, the colobus monkeys shrieked and screamed in the trees, shaking the branches. Kruger glanced upward, wondering what had set them going. But it was normal for colobus monkeys to fight in the morning.

Something struck him lightly in the chest. At first he thought it was an insect but, glancing down at his khaki shirt, he saw a spot of red, and a fleshy bit of red fruit rolled down his shirt to the muddy ground. The damned monkeys were throwing berries. He bent over to pick it up. And then he realized that it was not a piece of fruit at all. It was a human eyeball, crushed and slippery in his fingers, pinkish white with a shred of white optic nerve still attached at the back.

He swung his gun around and looked over to where Misulu was sitting on the rock. Misulu was not there.

Kruger moved across the campsite. Overhead, the colobus monkeys fell silent. He heard his boots squish in the mud as he moved past the tents of sleeping men. And then he heard the wheezing sound again. It was an odd, soft sound, carried on the swirling morning mist. Kruger wondered if he had been mistaken, if it was really a leopard.

And he saw Misulu. Misulu lay on his back, in a kind of halo of blood. His skull had been crushed from the sides, the facial bones shattered, the face narrowed and elongated, the mouth open in an obscene yawn, the one remaining eye wide and bulging. The other eye had exploded outward with the force of the impact.

Kruger felt his heart pounding as he bent to examine the body. He wondered what could have caused such an injury. And then he heard the soft wheezing sound again, and this time he felt quite sure it was not a leopard. Then the colobus monkeys began their shrieking, and Kruger leapt to his feet and screamed.

DAY 1: HOUSTON

JUNE 13, 1979

1. ERTS Houston

Ten thousand miles away, in the cold, windowless main data room of Earth Resources Technology Services, Inc., of Houston, Karen Ross sat hunched over a mug of coffee in front of a computer terminal, reviewing the latest Landsat images from Africa. Ross was the ERTS Congo Project Supervisor, and as she manipulated the satellite images in artificial contrast colors, blue and purple and green, she glanced at her watch impatiently. She was waiting for the next field transmission from Africa.

It was now 10:15 P.M. Houston time, but there was no indication of time or place in the room. Day or night, the main data facility of ERTS remained the same. Beneath banks of special kalon fluorescent lights, programming crews in sweaters worked at long rows of quietly clicking computer terminals, providing real-time inputs to the field parties that ERTS maintained around the world. This timeless quality was understood to be necessary for the computers, which required a constant temperature of 60 degrees, dedicated electrical lines, special color-corrected lights that did not interfere with circuitry. It was an environment made for machines; the needs of people were secondary.

But there was another rationale for the main facility design. ERTS wanted programmers in Houston to identify with the field parties, and if possible to live on their schedules. Inputting baseball games and other local events was discouraged; there was no clock which showed Houston time, although on the far wall eight large digital clocks recorded local time for the various field parties.

The clock marked CONGO FIELD PARTY read 06:15 A.M. when the overhead intercom said, "Dr. Ross, CCR bounce."

She left the console after punching in the digital password blocking codes. Every ERTS terminal had a password control, like a combination lock. It was part of an elaborate system to prevent outside sources tapping into their enormous data bank. ERTS dealt in information, and as R. B. Travis, the head of ERTS, was fond of saying, the easiest way to obtain information was to steal it.

She crossed the room with long strides. Karen Ross was nearly six feet tall, an attractive though ungainly girl. Only twenty-four years old, she was younger than most of the programmers, but despite her youth, she had a self-possession that most people found striking—even a little unsettling. Karen Ross was a genuine mathematical prodigy.

At the age of two, while accompanying her mother to the supermarket, she had worked out in her head whether a ten-ounce can at 19¢ was cheaper than a one-pound-twelve-ounce can at 79¢. At three, she startled her father by observing that, unlike other numbers, zero meant different things in different positions. By eight, she had mastered algebra and geometry; by ten, she had taught herself calculus; she entered M.I.T. at thirteen and proceeded to make a series of brilliant discoveries in abstract mathematics, culminating in a treatise, "Topological Prediction in n-Space," which was useful for decision matrices, critical path analyses, and multidimensional mapping. This interest had brought her to the attention of ERTS, where she was made the youngest field supervisor in the company.

Not everyone liked her. The years of isolation, of being the youngest person in any room, had left her aloof and rather distant. One co-worker described her as "logical to a fault." Her chilly demeanor had earned her the title "Ross Glacier," after the Antarctic formation.

And her youth still held her back—at least, age was Travis's excuse when he refused to let her lead the Congo expedition into the field, even though she had derived all the Congo database, and by rights should have been the onsite team leader. "I'm sorry," Travis had said, "but this contract's too big, and I just can't let you have it." She had pressed, reminding him of her successes leading teams the year before to Pahang and Zambia. Finally he had said, "Look, Karen, that site's ten thousand miles away, in four-plus terrain. We need more than a console hotdogger out there."

She bridled under the implication that that was all she was—a console hotdogger, fast at the keyboard, good at playing with Travis's toys. She wanted to prove herself in a four-plus field situation. And the next time she was determined to make Travis let her go.

Ross pressed the button for the third-floor elevator, marked "CX Access Only." She caught an envious glance from one of the programmers while she waited for the elevator to arrive. Within ERTS, status was not measured by salary, title, the size of one's office, or the other usual corporate indicators of power. Status at ERTS was purely a matter of access to information—and Karen Ross was one of eight people in the company who had access to the third floor at any time.

She stepped onto the third-floor elevator, glancing up at the scanner lens mounted over the door. At ERTS the elevators traveled only one floor, and all were equipped with passive scanners; it was one way that ERTS kept track of the movements of personnel while they were in the building. She said "Karen Ross" for the voice monitors, and turned in a full circle for the scanners. There was a soft electronic bleep, and the door slid open at the third floor.

She emerged into a small square room with a ceiling video monitor, and faced the unmarked outer door of the Communications Control Room. She repeated "Karen Ross," and inserted her electronic identicard in the slot, resting her fingers on the metallic edge of the card so the computer could record galvanic skin potentials. (This was a refinement instituted three months earlier, after Travis learned that Army experiments with vocal cord surgery had altered voice characteristics precisely enough to false-positive Voiceident programs.) After a cycling pause, the door buzzed open. She went inside.

With its red night lights, Communications Control was like a soft, warm womb—an impression heightened by the cramped, almost claustrophobic quality of the room, packed with electronic equipment. From floor to ceiling, dozens of video monitors and LEDs flickered and glowed as the technicians spoke in hushed tones, setting dials and twisting knobs. The CCR was the electronic nerve center of ERTS: all communications from field parties around the world were routed through here. Everything in the CCR was recorded, not only incoming data but room voice responses, so the exact conversation on the night of June 13, 1979, is known.

One of the technicians said to her, "We'll have the transponders hooked in in a minute. You want coffee?"

"No," Ross said.

"You want to be out there, right?"

"I earned it," she said. She stared at the video screens, at the bewildering display of rotating and shifting forms as the technicians began the litany of locking in the bird bounce, a transmission from a satellite in orbit, 720 miles over their heads.

"Signal key."

"Signal key. Password mark."

"Password mark."

"Carrier fix."

"Carrier fix. We're rolling."

She paid hardly any attention to the familiar phrases. She watched as the screens displayed gray fields of crackling static.

"Did we open or did they open?" she asked.

"We initiated," a technician said. "We had it down on the call sheet to check them at dawn local time. So when they didn't initiate, we did."

"I wonder why they didn't initiate," Ross said. "Is something wrong?"

"I don't think so. We put out the initiation trigger and they picked it up and locked in within fifteen seconds, all the appropriate codes. Ah, here we go."

At 6:22 A.M. Congo time, the transmission came through: there was a final blur of gray static and then the screens cleared. They were looking at a part of the camp in the Congo, apparently a view from a tripod-mounted video camera. They saw two tents, a low smoldering fire, the lingering wisps of a foggy dawn. There was no sign of activity, no people.

One of the technicians laughed. "We caught them still sleeping. Guess they do need you there." Ross was known for her insistence on formalities.

"Lock your remote," she said.

The technician punched in the remote override. The field camera, ten thousand miles away, came under their control in Houston.

"Pan scan," she said.

At the console, the technician used a joystick. They watched as the video images shifted to the left, and they saw more of the camp. The camp was destroyed: tents crushed and torn, supply tarp pulled away, equipment scattered in the mud. One tent burned brightly, sending up clouds of black smoke. They saw several dead bodies.

"Jesus," one technician said.

"Back scan," Ross said. "Spot resolve to six-six."

On the screens, the camera panned back across the camp. They looked at the jungle. They still saw no sign of life.

"Down pan. Reverse sweep."

Onscreen, the camera panned down to show the silver dish of the portable antenna, and the black box of the transmitter. Nearby was another body, one of the geologists, lying on his back.

"Jesus, that's Roger. . . ."

"Zoom and T-lock," Ross said. On the tape, her voice sounds cool, almost detached.

The camera zoomed in on the face. What they saw was grotesque, the head crushed and leaking blood from eyes and nose, mouth gaping toward the sky.

"What did *that?*"

At that moment, a shadow fell across the dead face onscreen. Ross jumped forward, grabbing the joystick and hitting the zoom control. The image widened swiftly; they could see the outline of the shadow now. It was a man. And he was moving.

"Somebody's there! Somebody's still alive!"

"He's limping. Looks wounded."

Ross stared at the shadow. It did not look to her like a limping man; something was wrong, she couldn't put her finger on what it was. . . .

"He's going to walk in front of the lens," she said. It was almost too much to hope for. "What's that audio static?"

They were hearing an odd sound, like a hissing or a sighing.

"It's not static, it's in the transmission."

"Resolve it," Ross said. The technicians punched buttons, altering the audio frequencies, but the sound remained peculiar and indistinct. And then the shadow moved, and the man stepped in front of the lens.

"Diopter," Ross said, but it was too late. The face had already appeared, very near the lens. It was too close to focus without a diopter. They saw a blurred, dark shape, nothing more. Before they could click in the diopter, it was gone.

"A native?"

22

"This region of the Congo is uninhabited," Ross said.

"*Something* inhabits it."

"Pan scan," Ross said. "See if you can get him onscreen again."

The camera continued to pan. She could imagine it sitting on its tripod in the jungle, motor whirring as the lens head swung around. Then suddenly the image tilted and fell sideways.

"He knocked it over."

"Damn!"

The video image crackled, shifting lines of static. It became very difficult to see.

"Resolve it! Resolve it!"

They had a final glimpse of a large face and a dark hand as the silver dish antenna was smashed. The image from the Congo shrank to a spot, and was gone.

2. Interference Signature

During June of 1979, Earth Resources Technology had field teams studying uranium deposits in Bolivia, copper deposits in Pakistan, agricultural field utilization in Kashmir, glacier advance in Iceland, timber resources in Malaysia, and diamond deposits in the Congo. This was not unusual for ERTS; they generally had between six and eight groups in the field at any time.

Since their teams were often in hazardous or politically unstable regions, they were vigilant in watching for the first signs of "interference signatures." (In remote-sensing terminology, a "signature" is the characteristic appearance of an object or geological feature in a photograph or video image.) Most interference signatures were political. In 1977, ERTS had airlifted a team out of Borneo during a local Communist uprising, and again from Nigeria in 1978 during a military coup. Occasionally the signatures were geological; they had pulled a team from Guatemala in 1976 after the earthquake there.

In the opinion of R. B. Travis, called out of bed in the late hours of June 13, 1979, the videotapes from the Congo were "the worst interference signature ever," but the problem remained mysterious. All they knew was that the camp had been destroyed in a mere six minutes—the time between the signal initiation from Houston and the reception in the Congo. The rapidity was frightening; Travis's first instruction to his team was to figure out "what the hell happened out there."

A heavyset man of forty-eight, Travis was accustomed to crises. By training he was an engineer with a background in satellite construction for RCA and later Rockwell; in his thirties he had shifted to management, becoming what aerospace engineers called a "rain dancer." Companies manufacturing satellites contracted eighteen to twenty-four months in advance for a launch rocket to put the satellite in orbit—and then hoped that the satellite, with its half-million working parts, would be ready on the assigned day. If it was not, the only alternative was to pray for bad weather delaying the launch, to dance for rain.

Travis had managed to keep a sense of humor after a decade of high-tech problems; his management philosophy was summarized by a large sign mounted behind his desk, which read "S.D.T.A.G.W." It stood for "Some Damn Thing Always Goes Wrong."

But Travis was not amused on the night of June 13. His entire expedition had been lost, all the ERTS party killed—eight of his people, and however many local porters were with them. The worst disaster in ERTS history, worse even than Nigeria in '78. Travis felt fatigued, mentally drained, as he thought of all the phone calls ahead of him. Not the calls he would make, but those he would receive. Would so-and-so be back in time for a daughter's graduation, a son's Little League playoff? Those calls would be routed to Travis, and he would have to listen to the bright expectation in the voices, the hopefulness, and his own careful answers—he wasn't sure, he understood the problem, he would do his best, of course, of course. . . . The coming deception exhausted him in advance.

Because Travis couldn't tell anyone what had happened for at least two weeks, perhaps a month. And then he would be making phone calls himself, and visits to the homes, and attending the memorial services where there would be no casket, a deadly blank space, a gap, and the inevitable questions from families and relatives that he couldn't answer while they scrutinized his face, looking for the least muscle twitch, or hesitation, or sign.

What could he tell them?

That was his only consolation—perhaps in a few weeks, Travis could tell them more. One thing was certain: if he were to make the dreadful calls tonight, he could tell the families nothing at all, for ERTS had no idea what had gone wrong. That fact added to Travis's sense of exhaustion. And there were details: Morris, the insurance auditor, came in and said, "What do you want to do about the terms?" ERTS took out term life insurance policies for every expedition member, and also for local porters. African porters received U.S. $15,000 each in insurance, which seemed trivial until one recognized that African per capita income averaged U.S. $180 per year. But Travis had always argued that local expedition people should share risk benefits—even if it meant paying widowed families a small fortune, in their terms. Even if it cost ERTS a small fortune for the insurance.

"Hold them," Travis said.

"Those policies are costing us *per day*—"

"Hold them," Travis said.

"For how long?"

"Thirty days," Travis said.

"Thirty *more* days?"

"That's right."

"But we know the holders are dead." Morris could not reconcile himself to the waste of money. His actuarial mind rebelled.

"That's right," Travis said. "But you'd better slip the porters' families some cash to keep them quiet."

"Jesus. How much are we talking about?"

"Five hundred dollars each."

"How do we account that?"

"Legal fees," Travis said. "Bury it in legal, local disposition."

"And the American team people that we've lost?"

"They have MasterCard," Travis said. "Stop worrying."

Roberts, the British-born ERTS press liaison, came into his office. "You want to open this can up?"

"No," Travis said. "I want to kill it."

"For how long?"

"Thirty days."

"Bloody hell. Your own staff will leak inside thirty days," Roberts said. "I promise you."

"If they do, you'll squash it," Travis said. "I need another thirty days to make this contract."

"Do we know what happened out there?"

"No," Travis said. "But we will."

"How?"

"From the tapes."

"Those tapes are a mess."

"So far," Travis said. And he called in the specialty teams of console hot-doggers. Travis had long since concluded that although ERTS could wake up political advisers around the world, they were most likely to get information in-house. "Everything we know from the Congo field expedition," he said, "is registered on that final videotape. I want a seven-band visual and audio salvage, starting right now. Because that tape is all we have."

The specialty teams went to work.

3. Recovery

ERTS referred to the process as "data recovery," or sometimes as "data salvage." The terms evoked images of deep-sea operations, and they were oddly appropriate.

To recover or salvage data meant that coherent meaning was pulled to the surface from the depths of massive electronic information storage. And, like salvage from the sea, it was a slow and delicate process, where a single false step meant the irretrievable loss of the very elements one was trying to bring up. ERTS had whole salvage crews skilled in the art of data recovery. One crew immediately went to work on the audio recovery, another on the visual recovery.

But Karen Ross was already engaged in a visual recovery. The procedures she followed were highly sophisticated, and only possible at ERTS.

Earth Resources Technology was a relatively new company, formed in 1975 in response to the explosive growth of information on the Earth and its resources. The amount of material handled by ERTS was staggering: just the Landsat imagery alone amounted to more than five hundred thousand pictures, and sixteen new images were acquired every hour, around the clock. With the addition of conventional and draped aerial photography, infrared photography, and artificial aperture side-looking radar, the total information available to ERTS exceeded two million images, with new input on the order of thirty images an hour. All this information had to be catalogued, stored, and made available for instantaneous retrieval. ERTS was like a library which acquired seven hundred new books a day. It was not surprising that the librarians worked at fever pitch around the clock.

Visitors to ERTS never seemed to realize that even with computers, such data-handling capacity would have been impossible ten years earlier. Nor did visitors understand the basic nature of the ERTS information—they assumed that the pictures on the screens were photographic, although they were not.

Photography was a nineteenth-century chemical system for recording information using light-sensitive silver salts. ERTS utilized a twentieth-century electronic system for recording information, analogous to chemical photographs, but very different. Instead of cameras, ERTS used multi-spectral scanners; instead of film, they used CCTs—computer compatible tapes. In fact, ERTS did not bother with "pictures" as they were ordinarily understood from

26

old-fashioned photographic technology. ERTS bought "data scans" which they converted to "data displays," as the need arose.

Since the ERTS images were just electrical signals recorded on magnetic tape, a great variety of electrical image manipulation was possible. ERTS had 837 computer programs to alter imagery: to enhance it, to eliminate unwanted elements, to bring out details. Ross used fourteen programs on the Congo videotape—particularly on the static-filled section in which the hand and face appeared, just before the antenna was smashed.

First she carried out what was called a "wash cycle," getting rid of the static. She identified the static lines as occurring at specific scan positions, and having a specific gray-scale value. She instructed the computer to cancel those lines.

The resulting image showed blank spaces where the static was removed. So she did "fill-in-the-blanks"—instructing the computer to introject imagery, according to what was around the blank spaces. In this operation the computer made a logical guess about what was missing.

She now had a static-free image, but it was muddy and indistinct, lacking definition. So she did a "high-priced spread"—intensifying the image by spreading the gray-scale values. But for some reason she also got a phase distortion that she had to cancel, and that released spiking glitches previously suppressed, and to get rid of the glitches she had to run three other programs. . . .

Technical details preoccupied her for an hour, until suddenly the image "popped," coming up bright and clean. She caught her breath as she saw it. The screen showed a dark, brooding face with heavy brows, watchful eyes, a flattened nose, prognathous lips.

Frozen on the video screen was the face of a male gorilla.

Travis walked toward her from across the room, shaking his head. "We finished the audio recovery on that hissing noise. The computer confirms it as human breathing, with at least four separate origins. But it's damned strange. According to the analysis, the sound is coming from inhalation, not exhalation, the way people usually make sounds."

"The computer is wrong," Ross said. "It's not human." She pointed to the screen, and the face of the gorilla.

Travis showed no surprise. "Artifact," he said.

"It's no artifact."

"You did fill-in-the-blanks, and you got an artifact. The tag team's been screwing around with the software at lunch again." The tag team—the young software programmers—had a tendency to convert data to play highly sophisticated versions of pinball games. Their games sometimes got subrouted into other programs.

Ross herself had complained about it. "But this image is real," she insisted, pointing to the screen.

"Look," Travis said, "last week Harry did fill-in-the-blanks on the Karakorum Mountains and he got back a lunar landing game. You're supposed to land next to the McDonald's stand, all very amusing." He walked off. "You'd better meet the others in my office. We're setting advance times to get back in."

"I'm leading the next team."

Travis shook his head. "Out of the question."

"But what about this?" she said, pointing to the screen.

"I'm not buying that image," Travis said. "Gorillas don't behave that way. It's got to be an artifact." He glanced at his watch. "Right now, the only question I have is how fast we can put a team back in the Congo."

4. Return Expedition

Travis had never had any doubts in his mind about going back in; from the first time he saw the videotapes from the Congo, the only question was how best to do it. He called in all the section heads: Accounts, Diplo, Remote, Geo, Logistics, Legal. They were all yawning and rubbing their eyes. Travis began by saying, "I want us back in the Congo in ninety-six hours."

Then he leaned back in his chair and let them tell him why it couldn't be done. There were plenty of reasons.

"We can't assemble the air cargo units for shipment in less than a hundred and sixty hours," Cameron, the logistics man said.

"We can postpone the Himalaya team, and use their units," Travis said.

"But that's a mountain expedition."

"You can modify the units in nine hours," Travis said.

"But we can't get equipment to fly it out," Lewis, the transport master, said.

"Korean Airlines has a 747 cargo jet available at SFX. They tell me it can be down here in nine hours."

"They have a plane just sitting there?" Lewis said, incredulous.

"I believe," Travis said, "that they had a last-minute cancellation from another customer."

Irwin, the accountant, groaned. "What'd that cost?"

"We can't get visas from the Zaire Embassy in Washington in time," Martin, the diplomatic man, said. "And there is serious doubt they'd issue them to us at all. As you know, the first set of Congo visas were based on our mineral exploration rights with the Zaire government, and our MERs are non-exclusive. We were granted permission to go in, and so were the Japanese, the Germans, and the Dutch, who've formed a mining consortium. The first ore-body strike takes the contract. If Zaire suspects that our expedition is in trouble, they'll just cancel us out and let the Euro-Japanese consortium try their luck. There are thirty Japanese trade officials in Kinshasa right now, spending yen like water."

"I think that's right," Travis said. "If it became known that our expedition is in trouble."

"It'll become known the minute we apply for visas."

"We won't apply for them. As far as anybody knows," Travis said, "we still have an expedition in Virunga. If we put a second small team into the field fast enough, nobody will ever know that it wasn't the original team."

"But what about the specific personnel visas to cross the borders, the manifests—"

"Details," Travis said. "That's what liquor is for," referring to bribes, which were often liquor. In many parts of the world, expedition teams went in with crates of liquor and boxes of those perennial favorites, transistor radios and Polaroid cameras.

"Details? How're you going to cross the border?"

"We'll need a good man for that. Maybe Munro."

"Munro? That's playing rough. The Zaire government hates Munro."

"He's resourceful, and he knows the area."

Martin, the diplomatic expert, cleared his throat and said, "I'm not sure I should be here for this discussion. It looks to me as if you are proposing to enter a sovereign state with an illegal party led by a former Congo mercenary soldier. . . ."

"Not at all," Travis said. "I'm obliged to put a support party into the field to assist my people already there. Happens all the time. I have no reason to think anybody is in trouble; just a routine support party. I haven't got time to go through official channels. I may not be showing the best judgment in whom I hire, but it's nothing more serious than that."

By 11:45 P.M. on the night of June 13, the main sequencing of the next ERTS expedition had been worked out and confirmed by the computer. A fully loaded 747 could leave Houston at 8 P.M. the following evening, June 14; the plane could be in Africa on June 15 to pick up Munro "or someone like him"; and the full team could be in place in the Congo on June 17.

In ninety-six hours.

From the main data room, Karen Ross could look through the glass walls into Travis's office and see the arguments taking place. In her logical way, she concluded that Travis had "Q'd" himself, meaning that he had drawn false conclusions from insufficient data, and had said Q.E.D. too soon. Ross felt there was no point in going back into the Congo until they knew what they were up against. She remained at her console, checking the image she had recovered.

Ross bought this image—but how could she make Travis buy it?

In the highly sophisticated data-processing world of ERTS, there was a constant danger that extracted information would begin to "float"—that the images would cut loose from reality, like a ship cut loose from its moorings. This was true particularly when the database was put through multiple manipulations—when you were rotating 10^6 pixels in computer-generated hyperspace.

So ERTS evolved other ways to check the validity of images they got back from the computer. Ross ran two check programs against the gorilla image. The first was called APNF, for Animation Predicted Next Frame.

It was possible to treat videotape as if it were movie film, a succession of stills. She showed the computer several "stills" in succession, and then asked it to create the Predicted Next Frame. This PNF was then checked against the actual next frame.

She ran eight PNFs in a row, and they worked. If there was an error in the data handling, it was at least a consistent error.

Encouraged, she next ran a "fast and dirty three-space." Here the flat video image was assumed to have certain three-dimensional characteristics, based on gray-scale patterns. In essence, the computer decided that the shadow of a nose, or a mountain range, meant that the nose or mountain range protruded above the surrounding surface. Succeeding images could be checked against these assumptions. As the gorilla moved, the computer verified that the flat image was, indeed, three-dimensional and coherent.

This proved beyond a doubt that the image was real.

She went to see Travis.

"Let's say I buy this image," Travis said, frowning. "I still don't see why you should take the next expedition in."

Ross said, "What did the other team find?"

"The other team?" Travis asked innocently.

"You gave that tape to another salvage team to confirm my recovery," Ross said.

Travis glanced at his watch. "They haven't pulled anything out yet." And he added, "We all know you're fast with the database."

Ross smiled. "That's why you need me to take the expedition in," she said. "I know the database, because I generated the database. And if you intend to send another team in right away, before this gorilla thing is solved, the only hope you have is for the team leader to be fast onsite with the data. This time, you *need* a console hotdogger in the field. Or the next expedition will end up like the last one. Because you still don't know what happened to the last expedition."

Travis sat behind his desk, and stared at her for a long time. She recognized his hesitation as a sign that he was weakening.

"And I want to go outside," Ross said.

"To an outside expert?"

"Yes. Somebody on our grant list."

"Risky," Travis said. "I hate to involve outside people at this point. You know the consortium is breathing down our necks. You up the leak averages."

"It's important," Ross insisted.

Travis sighed. "Okay, if you think it's important." He sighed again. "Just don't delay your team."

Ross was already packing up her hard copy.

Alone, Travis frowned, turning over his decision in his mind. Even if they ran the next Congo expedition slambam, in and out in less than fifteen days, their fixed costs would still exceed three hundred thousand dollars. The Board was going to scream—sending an untried, twenty-four-year-old kid, a *girl*, into the field with this kind of responsibility. Especially on a project as important as this one, where the stakes were enormous, and where they had already fallen behind on every timeline and cost projection. And Ross was so cold, she was likely to prove a poor field leader, alienating the others in the team.

Yet Travis had a hunch about the Ross Glacier. His management philosophy, tempered in his rain-dancing days, was always to give the project to whoever had the most to gain from success—or the most to lose from failure.

He turned to face his console, mounted beside his desk. "Travis," he said, and the screen glowed.

"Psychograph file," he said.

The screen showed call prompts.

"Ross, Karen," Travis said.

The screen flashed THINKING A MOMENT. That was the programmed response which meant that information was being extracted. He waited.

Then the psychograph summary printed out across the screen. Every ERTS employee underwent three days of intensive psychological testing to determine not only skills but potential biases. The assessment of Ross would, he felt, be reassuring to the Board.

HIGHLY INTELLIGENT / LOGICAL / FLEXIBLE / RESOURCEFUL / DATA INTUITIVE / THOUGHT PROCESSES SUITED TO RAPIDLY CHANGING REALTIME CONTEXTS / DRIVEN TO SUCCEED AT DEFINED GOALS / CAPABLE SUSTAINED MENTAL EFFORT /

It looked like the perfect description of the next Congo team leader. He scanned down the screen, looking for the negatives. These were less reassuring.

YOUTHFUL-RUTHLESS / TENUOUS HUMAN RAPPORT / DOMINEERING / INTEL-LECTUALLY ARROGANT / INSENSITIVE / DRIVEN TO SUCCEED AT ANY COST /

And there was a final "flopover" notation. The very concept of personality flopover had been evolved through ERTS testing. It suggested that any dominant personality trait could be suddenly reversed under stress conditions: parental personalities could flop over and turn childishly petulant, hysterical personalities could become icy calm—or logical personalities could become illogical.

FLOPOVER MATRIX: DOMINANT (POSSIBLY UNDESIRABLE) OBJECTIVITY MAY BE LOST ONCE DESIRED GOAL IS PERCEIVED CLOSE AT HAND / DESIRE FOR SUCCESS MAY PROVOKE DANGEROUSLY ILLOGICAL RESPONSES / PAREN-TAL FIGURES WILL BE ESPECIALLY DENIGRATED / SUBJECT MUST BE MONI-TORED IN LATE STAGE GOAL-ORIENTED PROCEDURES /

Travis looked at the screen, and decided that such a circumstance was highly unlikely in the coming Congo expedition. He turned the computer off.

Karen Ross was exhilarated by her new authority. Shortly before midnight, she called up the grant lists on her office terminal. ERTS had animal experts in various areas whom they supported with nominal grants from a non-profit foundation called the Earth Resources Wildlife Fund. The grant lists were arranged taxonomically. Under "Primates" she found fourteen names, including several in Borneo, Malaysia, and Africa as well as the United States. In the United States there was only one gorilla researcher available, a primatologist named Dr. Peter Elliot, at the University of California at Berkeley.

The file onscreen indicated that Elliot was twenty-nine years old, unmarried, an associate professor without tenure in the Department of Zoology. Principal Research Interest was listed as "Primate Communications (Gorilla)." Funding was made to something called Project Amy.

She checked her watch. It was just midnight in Houston, 10 P.M. in California. She dialed the home number on the screen.

"Hello," a wary male voice said.

"Dr. Peter Elliot?"

"Yes . . ." The voice was still cautious, hesitant. "Are you a reporter?"

"No," she said. "This is Dr. Karen Ross in Houston; I'm associated with the Earth Resources Wildlife Fund, which supports your research."

"Oh, yes . . ." The voice remained cautious. "You're sure you're not a reporter? It's only fair to tell you I'm recording this telephone call as a potential legal document."

Karen Ross hesitated. The last thing she needed was some paranoid academic recording ERTS developments. She said nothing.

"You're American?" he said.

"Of course."

Karen Ross stared at the computer screens, which flashed VOICE IDENTIFICATION CONFIRMED: ELLIOT, PETER, 29 YEARS.

"State your business," Elliot said.

"Well, we're about to send an expedition into the Virunga region of the Congo, and—"

"Really? When are you going?" The voice suddenly sounded excited, boyish.

"Well, as a matter of fact we're leaving in two days, and—"

"I want to go," Elliot said.

Ross was so surprised she hardly knew what to say. "Well, Dr. Elliot, that's not why I'm calling you, as a matter of fact—"

"I'm planning to go there anyway," Elliot said. "With Amy."

"Who's Amy?"

"Amy is a gorilla," Peter Elliot said.

DAY 2: SAN FRANCISCO

JUNE 14, 1979

1. Project Amy

It is unfair to suggest, as some primatologists later did, that Peter Elliot had to "get out of town" in June, 1979. His motives, and the planning behind the decision to go to the Congo, are a matter of record. Professor Elliot and his staff had decided on an African trip at least two days before Ross called him.

But it is certainly true that Peter Elliot was under attack: from outside groups, the press, academic colleagues, and even members of his own department at Berkeley. Toward the end, Elliot was accused of being a "Nazi criminal" engaged in the "torture of dumb [*sic*] animals." It is no exaggeration to say that Elliot had found himself, in the spring of 1979, fighting for his professional life.

Yet his research had begun quietly, almost accidentally. Peter Elliot was a twenty-three-year-old graduate student in the Department of Anthropology at Berkeley when he first read about a year-old gorilla with amoebic dysentery who had been flown from the Minneapolis zoo to the San Francisco School of Veterinary Medicine for treatment. That was in 1973, in the exciting early days of primate language research.

The idea that primates might be taught language was very old. In 1661, Samuel Pepys saw a chimpanzee in London and wrote in his diary that it was "so much like a man in most things that . . . I do believe that it already understands much English, and I am of the mind it might be taught to speak or make signs." Another seventeenth-century writer went further, saying, "Apes and Baboons . . . can speak but will not for fear they should be imployed, and set to work."

Yet for the next three hundred years attempts to teach apes to talk were notably unsuccessful. They culminated in an ambitious effort by a Florida couple, Keith and Kathy Hayes, who for six years in the early 1950s raised a chimpanzee named Vicki as if she were a human infant. During that time, Vicki learned four words—"mama," "papa," "cup," and "up." But her pronunciation was labored and her progress slow. Her difficulties seemed to support the growing conviction among scientists that man was the only animal capable of language. Typical was the pronouncement of George Gaylord Simpson: "Language is . . . the most diagnostic single trait of man: all normal men have language; no other now living organisms do."

This seemed so self-evident that for the next fifteen years nobody bothered to try teaching language to an ape. Then in 1966, a Reno, Nevada, couple named Beatrice and Allen Gardner reviewed movies of Vicki speaking. It seemed to them that Vicki was not so much incapable of language as incapable of speech. They noticed that while her lip movements were awkward, her hand gestures were fluid and expressive. The obvious conclusion was to try sign language.

In June, 1966, the Gardners began teaching American Sign Language (Ameslan), the standardized language of the deaf, to an infant chimpanzee named Washoe. Washoe's progress with ASL was rapid; by 1971, she had a vocabulary of 160 signs, which she used in conversation. She also made up new word combinations for things she had never seen before: when shown watermelon for the first time, she signed it "water fruit."

The Gardners' work was highly controversial; it turned out that many scientists had an investment in the idea that apes were incapable of language. (As one researcher said, "My God, think of all those eminent names attached to all those scholarly papers for all those decades—and everyone agreeing that only man had language. What a mess.")

Washoe's skills provoked a variety of other experiments in teaching language. A chimpanzee named Lucy was taught to communicate through a computer; another, Sarah, was taught to use plastic markers on a board. Other apes were studied as well. An orangutan named Alfred began instruction in 1971; a lowland gorilla named Koko in 1972; and in 1973 Peter Elliot began with a mountain gorilla, Amy.

At his first visit to the hospital to meet Amy, he found a pathetic little creature, heavily sedated, with restraining straps on her frail black arms and legs. He stroked her head and said gently, "Hello, Amy, I'm Peter."

Amy promptly bit his hand, drawing blood.

From this inauspicious beginning emerged a singularly successful research program. In 1973, the basic teaching technique, called molding, was well understood. The animal was shown an object and the researcher simultaneously molded the animal's hand into the correct sign, until the association was firmly made. Subsequent testing confirmed that the animal understood the meaning of the sign.

But if the basic methodology was accepted, the application was highly competitive. Researchers competed over the rate of sign acquisition, or vocabulary. (Among human beings, vocabulary was considered the best measure of intelligence.) The rate of sign acquisition could be taken as a measure of either the scientist's skill or the animal's intelligence.

It was by now clearly recognized that different apes had different personalities. As one researcher commented, "Pongid studies are perhaps the only field in which academic gossip centers on the students and not the teachers." In the increasingly competitive and disputatious world of primate research, it was said that Lucy was a drunk, that Koko was an ill-mannered brat, that

Lana's head was turned by her celebrity ("she only works when there is an interviewer present"), and that Nim was so stupid he should have been named Dim.

At first glance, it may seem odd that Peter Elliot should have come under attack, for this handsome, rather shy man—the son of a Marin County librarian—had avoided controversy during his years of work with Amy. Elliot's publications were modest and temperate; his progress with Amy was well documented; he showed no interest in publicity, and was not among those researchers who took their apes on the Carson or the Griffin show.

But Elliot's diffident manner concealed not only a quick intelligence, but a fierce ambition as well. If he avoided controversy, it was only because he didn't have time for it—he had been working nights and weekends for years, and driving his staff and Amy just as hard. He was very good at the business of science, getting grants; at all the animal behaviorist conferences, where others showed up in jeans and plaid lumberjack shirts, Elliot arrived in a three-piece suit. Elliot intended to be the foremost ape researcher, and he intended Amy to be the foremost ape.

Elliot's success in obtaining grants was such that by 1975, Project Amy had an annual budget of $160,000 and a staff of eight, including a child psychologist and a computer programmer. A staff member of the Bergren Institute later said that Elliot's appeal lay in the fact that he was "a good investment; for example, Project Amy got fifty percent more computer time for our money because he went on line with his time-sharing terminal at night and on weekends, when the time was cheaper. He was very cost-effective. And dedicated, of course: Elliot obviously cared about nothing in life except his work with Amy. That made him a boring conversationalist but a very good bet, from our standpoint. It's hard to decide who's truly brilliant; it's easier to see who's driven, which in the long run may be more important. We anticipated great things from Elliot."

Peter Elliot's difficulties began on the morning of February 2, 1979. Amy lived in a mobile home on the Berkeley campus; she spent nights there alone, and usually provided an effusive greeting the next day. However, on that morning the Project Amy staff found her in an uncharacteristic sullen mood; she was irritable and bleary-eyed, behaving as if she had been wronged in some fashion.

Elliot felt that something had upset her during the night. When asked, she kept making signs for "sleep box," a new word pairing he did not understand. That in itself was not unusual; Amy made up new word pairings all the time, and they were often hard to decipher. Just a few days before, she had bewildered them by talking about "crocodile milk." Eventually they realized that Amy's milk had gone sour, and that since she disliked crocodiles (which she had only seen in picture books), she somehow decided that sour milk was "crocodile milk."

Now she was talking about "sleep box." At first they thought she might be referring to her nestlike bed. It turned out she was using "box" in her usual sense, to refer to the television set.

Everything in her trailer, including the television, was controlled on a twenty-four-hour cycle by the computer. They ran a check to see if the television had been turned on during the night, disturbing her sleep. Since Amy liked to watch television, it was conceivable that she had managed to turn it on herself. But Amy looked scornful as they examined the actual television in the trailer. She clearly meant something else.

Finally they determined that by "sleep box" she meant "sleep pictures." When asked about these sleep pictures, Amy signed that they were "bad pictures" and "old pictures," and that they "make Amy cry."

She was dreaming.

The fact that Amy was the first primate to report dreams caused tremendous excitement among Elliot's staff. But the excitement was short-lived. Although Amy continued to dream on succeeding nights, she refused to discuss her dreams; in fact, she seemed to blame the researchers for this new and confusing intrusion into her mental life. Worse, her waking behavior deteriorated alarmingly.

Her word acquisition rate fell from 2.7 words a week to 0.8 words a week, her spontaneous word formation rate from 1.9 to 0.3. Monitored attention span was halved. Mood swings increased; erratic and unmotivated behavior became commonplace; temper tantrums occurred daily. Amy was four and a half feet tall, and weighed 130 pounds. She was an immensely strong animal. The staff began to wonder if they could control her.

Her refusal to talk about her dreams frustrated them. They tried a variety of investigative approaches; they showed her pictures from books and magazines; they ran the ceiling-mounted video monitors around the clock, in case she signed something significant while alone (like young children, Amy often "talked to herself"); they even administered a battery of neurological tests, including an EEG.

Finally they hit on finger painting.

This was immediately successful. Amy was enthusiastic about finger painting, and after they mixed cayenne pepper with the pigments, she stopped licking her fingers. She drew images swiftly and repetitively, and she seemed to become somewhat more relaxed, more her old self.

David Bergman, the child psychologist, noted that "what Amy actually draws is a cluster of apparently related images: inverted crescent shapes, or semicircles, which are always associated with an area of vertical green streaks. Amy says the green streaks represent 'forest,' and she calls the semi-circles 'bad houses' or 'old houses.' In addition she often draws black circles, which she calls 'holes.' "

Bergman cautioned against the obvious conclusion that she was drawing old buildings in the jungle. "Watching her make drawings one after another, again and again, convinces me of the obsessive and private nature of the imagery. Amy is troubled by these pictures, and she is trying to get them out, to banish them to paper."

In fact, the nature of the imagery remained mysterious to the Project Amy staff. By late April, 1979, they had concluded that her dreams could be explained in four ways. In order of seriousness, they were:

1. *The dreams are an attempt to rationalize events in her daily life.* This was the usual explanation of (human) dreams, but the staff doubted that it applied in Amy's case.

2. *The dreams are a transitional adolescent manifestation.* At seven years of age, Amy was a gorilla teenager, and for nearly a year she had shown many typical teenage traits, including rages and sulks, fussiness about her appearance, a new interest in the opposite sex.

3. *The dreams are a species-specific phenomenon.* It was possible that all gorillas had disturbing dreams, and that in the wild the resultant stresses were handled in some fashion by the behavior of the group. Although gorillas had been studied in the wild for the past twenty years, there was no evidence for this.

4. *The dreams are the first sign of incipient dementia.* This was the most feared possibility. To train an ape effectively, one had to begin with an infant; as the years progressed, researchers waited to see if their animal would grow up to be bright or stupid, recalcitrant or pliable, healthy or sickly. The health of apes was a constant worry; many programs collapsed after years of effort and expense when the apes died of physical or mental illness. Timothy, an Atlanta chimp, became psychotic in 1976 and committed suicide by coprophagia, choking to death on his own feces. Maurice, a Chicago orang, became intensely neurotic, developing phobias that halted work in 1977. For better or worse, the very intelligence that made apes worthwhile subjects for study also made them as unstable as human beings.

But the Project Amy staff was unable to make further progress. In May, 1979, they made what turned out to be a momentous decision: they decided to publish Amy's drawings, and submitted her images to the *Journal of Behavioral Sciences*.

2. Breakthrough

"**D**ream Behavior in a Mountain Gorilla" was never published. The paper was routinely forwarded to three scientists on the editorial board for review, and one copy somehow (it is still unclear just how) fell into the hands of the Primate Preservation Agency, a New York group formed in 1975 to prevent the "unwarranted and illegitimate exploitation of intelligent primates in unnecessary laboratory research."*

On June 3, the PPA began picketing the Zoology Department at Berkeley, and calling for the "release" of Amy. Most of the demonstrators were women, and several young children were present; videotapes of an eight-year-old boy holding a placard with Amy's photograph and shouting "Free Amy! Free Amy!" appeared on local television news.

In a tactical error, the Project Amy staff elected to ignore the protests except for a brief press release stating that the PPA was "misinformed." The release went out under the Berkeley Information Office letterhead.

On June 5, the PPA released comments on Professor Elliot's work from other primatologists around the country. (Many later denied the comments or claimed they were misquoted.) Dr. Wayne Turman, of the University of Oklahoma at Norman, was quoted as saying that Elliot's work was "fanciful and unethical." Dr. Felicity Hammond, of the Yerkes Primate Research Center in Atlanta, said that "neither Elliot nor his research is of the first rank." Dr. Richard Aronson at the University of Chicago called the research "clearly fascist in nature."

None of these scientists had read Elliot's paper before commenting; but the damage, particularly from Aronson, was incalculable. On June 8, Eleanor Vries, the spokesperson for the PPA, referred to the "criminal research of Dr. Elliot and his Nazi staff"; she claimed Elliot's research caused Amy to have nightmares, and that Amy was being subjected to torture, drugs, and electroshock treatments.

Belatedly, on June 10, the Project Amy staff prepared a lengthy press release, explaining their position in detail and referring to the unpublished

*The following account of Elliot's persecution draws heavily on J. A. Peebles, "Infringement of Academic Freedom by Press Innuendo and Hearsay: The Experience of Dr. Peter Elliot," in the *Journal of Academic Law and Psychiatry 52*, no. 12 (1979): 19–38.

paper. But the University Information Office was now "too busy" to issue the release.

On June 11, the Berkeley faculty scheduled a meeting to consider "issues of ethical conduct" within the university. Eleanor Vries announced that the PPA had hired the noted San Francisco attorney Melvin Belli "to free Amy from subjugation." Belli's office was not available for comment.

On the same day, the Project Amy staff had a sudden, unexpected breakthrough in their understanding of Amy's dreams.

Through all the publicity and commotion, the group had continued to work daily with Amy, and her continued distress—and flaring temper tantrums—was a constant reminder that they had not solved the initial problem. They persisted in their search for clues, although when the break finally came, it happened almost by accident.

Sarah Johnson, a research assistant, was checking prehistoric archaeological sites in the Congo, on the unlikely chance that Amy might have seen such a site ("old buildings in the jungle") in her infancy, before she was brought to the Minneapolis zoo. Johnson quickly discovered the pertinent facts about the Congo: the region had not been explored by Western observers until a hundred years ago; in recent times, hostile tribes and civil war had made scientific inquiry hazardous; and finally, the moist jungle environment did not lend itself to artifact preservation.

This meant remarkably little was known about Congolese prehistory, and Johnson completed her research in a few hours. But she was reluctant to return so quickly from her assignment, so she stayed on, looking at other books in the anthropology library—ethnographies, histories, early accounts. The earliest visitors to the interior of the Congo were Arab slave traders and Portuguese merchants, and several had written accounts of their travels. Because Johnson could read neither Arabic nor Portuguese, she just looked at the plates.

And then she saw a picture that, she said, "sent a chill up my spine."

It was a Portuguese engraving originally dated 1642 and reprinted in an 1842 volume. The ink was yellowing on frayed brittle paper, but clearly visible was a ruined city in the jungle, overgrown with creeper vines and giant ferns. The doors and windows were constructed with semicircular arches, exactly as Amy had drawn them.

"It was," Elliot said later, "the kind of opportunity that comes to a researcher once in his lifetime—if he's lucky. Of course we knew nothing about the picture; the caption was written in flowing script and included a word that looked like 'Zinj,' and the date 1642. We immediately hired translators skilled in archaic Arabic and seventeenth-century Portuguese, but that wasn't the point. The point was we had a chance to verify a major theoretical question. Amy's pictures seemed to be a clear case of specific genetic memory."

43

Genetic memory was first proposed by Marais in 1911, and it has been vigorously debated ever since. In its simplest form, the theory proposed that the mechanism of genetic inheritance, which governed the transmission of all physical traits, was not limited to physical traits alone. Behavior was clearly genetically determined in lower animals, which were born with complex behavior that did not have to be learned. But higher animals had more flexible behavior, dependent on learning and memory. The question was whether higher animals, particularly apes and men, had any part of their psychic apparatus fixed from birth by their genes.

Now, Elliot felt, with Amy they had evidence for such a memory. Amy had been taken from Africa when she was only seven months old. Unless she had seen this ruined city in her infancy, her dreams represented a specific genetic memory which could be verified by a trip to Africa. By the evening of June 11, the Project Amy staff was agreed. If they could arrange it—and pay for it—they would take Amy back to Africa.

On June 12, the team waited for the translators to complete work on the source material. Checked translations were expected to be ready within two days. But a trip to Africa for Amy and two staff members would cost at least thirty thousand dollars, a substantial fraction of their total annual operating budget. And transporting a gorilla halfway around the world involved a bewildering tangle of customs regulations and bureaucratic red tape.

Clearly, they needed expert help, but they were not sure where to turn. And then, on June 13, a Dr. Karen Ross from one of their granting institutions, the Earth Resources Wildlife Fund, called from Houston to say that she was leading an expedition into the Congo in two days' time. And although she showed no interest in taking Peter Elliot or Amy with her, she conveyed—at least over the telephone—a confident familiarity with the way expeditions were assembled and managed in faroff places around the world.

When she asked if she could come to San Francisco to meet with Dr. Elliot, Dr. Elliot replied that he would be delighted to meet with her, at her convenience.

3. Legal Issues

Peter Elliot remembered June 14, 1979, as a day of sudden reverses. He began at 8 A.M. in the San Francisco law firm of Sutherland, Morton & O'Connell, because of the threatened custody suit from the PPA—a suit which became all the more important now that he was planning to take Amy out of the country.

He met with John Morton in the firm's wood-paneled library overlooking Grant Street. Morton took notes on a yellow legal pad. "I think you're all right," Morton began, "but let me get a few facts. Amy is a gorilla?"

"Yes, a female mountain gorilla."

"Age?"

"She's seven now."

"So she's still a child?"

Elliot explained that gorillas matured in six to eight years, so that Amy was late adolescent, the equivalent of a sixteen-year-old human female.

Morton scratched notes on a pad. "Could we say she's still a minor?"

"Do we want to say that?"

"I think so."

"Yes, she's still a minor," Elliot said.

"Where did she come from? I mean originally."

"A woman tourist named Swenson found her in Africa, in a village called Bagimindi. Amy's mother had been killed by the natives for food. Mrs. Swenson bought her as an infant."

"So she was not bred in captivity," Morton said, writing on his pad.

"No. Mrs. Swenson brought her back to the States and donated her to the Minneapolis zoo."

"She relinquished her interest in Amy?"

"I assume so," Elliot said. "We've been trying to reach Mrs. Swenson to ask about Amy's early life, but she's out of the country. Apparently she travels constantly; she's in Borneo. Anyway, when Amy was sent to San Francisco, I called the Minneapolis zoo to ask if I could keep her for study. The zoo said yes, for three years."

"Did you pay any money?"

"No."

"Was there a written contract?"

"No, I just called the zoo director."

Morton nodded. "Oral agreement . . ." he said, writing. "And when the three years were up?"

"That was the spring of 1976. I asked the zoo for an extension of six years, and they gave it to me."

"Again orally?"

"Yes. I called on the phone."

"No correspondence?"

"No. They didn't seem very interested when I called. To tell you the truth, I think they had forgotten about Amy. The zoo has four gorillas, anyway."

Morton frowned. "Isn't a gorilla a pretty expensive animal? I mean, if you wanted to buy one for a pet or for the circus."

"Gorillas are on the endangered list; you can't buy them as pets. But yes, they'd be pretty expensive."

"How expensive?"

"Well, there's no established market value, but it would be twenty or thirty thousand dollars."

"And all during these years, you have been teaching her language?"

"Yes," Peter said. "American Sign Language. She has a vocabulary of six hundred and twenty words now."

"Is that a lot?"

"More than any known primate."

Morton nodded, making notes. "You work with her every day in ongoing research?"

"Yes."

"Good," Morton said. "That's been very important in the animal custody cases so far."

For more than a hundred years, there had been organized movements in Western countries to stop animal experimentation. They were led by the anti-vivisectionists, the RSPCA, the ASPCA. Originally these organizations were a kind of lunatic fringe of animal lovers, intent on stopping all animal research.

Over the years, scientists had evolved a standard defense acceptable to the courts. Researchers claimed that their experiments had the goal of bettering the health and welfare of mankind, a higher priority than animal welfare. They pointed out that no one objected to animals being used as beasts of burden or for agricultural work—a life of drudgery to which animals had been subjected for thousands of years. Using animals in scientific experiments simply extended the idea that animals were the servants of human enterprises.

In addition, animals were literally brutes. They had no self-awareness, no recognition of their existence in nature. This meant, in the words of philosopher George H. Mead, that "animals have no rights. We are at liberty to cut off their lives; there is no wrong committed when an animal's life is taken away. He has not lost anything. . . ."

Many people were troubled by these views, but attempts to establish guidelines quickly ran into logical problems. The most obvious concerned the perceptions of animals further down the phylogenetic scale. Few researchers operated on dogs, cats, and other mammals without anesthesia, but what about annelid worms, crayfish, leeches, and squid? Ignoring these creatures was a form of "taxonomic discrimination." Yet if these animals deserved consideration, shouldn't it also be illegal to throw a live lobster into a pot of boiling water?

The question of what constituted cruelty to animals was confused by the animal societies themselves. In some countries, they fought the extermination of rats; and in 1968 there was the bizarre Australian pharmaceutical case.* In the face of these ironies, the courts hesitated to interfere with animal experimentation. As a practical matter, researchers were free to do as they wished. The volume of animal research was extraordinary: during the 1970s, sixty-four million animals were killed in experiments in the United States each year.

But attitudes had slowly changed. Language studies with dolphins and apes made it clear that these animals were not only intelligent but self-aware; they recognized themselves in mirrors and photographs. In 1974, scientists themselves formed the International Primate Protection League to monitor research involving monkeys and apes. In March, 1978, the Indian government banned the export of rhesus monkeys to research laboratories around the world. And there were court cases which concluded that in some instances animals did, indeed, have rights.

The old view was analogous to slavery: the animal was the property of its owner, who could do whatever he wished. But now ownership became secondary. In February, 1977, there was a case involving a dolphin named Mary, released by a lab technician into the open ocean. The University of Hawaii prosecuted the technician, charging loss of a valuable research animal. Two trials resulted in hung juries; the case was dropped.

In November, 1978, there was a custody case involving a chimpanzee named Arthur, who was fluent in sign language. His owner, Johns Hopkins University, decided to sell him and close the program. His trainer, William Levine, went to court and obtained custody on the grounds that Arthur knew language and thus was no longer a chimpanzee.

"One of the pertinent facts," Morton said, "was that when Arthur was confronted by other chimpanzees, he referred to them as 'black things.' And when Arthur was twice asked to sort photographs of people and photographs of

---

*A new pharmaceutical factory was built in Western Australia. In this factory all the pills came out on a conveyor belt; a person had to watch the belt, and press buttons to sort the pills into separate bins by size and color. A Skinnerian animal behaviorist pointed out that it would be simple to teach pigeons to watch the pills and peck colored keys to do the sorting process. Incredulous factory managers agreed to a test; the pigeons indeed performed reliably, and were duly placed on the assembly line. Then the RSPCA stepped in and put a stop to it on the grounds that it represented cruelty to animals; the job was turned over to a human operator, for whom it did not, apparently, represent cruelty.

chimps, he sorted them correctly except that both times he put his own picture in the stack with the people. He obviously did not consider himself a chimpanzee, and the court ruled that he should remain with his trainer, since any separation would cause him severe psychic distress."

"Amy cries when I leave her," Elliot said.

"When you conduct experiments, do you obtain her permission?"

"Always," Elliot smiled. Morton obviously had no sense of day-to-day life with Amy. It was essential to obtain her permission for any course of action, even a ride in a car. She was a powerful animal, and she could be willful and stubborn.

"Do you keep a record of her acquiescence?"

"Videotapes."

"Does she understand the experiments you propose?"

He shrugged. "She says she does."

"You follow a system of rewards and punishments?"

"All animal behaviorists do."

Morton frowned. "What forms do her punishments take?"

"Well, when she's a bad girl I make her stand in the corner facing the wall. Or else I send her to bed early without her peanut-butter-and-jelly snack."

"What about torture and shock treatments?"

"Ridiculous."

"You never physically punish the animal?"

"She's a pretty damn big animal. Usually I worry that she'll get mad and punish *me.*"

Morton smiled and stood. "You're going to be all right," he said. "Any court will rule that Amy is your ward and that you must decide any ultimate disposition in her case." He hesitated. "I know this sounds strange, but could you put Amy on the stand?"

"I guess so," Elliot said. "Do you think it will come to that?"

"Not in this case," Morton said, "but sooner or later it will. You watch: within ten years, there will be a custody case involving a language-using primate, and the ape will be in the witness-box."

Elliot shook his hand, and said as he was leaving, "By the way, would I have any problem taking her out of the country?"

"If there *is* a custody case, you could have trouble taking her across state lines," Morton said. "Are you planning to take her out of the country?"

"Yes."

"Then my advice is to do it fast, and don't tell anyone," Morton said.

Elliot entered his office on the third floor of the Zoology Department building shortly after nine. His secretary, Carolyn, said: "A Dr. Ross called from that Wildlife Fund in Houston; she's on her way to San Francisco. A Mr. Morikawa called three times, says it's important. The Project Amy staff meeting is set for ten o'clock. And Windy is in your office."

"Really?"

James Weldon was a senior professor in the Department, a weak, blustery man. "Windy" Weldon was usually portrayed in departmental cartoons as holding a wet finger in the air: he was a master at knowing which way the wind was blowing. For the past several days, he had avoided Peter Elliot and his staff.

Elliot went into his office.

"Well, Peter my boy," Weldon said, reaching out to give his version of a hearty handshake. "You're in early."

Elliot was instantly wary. "I thought I'd beat the crowds," he said. The picketers did not show up until ten o'clock, sometimes later, depending on when they had arranged to meet the TV news crews. That was how it worked these days: protest by appointment.

"They're not coming anymore." Weldon smiled.

He handed Elliot the late city edition of the *Chronicle,* a front-page story circled in black pen. Eleanor Vries had resigned her position as regional director of the PPA, pleading overwork and personal pressures; a statement from the PPA in New York indicated that they had seriously misconstrued the nature and content of Elliot's research.

"Meaning what?" Elliot asked.

"Belli's office reviewed your paper and Vries's public statements about torture, and decided that the PPA was exposed to a major libel suit," Weldon said. "The New York office is terrified. They'll be making overtures to you later today. Personally, I hope you'll be understanding."

Elliot dropped into his chair. "What about the faculty meeting next week?"

"Oh, that's essential," Weldon said. "There's no question that the faculty will want to discuss unethical conduct—on the part of the media, and issue a strong statement in your support. I'm drawing up a statement now, to come from my office."

The irony of this was not lost on Elliot. "You sure you want to go out on a limb?" he asked.

"I'm behind you one thousand percent, I hope you know that," Weldon said. Weldon was restless, pacing around the office, staring at the walls, which were covered with Amy's finger paintings. Windy had something further on his mind. "She's still making these same pictures?" he asked, finally.

"Yes," Elliot said.

"And you still have no idea what they mean?"

Elliot paused; at best it was premature to tell Weldon what they thought the pictures meant. "No idea," he said.

"Are you sure?" Weldon asked, frowning. "I think somebody knows what they mean."

"Why is that?"

"Something very strange has happened," Weldon said. "Someone has offered to buy Amy."

"To *buy* her? What are you talking about, to buy her?"

"A lawyer in Los Angeles called my office yesterday and offered to buy her for a hundred and fifty thousand dollars."

"It must be some rich do-gooder," Elliot said, "trying to save Amy from torture."

"I don't think so," Weldon said. "For one thing, the offer came from Japan. Someone named Morikawa—he's in electronics in Tokyo. I found that out when the lawyer called back this morning, to increase his offer to two hundred and fifty thousand dollars."

"Two hundred and fifty thousand dollars?" Elliot said. "For Amy?" Of course it was out of the question. He would never sell her. But why would anyone offer so much money?

Weldon had an answer. "This kind of money, a quarter of a million dollars, can only be coming from private enterprise. Industry. Clearly, Morikawa has read about your work and found a use for speaking primates in an industrial context." Windy stared at the ceiling, a sure sign he was about to wax eloquent. "I think a new field might be opening up here, the training of primates for industrial applications in the real world."

Peter Elliot swore. He was not teaching Amy language in order to put a hard hat on her head and a lunch pail in her hand, and he said so.

"You're not thinking it through," Weldon said. "What if we are on the verge of a new field of applied behavior for the great apes? Think what it means. Not only funding to the Department, and an opportunity for applied research. Most important, there would be a reason to keep these animals alive. You know that the great apes are becoming extinct. The chimps in Africa are greatly reduced in number. The orangs of Borneo are losing their natural habitat to the timber cutters and will be extinct in ten years. The gorilla is down to three thousand in the central African forests. These animals will all disappear in our lifetime—*unless there is a reason to keep them alive,* as a species. You may provide that reason, Peter my boy. Think about it."

Elliot did think about it, and he discussed it at the Project Amy staff meeting at ten o'clock. They considered possible industrial applications for apes, and possible advantages to employers, such as the lack of unions and fringe benefits. In the late twentieth century, these were major considerations. (In 1978, for each new automobile that rolled off the Detroit assembly lines, the cost of worker health benefits exceeded the cost of all the steel used to build the car.)

But they concluded that a vision of "industrialized apes" was wildly fanciful. An ape like Amy was not a cheap and stupid version of a human worker. Quite the opposite: Amy was a highly intelligent and complex creature out of her element in the modern industrial world. She demanded a great deal of supervision; she was whimsical and unreliable; and her health was always at risk. It simply didn't make sense to use her in industry. If Morikawa had visions of apes wielding soldering irons on a microelectronic assembly line, building TVs and hi-fi sets, he was sorely misinformed.

The only note of caution came from Bergman, the child psychologist. "A quarter of a million is a lot of money," he said, "and Mr. Morikawa is probably no fool. He must have learned about Amy through her drawings, which imply she is neurotic and difficult. If he's interested in her, I'd bet it's *because of her drawings.* But I can't imagine why those drawings should be worth a quarter of a million dollars."

Neither could anyone else, and the discussion turned to the drawings themselves, and the newly translated texts. Sarah Johnson, in charge of research, started out with the flat comment "I have bad news about the Congo."*

For most of recorded history, she explained, nothing was known about the Congo. The ancient Egyptians on the upper Nile knew only that their river originated far to the south, in a region they called the Land of Trees. This was a mysterious place with forests so dense they were as dark as night in the middle of the day. Strange creatures inhabited this perpetual gloom, including little men with tails, and animals half black and half white.

For nearly four thousand years afterward, nothing more substantial was learned about the interior of Africa. The Arabs came to East Africa in the seventh century A.D., in search of gold, ivory, spices, and slaves. But the Arabs were merchant seamen and did not venture inland. They called the interior Zinj—the Land of the Blacks—a region of fable and fantasy. There were stories of vast forests and tiny men with tails; stories of mountains that spewed fire and turned the sky black; stories of native villages overwhelmed by monkeys, which would have congress with the women; stories of great giants with hairy bodies and flat noses; stories of creatures half leopard, half man; stories of native markets where the fattened carcasses of men were butchered and sold as a delicacy.

Such stories were sufficiently forbidding to keep the Arabs on the coast, despite other stories equally alluring: mountains of shimmering gold, riverbeds gleaming with diamonds, animals that spoke the language of men, great jungle civilizations of unimaginable splendor. In particular, one story was repeated again and again in early accounts: the story of the Lost City of Zinj.

According to legend, a city known to the Hebrews of Solomonic times had been a source of inconceivable wealth in diamonds. The caravan route to the city had been jealously guarded, passed from father to son, as a sacred trust for generation after generation. But the diamond mines were exhausted and the city itself now lay in crumbling ruins, somewhere in the dark heart of Africa. The arduous caravan routes were long since swallowed up by jungle,

---

*Johnson's principal reference was the definitive work by A. J. Parkinson, *The Congo Delta in Myth and History* (London: Peters, 1904).

and the last trader who remembered the way had carried his secret with him to the grave many hundreds of years before.

This mysterious and alluring place the Arabs called the Lost City of Zinj.* Yet despite its enduring fame, Johnson could find few detailed descriptions of the city. In 1187 Ibn Baratu, an Arab in Mombasa, recorded that "the natives of the region tell . . . of a lost city far inland, called Zinj. There the inhabitants, who are black, once lived in wealth and luxury, and even the slaves decorated themselves with jewels and especially blue diamonds, for a great store of diamonds is there."

In 1292, a Persian named Mohammed Zaid stated that "a large diamond [the size] of a man's clenched fist . . . was exhibited on the streets of Zanzibar, and all said it had come from the interior, where the ruins of a city called Zinj may be found, and it is here that such diamonds may be found in profusion, scattered upon the ground and also in rivers. . . ."

In 1334, another Arab, Ibn Mohammed, stated that "our number made arrangements to seek out the city of Zinj, but quitted our quest upon learning that the city was long since abandoned, and much ruined. It is said that the aspect of the city is wondrous strange, for doors and windows are built in the curve of a half-moon, and the residences are now overtaken by a violent race of hairy men who speak in whispers no known language. . . ."

Then the Portuguese, those indefatigable explorers, arrived. By 1544, they were venturing inland from the west coast up the mighty Congo River, but they soon encountered all the obstacles that would prevent exploration of central Africa for hundreds of years to come. The Congo was not navigable beyond the first set of rapids, two hundred miles inland (at what was once Léopoldville, and is now Kinshasa). The natives were hostile and cannibalistic. And the hot steaming jungle was the source of disease—malaria, sleeping sickness, bilharzia, blackwater fever—which decimated foreign intruders.

The Portuguese never managed to penetrate the central Congo. Neither did the English, under Captain Brenner, in 1644; his entire party was lost. The Congo would remain for two hundred years as a blank spot on the civilized maps of the world.

But the early explorers repeated the legends of the interior, including the story of Zinj. A Portuguese artist, Juan Diego de Valdez, drew a widely acclaimed picture of the Lost City of Zinj in 1642. "But," Sarah Johnson said, "he also drew pictures of men with tails, and monkeys having carnal knowledge of native women."

Somebody groaned.

"Apparently Valdez was crippled," she continued. "He lived all his life in

*The fabled city of Zinj formed the basis for H. Rider Haggard's popular novel *King Solomon's Mines*, first published in 1885. Haggard, a gifted linguist, had served on the staff of the Governor of Natal in 1875, and he presumably heard of Zinj from the neighboring Zulus at that time.

the town of Setúbal, drinking with sailors and drawing pictures based on his conversations."

Africa was not thoroughly explored until the mid-nineteenth century, by Burton and Speke, Baker and Livingstone, and especially Stanley. No trace of the Lost City of Zinj was found by any of them. Nor had any trace of the apocryphal city been found in the hundred years since.

The gloom that descended over the Project Amy staff meeting was profound. "I told you it was bad news," Sarah Johnson said.

"You mean," Peter Elliot said, "that this picture is based on a description, and we don't know whether the city actually exists or not."

"I'm afraid so," Sarah Johnson said. "There is no proof that the city in the picture exists at all. It's just a story."

4. Resolution

Peter Elliot's unquestioned reliance on twentieth-century hard data—facts, figures, graphs—left him unprepared for the possibility that the 1642 engraving, in all its detail, was merely the fanciful speculation of an uninhibited artist. The news came as a shock.

Their plans to take Amy to the Congo suddenly appeared childishly naïve; the resemblance of her sketchy, schematic drawings to the 1642 Valdez engraving was obviously coincidental. How could they ever have imagined that a Lost City of Zinj was anything but the stuff of ancient fable? In the seventeenth-century world of widening horizons and new wonders, the idea of such a city would have seemed perfectly reasonable, even compelling. But in the computerized twentieth century, the Lost City of Zinj was as unlikely as Camelot or Xanadu. They had been fools ever to take it seriously. "The lost city doesn't exist," he said.

"Oh, it exists, all right," she said. "There's no doubt about *that.*"

Elliot glanced up quickly, and then he saw that Sarah Johnson had not answered him. A tall gangly girl in her early twenties stood at the back of the room. She might have been considered beautiful except for her cold, aloof demeanor. This girl was dressed in a severe, businesslike suit, and she carried a briefcase, which she now set on the table, popping the latches.

"I'm Dr. Ross," she announced, "from the Wildlife Fund, and I'd like your opinion of these pictures."

She passed around a series of photographs, which were viewed by the staff with an assortment of whistles and sighs. At the head of the table, Elliot waited impatiently until the photographs came down to him.

They were grainy black-and-white images with horizontal scanning line streaks, photographed off a video screen. But the image was unmistakable: a ruined city in the jungle, with curious inverted crescent-shaped doors and windows.

5. Amy

"**B**y satellite?" Elliot repeated, hearing the tension in his voice.

"That's right, the pictures were transmitted by satellite from Africa two days ago."

"Then you know the location of this ruin?"

"Of course."

"And your expedition leaves in a matter of hours?"

"Six hours and twenty-three minutes, to be exact," Ross said, glancing at her digital watch.

Elliot adjourned the meeting, and talked privately with Ross for more than an hour. Elliot later claimed that Ross had "deceived" him about the purpose of the expedition and the hazards they would face. But Elliot was eager to go, and probably not inclined to be too fussy about the reasons behind Ross's coming expedition, or the dangers involved. As a skilled grantsman, he had long ago grown comfortable with situations where other peoples' money and his own motivations did not exactly coincide. This was the cynical side of academic life: how much pure research had been funded because it might cure cancer? A researcher promised anything to get his money.

Apparently it never occurred to Elliot that Ross might be using him as coldly as he was using her. From the start Ross was never entirely truthful; she had been instructed by Travis to explain the ERTS Congo mission "with a little data dropout." Data dropout was second nature to her; everyone at ERTS had learned to say no more than was necessary. Elliot treated her as if she were an ordinary funding agency, and that was a serious mistake.

In the final analysis, Ross and Elliot misjudged each other, for each presented a deceptive appearance, and in the same way. Elliot appeared so shy and retiring that one Berkeley faculty member had commented, "It's no wonder he's devoted his life to apes; he can't work up the nerve to talk to people." But Elliot had been a tough middle linebacker in college, and his diffident academic demeanor concealed a head-crunching ambitious drive.

Similarly, Karen Ross, despite her youthful cheerleader beauty and soft, seductive Texas accent, possessed great intelligence and a deep inner toughness. (She had matured early, and a high-school teacher had once appraised her as "the very flower of virile Texas womanhood.") Ross felt responsible for the previous ERTS expedition, and she was determined to rectify past errors. It was at least possible that Elliot and Amy could help her when she got onsite; that was reason enough to take them with her. Beyond that, Ross was concerned about the consortium, which was obviously seeking Elliot, since Morikawa was calling. If she took Elliot and Amy with her, she removed a possible advantage to the consortium—again, reason enough to take them with her. Finally, she needed a cover in case her expedition was stopped at one of the borders—and a primatologist and an ape provided a perfect cover.

But in the end Karen Ross wanted only the Congo diamonds—and she was prepared to say anything, do anything, sacrifice anything to get them.

In photographs taken at San Francisco airport, Elliot and Ross appeared as two smiling, youthful academics, embarking on a lark of an expedition to Africa. But in fact, their motivations were different, and grimly held. Elliot was reluctant to tell her how theoretical and academic his goals were—and Ross was reluctant to admit how pragmatic were hers.

In any case, by midday on June 14, Karen Ross found herself riding with Peter Elliot in his battered Fiat sedan along Hallowell Road, going past the University athletic field. She had some misgivings: they were going to meet Amy.

Elliot unlocked the door with its red sign DO NOT DISTURB ANIMAL EXPERIMENTATION IN PROGRESS. Behind the door, Amy was grunting and scratching impatiently. Elliot paused.

"When you meet her," he said, "remember that she is a gorilla and not a human being. Gorillas have their own etiquette. Don't speak loudly or make any sudden movements until she gets used to you. If you smile, don't show your teeth, because bared teeth are a threat. And keep your eyes downcast, because direct stares from strangers are considered hostile. Don't stand too close to me or touch me, because she's very jealous. If you talk to her, don't lie. Even though she uses sign language, she understands most human speech, and we usually just talk to her. She can tell when you're lying and she doesn't like it."

"She doesn't like it?"

"She dismisses you, won't talk to you, and gets bitchy."

"Anything else?"

"No, it should be okay." He smiled reassuringly. "We have this traditional greeting, even though she's getting a little big for it." He opened the door, braced himself, and said, "Good morning, Amy."

A huge black shape came leaping out through the open door into his arms. Elliot staggered back under the impact. Ross was astonished by the size of the animal. She had been imagining something smaller and cuter. Amy was as large as an adult human female.

Amy kissed Elliot on the cheek with her large lips, her black head seeming enormous alongside his. Her breath steamed his glasses. Ross smelled a sweet-ish odor, and watched as he gently unwrapped her long arms from around his shoulders. "Amy happy this morning?" he asked.

Amy's fingers moved quickly near her cheek, as if she were brushing away flies.

"Yes, I was late today," Elliot said.

She moved her fingers again, and Ross realized that Amy was signing. The speed was surprising; she had expected something much slower and more de-liberate. She noticed that Amy's eyes never left Elliot's face. She was extraor-dinarily attentive, focusing on him with total animal watchfulness. She seemed to absorb everything, his posture, his expression, his tone of voice, as well as his words.

"I had to work," Elliot said. She sighed again quickly, like human gestures of dismissal. "Yes, that's right, people work." He led Amy back into the trailer, and motioned for Karen Ross to follow. Inside the trailer, he said, "Amy, this is Dr. Ross. Say hello to Dr. Ross."

Amy looked at Karen Ross suspiciously.

"Hello, Amy," Karen Ross said, smiling at the floor. She felt a little foolish behaving this way, but Amy was large enough to frighten her.

Amy stared at Karen Ross for a moment, then walked away, across the trailer to her easel. She had been fingerpainting, and now resumed this activ-ity, ignoring them.

"What's that mean?" Ross said. She distinctly felt she was being snubbed.

"We'll see," Elliot said.

After a few moments, Amy ambled back, walking on her knuckles. She went directly to Karen Ross, sniffed her crotch, and examined her minutely. She seemed particularly interested in Ross's leather purse, which had a shiny brass clasp. Ross said later that "it was just like any cocktail party in Houston. I was being checked out by another woman. I had the feeling that any minute she was going to ask me where I bought my clothes."

That was not the outcome, however. Amy reached up and deliberately streaked globs of green finger paint on Ross's skirt.

"I don't think this is going too well," Karen Ross said.

* * *

56

Elliot had watched the progress of this first meeting with more apprehension than he was willing to admit. Introducing new humans to Amy was often difficult, particularly if they were women.

Over the years, Elliot had come to recognize many distinctly "feminine" traits in Amy. She could be coy, she responded to flattery, she was preoccupied with her appearance, loved makeup, and was very fussy about the color of the sweaters she wore in the winter. She preferred men to women, and she was openly jealous of Elliot's girl friends. He rarely brought them around to meet her, but sometimes in the morning she would sniff him for perfume, and she always commented if he had not changed his clothing overnight.

This situation might have been amusing if not for the fact that Amy made occasional unprovoked attacks on strange women. And an attack by Amy was never amusing.

Amy returned to the easel and signed, *No like woman no like Amy no like go away away.*

"Come on, Amy, be a good gorilla," Peter said.

"What did she say?" Ross asked, going to the sink to wash the finger paint from her dress. Peter noticed that she did not squeal and shriek as many visitors did when they received an unfriendly greeting from Amy.

"She said she likes your dress," he said.

Amy shot him a look, as she always did whenever Elliot mistranslated her. *Amy not lie. Peter not lie.*

"Be nice, Amy," he said. "Karen is a nice human person."

Amy grunted, and returned to her work, painting rapidly.

"What happens now?" Karen Ross said.

"Give her time." He smiled reassuringly. "She needs time to adjust."

He did not bother to explain that it was much worse with chimpanzees. Chimps threw feces at strangers, and even at workers they knew well; they sometimes attacked to establish dominance. Chimpanzees had a strong need to determine who was in charge. Fortunately, gorillas were much less formal in their dominance hierarchies, and less violent.

At that moment, Amy ripped the paper from the easel and shredded it noisily, flinging the pieces around the room.

"Is this part of the adjustment?" Karen Ross asked. She seemed more amused than frightened.

"Amy, cut it out," Peter said, allowing his tone to convey irritation. "Amy . . ."

Amy sat in the middle of the floor, surrounded by the paper. She tore it angrily and signed, *This woman. This woman.* It was classic displacement behavior. Whenever gorillas did not feel comfortable with direct aggression, they did something symbolic. In symbolic terms, she was now tearing Karen Ross apart.

And she was getting worked up, beginning what the Project Amy staff called "sequencing." Just as human beings first became red-faced, and then tensed their bodies, and then shouted and threw things before they finally resorted to direct physical aggression, so gorillas passed through a stereotyped behavioral sequence on the way to physical aggression. Tearing up paper, or grass, would be followed by lateral crablike movements and grunts. Then she would slap the ground, making as much noise as possible.

And then Amy would charge, if he didn't interrupt the sequence.

"Amy," he said sternly. "Karen button woman."

Amy stopped shredding. In her world, "button" was the acknowledged term for a person of high status.

Amy was extremely sensitive to individual moods and behavior, and she had no difficulty observing the staff and deciding who was superior to whom. But among strangers, Amy as a gorilla was utterly impervious to formal human status cues; the principal indicators—clothing, bearing, and speech—had no meaning to her.

As a young animal, she had inexplicably attacked policemen. After several biting episodes and threatened lawsuits, they finally learned that Amy found police uniforms with their shiny buttons clownlike and ridiculous; she assumed that anyone so foolishly dressed must be of inferior status and safe to attack. After they had taught her the concept of "button," she treated anyone in uniform with deference.

Amy now stared at "button" Ross with new respect. Surrounded by the torn paper, she seemed suddenly embarrassed, as if she had made a social error. Without being told, she went and stood in the corner, facing the wall.

"What's that about?" Ross said.

"She knows she's been bad."

"You make her stand in the corner, like a child? She didn't mean any harm." Before Elliot could warn against it, she went over to Amy. Amy stared steadfastly at the corner.

Ross unshouldered her purse and set it on the floor within Amy's reach. Nothing happened for a moment. Then Amy took the purse, looked at Karen, then looked at Peter.

Peter said, "She'll wreck whatever's inside."

"That's all right."

Amy immediately opened the brass clasp, and dumped the contents on the floor. She began sifting through, signing, *Lipstick lipstick, Amy like Amy want lipstick want.*

"She wants lipstick."

Ross bent over and found it for her. Amy removed the cap and smeared a red circle on Karen's face. She then smiled and grunted happily, and crossed the room to her mirror, which was mounted on the floor. She applied lipstick.

"I think we're doing better," Karen Ross said.

Across the room, Amy squatted by the mirror, happily making a mess of her face. She grinned at her smart image, then applied lipstick to her teeth. It seemed a good time to ask her the question. "Amy want take trip?" Peter said.

Amy loved trips, and regarded them as special treats. After an especially good day, Elliot often took her for a ride to a nearby drive-in, where she would have an orange drink, sucking it through the straw and enjoying the commotion she caused among the other people there. Lipstick and an offer of a trip was almost too much pleasure for one morning. She signed, *Car trip?*

"No, not in the car. A long trip. Many days."

Leave house?

"Yes, leave house. Many days."

This made her suspicious. The only times she had left the house for many days had been during hospitalizations for pneumonia and urinary-tract infections; they had not been pleasant trips. She signed, *Where go trip?*

"To the jungle, Amy."

There was a long pause. At first he thought she had not understood, but she knew the word for jungle, and she should be able to put it all together. Amy signed thoughtfully to herself, repetitively as she always did when she was mulling things over: *Jungle trip trip jungle go trip jungle go.* She set aside her lipstick. She stared at the bits of paper on the floor, and then she began to pick them up and put them in the wastebasket.

"What does that mean?" Karen Ross asked.

"That means Amy wants to take a trip," Peter Elliot said.

6. Departure

The hinged nose of the Boeing 747 cargo jet lay open like a jaw, exposing the cavernous, brightly lit interior. The plane had been flown up from Houston to San Francisco that afternoon; it was now nine o'clock at night, and puzzled workers were loading on the large aluminum travel cage, boxes of vitamin pills, a portable potty, and cartons of toys. One workman pulled out a Mickey Mouse drinking cup and stared at it, shaking his head.

Outside on the concrete, Elliot stood with Amy, who covered her ears against the whine of the jet engines. She signed to Peter, *Birds noisy.*

"We fly bird, Amy," he said.

Amy had never flown before, and had never seen an airplane at close hand. *We go car,* she decided, looking at the plane.

"We can't go by car. We fly."

Fly where fly? Amy signed.

"Fly jungle."

This seemed to perplex her, but he did not want to explain further. Like all gorillas, Amy had an aversion to water, refusing to cross even small streams. He knew she would be distressed to hear that they would be flying over large bodies of water. Changing the subject, he suggested they board the plane and look around. As they climbed the sloping ramp up the nose, Amy signed, *Where button woman?*

He had not seen Ross for the last five hours, and was surprised to discover that she was already on board, talking on a telephone mounted on a wall of the cargo hold, one hand cupped over her free ear to block the noise. Elliot overheard her say, "Well, Irving seems to think it's enough. . . . Yes, we have four nine-oh-seven units and we are prepared to match and absorb. Two micro HUDs, that's all. . . . Yes, why not?" She finished the call, turned to Elliot and Amy.

"Everything okay?" he asked.

"Fine. I'll show you around." She led him deeper into the cargo hold, with Amy at his side. Elliot glanced back and saw the chauffeur coming up the ramp with a series of numbered metal boxes marked INTEC, INC. followed by serial numbers.

"This," Karen Ross said, "is the main cargo hold." It was filled with four-wheel-drive trucks, Land Cruisers, amphibious vehicles, inflatable boats, and racks of clothing, equipment, food—all tagged with computer codes, all loaded in modules. Ross explained that ERTS could outfit expeditions to any geographical and climatic condition in a matter of hours. She kept emphasizing the speed possible with computer assembly.

"Why the rush?" Elliot asked.

"It's business," Karen Ross said. "Four years ago, there were no companies like ERTS. Now there are nine around the world, and what they all sell is competitive advantage, meaning speed. Back in the sixties, a company—say, an oil company—might spend months or years investigating a possible site. But that's no longer competitive; business decisions are made in weeks or days. The pace of everything has speeded up. We're already looking to the nineteen-eighties, where we'll provide answers in *hours*. Right now the average ERTS contract runs a little under three weeks, or five hundred hours. But by 1990 there will be 'close of business' data—an executive can call us in the morning for information anywhere in the world, and have a complete report transmitted by computer to his desk before close of business that evening, say ten to twelve hours."

As they continued the tour, Elliot noticed that although the trucks and vehicles caught the eye first, much of the aircraft storage space was given over to aluminum modules marked "C3I."

"That's right," Ross said. "Command-Control Communications and

Intelligence. They're micronic components, the most expensive budget item we carry. When we started outfitting expeditions, twelve percent of the cost went to electronics. Now it's up to thirty-one percent, and climbing every year. It's field communications, remote sensing, defense, and so on."

She led them to the rear of the plane, where there was a modular living area, nicely furnished, with a large computer console, and bunks for sleeping.

Amy signed, *Nice house.*

"Yes, it is nice."

They were introduced to Jensen, a young bearded geologist, and to Irving, who announced that he was the "triple E." The two men were running some kind of probability study on the computer but they paused to shake hands with Amy, who regarded them gravely, and then turned her attention to the screen. Amy was captivated by the colorful screen images and bright LEDs, and kept trying to punch the keys herself. She signed, *Amy play box.*

"Not now, Amy," Elliot said, and swatted her hands away.

Jensen asked, "Is she always this way?"

"I'm afraid so," Elliot said. "She likes computers. She's worked around them ever since she was very young, and she thinks of them as her private property." And then he added, "What's a triple E?"

"Expedition electronic expert," Irving said cheerfully. He was a short man with an impish quick smile. "Doing the best I can. We picked up some stuff from Intec, that's about all. God knows what the Japanese and the Germans will throw at us."

"Oh, damn, there she goes," Jensen said, laughing as Amy pushed the keyboard.

Elliot said, "Amy, no!"

"It's just a game. Probably not interesting to apes," Jensen said. And he added, "She can't hurt anything."

Amy signed, *Amy good gorilla,* and pushed the keys on the computer again. She appeared relaxed, and Elliot was grateful for the distraction the computer provided. He was always amused by the sight of Amy's heavy dark form before a computer console. She would touch her lower lip thoughtfully before pushing the keys, in what seemed a parody of human behavior.

Ross, practical as always, brought them back to mundane matters. "Will Amy sleep on one of the bunks?"

Elliot shook his head. "No. Gorillas expect to make a fresh bed each night. Give her some blankets, and she'll twist them into a nest on the floor and sleep there."

Ross nodded. "What about her vitamins and medications? Will she swallow pills?"

"Ordinarily you have to bribe her, or hide the pills in a piece of banana. She tends to gulp banana, without chewing it."

"Without chewing." Ross nodded as if that were important. "We have a standard issue," she said. "I'll see that she gets them."

"She takes the same vitamins that people do, except that she'll need lots of ascorbic acid."

"We issue three thousand units a day. That's enough? Good. And she'll tolerate anti-malarials? We have to start them right away."

"Generally speaking," Elliot said, "she has the same reaction to medication as people."

Ross nodded. "Will the cabin pressurization bother her? It's set at five thousand feet."

Elliot shook his head. "She's a mountain gorilla, and they live at five thousand to nine thousand feet, so she's actually altitude-adapted. But she's acclimated to a moist climate and she dehydrates quickly; we'll have to keep forcing fluids on her."

"Can she use the head?"

"The seat's probably too high for her," Elliot said, "but I brought her potty."

"She'll use her potty?"

"Sure."

"I have a new collar for her; will she wear it?"

"If you give it to her as a gift."

As they reviewed other details of Amy's requirements, Elliot realized that something had happened during the last few hours, almost without his knowing it: Amy's unpredictable, dream-driven neurotic behavior had fallen away. It was as if the earlier behavior was irrelevant; now that she was going on a trip, she was no longer moody and introspective, her interests were outgoing; she was once again a youthful female gorilla. He found himself wondering whether her dreams, her depression—finger paintings, everything—were a result of her confined laboratory environment for so many years. At first the laboratory had been agreeable, like a crib for young children. But perhaps in later years it pinched. Perhaps, he thought, Amy just needed a little excitement.

Excitement was in the air: as he talked with Ross, Elliot felt something remarkable was about to happen. This expedition with Amy was the first example of an event primate researchers had predicted for years—the Pearl thesis.

Frederick Pearl was a theoretical animal behaviorist. At a meeting of the American Ethnological Society in New York in 1972, he had said, "Now that primates have learned sign language, it is only a matter of time until someone takes an animal into the field to assist the study of wild animals of the same species. We can imagine language-skilled primates acting as interpreters or perhaps even as ambassadors for mankind, in contact with wild creatures."

Pearl's thesis attracted considerable attention, and funding from the U.S. Air Force, which had supported linguistic research since the 1960s. According to one story, the Air Force had a secret project called CONTOUR, involving possible contact with alien life forms. The official military position was that UFOs were of natural origin—but the military was covering its bets. Should alien contact occur, linguistic fundamentals were obviously critically important. And taking primates into the field was seen as an example of contact with "alien intelligence"; hence the Air Force funding.

Pearl predicted that fieldwork would be undertaken before 1976, but in fact no one had yet done it. The reason was that on closer examination, no one could figure out quite what the advantages were—most language-using primates were as baffled by wild primates as human beings were. Some, like the chimpanzee Arthur, denied any association with their own kind, referring to them as "black things." (Amy, who had been taken to the zoo to view other gorillas, recognized them but was haughty, calling them "stupid gorillas" once she found that when she signed to them, they did not reply.)

Such observations led another researcher, John Bates, to say in 1977 that "we are producing an educated animal élite which demonstrates the same snobbish aloofness that a Ph.D. shows toward a truck driver. . . . It is highly unlikely that the generation of language-using primates will be skillful ambassadors in the field. They are simply too disdainful."

But the truth was that no one really knew what would happen when a primate was taken into the field. Because no one had done it: Amy would be the first.

At eleven o'clock, the ERTS cargo plane taxied down the runway at San Francisco International, lifted ponderously into the air, and headed east through the darkness toward Africa.

DAY 3: TANGIER

JUNE 15, 1979

1. Ground Truth

Peter Elliot had known Amy since infancy. He prided himself on his ability to predict her responses, although he had only known her in a laboratory setting. Now, as she was faced with new situations, her behavior surprised him.

Elliot had anticipated Amy would be terrified of the takeoff, and had prepared a syringe with Thoralen tranquilizer. But sedation proved unnecessary. Amy watched Jensen and Irving buckle their seat belts, and she immediately buckled herself in, too; she seemed to regard the procedure as an amusing, if simpleminded, game. And although her eyes widened when she heard the full roar of the engines, the human beings around her did not seem disturbed, and Amy imitated their bored indifference, raising her eyebrows and sighing at the tedium of it all.

Once airborne, however, Amy looked out the window and immediately panicked. She released her seat belt and scurried back and forth across the passenger compartment, moving from window to window, knocking people aside in whimpering terror while she signed, *Where ground ground where ground?* Outside, the ground was black and indistinct. *Where ground?* Elliot shot her with Thoralen and then began grooming her, sitting her down and plucking at her hair.

In the wild, primates devoted several hours each day to grooming one another, removing ticks and lice. Grooming behavior was important in ordering the group's social dominance structure—there was a pattern by which animals groomed each other, and with what frequency. And, like back rubs for people, grooming seemed to have a soothing, calming effect. Within minutes, Amy had relaxed enough to notice that the others were drinking, and she promptly demanded a "green drop drink"—her term for a martini with an olive—and a cigarette. She was allowed this on special occasions such as departmental parties, and Elliot now gave her a drink and a cigarette.

But the excitement proved too much for her: an hour later, she was quietly looking out the window and signing *Nice picture* to herself when she vomited. She apologized abjectly, *Amy sorry Amy mess Amy Amy sorry.*

"It's all right, Amy," Elliot assured her, stroking the back of her head. Soon afterward, signing *Amy sleep now,* she twisted the blankets into a nest on the floor and went to sleep, snoring loudly through her broad nostrils. Lying next to her, Elliot thought, how do other gorillas get to sleep with this racket?

Elliot had his own reaction to the journey. When he had first met Karen Ross, he assumed she was an academic like himself. But this enormous airplane filled with computerized equipment, the acronymic complexity of the entire operation suggested that Earth Resources Technology had powerful resources behind it, perhaps even a military association.

Karen Ross laughed. "We're much too organized to be military." She then told him the background of the ERTS interest in Virunga. Like the Project Amy staff, Karen Ross had also stumbled upon the legend of the Lost City of Zinj. But she had drawn very different conclusions from the story.

During the last three hundred years, there had been several attempts to reach the lost city. In 1692, John Marley, an English adventurer, led an expedition of two hundred into the Congo; it was never heard from again. In 1744, a Dutch expedition went in; in 1804, another British party led by a Scottish aristocrat, Sir James Taggert, approached Virunga from the north, getting as far as the Rawana bend of the Ubangi River. He sent an advance party farther south, but it never returned.

In 1872, Stanley passed near the Virunga region but did not enter it; in 1899, a German expedition went in, losing more than half its party. A privately financed Italian expedition disappeared entirely in 1911. There had been no more recent searches for the Lost City of Zinj.

"So no one has ever found it," Elliot said.

Ross shook her head. "I think several expeditions found the city," she said. "But nobody ever got back out again."

Such an outcome was not necessarily mysterious. The early days of African exploration were incredibly hazardous. Even carefully managed expeditions lost half of their party or more. Those who did not succumb to malaria, sleeping sickness, and blackwater fever faced rivers teeming with crocodiles and hippos, jungles with leopards and suspicious, cannibalistic natives. And, for all its luxuriant growth, the rain forest provided little edible food; a number of expeditions had starved to death.

"I began," Ross said to Elliot, "with the idea that the city existed, after all. Assuming it existed, where would I find it?"

The Lost City of Zinj was associated with diamond mines, and diamonds were found with volcanoes. This led Ross to look along the Great Rift Valley—an enormous geological fault thirty miles wide, which sliced vertically up the eastern third of the continent for a distance of fifteen hundred miles. The Rift Valley was so huge that its existence was not recognized until the 1890s, when a geologist named Gregory noticed that the cliff walls thirty miles apart were composed of the same rocks. In modern terms the Great Rift was actually an abortive attempt to form an ocean, for the eastern third of the continent had begun splitting off from the rest of the African land mass two hundred million years ago; for some reason, it had stopped before the break was complete.

On a map the Great Rift depression was marked by two features: a series of thin vertical lakes—Malawi, Tanganyika, Kivu, Mobutu—and a series of volcanoes, including the only active volcanoes in Africa at Virunga. Three volcanoes in the Virunga chain were active: Mukenko, Mubuti, and Kanagarawi. They rose 11,000–15,000 feet above the Rift Valley to the east, and the Congo Basin to the west. Thus Virunga seemed a good place to look for diamonds. Her next step was to investigate the ground truth.

"What's ground truth?" Peter asked.

"At ERTS, we deal mostly in remote sensing," she explained. "Satellite photographs, aerial run-bys, radar side scans. We carry millions of remote images, but there's no substitute for ground truth, the experience of a team actually on the site, finding out what's there. I started with the preliminary expedition we sent in looking for gold. They found diamonds as well." She punched buttons on the console, and the screen images changed, glowing with dozens of flashing pinpoints of light.

"This shows the placer deposit locations in streambeds near Virunga. You see the deposits form concentric semicircles leading back to the volcanoes. The obvious conclusion is that diamonds were eroded from the slopes of the Virunga volcanoes, and washed down the streams to their present locations."

"So you sent in a party to look for the source?"

"Yes." She pointed to the screen. "But don't be deceived by what you see here. This satellite image covers fifty thousand square kilometers of jungle. Most of it has never been seen by white men. It's hard terrain, with visibility limited to a few meters in any direction. An expedition could search that area for years, passing within two hundred meters of the city and failing to see it. So I needed to narrow the search sector. I decided to see if I could find the city."

"Find the city? From satellite pictures?"

"Yes," she said. "And I found it."

The rain forests of the world had traditionally frustrated remote-sensing technology. The great jungle trees spread an impenetrable canopy of vegetation, concealing whatever lay beneath. In aerial or satellite pictures, the Congo rain forest appeared as a vast, undulating carpet of featureless and monotonous green. Even large features, rivers fifty or a hundred feet wide, were hidden beneath this leafy canopy, invisible from the air.

So it seemed unlikely she would find any evidence for a lost city in aerial photographs. But Ross had a different idea: she would utilize the very vegetation that obscured her vision of the ground.

The study of vegetation was common in temperate regions, where the foliage underwent seasonal changes. But the equatorial rain forest was unchanging: winter or summer, the foliage remained the same. Ross turned her attention to another aspect, the differences in vegetation albedo.

Albedo was technically defined as the ratio of electromagnetic energy reflected by a surface to the amount of energy incident upon it. In terms of the visible spectrum, it was a measure of how "shiny" a surface was. A river had a high albedo, since water reflected most of the sunlight striking it. Vegetation absorbed light, and therefore had a low albedo. Starting in 1977, ERTS developed computer programs which measured albedo precisely, making very fine distinctions.

Ross asked herself the question: If there was a lost city, what signature might appear in the vegetation? There was an obvious answer: late secondary jungle.

The untouched or virgin rain forest was called primary jungle. Primary jungle was what most people thought of when they thought of rain forests: huge hardwood trees, mahogany and teak and ebony, and underneath a lower layer of ferns and palms, clinging to the ground. Primary jungle was dark and forbidding, but actually easy to move through. However, if the primary jungle was cleared by man and later abandoned, an entirely different secondary growth took over. The dominant plants were softwoods and fast-growing trees, bamboo and thorny tearing vines, which formed a dense and impenetrable barrier.

But Ross was not concerned about any aspect of the jungle except its albedo. Because the secondary plants were different, secondary jungle had a different albedo from primary jungle. And it could be graded by age: unlike the hardwood trees of primary jungle, which lived hundreds of years, the softwoods of secondary jungle lived only twenty years or so. Thus as time went on, the secondary jungle was replaced by another form of secondary jungle, and later by still another form.

By checking regions where late secondary jungle was generally found—such as the banks of large rivers, where innumerable human settlements had been cleared and abandoned—Ross confirmed that the ERTS computers could, indeed, measure the necessary small differences in reflectivity.

She then instructed the ERTS scanners to search for albedo differences of .03 or less, with a unit signature size of a hundred meters or less, across the fifty thousand square kilometers of rain forest on the western slopes of the Virunga volcanoes. This job would occupy a team of fifty human aerial photographic analysts for thirty-one years. The computer scanned 129,000 satellite and aerial photographs in under nine hours.

And found her city.

In May, 1979, Ross had a computer image showing a very old secondary jungle pattern laid out in a geometric, gridlike form. The pattern was located 2 degrees north of the equator, longitude 3 degrees, on the western slopes of the active volcano Mukenko. The computer estimated the age of the secondary jungle at five hundred to eight hundred years.

"So you sent an expedition in?" Elliot said.

Ross nodded. "Three weeks ago, led by a South African named Kruger.

The expedition confirmed the placer diamond deposits, went on to search for the origin, and found the ruins of the city."

"And then what happened?" Elliot asked.

He ran the videotape a second time.

Onscreen he saw black-and-white images of the camp, destroyed, smoldering. Several dead bodies with crushed skulls were visible. As they watched, a shadow moved over the dead bodies, and the camera zoomed back to show the outline of the lumbering shadow. Elliot agreed that it looked like the shadow of a gorilla, but he insisted, "Gorillas couldn't do this. Gorillas are peaceful, vegetarian animals."

They watched as the tape ran to the end. And then they reviewed her final computer-reconstituted image, which clearly showed the head of a male gorilla.

"That's ground truth," Ross said.

Elliot was not so sure. He reran the last three seconds of videotape a final time, staring at the gorilla head. The image was fleeting, leaving a ghostly trail, but something was wrong with it. He couldn't quite identify what. Certainly this was atypical gorilla behavior, but there was something else. . . . He pushed the freeze-frame button and stared at the frozen image. The face and the fur were both gray: unquestionably gray.

"Can we increase contrast?" he asked Ross. "This image is washed out."

"I don't know," Ross said, touching the controls. "I think this is a pretty good image." She was unable to darken it.

"It's very gray," he said. "Gorillas are much darker."

"Well, this contrast range is correct for video."

Elliot was sure this creature was too light to be a mountain gorilla. Either they were seeing a new race of animal, *or a new species*. A new species of great ape, gray in color, aggressive in behavior, discovered in the eastern Congo. . . . He had come on this expedition to verify Amy's dreams—a fascinating psychological insight—but now the stakes were suddenly much higher.

Ross said, "You don't think this is a gorilla?"

"There are ways to test it," he said. He stared at the screen, frowning, as the plane flew onward in the night.

2. B-8 Problems

"**Y**ou want me to *what?*" Tom Seamans said, cradling the phone in his shoulder and rolling over to look at his bedside clock. It was 3 A.M.

"Go to the zoo," Elliot repeated. His voice sounded garbled, as if coming from under water.

"Peter, where are you calling from?"

"We're somewhere over the Atlantic now," Elliot said. "On our way to Africa."

"Is everything all right?"

"Everything is fine," Elliot said. "But I want you to go to the zoo first thing in the morning."

"And do what?"

"Videotape the gorillas. Try to get them in movement. That's very important for the discriminant function, that they be moving."

"I'd better write this down," Seamans said. Seamans handled the computer programming for the Project Amy staff, and he was accustomed to unusual requests, but not in the middle of the night. "What discriminant function?"

"While you're at it, run any films we have in the library of gorillas—any gorillas, wild or in zoos or whatever. The more specimens the better, so long as they're moving. And for a baseline, you'd better use chimps. Anything we have on chimps. Transfer it to tape and put it through the function."

"What function?" Seamans yawned.

"The function you're going to write," Elliot said. "I want a multiple variable discriminant function based on total imagery—"

"You mean a pattern-recognition function?" Seamans had written pattern-recognition functions for Amy's language use, enabling them to monitor her signing around the clock. Seamans was proud of that program; in its own way, it was highly inventive.

"However you structure it," Elliot said. "I just want a function that'll discriminate gorillas from other primates like chimps. A species-differentiating function."

"Are you kidding?" Seamans said. "That's a B-8 problem." In the developing field of pattern-recognition computer programs, so-called B-8 problems

72

were the most difficult; whole teams of researchers had devoted years to trying to teach computers the difference between "B" and "8"—precisely because the difference was so obvious. But what was obvious to the human eye was not obvious to the computer scanner. The scanner had to be told, and the specific instructions turned out to be far more difficult than anyone anticipated, particularly for handwritten characters.

Now Elliot wanted a program that would distinguish between similar visual images of gorillas and chimps. Seamans could not help asking, "Why? It's pretty obvious. A gorilla is a gorilla, and a chimp is a chimp."

"Just do it," Elliot said.

"Can I use size?" On the basis of size alone, gorillas and chimps could be accurately distinguished. But visual functions could not determine size unless the distance from the recording instrument to the subject image was known, as well as the focal length of the recording lens.

"No, you can't use size," Elliot said. "Element morphology only."

Seamans sighed. "Thanks a lot. What resolution?"

"I need ninety-five-percent confidence limits on species assignment, to be based on less than three seconds of black-and-white scan imagery."

Seamans frowned. Obviously, Elliot had three seconds of videotape imagery of some animal and he was not sure whether it was a gorilla or not. Elliot had seen enough gorillas over the years to know the difference: gorillas and chimps were utterly different animals in size, appearance, movement, and behavior. They were as different as intelligent oceanic mammals—say, porpoises and whales. In making such discriminations, the human eye was far superior to any computer program that could be devised. Yet Elliot apparently did not trust his eye. What was he thinking of?

"I'll try," Seamans said, "but it's going to take a while. You don't write that kind of program overnight."

"I need it overnight, Tom," Elliot said. "I'll call you back in twenty-four hours."

3. Inside the Coffin

In one corner of the 747 living module was a sound-baffled fiberglass booth, with a hinged hood and a small CRT screen; it was called "the coffin" because of the claustrophobic feeling that came from working inside it. As the airplane crossed the mid-Atlantic, Ross stepped inside the coffin. She had a last look at Elliot and Amy—both asleep, both snoring loudly—and Jensen and Irving playing "submarine chase" on the computer console, as she lowered the hood.

Ross was tired, but she did not expect to get much sleep for the next two weeks, which was as long as she thought the expedition would last. Within fourteen days—336 hours—Ross's team would either have beaten the Euro-Japanese consortium or she would have failed and the Zaire Virunga mineral exploration rights would be lost forever.

The race was already under way, and Karen Ross did not intend to lose it.

She punched Houston coordinates, including her own sender designation, and waited while the scrambler interlocked. From now on, there would be a signal delay of five seconds at both ends, because both she and Houston would be sending in coded burst transmissions to elude passive listeners.

The screen glowed: TRAVIS.

She typed back: ROSS. She picked up the telephone receiver.

"It's a bitch," Travis said, although it was not Travis's voice, but a computer-generated flat audio signal, without expression.

"Tell me," Ross said.

"The consortium's are rolling," Travis's surrogate voice said.

"Details," Ross said, and waited for the five-second delay. She could imagine Travis in the CCR in Houston, hearing her own computer-generated voice. That flat voice required a change in speech patterns; what was ordinarily conveyed by phrasing and emphasis had to be made explicit.

"They know you're on your way," Travis's voice whined. "They are pushing their own schedule. The Germans are behind it—your friend Richter. I'm arranging a feeding in a matter of minutes. That's the good news."

"And the bad news?"

"The Congo has gone to hell in the last ten hours," Travis said. "We have a nasty GPU."

"Print," she said.

On the screen, she saw printed GEOPOLITICAL UPDATE, followed by a dense paragraph. It read:

ZAIRE EMBASSY WASHINGTON STATES EASTERN BORDERS VIA RWANDA CLOSED / NO EXPLANATION / PRESUMPTION IDI AMIN TROOPS FLEEING TANZANIAN INVASION UGANDA INTO EASTERN ZAIRE / CONSEQUENT DISRUPTION / BUT FACTS DIFFER / LOCAL TRIBES {KIGANI} ON RAMPAGE / REPORTED ATROCITIES AND CANNIBALISM ETC / FOREST-DWELLING PYGMIES UNRELIABLE / KILLING ALL VISITORS CONGO RAIN FOREST / ZAIRE GOVERNMENT DISPATCHED GENERAL MUGURU (AKA BUTCHER OF STANLEYVILLE) / PUT DOWN KIGANI REBELLION 'AT ALL COSTS' / SITUATION HIGHLY UNSTABLE / ONLY LEGAL ENTRY INTO ZAIRE NOW WEST THROUGH KINSHASA / YOU ARE ON YOUR OWN / ACQUISITION WHITE HUNTER MUNRO NOW PARAMOUNT IMPORTANCE WHATEVER COST / KEEP HIM FROM CONSORTIUM WILL PAY ANYTHING / YOUR SITUATION EXTREME DANGER / MUST HAVE MUNRO TO SURVIVE /

She stared at the screen. It was the worst possible news. She said, "Have you got a time course?"

EURO-JAPANESE CONSORTIUM NOW COMPRISES HAKAMICHI (JAPAN) / GERLICH (GERMANY) / VOORSTER (AMSTERDAM) / UNFORTUNATELY HAVE RESOLVED DIFFERENCES NOW IN COMPLETE ACCORD / MONITORING US CANNOT ANTICIPATE SECURE TRANSMISSIONS ANYTIME HENCEFORTH / ANTICIPATE ELECTRONIC COUNTERMEASURES AND WARFARE TACTICS IN PURSUIT OF TWO-B GOAL / THEY WILL ENTER CONGO (RELIABLE SOURCE) WITHIN 48 HOURS NOW SEEKING MUNRO /

"When will they reach Tangier?" she asked.
"In six hours. You?"
"Seven hours. And Munro?"
"We don't know about Munro," Travis said. "Can you booby him?"
"Absolutely," Ross said. "I'll arrange the booby now. If Munro doesn't see things our way, I promise you it'll be seventy-two hours before he's allowed out of the country."
"What've you got?" Travis asked.
"Czech submachine guns. Found on the premises, with his prints on them, carefully applied. That should do it."
"That should do it," Travis agreed. "What about your passengers?" He was referring to Elliot and Amy.
"They're fine," Ross said. "They know nothing."
"Keep it that way," Travis said, and hung up.

4. Feeding Time

"It's feeding time," Travis called cheerfully. "Who's at the trough?"

"We've got five tap dancers on Beta dataline," Rogers said. Rogers was the electronic surveillance expert, the bug catcher.

"Anybody we know?"

"Know them all," Rogers said, slightly annoyed. "Beta line is our main cross-trunk line in-house, so whoever wants to tap in to our system will naturally plug in there. You get more bits and pieces that way. Of course we aren't using Beta anymore except for routine uncoded garbage—taxes and payroll, that stuff."

"We have to arrange a feed," Travis said. A feed meant putting false data out over a tapped line, to be picked up. It was a delicate operation. "You have the consortium on the line?"

"Sure. What do you want to feed them?"

"Coordinates for the lost city," Travis said.

Rogers nodded, mopping his brow. He was a portly man who sweated profusely. "How good do you want it?"

"Damned good," Travis said. "You won't fool the Japanese with static."

"You don't want to give them the actual co-ords?"

"God, no. But I want them reasonably close. Say, within two hundred kilometers."

"Can do," Rogers said.

"Coded?" Travis said.

"Of course."

"You have a code they can break in twelve to fifteen hours?"

Rogers nodded. "We've got a dilly. Looks like hell, but then when you work it, it pops out. Got an internal weakness in concealed lettering frequency. At the other end, looks like we made a mistake, but it's very breakable."

"It can't be too easy," Travis warned.

"Oh, no, they'll earn their yen. They'll never suspect a feed. We ran it past the army and they came back all smiles, teaching us a lesson. Never knew it was a setup."

"Okay," Travis said, "put the data out, and let's feed them. I want something that'll give them a sense of confidence for the next forty-eight hours or more—until they figure out that we've screwed them."

"Delighted," Rogers said, and he moved off to Beta terminal.

Travis sighed. The feeding would soon begin, and he hoped it would protect his team in the field—long enough for them to get to the diamonds first.

5. Dangerous Signatures

The soft murmur of voices woke him.

"How unequivocal is that signature?"

"Pretty damn unequivocal. Here's the pissup, nine days ago, and it's not even epicentered."

"That's cloud cover?"

"No, that's not cloud cover, it's too black. That's ejecta from the signature."

"Hell."

Elliot opened his eyes to see dawn breaking as a thin red line against blue-black through the windows of the passenger compartment. His watch read 5:11—five in the morning, San Francisco time. He had slept only two hours since calling Seamans. He yawned and glanced down at Amy, curled up in her nest of blankets on the floor. Amy snored loudly. The other bunks were unoccupied.

He heard soft voices again, and looked toward the computer console. Jensen and Irving were staring at a screen and talking quietly. "Dangerous signature. We got a computer projection on that?"

"Coming. It'll take a while. I asked for a five-year runback, as well as the other pissups."

Elliot climbed out of his cot and looked at the screen. "What's pissups?" he said.

"PSOPs are prior significant orbital passes by the satellite," Jensen explained. "They're called pissups because we usually ask for them when we're already pissing upwind. We've been looking at this volcanic signature here," Jensen said, pointing to the screen. "It's not too promising."

"What volcanic signature?" Elliot asked.

They showed him the billowing plumes of smoke—dark green in artificial computer-generated colors—which belched from the mouth of Mukenko, one of the active volcanoes of the Virunga range. "Mukenko erupts on the average of once every three years," Irving said. "The last eruption was March, 1977, but it looks like it's gearing up for another full eruption in the next week or so. We're waiting now for the probability assessment."

"Does Ross know about this?"

They shrugged. "She knows, but she doesn't seem worried. She got an urgent GPU—geopolitical update—from Houston about two hours ago, and she went directly into the cargo bay. Haven't seen her since."

Elliot went into the dimly lit cargo bay of the jet. The cargo bay was not insulated and it was chilly: the trucks had a thin frost on metal and glass, and his breath hissed from his mouth. He found Karen Ross working at a table under low pools of light. Her back was turned to him, but when he approached, she dropped what she was doing and turned to face him.

"I thought you were asleep," she said.

"I got restless. What's going on?"

"Just checking supplies. This is our advanced technology unit," she said, lifting up a small backpack. "We've developed a miniaturized package for field parties; twenty pounds of equipment contains everything a man needs for two weeks: food, water, clothing, everything."

"Even water?" Elliot asked.

Water was heavy: seven-tenths of human body weight was water, and most of the weight of food was water; that was why dehydrated food was so light. But water was far more critical to human life than food. Men could survive for weeks without food, but they would die in a matter of hours without water. And water was heavy.

Ross smiled. "The average man consumes four to six liters a day, which is eight to thirteen pounds of weight. On a two-week expedition to a desert region, we'd have to provide two hundred pounds of water for each man. But we have a NASA water-recycling unit which purifies all excretions, including urine. It weighs six ounces. That's how we do it."

Seeing his expression, she said, "It's not bad at all. Our purified water is cleaner than what you get from the tap."

"I'll take your word for it." Elliot picked up a pair of strange-looking sunglasses. They were very dark and thick, and there was a peculiar lens mounted over the forehead bridge.

"Holographic night goggles," Ross said. "Employing thin-film diffraction optics." She then pointed out a vibration-free camera lens with optical systems that compensated for movement, strobe infrared lights, and miniature survey lasers no larger than a pencil eraser. There was also a series of small tripods with rapid-geared motors mounted on the top, and brackets to hold something, but she did not explain these devices beyond saying they were "defensive units."

Elliot drifted toward the far table, where he found six submachine guns set out under the lights. He picked one up; it was heavy, and gleaming with grease. Clips of ammunition lay stacked nearby. Elliot did not notice the lettering on the stock; the machine guns were Russian AK-47s manufactured under license in Czechoslovakia.

He glanced at Ross.

"Just precautions," Ross said. "We carry them on every expedition. It doesn't mean anything."

Elliot shook his head. "Tell me about your GPU from Houston," he said.

"I'm not worried about it," she said.

"I am," Elliot said.

As Ross explained it, the GPU was just a technical report. The Zaire government had closed its eastern borders during the previous twenty-four hours; no tourist or commercial traffic could enter the country from Rwanda or Uganda; everyone now had to enter the country from the west, through Kinshasa.

No official reason was given for closing the eastern border, although sources in Washington speculated that Idi Amin's troops, fleeing across the Zaire border from the Tanzanian invasion of Uganda, might be causing "local difficulties." In central Africa, local difficulties usually meant cannibalism and other atrocities.

"Do you believe that?" Elliot asked. "Cannibalism and atrocities?"

"No," Ross said. "It's all a lie. It's the Dutch and the Germans and the Japanese—probably your friend Morikawa. The Euro-Japanese electronics consortium knows that ERTS is close to discovering important diamond reserves in Virunga. They want to slow us down as much as they can. They've got the fix in somewhere, probably in Kinshasa, and closed the eastern borders. It's nothing more than that."

"If there's no danger, why the machine guns?"

"Just precautions," she said again. "We'll never use machine guns on this trip, believe me. Now why don't you get some sleep? We'll be landing in Tangier soon."

"Tangier?"

"Captain Munro is there."

6. Munro

The name of "Captain" Charles Munro was not to be found on the list of the expedition leaders employed by any of the usual field parties. There were several reasons for this, foremost among them his distinctly unsavory reputation.

Munro had been raised in the wild Northern Frontier Province of Kenya, the illegitimate son of a Scottish farmer and his handsome Indian house-keeper. Munro's father had the bad luck to be killed by Mau Mau guerillas in 1956.* Soon afterward, Munro's mother died of tuberculosis, and Munro made his way to Nairobi where in the late 1950s he worked as a white hunter, leading parties of tourists into the bush. It was during this time that Munro awarded himself the title of "Captain," although he had never served in the military.

Apparently, Captain Munro found humoring tourists uncongenial; by 1960, he was reported running guns from Uganda into the newly independent Congo. After Moise Tshombe went into exile in 1963, Munro's activities became politically embarrassing, and ultimately forced him to disappear from East Africa in late 1963.

He appeared again in 1964, as one of General Mobutu's white mercenaries in the Congo, under the leadership of Colonel "Mad Mike" Hoare. Hoare assessed Munro as a "hard, lethal customer who knew the jungle and was highly effective, when we could get him away from the ladies." Following the capture of Stanleyville in Operation Dragon Rouge, Munro's name was associated with the mercenary atrocities at a village called Avakabi. Munro again disappeared for several years.

In 1968, he re-emerged in Tangier, where he lived splendidly and was something of a local character. The source of Munro's obviously substantial income was unclear, but he was said to have supplied Communist Sudanese rebels with East German light arms in 1971, to have assisted the royalist Ethiopians in their rebellion in 1974–1975, and to have assisted the French paratroopers who dropped into Zaire's Shaba province in 1978.

*Although more than nineteen thousand people were killed in the Mau Mau uprisings, only thirty-seven whites were killed during seven years of terrorism. Each dead white was properly regarded more as a victim of circumstance than of emerging black politics.

His mixed activities made Munro a special case in Africa in the 1970s; although he was *persona non grata* in a half-dozen African states, he traveled freely throughout the continent, using various passports. It was a transparent ruse: every border official recognized him on sight, but these officials were equally afraid to let him enter the country or to deny him entry.

Foreign mining and exploration companies, sensitive to local feeling, were reluctant to hire Munro as an expedition leader for their parties. It was also true that Munro was by far the most expensive of the bush guides. Nevertheless, he had a reputation for getting tough, difficult jobs done. Under an assumed name, he had taken two German tin-mining parties into the Cameroons in 1974; and he had led one previous ERTS expedition into Angola during the height of the armed conflict in 1977. He quit another ERTS field group headed for Zambia the following year after Houston refused to meet his price: Houston had canceled the expedition.

In short, Munro was acknowledged as the best man for dangerous travel. That was why the ERTS jet stopped in Tangier.

At the Tangier airport, the ERTS cargo jet and its contents were bonded, but all ongoing personnel except Amy passed through customs, carrying their personal belongings. Jensen and Irving were pulled aside for searches; trace quantities of heroin were discovered in their hand baggage.

This bizarre event occurred through a series of remarkable coincidences. In 1977, United States customs agents began to employ neutron backscatter devices, as well as chemical vapor detectors, or sniffers. Both were hand-held electronic devices manufactured under contract by Morikawa Electronics in Tokyo. In 1978, questions arose about the accuracy of these devices; Morikawa suggested that they be tested at other ports of entry around the world, including Singapore, Bangkok, Delhi, Munich, and Tangier.

Thus Morikawa Electronics knew the capabilities of the detectors at Tangier airport, and they also knew that a variety of substances, including ground poppy seeds and shredded turnip, would produce a false-positive registration on airport sensors. And the "false-positive net" required forty-eight hours to untangle. (It was later shown that both men had somehow acquired traces of turnip on their briefcases.)

Both Irving and Jensen vigorously denied any knowledge of illicit material, and appealed to the local U.S. consular office. But the case could not be resolved for several days; Ross telephoned Travis in Houston, who determined that it was a "Dutch herring." There was nothing to be done except to carry on, and continue with the expedition as best they could.

"They think this will stop us," Travis said, "but it won't."

"Who's going to do the geology?" Ross asked.

"You are," Travis said.

"And the electronics?"

"You're the certified genius," Travis said. "Just make sure you have Munro. He's the key to everything."

The song of the muezzin floated over the pastel jumble of houses in the Tangier Casbah at twilight, calling the faithful to evening prayer. In the old days, the muezzin himself appeared in the minaret of the mosque, but now a recording played over loudspeakers: a mechanized call to the Muslim ritual of obeisance.

Karen Ross sat on the terrace of Captain Munro's house overlooking the Casbah and waited for her audience with the man himself. Beside her, Peter Elliot sat in a chair and snored noisily, exhausted from the long flight.

They had been waiting nearly three hours, and she was worried. Munro's house was of Moorish design, and open to the outdoors. From the interior she could hear voices, faintly carried by the breeze, speaking some Oriental language.

One of the graceful Moroccan servant girls that Munro seemed to have in infinite supply came onto the terrace carrying a telephone. She bowed formally. Ross saw that the girl had violet eyes; she was exquisitely beautiful, and could not have been more than sixteen. In careful English the girl said, "This is your telephone to Houston. The bidding will now begin."

Karen nudged Peter, who awoke groggily. "The bidding will now begin," she said.

Peter Elliot was surprised from the moment of his first entrance into Munro's house. He had anticipated a tough military setting and was amazed to see delicate carved Moroccan arches and soft gurgling fountains with sunlight sparkling on them.

Then he saw the Japanese and Germans in the next room, staring at him and at Ross. The glances were distinctly unfriendly, but Ross stood and said, "Excuse me a moment," and she went forward and embraced a young blond German man warmly. They kissed, chattered happily, and in general appeared to be intimate friends.

Elliot did not like this development, but he was reassured to see that the Japanese—identically dressed in black suits—were equally displeased. Noticing this, Elliot smiled benignly, to convey a sense of approval for the reunion.

But when Ross returned, he demanded, "Who was that?"

"That's Richter," she said. "The most brilliant topologist in Western Europe; his field is n-space extrapolation. His work's extremely elegant." She smiled. "Almost as elegant as mine."

"But he works for the consortium?"

"Naturally. He's German."

"And you're talking with him?"

"I was delighted for the opportunity," she said. "Karl has a fatal limitation.

He can only deal with pre-existing data. He takes what he is given, and does cartwheels with it in *n*-space. But he cannot imagine anything new at all. I had a professor at M.I.T. who was the same way. Tied to facts, a hostage to reality." She shook her head.

"Did he ask about Amy?"

"Of course."

"And what did you tell him?"

"I told him she was sick and probably dying."

"And he believed that?"

"We'll see. There's Munro."

Captain Munro appeared in the next room, wearing khakis, smoking a cigar. He was a tall, rugged-looking man with a mustache, and soft dark watchful eyes that missed nothing. He talked with the Japanese and Germans, who were evidently unhappy with what he was saying. Moments later, Munro entered their room, smiling broadly.

"So you're going to the Congo, Dr. Ross."

"We are, Captain Munro," she said.

Munro smiled. "It seems as though everyone is going."

There followed a rapid exchange which Elliot found incomprehensible. Karen Ross said, "Fifty thousand U.S. in Swiss francs against point oh two of first-year adjusted extraction returns."

Munro shook his head. "A hundred in Swiss francs and point oh six of first-year return on the primary deposits, crude-grade accounting, no discounting.

"A hundred in U.S. dollars against point oh one of the first-year return on all deposits, with full discounting from point of origin."

"Point of origin? In the middle of the bloody Congo? I would want three years from point of origin: what if you're shut down?"

"You want a piece, you gamble. Mobutu's clever."

"Mobutu's barely in control, and I am still alive because I am no gambler," Munro said. "A hundred against point oh four of first year on primary with front-load discount only. Or I'll take point oh two of yours."

"If you're no gambler, I'll give you a straight buy-out for two hundred."

Munro shook his head. "You've paid more than that for your MER in Kinshasa."

"Prices for everything are inflated in Kinshasa, including mineral exploration rights. And the current exploration limit, the computer CEL, is running well under a thousand."

"If you say so." He smiled, and headed back into the other room, where the Japanese and Germans were waiting for his return.

Ross said quickly, "That's not for them to know."

"Oh, I'm sure they know it anyway," Munro said, and walked into the other room.

"Bastard," she whispered to his back. She talked in low tones on the telephone. "He'll never accept that. . . . No, no, he won't go for it . . . they want him bad. . . ."

Elliot said, "You're bidding very high for his services."

"He's the best," Ross said, and continued whispering into the telephone. In the next room, Munro was shaking his head sadly, turning down an offer. Elliot noticed that Richter was very red in the face.

Munro came back to Karen Ross. "What was your projected CEL?"

"Under a thousand."

"So you say. Yet you know there's an ore intercept."

"I don't know there's an ore intercept."

"Then you're foolish to spend all this money to go to the Congo," Munro said. "Aren't you?"

Karen Ross made no reply. She stared at the ornate ceiling of the room.

"Virunga's not exactly a garden spot these days," Munro continued. "The Kigani are on the rampage, and they're cannibals. Pygmies aren't friendly anymore either. Likely to find an arrow in your back for your troubles. Volcanoes always threatening to blow. Tsetse flies. Bad water. Corrupt officials. Not a place to go without a very good reason, hmm? Perhaps you should put off your trip until things settle down."

Those were precisely Peter Elliot's sentiments, and he said so.

"Wise man," Munro said, with a broad smile that annoyed Karen Ross.

"Evidently," Karen Ross said, "we will never come to terms."

"That seems clear." Munro nodded.

Elliot understood that negotiations were broken off. He got up to shake Munro's hand and leave—but before he could do that, Munro walked into the next room and conferred with the Japanese and Germans.

"Things are looking up," Ross said.

"Why?" Elliot said. "Because he thinks he's beaten you down?"

"No. Because he thinks we know more than they do about the site location and are more likely to hit an ore body and pay off."

In the next room, the Japanese and Germans abruptly stood, and walked to the front door. At the door, Munro shook hands with the Germans, and bowed elaborately to the Japanese.

"I guess you're right," Elliot said to Ross. "He's sending them away."

But Ross was frowning, her face grim. "They can't do this," she said. "They can't just quit this way."

Elliot was confused again. "I thought you wanted them to quit."

"Damn," Ross said. "We've been screwed." She whispered into the telephone, talking to Houston.

Elliot didn't understand it at all. And his confusion was not resolved when Munro locked the door behind the last of the departing men, then came back to Elliot and Ross to say that supper was served.

* * *

They ate Moroccan-style, sitting on the floor and eating with their fingers. The first course was a pigeon pie, and it was followed by some sort of stew.

"So you sent the Japanese off?" Ross said. "Told them no?"

"Oh, no," Munro said. "That would be impolite. I told them I would think about it. And I will."

"Then why did they leave?"

Munro shrugged. "Not my doing, I assure you. I think they heard something on the telephone which changed their whole plan."

Karen Ross glanced at her watch, making a note of the time. "Very good stew," she said. She was doing her best to be agreeable.

"Glad you like it. It's *tajin*. Camel meat."

Karen Ross coughed. Peter Elliot noticed that his own appetite had diminished. Munro turned to him. "So you have the gorilla, Professor Elliot?"

"How did you know that?"

"The Japanese told me. The Japanese are fascinated by your gorilla. Can't figure the point of it, drives them mad. A young man with a gorilla, and a young woman who is searching for—"

"Industrial-grade diamonds," Karen Ross said.

"Ah, industrial-grade diamonds." He turned to Elliot. "I enjoy a frank conversation. Diamonds, fascinating." His manner suggested that he had been told nothing of importance.

Ross said, "You've got to take us in, Munro."

"World's full of industrial-grade diamonds," Munro said. "You can find them in Africa, India, Russia, Brazil, Canada, even in America—Arkansas, New York, Kentucky—everywhere you look. But you're going to the Congo."

The obvious question hung in the air.

"We are looking for Type IIb boron-coated blue diamonds," Karen Ross said, "which have semiconducting properties important to microelectronics applications."

Munro stroked his mustache. "Blue diamonds," he said, nodding. "It makes sense."

Ross said that of course it made sense.

"You can't dope them?" Munro asked.

"No. It's been tried. There was a commercial boron-doping process, but it was too unreliable. The Americans had one and so did the Japanese. Everyone gave it up as hopeless."

"So you've got to find a natural source."

"That's right. I want to get there as soon as possible," Ross said, staring at him, her voice flat.

"I'm sure you do," Munro said. "Nothing but business for our Dr. Ross, eh?" He crossed the room and, leaning against one of the arches, looked out on the dark Tangier night. "I'm not surprised at all," he said. "As a matter of—"

At the first blast of machine-gun fire, Munro dived for cover, the glassware on the table splattered, one of the girls screamed, and Elliot and Ross threw themselves to the marble floor as the bullets whined around them, chipping the plaster overhead, raining plaster dust down upon them. The blast lasted thirty seconds or so, and it was followed by complete silence.

When it was over, they got up hesitantly, staring at one another.

"The consortium plays for keeps." Munro grinned. "Just my sort of people."

Ross brushed plaster dust off her clothes. She turned to Munro. "Five point two against the first two hundred, no deductions, in Swiss francs, adjusted."

"Five point seven, and you have me."

"Five point seven. Done."

Munro shook hands with them, then announced that he would need a few minutes to pack his things before leaving for Nairobi.

"Just like that?" Ross asked. She seemed suddenly concerned, glancing again at her watch.

"What's your problem?" Munro asked.

"Czech AK-47s," she said. "In your warehouse."

Munro showed no surprise. "Better get them out," he said. "The consortium undoubtedly has something similar in the works, and we've got a lot to do in the next few hours." As he spoke, they heard the police Klaxons approaching from a distance. Munro said, "We'll take the back stair."

An hour later, they were airborne, heading toward Nairobi.

DAY 4: NAIROBI

JUNE 16, 1979

1. Timeline

It was farther across Africa from Tangier to Nairobi than it was across the Atlantic Ocean from New York to London—3,600 miles, an eight-hour flight. Ross spent the time at the computer console, working out what she called "hyperspace probability lines."

The screen showed a computer-generated map of Africa, with streaking multicolored lines across it. "These are all timelines," Ross said. "We can weight them for duration and delay factors." Beneath the screen was a total-elapsed-time clock, which kept shifting numbers.

"What's that mean?" Elliot asked.

"The computer's picking the fastest route. You see it's just identified a timeline that will get us on-site in six days eighteen hours and fifty-one minutes. Now it's trying to beat that time."

Elliot had to smile. The idea of a computer predicting *to the minute* when they would reach their Congo location seemed ludicrous to him. But Ross was totally serious.

As they watched, the computer clock shifted to 5 days 22 hours 24 minutes.

"Better," Ross said, nodding. "But still not very good." She pressed another key and the lines shifted, stretching like rubber bands over the African continent. "This is the consortium route," she said, "based on our assumptions about the expedition. They're going in big—thirty or more people, a full-scale undertaking. And they don't know the exact location of the city; at least, we don't think they know. But they have a substantial start on us, at least twelve hours, since their aircraft is already forming up in Nairobi."

The clock registered total elapsed time: 5 days 09 hours 19 minutes. Then she pressed a button marked DATE and it shifted to 06 21 79 0814. "According to this, the consortium will reach the Congo site a little after eight o'clock in the morning on June 21."

The computer clicked quietly; the lines continued to stretch and pull, and the clock read a new date: 06 21 79 1224.

"Well," she said, "that's where we are now. Given maximum favorable movements for us and them, the consortium will beat us to the site by slightly more than four hours, five days from now."

Munro walked past, eating a sandwich. "Better lock another path," he said. "Or go radical."

"I hesitate to go radical with the ape."

Munro shrugged. "Have to do something, with a timeline like that."

Elliot listened to them with a vague sense of unreality: they were discussing a difference of hours, five days in the future. "But surely," Elliot said, "over the next few days, with all the arrangements at Nairobi, and then getting into the jungle—you can't put too much faith in those figures."

"This isn't like the old days of African exploration," Ross said, "where parties disappeared into the wilds for months. At most, the computer is off by minutes—say, roughly half an hour in the total five-day projection." She shook her head. "No. We have a problem here, and we've got to do something about it. The stakes are too great."

"You mean the diamonds."

She nodded, and pointed to the bottom of the screen, where the words BLUE CONTRACT appeared. He asked her what the Blue Contract was.

"One hell of a lot of money," Ross said. And she added, "I think." For in truth she did not really know.

Each new contract at ERTS was given a code name. Only Travis and the computer knew the name of the company buying the contract; everyone else at ERTS, from computer programmers to field personnel, knew the projects only by their color-code names: Red Contract, Yellow Contract, White Contract. This was a business protection for the firms involved. But the ERTS mathematicians could not resist a lively guessing game about contract sources, which was the staple of daily conversation in the company canteen.

The Blue Contract had come to ERTS in December, 1978. It called for ERTS to locate a natural source of industrial-grade diamonds in a friendly or neutralist country. The diamonds were to be Type IIb, "nitrogen-poor" crystals. No dimensions were specified, so crystal size did not matter; nor were recoverable quantities specified: the contractor would take what he could get. And, most unusual, there was no UECL.

Nearly all contracts arrived with a unit extraction cost limit. It was not enough to find a mineral source; the minerals had to be extractable at a specified unit cost. This unit cost in turn reflected the richness of the ore body, its remoteness, the availability of local labor, political conditions, the possible need to build airfields, roads, hospitals, mines, or refineries.

For a contract to come in without a UECL meant only one thing: somebody wanted blue diamonds so badly he didn't care what they cost.

Within forty-eight hours, the ERTS canteen had explained the Blue Contract. It turned out that Type IIb diamonds were blue from trace quantities of the element boron, which rendered them worthless as gemstones but altered their electronic properties, making them semiconductors with a resistivity on the order of 100 ohms centimeters. They also had light-transmissive properties.

Someone then found a brief article in *Electronic News* for November 17,

1978: "McPhee Doping Dropped." It explained that the Waltham, Massachusetts, firm of Silec, Inc., had abandoned the experimental McPhee technique to dope diamonds artificially with a monolayer boron coating. The McPhee process had been abandoned as too expensive and too unreliable to produce "desirable semiconducting properties." The article concluded that "other firms have underestimated problems in boron monolayer doping; Morikawa (Tokyo) abandoned the Nagaura process in September of this year." Working backward, the ERTS canteen fitted additional pieces of the puzzle into place.

Back in 1971, Intec, the Santa Clara microelectronics firm, had first predicted that diamond semiconductors would be important to a future generation of "superconducting" computers in the 1980s.

The first generation of electronic computers, ENIAC and UNIVAC, built in the wartime secrecy of the 1940s, employed vacuum tubes. Vacuum tubes had an average life span of twenty hours, but with thousands of glowing hot tubes in a single machine, some computers shut down every seven to twelve minutes. Vacuum-tube technology imposed a limit on the size and power of planned second-generation computers.

But the second generation never used vacuum tubes. In 1947, the invention of the transistor—a thumbnail-sized sandwich of solid material which performed all the functions of a vacuum tube—ushered in an era of "solid state" electronic devices which drew little power, generated little heat, and were smaller and more reliable than the tubes they replaced. Silicon technology provided the basis for three generations of increasingly compact, reliable, and cheap computers over the next twenty years.

But by the 1970s, computer designers began to confront the inherent limitations of silicon technology. Although circuits had been shrunk to microscopic dimensions, computation speed was still dependent on circuit length. To miniaturize circuits still more, where distances were already on the order of millionths of an inch, brought back an old problem: heat. Smaller circuits would literally melt from the heat produced. What was needed was some method to eliminate heat and reduce resistance at the same time.

It had been known since the 1950s that many metals when cooled to extremely low temperatures became "superconducting," permitting the unimpeded flow of electrons through them. In 1977, IBM announced it was designing an ultra-high-speed computer the size of a grapefruit, chilled with liquid nitrogen. The superconducting computer required a radically new technology, and a new range of low-temperature construction materials.

Doped diamonds would be used extensively throughout.

Several days later, the ERTS canteen came up with an alternative explanation. According to the new theory, the 1970s had been a decade of unprecedented growth in computers. Although the first computer manufacturers in the 1940s had predicted that four computers would do the computing work of the entire world for the foreseeable future, experts anticipated that by 1990 there would actually be *one billion* computers—most of them linked by communications networks to other computers. Such networks didn't exist, and might even be theoretically impossible. (A 1975 study by the Hanover Institute concluded there was insufficient metal in the earth's crust to construct the necessary computer transmission lines.)

According to Harvey Rumbaugh, the 1980s would be characterized by a critical shortage of computer data transmission systems: "Just as the fossil fuel shortage took the industrialized world by surprise in the 1970s, so will the data transmission shortage take the world by surprise in the next ten years. People were denied *movement* in the 1970s; but they will be denied *information* in the 1980s, and it remains to be seen which shortage will prove more frustrating."

Laser light represented the only hope for handling these massive data requirements, since laser channels carried twenty thousand times the information of an ordinary metal coaxial trunk line. Laser transmission demanded whole new technologies—including thin-spun fiber optics, and doped semiconducting diamonds, which Rumbaugh predicted would be "more valuable than oil" in the coming years.

Even further, Rumbaugh anticipated that within ten years *electricity itself would become obsolete*. Future computers would utilize only light circuits, and interface with light-transmission data systems. The reason was speed. "Light," Rumbaugh said, "moves at the speed of light. Electricity doesn't. We are living in the final years of microelectronic technology."

Certainly microelectronics did not look like a moribund technology. In 1979, microelectronics was a major industry throughout the industrialized world, accounting for eighty billion dollars annually in the United States alone; six of the top twenty corporations in the Fortune 500 were deeply involved in microelectronics. These companies had a history of extraordinary competition and advance, over a period of less than thirty years.

In 1958, a manufacturer could fit 10 electronic components onto a single silicon chip. By 1970, it was possible to fit 100 units onto a chip of the same size—a tenfold increase in slightly more than a decade.

But by 1972, it was possible to fit 1,000 units on a chip, and by 1974, 10,-000 units. It was expected that by 1980, there would be one million units on a single chip the size of a thumbnail, but, using electronic photoprojection, this goal was actually realized in 1978. By the spring of 1979, the new goal was ten million units—or, even better, one billion units—on a single silicon chip by 1980. But nobody expected to wait past June or July of 1979 for this development.

Such advances within an industry are unprecedented. Comparison to older manufacturing technologies makes this clear. Detroit was content to make trivial product design changes at three-year intervals, but the electronics industry routinely expected *order of magnitude* advances in the same time. (To keep pace, Detroit would have had to increase automobile gas mileage from 8 miles per gallon in 1970 to 80,000,000 miles per gallon in 1979. Instead, Detroit went from 8 to 16 miles per gallon during that time, further evidence of the coming demise of the automotive industry as the center of the American economy.)

In such a competitive market, everyone worried about foreign powers, particularly Japan, which since 1973 had maintained a Japanese Cultural Exchange in San José—which some considered a cover organization for well-financed industrial espionage.

The Blue Contract could only be understood in the light of an industry making major advances every few months. Travis had said that the Blue Contract was "the biggest thing we'll see in the next ten years. Whoever finds those diamonds has a jump on the technology for at least five years. *Five years.* Do you know what that means?"

Ross knew what it meant. In an industry where competitive edges were measured in months, companies had made fortunes by beating competitors by a matter of weeks with some new techniques or device; Syntel in California had been the first to make a 256K memory chip while everyone else was still making 16K chips and dreaming of 64K chips. Syntel kept their advantage for only sixteen weeks, but realized a profit of more than a hundred and thirty million dollars.

"And we're talking about *five years,*" Travis said. "That's an advantage measured in billions of dollars, maybe tens of billions of dollars. If we can get to those diamonds."

These were the reasons for the extraordinary pressure Ross felt as she continued to work with the computer. At the age of twenty-four, she was team leader in a high-technology race involving a half-dozen nations around the globe, all secretly pitting their business and industrial resources against one another.

The stakes made any conventional race seem ludicrous. Travis told her before she left, "Don't be afraid when the pressure makes you crazy. You have *billions of dollars* riding on your shoulders. Just do the best you can."

Doing the best she could, she managed to reduce the expedition timeline by another three hours and thirty-seven minutes—but they were still slightly behind the consortium projection. Not too far to make up the time, especially with Munro's cold-blooded shortcuts, but nevertheless behind—which could mean total disaster in a winner-take-all race.

And then she received bad news.

The screen printed PIGGYBACK SLURP / ALL BETS OFF.

"Hell," Ross said. She felt suddenly tired. Because if there really had been a piggyback slurp, their chances of winning the race were vanishing—before any of them had even set foot in the rain forests of central Africa.

2. Piggyback Slurp

Travis felt like a fool.

He stared at the hard copy from Goddard Space Flight Center, Greenbelt, Maryland.

ERTS WHY ARE YOU SENDING US ALL THIS MUKENKO DATA WE DON'T RE-
ALLY CARE THANKS ANYWAY.

That had arrived an hour ago from GSFC/Maryland, but it was already too late by more than five hours.

"Damn!" Travis said, staring at the telex.

The first indication to Travis that anything was wrong was when the Japanese and Germans broke off negotiations with Munro in Tangier. One minute they had been willing to pay anything; the next minute they could hardly wait to leave. The break-off had come abruptly, discontinuously; it implied the sudden introduction of new data into the consortium computer files.

New data from where?

There could be only one explanation—and now it was confirmed in the GSFC telex from Greenbelt.

ERTS WHY ARE YOU SENDING ALL THIS MUKENKO DATA

There was a simple answer to that: ERTS *wasn't* sending any data. At least, not willingly. ERTS and GSFC had an arrangement to exchange data updates—Travis had made that deal in 1978 to obtain cheaper satellite imagery from orbiting Landsats. Satellite imagery was his company's single greatest expense. In return for a look at derived ERTS data, GSFC agreed to supply satellite CCTs at 30 percent below gross rate.

It seemed like a good deal at the time, and the coded locks were specified in the agreement.

But now the potential drawbacks loomed large before Travis; his worst fears were confirmed. Once you put a line over two thousand miles from Houston to Greenbelt, you begged for a piggyback data slurp. Somewhere between Texas and Maryland someone had inserted a terminal linkup—probably in the carrier telephone lines—and had begun to slurp out data on a piggyback terminal. This was the form of industrial espionage they most feared.

A piggyback-slurp terminal tapped in between two legitimate terminals, monitoring the back and forth transmissions. After a time, the piggyback operator knew enough to begin making transmissions on line, slurping out data from both ends, pretending to be GSFC to Houston, and Houston to GSFC. The piggyback terminal could continue to function until one or both legitimate terminals realized that they were being slurped.

Now the question was: how much data had been slurped out in the last seventy-two hours?

He called for twenty-four-hour scanner checks, and the readings were disheartening. It looked as though the ERTS computer had yielded up not only original database elements, but also data-transformation histories—the sequence of operations performed on the data by ERTS over the last four weeks.

If that was true, it meant that the Euro-Japanese consortium piggyback knew what transformations ERTS had carried out on the Mukenko data—and therefore they knew where the lost city was located, with pinpoint accuracy. They now knew the location of the city as precisely as Ross did.

Timelines had to be adjusted, unfavorably to the ERTS team. And the updated computer projections were unequivocal—Ross or no Ross, the likelihood of the ERTS team reaching the site ahead of the Japanese and Germans was now almost nil.

From Travis's viewpoint, the entire ERTS expedition was now a futile exercise, and a waste of time. There was no hope of success. The only unfactorable element was the gorilla Amy, and Travis's instincts told him that a gorilla named Amy would not prove decisive in the discovery of mineral deposits in the northeastern Congo.

It was hopeless.

Should he recall the ERTS team? He stared at the console by his desk. "Call cost-time," he said.

The computer blinked COST-TIME AVAILABLE.

"Congo Field Survey," he said.

The screen printed out numbers for the Congo Field Survey: expenditures by the hour, accumulated costs, committed future costs, cutoff points, future branch-point deletions. . . . The project was now just outside Nairobi, and was running at an accumulated cost of slightly over $189,000.

Cancellation would cost $227,455.

"Factor BF," he said.

The screen changed. BF. He now saw a series of probabilities. "Factor BF" was *bona fortuna,* good luck—the imponderable in all expeditions, especially remote, dangerous expeditions.

THINKING A MOMENT, the computer flashed.

Travis waited. He knew that the computer would require several seconds to perform the computations to assign weights to random factors that might influence the expedition, still five or more days from the target site.

His beeper buzzed. Rogers, the tap dancer, said, "We've traced the pig-gyback slurp. It's in Norman, Oklahoma, nominally at the North Central Insur-ance Corporation of America. NCIC is fifty-one percent owned by a Hawaiian holding company, Halekuli, Inc., which is in turn owned by mainland Japa-nese interests. What do you want?"

"I want a very bad fire," Travis said.

"Got you," Rogers said. He hung up the phone.

The screen flashed **ASSESSED FACTOR BF** and a probability: .449. He was surprised: that figure meant that ERTS had an almost even chance of attaining the target site before the consortium. Travis didn't question the mathematics; .449 was good enough.

The ERTS expedition would continue to the Congo, at least for the time being. And in the meantime he would do whatever he could to slow down the consortium. Off the top of his head, Travis could think of one or two ideas to accomplish that.

3. Additional Data

The jet was moving south over Lake Rudolph in northern Kenya when Tom Seamans called Elliot.

Seamans had finished his computer analysis to discriminate gorillas from other apes, principally chimpanzees. He had then obtained from Houston a videotape of three seconds of a garbled video transmission which seemed to show a gorilla smashing a dish antenna and staring into a camera.

"Well?" Elliot said, looking at the computer screen. The data flashed up:

```
DISCRIMINANT FUNCTION GORILLA / CHIMP
FUNCTIONAL GROUPINGS DISTRIBUTED AS:
GORILLA: .9934
CHIMP: .1132
TEST VIDEOTAPE (HOUSTON): .3349
```

"Hell," Elliot said. At those figures, the study was equivocal, useless.

"Sorry about that," Seamans said over the phone. "But part of the trouble comes from the test material itself. We had to factor in the computer derivation of that image. The image has been cleaned up, and that means it's been regularized; the critical stuff has been lost. I'd like to work with the original digitized matrix. Can you get me that?"

Karen Ross was nodding yes. "Sure," Elliot said.

"I'll go another round with it," Seamans said. "But if you want my gut opinion, it is never going to turn out. The fact is that gorillas show a considerable individual variation in facial structure, just as people do. If we increase our sample base, we're going to get more variation, and a larger population interval. I think you're stuck. You can never prove it's not a gorilla—but for my money, it's not."

"Meaning what?" Elliot asked.

"It's something new," Seamans said. "I'm telling you, if this was really a gorilla, it would have showed up .89 or .94, somewhere in there, on this function. But the image comes out at .39. That's just not good enough. It's not a gorilla, Peter."

"Then what is it?"

"It's a transitional form. I ran a function to measure where the variation was. You know what was the major differential? Skin color. Even in black-and-white, it's not dark enough to be a gorilla, Peter. This is a whole new animal, I promise you."

Elliot looked at Ross. "What does this do to your timeline?"

"For the moment, nothing," she said. "Other elements are more critical, and this is unfactorable."

The pilot clicked on the intercom. "We are beginning our descent into Nairobi," he said.

4. Nairobi

Five miles outside Nairobi, one can find wild game of the East African savannah. And within the memory of many Nairobi residents the game could be found closer still—gazelles, buffalo, and giraffe wandering around backyards, and the occasional leopard slipping into one's bedroom. In those days, the city still retained the character of a wild colonial station; in its heyday, Nairobi was a fast-living place indeed: "Are you married or do you live in Kenya?" went the standard question. The men were hard-drinking and rough, the women beautiful and loose, and the pattern of life no more predictable than the fox hunts that ranged over the rugged countryside each weekend.

But modern Nairobi is almost unrecognizable from the time of those free-wheeling colonial days. The few remaining Victorian buildings lie stranded in a modern city of half a million, with traffic jams, stoplights, skyscrapers, supermarkets, same-day dry cleaners, French restaurants, and air pollution.

The ERTS cargo plane landed at Nairobi International Airport at dawn on the morning of June 16, and Munro contacted porters and assistants for the expedition. They intended to leave Nairobi within two hours—until Travis called from Houston to inform them that Peterson, one of the geologists on the first Congo expedition, had somehow made it back to Nairobi.

Ross was excited by the news. "Where is he now?" she asked.

"At the morgue," Travis said.

Elliot winced as he came close: the body on the stainless steel table was a blond man his own age. The man's arms had been crushed; the skin was swollen, a ghastly purple color. He glanced at Ross. She seemed perfectly cool, not blinking or turning away. The pathologist stepped on a foot petal, activating a microphone overhead. "Would you state your name, please."

"Karen Ellen Ross."

"Your nationality and passport number?"

"American, F 1413649."

"Can you identify the man before you, Miss Ross?"

"Yes," she said. "He is James Robert Peterson."

"What is your relation to the deceased James Robert Peterson?"

"I worked with him," she said dully. She seemed to be examining a geological specimen, scrutinizing it unemotionally. Her face showed no reaction.

The pathologist faced the microphone. "Identity confirmed as James Robert Peterson, male Caucasian, twenty-nine years old, nationality American." He turned back to Ross. "When was the last time you saw Mr. Peterson?"

"In May of this year. He was leaving for the Congo."

"You have not seen him in the last month?"

"No," she said. "What happened?"

The pathologist touched the puffy purple injuries on his arms. His fingertips sank in, leaving indentations like teeth in the flesh. "Damned strange story," the pathologist said.

The previous day, June 15, Peterson had been flown to Nairobi airport aboard a small charter cargo plane, in endstage terminal shock. He died several hours later without regaining consciousness. "Extraordinary he made it at all. Apparently the aircraft made an unscheduled stop for a mechanical problem at Garona field, a dirt track in Zaire. And then this fellow comes stumbling out of the woods, collapsing at their feet." The pathologist pointed out that the bones had been shattered in both arms. The injuries, he explained, were not new; they had occurred at least four days earlier, perhaps more. "He must have been in incredible pain."

Elliot said, "What could cause that injury?"

The pathologist had never seen anything like it. "Superficially, it resembles mechanical trauma, a crush injury from an automobile or truck. We see a good deal of those here; but mechanical crush injuries are never bilateral, as they are in this case."

"So it wasn't a mechanical injury?" Karen Ross asked.

"Don't know what it was. It's unique in my experience," the pathologist said briskly. "We also found traces of blood under his nails, and a few strands of gray hair. We're running a test now."

Across the room, another pathologist looked up from his microscope. "The hair is definitely not human. Cross section doesn't match. Some kind of animal hair, close to human."

"The cross section?" Ross said.

"Best index we have of hair origin," the pathologist said. "For instance, human pubic hair is more elliptical in cross section than other body hair, or facial hair. It's quite characteristic—admissible in court. But especially in this laboratory, we come across a great deal of animal hair, and we're expert in that as well."

A large stainless-steel analyzer began pinging. "Blood's coming through," the pathologist said.

On a video screen they saw twin patterns of pastel-colored streaks. "This is the electrophoresis pattern," the pathologist explained. "To check serum proteins. That's ordinary human blood on the left. On the right we have the blood sample from under the nails. You can see it's definitely not human blood."

"Not human blood?" Ross said, glancing at Elliot.

"It's *close* to human blood," the pathologist said, staring at the pattern. "But it's not human. Could be a domestic or farm animal—a pig, perhaps. Or else a primate. Monkeys and apes are very close serologically to human beings. We'll have a computer analysis in a minute."

On the screen, the computer printed ALPHA AND BETA SERUM GLOBULINS MATCH: GORILLA BLOOD.

The pathologist said, "There's your answer to what he had under his nails. Gorilla blood."

5. Examination

"**S**he won't hurt you," Elliot told the frightened orderly. They were in the passenger compartment of the 747 cargo jet. "See, she's smiling at you."

Amy was indeed giving her most winning smile, being careful not to expose her teeth. But the orderly from the private clinic in Nairobi was not familiar with these fine points of gorilla etiquette. His hands shook as he held the syringe.

Nairobi was the last opportunity for Amy to receive a thorough checkup. Her large, powerful body belied a constitutional fragility, as her heavy-browed, glowering face belied a meek, rather tender nature. In San Francisco, the Project Amy staff subjected her to a thorough medical regimen—urine samples every other day, stool samples checked weekly for occult blood, complete blood studies monthly, and a trip to the dentist every three months for removal of the black tartar that accumulated from her vegetarian diet.

Amy took it all in stride, but the terrified orderly did not know that. He approached her holding the syringe in front of him like a weapon. "You sure he won't bite?"

Amy, trying to be helpful, signed, *Amy promise no bite.* She was signing slowly, deliberately, as she always did when confronted by someone who did not know her language.

"She promises not to bite you," Elliot said.

"So you say," the orderly said. Elliot did not bother to explain that he hadn't said it; she had.

After the blood samples were drawn, the orderly relaxed a little. Packing up, he said, "Certainly is an ugly brute."

"You've hurt her feelings," Elliot said.

And, indeed, Amy was signing vigorously, *What ugly?* "Nothing, Amy," Elliot said. "He's just never seen a gorilla before."

The orderly said, "I beg your pardon?"

"You've hurt her feelings. You'd better apologize."

The orderly snapped his medical case shut. He stared at Elliot and then at Amy. "Apologize to *him?*"

"Her," Elliot said. "Yes. How would you like to be told you're ugly?"

Elliot felt strongly about this. Over the years, he had come to feel acutely

100

the prejudices that human beings showed toward apes, considering chimpan-zees to be cute children, orangs to be wise old men, and gorillas to be hulking, dangerous brutes. They were wrong in every case.

Each of these animals were unique, and did not fit the human stereotypes at all. Chimps, for example, were much more callous than gorillas ever were. Because chimps were extroverts, an angry chimp was far more dangerous than an angry gorilla; at the zoo, Elliot would watch in amazement as human mothers pushed their children closer to look at the chimps, but recoiled pro-tectively at the sight of the gorillas. These mothers obviously did not know that wild chimpanzees caught and ate human infants—something gorillas never did.

Elliot had witnessed repeatedly the human prejudice against gorillas, and had come to recognize its effect on Amy. Amy could not help the fact that she was huge and black and heavy-browed and squash-faced. Behind the face people considered so repulsive was an intelligent and sensitive conscious-ness, sympathetic to the people around her. It pained her when people ran away, or screamed in fear, or made cruel remarks.

The orderly frowned. "You mean that he understands English?"

"Yes, *she* does." The gender change was something else Elliot didn't like. People who were afraid of Amy always assumed she was male.

The orderly shook his head. "I don't believe it."

"Amy, show the man to the door."

Amy lumbered over to the door and opened it for the orderly, whose eyes widened as he left. Amy closed the door behind him.

Silly human man, Amy signed.

"Never mind," Elliot said. "Come, Peter tickle Amy." And for the next fif-teen minutes, he tickled her as she rolled on the floor and grunted in deep satisfaction. Elliot never noticed the door open behind him, never noticed the shadow falling across the floor, until it was too late and he turned his head to look up and saw the dark cylinder swing down, and his head erupted with blinding white pain and everything went black.

6. Kidnapped

He awoke to a piercing electronic shriek.

"Don't move, sir," a voice said.

Elliot opened his eyes and stared into a bright light shining down on him. He was still lying on his back in the aircraft; someone was bent over him.

"Look to the right . . . now to the left. . . . Can you flex your fingers?"

He followed the instructions. The light was taken away and he saw a black man in a white suit crouched beside him. The man touched Elliot's head; his fingers came away red with blood. "Nothing to be alarmed about," the man said; "it's quite superficial." He looked off. "How long would you estimate he was unconscious?"

"Couple of minutes, no more," Munro said.

The high-pitched squeal came again. He saw Ross moving around the passenger section, wearing a shoulder pack, and holding a wand in front of her. There was another squeal. "Damn," she said, and plucked something from the molding around the window. "That's five. They really did a job."

Munro looked down at Elliot. "How do you feel?" he asked.

"He should be put under observation for twenty-four hours," the black man said. "Just as a precaution."

"Twenty-four hours!" Ross said, moving around the compartment.

Elliot said, "Where is she?"

"They took her," Munro said. "They opened the rear door, inflated the pneumatic slide, and were gone before anyone realized what happened. We found this next to you."

Munro gave him a small glass vial with Japanese markings. The sides of the vial were scratched and scored; at one end was a rubber plunger, at the other end a broken needle.

Elliot sat up.

"Easy there," the doctor said.

"I feel fine," Elliot said, although his head was throbbing. He turned the vial over in his hand. "There was frost on it when you found it?"

Munro nodded. "Very cold."

"CO_2," Elliot said. It was a dart from a gas gun. He shook his head. "They broke the needle off in her." He could imagine Amy's screams of outrage. She was unaccustomed to anything but the tenderest treatment. Perhaps that was one of the shortcomings of his work with her; he had not prepared her well enough for the real world. He sniffed the vial, smelled a pungent odor. "Lobaxin. Fast-acting soporific, onset within fifteen seconds. It's what they'd use." Elliot was angry. Lobaxin was not often used on animals because it caused liver damage. And they had broken the needle—

He got to his feet and leaned on Munro, who put his arm around him. The doctor protested.

"I'm fine," Elliot said.

Across the room, there was another squeal, this one loud and prolonged. Ross was moving her wand over the medicine cabinet, past the bottles of pills and supplies. The sound seemed to embarrass her; quickly she moved away, shutting the cabinet.

She crossed the passenger compartment, and a squeal was heard again. Ross removed a small black device from the underside of one seat. "Look at this. They must have brought an extra person just to plant the bugs. It'll take hours to sterilize the plane. We can't wait."

She went immediately to the computer console and began typing.

Elliot said, "Where are they now? The consortium?"

"The main party left from Kubala airport outside Nairobi six hours ago," Munro said.

"Then they didn't take Amy with them."

"Of course they didn't take her," Ross said, sounding annoyed. "They've got no use for her."

"Have they killed her?" Elliot asked.

"Maybe," Munro said quietly.

"Oh, *Jesus* . . ."

"But I doubt it," Munro continued. "They don't want any publicity, and Amy's famous—as famous in some circles as an ambassador or a head of state. She's a talking gorilla, and there aren't many of those. She's been on television news, she's had her picture in the newspapers. . . . They'd kill you before they killed her."

"Just so they don't kill her," Elliot said.

"They won't," Ross said, with finality. "The consortium isn't interested in Amy. They don't even know why we brought her. They're just trying to blow our timeline—but they won't succeed."

Something in her tone suggested that she planned to leave Amy behind. The idea appalled Elliot. "We've got to get her back," he said. "Amy is my responsibility, I can't possibly abandon her here—"

"Seventy-two minutes," Ross said, pointing to the screen. "We have exactly one hour and twelve minutes before we blow the timeline." She turned to Munro. "And we have to switch over to the second contingency."

"Fine," Munro said. "I'll get the men working on it."

"In a new plane," Ross said. "We can't take this one, it's contaminated."

She was punching in call letters to the computer console, her fingers clicking on the keys. "We'll take it straight to point M," Ross said. "Okay?"

"Absolutely," Munro said.

Elliot said, "I won't leave Amy. If you're going to leave her behind, you'll have to leave me as well—" Elliot stopped.

Printed on the screen was the message FORGET GORILLA PROCEED TO NEXT CHECKPOINT URGENT APE NOT SIGNIFICANT TIMELINE OUTCOME COMPUTER VERIFI-CATION REPEAT PROCEED WITHOUT AMY.

"You can't leave her behind," Elliot said. "I'll stay behind, too."

"Let me tell you something," Ross said. "I never believed that Amy was important to this expedition—or you either. From the very beginning she was just a diversion. When I came to San Francisco, I was followed. You and Amy provided a diversion. You threw the consortium into a spin. It was worth it. Now it's not worth it. We'll leave you both behind if we have to. I couldn't care less."

7. Bugs

"Well, goddamn it," Elliot began, "do you mean to tell me that . . ."

"That's right," Ross said coldly. "You're expendable." But even as she spoke, she grabbed his arm firmly and led him out of the airplane while she held her finger to her lips.

Elliot realized that she intended to pacify him in private, Amy was his responsibility, and to hell with all the diamonds and international intrigue. Outside on the concrete runway he repeated stubbornly, "I'm not leaving without Amy."

"Neither am I." Ross walked quickly across the runway toward a police helicopter.

Elliot hurried to catch up. "What?"

"Don't you understand *anything?*" Ross said. "That airplane's *not clean.* It's full of bugs, and the consortium's listening in. I made that speech for their benefit."

"But who was following you in San Francisco?"

"Nobody. They're going to spend hours trying to figure out who was."

"Amy and I weren't just a diversion?"

"Not at all," she said. "Look: we don't know what happened to the last ERTS Congo team, but no matter what you or Travis or anyone else says, *I* think gorillas were involved. And I think that Amy will help us when we get there."

"As an ambassador?"

"We need information," Ross said. "And she knows more about gorillas than we do."

"But can you find her in an hour and ten minutes?"

"Hell, no," Ross said, checking her watch. "This won't take more than twenty minutes."

"**L**ower! Lower!"

Ross was shouting into her radio headset as she sat alongside the police helicopter pilot. The helicopter was circling the tower of Government House, turning and moving north, toward the Hilton.

"This is not acceptable, madam," the pilot said politely. "We fly below airspace limitations."

"You're too damn high!" Ross said. She was looking at a box on her knees, with four compass-point digital readouts. She flicked switches quickly, while the radio crackled with angry complaints from Nairobi tower.

"East now, due east," she instructed, and the helicopter tilted and moved east, toward the poor outskirts of the city.

In the back, Elliot felt his stomach twist with each banking turn on the helicopter. His head pounded and he felt awful, but he had insisted on coming. He was the only person knowledgeable enough to minister to Amy if she was in medical trouble.

Now, sitting alongside the pilot, Ross said, "Get a reading," and she pointed to the northeast. The helicopter thumped over crude shacks, junked automobile lots, dirt roads. "Slower now, slower . . ."

The readouts glowed, the numbers shifting. Elliot saw them all go to zero, simultaneously.

"Down!" Ross shouted, and the helicopter descended in the center of a vast garbage dump.

The pilot remained with the helicopter; his final words were disquieting. "Where there's garbage, there's rats," he said.

"Rats don't bother me," Ross said, climbing out with her box in her hand.

"Where there's rats, there's cobras," the pilot said.

"Oh," Ross said.

She crossed the dump with Elliot. There was a stiff breeze; papers and debris ruffled at their feet. Elliot's head ached, and the odors arising from the dump nauseated him.

"Not far now," Ross said, watching the box. She was excited, glancing at her watch.

"Here?"

She bent over and picked through the trash, her hand making circles, digging deeper in frustration, elbow-deep in the trash.

Finally she came up with a necklace—a necklace she had given Amy when they first boarded the airplane in San Francisco. She turned it over, examining the plastic name tag on it, which Elliot noticed was unusually thick. There were fresh scratches on the back.

"Hell," Ross said. "Sixteen minutes shot." And she hurried back to the waiting helicopter.

Elliot fell into step beside her. "But how can you find her if they got rid of her necklace bug?"

"Nobody," Ross said, "plants only one bug. This was just a decoy, they were supposed to find it." She pointed to the scratches on the back. "But they're clever, they reset the frequencies."

"Maybe they got rid of the second bug, too," Elliot said.

"They didn't," Ross said. The helicopter lifted off, a thuddering whirr of blades, and the paper and trash of the dump swirled in circles beneath them. She pressed her mouthpiece to her lips and said to the pilot, "Take me to the largest scrapmetal source in Nairobi."

Within nine minutes, they had picked up another very weak signal, located within an automobile junkyard. The helicopter landed in the street outside, drawing dozens of shouting children. Ross went with Elliot into the junkyard, moving past the rusting hulks of cars and trucks.

"You're sure she's here?" Elliot said.

"No question. They have to surround her with metal, it's the only thing they can do."

"Why?"

"Shielding." She picked her way around the broken cars, pausing frequently to refer to her electronic box.

Then Elliot heard a grunt.

It came from inside an ancient rust-red Mercedes bus. Elliot climbed through the shattered doors, the rubber gaskets crumbling in his hands, into the interior. He found Amy on her back, tied with adhesive tape. She was groggy, but complained loudly when he tore the tape off her hair.

He located the broken needle in her right chest and plucked it out with forceps, Amy shrieked, then hugged him. He heard the far-off whine of a police siren.

"It's all right, Amy, it's all right," he said. He set her down and examined her more carefully. She seemed to be okay.

And then he said, "Where's the second bug?"

Ross grinned. "She swallowed it."

Now that Amy was safe, Elliot felt a wave of anger. "You made her swallow it? An electronic bug? Don't you realize that she is a very delicate animal and her health is extremely precarious—"

"Don't get worked up," Ross said. "Remember the vitamins I gave you? You swallowed one, too." She glanced at her watch. "Thirty-two minutes," she said. "Not bad at all. We have forty minutes before we have to leave Nairobi."

8. Present Point

Munro sat in the 747, punching keys on the computer. He watched as the lines crisscrossed over the maps, ticking out datalines, timelines, information lock coordinates.

The computer ran through possible expedition routines quickly, testing a new one every ten seconds. After each data fit, outcomes were printed—cost, logistical difficulties, supply problems, total elapsed times from Houston, from Present Point (Nairobi), where they were now.

Looking for a solution.

It wasn't like the old days, Munro thought. Even five years ago, expeditions were still run on guesswork and luck. But now every expedition employed real-time computer planning; Munro had long since been forced to learn BASIC and TW/GESHUND and other major interactive languages. Nobody did it by the seat of the pants anymore. The business had changed.

Munro had decided to join the ERTS expedition precisely because of those changes. Certainly he hadn't joined because of Karen Ross, who was stubborn and inexperienced. But ERTS had the most elaborate working database, and the most sophisticated planning programs. In the long run, he expected those programs to make the crucial difference. And he liked a smaller team; once the consortium was in the field, their working party of thirty was going to prove unwieldy.

But he had to find a faster timeline to get them in. Munro pressed the buttons, watching the data flash up. He set trajectories, intersections, junctions. Then, with a practiced eye, he began to eliminate alternatives. He closed out pathways, shut down airfields, eliminated truck routes, avoided river crossings.

The computer kept coming back with reduced times, but from Present Point (Nairobi) the total elapsed times were always too long. The best projection beat the consortium by thirty-seven minutes—which was nothing to rely on. He frowned, and smoked a cigar. Perhaps if he crossed the Liko River at Mugana . . .

He punched the buttons.

It didn't help. Crossing the Liko was *slower.* He tried trekking through the Goroba Valley, even though it was probably too hazardous to execute.

PROPOSED ROUTING EXCESSIVELY HAZARDOUS

"Great minds think alike," Munro said, smoking his cigar. But it started him wondering: were there other, unorthodox approaches they had overlooked? And then he had an idea.

The others wouldn't like it, but it might work. . . .

Munro called the logistics equipment list. Yes, they were equipped for it. He punched in the routing, smiling as he saw the line streak straight across Africa, within a few miles of their destination. He called for outcomes.

PROPOSED ROUTING UNACCEPTABLE.

He pressed the override button, got the data outcomes anyway. It was just as he thought—they could beat the consortium by a full forty hours. Nearly two full days!

The computer went back to the previous statement:

PROPOSED ROUTING UNACCEPTABLE / ALTITUDE FACTORS / HAZARDS TO PERSONNEL EXCESSIVE / PROBABILITY SUCCESS UNDER LIMITS /

Munro didn't think that was true. He thought they could pull it off, especially if the weather was good. The altitude wouldn't be a problem, and the ground although rough would be reasonably yielding.

In fact, the more Munro thought about it, the more certain he was that it would work.

9. Departure

The little Fokker S-144 prop plane was pulled up alongside the giant 747 cargo jet, like an infant nursing at its mother's breast. Two cargo ramps were in constant motion as men transferred equipment from the larger plane to the smaller one. Returning to the airfield, Ross explained to Elliot that they would be taking the smaller plane, since the 747 had to be debugged, and since it was "too large" for their needs now.

"But the jet must be faster," Elliot said.

"Not necessarily," Ross said, but she did not explain further.

In any case, things were now happening very fast, and Elliot had other concerns. He helped Amy aboard the Fokker, and checked her thoroughly. She seemed to be bruised all over her body—at least she complained that everything hurt when he touched her—but she had no broken bones, and she was in good spirits.

Several black men were loading equipment into the airplane, laughing and slapping each other on the back, having a fine time. Amy was intrigued with the men, demanding to know *What joke?* But they ignored her, concentrating on the work at hand. And she was still groggy from her medication. Soon she fell asleep.

Ross supervised the loading, and Elliot moved toward the rear of the plane, where she was talking with a jolly black man, whom she introduced as Kahega.

"Ah," Kahega said, shaking Elliot's hand. "Dr. Elliot. Dr. Ross and Dr. Elliot, two doctors, very excellent."

Elliot was not sure why it was excellent.

Kahega laughed infectiously. "Very good *cover,*" he announced. "Not like the old days with Captain Munro. Now two doctors—a medical mission, yes? Very excellent. Where are the 'medical supplies'?" He cocked an eyebrow.

"We have no medical supplies." Ross sighed.

"Oh, very excellent, Doctor, I like your manner," Kahega said. "You are American, yes? We take what, M-16s? Very good rifle, M-16. I prefer it myself."

"Kahega thinks we are running guns," Ross said. "He just can't believe we aren't."

Kahega was laughing. "You are with Captain Munro!" he said, as if this explained everything. And then he went off to see about the other workmen.

"You sure we aren't running guns?" Elliot asked when they were alone.

"We're after something more valuable than guns," Ross said. She was re-packing the equipment, working quickly. Elliot asked if he could help, but she shook her head. "I've got to do this myself. We have to get it down to forty pounds per person."

"Forty pounds? For everything?"

"That's what the computer projection allows. Munro's brought in Kahega and seven other Kikuya assistants. With the three of us, that makes eleven people all together, plus Amy—she gets her full forty pounds. But it means a total of four hundred eighty pounds." Ross continued to weigh packs and parcels of food.

The news gave Elliot serious misgivings. The expedition was taking yet an-other turn, into still greater danger. His immediate desire to back out was checked by his memory of the video screen, and the gray gorillalike creature that he suspected was a new, unknown animal. That was a discovery worth risk. He stared out the window at the porters. "They're Kikuyu?"

"Yes," she said. "They're good porters, even if they never shut up. Kikuyu tribesmen love to talk. They're all brothers, by the way, so be careful what you say. I just hope Munro didn't have to tell them too much."

"The Kikuyu?"

"No, the NCNA."

"The NCNA," Elliot repeated.

"The Chinese. The Chinese are very interested in computers and elec-tronic technology," Ross said. "Munro must be telling them something in ex-change for the advice they're giving him." She gestured to the window, and Elliot looked out. Sure enough, Munro stood under the shadow of the 747 wing, talking with four Chinese men.

"Here," Ross said, "stow these in that corner." She pointed to three large Styrofoam cartons marked AMERICAN SPORTS DIVERS, LAKE ELSINORE, CALIF.

"We doing underwater work?" Elliot asked, puzzled.

But Ross wasn't paying attention. "I just wish I knew what he was telling them," she said. But as it turned out, Ross needn't have worried, for Munro paid the Chinese in something more valuable to them than electronics infor-mation.

The Fokker lifted off from the Nairobi runway at 14:24 hours, three min-utes ahead of their new timeline schedule.

During the sixteen hours following Amy's recovery, the ERTS expedition trav-eled 560 miles across the borders of four countries—Kenya, Tanzania, Rwanda, and Zaire—as they went from Nairobi to the Barawana Forest, at the edge of the Congo rain forest. The logistics of this complex move would have been impossible without the assistance of an outside ally. Munro said that he "had friends in low places," and in this case he had turned to the Chinese Secret Service, in Tanzania.

The Chinese had been active in Africa since the early 1960s, when their spy networks attempted to influence the course of the Congolese civil war because China wanted access to the Congo's rich supplies of uranium. Field operatives were run out of the Bank of China or, more commonly, the New China News Agency. Munro had dealt with a number of NCNA "war correspondents" when he was running arms from 1963 to 1968, and he had never lost his contacts.

The Chinese financial commitment to Africa was considerable. In the late 1960s, more than half of China's two billion dollars in foreign aid went to African nations. An equal sum was spent secretly; in 1973, Mao Tse-tung complained publicly about the money he had wasted trying to overthrow the Zaire government of President Mobutu.

The Chinese mission in Africa was meant to counter the Russian influence, but since World War II the Chinese bore no great love for the Japanese, and Munro's desire to beat the Euro-Japanese consortium fell on sympathetic ears. To celebrate the alliance, Munro had brought three grease-stained cardboard cartons from Hong Kong.

The two chief Chinese operatives in Africa, Li T'ao and Liu Shu-wen, were both from Hunan province. They found their African posting tedious because of the bland African food, and gratefully accepted Munro's gift of a case of tree ears fungus, a case of hot bean sauce, and a case of chili paste with garlic. The fact that these spices came from neutral Hong Kong, and were not the inferior condiments produced in Taiwan, was a subtle point; in any case, the gift struck exactly the proper note for an informal exchange.

NCNA operatives assisted Munro with paperwork, some difficult-to-obtain equipment, and information. The Chinese possessed excellent maps, and remarkably detailed information about conditions along the northeast Zaire border—since they were assisting the Tanzanian troops invading Uganda. The Chinese had told him that the jungle rivers were flooding, and had advised him to procure a balloon for crossings. But Munro did not bother to take their advice; indeed, he seemed to have some plan to reach his destination without crossing any rivers at all. Although how, the Chinese could not imagine.

At 10 P.M. on June 16, the Fokker stopped to refuel at Rawamagena airport, outside Kigali in Rwanda. The local traffic control officer boarded the plane with a clipboard and forms, asking their next destination. Munro said that it was Rawamagena airport, meaning that the aircraft would make a loop, then return.

Elliot frowned. "But we're going to land somewhere in the—"

"Sh-h-h," Ross said, shaking her head. "Leave it alone."

Certainly the traffic officer seemed content with this flight plan; once the pilot signed the clipboard, he departed. Ross explained that flight controllers in Rwanda were accustomed to aircraft that did not file full plans. "He just wants to know when the plane will be back at his field. The rest is none of his business."

Rawamagena airport was sleepy; they had to wait two hours for petrol to be brought, yet the normally impatient Ross waited quietly. And Munro dozed, equally indifferent to the delay.

"What about the timeline?" Elliot asked.

"No problem," she said. "We can't leave for three hours anyway. We need the light over Mukenko."

"That's where the airfield is?" Elliot asked.

"If you call it an airfield," Munro said, and he pulled his safari hat down over his eyes and went back to sleep.

This worried Elliot until Ross explained to him that most outlying African airfields were just dirt strips cut into the bush. The pilots couldn't land at night, or in the foggy morning, because there were often animals on the field, or encamped nomads, or another plane that had put down and was unable to take off again. "We need the light," she explained. "That's why we're waiting. Don't worry: it's all factored in."

Elliot accepted her explanation, and went back to check on Amy. Ross sighed. "Don't you think we'd better tell him?" she asked.

"Why?" Munro said, not lifting his hat.

"Maybe there's a problem with Amy."

"I'll take care of Amy," Munro said.

"It's going to upset Elliot when he finds out," Ross said.

"Of course it's going to upset him," Munro said. "But there's no point upsetting him until we have to. After all, what's this jump worth to us?"

"Forty hours, at least. It's dangerous, but it'll give us a whole new timeline. We could still beat them."

"Well, there's your answer," Munro said. "Now keep your mouth shut, and get some rest."

DAY 5: MORUTI

JUNE 17, 1979

1. Zaire

Five hours out of Rawamagena, the landscape changed. Once past Goma, near the Zaire border, they found themselves flying over the easternmost fingers of the Congo rain forest. Elliot stared out the window, fascinated.

Here and there in the pale morning light, a few fragile wisps of fog clung like cotton to the canopy of trees. And occasionally they passed the dark snaking curve of a muddy river, or the straight deep red gash of a road. But for the most part they looked down upon an unbroken expanse of dense forest, extending away into the distance as far as the eye could see.

The view was boring, and simultaneously frightening—it was frightening to be confronted by what Stanley had called "the indifferent immensity of the natural world." As one sat in the air-conditioned comfort of an airplane seat, it was impossible not to recognize that this vast, monotonous forest was a giant creation of nature, utterly dwarfing in scale the greatest cities or other creations of mankind. Each individual green puff of a tree had a trunk forty feet in diameter, soaring two hundred feet into the air; a space the size of a Gothic cathedral was concealed beneath its billowing foliage. And Elliot knew that the forest extended to the west for nearly two thousand miles, until it finally stopped at the Atlantic Ocean, on the west coast of Zaire.

Elliot had been anticipating Amy's reaction to this first view of the jungle, her natural environment. She looked out the window with a fixed stare. She signed *Here jungle* with the same emotional neutrality that she named color cards, or objects spread out on her trailer floor in San Francisco. She was identifying the jungle, giving a name to what she saw, but he sensed no deeper recognition.

Elliot said to her, "Amy like jungle?"

Jungle here, she signed. *Jungle is.*

He persisted, probing for the emotional context that he was sure must be there. Amy like jungle?

Jungle here. Jungle is. Jungle place here Amy see jungle here.

He tried another approach. "Amy live jungle here?"

No. Expressionless.

"Where Amy live?"

Amy live Amy house. Referring to her trailer in San Francisco.

Elliot watched her loosen her seat belt, cup her chin on her hand as she stared lazily out the window. She signed, *Amy want cigarette*.

She had noticed Munro smoking.

"Later, Amy," Elliot said.

At seven in the morning, they flew over the shimmering metal roofs of the tin and tantalum mining complex at Masisi. Munro, Kahega, and the other porters went to the back of the plane, where they worked on the equipment, chattering excitedly in Swahili.

Amy, seeing them go, signed, *They worried*.

"Worried about what, Amy?"

They worried men worry they worried problems. After a while, Elliot moved to the rear of the plane to find Munro's men half buried under great heaps of straw, stuffing equipment into oblong torpedo-shaped muslin containers, then packing straw around the supplies. Elliot pointed to the muslin torpedoes. "What are these?"

"They're called Crosslin containers," Munro said. "Very reliable."

"I've never seen equipment packed this way," Elliot said, watching the men work. "They seem to be protecting our supplies very carefully."

"That's the idea," Munro said. And he moved up the aircraft to the cockpit, to confer with the pilot.

Amy signed, *Nosehair man lie Peter*. "Nosehair man" was her term for Munro, but Elliot ignored her. He turned to Kahega. "How far to the airfield?"

Kahega glanced up. "Airfield?"

"At Mukenko."

Kahega paused, thinking it over. "Two hours," he said. And then he giggled. He said something in Swahili and all his brothers laughed, too.

"What's funny?" Elliot said.

"Oh, Doctor," Kahega said, slapping him on the back. "You are humorous by your nature."

The airplane banked, making a slow wide circle in the air. Kahega and his brothers peered out the windows, and Elliot joined them. He saw only unbroken jungle—and then a column of green jeeps, moving down a muddy track far below. It looked like a military formation. He heard the word "Muguru" repeated several times.

"What's the matter?" Elliot said. "Is this Muguru?"

Kahega shook his head vigorously. "No hell. This damn pilot, I warn Captain Munro, this damn pilot lost."

"Lost?" Elliot repeated. Even the word was chilling.

Kahega laughed. "Captain Munro set him right, give him dickens."

The airplane now flew east, away from the jungle toward a wooded highland area, rolling hills and stands of deciduous trees. Kahega's brothers chattered excitedly, and laughed and slapped one another; they seemed to be having a fine time.

116

Then Ross came back, moving quickly down the aisle, her face tense. She unpacked cardboard boxes, withdrawing several basketball-sized spheres of tightly wrapped metal foil.

The foil reminded him of Christmas-tree tinsel. "What's that for?" Elliot asked.

And then he heard the first explosion, and the Fokker shuddered in the air.

Running to the window, he saw a straight thin white vapor trail terminating in a black smoke cloud off to their right. The Fokker was banking, tilting toward the jungle. As he watched, a second trail streaked up toward them from the green forest below.

It was a missile, he realized. A guided missile.

"Ross!" Munro shouted.

"Ready!" Ross shouted back.

There was a bursting red explosion, and his view through the windows was obscured by dense smoke. The airplane shook with the blast, but continued the turn. Elliot couldn't believe it: *someone was shooting missiles at them.*

"Radar!" Munro shouted. "Not optical! Radar!"

Ross gathered up the silver basketballs in her arms and moved back down the aisle. Kahega was opening the rear door, the wind whipping through the compartment.

"What the hell's happening?" Elliot said.

"Don't worry," Ross said over her shoulder. "We'll make up the time." There was a loud whoosh, followed by a third explosion. With the airplane still banked steeply, Ross tore the wrappings from the basketballs and threw them out into the open sky.

Engines roaring, the Fokker swung eight miles to the south and climbed to twelve thousand feet, then circled the forest in a holding pattern. With each revolution, Elliot could see the foil strips hanging in the air like a glinting metallic cloud. Two more rockets exploded within the cloud. Even from a distance, the noise and the shock waves disturbed Amy; she was rocking back and forth in her seat, grunting softly.

"That's chaff," Ross explained, sitting in front of her portable computer console, punching keys. "It confuses radar weapons systems. Those radar-guided SAMs read us as somewhere in the cloud."

Elliot heard her words slowly, as if in a dream. It made no sense to him. "But who's shooting at us?"

"Probably the FZA," Munro said. "Forces Zairoises Armoises—the Zaire army."

"The Zaire army? Why?"

"It's a mistake," Ross said, still punching buttons, not looking up.

"A mistake? They're shooting surface-to-air missiles at us and *it's a mis-*

take? Don't you think you'd better call them and tell them it's a mistake?"

"Can't," Ross said.

"Why not?"

"Because," Munro said, "we didn't want to file a flight plan in Rawamagena. That means we are technically in violation of Zaire airspace."

"Jesus Christ," Elliot said.

Ross said nothing. She continued to work at the computer console, trying to get the static to resolve on the screen, pressing one key after another.

"When I agreed to join this expedition," Elliot said, beginning to shout, "I didn't expect to get into a shooting war."

"Neither did I," Ross said. "It looks as if we both got more than we bargained for."

Before Elliot could reply, Munro put an arm around his shoulder and took him aside. "It's going to be all right," he told Elliot. "They're outdated sixties SAMs and most of them are blowing up because the solid propellant's cracked with age. We're in no danger. Just look after Amy, she needs your help now. Let me work with Ross."

Ross was under intense pressure. With the airplane circling eight miles from the chaff cloud, she had to make a decision quickly. But she had just been dealt a devastating—and wholly unexpected—setback.

The Euro-Japanese consortium had been ahead of them from the very start, by approximately eighteen hours and twenty minutes. On the ground in Nairobi, Munro had worked out a plan with Ross which would erase that difference and put the ERTS expedition on-site *forty hours* ahead of the consortium team. This plan—which for obvious reasons she had not told Elliot—called for them to parachute onto the barren southern slopes of Mount Mukenko.

From Mukenko, Munro estimated it was thirty-six hours to the ruined city; Ross expected to jump at two o'clock that afternoon. Depending on cloud cover over Mukenko and the specific drop zone, they might reach the city as early as noon on June 19.

The plan was extremely hazardous. They would be jumping untrained personnel into a wilderness area, more than three days' walk from the nearest large town. If anyone suffered a serious injury, the chances of survival were slight. There was also a question about the equipment: at altitudes of 8,000– 10,000 feet on the volcanic slopes, air resistance was reduced, and the Crosslin packets might not provide enough protection.

Initially Ross had rejected Munro's plan as too risky, but he convinced her it was feasible. He pointed out that the parafoils were equipped with automated altimeter-release devices; that the upper volcanic scree was as yielding as a sandy beach; that the Crosslin containers could be over-packed; and that he could carry Amy down himself.

Ross had double-checked outcome probabilities from the Houston computer, and the results were unequivocal. The probability of a successful jump was .7980, meaning there was one chance in five that someone would be badly hurt. However, *given a successful jump,* the probability of expedition success was .9934, making it virtually certain they would beat the consortium to the site.

No alternate plan scored so high. She had looked at the data and said, "I guess we jump."

"I think we do," Munro had said.

The jump solved many problems, for the geopolitical updates were increasingly unfavorable. The Kigani were now in full rebellion; the pygmies were unstable; the Zaire army had sent armored units into the eastern border area to put down the Kigani—and African field armies were notoriously trigger-happy. By jumping onto Mukenko, they expected to bypass all these hazards.

But that was before the Zaire army SAMs began exploding all around them. They were still eighty miles south of the intended drop zone, circling over Kigani territory, wasting time and fuel. It looked as if their daring plan, so carefully worked out and confirmed by computer, was suddenly irrelevant.

And to add to her difficulties, she could not confer with Houston; the computer refused to link up by satellite. She spent fifteen minutes working with the portable unit, boosting power and switching scrambler codes, until she finally realized that her transmission was being electronically jammed.

For the first time in her memory, Karen Ross wanted to cry.

"Easy now," Munro said quietly, lifting her hand away from the keyboard. "One thing at a time, no point in getting upset." Ross had been pressing the keys over and over again, unaware of what she was doing.

Munro was conscious of the deteriorating situation with both Elliot and Ross. He had seen it happen on expeditions before, particularly when scientists and technical people were involved. Scientists worked all day in laboratories where conditions could be rigorously regulated and monitored. Sooner or later, scientists came to believe that the outside world was just as controllable as their laboratories. Even though they knew better, the shock of discovering that the natural world followed its own rules and was indifferent to them represented a harsh psychic blow. Munro could read the signs.

"But this," Ross said, "is obviously a non-military aircraft, how can they do it?"

Munro stared at her. In the Congolese civil war, civilian aircraft had been routinely shot down by all sides. "These things happen," he said.

"And the jamming? Those bastards haven't got the capability to jam us. We're being jammed between our transmitter and our satellite transponder. To do that requires another satellite somewhere, and—" She broke off, frowning.

"You didn't expect the consortium to sit by idly," Munro said. "The question is, can you fix it? Have you got countermeasures?"

"Sure, I've got countermeasures," Ross said. "I can encode a burst bounce, I can transmit optically on an IR carrier, I can link a ground-base cable—but there's nothing I can put together in the next few minutes, and we need information now. Our plan is shot."

"One thing at a time," Munro repeated quietly. He saw the tension in her features, and he knew she was not thinking clearly. He also knew he could not do her thinking for her; he had to get her calm again.

In Munro's judgment, the ERTS expedition was already finished—they could not possibly beat the consortium to the Congo site. But he had no intention of quitting; he had led expeditions long enough to know that anything could happen, so he said, "We can still make up the lost time."

"Make it up? How?"

Munro said the first thing that came to mind: "We'll take the Ragora north. Very fast river, no problem."

"The Ragora's too dangerous."

"We'll have to see," Munro said, although he knew that she was right. The Ragora was much too dangerous, particularly in June. Yet he kept his voice calm, soothing, reassuring. "Shall I tell the others?" he asked finally.

"Yes," Ross said. In the distance, they heard another rocket explosion. "Let's get out of here."

Munro moved swiftly to the rear of the Fokker and said to Kahega, "Prepare the men."

"Yes, boss," Kahega said. A bottle of whiskey was passed around, and each of the men took a long swallow.

Elliot said, "What the hell is this?"

"The men are getting prepared," Munro said.

"Prepared for what?" Elliot asked.

At that moment, Ross came back, looking grim. "From here on, we'll continue on foot," she said.

Elliot looked out the window. "Where's the airfield?"

"There is no airfield," Ross said.

"What do you mean?"

"I mean there is no airfield."

"Is the plane going to put down in the fields?" Elliot asked.

"No," Ross said. "The plane is not going to put down at all."

"Then how do we get down?" Elliot asked, but even as he asked the question, his stomach sank, because he knew the answer.

"**A**my will be fine," Munro said cheerfully, cinching Elliot's straps tightly around his chest. "I gave her a shot of your Thoralen tranquilizer, and she'll be quite calm. No problem at all, I'll keep a good grip on her."

"Keep a good grip on her?" Elliot asked.

"She's too small to fit a harness," Munro said. "I'll have to carry her down." Amy snored loudly, and drooled on Munro's shoulder. He set Amy on the floor; she lay limply on her back, still snoring.

"Now, then," Munro said. "Your parafoil opens automatically. You'll find you have lines in both hands, left and right. Pull left to go left, right to go right, and—"

"What happens to her?" Elliot asked, pointing to Amy.

"I'll take her. Pay attention now. If anything goes wrong, your reserve chute is here, on your chest." He tapped a cloth bundle with a small black digital box, which read 4757. "That's your rate-of-fall altimeter. Automatically pops your reserve chute if you hit thirty-six hundred feet and are still falling faster than two feet per second. Nothing to worry about; whole thing's automatic."

Elliot was chilled, drenched in sweat. "What about landing?"

"Nothing to it," Munro grinned. "You'll land automatically too. Stay loose and relax, take the shock in the legs. Equivalent of jumping off a ten-foot ledge. You've done it a thousand times."

Behind him Elliot saw the open door, bright sunlight glaring into the plane. The wind whipped and howled. Kahega's men jumped in quick succession, one after another. He glanced at Ross, who was ashen, her lower lip trembling as she gripped the doorway.

"Karen, you're not going to go along with—"

She jumped, disappearing into the sunlight. Munro said, "You're next."

"I've never jumped before," Elliot said.

"That's the best way. You won't be frightened."

"But I *am* frightened."

"I can help you with that," Munro said, and he pushed Elliot out of the plane.

Munro watched him fall away, his grin instantly gone. Munro had adopted his hearty demeanor only for Elliot's benefit. "If a man has to do something dangerous," he said later, "it helps to be angry. It's for his own protection, really. Better he should hate someone than fall apart. I wanted Elliot to hate me all the way down."

Munro understood the risks. The minute they left the aircraft, they also left civilization, and all the unquestioned assumptions of civilization. They were jumping not only through the air, but through time, backward into a more primitive and dangerous way of life—the eternal realities of the Congo, which had existed for centuries before them. "Those were the facts of life," Munro said, "but I didn't see any reason to worry the others before they jumped. My job was to get those people into the Congo, not scare them to death. There was plenty of time for that."

Elliot fell, scared to death.

His stomach jumped into his throat, and he tasted bile; the wind screamed around his ears and tugged at his hair; and the air was so cold—he was instantly chilled and shivering. Below him the Barawana Forest lay spread across rolling hills. He felt no appreciation for the beauty before him, and in fact he closed his eyes, for he was plummeting at hideous speed toward the ground. But with his eyes shut he was more aware of the screaming wind.

Too much time had passed. Obviously the parafoil (whatever the hell that was) was not going to open. His life now depended on the parachute attached to his chest. He clutched it, a small tight bundle near his churning stomach. Then he pulled his hands away: he didn't want to interfere with its opening. He dimly remembered that people had died that way, when they interfered with the opening of their parachute.

The screaming wind continued; his body rushed sickeningly downward. *Nothing was happening.* He felt the fierce wind tugging at his feet, whipping his trousers, flapping his shirt against his arms. *Nothing was happening.* It had been at least three minutes since he'd jumped from the plane. He dared not open his eyes, for fear of seeing the trees rushing up close as his body crashed downward toward them in his final seconds of conscious life. . . .

He was going to throw up.

Bile dribbled from his mouth, but since he was falling head downward, the liquid ran up his chin to his neck and then inside his shirt. It was freezing cold. His shivering was becoming uncontrollable.

He snapped upright with a bone-twisting jolt.

For an instant he thought he had hit the ground, and then he realized that he was still descending through the air, but more slowly. He opened his eyes and stared at pale blue sky.

He looked down, and was shocked to see that he was still thousands of feet from the earth. Obviously he had only been falling a few seconds from the airplane above him—

Looking up, he could not see the plane. Directly overhead was a giant rectangular shape, with brilliant red, white, and blue stripes: the parafoil. Finding it easier to look up than down, he studied the parafoil intently. The leading edge was curved and puffy; the rear edge thin, fluttering in the breeze. The parafoil looked very much like an airplane wing, with cords running down to his body.

He took a deep breath and looked down. He was still very high over the landscape. There was some comfort in the slowness with which he was descending. It was really rather peaceful.

And then he noticed he wasn't moving down; he was moving sideways. He could see the other parafoils below, Kahega and his men and Ross; he tried to count them, and thought there were six, but he had difficulty concentrating. He appeared to be moving laterally away from them.

He tugged on the lines in his left hand, and he felt his body twist as the parafoil moved, taking him to the left.

Not bad, he thought.

He pulled harder on the left cords, ignoring the fact that this seemed to make him move faster. He tried to stay near the rectangles descending beneath him. He heard the scream of the wind in his ears. He looked up, hoping to see Munro, but all he could see was the stripes of his own parafoil.

He looked back down, and was astonished to find that the ground was a great deal closer. In fact, it seemed to be rushing up to him at brutal speed. He wondered where he had got the idea that he was drifting gently downward. There was nothing gentle about his descent at all. He saw the first of the parafoils crumple gently as Kahega touched ground, then the second, and the third.

It wouldn't be long before he landed. He was approaching the level of the trees, but his lateral movement was very fast. He realized that his left hand was rigidly pulling on the cords. He released his grip, and his lateral movement ceased. He drifted forward.

Two more parafoils crumpled on impact. He looked back to see Kahega and his men, already down, gathering up the cloth. They were all right; that was encouraging.

He was sliding right into a dense clump of trees. He pulled his cords and twisted to the right, his whole body tilting. He was moving very fast now. The trees could not be avoided. He was going to smash into them. The branches seemed to reach up like fingers, grasping for him.

He closed his eyes, and felt the branches scratching at his face and body as he crashed down, knowing that any second he was going to hit, that he was going to hit the ground and roll—

He never hit.

Everything became silent. He felt himself bobbing up and down. He opened his eyes and saw that he was swinging four feet above the ground. His parafoil had caught in the trees.

He fumbled with his harness buckles, and fell out onto the earth. As he picked himself up, Kahega and Ross came running over to ask if he was all right.

"I'm fine," Elliot said, and indeed he felt extraordinarily fine, more alive than he could ever remember feeling. The next instant he fell over on rubber legs and promptly threw up.

Kahega laughed. "Welcome to the Congo," he said.

Elliot wiped his chin and said, "Where is Amy?"

A moment later Munro landed, with a bleeding ear where Amy had bitten him in terror. But Amy was not the worse for the experience, and came running on her knuckles over to Elliot, making sure that he was all right, and then signing, *Amy fly no like.*

"Look out!"

The first of the torpedo-shaped Crosslin packets smashed down, exploding like a bomb when it hit the ground, spraying equipment and straw in all directions.

123

"There's the second one!"

Elliot dived for safety. The second bomb hit just a few yards away; he was pelted with foil containers of food and rice. Overhead, he heard the drone of the circling Fokker airplane. He got to his feet in time to see the final two Crosslin containers crash down, and Kahega's men running for safety, with Ross shouting, "Careful, those have the lasers!"

It was like being in the middle of a blitz, but as swiftly as it had begun it was over. The Fokker above them flew off, and the sky was silent; the men began repacking the equipment and burying the parafoils, while Munro barked instructions in Swahili.

Twenty minutes later, they were moving single-file through the forest, starting a two-hundred-mile trek that would lead them into the unexplored eastern reaches of the Congo, to a fabulous reward.

If they could reach it in time.

2. Kigani

Once past the initial shock of his jump, Elliot enjoyed the walk through the Barawana Forest. Monkeys chattered in the trees, and birds called in the cool air; the Kikuyu porters were strung out behind them, smoking cigarettes and joking with one another in an exotic tongue. Elliot found all his emotions agreeable—the sense of freedom from a crass civilization; the sense of adventure, of unexpected events that might occur at any future moment; and finally the sense of romance, of a quest for the poignant past while omnipresent danger kept sensation at a peak of intense feeling. It was in this heightened mood that he listened to the forest animals around him, viewed the play of sunlight and shadow, felt the springy ground beneath his boots, and looked over at Karen Ross, whom he found beautiful and graceful in an utterly unexpected way.

Karen Ross did not look back at him.

As she walked, she twisted knobs on one of her black electronic boxes, trying to establish a signal. A second electronic box hung from a shoulder strap, and since she did not turn to look at him, he had time to notice that there was already a dark stain of sweat at her shoulder, and another running

down the back of her shirt. Her dark blonde hair was damp, clinging unattrac-
tively to the back of her head. And he noticed that her trousers were wrinkled,
streaked with dirt from the fall. She still did not look back.

"Enjoy the forest," Munro advised him. "This is the last time you'll feel
cool and dry for quite a while."

Elliot agreed that the forest was pleasant.

"Yes, very pleasant." Munro nodded, with an odd expression on his face.

The Barawana Forest was not virginal. From time to time, they passed
cleared fields and other signs of human habitation, although they never saw
farmers. When Elliot mentioned that fact, Munro just shook his head. As they
moved deeper into the forest Munro turned self-absorbed, unwilling to talk.
Yet he showed an interest in the fauna, frequently pausing to listen intently to
bird cries before signaling the expedition to continue on.

During these pauses, Elliot would look back down the line of porters with
loads balanced on their heads, and feel acutely his kinship with Livingstone
and Stanley and the other explorers who had ventured through Africa a century before. And in this, his romantic associations were accurate. Central African life was little changed since Stanley explored the Congo in the 1870s, and
neither was the basic nature of expeditions to that region. Serious exploration
was still carried out on foot; porters were still necessary; expenses were still
daunting—and so were the dangers.

By midday, Elliot's boots had begun to hurt his feet, and he found that he was
exceedingly tired. Apparently the porters were tired too, because they had
fallen silent, no longer smoking cigarettes and shouting jokes to one another
up and down the line. The expedition proceeded in silence until Elliot asked
Munro if they were going to stop for lunch.

"No," Munro said.

"Good," Karen Ross said, glancing at her watch.

Shortly after one o'clock, they heard the thumping of helicopters. The reaction of Munro and the porters was immediate—they dived under a stand of
large trees and waited, looking upwards. Moments later, two large green helicopters passed overhead; Elliot clearly read white stenciling: "FZA."

Munro squinted at the departing craft. They were American-made Hueys;
he had not been able to see the armament. "It's the army," he said. "They're
looking for Kigani."

An hour later, they arrived at a clearing where manioc was being grown. A
crude wooden farmhouse stood in the center, with pale smoke issuing from a
chimney and laundry on a wash line flapping in the gentle breeze. But they
saw no inhabitants.

The expedition had circled around previous farm clearings, but this time
Munro raised his hand to call for a halt. The porters dropped their loads and
sat in the grass, not speaking.

The atmosphere was tense, although Elliot could not understand why.

Munro squatted with Kahega at the edge of the clearing, watching the farmhouse and the surrounding fields. After twenty minutes, when there was still no sign of movement, Ross, who was crouched near Munro, became impatient. "I don't see why we are—"

Munro clapped his hand over her mouth. He pointed to the clearing, and mouthed one word: Kigani.

Ross's eyes went wide. Munro took his hand away.

They all stared at the farmhouse. Still there was no sign of life. Ross made a circular movement with her arm, suggesting that they circle around the clearing and move on. Munro shook his head, and pointed to the ground, indicating that she should sit. Munro looked questioningly at Elliot, and pointed to Amy, who foraged in the tall grass off to one side. He seemed to be concerned that Amy would make noise. Elliot signed to Amy to be quiet, but it was not necessary. Amy had sensed the general tension, and glanced warily from time to time toward the farmhouse.

Nothing happened for several more minutes; they listened to the buzz of the cicadas in the hot midday sun, and they waited. They watched the laundry flutter in the breeze.

Then the thin wisp of blue smoke from the chimney stopped.

Munro and Kahega exchanged glances. Kahega slipped back to where the porters sat, opened one load, and brought out a machine gun. He covered the safety with his hand, muffling the click as he released it. It was incredibly quiet in the clearing. Kahega resumed his place next to Munro and handed him the gun. Munro checked the safety, then set the gun on the ground. They waited several minutes more. Elliot looked at Ross but she was not looking at him.

There was a soft creak as the farmhouse door opened. Munro picked up the machine gun.

No one came out. They all stared at the open door, waiting. And then finally the Kigani stepped into the sunlight.

Elliot counted twelve tall muscular men armed with bows and arrows, and carrying long *pangas* in their hands. Their legs and chests were streaked with white, and their faces were solid white, which gave their heads a menacing, skull-like appearance. As the Kigani moved off through the tall manioc, only their white heads were visible, looking around tensely.

Even after they were gone, Munro remained watching the silent clearing for another ten minutes. Finally he stood and sighed. When he spoke, his voice seemed incredibly loud. "Those were Kigani," Munro said.

"What were they doing?" Ross said.

"Eating," Munro said. "They killed the family in that house, and then ate them. Most farmers have left, because the Kigani are on the rampage."

He signaled Kahega to get the men moving again, and they set off, skirting around the clearing. Elliot kept looking at the farmhouse, wondering what he would see if he went inside. Munro's statement had been so casual; *They killed the family . . . and then ate them.*

126

"I suppose," Ross said, looking over her shoulder, "that we should consider ourselves lucky. We're probably among the last people in the world to see these things."

Munro shook his head. "I doubt it," he said. "Old habits die hard."

During the Congolese civil war in the 1960s, reports of widespread cannibalism and other atrocities shocked the Western world. But in fact cannibalism had always been openly practiced in central Africa.

In 1897, Sidney Hinde wrote that "nearly all the tribes in the Congo Basin either are, or have been, cannibals; and among some of them the practice is on the increase." Hinde was impressed by the undisguised nature of Congolese cannibalism: "The captains of steamers have often assured me that whenever they try to buy goats from the natives, slaves are demanded in exchange; the natives often come aboard with tusks of ivory with the intention of buying a slave, complaining that *meat is now scarce in their neighborhood.*"

In the Congo, cannibalism was not associated with ritual or religion or war; it was a simple dietary preference. The Reverend Holman Bentley, who spent twenty years in the region, quoted a native as saying, "You white men consider pork to be the tastiest of meat, but pork is not to be compared with human flesh." Bentley felt that the natives "could not understand the objections raised to the practice. 'You eat fowls and goats, and we eat men; why not? What is the difference?' "

This frank attitude astonished observers, and led to bizarre customs. In 1910, Herbert Ward wrote of markets where slaves were sold "piecemeal whilst still alive. Incredible as it may appear, captives are led from place to place in order that individuals may have the opportunity of indicating, by external marks on the body, the portion they desire to acquire. The distinguishing marks are generally made by means of coloured clay or strips of grass tied in a peculiar fashion. The astounding stoicism of the victims, who thus witness the bargaining for their limbs piecemeal, is only equalled by the callousness with which they walk forward to meet their fate."

Such reports cannot be dismissed as late-Victorian hysteria, for all observers found the cannibals likable and sympathetic. Ward wrote that "the cannibals are not schemers and they are not mean. In direct opposition to all natural conjectures, they are among the best types of men." Bentley described them as "merry, manly fellows, very friendly in conversation and quite demonstrative in their affection."

Under Belgian colonial administration, cannibalism became much rarer—by the 1950s, there were even a few graveyards to be found—but no one seriously thought it had been eradicated. In 1956, H. C. Engert wrote, "Cannibalism is far from being dead in Africa. . . . I myself once lived in a cannibal village for a time, and found some [human] bones. The natives . . . were pleasant enough people. It was just an old custom which dies hard."

* * *

Munro considered the 1979 Kigani uprising a political insurrection. The tribesmen were rebelling against the demand by the Zaire government that the Kigani change from hunting to farming, as if that were a simple matter. The Kigani were a poor and backward people; their knowledge of hygiene was rudimentary, their diet lacked proteins and vitamins, and they were prey to malaria, hookworm, bilharzia, and African sleeping sickness. One child in four died at birth, and few Kigani adults lived past the age of twenty-five. The hardships of their life required explanation, supplied by Angawa, or sorcerers. The Kigani believed that most deaths were supernatural: either the victim was under a sorcerer's spell, had broken some taboo, or was killed by vengeful spirits from the dead. Hunting also had a supernatural aspect: game was strongly influenced by the spirit world. In fact, the Kigani considered the supernatural world far more real than the day-to-day world, which they felt to be a "waking dream," and they attempted to control the supernatural through magical spells and potions, provided by the Angawa. They also carried out ritual body alterations, such as painting the face and hands white, to render an individual more powerful in battle. The Kigani believed that magic also resided in the bodies of their adversaries, and so to overcome spells cast by other Angawa they ate the bodies of their enemies. The magical power invested in the enemy thus became their own, frustrating enemy sorcerers.

These beliefs were very old, and the Kigani had long since settled on a pattern of response to threat, which was to eat other human beings. In 1890, they went on the rampage in the north, following the first visits by foreigners bearing firearms, which had frightened off the game. During the civil war in 1961, starving, they attacked and ate other tribes.

"And why are they eating people now?" Elliot asked Munro.

"They want their right to hunt," Munro said. "Despite the Kinshasa bureaucrats."

In the early afternoon, the expedition mounted a hill from which they could overlook the valleys behind them to the south. In the distance they saw great billowing clouds of smoke and licking flames; there were the muffled explosions of air-to-ground rockets, and the helicopters wheeling like mechanical vultures over a kill.

"Those are Kigani villages," Munro said, looking back, shaking his head. "They haven't a prayer, especially since the men in those helicopters and the troops on the ground are all from the Abawe tribe, the traditional enemy of the Kigani."

The twentieth-century world did not accommodate man-eating beliefs; indeed, the government in Kinshasa, two thousand miles away, had already decided to "expunge the embarrassment" of cannibals within its borders. In June, the Zaire government dispatched five thousand armed troops, six rocket-armed American UH-2 helicopters, and ten armored personnel carriers to put down the Kigani rebellion. The military leader in charge, General Ngo

Muguru, had no illusions about his directive. Muguru knew that Kinshasa wanted him to eliminate the Kigani as a tribe. And he intended to do exactly that.

During the rest of the day, they heard distant explosions of mortar and rockets. It was impossible not to contrast the modernity of this equipment with the bows and arrows of the Kigani they had seen. Ross said it was sad, but Munro replied that it was inevitable.

"The purpose of life," Munro said, "is to stay alive. Watch any animal in nature—all it tries to do is stay alive. It doesn't care about beliefs or philosophy. Whenever any animal's behavior puts it out of touch with the realities of its existence, it becomes extinct. The Kigani haven't seen that times have changed and their beliefs don't work. And they're going to be extinct."

"Maybe there is a higher truth than merely staying alive," Ross said.

"There isn't," Munro said.

They saw several other parties of Kigani, usually from a distance of many miles. At the end of the day, after they had crossed the swaying wooden bridge over the Moruti Gorge, Munro announced that they were now beyond the Kigani territory and, at least for the time being, safe.

3. Moruti Camp

In a high clearing above Moruti, the "place of soft winds," Munro shouted Swahili instructions and Kahega's porters began to unpack their loads. Karen Ross looked at her watch. "Are we stopping?"

"Yes," Munro said.

"But it's only five o'clock. There's still two hours of light left."

"We stop here," Munro said. Moruti was located at 1,500 feet; another two hours' walking would put them down in the rain forest below. "It's much cooler and more pleasant here."

Ross said that she did not care about pleasantness.

"You will," Munro said.

To make the best time, Munro intended to keep out of the rain forest wherever possible. Progress in the jungle was slow and uncomfortable; they would have more than enough experience with mud and leeches and fevers.

Kahega called to him in Swahili; Munro turned to Ross and said, "Kahega wants to know how to pitch the tents."

Kahega was holding a crumpled silver ball of fabric in his outstretched hand; the other porters were just as confused, rummaging through their loads, looking for familiar tent poles or stakes, finding none.

The ERTS camp had been designed under contract by a NASA team in 1977, based on the recognition that wilderness expedition equipment was fundamentally unchanged since the eighteenth century. "Designs for modern exploration are long overdue," ERTS said, and asked for state-of-the-art improvements in lightness, comfort, and efficiency of expedition gear. NASA had redesigned everything, from clothing and boots to tents and cooking gear, food and menus, first-aid kits, and communications systems for ERTS wilderness parties.

The redesigned tents were typical of the NASA approach. NASA had determined that tent weight consisted chiefly of the structural supports. In addition, single-ply tents were poorly insulated. If tents could be properly insulated, clothing and sleeping-bag weight could be reduced, as could the daily caloric requirements of expedition members. Since air was an excellent insulator, the obvious solution was an unsupported, pneumatic tent: NASA designed one that weighed six ounces.

Using a little hissing foot pump, Ross inflated the first tent. It was made from double-layer silvered Mylar, and looked like a gleaming ribbed Quonset hut. The porters clapped their hands with delight; Munro shook his head, amused; Kahega produced a small silver unit, the size of a shoebox. "And this, Doctor? What is this?"

"We won't need that tonight. That's an air conditioner," Ross said.

"Never go anywhere without one," Munro said, still amused.

Ross glared at him. "Studies show," she said, "that the single greatest factor limiting work efficiency is ambient temperature, with sleep deprivation as the second factor."

"Really."

Munro laughed and looked to Elliot, but Elliot was studiously examining the view of the rain forest in the evening sun. Amy came up and tugged at his sleeve.

Woman and nosehair man fight, she signed.

Amy had liked Munro from the beginning, and the feeling was mutual. Instead of patting her on the head and treating her like a child, as most people did, Munro instinctively treated her like a female. Then, too, he had been around enough gorillas to have a feeling for their behavior. Although he didn't know ASL, when Amy raised her arms, he understood that she wanted to be tickled, and would oblige her for a few moments, while she rolled grunting with pleasure on the ground.

But Amy was always distressed by conflict, and she was frowning now. "They're just talking," Elliot assured her.

She signed, *Amy want eat.*

"In a minute." Turning back, he saw Ross setting up the transmitting equipment; this would be a daily ritual during the rest of the expedition, and one which never failed to fascinate Amy. Altogether, the equipment to send a transmission ten thousand miles by satellite weighed six pounds, and the electronic countermeasures, or ECM devices, weighed an additional three pounds.

First, Ross popped open the collapsed umbrella of the silver dish antenna, five feet in diameter. (Amy particularly liked this; as each day progressed, she would ask Ross when she would "open metal flower.") Then Ross attached the transmitter box, plugging in the krylon-cadmium fuel cells. Next she linked the anti-jamming modules, and finally she hooked up the miniaturized computer terminal with its tiny keyboard and three-inch video screen.

This miniature equipment was highly sophisticated. Ross's computer had a 189K memory and all circuitry was redundant; housings were hermetically sealed and shockproof; even the keyboard was impedance-operated, so there were no moving parts to get gummed up, or admit water or dust.

And it was incredibly rugged. Ross remembered their "field tests." In the ERTS parking lot, technicians would throw new equipment against the wall, kick it across the concrete, and leave it in a bucket of muddy water overnight. Anything found working the next day was certified as field-worthy.

Now, in the sunset at Moruti, she punched in code coordinates to lock the transmission to Houston, checked signal strength, and waited the six minutes until the transponders matched up. But the little screen continued to show only gray static, with intermittent pulses of color. That meant someone was jamming them with a "symphony."

In ERTS slang, the simplest level of electronic jamming was called "tuba." Like a kid next door practicing his tuba, this jamming was merely annoying; it occurred within limited frequencies, and was often random or accidental, but transmissions could generally pass through it. At the next level was "string quartet," where multiple frequencies were jammed in an orderly fashion; next was "big band," where the electronic music covered a wider frequency range; and finally "symphony," where virtually the full transmission range was blocked.

Ross was now getting hit by a "symphony." To break through demanded coordination with Houston—which she was unable to arrange—but ERTS had several prearranged routines. She tried them one after another and finally broke the jamming with a technique called interstitial coding. (Interstitial coding utilized the fact that even dense music had periods of silence, or interstices, lasting microseconds. It was possible to monitor the jamming signals, identify regularities in the interstices, and then transmit in bursts during the silences.)

131

Ross was gratified to see the little screen glow in a multicolored image—a map of their position in the Congo. She punched in the field position lock, and a light blinked on the screen. Words appeared in "shortline," the compressed language devised for small-screen imagery. FILD TME-POSITN CHEK; PLS CONFRM LOCL TME 18:04 H 6/17/79. She confirmed that it was indeed just after 6 P.M. at their location. Immediately, overlaid lines produced a scrambled pattern as their Field Time-Position was measured against the computer simulation run in Houston before their departure.

Ross was prepared for bad news. According to her mental calculations, they had fallen some seventy-odd hours behind their projected timeline, and some twenty-odd hours behind the consortium.

Their original plan had called for them to jump onto the slopes of Mukenko at 2 P.M. on June 17, arriving at Zinj approximately thirty-six hours later, around midday of June 19. This would have put them onsite nearly two days before the consortium.

However, the SAM attack forced them to jump eighty miles south of their intended drop zone. The jungle terrain before them was varied, and they could expect to pick up time rafting on rivers, but it would still take a minimum of three days to go eighty miles.

That meant that they could no longer expect to beat the consortium to the site. Instead of arriving forty-eight hours ahead, they would be lucky if they arrived only twenty-four hours too late.

To her surprise, the screen blinked: FILD TME—POSITN CHEK:-09:04 H WEL DUN. They were only nine hours off their simulation timeline.

"What does that mean?" Munro asked, looking at the screen.

There was only one possible conclusion. "Something has slowed the consortium," Ross said.

On the screen they read EURO / NIPON CONSRTIM LEGL TRUBL GOMA AIRPRT ZAIR THEIR AIRCRFT FOUND RADIOACTIVE TUF LUK FOR THEM.

"Travis has been working back in Houston," Ross said. She could imagine what it must have cost ERTS to put in the fix at the rural airport in Goma. "But it means we can still do it, if we can make up the nine hours."

"We can do it," Munro said.

In the light of the setting equatorial sun, Moruti camp gleamed like a cluster of dazzling jewels—a silver dish antenna, and five silver-domed tents, all reflecting the fiery sun. Peter Elliot sat on the hilltop with Amy and stared at the rain forest spread out below them. As night fell, the first hazy strands of mist appeared; and as the darkness deepened and water vapor condensed in the cooling air, the forest became shrouded in dense, darkening fog.

DAY 6: LIKO

JUNE 18, 1979

1. Rain Forest

The next morning they entered the humid perpetual gloom of the Congo rain forest.

Munro noted the return of old feelings of oppression and claustrophobia, tinged with a strange, overpowering lassitude. As a Congo mercenary in the 1960s, he had avoided the jungle wherever possible. Most military engagements had occurred in open spaces—in the Belgian colonial towns, along riverbanks, beside the red dirt roads. Nobody wanted to fight in the jungle; the mercenaries hated it, and the superstitious Simbas feared it. When the mercenaries advanced, the rebels often fled into the bush, but they never went very far, and Munro's troops never pursued them. They just waited for them to come out again.

Even in the 1960s the jungle remained *terra incognita,* an unknown land with the power to hold the technology of mechanized warfare beyond its periphery. And with good reason, Munro thought. Men just did not belong there. He was not pleased to be back.

Elliot, never having been in a rain forest, was fascinated. The jungle was different from the way he had imagined it to be. He was totally unprepared for the scale—the gigantic trees soaring over his head, the trunks as broad as a house, the thick snaking moss-covered roots. To move in the vast space beneath these trees was like being in a very dark cathedral: the sun was completely blocked, and he could not get an exposure reading on his camera.

He had also expected the jungle to be much denser than it was. Their party moved through it freely; in a surprising way it seemed barren and silent—there were occasional birdcalls and cries from monkeys, but otherwise a profound stillness settled over them. And it was oddly monotonous: although he saw every shade of green in the foliage and the clinging creeper vines, there were few flowers or blooms. Even the occasional orchids seemed pale and muted.

He had expected rotting decay at every turn, but that was not true either. The ground underfoot was often firm, and the air had a neutral smell. But it was incredibly hot, and it seemed as though everything was wet—the leaves, the ground, the trunks of the trees, the oppressively still air itself, trapped under the overhanging trees.

Elliot would have agreed with Stanley's description from a century before:

"Overhead the wide-spreading branches absolutely shut out the daylight. . . . We marched in a feeble twilight. . . . The dew dropped and pattered on us incessantly. . . . Our clothes were heavily saturated with it. . . . Perspiration exuded from every pore, for the atmosphere was stifling. . . . What a forbidding aspect had the Dark Unknown which confronted us!"

Because Elliot had looked forward to his first experience of the equatorial African rain forest, he was surprised at how quickly he felt oppressed—and how soon he entertained thoughts of leaving again. Yet the tropical rain forests had spawned most new life forms, including man. The jungle was not one uniform environment but many different microenvironments, arranged vertically like a layer cake. Each microenvironment supported a bewildering profusion of plant and animal life, but there were typically few members of each species. The tropical jungle supported four times as many species of animal life as a comparable temperate forest. As he walked through the forest, Elliot found himself thinking of it as an enormous hot, dark womb, a place where new species were nourished in unchanging conditions until they were ready to migrate out to the harsher and more variable temperate zones. That was the way it had been for millions of years.

Amy's behavior immediately changed as she entered the vast humid darkness of her original home. In retrospect, Elliot believed he could have predicted her reaction, had he thought it through clearly.

Amy no longer kept up with the group.

She insisted on foraging along the trail, pausing to sit and chew tender shoots and grasses. She could not be budged or hurried, and ignored Elliot's requests that she stay with them. She ate lazily, a pleasant, rather vacant expression on her face. In shafts of sunlight, she would lie on her back, and belch, and sigh contentedly.

"What the hell is this all about?" Ross asked, annoyed. They were not making good time.

"She's become a gorilla again," Elliot said. "Gorillas are vegetarians, and they spend nearly all day eating; they're large animals, and they need a lot of food." Amy had immediately reverted to these traits.

"Well, can't you make her keep up with us?"

"I'm trying. She won't pay attention to me." And he knew why—Amy was finally back in a world where Peter Elliot was irrelevant, where she herself could find food and security and shelter, and everything else that she wanted.

"School's out," Munro said, summarizing the situation. But he had a solution. "Leave her," he said crisply, and he led the party onward. He took Elliot firmly by the elbow. "Don't look back," he said. "Just walk on. Ignore her."

They continued for several minutes in silence.

Elliot said, "She may not follow us."

"Come, come, Professor," Munro said. "I thought you knew about gorillas."

"I do," Elliot said.

"Then you know there are none in this part of the rain forest."

Elliot nodded; he had seen no nests or spoor. "But she has everything she needs here."

"Not everything," Munro said. "Not without other gorillas around."

Like all higher primates, gorillas were social animals. They lived in a group, and they were not comfortable—or safe—in isolation. In fact, most primatologists assumed that there was a need for social contact as strongly perceived as hunger, thirst, or fatigue.

"We're her troop," Munro said. "She won't let us get far."

Several minutes later, Amy came crashing through the underbrush fifty yards ahead. She watched the group, and glared at Peter.

"Now come here, Amy," Munro said, "and I'll tickle you." Amy bounded up and lay on her back in front of him. Munro tickled her.

"You see, Professor? Nothing to it."

Amy never strayed far from the group again.

If Elliot had an uncomfortable sense of the rain forest as the natural domain of his own animal, Karen Ross viewed it in terms of earth resources—in which it was poor. She was not fooled by the luxuriant, oversized vegetation, which she knew represented an extraordinarily efficient ecosystem built in virtually barren soil.*

The developing nations of the world did not understand this fact; once cleared, the jungle soil yielded disappointing crops. Yet the rain forests were being cleared at the incredible rate of fifty acres a minute, day and night. The rain forests of the world had circled the equator in a green belt for at least sixty million years—but man would have cleared them within twenty years.

This widespread destruction had caused some alarm Ross did not share. She doubted that the world climate would change or the atmospheric oxygen be reduced. Ross was not an alarmist, and not impressed by the calculations of those who were. The only reason she felt uneasy was that the forest was so little understood. A clearing rate of fifty acres a minute meant that plant and animal species were becoming extinct at the incredible rate of *one species per hour*. Life forms that had evolved for millions of years were being wiped out every few minutes, and no one could predict the consequences of this stupendous rate of destruction. The extinction of species was proceeding much faster than anybody recognized, and the publicized lists of "endangered" species told only a fraction of the story; the disaster extended all the way down the animal phyla to insects, worms, and mosses.

The reality was that entire ecosystems were being destroyed by man with-

---

*The rain forest ecosystem is an energy utilization complex far more efficient than any energy conversion system developed by man. See C. F. Higgins et al., *Energy Resources and Ecosystem Utilization* (Englewood Cliffs, N.J.: Prentice Hall, 1977), pp. 232–255.

out a care or a backward glance. And these ecosystems were for the most part mysterious, poorly understood. Karen Ross felt herself plunged into a world entirely different from the exploitable world of mineral resources; this was an environment in which plant life reigned supreme. It was no wonder, she thought, that the Egyptians called this the Land of Trees. The rain forest provided a hothouse environment for plant life, an environment in which gigantic plants were much superior to—and much favored over—mammals, including the insignificant human mammals who were now picking their way through its perpetual darkness.

The Kikuyu porters had an immediate reaction to the forest: they began to laugh and joke and make as much noise as possible. Ross said to Kahega, "They certainly are jolly."

"Oh, no," Kahega said. "They are warning."

"Warning?"

Kahega explained that the men made noise to warn off the buffalo and leopards. And the *tembo,* he added, pointing to the trail.

"Is this a *tembo* trail?" she asked.

Kahega nodded.

"The *tembo* live nearby?"

Kahega laughed. "I hope no," Kahega said. "*Tembo.* Elephant."

"So this is a game trail. Will we see elephants?"

"Maybe yes, maybe no," Kahega said. "I hope no. They are very big, elephants."

There was no arguing with his logic. Ross said, "They tell me these are your brothers," nodding down the line of porters.

"Yes, they are my brothers."

"Ah."

"But you mean that my brothers, we have the same mother?"

"Yes, you have the same mother."

"No," Kahega said.

Ross was confused. "You are not real brothers?"

"Yes, we are real brothers. But we do not have the same mother."

"Then why are you brothers?"

"Because we live in the same village."

"With your father and mother?"

Kahega looked shocked. "*No,*" he said emphatically. "Not the same village."

"A different village, then?"

"Yes, of course—we are Kikuyu."

Ross was perplexed. Kahega laughed.

Kahega offered to carry the electronic equipment that Ross had slung over her shoulder, but she declined. Ross was obliged to try and link up with

Houston at intervals throughout the day, and at noon she found a clear window, probably because the consortium jamming operator took a break for lunch. She managed to link through and register another Field Time—Position.

The console read: FILD TME—POSITN CHEK—10:03 H

They had lost nearly an hour since the previous check the night before. "We've got to go faster," she told Munro.

"Perhaps you'd prefer to jog," Munro said. "Very good exercise." And then, because he decided he was being too hard on her, he added, "A lot can happen between here and Virunga."

They heard the distant growl of thunder and minutes later were drenched in a torrential rain, the drops so dense and heavy that they actually hurt. The rain fell solidly for the next hour, then stopped as abruptly as it had begun. They were all soaked and miserable, and when Munro called a halt for food, Ross did not protest.

Amy promptly went off into the forest to forage; the porters cooked curried meat gravy on rice; Munro, Ross, and Elliot burned leeches off their legs with cigarettes. The leeches were swollen with blood. "I didn't even notice them," Ross said.

"Rain makes 'em worse," Munro said. Then he looked up sharply, glancing at the jungle.

"Something wrong?"

"No, nothing," Munro said, and he went into an explanation of why leeches had to be burned off; if they were pulled off, a part of the head remained lodged in the flesh and caused an infection.

Kahega brought them food, and Munro said in a low voice, "Are the men all right?"

"Yes," Kahega said. "The men are all right. They will not be afraid."

"Afraid of what?" Elliot said.

"Keep eating. Just be natural," Munro said.

Elliot looked nervously around the little clearing.

"Eat!" Munro whispered. "Don't insult them. You're not supposed to know they're here."

The group ate in silence for several minutes. And then the nearby brush rustled and a pygmy stepped out.

2. The Dancers of God

He was a light-skinned man about four and a half feet tall, barrel-chested, wearing only a loincloth, with a bow and arrow over his shoulder. He looked around the expedition, apparently trying to determine who was the leader.

Munro stood, and said something quickly in a language that was not Swahili. The pygmy replied. Munro gave him one of the cigarettes they had been using to burn off the leeches. The pygmy did not want it lit; instead he dropped it into a small leather pouch attached to his quiver. A brief conversation followed. The pygmy pointed off into the jungle several times.

"He says a white man is dead in their village," Munro said. He picked up his pack, which contained the first-aid kit. "I'll have to hurry."

Ross said, "We can't afford the time."

Munro frowned at her.

"Well, the man's dead anyway."

"He's not *completely* dead," Munro said. "He's not dead-for-ever."

The pygmy nodded vigorously. Munro explained that pygmies graded illness in several stages. First a person was hot, then he was with fever, then ill, then dead, then completely dead—and finally dead-for-ever.

From the bush, three more pygmies appeared. Munro nodded. "Knew he wasn't alone," he said. "These chaps never are alone. Hate to travel alone. The others were watching us; if we'd made a wrong move, we'd get an arrow for our trouble. See those brown tips? Poison."

Yet the pygmies appeared relaxed now—at least until Amy came crashing back through the underbrush. Then there were shouts and swiftly drawn bows; Amy was terrified and ran to Peter, jumping up on him and clutching his chest—and making him thoroughly muddy.

The pygmies engaged in a lively discussion among themselves, trying to decide what Amy's arrival meant. Several questions were asked of Munro. Finally, Elliot set Amy back down on the ground and said to Munro, "What did you tell them?"

"They wanted to know if the gorilla was yours, and I said yes. They wanted to know if the gorilla was female, and I said yes. They wanted to know if you had relations with the gorilla; I said no. They said that was good, that you should not become too attached to the gorilla, because that would cause you pain."

"Why pain?"

"They said when the gorilla grows up, she will either run away into the forest and break your heart or kill you."

Ross still opposed making a detour to the pygmy village, which was several miles away on the banks of the Liko River. "We're behind on our timeline," she said, "and slipping further behind every minute."

For the first and last time during the expedition, Munro lost his temper. "Listen, Doctor," he said, "this isn't downtown Houston, this is the middle of the goddamn Congo and it's no place to be injured. We have medicines. That man may need it. You don't leave him behind. You just don't."

"If we go to that village," Ross said, "we blow the rest of the day. It puts us nine or ten hours further back. Right now we can still make it. With another delay, we won't have a chance."

One of the pygmies began talking quickly to Munro. He nodded, glancing several times at Ross. Then he turned to the others.

"He says that the sick white man has some writing on his shirt pocket. He's going to draw the writing for us."

Ross glanced at her watch and sighed.

The pygmy picked up a stick and drew large characters in the muddy earth at their feet. He drew carefully, frowning in concentration as he reproduced the alien symbols: E R T S.

"Oh, God," Ross said softly.

The pygmies did not walk through the forest: they ran at a brisk trot, slipping through the forest vines and branches, dodging rain puddles and gnarled tree roots with deceptive ease. Occasionally they glanced over their shoulders and giggled at the difficulties of the three white people who followed.

For Elliot, it was a difficult pace—a succession of roots to stumble over, tree limbs to strike his head on, thorny vines to tear at his flesh. He was gasping for breath, trying to keep up with the little men who padded effortlessly ahead of him. Ross was doing no better than he, and even Munro, although surprisingly agile, showed signs of fatigue.

Finally they came to a small stream and a sunlit clearing. The pygmies paused on the rocks, squatting and turning their faces up to the sun. The white people collapsed, panting and gasping. The pygmies seemed to find this hilarious, their laughter good-natured.

The pygmies were the earliest human inhabitants of the Congo rain forest. Their small size, distinctive manner, and deft agility had made them famous centuries before. More than four thousand years ago, an Egyptian commander named Herkouf entered the great forest west of the Mountains of the Moon; there he found a race of tiny men who sang and danced to their god. Herkouf's amazing report had the ring of fact, and Herodotus and later Aristotle insisted that these stories of the tiny men were true, and not fabulous. The

Dancers of God inevitably acquired mythical trappings as the centuries passed.

As late as the seventeenth century, Europeans remained unsure whether tiny men with tails who had the power to fly through the trees, make themselves invisible, and kill elephants actually existed. That skeletons of chimpanzees were sometimes mistaken for pygmy skeletons added to the confusion. Colin Turnbull notes that many elements of the fable are actually true: the pounded-bark loincloths hang down and look like tails; the pygmies can blend into the forest and become virtually invisible; and they have always hunted and killed elephants.

The pygmies were laughing now as they got to their feet and padded off again. Sighing, the white people struggled up and lumbered after them. They ran for another half hour, never pausing or hesitating, and then Elliot smelled smoke and they came into a clearing beside a stream where the village was located.

He saw ten low rounded huts no more than four feet high, arranged in a semicircle. The villagers were all outside in the afternoon light, the women cleaning mushrooms and berries picked during the day, or cooking grubs and turtles on crackling fires; children tottered around, bothering the men who sat before their houses and smoked tobacco while the women worked.

At Munro's signal, they waited at the edge of the camp until they were noticed, and then they were led in. Their arrival provoked great interest; the children giggled and pointed; the men wanted tobacco from Munro and Elliot; the women touched Ross's blonde hair, and argued about it. A little girl crawled between Ross's legs, peering up her trousers. Munro explained that the women were uncertain whether Ross painted her hair, and the girl had taken it upon herself to settle the question of artifice.

"Tell them it's natural," Ross said, blushing.

Munro spoke briefly to the women. "I told them it was the color of your father's hair," he told Ross. "But I'm not sure they believe it." He gave Elliot cigarettes to pass out, one to each man; they were received with broad smiles and odd girlish giggles.

Preliminaries concluded, they were taken to a newly constructed house at the far end of the village where the dead white man was said to be. They found a filthy, bearded man of thirty, sitting cross-legged in the small doorway, staring outward. After a moment Elliot realized the man was catatonic—he was not moving at all.

"Oh, my God," Ross said. "It's Bob Driscoll."

"You know him?" Munro said.

"He was a geologist on the first Congo expedition." She leaned close to him, waved her hand in front of his face. "Bobby, it's me, Karen. Bobby, what happened to you?"

Driscoll did not respond, did not even blink. He continued to stare forward.

One of the pygmies offered an explanation to Munro. "He came into their camp four days ago," Munro said. "He was wild and they had to restrain him. They thought he had blackwater fever, so they made a house for him and gave him some medicines, and he was not wild anymore. Now he lets them feed him, but he never speaks. They think perhaps he was captured by General Muguru's men and tortured, or else he is *agudu*—a mute."

Ross moved back in horror.

"I don't see what we can do for him," Munro said. "Not in his condition. Physically he's okay but . . ." He shook his head.

"I'll give Houston the location," Ross said, "and they'll send help from Kinshasa."

During all this, Driscoll never moved. Elliot leaned forward to look at his eyes, and as he approached, Driscoll wrinkled his nose. His body tensed. He broke into a high-pitched wail—"Ah-ah-ah-ah"—like a man about to scream.

Appalled, Elliot backed off, and Driscoll relaxed, falling silent again. "What the hell was that all about?"

One of the pygmies whispered to Munro. "He says," Munro said, "that you smell like gorilla."

3. Ragora

Two hours later, they were reunited with Kahega and the others, led by a pygmy guide across the rain forest south of Gabutu. They were all sullen, uncommunicative—and suffering from dysentery.

The pygmies had insisted they stay for an early dinner, and Munro felt they had no choice but to accept. The meal was mostly a slender wild potato called *kitsombe,* which looked like a shriveled asparagus; forest onions, called *otsa;* and *modoke,* wild manioc leaves, along with several kinds of mushrooms. There were also small quantities of sour, tough turtle meat and occasional grasshoppers, caterpillars, worms, frogs, and snails.

This diet actually contained twice as much protein by weight as beefsteak, but it did not sit well on unaccustomed stomachs. Nor was the news around the campfire likely to improve their spirits.

According to the pygmies, General Muguru's men had established a supply camp up at the Makran escarpment, which was where Munro was headed. It seemed wise to avoid the troops. Munro explained there was no Swahili word for chivalry or sportsmanship, and the same was true of the Congolese variant, Lingala. "In this part of the world, it's kill or be killed. We'd best stay away."

Their only alternate route took them west, to the Ragora River. Munro frowned at his map, and Ross frowned at her computer console.

"What's wrong with the Ragora River?" Elliot asked.

"Maybe nothing," Munro said. "Depends on how hard it's rained lately."

Ross glanced at her watch. "We're now twelve hours behind," she said. "The only thing we can do is continue straight through the night on the river."

"I'd do that anyway," Munro said.

Ross had never heard of an expedition guide leading a party through a wilderness area at night. "You would? Why?"

"Because," Munro said, "the obstacles on the lower river will be much easier at night."

"What obstacles?"

"We'll discuss them when we come to them," Munro said.

A mile before they reached the Ragora, they heard the distant roar of powerful water. Amy was immediately anxious, signing *What water?* again and again. Elliot tried to reassure her, but he was not inclined to do much; Amy was going to have to put up with the river, despite her fears.

But when they got to the Ragora they found that the sound came from tumbling cataracts somewhere upstream; directly before them, the river was fifty feet wide and a placid muddy brown.

"Doesn't look too bad," Elliot said.

"No," Munro said, "it doesn't."

But Munro understood about the Congo. The fourth largest river in the world (after the Nile, the Amazon, and the Yangtze) was unique in many ways. It twisted like a giant snake across the face of Africa, twice crossing the equator—the first time going north, toward Kisangani, and later going south, at Mbandaka. This fact was so remarkable that even a hundred years ago geographers did not believe it was true. Because the Congo flowed both north and south of the equator, there was always a rainy season somewhere along its path; the river was not subject to the seasonal fluctuations that characterized rivers such as the Nile. The Congo poured a steady 1,500,000 cubic feet of water every second into the Atlantic Ocean, a flow greater than any river except the Amazon.

But this tortuous course also made the Congo the least navigable of the great rivers. Serious disruptions began with the rapids of Stanley Pool, three hundred miles from the Atlantic. Two thousand miles inland, at Kisangani, where the river was still a mile wide, the Wagenia Cataract blocked all navigation. And as one moved farther upriver along the fan of tributaries, the impediments became even more pronounced, for above Kisangani the tributaries were descending rapidly into the low jungle from their sources—the highland savannahs to the south, and the 16,000-foot snowcapped Ruwenzori Mountains to the east.

The tributaries cut a series of gorges, the most striking of which was the Portes d'Enfer—the Gates of Hell—at Kongolo. Here the placid Lualaba River funneled through a gorge half a mile deep and a hundred yards wide.

The Ragora was a minor tributary of the Lualaba, which it joined near Kisangani. The tribes along the river referred to it as *baratawani,* "the deceitful road," for the Ragora was notoriously changeable. Its principal feature was the Ragora Gorge, a limestone cut two hundred feet deep and in places only ten feet wide. Depending on recent rainfall, the Ragora Gorge was either a pleasant scenic spectacle or a boiling whitewater nightmare.

At Abutu, they were still fifteen miles upriver from the gorge, and conditions on the river told them nothing about conditions within the gorge. Munro knew all that, but he did not feel it necessary to explain it to Elliot, particularly since at the moment Elliot was fully occupied with Amy.

Amy had watched with growing uneasiness as Kahega's men inflated the two Zodiac rafts. She tugged Elliot's sleeve and demanded to know *What balloons?*

"They're boats, Amy," he said, although he sensed she had already figured that out, and was being euphemistic. "Boat" was a word she had learned with difficulty; since she disliked water, she had no interest in anything intended to ride upon it.

Why boat? she asked.

"We ride boat now," Elliot said.

Indeed, Kahega's men were pushing the boats to the edge of the water, and loading the equipment on, lashing it to the rubber stanchions at the gunwales.

Who ride? she asked.

"We all ride," Elliot said.

Amy watched a moment longer. Unfortunately, everyone was nervous, Munro barking orders, the men working hastily. As she had often shown, Amy was sensitive to the moods of those around her. Elliot always remembered how she had insisted that something was wrong with Sarah Johnson for days before Sarah finally told the Project Amy staff that she had split up with her husband. Now Elliot was certain that Amy sensed their apprehension. *Cross water in boat?* she asked.

"No, Amy," he said. "Not cross. Ride boat."

No, Amy signed, stiffening her back, tightening her shoulders.

"Amy," he said, "we can't leave you here."

She had a solution for that. *Other people go. Peter stay Amy.*

"I'm sorry, Amy," he said. "I have to go. You have to go."

No, she signed. *Amy no go.*

"Yes, Amy." He went to his pack and got his syringe and a bottle of Thoralen.

With her body stiff and angry, she tapped the underside of her chin with a clenched fist.

"Watch your language, Amy," he warned her.

Ross came over with orange life vests for him and Amy. "Something wrong?"

"She's swearing," Elliot said. "Better leave us alone." Ross took one look at Amy's tense, rigid body, and left hurriedly.

Amy signed Peter's name, then tapped the underside of her chin again. This was the Ameslan sign politely translated in scholarly reports as "dirty," although it was most often employed by apes when they needed to go to the potty. Primate investigators were under no illusions about what the animals really meant. Amy was saying, *Peter shitty.*

Nearly all language-skilled primates swore, and they employed a variety of words for swearing. Sometimes the pejorative seemed to be chosen at random, "nut" or "bird" or "wash." But at least eight primates in different laboratories had independently settled on the clenched-fist sign to signify extreme displeasure. The only reason this remarkable coincidence hadn't been written up was that no investigator was willing to try and explain it. It seemed to prove that apes, like people, found bodily excretions suitable terms to express denigration and anger.

Peter shitty, she signed again.

"Amy . . ." He doubled the Thoralen dose he was drawing into the syringe.

Peter shitty boat shitty people shitty.

"Amy, cut it out." He stiffened his own body and hunched over, imitating a gorilla's angry posture; that often made her back off, but this time it had no effect.

Peter no like Amy. Now she was sulking, turned away from him, signing to nobody.

"Don't be ridiculous," Elliot said, approaching her with the syringe held ready. "Peter like Amy."

She backed away and would not let him come close to her. In the end he was forced to load the CO_2 gun and shoot a dart into her chest. He had only done this three or four times in all their years together. She plucked out the dart with a sad expression. *Peter no like Amy.*

"Sorry," Peter Elliot said, and ran forward to catch her as her eyes rolled back and she collapsed into his arms.

Amy lay on her back in the second boat at Elliot's feet, breathing shallowly. Ahead, Elliot saw Munro standing in the first boat, leading the way as the Zodiacs slid silently downstream.

Munro had divided the expedition into two rafts of six each; Munro went in the first, and Elliot, Ross, and Amy went in the second, under Kahega's command. As Munro put it, the second boat would "learn from our misfortunes."

But for the first two hours on the Ragora, there were no misfortunes. It was an extraordinarily peaceful experience to sit in the front of the boat and watch the jungle on both sides of the river glide past them in timeless, hypnotic silence. It was idyllic, and very hot; Ross began to trail her hand over the side in the muddy water, until Kahega put a stop to it.

"Where there is water, there is always *mamba,*" he said.

Kahega pointed to the muddy banks, where crocodiles basked in the sunshine, indifferent to their approach. Occasionally one of the huge reptiles yawned, lifting jagged jaws into the air, but for the most part they seemed sluggish, hardly noticing the boats.

Elliot was secretly disappointed. He had grown up on the jungle movies where the crocodiles slithered menacingly into the water at the first approach of boats. "Aren't they going to bother us?" he asked.

"Too hot," Kahega said. "*Mamba* sleepy except at cool times, eat morning and night, not now. In daytime, Kikuyu say *mamba* have joined army, one-two-three-four." And he laughed.

It took some explaining before it was clear that Kahega's tribesmen had noticed that during the day the crocodiles did pushups, periodically lifting their heavy bodies off the ground on their stubby legs in a movement that reminded Kahega of army calisthenics.

"What is Munro so worried about?" Elliot asked. "The crocodiles?"

"No," Kahega said.

"The Ragora Gorge?"

"No," Kahega said.

"Then what?"

"*After* the gorge," Kahega said.

Now the Ragora twisted, and they came around a bend, and they heard the growing roar of the water. Elliot felt the boat gathering speed, the water rippling along the rubber gunwales. Kahega shouted, "Hold fast, Doctors!"

And they were into the gorge.

Afterward, Elliot had only fragmented, kaleidoscopic impressions: the churning muddy water that boiled white in the sunlight; the erratic wrenching of his own boat, and the way Munro's boat up ahead seemed to reel and upend, yet miraculously remain upright.

They were moving so fast it was hard to focus on the passing blur of craggy red canyon walls, bare rock except for sparse green clinging scrub; the hot humid air and the shockingly cold muddy water that smashed over them, drenching them time and again; the pure white surge of water boiling around the black protruding rocks, like the bald heads of drowned men.

Everything was happening too fast.

Ahead, Munro's boat was often lost from sight for minutes at a time, concealed by giant standing waves of leaping, roaring muddy water. The roar echoed off the rock walls, reverberating, becoming a constant feature of their world; in the depths of the gorge, where the afternoon sun did not reach the narrow strip of dark water, the boats moved through a rushing, churning inferno, careening off rocky walls, spinning end around end, while the boatmen shouted and cursed and fended off the rock walls with paddles.

Amy lay on her back, lashed to the side of the boat, and Elliot was in constant fear that she would drown from the muddy waves that crashed over the gunwales. Not that Ross was doing much better; she kept repeating "Oh my God oh my God oh my God" over and over, in a low monotone, as the water smashed down on them in successive waves, soaking them to the skin.

Other indignities were forced upon them by nature. Even in the boiling, pounding heart of the gorge, black clouds of mosquitoes hung in the air, stinging them again and again. Somehow it did not seem possible that there could be mosquitoes in the midst of the roaring chaos of the Ragora Gorge, but they were there. The boats moved with gut-wrenching fury through the standing waves, and in the growing darkness the passengers baled out the boats and slapped at the mosquitoes with equal intensity.

And then suddenly the river broadened, the muddy water slowed, and the walls of the canyon moved apart. The river became peaceful again. Elliot slumped back in the boat, exhausted, feeling the fading sun on his face and the water moving beneath the inflated rubber of the boat.

"We made it," he said.

"So far," Kahega said. "But we Kikuyu say no one escapes from life alive. No relaxing now, Doctors!"

"Somehow," Ross said wearily, "I believe him."

They drifted gently downstream for another hour, and the rock walls receded farther away on each side, until finally they were in flat African rain forest once more. It was as if the Ragora Gorge had never existed; the river was wide and sluggish gold in the descending sun.

Elliot stripped off his soaking shirt and changed it for a pullover, for the evening air was chilly. Amy snored at his feet, covered with a towel so she would not get too cold. Ross checked her transmitting equipment, making sure it was all right. When she was finished, the sun had set and it was rapidly growing dark. Kahega broke out a shotgun and inserted yellow stubby shells.

"What's that for?" Elliot said.

"*Kiboko,*" Kahega said. "I do not know the word in English." He shouted, "*Mzee! Nini maana kiboko?*"

In the lead boat, Munro glanced back. "Hippopotamus," he said.

"Hippo," Kahega said.

"Are they dangerous?" Elliot asked.

"At night, we hope no," Kahega said. "But me, I think yes."

* * *

The twentieth century had been a period of intensive wildlife study, which overturned many long-standing conceptions about animals. It was now recognized that the gentle, soft-eyed deer actually lived in a ruthless, nasty society, while the supposedly vicious wolf was devoted to family and offspring in exemplary fashion. And the African lion—the proud king of beasts—was relegated to the status of slinking scavenger, while the loathed hyena assumed new dignity. (For decades, observers had come upon a dawn kill to find lions feeding on the carcass, while the scavenging hyenas circled at the periphery, awaiting their chance. Only after scientists began night tracking the animals did a new interpretation emerge: hyenas actually made the kill, only to be driven off by opportunistic and lazy lions; hence the traditional dawn scene. This coincided with the discovery that lions were in many ways erratic and mean, while the hyenas had a finely developed social structure—yet another instance of long-standing human prejudice toward the natural world of animals.)

But the hippopotamus remained a poorly understood animal. Herodotus's "river horse" was the largest African mammal after the elephant, but its habit of lying in the water with just eyes and nostrils protruding made it difficult to study. Hippos were organized around a male. A mature male had a harem of several females and their offspring, a group of eight to fourteen animals altogether.

Despite their obese, rather humorous appearance, hippos were capable of unusual violence. The bull hippopotamus was a formidable creature, fourteen feet long and weighing nearly ten thousand pounds. Charging, he moved with extraordinary speed for such a large animal, and his four stubby blunted tusks were actually razor sharp on the sides. A hippo attacked by slashing, moving his cavernous mouth from side to side, rather than biting. And, unlike most animals, a fight between bulls often resulted in the death of one animal from deep slashing wounds. There was nothing symbolic about a hippopotamus fight.

The animal was dangerous to man, as well. In river areas where herds were found, half of native deaths were attributed to hippos; elephants and predatory cats accounted for the remainder. The hippopotamus was vegetarian, and at night the animals came onto the land, where they ate enormous quantities of grass to sustain their great bulk. A hippo separated from the water was especially dangerous; anyone finding himself between a landed hippo and the river he was rushing to return to did not generally survive the experience.

But the hippo was essential to Africa's river ecology. His fecal matter, produced in prodigious quantities, fertilized the river grasses, which in turn allowed river fish and other creatures to live. Without the hippopotamus African rivers would be sterile, and where they had been driven away, the rivers died.

This much was known, and one thing more. The hippopotamus was fiercely territorial. Without exception, the male defended his river against any intruder. And as had been recorded on many occasions, intruders included other hippos, crocodiles, and passing boats. And the people in them.

DAY 7: MUKENKO

JUNE 19, 1979

1. Kiboko

Munro's intention in continuing through the night was two-fold. First, he hoped to make up precious time, for all the computer projections assumed that they would stop each night. But it took no effort to ride the river in the moonlight; most of the party could sleep, and they would advance themselves another fifty or sixty miles by dawn.

But more important, he hoped to avoid the Ragora hippos, which could easily destroy their flimsy rubber boats. During the day, the hippos were found in pools beside the riverbanks, and the bulls would certainly attack any passing boat. At night, when the animals went ashore to forage, the expedition could slip down the river and avoid a confrontation entirely.

It was a clever plan, but it ran into trouble for an unexpected reason— their progress on the Ragora was too rapid. It was only nine o'clock at night when they reached the first hippo areas, too early for the animals to be eating. The hippos would attack the boats—but they would attack in the dark.

The river twisted and turned in a series of curves. At each curve there was a still pool, which Kahega pointed out as the kind of quiet water that hippos liked to inhabit. And he pointed to the grass on the banks, cut short as if the banks had been mown.

"Soon now," Kahega said.

They heard a low grunting, *"Haw-huh-huh-huh."* It sounded like an old man trying to clear his throat of phlegm. Munro tensed in the lead boat. They drifted around another curve, carried smoothly in the flow of current. The two boats were now about ten yards apart. Munro held his loaded shotgun ready.

The sound came again, this time in a chorus: *"Haw-huh-huh-huh."*

Kahega plunged his paddle into the water. It struck bottom quickly. He pulled it out; only three feet of it was wet. "Not deep," he said, shaking his head.

"Is that bad?" Ross said.

"Yes, I think it is bad."

They came around the next bend, and Elliot saw a half-dozen partially submerged black rocks near the shore, gleaming in the moonlight. Then one of the "rocks" crashed upward and he saw an enormous creature lift entirely out of the shallow water so that he could see the four stubby legs, and the hippo churned forward toward Munro's boat.

Munro fired a low magnesium flare as the animal charged; in the harsh white light Elliot saw a gigantic mouth, four huge glistening blunted teeth, the head lifted upward as the animal roared. And then the hippo was engulfed in a cloud of pale yellow gas. The gas drifted back, and stung their eyes.

"He's using tear gas," Ross said.

Munro's boat had already moved on. With a roar of pain the male hippo had plunged down into the water and disappeared from sight. In the second boat, they blinked back tears and watched for him as they approached the pool. Overhead, the magnesium flare sizzled and descended, lengthening sharp shadows, glaring off the water.

"Perhaps he's given up," Elliot said. They could not see the hippo anywhere. They drifted in silence.

And suddenly the front of the boat bucked up, and the hippo roared and Ross screamed. Kahega toppled backward, discharging his gun into the air. The boat slapped down with a wrenching crash and a spray of water over the sides, and Elliot scrambled to his feet to check Amy and found himself staring into a huge pink cavernous mouth and hot breath. The mouth came down with a lateral slash on the side of the rubber boat, and the air began to hiss and sizzle in the water.

The mouth opened again, and the hippo grunted, but by then Kahega had got to his feet and fired a stinging cloud of gas. The hippo backed off and splashed down, rocking the boat and propelling them onward, down the river. The whole right side of the boat was collapsing swiftly as the air leaked out of the huge cuts in the rubber. Elliot tried to pull them shut with his hands; the hissing continued unabated. They would sink within a minute.

Behind them, the bull hippo charged, racing down the shallow river like a powerboat, churning water in a wake from both sides of his body, bellowing in anger.

"Hold on, hold on!" Kahega shouted, and fired again. The hippo disappeared behind a cloud of gas, and the boat drifted around another curve. When the gas cleared the animal was gone. The magnesium flare sputtered into the water and they were plunged into darkness again. Elliot grabbed Amy as the boat sank, and they found themselves standing knee-deep in the muddy water.

They managed to beach the Zodiac on the dark riverbank. In the lead boat, Munro paddled over, surveyed the damage, and announced that they would inflate another boat and go on. He called for a rest, and they all lay in the moonlight on the river's edge swatting mosquitoes away.

Their reverie was interrupted by the screaming whine of ground-to-air rockets, blossoming explosions in the sky overhead. With each explosion, the riverbank glowed bright red, casting long shadows, then fading black once more.

"Muguru's men firing from the ground," Munro said, reaching for his field glasses.

"What're they shooting at?" Elliot said, staring up into the sky.

"Beats me," Munro said.

Amy touched Munro's arm, and signed, *Bird come.* But they heard no sound of an aircraft, only the bursting of rockets in the sky.

Munro said, "You think she hears something?"

"Her hearing is very acute."

And then they heard the drone of a distant aircraft, approaching from the south. As it came into view, they saw it twist, maneuvering among the brilliant yellow-red explosions that burst in the moonlight and glinted off the metal body of the aircraft.

"Those poor bastards are trying to make time," Munro said, scanning the plane through field glasses. "That's a C-130 transport with Japanese markings on the tail. Supply plane for the consortium base camp—if it makes it through."

As they watched, the transport twisted left and right, running a zigzag course through the bursting fireballs of exploding missiles.

"Breaking a snake's back," Munro said. "The crew must be terrified; they didn't buy into this."

Elliot felt a sudden sympathy for the crew; he imagined them staring out the windows as the fireballs exploded with brilliant light, illuminating the interior of the plane. Were they chattering in Japanese? Wishing they had never come?

A moment later, the aircraft droned onward to the north, out of sight, a final missile with a red-hot tail chasing after it, but it was gone over the jungle trees, and he listened to the distant explosion of the missile.

"Probably got through," Munro said, standing. "We'd better move on." And he shouted in Swahili for Kahega to put the men on the river once more.

2. Mukenko

Elliot shivered, zipped his parka tighter, and waited for the hailstorm to stop. They were huddled beneath a stand of evergreen trees above 8,000 feet on the alpine slopes of Mount

Mukenko. It was ten o'clock in the morning, and the air temperature was 38 degrees. Five hours before, they had left the river behind and begun their predawn climb in 100-degree steaming jungle.

Alongside him, Amy watched the golfball-sized white pellets bounce on the grass and slap the branches of the tree over their heads. She had never seen hail before.

She signed, *What name?*

"Hail," he told her.

Peter make stop.

"I wish I could, Amy."

She watched the hail for a moment, then signed, *Amy want go home.*

She had begun talking about going home the night before. Although the Thoralen had worn off, she remained depressed and withdrawn. Elliot had offered her some food to cheer her up. She signed that she wanted milk. When he told her they had none (which she knew perfectly well), she signed that she wanted a banana. Kahega had produced a bunch of small, slightly sour jungle bananas. Amy had eaten them without objection on previous days, but she now threw them into the water contemptuously, signing she wanted "real bananas."

When Elliot told her that they had no real bananas, she signed, *Amy want go home.*

"We can't go home now, Amy."

Amy good gorilla Peter take Amy home.

She had only known him as the person in charge, the final arbiter of her daily life in the experimental setting of Project Amy. He could think of no way to make clear to her that he was no longer in charge, and that he was not punishing her by keeping her here.

In fact, they were all discouraged. Each of the expedition members had looked forward to escaping the oppressive heat of the rain forest, but now that they were climbing Mukenko, their enthusiasm had quickly faded. "Christ," Ross said. "From hippos to hail."

As if on cue, the hail stopped. "All right," Munro said, "let's get moving."

Mukenko had never been climbed until 1933. In 1908, a German party under von Ranke ran into storms and had to descend; a Belgian team in 1913 reached 10,000 feet but could not find a route to the summit; and another German team was forced to quit in 1919 when two team members fell and died, about 12,000 feet. Nevertheless Mukenko was classified as a fairly easy (non-technical) climb by most mountaineers, who generally devoted a day to the ascent; after 1943, a new route up the southeast was found which was frustratingly slow but not dangerous, and it was this route that most climbers followed.

Above 9,000 feet, the pine forest disappeared and they crossed weak grassy fields cloaked in chilly mist; the air was thinner, and they called frequently for a rest. Munro had no patience with the complaints of his charges. "What did you expect?" he demanded. "It's a mountain. Mountains are high." He was especially merciless with Ross, who seemed the most easily fatigued. "What about your timetable?" he would ask her. "We're not even to the difficult part. It's not even interesting until eleven thousand feet. You quit now and we'll never make it to the summit before nightfall, and that means we lose a full day."

"I don't care," Ross said finally, dropping to the ground, gasping for breath.

"Just like a woman," Munro said scornfully, and smiled when Ross glared at him. Munro humiliated them, chided them, encouraged them—and somehow kept them moving.

Above 10,000 feet, the grass disappeared and there was only mossy ground cover; they came upon the solitary peculiar fat-leafed lobelia trees, emerging suddenly from the cold gray mist. There was no real cover between 10,000 feet and the summit, which was why Munro pushed them; he did not want to get caught in a storm on the barren upper slopes.

The sun broke out at 11,000 feet, and they stopped to position the second of the directional lasers for the ERTS laser-fix system. Ross had already set the first laser several miles to the south that morning, and it had taken thirty minutes.

The second laser was more critical, since it had to be matched to the first. Despite the electronic jamming, the transmitting equipment had to be connected with Houston, in order that the little laser—it was the size of a pencil eraser, mounted on a tiny steel tripod—could be accurately aimed. The two lasers on the volcano were positioned so that their beams crossed many miles away, above the jungle. And if Ross's calculations were correct, that intersection point was directly over the city of Zinj.

Elliot wondered if they were inadvertently assisting the consortium, but Ross said no. "Only at night," she said, "when they aren't moving. During the day, they won't be able to lock on our beacons—that's the beauty of the system."

Soon they smelled sulfurous volcanic fumes drifting down from the summit, now 1,500 feet above them. Up here there was no vegetation at all, only bare hard rock and scattered patches of snow tinged yellow from the sulfur. The sky was clear dark blue, and they had spectacular views of the south Virunga range—the great cone of Nyiragongo, rising steeply from the deep green of the Congo forests, and, beyond that, Mukenko, shrouded in fog.

The last thousand feet were the most difficult, particularly for Amy, who had to pick her way barefoot among the sharp lava rocks. Above 12,000 feet, the ground was loose volcanic scree. They reached the summit at five in the afternoon, and gazed over the eight-mile-wide lava lake and smoking crater of the volcano. Elliot was disappointed in the landscape of black rock and gray steam clouds. "Wait until night," Munro said.

That night the lava glowed in a network of hot red through the broken dark crust; hissing red steam slowly lost its color as it rose into the sky. On the crater rim, their little tents reflected the red glow of the lava. To the west scattered clouds were silver in the moonlight, and beneath them the Congo jungle stretched away for miles. They could see the straight green laser beams, intersecting over the black forest. With any luck they would reach that intersection tomorrow.

Ross connected her transmitting equipment to make the nightly report to Houston. After the regular six-minute delay, the signal linked directly through to Houston, without interstitial encoding or other evasive techniques.

"Hell," Munro said.

"But what does it mean?" Elliot asked.

"It means," Munro said gloomily, "the consortium has stopped jamming us."

"Isn't that good?"

"No," Ross said. "It's bad. They must already be on the site, and they've found the diamonds." She shook her head, and adjusted the video screen:

HUSTN CONFRMS CONSRTUM ONSITE ZINJ PROBABILITY 1.000. TAK NO FURTHR RSKS. SITUTN HOPELSS.

"I can't believe it," Ross said. "It's all over."

Elliot sighed. "My feet hurt," he said.

"I'm tired," Munro said.

"The hell with it," Ross said.

Utterly exhausted, they all went to bed.

DAY 8: KANYAMAGUFA

JUNE 20, 1979

1. Descent

Everyone slept late on the morning of June 20. They had a leisurely breakfast, taking the time to cook a hot meal. They relaxed in the sun, and played with Amy, who was delighted by this unexpected attention. It was past ten o'clock before they started down Mukenko to the jungle.

Because the western slopes of Mukenko are sheer and impassible, they descended inside the smoking volcanic crater to a depth of half a mile. Munro led the way, carrying a porter's load on his head; Asari, the strongest porter, had to carry Amy, because the rocks were much too hot for her bare feet.

Amy was terrified, and regarded the human persons trekking single-file down the steep inner cone to be mad. Elliot was not sure she was wrong: the heat was intense; as they approached the lava lake, the acrid fumes made eyes water and nostrils burn; they heard the lava pop and crackle beneath the heavy black crust.

Then they reached the formation called Naragema—the Devil's Eye. It was a natural arch 150 feet high, and so smooth it appeared polished on the inside. Through this arch a fresh breeze blew, and they saw the green jungle below. They paused to rest in the arch, and Ross examined the smooth inner surface. It was part of a lava tube formed in some earlier eruption; the main body of the tube had been blown away, leaving just the slender arch.

"They call it the Devil's Eye," Munro said, "because from below, during an eruption, it glows like a red eye."

From the Devil's Eye they descended rapidly through an alpine zone, and from there across the unworldly jagged terrain of a recent lava flow. Here they encountered black craters of scorched earth, some as deep as five or six feet. Munro's first thought was that the Zaire army had used this field for mortar practice. But on closer examination, they saw a scorched pattern etched into the rock, extending like tentacles outward from the craters. Munro had never seen anything like it; Ross immediately set up her antenna, hooked in the computer, and got in touch with Houston. She seemed very excited.

The party rested while she reviewed the data on the little screen, Munro said, "What are you asking them?"

"The date of the last Mukenko eruption, and the local weather. It was in March—Do you know somebody named Seamans?"

"Yes," Elliot said. "Tom Seamans is the computer programmer for Project Amy. Why?"

"There's a message for you," she said, pointing to the screen.

Elliot came around to look: SEMNS MESG FOR ELYT STNDBY.

"What's the message?" Elliot asked.

"Push the transmit button," she said.

He pushed the button and the message flashed: REVUWD ORGNL TAPE HUSTN NU M.

"I don't understand," Elliot said. Ross explained that the "M" meant that there was more message, and he had to press the transmit button again. He pushed the button several times before he got the message, which in its entirety read:

REVUWD ORGNL TAPE HUSTON NU FINDNG RE AURL SIGNL INFO—COMPUTR ANLYSS COMPLTE THINK ITS LNGWGE.

Elliot found he could read the compressed shortline language by speaking it aloud: "Reviewed original tape Houston, new finding regarding aural signal information, computer analysis complete think it's language." He frowned. "Language?"

Ross said, "Didn't you ask him to review Houston's original tape material from the Congo?"

"Yes, but that was for visual identification of the animal on the screen. I never said anything to him about aural information." Elliot shook his head. "I wish I could talk to him."

"You can," Ross said. "If you don't mind waking him up." She pushed the interlock button, and fifteen minutes later Elliot typed, Hello Tom How Are You? The screen printed HLO TOM HOWRU.

"We don't usually waste satellite time with that kind of thing," Ross said.

The screen printed SLEPY WHRERU.

He typed, Virunga. VIRNGA.

"Travis is going to scream when he sees this transcript," Ross said. "Do you realize what the transmission costs are?" But Ross needn't have worried; the conversation soon became technical:

RECVD MESG AURL INFO PLS XPLN.

AXIDENTL DISKVRY VRY XCITNG—DISCRIMNT FUNXN COMPTR ANLSS 99 CONFDNCE LIMTS TAPD AURL INFO {BRETHNG SOUNS} DEMNSTRTS CHRCTRISTX SPECH.

SPSFY CHRCTRISTX.

REPETNG ELMNTS—ARBTRARY PATRN—STRXRAL RLATNSHPS—PROBLY THRFOR SPOKN LNGWGE.

KN U TRNSLTE?

NOT SOFR.

WHT RESN?

COMPUTR HAS INSFSNT INFO IN AURL MESG—WNT MOR DATA—ST WORKNG—MAYB MOR TOMORO—FINGRS X.

RLY THNK GORILA LNGWGE?

YES IF GORILA.

"I'll be damned," Elliot said. He ended the satellite transmission, but the final message from Seamans remained on the screen, glowing bright green:

YES IF GORILA.

2. The Hairy Men

Within two hours of receiving this unexpected news, the expedition had its first contact with gorillas.

They were by now back in the darkness of the equatorial rain forest. They proceeded directly toward the site, following the overhead laser beams. They could not see these beams directly, but Ross had brought a weird optical track guide, a cadmium photocell filtered to record the specific laser wavelength emission. Periodically during the day, she inflated a small helium balloon, attached the track guide with a wire, and released it. Lifted by the helium, the guide rose into the sky above the trees. There it rotated, sighted one of the laser lines, and transmitted coordinates down the wire to the computer. They followed the track of diminishing laser intensity from a single beam, and waited for the "blip reading," the doubled intensity value that would signal the intersection of two beams above them.

This was a slow job and their patience was wearing thin when, toward midday, they came upon the characteristic three-lobed feces of gorilla, and they saw several nests made of eucalyptus leaves on the ground and in the trees.

Fifteen minutes later, the air was shattered by a deafening roar. "Gorilla," Munro announced. "That was a male telling somebody off."

Amy signed, *Gorillas say go away.*

"We have to continue, Amy," he said.

Gorilla no want human people come.

"Human people won't harm gorillas," Elliot assured her. But Amy just looked blank at this, and shook her head, as if Elliot had missed the point.

Days later he realized that he had indeed missed the point. Amy was not telling him that the gorillas were afraid of being harmed by people. She was saying that the gorillas were afraid that the people would be harmed, by gorillas.

They had progressed halfway across a small jungle clearing when the large silverback male reared above the foliage and bellowed at them.

Elliot was leading the group, because Munro had gone back to help one of the porters with his pack. He saw six animals at the edge of the clearing, dark black shapes against the green, watching the human intruders. Several of the females cocked their heads and compressed their lips in a kind of disapproval. The dominant male roared again.

He was a large male with silver hair down his back. His massive head stood more than six feet above the ground, and his barrel chest indicated that he weighed more than four hundred pounds. Seeing him, Elliot understood why the first explorers to the Congo had believed gorillas to be "hairy men," for this magnificent creature looked like a gigantic man, both in size and shape.

At Elliot's back Ross whispered, "What do we do?"

"Stay behind me," Elliot said, "and don't move."

The silverback male dropped to all fours briefly, and began a soft *ho-ho-ho* sound, which grew more intense as he leapt to his feet again, grabbing handfuls of grass as he did so. He threw the grass in the air, and then beat his chest with flat palms, making a hollow thumping sound.

"Oh, no," Ross said.

The chest-beating lasted five seconds, and then the male dropped to all fours again. He ran sideways across the grass, slapping the foliage and making as much noise as possible, to frighten the intruders off. Finally he began the *ho-ho-ho* sound once more.

The male stared at Elliot, expecting that this display would send him running. When it did not, the male leapt to his feet, pounded his chest, and roared with even greater fury.

And then he charged.

With a howling scream he came crashing forward at frightening speed, directly toward Elliot. Elliot heard Ross gasp behind him. He wanted to turn and run, his every bodily instinct screamed that he should run, but he forced himself to stand absolutely still—and to look down at the ground.

Staring at his feet while he listened to the gorilla crashing through the tall grass toward him, he had the sudden sensation that all his abstract book knowledge was wrong, that everything that scientists around the world thought about gorillas was wrong. He had a mental image of the huge head and the deep chest and the long arms swinging wide as the powerful animal rushed toward an easy kill, a stationary target foolish enough to believe all the academic misinformation sanctified by print. . . .

The gorilla (who must have been quite close) made a snorting noise, and

Elliot could see his heavy shadow on the grass near his feet. But he did not look up until the shadow moved away.

When Elliot raised his head, he saw the male gorilla retreating backward, toward the far edge of the clearing. There the male turned, and scratched his head in a puzzled way, as if wondering why his terrifying display had not driven off the intruders. He slapped the ground a final time, and then he and the rest of the troop melted away into the tall grass. It was silent in the clearing until Ross collapsed into Elliot's arms.

"Well," Munro said as he came up, "it seems you know a thing or two about gorillas after all." Munro patted Ross's arm. "It's all right. They don't do anything unless you run away. Then they bite you on the ass. That's the mark for cowardice in these regions—because it means you ran away."

Ross was sobbing quietly, and Elliot discovered that his own knees were shaky; he went to sit down. It had all happened so fast that it was a few moments before he realized that these gorillas had behaved in exactly the textbook manner, which included not making any verbalizations even remotely like speech.

3. The Consortium

An hour later they found the wreckage of the C-130 transport. The largest airplane in the world appeared in correct scale as it lay half buried in the jungle, the gigantic nose crushed against equally gigantic trees, the enormous tail section twisted toward the ground, the massive wings buckled casting shadows on the jungle floor.

Through the shattered cockpit windshield, they saw the body of the pilot, covered with black flies. The flies buzzed and thumped against the glass as they peered in. Moving aft, they tried to look into the fuselage windows, but even on crumpled landing gear the body of the plane stood too high above the jungle floor.

Kahega managed to climb an overturned tree, and from there moved onto one wing and looked into the interior. "No people," he said.

"Supplies?"

"Yes, many supplies. Boxes and containers."

Munro left the others, walking beneath the crushed tail section to examine the far side of the plane. The port wing, concealed from their view, was blackened and shattered, the engines gone. That explained why the plane crashed—the last FZA missile had found its target, blowing away most of the port wing. Yet the wreck remained oddly mysterious to Munro; something about its appearance was wrong. He looked along the length of the fuselage, from the crushed nose, down the line of windows, past the stump of wing, past the rear exit doors. . . .

"I'll be damned," Munro said softly.

He hurried back to the others, who were sitting on one of the tires, in the shadow of the starboard wing. The tire was so enormous that Ross could sit on it and swing her feet in the air without touching the ground.

"Well," Ross said, with barely concealed satisfaction. "They didn't get their damn supplies."

"No," Munro said. "And we saw this plane the night before last, which means it's been down at least thirty-six hours."

Munro waited for Ross to figure it out.

"Thirty-six hours?"

"That's right. Thirty-six hours."

"And they never came back to get their supplies. . . ."

"They didn't even *try* to get them," Munro said. "Look at the main cargo doors, fore and aft—no one has tried to open them. I wonder why they never came back?"

In a section of dense jungle, the ground underfoot crunched and crackled. Pushing aside the palm fronds, they saw a carpeting of shattered white bones.

"*Kanyamagufa,*" Munro said. The place of bones. He glanced quickly at the porters to see what their reaction was, but they showed only puzzlement, no fear. They were East African Kikuyu and they had none of the superstitions of the tribes that bordered the rain forest.

Amy lifted her feet from the sharp bleached fragments. She signed, *Ground hurt.*

Elliot signed, What place this?

We come bad place.

What bad place?

Amy had no reply.

"These are bones!" Ross said, staring down at the ground.

"That's right," Munro said quickly, "but they're not human bones. Are they, Elliot?"

Elliot was also looking at the ground. He saw bleached skeletal remains from several species, although he could not immediately identify any of them.

"Elliot? Not human?"

"They don't look human," Elliot agreed, staring at the ground. The first thing he noticed was that the majority of the bones came from distinctly small animals—birds, monkeys, and tiny forest rodents. Other small pieces were actually fragments from larger animals, but how large was hard to say. Perhaps large monkeys—but there weren't any large monkeys in the rain forest.

Chimpanzees? There were no chimps in this part of the Congo. Perhaps they might be gorillas: he saw one fragment from a cranium with heavy frontal sinuses, and he saw the beginning of the characteristic sagittal crest.

"Elliot?" Munro said, his voice tense, insistent. "Non-human?"

"Definitely non-human," Elliot said, staring. *What could shatter a gorilla skull?* It must have happened after death, he decided. A gorilla had died and after many years the bleached skeleton had been crushed in some fashion. Certainly it could not have happened during life.

"Not human," Munro said, looking at the ground. "Hell of a lot of bones, but nothing human." As he walked past Elliot, he gave him a look. *Keep your mouth shut.* "Kahega and his men know that you are expert in these matters," Munro said, looking at him steadily.

What had Munro seen? Certainly he had been around enough death to know a human skeleton when he saw one. Elliot's glance fell on a curved bone. It looked a bit like a turkey wishbone, only much larger and broader, and white with age. He picked it up. It was a fragment of the zygomatic arch from a human skull. A cheekbone, from beneath the eye.

He turned the fragment in his hands. He looked back at the jungle floor, and the creepers that spread reaching tentacles over the white carpet of bones. He saw many very fragile bones, some so thin they were translucent—bones that he assumed had come from small animals.

Now he was not sure.

A question from graduate school returned to him. What seven bones compose the orbit of the human eye? Elliot tried to remember. The zygoma, the nasal, the inferior orbital, the sphenoid—that was four—the ethmoid, five—something must come from beneath, from the mouth—the palatine, six—one more to go—he couldn't think of the last bone. Zygoma, nasal, inferior orbital, sphenoid, ethmoid, palatine . . . delicate bones, translucent bones, small bones.

Human bones.

"At least these aren't human bones," Ross said.

"No," Elliot agreed. He glanced at Amy.

Amy signed, *People die here.*

"What did she say?"

"She said people don't benefit from the air here."

"Let's push on," Munro said.

Munro led him a little distance ahead of the others. "Well done," he said. "Have to be careful about the Kikuyu. Don't want to panic them. What'd your monkey say?"

"She said people died there."

"That's more than the others know," Munro said, nodding grimly. "Although they suspect."

Behind them, the party walked single-file, nobody talking.

"What the hell happened back there?" Elliot said.

"Lots of bones," Munro said. "Leopard, colobus, forest rat, maybe a bush baby, human . . ."

"And gorilla," Elliot said.

"Yes," Munro said. "I saw that, too. Gorilla." He shook his head. "What can kill a gorilla, Professor?"

Elliot had no answer.

The consortium camp lay in ruins, the tents shredded and shattered, the dead bodies covered with dense black clouds of flies. In the humid air, the stench was overpowering, the buzzing of the flies an angry monotonous sound. Everybody except Munro hung back at the edge of the camp.

"No choice," he said. "We've got to know what happened to these—" He went inside the camp itself, stepping over the flattened fence.

As Munro moved inside, the perimeter defenses were set off, emitting a screaming high-frequency signal. Outside the fence, the others cupped their hands over their ears and Amy snorted her displeasure.

Bad noise.

Munro glanced back at them. "Doesn't bother me," he said. "That's what you get for staying outside." Munro went to one dead body, turning it over with his foot. Then he bent down, swatting away the cloud of buzzing flies, and carefully examined the head.

Ross glanced over at Elliot. He seemed to be in shock, the typical scientist, immobilized by disaster. At his side, Amy covered her ears and winced. But Ross was not immobilized; she took a deep breath and crossed the perimeter. "I have to know what defenses they installed."

"Fine," Elliot said. He felt detached, light-headed, as if he might faint; the sight and the smells made him dizzy. He saw Ross pick her way across the compound, then lift up a black box with an odd baffled cone. She traced a wire back toward the center of the camp. Soon afterward the high-frequency signal ceased; she had turned it off at the source.

Amy signed, *Better now.*

With one hand, Ross rummaged through the electronics equipment in the center of the units in the camp, while with the other she held her nose against the stench.

Kahega said, "I'll see if they have guns, Doctor," and he, too, moved into the camp. Hesitantly, the other porters followed him.

Alone, Elliot remained with Amy. She impassively surveyed the destruction, although she reached up and took his hand. He signed, Amy what happened this place?

Amy signed, *Things come.*
What things?
Bad things.
What things?
Bad things come things come bad.
What things?
Bad things.

Obviously he would get nowhere with this line of questioning. He told her to remain outside the camp, and went in himself, moving among the bodies and the buzzing flies.

Ross said, "Anybody find the leader?"

Across the camp, Munro said, "Menard."

"Out of Kinshasa?"

Munro nodded. "Yeah."

"Who's Menard?" Elliot asked.

"He's got a good reputation, knows the Congo." Ross picked her way through the debris. "But he wasn't good enough." A moment later she paused.

Elliot went over to her. She stared at a body lying face down on the ground.

"Don't turn it over," she said. "It's Richter."

Elliot did not understand how she could be sure. The body was covered with black flies. He bent over.

"Don't touch him!"

"Okay," Elliot said.

"Kahega," Munro shouted, raising a green plastic twenty-liter can. The can sloshed with liquid in his hand. "Let's get this done."

Kahega and his men moved swiftly, splashing kerosene over the tents and dead bodies. Elliot smelled the sharp odor.

Ross, crouched under a torn nylon supply tent, shouted, "Give me a minute!"

"Take all the time you want," Munro said. He turned to Elliot, who was watching Amy outside the camp.

Amy was signing to herself: *People bad. No believe people bad things come.*

"She seems very calm about it," Munro said.

"Not really," Elliot said. "I think she knows what took place here."

"I hope she'll tell us," Munro said. "Because all these men died in the same way. Their skulls were crushed."

The flames from the consortium camp licked upward into the air, and the black smoke bellowed as the expedition moved onward through the jungle. Ross was silent, lost in thought. Elliot said, "What did you find?"

"Nothing good," she said. "They had a perfectly adequate peripheral system, quite similar to our ADP—animal defense perimeter. Those cones I found are audio-sensing units, and when they pick up a signal, they emit an ultra-high-frequency signal that is very painful to auditory systems. Doesn't work for reptiles, but it's damn effective on mammalian systems. Send a wolf or a leopard running for the hills."

"But it didn't work here," Elliot said.

"No," Ross said. "And it didn't bother Amy very much."

Elliot said, "What does it do to human auditory systems?"

"You felt it. It's annoying, but that's all." She glanced at Elliot. "But there aren't any human beings in this part of the Congo. Except us."

Munro asked, "Can we make a better perimeter defense?"

"Damn right we can," Ross said. "I'll give you the next generation perimeter—it'll stop anything except elephants and rhinos." But she didn't sound convinced.

Late in the afternoon, they came upon the remains of the first ERTS Congo camp. They nearly missed it, for during the intervening eight days the jungle vines and creepers had already begun to grow back over it, obliterating all traces. There was not much left—a few shreds of orange nylon, a dented aluminum cooking pan, the crushed tripod, and the broken video camera, its green circuit boards scattered across the ground. They found no bodies, and since the light was fading they pressed on.

Amy was distinctly agitated, She signed, *No go.*

Peter Elliot paid no attention.

Bad place old place no go.

"We go, Amy," he said.

Fifteen minutes later they came to a break in the overhanging trees. Looking up, they saw the dark cone of Mukenko rising above the forest, and the faint crossed green beams of the lasers glinting in the humid air. And directly beneath the beams were the moss-covered stone blocks, half concealed in jungle foliage, of the Lost City of Zinj.

Elliot turned to look at Amy.

Amy was gone.

4. Weird

He could not believe it.

At first he thought she was just punishing him, running off to make him sorry for shooting the dart at her on the river. He explained to Munro and Ross that she was capable of such things, and they spent the next half hour wandering through the jungle, calling her name. But there was no response, just the eternal silence of the rain forest. The half hour became an hour, then almost two hours.

Elliot was panic-stricken.

When she still did not emerge from the foliage, another possibility had to be considered. "Maybe she ran off with the last group of gorillas," Munro said.

"Impossible," Elliot said.

"She's seven, she's near maturity." Munro shrugged. "She *is* a gorilla."

"Impossible," Elliot insisted.

But he knew what Munro was saying. Inevitably, people who raised apes found at a certain point they could no longer keep them. With maturity the animals became too large, too powerful, too much their own species to be controllable. It was no longer possible to put them in diapers and pretend they were cute humanlike creatures. Their genes coded inevitable differences that ultimately became impossible to overlook.

"Gorilla troops aren't closed," Munro reminded him. "They accept strangers, particularly female strangers."

"She wouldn't do that," Elliot insisted. "She couldn't."

Amy had been raised from infancy among human beings. She was much more familiar with the Westernized world of freeways and drive-ins than she was with the jungle. If Elliot drove his car past her favorite drive-in, she was quick to tap his shoulder and point out his error. What did she know of the jungle? It was as alien to her as it was to Elliot himself. And not only that—

"We'd better make camp," Ross said, glancing at her watch. "She'll come back—if she wants to. After all," she said, "we didn't leave her. She left us."

They had brought a bottle of Dom Pérignon champagne but nobody was in a mood to celebrate. Elliot was remorseful over the loss of Amy; the others were horrified by what they had seen of the earlier camp; with night rapidly falling,

171

there was much to do to set up the ERTS system known as WEIRD (Wilderness Environment Intruder Response Defenses).

The exotic WEIRD technology recognized the fact that perimeter defenses were traditional throughout the history of Congo exploration. More than a century before, Stanley observed that "no camp is to be considered complete until it is fenced around by bush or trees." In the years since there was little reason to alter the essential nature of that instruction. But defensive technology had changed, and the WEIRD system incorporated all the latest innovations.

Kahega and his men inflated the silvered Mylar tents, arranging them close together. Ross directed the placement of the tubular infrared night lights on telescoping tripods. These were positioned shining outward around the camp.

Next the perimeter fence was installed. This was a lightweight metalloid mesh, more like cloth than wire. Attached to stakes, it completely enclosed the campsite, and when hooked to the transformer carried 10,000 volts of electrical current. To reduce drain on the fuel cells, the current was pulsed at four cycles a second, creating a throbbing, intermittent hum.

Dinner on the night of June 21 was rice with rehydrated Creole shrimp sauce. The shrimps did not rehydrate well, remaining little cardboard-tasting chunks in the mix, but nobody complained about this failure of twentieth-century technology as they glanced around them at the deepening jungle darkness.

Munro positioned the sentries. They would stand four-hour watches; Munro announced that he, Kahega, and Elliot would take the first watch.

With night goggles in place, the sentries looked like mysterious grasshoppers peering out at the jungle. The night goggles intensified ambient light and overlaid this on the pre-existing imagery, rimming it in ghostly green. Elliot found the goggles heavy, and the electronic view through them difficult to adjust to. He pulled them off after several minutes, and was astonished to see that the jungle was inky black around him. He put them back on hastily.

The night passed quietly, without incident.

DAY 9: ZINJ

JUNE 21, 1979

1. Tiger Tail

Their entrance into the Lost City of Zinj on the morning of June 21 was accomplished with none of the mystery and romance of nineteenth-century accounts of similar journeys. These twentieth-century explorers sweated and grunted under a burdensome load of technical equipment—optical range finders, data-lock compasses, RF directionals with attached transmitters, and microwave transponders—all deemed essential to the modern high-speed evaluation of a ruined archaeological site.

They were only interested in diamonds. Schliemann had been only interested in gold when he excavated Troy, and he had devoted three years to it. Ross expected to find her diamonds in three days.

According to the ERTS computer simulation the best way to do this was to draw up a ground plan of the city. With a plan in hand, it would be relatively simple to deduce mine locations from the arrangement of urban structures.

They expected a usable plan of the city within six hours. Using RF transponders, they had only to stand in each of the four corners of a building, pressing the radio beeper at each corner. Back in camp, two widely spaced receivers recorded their signals so that their computer could plot them in two dimensions. But the ruins were extensive, covering more than three square kilometers. A radio survey would separate them widely in dense foliage—and, considering what had happened to the previous expedition, this seemed unwise.

Their alternative was what ERTS called the non-systematic survey, or "the tiger-tail approach." (It was a joke at ERTS that one way to find a tiger was to keep walking until you stepped on its tail.) They moved through the ruined buildings, avoiding slithering snakes and giant spiders that scurried into dark recesses. The spiders were the size of a man's hand, and to Ross's astonishment made a loud clicking noise.

They noticed that the stonework was of excellent quality, although the limestone in many places was pitted and crumbling. And everywhere they saw the half-moon curve of doors and windows, which seemed to be a cultural design motif.

But aside from that curved shape, they found almost nothing distinctive about the rooms they passed through. In general, the rooms were rectangular and roughly the same size; the walls were bare, lacking decoration. After so many intervening centuries they found no artifacts at all—although Elliot finally came upon a pair of disc-shaped stone paddles, which they presumed had been used to grind spices or grain.

The bland, characterless quality of the city grew more disturbing as they continued; it was also inconvenient, since they had no way to refer to one place or another; they began assigning arbitrary names to different buildings. When Karen Ross found a series of cubby holes carved into the wall of one room, she announced that this must be a post office, and from then on it was referred to as "the post office."

They came upon a row of small rooms with postholes for wooden bars. Munro thought these were cells of a jail, but the cells were extremely small. Ross said that perhaps the people were small, or perhaps the cells were intentionally small for punishment. Elliot thought perhaps they were cages for a zoo. But in that case, why were all the cages of the same size? And Munro pointed out there was no provision for viewing the animals; he repeated his conviction that it was a jail, and the rooms became known as "the jail."

Near to the jail they found an open court they called "the gymnasium." It was apparently an athletic field or training ground. There were four tall stone stakes with a crumbling stone ring at the top; evidently these had been used for some kind of game like tetherball. In a corner of the court stood a horizontal overhead bar, like a jungle gym, no more than five feet off the ground. The low bar led Elliot to conclude that this was a playground for children. Ross repeated her belief that the people were small. Munro wondered if the gymnasium was a training area for soldiers.

As they continued their search, they were all aware that their reactions simply mirrored their preoccupations. The city was so neutral, so uninformative, that it became a kind of Rorschach for them. What they needed was objective information about the people who had built the city, and their life.

It was there all along, although they were slow to realize it. In many rooms, one wall or another was overgrown with black-green mold. Munro noticed that this mold did not grow in relation to light from a window, or air currents, or any other factor they could identify. In some rooms, the mold grew thickly halfway down a wall, only to stop in a sharp horizontal line, as if cut by a knife.

"Damn strange," Munro said, peering at the mold, rubbing his finger against it. His finger came away with traces of blue paint.

That was how they discovered the elaborate bas-reliefs, once painted, that appeared throughout the city. However, the overgrowth of mold on the irregular carved surface and the pitting of the limestone made any interpretation of the images impossible.

At lunch, Munro mentioned that it was too bad they hadn't brought along a group of art historians to recover the bas-relief images. "With all their lights and machines, they could see what's there in no time," he said.

The most recent examination techniques for artwork, as devised by

Degusto and others, employed infrared light and image intensification, and the Congo expedition had the necessary equipment to contrive such a method on the spot. At least it was worth a try. After lunch they returned to the ruins, lugging in the video camera, one of the infrared night lights, and the tiny computer display screen.

After an hour of fiddling they had worked out a system. By shining infrared light on the walls and recording the image with the video camera—and then feeding that image via satellite through the digitizing computer programs in Houston, and returning it back to their portable display unit—they were able to reconstitute the pictures on the walls.

Seeing the bas-reliefs in this way reminded Peter Elliot of the night goggles. If you looked directly at the walls, you saw nothing but dark moss and lichen and pitted stone. But if you looked at the little computer screen, you saw the original painted scenes, vibrant and lifelike. It was, he remembered, "very peculiar. There we were in the middle of the jungle, but we could only examine our environment indirectly, with the machines. We used goggles to see at night, and video to see during the day. We were using machines to see what we could not see otherwise, and we were totally dependent on them."

He also found it odd that the information recorded by the video camera had to travel more than twenty thousand miles before returning to the display screen, only a few feet away. It was, he said later, the "world's longest spinal cord," and it produced an odd effect. Even at the speed of light, the transmission required a tenth of a second, and since there was a short processing time in the Houston computer, the images did not appear on the screen instantaneously, but arrived about half a second late. The delay was just barely noticeable. The scenes they saw provided them with their first insight into the city and its inhabitants.

The people of Zinj were relatively tall blacks, with round heads and muscular bodies; in appearance they resembled the Bantu-speaking people who had first entered the Congo from the highland savannahs to the north, two thousand years ago. They were depicted here as lively and energetic: despite the climate, they favored elaborately decorated, colorful long robes; their attitudes and gestures were expansive; in all ways they contrasted sharply with the bland and crumbling structures, now all that remained of their civilization.

The first decoded frescoes showed marketplace scenes: sellers squatted on the ground beside beautiful woven baskets containing round objects, while buyers stood and bargained with them. At first they thought the round objects were fruit, but Ross decided they were stones.

"Those are uncut diamonds in a surrounding matrix," she said, staring at the screen. "They're selling diamonds."

The frescoes led them to consider what had happened to the inhabitants of the city of Zinj, for the city was clearly abandoned, not destroyed—there was no sign of war or invaders, no evidence of any cataclysm or natural disaster.

Ross, voicing her deepest fears, suspected the diamond mines had given out, turning this city into a ghost town like so many other mining settlements in history. Elliot thought that a plague or disease had overcome the inhabitants. Munro said he thought the gorillas were responsible.

"Don't laugh," he said. "This is a volcanic area. Eruptions, earthquakes, drought, fires on the savannah—the animals go berserk, and don't behave in the ordinary way at all."

"Nature on the rampage?" Elliot asked, shaking his head. "There are volcanic eruptions here every few years, and we know this city existed for centuries. It can't be that."

"Maybe there was a palace revolution, a coup."

"What would that matter to gorillas?" Elliot laughed.

"It happens," Munro said. "In Africa, the animals always get strange when there's a war on, you know." He then told them stories of baboons attacking farmhouses in South Africa and buses in Ethiopia.

Elliot was unimpressed. These ideas of nature mirroring the affairs of man were very old—at least as old as Aesop, and about as scientific. "The natural world is indifferent to man," he said.

"Oh, no question," Munro said, "but there isn't much natural world left."

Elliot was reluctant to agree with Munro, but in fact a well-known academic thesis argued just that. In 1955, the French anthropologist Maurice Cavalle published a controversial paper entitled "The Death of Nature." In it he said:

One million years ago the earth was characterized by a pervasive wilderness which we may call "nature." In the midst of this wild nature stood small enclaves of human habitation. Whether caves with artificial fire to keep men warm, or later cities with dwellings and artificial fields of cultivation, these enclaves were distinctly unnatural. In the succeeding millennia, the area of untouched nature surrounding artificial human enclaves progressively declined, although for centuries the trend remained invisible.

Even 300 years ago in France or England, the great cities of man were isolated by hectares of wilderness in which untamed beasts roamed, as they had for thousands of years before. And yet the expansion of man continued inexorably.

One hundred years ago, in the last days of the great European explorers, nature had so radically diminished that it was a novelty: it is for this reason that African explorations captured the imagination of nineteenth-century man. To enter a truly natural world was exotic, beyond the experience of most mankind, who lived from birth to death in entirely man-made circumstances.

In the twentieth century the balance has shifted so far that for all practical purposes one may say that nature has disappeared. Wild plants are preserved in hothouses, wild animals in zoos and game parks: artificial settings created by man as a souvenir of the once-prevalent natural world. But an animal in a zoo or a game park does not live its natural life, any more than a man in a city lives a natural life.

Today we are surrounded by man and his creations. Man is inescapable, everywhere on the globe, and nature is a fantasy, a dream of the past, long gone.

Ross called Elliot away from his dinner. "It's for you," she said, pointing to the computer next to the antenna. "That friend of yours again."

Munro grinned, "Even in the jungle, the phone never stops ringing."

Elliot went over to look at the screen: COMPUTR LNGWAGE ANALYSS NG REQUIR MOR INPUT KN PROVIDE?

WHT INPUT? Elliot typed back.

MOR AURL INPUT—TRNSMIT RECORDNGS.

Elliot typed back, Yes If Occurs. YES IF OCRS.

RCORD FREQNCY 22-50,000 CYCLS-CRITICL

Elliot typed back, Understood. UNDRSTOD.

There was a pause, then the screen printed: HOWS AMY?

Elliot hesitated. FINE.

STAF SNDS LOV came the reply, and the transmission was momentarily interrupted.

HOLD TRSNMSN.

There was a long pause.

INCREDIBL NWZ, Seamans printed. HAV FOUND MRS SWENSN.

2. Swensn NWZ

For a moment Elliot did not recognize the name. Swensn? Who was Swensn? A transmission error? And then he realized: *Mrs. Swenson!* Amy's discoverer, the woman who had brought her from Africa and had donated her to the Minneapolis zoo. The woman who had been in Borneo all these weeks. IF WE HAD ONLY KNON AMY MOTHR NOT KILD BY NATIVS.

Elliot waited impatiently for the next message from Seamans.

Elliot stared at the message. He had always been told that Amy's mother had been killed by natives in a village called Bagimindi. The mother had been killed for food, and Amy was orphaned. . . .

WHT MEANS?

MOTHR ALREDY DED NOT EATN.

The natives hadn't killed Amy's mother? She was already dead?

XPLN.

SWENSN HAS PICTR CAN TRANSMT?

Hastily, Elliot typed, his fingers fumbling at the keyboard.

TRANSMT.

There was a pause that seemed interminable, and then the video screen received the transmission, scanning it from top to bottom. Long before the picture filled the screen, Elliot realized what it showed.

A crude snapshot of a gorilla corpse with a crushed skull. The animal lay on its back in a packed-earth clearing, presumably in a native village.

In that moment Elliot felt as if the puzzle that preoccupied him, that had caused so much anguish for so many months, was explained. If only they had been able to reach her before . . .

The glowing electronic image faded to black.

Elliot was confronted by a rush of sudden questions. Crushed skulls occurred in the remote—and supposedly uninhabited—region of the Congo, *kanyamagufa,* the place of bones. But Bagimindi was a trading village on the Lubula River, more than a hundred miles away. How had Amy and her dead mother reached Bagimindi?

Ross said, "Got a problem?"

"I don't understand the sequence. I need to ask—"

"Before you do," she said, "review the transmission. It's all in memory." She pressed a button marked REPEAT.

The earlier transmitted conversation was repeated on the screen. As Elliot watched Seaman's answers, one line struck him: MOTHR ALREDY DED NOT EATN.

Why wasn't the mother eaten? Gorilla meat was an acceptable—indeed a prized—food in this part of the Congo basin. He typed in a question:

WHY MOTHR NOT EATN.

MOTHR / INFNT FWND BY NATIV ARMY PATRL DOWN FRM SUDAN CARRIED CRPSE / INFNT 5 DAYS TO BAGMINDI VILLAG FOR SALE TOURISTS. SWENSN THERE.

Five days! Quickly, Elliot typed the important question:

WHER FWND?

The answer came back: UNKNWN AREA CONGO.

SPECFY.

NO DETALS. A short pause, then: THERS MOR PICTRS.

SND, he typed back.

The screen went blank, and then filled once more, from top to bottom. Now he saw a closer view of the female gorilla's crushed skull. And alongside the huge skull, a small black creature lying on the ground, hands and feet clenched, mouth open in a frozen scream.

Amy.

Ross repeated the transmission several times, finishing on the image of Amy as an infant—small, black, screaming.

"No wonder she's been having nightmares," Ross said. "She probably saw her mother killed."

Elliot said, "Well, at least we can be sure it wasn't gorillas. They don't kill each other."

"Right now," Ross said, "we can't be sure of anything at all."

The night of June 21 was so quiet that by ten o'clock they switched off the infrared night lights to save power. Almost at once they became aware of movement in the foliage outside the compound. Munro and Kahega swung their guns around. The rustling increased, and they heard an odd sighing sound, a sort of wheeze.

Elliot heard it too, and felt a chill: it was the same wheezing that had been recorded on the tapes from the first Congo expedition. He turned on the tape recorder, and swung the microphone around. They were all tense, alert, waiting.

But for the next hour nothing further happened. The foliage moved all around them, but they saw nothing. Then shortly before midnight the electrified perimeter fence erupted in sparks. Munro swung his gun around and fired; Ross hit the switch for the night lights and the camp was bathed in deep red.

"Did you see it?" Munro said. "Did you see what it was?"

They shook their heads. Nobody had seen anything. Elliot checked his tapes; he had only the harsh rattle of gunfire, and the sounds of sparks. No breathing.

The rest of the night passed uneventfully.

DAY 10: ZINJ

JUNE 22, 1979

1. Return

The morning of June 22 was foggy and gray. Peter Elliot awoke at 6 A.M. to find the camp already up and active. Munro was stalking around the perimeter of the camp, his clothing soaked to the chest by the wet foliage. He greeted Elliot with a look of triumph, and pointed to the ground.

There, on the ground, were fresh footprints. They were deep and short, rather triangular-shaped, and there was a wide space between the big toe and the other four toes—as wide as the space between a human thumb and fingers.

"Definitely not human," Elliot said, bending to look closely.

Munro said nothing.

"Some kind of primate."

Munro said nothing.

"It can't be a gorilla," Elliot finished, straightening. His video communications from the night before had hardened his belief that gorillas were not involved. Gorillas did not kill other gorillas as Amy's mother had been killed. "It can't be a gorilla," he repeated.

"It's a gorilla, all right," Munro said. "Have a look at this." He pointed to another area of the soft earth. There were four indentations in a row. "Those are the knuckles, when they walk on their hands."

"But gorillas," Elliot said, "are shy animals that sleep at night and avoid contact with men."

"Tell the one that made this print."

"It's small for a gorilla," Elliot said. He examined the fence nearby, where the electrical short had occurred the night before. Bits of gray fur clung to the fence. "And gorillas don't have gray fur."

"Males do," Munro said. "Silverbacks."

"Yes, but the silverback coloring is whiter than this. This fur is distinctly gray." He hesitated. "Maybe it's a *kakundakari.*"

Munro looked disgusted.

The *kakundakari* was a disputed primate in the Congo. Like the yeti of the Himalayas and bigfoot of North America, he had been sighted but never captured. There were endless native stories of a six-foot-tall hairy ape that walked on his hind legs and otherwise behaved in a manlike fashion.

185

Many respected scientists believed the *kakundakari* existed; perhaps they remembered the authorities who had once denied the existence of the gorilla.

In 1774, Lord Monboddo wrote of the gorilla that "this wonderful and fright-ful production of nature walks upright like man; is from 7 to 9 feet high . . . and amazingly strong; covered with longish hair, jet black over the body, but longer on the head; the face more like the human than the Chimpenza, but the complexion black; and has no tail."

Forty years later, Bowditch described an African ape "generally five feet high, and four across the shoulders; its paw was said to be even more dispro-portionate than its breadth, and one blow of it to be fatal." But it was not until 1847 that Thomas Savage, an African missionary, and Jeffries Wyman, a Bos-ton anatomist, published a paper describing "a second species in Africa . . . not recognized by naturalists," which they proposed to call *Troglodytes go-rilla.* Their announcement caused enormous excitement in the scientific world, and a rush in London, Paris, and Boston to procure skeletons; by 1855, there was no longer any doubt—a second, very large ape existed in Africa.

Even in the twentieth century, new animal species were discovered in the rain forest: the blue pig in 1944, and the red-breasted grouse in 1961. It was perfectly possible that a rare, reclusive primate might exist in the jungle depths. But there was still no hard evidence for the *kakundakari.*

"This print is from a gorilla," Munro insisted. "Or rather a group of gorillas. They're all around the perimeter fence. They've been scouting our camp."

"Scouting our camp," Elliot repeated, shaking his head.

"That's right," Munro said. "Just look at the bloody prints."

Elliot felt his patience growing short. He said something about white-hunter campfire tales, to which Munro said something unflattering about peo-ple who knew everything from books.

At that point, the colobus monkeys in the trees overhead began to shriek and shake the branches.

They found Malawi's body just outside the compound. The porter had been going to the stream to get water when he had been killed; the collapsible buckets lay on the ground nearby. The bones of his skull had been crushed; the purple, swelling face was distorted, the mouth open.

The group was repelled by the manner of death; Ross turned away, nau-seated; the porters huddled with Kahega, who tried to reassure them; Munro bent to examine the injury. "You notice these flattened areas of compression, as if the head was squeezed between something. . . ."

Munro then called for the stone paddles that Elliot had found in the city the day before. He glanced back at Kahega.

Kahega stood at his most erect and said, "We go home now, boss."

"That's not possible," Munro said.

"We go home. We must go home, one of our brothers is dead, we must make ceremony for his wife and his children, boss."

"Kahega . . ."

"Boss, we must go now."

"Kahega, we will talk." Munro straightened, put his arm over Kahega and led him some distance away, across the clearing. They talked in low voices for several minutes.

"It's awful," Ross said. She seemed genuinely affected with human feeling and instinctively Elliot turned to comfort her, but she continued, "The whole expedition is falling apart. It's awful. We have to hold it together somehow, or we'll *never* find the diamonds."

"Is that all you care about?"

"Well, they *do* have insurance. . . ."

"For Christ's sake," Elliot said.

"You're just upset because you've lost your damned monkey," Ross said. "Now get hold of yourself. They're watching us."

The Kikuyu were indeed watching Ross and Elliot, trying to sense the drift of sentiment. But they all knew that the real negotiations were between Munro and Kahega, standing off to one side. Several minutes later Kahega returned, wiping his eyes. He spoke quickly to his remaining brothers, and they nodded. He turned back to Munro.

"We stay, boss."

"Good," Munro said, immediately resuming his former imperious tone. "Bring the paddles."

When they were brought, Munro placed the paddles to either side of Malawi's head. They fitted the semicircular indentations on the head perfectly.

Munro then said something quickly to Kahega in Swahili, and Kahega said something to his brothers, and they nodded. Only then did Munro take the next horrible step. He raised his arms wide, and then swung the paddles back hard against the already crushed skull. The dull sound was sickening; droplets of blood spattered over his shirt, but he did not further damage the skull.

"A man hasn't the strength to do this," Munro said flatly. He looked up at Peter Elliot. "Care to try?"

Elliot shook his head.

Munro stood. "Judging by the way he fell, Malawi was standing when it happened." Munro faced Elliot, looking him in the eye. "Large animal, the size of a man. Large, strong animal. A gorilla."

Elliot had no reply.

There is no doubt that Peter Elliot felt a personal threat in these developments, although not a threat to his safety. "I simply couldn't accept it," he said later. "I knew my field, and I simply couldn't accept the idea of some unknown, radically violent behavior displayed by gorillas in the wild. And in any case, it didn't make sense. Gorillas making stone paddles that they used to crush human skulls? It was impossible."

After examining the body, Elliot went to the stream to wash the blood

187

from his hands. Once alone, away from the others, he found himself staring into the clear running water and considering the possibility that he might be wrong. Certainly primate researchers had a long history of misjudging their subjects.

Elliot himself had helped eradicate one of the most famous misconceptions—the brutish stupidity of the gorilla. In their first descriptions, Savage and Wyman had written, "This animal exhibits a degree of intelligence inferior to that of the Chimpanzee; this might be expected from its wider departure from the organization of the human subject." Later observers saw the gorilla as "savage, morose, and brutal." But now there was abundant evidence from field and laboratory studies that the gorilla was in many ways brighter than the chimpanzee.

Then, too, there were the famous stories of chimpanzees kidnapping and eating human infants. For decades, primate researchers had dismissed such native tales as "wild and superstitious fantasy." But there was no longer any doubt that chimpanzees occasionally kidnapped—and ate—human infants; when Jane Goodall studied Gombe chimpanzees, she locked away her own infant to prevent his being taken and killed by the chimps.

Chimpanzees hunted a variety of animals, according to a complicated ritual. And field studies by Dian Fossey suggested that gorillas also hunted from time to time, killing small game and monkeys, whenever—

He heard a rustling in the bushes across the stream, and an enormous silverback male gorilla reared up in chest-high foliage. Peter was startled, although as soon as he got over his fright he realized that he was safe. Gorillas never crossed open water, even a small stream. Or was that a misconception, too?

The male stared at him across the water. There seemed to be no threat in his gaze, just a kind of watchful curiosity. Elliot smelled the musty odor of the gorilla, and he heard the breath hiss through his flattened nostrils. He was wondering what he should do when suddenly the gorilla crashed noisily away through the underbrush, and was gone.

This encounter perplexed him, and he stood, wiping the sweat from his face. Then he realized that there was still movement in the foliage across the stream. After a moment, another gorilla rose up, this one smaller: a female, he thought, though he couldn't be sure. The new gorilla gazed at him as implacably as the first. Then the hand moved.

Peter come give tickle.

"Amy!" he shouted, and a moment later he had splashed across the stream, and she had leapt into his arms, hugging him and delivering sloppy wet kisses and grunting happily.

Amy's unexpected return to camp nearly got her shot by the jumpy Kikuyu porters. Only by blocking her body with his own did Elliot prevent gunfire.

Twenty minutes later, however, everyone had adjusted to her presence—and Amy promptly began making demands.

She was unhappy to learn that they had not acquired milk or cookies in her absence, but when Munro produced the bottle of warm Dom Pérignon, she agreed to accept champagne instead.

They all sat around her, drinking champagne from tin cups. Elliot was glad for the mitigating presence of the others, for now that Amy was sitting there, safely restored to him, calmly sipping her champagne and signing *Tickle drink Amy like,* he found himself overcome with anger toward her.

Munro grinned at Elliot as he gave him his champagne. "Calmly, Professor, calmly. She's just a child."

"The hell she is," Elliot said. He conducted the subsequent conversation entirely in sign language, not speaking.

Amy, he signed. Why Amy leave?

She buried her nose in her cup, singing *Tickle drink good drink.*

Amy, he signed. Amy tell Peter why leave.

Peter not like Amy.

Peter like Amy.

Peter hurt Amy Peter fly ouch pin Amy no like Peter no like Amy Amy sad sad.

In a detached corner of his mind, he thought he would have to remember that "ouch pin" had now been extended to the Thoralen dart. Her generalization pleased him, but he signed sternly, Peter like Amy. Amy know Peter like Amy. Amy tell Peter why—

Peter no tickle Amy Peter not nice Amy Peter not nice human person Peter like woman no like Amy Peter not like Amy Amy sad Amy sad.

This increasingly rapid signing was itself an indication that she was upset. Where Amy go?

Amy go gorillas good gorillas. Amy like.

Curiosity overcame his anger. Had she joined a troop of wild gorillas for several days? If so, it was an event of major importance, a crucial moment in modern primate history—a language-skilled primate had joined a wild troop and had come back again. He wanted to know more.

Gorillas nice to Amy?

With a smug look: *Yes.*

Amy tell Peter.

She stared off into the distance, not answering.

To catch her attention Elliot snapped his fingers. She turned to him slowly, her expression bored.

Amy tell Peter, Amy stay gorillas?

Yes.

In her indifference was the clear recognition that Elliot was desperate to

189

learn what she knew. Amy was always very astute at recognizing when she had the upper hand—and she had it now.

Amy tell Peter, he signed as calmly as he could.

Good gorillas like Amy Amy good gorilla.

That told him nothing at all. She was composing phrases by rote: another way of ignoring him.

Amy.

She glanced at him.

Amy tell Peter. Amy come see gorillas?

Yes.

Gorillas do what?

Gorillas sniff Amy.

All gorillas?

Big gorillas white back gorillas sniff Amy baby sniff Amy all gorillas sniff gorillas like Amy.

So silverback males had sniffed her, then infants, then all the members of the troop. That much was clear—remarkably clear, he thought, making a mental note of her extended syntax. Afterward had she been accepted in the troop? He signed, What happen Amy then?

Gorillas give food.

What food?

No name Amy food give food.

Apparently they had shown her food. Or had they actually fed her? Such a thing had never been reported in the wild, but then no one had ever witnessed the introduction of a new animal into a troop. She was a female, and nearly of productive age. . . .

What gorillas give food?

All give food Amy take food Amy like.

Apparently it was not males, or males exclusively. But what had caused her acceptance? Granted that gorilla troops were not as closed to outsiders as monkey troops—what actually had happened?

Amy stay with gorillas?

Gorillas like Amy.

Yes. What Amy do?

Amy sleep Amy eat Amy live gorillas gorillas good gorillas Amy like.

So she had joined in the life of the troop, living the daily existence. Had she been totally accepted?

Amy like gorillas?

Gorillas dumb.

Why dumb?

Gorillas no talk.

No talk sign talk?

Gorillas no talk.

Evidently she had experienced frustration with the gorillas because they did not know her sign language. (Language-using primates were commonly frustrated and annoyed when thrown among animals who did not understand the signs.)

Gorillas nice to Amy?

Gorillas like Amy Amy like gorillas like Amy like gorillas.

Why Amy come back?

Want milk cookies.

"Amy," he said, "you know we don't have any damn milk or cookies." His sudden verbalization startled the others. They looked questioningly at Amy.

For a long time she did not answer. *Amy like Peter. Amy sad want Peter.*

He felt like crying.

Peter good human person.

Blinking his eyes he signed, Peter tickle Amy. She jumped into his arms.

Later, he questioned her in more detail. But it was a painstakingly slow process, chiefly because of Amy's difficulty in handling concepts of time.

Amy distinguished past, present, and future—she remembered previous events, and anticipated future promises—but the Project Amy staff had never succeeded in teaching her exact differentiations. She did not, for example, distinguish yesterday from the day before. Whether this reflected a failing in teaching methods or an innate feature of Amy's conceptual world was an open question. (There was evidence for a conceptual difference. Amy was particularly perplexed by spatial metaphors for time, such as "that's behind us" or "that's coming up." Her trainers conceived of the past as behind them and the future ahead. But Amy's behavior seemed to indicate that she conceived of the past as in front of her—because she could see it—and the future behind her—because it was still invisible. Whenever she was impatient for the promised arrival of a friend, she repeatedly looked over her shoulder, even if she was facing the door.)

In any case, the time problem was a difficulty in talking to her now, and Elliot phrased his questions carefully. He asked, "Amy, what happened at night? With the gorillas?"

She gave him the look she always gave him when she thought a question was obvious. *Amy sleep night.*

"And the other gorillas?"

Gorillas sleep night.

"All the gorillas?"

She disdained to answer.

"Amy," he said, "gorillas come to our camp at night."

Come this place?

"Yes, this place. Gorillas come at night."

She thought that over. *No.*

Munro said, "What did she say?"

Elliot said, "She said 'No.' Yes, Amy, they come."

She was silent a moment, and then she signed, *Things come.*

Munro again asked what she had said.

"She said, 'Things come.' " Elliot translated the rest of her responses for them.

Ross asked, "What things, Amy?"

Bad things.

Munro said, "Were they gorillas, Amy?"

Not gorillas. Bad things. Many bad things come forest come. Breath talk. Come night come.

Munro said, "Where are they now, Amy?"

Amy looked around at the jungle. *Here. This bad old place things come.*

Ross said, "What things, Amy? Are they animals?"

Elliot told them that Amy could not abstract the category "animals." "She thinks people are animals," he explained. "Are the bad things people, Amy? Are they human persons?"

No.

Munro said, "Monkeys?"

No. Bad things, not sleep night.

Munro said, "Is she reliable?"

What means?

"Yes," Elliot said. "Perfectly."

"She knows what gorillas are?"

Amy good gorilla, she signed.

"Yes, you are," Elliot said. "She's saying she's a good gorilla."

Munro frowned. "So she knows what gorillas are, but she says these things are not gorillas?"

"That's what she says."

2. Missing Elements

Elliot got Ross to set up the video camera at the outskirts of the city, facing the campsite. With the videotape running he led Amy to the edge of the camp to look at the ruined buildings. Elliot wanted to confront Amy with the lost city, the reality behind her dreams—and

he wanted a record of her responses to that moment. What happened was totally unexpected.

Amy had no reaction at all.

Her face remained impassive, her body relaxed. She did not sign. If anything she gave the impression of boredom, of suffering through another of Elliot's enthusiasms that she did not share. Elliot watched her carefully. She
wasn't displacing; she wasn't repressing; she wasn't doing anything. She stared
at the city with equanimity.

"Amy know this place?"

Yes.

"Amy tell Peter what place."

Bad place old place.

"Sleep pictures?"

This bad place.

"Why is it bad, Amy?"

Bad place old place.

"Yes, but why, Amy?"

Amy fear.

She showed no somatic indication of fear. Squatting on the ground alongside him she gazed forward, perfectly calm.

"Why Amy fear?"

Amy want eat.

"Why Amy fear?"

She would not answer, in the way that she did not deign to answer him
whenever she was completely bored; he could not provoke her to discuss her
dreams further. She was as closed on the subject as she had been in San Francisco. When he asked her to accompany them into the ruins, she calmly refused to do so. On the other hand, she did not seem distressed that Elliot was
going into the city, and she cheerfully waved goodbye before going to demand more food from Kahega.

Only after the expedition was concluded and Elliot had returned to Berkeley did he find the explanation to this perplexing event—in Freud's *Interpretation of Dreams,* first published in 1887.

It may happen on rare occasions that a patient may be confronted by
the reality behind his dreams. Whether a physical edifice, a person, or a
situation that has the tenor of deep familiarity, the subjective response of
the dreamer is uniformly the same. The emotive content held in the
dream—whether frightening, pleasurable, or mysterious—is drained
away upon sight of the reality. . . . We may be certain that the apparent
boredom of the subject does not prove the dream-content is false. Boredom may be most strongly felt when the dream-content is *real.* The subject recognizes on some deep level his inability to alter the conditions
that he feels, and so finds himself overcome by fatigue, boredom, and

indifference, to conceal from him *his fundamental helplessness in the face of a genuine problem which must be rectified.*

Months later, Elliot would conclude that Amy's bland reaction only indicated the depth of her feeling, and that Freud's analysis was correct; it protected her from a situation that had to be changed, but that Amy felt powerless to alter, especially considering whatever infantile memories remained from the traumatic death of her mother.

Yet at the time, Elliot felt disappointment with Amy's neutrality. Of all the possible reactions he had imagined when he first set out for the Congo, boredom was the least expected, and he utterly failed to grasp its significance— that the city of Zinj was so fraught with danger that Amy felt obliged in her own mind to push it aside, and to ignore it.

Elliot, Munro, and Ross spent a hot, difficult morning hacking their way through the dense bamboo and the clinging, tearing vines of secondary jungle growth to reach new buildings in the heart of the city. By midday, their efforts were rewarded as they entered structures unlike any they had seen before. These buildings were impressively engineered, enclosing vast cavernous spaces descending three and four stories beneath the ground.

Ross was delighted by the underground constructions, for it proved to her that the Zinj people had evolved the technology to dig into the earth, as was necessary for diamond mines. Munro expressed a similar view: "These people," he said, "could do anything with earthworks."

Despite their enthusiasm, they found nothing of interest in the depths of the city. They ascended to higher levels later in the day, coming upon a building so filled with reliefs that they termed it "the gallery." With the video camera hooked to the satellite linkup, they examined the pictures in the gallery.

These showed aspects of ordinary city life. There were domestic scenes of women cooking around fires, children playing a ball game with sticks, scribes squatting on the ground as they kept records on clay tablets. A whole wall of hunting scenes, the men in brief loincloths, armed with spears. And finally scenes of mining, men carrying baskets of stones from tunnels in the earth.

In this rich panorama, they noticed certain missing elements. The people of Zinj had dogs, used for hunting, and a variety of civet cat, kept as household pets—yet it had apparently never occurred to them to use animals as beasts of burden. All manual labor was done by human slaves. And they apparently never discovered the wheel for there were no carts or rolling vehicles. Everything was carried by hand in baskets.

Munro looked at the pictures for a long time and finally said, "Something else is missing."

They were looking at a scene from the diamond mines, the dark pits in the ground from which men emerged carrying baskets heaped with gems.

"Of course!" Munro said, snapping his fingers. "No police!"

Elliot suppressed a smile: he considered it only too predictable that a character like Munro would wonder about police in this long-dead society.

But Munro insisted his observation was significant. "Look here," he said. "This city existed because of its diamond mines. It had no other reason for being, out here in the jungle. Zinj was a mining civilization—its wealth, its trade, its daily life, everything depended upon mining. It was a classic one-crop economy—and yet they didn't guard it, didn't regulate it, didn't control it?"

Elliot said, "There are other things we haven't seen—pictures of people eating, for example. Perhaps it was taboo to show the guards."

"Perhaps," Munro said, unconvinced. "But in every other mining complex in the world guards are ostentatiously prominent, as proof of control. Go to the South African diamond mines or the Bolivian emerald mines and the first thing you are made aware of is the security. But here," he said, pointing to the reliefs, *"there are no guards."*

Karen Ross suggested that perhaps they didn't need guards, perhaps the Zinjian society was orderly and peaceful. "After all, it was a long time ago," she said.

"Human nature doesn't change," Munro insisted.

When they left the gallery, they came to an open courtyard, overgrown with tangled vines. The courtyard had a formal quality, heightened by the pillars of a temple-like building to one side. Their attention was immediately drawn to the courtyard floor. Strewn across the ground were dozens of stone paddles, of the kind Elliot had previously found.

"I'll be damned," Elliot said. They picked their way through this field of paddles, and entered the building they came to call "the temple."

It consisted of a single large square room. The ceiling had been broken in several places, and hazy shafts of sunlight filtered down. Directly ahead, they saw an enormous mound of vines perhaps ten feet high, a pyramid of vegetation. Then they recognized it was a statue.

Elliot climbed up on the statue and began stripping away the clinging foliage. It was hard work; the creepers had dug tenaciously into the stone. He glanced back at Munro. "Better?"

"Come and look," Munro said, with an odd expression on his face.

Elliot climbed down, stepped back to look. Although the statue was pitted and discolored, he could clearly see an enormous standing gorilla, the face fierce, the arms stretched wide. In each hand, the gorilla held stone paddles like cymbals, ready to swing them together.

"My God," Peter Elliot said.

"Gorilla," Munro said with satisfaction.

Ross said, "It's all clear now. These people worshiped gorillas. It was their religion."

"But why would Amy say they weren't gorillas?"

"Ask her," Munro said, glancing at his watch. "I have to get us ready for tonight."

3. Attack

They dug a moat outside the perimeter fence with collapsible metalloid shovels. The work continued long after sundown; they were obliged to turn on the red night lights while they filled the moat with water diverted from the nearby stream. Ross considered the moat a trivial obstacle—it was only a few inches deep and a foot wide. A man could step easily across it. In reply, Munro stood outside the moat and said, "Amy, come here, I'll tickle you."

With a delighted grunt, Amy came bounding toward him, but stopped abruptly on the other side of the water. "Come on, I'll tickle you," Munro said again, holding out his arms. "Come on, girl."

Still she would not cross. She signed irritably; Munro stepped over and lifted her across. "Gorillas hate water," he told Ross. "I've seen them refuse to cross a stream smaller than this." Amy was reaching up and scratching under his arms, then pointing to herself. The meaning was perfectly clear. "Women," Munro sighed, and bent over and tickled her vigorously. Amy rolled on the ground, grunting and snuffling and smiling broadly. When he stopped, she lay expectantly on the ground, waiting for more.

"That's all," Munro said.

She signed to him.

"Sorry, I don't understand. No," he laughed, "signing slower doesn't help." And then he understood what she wanted, and he carried her back across the moat again, into the camp. She kissed him wetly on the cheek.

"Better watch your monkey," Munro said to Elliot as he sat down to dinner. He continued in this light bantering fashion, aware of the need to loosen everybody up; they were all nervous, crouching around the fire. But when the dinner was finished, and Kahega was off setting out the ammunition and checking the guns, Munro took Elliot aside and said, "Chain her in your tent. If we start shooting tonight, I'd hate to have her running around in the dark.

Some of the lads may not be too particular about telling one gorilla from another. Explain to her that it may get very noisy from the guns but she should not be frightened."

"Is it going to get very noisy?" Elliot said.

"I imagine," Munro said.

He took Amy into his tent and put on the sturdy chain leash she often wore in California. He tied one end to his cot, but it was a symbolic gesture; Amy could move it easily if she chose to. He made her promise to stay in the tent.

She promised. He stepped to the tent entrance, and she signed, *Amy like Peter*.

"Peter like Amy," he said, smiling. "Everything's going to be fine."

He emerged into another world.

The red night lights had been doused, but in the flickering glow of the campfire he saw the goggle-eyed sentries in position around the compound. With the low throbbing pulse of the electrified fence, this sight created an unearthly atmosphere. Peter Elliot suddenly sensed the precariousness of their position—a handful of frightened people deep in the Congo rain forest, more than two hundred miles from the nearest human habitation.

Waiting.

He tripped over a black cable on the ground. Then he saw a network of cables, snaking over the compound, running to the guns of each sentry. He noticed then that the guns had an unfamiliar shape—they were somehow too slender, too insubstantial—and that the black cables ran from the guns to squat, snub-nosed mechanisms mounted on short tripods at intervals around the camp.

He saw Ross near the fire, setting up the tape recorder. "What the hell is all this?" he whispered, pointing to the cables.

"That's a LATRAP. For laser-tracking projectile," she whispered. "The LATRAP system consists of multiple LGSDs attached to sequential RFSDs."

She told him that the sentries held guns which were actually laser-guided sight devices, linked to rapid-firing sensor devices on tripods. "They lock onto the target," she said, "and do the actual shooting once the target is identified. It's a jungle warfare system. The RFSDs have marlan-baffle silencers so the enemy won't know where the firing is coming from. Just make sure you don't step in front of one, because they automatically lock onto body heat."

Ross gave him the tape recorder, and went off to check the fuel cells powering the perimeter fence. Elliot glanced at the sentries in the outer darkness; Munro waved cheerfully to him. Elliot realized that the sentries with their grasshopper goggles and their acronymic weapons could see him far better than he could see them. They looked like beings from another universe, dropped into the timeless jungle.

Waiting.

The hours passed. The jungle perimeter was silent except for the murmur of water in the moat. Occasionally the porters called to one another softly, making some joke in Swahili; but they never smoked because of the heat-sensing machinery. Eleven o'clock passed, and then midnight, and then one o'clock.

He heard Amy snoring in his tent, her noisy rasping audible above the throb of the electrified fence. He glanced over at Ross sleeping on the ground, her finger on the switch for the night lights. He looked at his watch and yawned; nothing was going to happen tonight; Munro was wrong.

Then he heard the breathing sound.

The sentries heard it too, swinging their guns in the darkness. Elliot pointed the recorder microphone toward the sound but it was hard to determine its exact location. The wheezing sighs seemed to come from all parts of the jungle at once, drifting with the night fog, soft and pervasive.

He watched the needles wiggle on the recording gauges. And then the needles bounced into the red, as Elliot heard a dull thud, and the gurgle of water. Everyone heard it; the sentries clicked off their safeties.

Elliot crept with his tape recorder toward the perimeter fence and looked out at the moat. Foliage moved beyond the fence. The sighing grew louder. He heard the gurgle of water and saw a dead tree trunk lying across the moat.

That was what the slapping sound had been: a bridge being placed across the moat. In that instant Elliot realized they had vastly underestimated whatever they were up against. He signaled to Munro to come and look, but Munro was waving him away from the fence and pointing emphatically to the squat tripod on the ground near his feet. Before Elliot could move, the colobus monkeys began to shriek in the trees overhead—and the first of the gorillas silently charged.

He had a glimpse of an enormous animal, distinctly gray in color, racing up to him as he ducked down; a moment later, the gorillas hit the electrified fence with a shower of spitting sparks and the odor of burning flesh.

It was the start of an eerie, silent battle.

Emerald laser beams flashed through the air; the tripod-mounted machine guns made a soft *thew-thew-thew* as the bullets spit outward, the aiming mechanisms whining as the barrels spun and fired, spun and fired again. Every tenth bullet was a white phosphorous tracer; the air was crisscrossed green and white over Elliot's head.

The gorillas attacked from all directions; six of them simultaneously hit the fence and were repelled in a crackling burst of sparks. Still more charged, throwing themselves on the flimsy perimeter mesh, yet the sizzle of sparks and the shriek of the colobus monkeys was the loudest sound they heard. And then he saw gorillas in the trees overhanging the campsite. Munro and Kahega began firing upward, silent laser beams streaking into the foliage. He heard the sighing sound again. Elliot turned and saw more gorillas tearing at the fence, which had gone dead—there were no more sparks.

And he realized that this swift, sophisticated equipment was not holding the gorillas back—they needed the noise. Munro had the same thought, because he shouted in Swahili for the men to hold their fire, and called to Elliot, "Pull the silencers! The silencers!"

Elliot grabbed the black barrel on the first tripod mechanism and plucked it away, swearing—it was very hot. Immediately as he stepped away from the tripod, a stuttering sound filled the air, and two gorillas fell heavily from the trees, one still alive. The gorilla charged him as he pulled away the silencer from the second tripod. The stubby barrel swung around and blasted the gorilla at very close range; warm liquid spattered Elliot's face. He pulled the silencer from the third tripod and threw himself to the ground.

Deafening machine-gun fire and clouds of acrid cordite had an immediate effect on the gorillas; they backed off in disorder. There was a period of silence, although the sentries fired laser shots that set the tripod machines scanning rapidly across the jungle landscape, whirring back and forth, searching for a target.

Then the machines stopped hunting, and paused. The jungle around them was still.

The gorillas were gone.

DAY 11: ZINJ

JUNE 23, 1979

1. Gorilla Elliotensis

The gorilla corpses lay stretched on the ground, the bodies already stiffening in the morning warmth. Elliot spent two hours examining the animals, both adult males in the prime of life.

The most striking feature was the uniform gray color. The two known races of gorilla, the mountain gorilla in Virunga, and the lowland gorilla near the coast, both had black hair. Infants were often brown with a white tuft of hair at the rump, but their hair darkened within the first five years. By the age of twelve, adult males had developed the silver patch along their back and rump, the sign of sexual maturity.

With age, gorillas turned gray in much the same way as people. Male gorillas first developed a spot of gray above each ear, and as the years passed more body hair turned gray. Old animals in their late twenties and thirties sometimes turned entirely gray except for their arms, which remained black.

But from their teeth Elliot estimated that these males were no more than ten years old. All their pigmentation seemed lighter, eye and skin color as well as hair. Gorilla skin was black, and eyes were dark brown. But here the pigmentation was distinctly gray, and the eyes were light yellow brown.

As much as anything it was the eyes that set him thinking.

Next Elliot measured the bodies. The crown-heel length was 139.2 and 141.7 centimeters. Male mountain gorillas had been recorded from 147 to 205 centimeters, with an average height of 175 centimeters—five feet eight inches. But these animals stood about four feet six inches tall. They were distinctly small for gorillas. He weighed them: 255 pounds and 347 pounds. Most mountain gorillas weighed between 280 and 450 pounds.

Elliot recorded thirty additional skeletal measurements for later analysis by the computer back in San Francisco. Because now he was convinced that he was onto something. With a knife, he dissected the head of the first animal, cutting away the gray skin to reveal the underlying muscle and bone. His interest was the sagittal crest, the bony ridge running along the center of the skull from the forehead to the back of the neck. The sagittal crest was a distinctive feature of gorilla skull architecture not found in other apes or man; it was what gave gorillas a pointy-headed look.

Elliot determined that the sagittal crest was poorly developed in these males. In general, the cranial musculature resembled a chimpanzee's far more than a gorilla's. Elliot made additional measurements of the molar cusps, the jaw, the simian shelf, and the brain case.

By midday, his conclusion was clear: this was at least a new race of gorilla, equal to the mountain and lowland gorilla—and it was possibly a new species of animal entirely.

"**S**omething happens to the man who discovers a new species of animal," wrote Lady Elizabeth Forstmann in 1879. "At once he forgets his family and friends, and all those who were near and dear to him; he forgets colleagues who supported his professional efforts; most cruelly he forgets parents and children; in short, he abandons all who knew him prior to his insensate lust for fame at the hands of the demon called Science."

Lady Forstmann understood, for her husband had just left her after discovering the Norwegian blue-crested grouse in 1878. "In vain," she observed, "does one ask what it matters that another bird or animal is added to the rich panoply of God's creations, which already number—by Linnaean reckoning—in the millions. There is no response to such a question, for the discoverer has joined the ranks of the immortals, at least as he imagines it, and he lies beyond the power of mere people to dissuade him from his course."

Certainly Peter Elliot would have denied that his own behavior resembled that of the dissolute Scottish nobleman. Nevertheless he found he was bored by the prospect of further exploration of Zinj; he had no interest in diamonds, or Amy's dreams; he wished only to return home with a skeleton of the new ape, which would astonish colleagues around the world. He suddenly remembered he did not own a tuxedo, and he found himself preoccupied with matters of nomenclature; he imagined in the future three species of African apes:

Pan troglodytes, the chimpanzee.
Gorilla gorilla, the gorilla.
Gorilla elliotensis, a new species of gray gorilla.

Even if the species category and name were ultimately rejected, he would have accomplished far more than most scientists studying primates could ever hope to achieve.

Elliot was dazzled by his own prospects.

In retrospect, no one was thinking clearly that morning. When Elliot said he wanted to transmit the recorded breathing sounds to Houston, Ross replied it was a trivial detail that could wait. Elliot did not press her; they both later regretted their decision.

And when they heard booming explosions like distant artillery fire that morning, they paid no attention. Ross assumed it was General Muguru's men fighting the Kigani. Munro told her that the fighting was at least fifty miles away, too far for the sound to carry, but offered no alternative explanation for the noise.

And because Ross skipped the morning transmission to Houston, she was not informed of new geological changes that might have given new significance to the explosive detonations.

They were seduced by the technology employed the night before, secure in their sense of indomitable power. Only Munro remained immune. He had checked their ammunition supplies with discouraging results. "That laser system is splendid but it uses up bullets like there's no tomorrow," Munro said. "Last night consumed half of our total ammunition."

"What can we do?" Elliot asked.

"I was hoping you'd have an answer for that," Munro said. "You examined the bodies."

Elliot stated his belief that they were confronted with a new species of primate. He summarized the anatomical findings, which supported his beliefs.

"That's all well and good," Munro said. "But I'm interested in how they act, not how they look. You said it yourself—gorillas are usually diurnal animals, and these are nocturnal. Gorillas are usually shy and avoid men, while these are aggressive and attack men fearlessly. Why?"

Elliot had to admit that he didn't know.

"Considering our ammunition supplies, I think we'd better find out," Munro said.

2. The Temple

The logical place to begin was the temple, with its enormous, menacing gorilla statue. They returned that afternoon, and found behind the statue a succession of small cubicle-like rooms. Ross thought that priests who worshiped the cult of the gorilla lived here.

She had an elaborate explanation: "The gorillas in the surrounding jungle terrorized the people of Zinj, who offered sacrifices to appease the gorillas. The priests were a separate class, secluded from society. Look here, at the entrance to the line of cubicles, there is this little room. A guard stayed here to keep people away from the priests. It was a whole system of belief."

Elliot was not convinced, and neither was Munro. "Even religion is practical," Munro said. "It's supposed to benefit you."

"People worship what they fear," Ross said, "hoping to control it."

"But how could they control the gorillas?" Munro asked. "What could they do?"

When the answer finally came it was startling, for they had it all backward.

They moved past the cubicles to a series of long corridors, decorated with bas-reliefs. Using their infrared computer system, they were able to see the reliefs, which were scenes arranged in a careful order like a picture textbook.

The first scene showed a series of caged gorillas. A black man stood near the cages holding a stick in his hand.

The second picture showed an African standing with two gorillas, holding ropes around their necks.

A third showed an African instructing the gorillas in a courtyard. The gorillas were tethered to vertical poles, each with a ring at the top.

The final picture showed the gorillas attacking a line of straw dummies, which hung from an overhead stone support. They now knew the meaning of what they had found in the courtyard of the gymnasium, and the jail.

"My God," Elliot said. "They *trained* them."

Munro nodded. "Trained them as guards to watch over the mines. An animal élite, ruthless and incorruptible. Not a bad idea when you think about it."

Ross looked at the building around her again, realizing it wasn't a temple but a school. An objection occurred to her: these pictures were hundreds of years old, the trainers long gone. Yet the gorillas were still here. "Who teaches them now?"

"They do," Elliot said. "They teach each other."

"Is that possible?"

"Perfectly possible. Conspecific teaching occurs among primates."

This had been a longstanding question among researchers. But Washoe, the first primate in history to learn sign language, taught ASL to her offspring. Language-skilled primates freely taught other animals in captivity; for that matter, they would teach people, signing slowly and repeatedly until the stupid uneducated human person got the point.

So it was possible for a primate tradition of language and behavior to be carried on for generations. "You mean," Ross said, "that the people in this city have been gone for centuries, but the gorillas they trained are still here?"

"That's the way it looks," Elliot said.

"And they use stone tools?" she asked. "Stone paddles."

"Yes," Elliot said. The idea of tool use was not as farfetched as it first seemed. Chimpanzees were capable of elaborate tool use, of which the most striking example was "termite fishing." Chimps would make a twig, carefully bending it to their specifications, and then spend hours over a termite mound, fishing with the stick to catch succulent grubs.

Human observers labeled this activity "primitive tool use" until they tried it themselves. It turned out that making a satisfactory twig and catching termites was not primitive at all; at least it proved to be beyond the ability of people who tried to duplicate it. Human fishermen quit, with a new respect for the chimpanzees, and a new observation—they now noticed that younger chimps spent days watching their elders make sticks and twirl them in the mound. Young chimps literally *learned* how to do it, and the learning process extended over a period of years.

This began to look suspiciously like culture; the apprenticeship of young Ben Franklin, printer, was not so different from the apprenticeship of young Chimpanzee, termite fisher. Both learned their skills over a period of years by observing their elders; both made mistakes on the way to ultimate success.

Yet manufactured stone tools implied a quantum jump beyond twigs and termites. The privileged position of stone tools as the special province of mankind might have remained sacrosanct were it not for a single iconoclastic researcher. In 1971, the British scientist R. V. S. Wright decided to teach an ape to make stone tools. His pupil was a five-year-old orangutan named Abang in the Bristol zoo. Wright presented Abang with a box containing food, bound with a rope; he showed Abang how to cut the rope with a flint chip to get the food. Abang got the point in an hour.

Wright then showed Abang how to make a stone chip by striking a pebble against a flint core. This was a more difficult lesson; over a period of weeks, Abang required a total of three hours to learn to grasp the flint core between his toes, strike a sharp chip, cut the rope, and get the food.

The point of the experiment was not that apes used stone tools, but that the ability to make stone tools was literally within their grasp. Wright's experiment was one more reason to think that human beings were not as unique as they had previously imagined themselves to be.

"**B**ut why would Amy say they weren't gorillas?"

"Because they're not," Elliot said. "These animals don't look like gorillas and they don't act like gorillas. They are physically and behaviorally different." He went on to voice his suspicion that not only had these animals been trained, they had been *bred*—perhaps interbred with chimpanzees or, more strangely still, with men.

They thought he was joking. But the facts were disturbing. In 1960, the first blood protein studies quantified the kinship between man and ape. Biochemically man's nearest relative was the chimpanzee, much closer than the gorilla. In 1964, chimpanzee kidneys were successfully transplanted into men; blood transfusions were also possible.

But the degree of similarity was not fully known until 1975, when biochemists compared the DNA of chimps and men. It was discovered that chimps differed from men by only 1 percent of their DNA strands. And almost no one wanted to acknowledge one consequence: with modern DNA hybridization techniques and embryonic implantation, ape-ape crosses were certain, and man-ape crosses were possible.

Of course, the fourteenth-century inhabitants of Zinj had no way to mate DNA strands. But Elliot pointed out that they had consistently underestimated the skills of the Zinj people, who at the very least had managed, five hundred years ago, to carry out sophisticated animal-training procedures only duplicated by Western scientists within the last ten years.

And as Elliot saw it, the animals the Zinjians had trained presented an awesome problem.

"We have to face the realities," he said. "When Amy was given a human IQ test, she scored ninety-two. For all practical purposes, Amy is as smart as a human being, and in many ways she is smarter—more perceptive and sensitive. She can manipulate us at least as skillfully as we can manipulate her.

"These gray gorillas possess that same intelligence, yet they have been single-mindedly bred to be the primate equivalent of Doberman pinschers—guard animals, attack animals, trained for cunning and viciousness. But they are much brighter and more resourceful than dogs. And they will continue their attacks until they succeed in killing us all, as they have killed everyone who has come here before."

3. Looking Through the Bars

In 1975, the mathematician S. L. Berensky reviewed the literature on primate language and reached a startling conclusion. "There is no doubt," he announced, "that primates are far superior in intelligence to man."

In Berensky's mind, "The salient question—which every human visitor to the zoo intuitively asks—is, who is behind the bars? Who is caged, and who is free? . . . On both sides of the bars primates can be observed making faces at each other. It is too facile to say that man is superior because he has made the zoo. We impose our special horror of barred captivity—a form of punishment among our species—and assume that other primates feel as we do."

Berensky likened primates to foreign ambassadors. "Apes have for centuries managed to get along with human beings, as ambassadors from their species. In recent years, they have even learned to communicate with human beings using sign language. But it is a one-sided diplomatic exchange; no human being has attempted to live in ape society, to master their language and customs, to eat their food, to live as they do. The apes have learned to talk to us, but we have never learned to talk to them. Who, then, should be judged the greater intellect?"

Berensky added a prediction. "The time will come," he said, "when circumstances may force some human beings to communicate with a primate society on its own terms. Only then human beings will become aware of their complacent egotism with regard to other animals."

The ERTS expedition, isolated deep in the Congo rain forest, now faced just such a problem. Confronted by a new species of gorilla-like animal, they somehow had to deal with it on its own terms.

During the evening, Elliot transmitted the taped breath sounds to Houston, and from there they were relayed to San Francisco. The transcript which followed the transmission was brief:

Seamans wrote: RECVD TRNSMISN. SHLD HELP.

IMPORTNT—NEED TRNSLATION SOON, Elliot typed back. WHN HAVE?

COMPUTR ANALYSS DIFICLT—PROBLEMS XCEED MGNITUDE CSL / JSL TRNSLATN.

"What does that mean?" Ross said.

"He's saying that the translation problems exceed the problem of translating Chinese or Japanese sign language."

She hadn't known there was a Chinese or Japanese sign language, but Elliot explained that there were sign languages for all major languages, and each followed its own rules. For instance, BSL, British sign language, was totally different from ASL, American sign language, even though spoken and written English language was virtually identical in the two countries.

Different sign languages had different grammar and syntax, and even obeyed different sign traditions. Chinese sign language used the middle finger pointing outward for several signs, such as TWO WEEKS FROM NOW and BROTHER, although this configuration was insulting and unacceptable in American sign language.

"But this is a spoken language," Ross said.

"Yes," Elliot said, "but it's a complicated problem. We aren't likely to get it translated soon."

By nightfall, they had two additional pieces of information. Ross ran a computer simulation through Houston which came back with a probability course of three days and a standard deviation of two days to find the diamond mines. That meant they should be prepared for five more days at the site. Food was not a problem, but ammunition was: Munro proposed to use tear gas.

They expected the gray gorillas to try a different approach, and they did, attacking immediately after dark. The battle on the night of June 23 was punctuated by the coughing explosions of canisters and the sizzling hiss of the gas. The strategy was effective; the gorillas were driven away, and did not return again that night.

Munro was pleased. He announced that they had enough tear gas to hold off the gorillas for a week, perhaps more. For the moment, their problems appeared to be solved.

DAY 12: ZINJ

JUNE 24, 1979

1. The Offensive

Shortly after dawn, they discovered the bodies of Mulewe and Akari near their tent. Apparently the attack the night before had been a diversion, allowing one gorilla to enter the compound, kill the porters, and slip out again. Even more disturbing, they could find no clue to how the gorilla had got through the electrified fence and back out again.

A careful search revealed a section of fence torn near the bottom. A long stick lay on the ground nearby. The gorillas had used the stick to lift the bottom of the fence, enabling one to crawl through. And before leaving, the gorillas had carefully restored the fence to its original condition.

The intelligence implied by such behavior was hard to accept. "Time and again," Elliot said later, "we came up against our prejudices about animals. We kept expecting the gorillas to behave in stupid, stereotyped ways but they never did. We never treated them as flexible and responsive adversaries, though they had already reduced our numbers by one fourth."

Munro had difficulty accepting the calculated hostility of the gorillas. His experience had taught him that animals in nature were indifferent to man. Finally he concluded that "these animals had been trained by men, and I had to think of them as men. The question became what would I do if they were men?"

For Munro the answer was clear: take the offensive.

Amy agreed to lead them into the jungle where she said the gorillas lived. By ten o'clock that morning, they were moving up the hillsides north of the city armed with machine guns. It was not long before they found gorilla spoor—quantities of dung, and nests on the ground and in the trees. Munro was disturbed by what he saw; some trees held twenty or thirty nests, suggesting a large population of animals.

Ten minutes later, they came upon a group of ten gray gorillas feeding on succulent vines: four males and three females, a juvenile, and two scampering infants. The adults were lazy, basking in the sun, eating in desultory fashion. Several other animals slept on their backs, snoring loudly. They all seemed remarkably unguarded.

Munro gave a hand signal; the safeties clicked off the guns. He prepared to fire into the group when Amy tugged at his trouser leg. He looked off and "had the shock of my bloody life. Up the slope was another group, perhaps ten or twelve animals—and then I saw another group—and another—and another still. There must have been three hundred or more. The hillside was *crawling* with gray gorillas."

The largest gorilla group ever sighted in the wild had been thirty-one individuals, in Kabara in 1971, and even that sighting was disputed. Most researchers thought it was actually two groups seen briefly together, since the usual group size was ten to fifteen individuals. Elliot found three hundred animals "an awesome sight." But he was even more impressed by the behavior of the animals. As they browsed and fed in the sunlight, they behaved very much like ordinary gorillas in the wild, but there were important differences.

"From the first sighting, I never had any doubt that they had language. Their wheezing vocalizations were striking and clearly constituted a form of language. In addition they used sign language, although nothing like what we knew. Their hand gestures were delivered with outstretched arms in a graceful way, rather like Thai dancers. These hand movements seemed to complement or add to the sighing vocalizations. Obviously the gorillas had been taught, or had elaborated on their own, a language system far more sophisticated than the pure sign language of laboratory apes in the twentieth century."

Some abstract corner of Elliot's mind considered this discovery tremendously exciting, while at the same time he shared the fear of the others around him. Crouched behind the dense foliage they held their breath and watched the gorillas feed on the opposite hillside. Although the gorillas seemed peaceful, the humans watching them felt a tension approaching panic at being so close to such great numbers of them. Finally, at Munro's signal, they slipped back down the trail, and returned to the camp.

The porters were digging graves for Akari and Mulewe in camp. It was a grim reminder of their jeopardy as they discussed their alternatives. Munro said to Elliot, "They don't seem to be aggressive during the day."

"No," Elliot said. "Their behavior looks quite typical—if anything, it's more sluggish than that of ordinary gorillas in daytime. Probably most of the males are sleeping during the day."

"How many animals on the hillside are males?" Munro asked. They had already concluded that only male animals participated in the attacks; Munro was asking for odds.

Elliot said, "Most studies have found that adult males constitute fifteen percent of gorilla groupings. And most studies show that isolated observations underestimate troop size by twenty-five percent. There are more animals than you see at any given moment."

The arithmetic was disheartening. They had counted three hundred gorillas on the hillside, which meant there were probably four hundred, of which 15 percent were males. That meant that there were sixty attacking animals—and only nine in their defending group.

"Hard," Munro said, shaking his head.

Amy had one solution. She signed, *Go now.*

Ross asked what she said and Elliot told her, "She wants to leave. I think she's right."

"Don't be ridiculous," Ross said. "We haven't found the diamonds. We can't leave now."

Go now, Amy signed again.

They looked at Munro. Somehow the group had decided that Munro would make the decision of what to do next. "I want the diamonds as much as anyone," he said. "But they won't be much use to us if we're dead. We have no choice. We must leave if we can."

Ross swore, in florid Texan style.

Elliot said to Munro, "What do you mean, if we can?"

"I mean," Munro said, "that they may not let us leave."

2. Departure

Following Munro's instructions, they carried only minimal supplies of food and ammunition. They left everything else—the tents, the perimeter defenses, the communications equipment, everything, in the sunlit clearing at midday.

Munro glanced back over his shoulder and hoped he was doing the right thing. In the 1960s, the Congo mercenaries had had an ironic rule: "Don't leave home." It had multiple meanings, including the obvious one that none of them should ever have come to the Congo in the first place. It also meant that once established in a fortified camp or colonial town you were unwise to step out into the surrounding jungle, whatever the provocation. Several of Munro's friends had bought it in the jungle because they had foolishly left home. The news would come to them: "Digger bought it last week outside Stanleyville." "Outside? Why'd he leave home?"

Munro was leading the expedition outside now, and home was the little silver camp with its perimeter defense behind them. Back in that camp, they were sitting ducks for the attacking gorillas. The mercenaries had had something to say about that, too: "Better a sitting duck than a dead duck."

As they marched through the rain forest, Munro was painfully aware of the single-file column strung out behind him, the least defensible formation. He watched the jungle foliage move in as their path narrowed. He did not remember this track being so narrow when they had come to the city. Now they were hemmed in by close ferns and spreading palms. The gorillas might be only a few feet away, concealed in the dense foliage, and they wouldn't know it until it was too late.

They walked on.

Munro thought if they could reach the eastern slopes of Mukenko, they would be all right. The gray gorillas were localized near the city, and would not follow them far. One or two hours walking, and they would be beyond danger.

He checked his watch: they had been gone ten minutes.

And then he heard the sighing sound. It seemed to come from all directions. He saw the foliage moving before him, shifting as if blown by a wind. Only there was no wind. He heard the sighing grow louder.

The column halted at the edge of a ravine, which followed a streambed past sloping jungle walls on both sides. It was the perfect spot for an ambush. Along the line he heard the safeties click on the machine guns. Kahega came up. "Captain, what do we do?"

Munro watched the foliage move, and heard the sighing. He could only guess at the numbers concealed in the bush. Twenty? Thirty? Too many, in any case.

Kahega pointed up the hillside to a track that ran above the ravine. "Go up there?"

For a long time, Munro did not answer. Finally, he said, "No, not up there."

"Then where, Captain?"

"Back," Munro said. "We go back."

When they turned away from the ravine, the sighing faded and the foliage ceased its movement. When he looked back over his shoulder for a last glimpse, the ravine appeared an ordinary passage in the jungle, without threat of any kind. But Munro knew the truth. They could not leave.

3. Return

Elliot's idea came in a flash of insight. "In the middle of the camp," he later related, "I was looking at Amy signing to Kahega. Amy was asking him for a drink, but Kahega didn't know Ameslan, and he kept shrugging helplessly. It occurred to me that the linguistic skill of the gray gorillas was both their great advantage and their Achilles' heel."

Elliot proposed to capture a single gray gorilla, learn its language, and use that language to establish communication with the other animals. Under normal circumstances it would take several months to learn a new ape language, but Elliot thought he could do it in a matter of hours.

Seamans was already at work on the gray-gorilla verbalizations; all he needed was further input. But Elliot had decided that the gray gorillas employed a combination of spoken sounds and sign language. And the sign language would be easy to work out.

Back at Berkeley, Seamans had developed a computer program called APE, for animal pattern explanation. APE was capable of observing Amy and assigning meanings to her signs. Since the APE program utilized declassified army software subroutines for code-breaking, it was capable of identifying new signs, and translating these as well. Although APE was intended to work with Amy in ASL, there was no reason why it would not work with an entirely new language.

If they could forge satellite links from the Congo to Houston to Berkeley, they could feed video data from a captive animal directly into the APE program. And APE promised a speed of translation far beyond the capacity of any human observer. (The army software was designed to break enemy codes in minutes.)

Elliot and Ross were convinced it would work; Munro was not. He made some disparaging comments about interrogating prisoners of war. "What do you intend to do," he said, "torture the animal?"

"We will employ situational stress," Elliot said, "to elicit language usage." He was laying out test materials on the ground: a banana, a bowl of water, a piece of candy, a stick, a succulent vine, stone paddles. "We'll scare the hell out of her if we have to."

"Her?"

"Of course," Elliot said, loading the Thoralen dart gun. "Her."

4. Capture

He wanted a female without an infant. An infant would create difficulties.

Pushing through waist-high undergrowth, he found himself on the edge of a sharp ridge and saw nine animals grouped below him: two males, five females, and two juveniles. They were foraging through the jungle twenty feet below. He watched the group long enough to be sure that all the females used language, and that there were no infants concealed in the foliage. Then he waited for his chance.

The gorillas fed casually among the ferns, plucking up tender shoots, which they chewed lazily. After several minutes, one female moved up from the group to forage nearer the top of the ridge where he was crouching. She was separated from the rest of the group by more than ten yards.

Elliot raised the dart pistol in both hands and squinted down the sight at the female. She was perfectly positioned. He watched, squeezed the trigger slowly—and lost his footing on the ridge. He fell crashing down the slope, right into the midst of the gorillas.

Elliot lay unconscious on his back, twenty feet below, but his chest was moving, and his arm twitched; Munro felt certain that he was all right. Munro was only concerned about the gorillas.

The gray gorillas had seen Elliot fall and now moved toward the body. Eight or nine animals clustered around him, staring impassively, signing.

Munro slipped the safety off his gun.

Elliot groaned, touched his head, and opened his eyes. Munro saw Elliot stiffen as he saw the gorillas, but he did not move. Three mature males crouched very close to him, and he understood the precariousness of his situation. Elliot lay motionless on the ground for nearly a minute. The gorillas whispered and signed, but they did not come any closer.

Finally Elliot sat up on one elbow, which caused a burst of signing but no direct threatening behavior.

On the hillside above, Amy tugged at Munro's sleeve, signing emphatically. Munro shook his head: he did not understand; he raised his machine gun again, and Amy bit his kneecap. The pain was excruciating. It was all Munro could do to keep from screaming.

*   *   *

218

Elliot, lying on the ground below, tried to control his breathing. The gorillas were very close—close enough for him to touch them, close enough to smell the sweet, musty odor of their bodies. They were agitated; the males had started grunting, a rhythmic *ho-ho-ho*.

He decided he had better get to his feet, slowly and methodically. He thought that if he could put some distance between himself and the animals, their sense of threat would be reduced. But as soon as he began to move the grunting grew louder, and one of the males began a sideways crablike movement, slapping the ground with his flat palms.

Immediately Elliot lay back down. The gorillas relaxed, and he decided he had done the correct thing. The animals were confused by this human being crashing down in their midst; they apparently did not expect contact with men in foraging areas.

He decided to wait them out, if necessary remaining on his back for several hours until they lost interest and moved off. He breathed slowly, regularly, aware that he was sweating. Probably he smelled of fear—but like men, gorillas had a poorly developed sense of smell. They did not react to the odor of fear. He waited. The gorillas were sighing and signing swiftly, trying to decide what to do. Then one male abruptly resumed his crabwise movements, slapping the ground and staring at Elliot. Elliot did not move. In his mind, he reviewed the stages of attack behavior: grunting, sideways movement, slapping, tearing up grass, beating chest—

Charging.

The male gorilla began tearing up grass. Elliot felt his heart pounding. The gorilla was a huge animal, easily three hundred pounds. He reared up on his hind legs and beat his chest with flat palms, making a hollow sound. Elliot wondered what Munro was doing above. And then he heard a crash, and he looked to see Amy tumbling down the hillside, breaking her fall by grabbing at branches and ferns. She landed at Elliot's feet.

The gorillas could not have been more surprised. The large male ceased beating his chest, dropped down from his upright posture, and glowered at Amy.

Amy grunted.

The large male moved menacingly toward Peter, but he never took his eyes off Amy. Amy watched him without response. It was a clear test of dominance. The male moved closer and closer, without hesitation.

Amy bellowed, a deafening sound; Elliot jumped in surprise. He had only heard her do it once or twice before in moments of extreme rage. It was unusual for females to roar, and the other gorillas were alarmed. Amy's forearms stiffened, her back went rigid, her face became tense. She stared aggressively at the male and roared again.

The male paused, tilted his head to one side. He seemed to be thinking it over. Finally he backed off, rejoining the semicircle of gray apes around Elliot's head.

Amy deliberately rested her hand on Elliot's leg, establishing possession. A juvenile male, four or five years old, impulsively scurried forward, baring his teeth. Amy slapped him across the face, and the juvenile whined and scrambled back to the safety of his group.

Amy glowered at the other gorillas. And then she began signing. *Go away leave Amy go away.*

The gorillas did not respond.

Peter good human person. But she seemed to be aware that the gorillas did not understand, for she then did something remarkable: she sighed, making the same wheezing sound that the gorillas made.

The gorillas were startled, and stared at one another.

But if Amy was speaking their language, it was without effect: they remained where they were. And the more she sighed, the more their reaction diminished, until finally they stared blandly at her.

She was not getting through to them.

Amy now came alongside Peter's head and began to groom him, plucking at his beard and scalp. The gray gorillas signed rapidly. Then the male began his rhythmic *ho-ho-ho* once more. When she saw this Amy turned to Peter and signed, *Amy hug Peter.* He was surprised: Amy never volunteered to hug Peter. Ordinarily she only wanted Peter to hug and tickle Amy.

Elliot sat up and she immediately pulled him to her chest, pressing his face into her hair. At once the male gorilla ceased grunting. The gray gorillas began to backpedal, as if they had committed some error. In that moment, Elliot understood: *she was treating him like her infant.*

This was classic primate behavior in aggressive situations. Primates carried strong inhibitions against harming infants, and this inhibition was invoked by adult animals in many contexts. Male baboons often ended their fight when one male grabbed an infant and clutched it to his chest; the sight of the small animal inhibited further attack. Chimpanzees showed more subtle variations of the same thing. If juvenile chimp play turned too brutal, a male would grab one juvenile and clutch it maternally, even though in this case both parent and child were symbolic. Yet the posture was sufficient to evoke the inhibition against further violence. In this case Amy was not only halting the male's attack but protecting Elliot as well, by treating him as an infant—if the gorillas would accept a bearded six-foot-tall infant.

They did.

They disappeared back into the foliage. Amy released Elliot from her fierce grip. She looked at him and signed, *Dumb things.*

"Thank you, Amy," he said and kissed her.

Peter tickle Amy Amy good gorilla.

"You bet," he said, and he tickled her for the next several minutes, while she rolled on the ground, grunting happily.

* * *

It was two o'clock in the afternoon when they returned to camp. Ross said, "Did you get a gorilla?"

"No," Elliot said.

"Well, it doesn't matter," Ross said, "because I can't raise Houston."

Elliot was stunned: "More electronic jamming?"

"Worse than that," Ross said. She had spent an hour trying to establish a satellite link with Houston, and had failed. Each time the link was broken within seconds. Finally, after confirming that there was no fault with her equipment, she had checked the date. "It's June 24," she said. "And we had communications trouble with the last Congo expedition on May 28. That's twenty-seven days ago."

When Elliot still didn't get it, Munro said, "She's telling you it's solar."

"That's right," Ross said. "This is an ionospheric disturbance of solar origin." Most disruptions of the earth's ionosphere—the thin layer of ionized molecules 50–250 miles up—were caused by phenomena such as sunspots on the surface of the sun. Since the sun rotated every twenty-seven days, these disturbances often recurred a month later.

"Okay," Elliot said, "it's solar. How long will it last?"

Ross shook her head. "Ordinarily, I would say a few hours, a day at most. But this seems to be a severe disturbance and it's come up very suddenly. Five hours ago we had perfect communications—and now we have none at all. Something unusual is going on. It could last a week."

"No communications for a week? No computer tie-ins, no nothing?"

"That's right," Ross said evenly. "From this moment on, we are entirely cut off from the outside world."

5. Isolation

The largest solar flare of 1979 was recorded on June 24, by the Kitt Peak Observatory near Tucson, Arizona, and duly passed on to the Space Environment Services Center in Boulder, Colorado. At first the SESC did not believe the incoming data: even by the gigantic standards of solar astronomy, this flare, designated 78/06/414aa, was a monster.

The cause of solar flares is unknown, but they are generally associated with sunspots. In this case the flare appeared as an extremely bright spot ten thousand miles in diameter, affecting not only alpha hydrogen and ionized calcium spectral lines but also the white light spectrum from the sun. Such a "continuous spectrum" flare was extremely rare.

Nor could the SESC believe the computed consequences. Solar flares release an enormous amount of energy; even a modest flare can double the amount of ultraviolet radiation emitted by the entire solar surface. But flare 78/06/414aa was almost *tripling* ultraviolet emissions. Within 8.3 minutes of its first appearances along the rotating rim—the time it takes light to reach the earth from the sun—this surge of ultraviolet radiation began to disrupt the ionosphere of the earth.

The consequence of the flare was that radio communications on a planet ninety-three million miles away were seriously disrupted. This was especially true for radio transmissions which utilized low signal strengths. Commercial radio stations generating kilowatts of power were hardly inconvenienced, but the Congo Field Survey, transmitting signals on the order of twenty thousand watts, was unable to establish satellite links. And since the solar flare also ejected X-rays and atomic particles which would not reach the earth for a full day, the radio disruption would last at least one day, and perhaps longer. At ERTS in Houston, technicians reported to Travis that the SESC predicted a time course of ionic disruption of four to eight days.

"That's how it looks. Ross'll probably figure it out," the technician said, "when she can't re-establish today."

"They need that computer hookup," Travis said. The ERTS staff had run five computer simulations and the outcome was always the same—short of airlifting in a small army, Ross's expedition was in serious trouble. Survival projections were running "point two four four and change"—only one chance in four that the Congo expedition would get out alive, assuming the help of the computer link which was now broken.

Travis wondered if Ross and the others realized how grave their situation was. "Any new Band Five on Mukenko?" Travis asked.

Band 5 on Landsat satellites recorded infrared data. On its last pass over the Congo, Landsat had acquired significant new information on Mukenko. The volcano had become much hotter in the nine days since the previous Landsat pass; the temperature increase was on the order of 8 degrees.

"Nothing new," the technician said. "And the computers don't project an eruption. Four degrees of orbital change are within sensor error on that system, and the additional four degrees have no predictive value."

"Well, that's something," Travis said. "But what are they going to do about the apes now that they're cut off from the computer?"

That was the question the Congo Field Survey had been asking themselves for the better part of an hour. With communications disrupted the only computers available were the computers in their own heads. And those computers were not powerful enough.

Elliot found it strange to think that his own brain was inadequate. "We had all become accustomed to the availability of computing power," he said later. "In any decent laboratory you can get all the memory and all the computation speed you could want, day or night. We were so used to it we had come to take it for granted.

Of course they could have eventually worked out the ape language, but they were up against a time factor: they didn't have months to puzzle it out; they had hours. Cut off from the APE program their situation was ominous. Munro said that they could not survive another night of frontal attack, and they had every reason to expect an attack that night.

Amy's rescue of Elliot suggested their plan. Amy had shown some ability to communicate with the gorillas; perhaps she could translate for them as well. "It's worth a try," Elliot insisted.

Unfortunately, Amy herself denied that this was possible. In response to the question "Amy talk thing talk?" She signed, *No talk.*

"Not at all?" Elliot said, remembering the way she had signed. "Peter see Amy talk thing talk."

No talk. Make noise.

He concluded from this that she was able to mimic the gorilla verbalizations but had no knowledge of their meaning. It was now past two; they had only four or five hours until nightfall.

Munro said, "Give it up. She obviously can't help us." Munro preferred to break camp and fight their way out in daylight. He was convinced that they could not survive another night among the gorillas.

But something nagged at Elliot's mind.

After years of working with Amy, he knew she had the maddening literal-mindedness of a child. With Amy, especially when she was feeling uncooperative, it was necessary to be exact to elicit the appropriate response. Now he looked at Amy and said, "Amy talk thing talk?"

No talk.

"Amy understand thing talk?"

Amy did not answer. She was chewing on vines, preoccupied.

"Amy, listen to Peter."

She stared at him.

"Amy understand thing talk?"

Amy understand thing talk, she signed back. She did it so matter-of-factly that at first he wondered if she realized what he was asking her.

"Amy watch thing talk, Amy understand talk?"

Amy understand.

"Amy sure?"

Amy sure.

"I'll be goddamned," Elliot said.

Munro was shaking his head. "We've only got a few hours of daylight left," he said. "And even if you do learn their language, how are you going to talk to them?"

6. Amy Talk Thing Talk

At 3 P.M., Elliot and Amy were completely concealed in the foliage along the hillside. The only sign of their presence was the slender cone of the microphone that protruded through the foliage. The microphone was connected to the videotape recorder at Elliot's feet, which he used to record the sounds of the gorillas on the hills beyond.

The only difficulty was trying to determine which gorilla the directional microphone had focused on—and which gorilla Amy had focused on, and whether they were the same gorilla. He could never be quite sure that Amy was translating the verbal utterances of the same animal that he was recording. There were eight gorillas in the nearest group and Amy kept getting distracted. One female had a six-month-old infant, and at one point, when the baby was bitten by a bee, Amy signed, *Baby mad.* But Elliot was recording a male.

Amy, he signed. Pay attention.

Amy pay attention. Amy good gorilla.

Yes, he signed. Amy good gorilla. Amy pay attention man thing.

Amy not like.

He swore silently, and erased half an hour of translations from Amy. She had obviously been paying attention to the wrong gorilla. When he started the tape again, he decided that this time he would record whatever Amy was watching. He signed, What thing Amy watch?

Amy watch baby.

That wouldn't work, because the baby didn't speak. He signed, Amy watch woman thing.

Amy like watch baby.

This dependency on Amy was like a bad dream. He was in the hands of an animal whose thinking and behavior he barely understood; he was cut off from the wider society of human beings and human machinery, thus increasing his dependency on the animal; and yet he had to trust her.

After another hour, with the sunlight fading, he took Amy back down the hillside to the camp.

Munro had planned as best he could.

First he dug a series of holes like elephant traps outside the camp; they were deep pits lined with sharp stakes, covered with leaves and branches.

He widened the moat in several places, and cleared away dead trees and underbrush that might be used as bridges.

He cut down the low tree branches overhanging the camp, so that if gorillas went into the trees, they would be kept at least thirty feet above the ground—too high to jump down.

He gave three of the remaining porters, Muzezi, Amburi, and Harawi, shotguns along with a supply of tear-gas canisters.

With Ross, he boosted power on the perimeter fence to almost 200 amps. This was the maximum the thin mesh could handle without melting; they had been obliged to reduce the pulses from four to two per second. But the additional current changed the fence from a deterrent to a lethal barrier. The first animals to hit that fence would be immediately killed, although the likelihood of shorts and a dead fence was considerably increased.

At sunset, Munro made his most difficult decision. He loaded the stubby tripod-mounted RFSDs with half their remaining ammunition. When that was gone, the machines would simply stop firing. From that point on, Munro was counting on Elliot and Amy and their translation.

And Elliot did not look very happy when he came back down the hill.

7. Final Defense

"**H**ow long until you're ready?" Munro asked him.

"Couple of hours, maybe more." Elliot asked Ross to help him, and Amy went to get food from Kahega. She seemed very proud of herself, and behaved like an important person in the group.

Ross said, "Did it work?"

"We'll know in a minute," Elliot said. His first plan was to run the only kind of internal check on Amy that he could, by verifying repetitions of sounds. If she had consistently translated sounds in the same way, they would have a reason for confidence.

But it was painstaking work. They had only the half-inch VTR and the small pocket tape recorder; there were no connecting cables. They called for silence from the others in the camp and proceeded to run the checks, taping, retaping, listening to the whispering sounds.

At once they found that their ears simply weren't capable of discriminating the sounds—everything sounded the same. Then Ross had an idea.

"These sounds taped," she said, "as electrical signals."

"Yes . . ."

"Well, the linkup transmitter has a 256K memory."

"But we can't link up to the Houston computer."

"I don't mean that," Ross said. She explained that the satellite linkup was made by having the 256K computer onsite match an internally generated signal—like a video test pattern—to a transmitted signal from Houston. That was how they locked on. The machine was built that way, but they could use the matching program for other purposes.

"You mean we can use it to compare these sounds?" Elliot said.

They could, but it was incredibly slow. They had to transfer the taped sounds to the computer memory, and rerecord it in the VTR, on another portion of the tape bandwidth. Then they had to input that signal into the computer memory, and run a second comparison tape on the VTR. Elliot found that he was standing by, watching Ross shuffle tape cartridges and mini floppy discs. Every half hour, Munro would wander over to ask how it was coming; Ross became increasingly snappish and irritable. "We're going as fast as we can," she said.

It was now eight o'clock.

But the first results were encouraging: Amy was indeed consistent in her translations. By nine o'clock they had quantified matching on almost a dozen words:

FOOD	.9213	.112
EAT	.8844	.334
WATER	.9978	.004
DRINK	.7743	.334
{AFFIRMATION} YES	.6654	.441
{NEGATION} NO	.8883	.220
COME	.5459	.440
GO	.5378	.404
SOUND COMPLEX: ? AWAY	.5444	.343
SOUND COMPLEX: ? HERE	.6344	.344
SOUND COMPLEX: ? ANGER		
? BAD	.4232	.477

Ross stepped away from the computer. "All yours," she said to Elliot.

Munro paced across the compound. This was the worst time. Everyone waiting, on edge, nerves shot. He would have joked with Kahega and the other porters, but Ross and Elliot needed silence for their work. He glanced at Kahega.

Kahega pointed to the sky and rubbed his fingers together.

Munro nodded.

He had felt it too, the heavy dampness in the air, the almost palpable feeling of electrical charge. Rain was coming. That was all they needed, he thought. During the afternoon, there had been more booming and distant explosions, which he had thought were far-off lightning storms. But the sound was not right; these were sharp, single reports, more like a sonic boom than anything else. Munro had heard them before, and he had an idea about what they meant.

He glanced up at the dark cone of Mukenko, and the faint glow of the Devil's Eye. He looked at the crossed green laser beams overhead. And he noticed one of the beams was moving where it struck foliage in the trees above.

At first he thought it was an illusion, that the leaf was moving and not the beam. But after a moment he was sure: the beam itself was quivering, shifting up and down in the night air.

Munro knew this was an ominous development, but it would have to wait until later; at the moment, there were more pressing concerns. He looked across the compound at Elliot and Ross bent over their equipment, talking quietly and in general behaving as if they had all the time in the world.

* * *

Elliot actually was going as fast as he could. He had eleven reliable vocabulary words recorded on tape. His problem now was to compose an unequivocal message. This was not as easy as it first appeared.

For one thing, the gorilla language was not a pure verbal language. The gorillas used sign and sound combinations to convey information. This raised a classic problem in language structure—how was the information actually conveyed? (L. S. Verinski once said that if alien visitors watched Italians speaking they would conclude that Italian was basically a gestural sign language, with sounds added for emphasis only.) Elliot needed a simple message that did not depend on accompanying hand signs.

But he had no idea of gorilla syntax, which could critically alter meaning in most circumstances—the difference between "me beat" and "beat me." And even a short message could be ambiguous in another language. In English, "Look out!" generally meant the opposite of its literal meaning.

Faced with these uncertainties, Elliot considered broadcasting a single word. But none of the words on his list was suitable. His second choice was to broadcast several short messages, in case one was inadvertently ambiguous. He eventually decided on three messages; GO AWAY, NO COME, and BAD HERE; two of these combinations had the virtue of being essentially independent of word order.

By nine o'clock, they had already isolated the specific sound components. But they still had a complicated task ahead. What Elliot needed was a loop, repeating the sounds over and over. The closest they would come was the VCR, which rewound automatically to play its message again. He could hold the six sounds in the 256K memory and play them out, but the timing was critical. For the next hour, they frantically worked at the keyboard, trying to bring the word combinations close enough together to sound—to their ears—correct.

By then it was after ten.

Munro came over with his laser gun. "You think all this will work?"

Elliot shook his head. "There's no way to know." A dozen objections had come to mind. They had recorded a female voice, but would the gorillas respond to a female? Would they accept voice sounds without accompanying hand signals? Would the message be clear? Would the spacing of the sounds be acceptable? Would the gorillas pay attention at all?

There was no way to know. They would simply have to try.

Equally uncertain was the problem of broadcasting. Ross had made a speaker, removing the tiny speaker from the pocket tape recorder and gluing it to an umbrella on a collapsible tripod. This makeshift speaker produced surprisingly loud volume, but reproduction was muffled and unconvincing.

Shortly afterward, they heard the first sighing sounds.

Munro swung the laser gun through the darkness, the red activation light glowing on the electronic pod at the end of the barrel. Through his night goggles he surveyed the foliage. Once again, the sighing came from all directions; and although he heard the jungle foliage shifting, he saw no movement close to the camp. The monkeys overhead were silent. There was only the soft, ominous sighing. Listening now, Munro was convinced that the sounds represented a language of some form, and—

. A single gorilla appeared and Kahega fired, his laser beam streaking arrow-straight through the night. The RFSD chattered and the foliage snapped with bullets. The gorilla ducked silently back into a stand of dense ferns.

Munro and the others quickly took positions along the perimeter, crouching tensely, the infrared night lights casting their shadows on the mesh fence and the jungle beyond.

The sighing continued for several minutes longer, and then slowly faded away, until all was silent again.

"What was that about?" Ross said.

Munro frowned. "They're waiting."

"For what?"

Munro shook his head. He circled the compound, looking at the other guards, trying to work it out. Many times he had anticipated the behavior of animals—a wounded leopard in the bush, a cornered buffalo—but this was different. He was forced to admit he didn't know what to expect. Had the single gorilla been a scout to look at their defenses? Or had an attack actually begun, only for some reason to be halted? Was it a maneuver designed to fray nerves? Munro had watched parties of hunting chimpanzees make brief threatening forays toward baboons, to raise the anxiety level of the entire troop before the actual assault, isolating some young animal for killing.

Then he heard the rumble of thunder. Kahega pointed to the sky, shaking his head. That was their answer.

"Damn," Munro said.

At 10:30 a torrential tropical rain poured down on them. Their fragile speaker was immediately soaked and drooping. The rain shorted the electrical cables and the perimeter fence went dead. The night lights flickered, and two bulbs exploded. The ground turned to mud; visibility was reduced to five yards. And worst of all, the rain splattering the foliage was so noisy they had to shout to each other. The tapes were unfinished; the loudspeaker probably would not work, and certainly would not carry over the rain. The rain would interfere with the lasers and prevent the dispersal of tear gas. Faces in camp were grim.

Five minutes later, the gorillas attacked.

The rain masked their approach; they seemed to burst out of nowhere, striking the fence from three directions simultaneously. From that first moment, Elliot realized the attack would be unlike the others. The gorillas had learned from the earlier assaults, and now were intent on finishing the job.

Primate attack animals, trained for cunning and viciousness: even though that was Elliot's own assessment, he was astonished to see the proof in front of him. The gorillas charged in waves, like disciplined shock troops. Yet he found it more horrifying than an attack by human troops. To them we are just animals, he thought. An alien species, for which they have no feeling. We are just pests to be eliminated.

These gorillas did not care why human beings were there, or what reasons had brought them to the Congo. They were not killing for food, or defense, or protection of their young. They were killing because they were trained to kill.

The attack proceeded with stunning swiftness. Within seconds, the gorillas had breached the perimeter and trampled the mesh fence into the mud. Unchecked, they rushed into the compound, grunting and roaring. The driving rain matted their hair, giving them a sleek, menacing appearance in the red night lights. Elliot saw ten or fifteen animals inside the compound, trampling the tents and attacking the people. Azizi was killed immediately, his skull crushed between paddles.

Munro, Kahega, and Ross all fired laser bursts, but in the confusion and poor visibility their effectiveness was limited. The laser beams fragmented in the slashing rain; the tracer bullets hissed and sputtered. One of the RFSDs went haywire, the barrel swinging in wide arcs, bullets spitting out in all directions, while everyone dived into the mud. Several gorillas were killed by the RFSD bursts, clutching their chests in a bizarre mimicry of human death.

Elliot turned back to the recording equipment and Amy flung herself on him, panicked, grunting in fear. He pushed her away and switched on the tape replay.

By now the gorillas had overwhelmed everyone in the camp. Munro lay on his back, a gorilla on top of him. Ross was nowhere to be seen. Kahega had a gorilla clinging to his chest as he rolled in the mud. Elliot was hardly aware of the hideous scratching sounds now emanating from the loudspeaker, and the gorillas themselves paid no attention.

Another porter, Muzezi, screamed as he stepped in front of a firing RFSD; his frame shook with the impact of the bullets and he fell backward to the ground, his body smoking from the tracers. At least a dozen gorillas were dead or lying wounded in the mud, groaning. The haywire RFSD had run out of ammunition; the barrel swung back and forth, the empty chamber clicking. A gorilla kicked it over, and it lay writhing on its side in the mud like a living thing as the barrel continued to swing.

Elliot saw one gorilla crouched over, methodically tearing a tent apart, shredding the silver Mylar into strips. Across the camp, another arrival banged aluminum cook pans together, as if they were metal paddles. More gorillas poured into the compound, ignoring the rasping broadcast sounds. He saw a gorilla pass beneath the loudspeaker, very close, and pay no attention at all. Elliot had the sickening realization that their plan had failed.

They were finished; it was only a matter of time.

A gorilla charged him, bellowing in rage, swinging stone paddles wide.

Terrified, Amy threw her hands over Elliot's eyes. "Amy!" he shouted, pulling her fingers away, expecting to feel at any moment the impact of the paddles and the instant of blinding pain.

He saw the gorilla bearing down on him. He tensed his body. Six feet away, the charging gorilla stopped so abruptly that he literally skidded in the mud and fell backward. He sat there surprised, cocking his head, listening.

Then Elliot realized that the rain had nearly stopped, that there was now only a light drizzle sifting down over the campsite. Looking across the compound, Elliot saw another gorilla stop to listen—then another—and another—and another. The compound took on the quality of a frozen tableau, as the gorillas stood silent in the mist.

They were listening to the broadcast sounds.

He held his breath, not daring to hope. The gorillas seemed uncertain, confused by the sounds they heard. Yet Elliot sensed that at any moment they could arrive at some group decision and resume their attack with the same intensity as before.

That did not happen. The gorillas stepped away from the people, listening. Munro scrambled to his feet, raising his gun from the mud, but he did not shoot; the gorilla standing over him seemed to be in a trance, to have forgotten all about the attack.

In the gentle rain, with the flickering night lights, the gorillas moved away, one by one. They seemed perplexed, off balance. The rasping continued over the loudspeaker.

The gorillas left, moving back across the trampled perimeter fence, disappearing once more into the jungle. And then the expedition members were alone, staring at each other, shivering in the misty rain. The gorillas were gone.

Twenty minutes later, as they were trying to rebuild their shattered campsite, the rain poured down again with unabated fury.

DAY 13: MUKENKO

JUNE 25, 1979

1. Diamonds

In the morning a fine layer of black ash covered the campsite, and in the distance Mukenko was belching great quantities of black smoke. Amy tugged at Elliot's sleeve.

Leave now, she signed insistently.

"No, Amy," he said.

Nobody in the expedition was in a mood to leave, including Elliot. Upon arising, he found himself thinking of additional data he needed before leaving Zinj. Elliot was no longer satisfied with a skeleton of one of these creatures; like men, their uniqueness went beyond the details of physical structure to their behavior. Elliot wanted videotapes of the gray apes, and more recordings of verbalizations. And Ross was more determined than ever to find the diamonds, with Munro no less interested.

Leave now.

"Why leave now?" he asked her.

Earth bad. Leave now.

Elliot had no experience with volcanic activity, but what he saw did not impress him. Mukenko was more active than it had been in previous days, but the volcano had ejected smoke and gas since their first arrival in Virunga.

He asked Munro, "Is there any danger?"

Munro shrugged. "Kahega thinks so, but he probably just wants an excuse to go home."

Amy came running over to Munro raising her arms, slapping them down on the earth in front of him. Munro recognized this as her desire to play; he laughed and began to tickle Amy. She signed to him.

"What's she saying?" Munro asked. "What are you saying, you little devil?"

Amy grunted with pleasure, and continued to sign.

"She says leave now," Elliot translated.

Munro stopped tickling her. "Does she?" he asked sharply. "What *exactly* does she say?"

Elliot was surprised at Munro's seriousness—although Amy accepted his interest in her communication as perfectly proper. She signed again, more slowly, for Munro's benefit, her eyes on his face.

"She says the earth is bad."

"Hmm," Munro said. "Interesting." He glanced at Amy and then at his watch.

Amy signed, *Nosehair man listen Amy go home now.*

"She says you listen to her and go home now," Elliot said.

Munro shrugged. "Tell her I understand."

Elliot translated. Amy looked unhappy, and did not sign again.

"Where is Ross?" Munro asked.

"Here," Ross said.

"Let's get moving," Munro said, and they headed for the lost city. Now they had another surprise—Amy signed she was coming with them, and she hurried to catch up with them.

This was their final day in the city, and all the participants in the Congo expedition described a similar reaction: the city, which had been so mysterious before, was somehow stripped of its mystery. On this morning, they saw the city for what it was: a cluster of crumbling old buildings in a hot stinking uncomfortable jungle.

They all found it tedious, except for Munro. Munro was worried.

Elliot was bored, talking about verbalizations and why he wanted tape recordings, and whether it was possible to preserve a brain from one of the apes to take back with them. It seemed there was some academic debate about where language came from; people used to think language was a development of animal cries, but now they knew that animal barks and cries were controlled by the limbic system of the brain, and that real language came from some other part of the brain called Broca's area. . . . Munro couldn't pay attention. He kept listening to the distant rumbling of Mukenko.

Munro had firsthand experience with volcanoes; he had been in the Congo in 1968, when Mbuti, another of the Virunga volcanoes, erupted. When he had heard the sharp explosions the day before, he had recognized them as brontides, the unexplained accompaniments of coming earthquakes. Munro had assumed that Mukenko would soon erupt, and when he had seen the flickering laser beam the night before, he had known there was new rumbling activity on the upper slopes of the volcano.

Munro knew that volcanoes were unpredictable—as witnessed by the fact that this ruined city at the base of an active volcano had been untouched after more than five hundred years. There were recent lava fields on the mountain slopes above, and others a few miles to the south, but the city itself was spared. This in itself was not so remarkable—the configuration of Mukenko was such that most eruptions occurred on the gentle south slopes. But it did not mean that they were now in any less danger. The unpredictability of volcanic eruptions meant that they could become lifethreatening in a matter of minutes. The danger was not from lava, which rarely flowed faster than a man could walk; it would take hours for lava to flow down from Mukenko's summit. The real danger from volcanic eruptions was ash and gas.

Just as most people killed by fires actually died from smoke inhalation, most deaths from volcanoes were caused by asphyxiation from dust and carbon monoxide. Volcanic gases were heavier than air; the Lost City of Zinj, located in a valley, could be filled in minutes with a heavy, poisonous atmosphere, should Mukenko discharge a large quantity of gas.

The question was how rapidly Mukenko was building toward a major eruptive phase. That was why Munro was so interested in Amy's reactions: it was well known that primates could anticipate geological events such as earthquakes and eruptions. Munro was surprised that Elliot, babbling away about freezing gorilla brains, didn't know about that. And he was even more surprised that Ross, with her extensive geological knowledge, did not regard the morning ashfall as the start of a major volcanic eruption.

Ross knew a major eruption was building. That morning, she had routinely tried to establish contact with Houston; to her surprise, the transmission keys immediately locked through. After the scrambler notations registered, she began typing in field updates, but the screen went blank, and flashed:

HUSTN STATN OVRIDE CLR BANX.

This was an emergency signal; she had never seen it before on a field expedition. She cleared the memory banks and pushed the transmit button. There was a burst transmission delay, then the screen printed:

COMPUTR DESIGNATN MAJR ERUPTN SIGNATR MUKENKO ADVIS LEAV SITE NOW EXPEDN JEPRDY DANGR REPET ALL LEAV SITE NOW.

Ross glanced across the campsite. Kahega was making breakfast; Amy squatted by the fire, eating a roasted banana (she had got Kahega to make special treats for her); Munro and Elliot were having coffee. Except for the black ashfall, it was a perfectly normal morning at the camp. She looked back at the screen.

MAJR ERUPTN SIGNATR MUKENKO ADVIS LEAV SITE NOW.

Ross glanced up at the smoking cone of Mukenko. The hell with it, she thought. She wanted the diamonds, and she had gone too far to quit now.

The screen blinked: PLS SIGNL REPLY.

Ross turned the transmitter off.

As the morning progressed they felt several sharp jolting earth tremors, which released clouds of dust from the crumbling buildings. The rumblings of Mukenko became more frequent. Ross paid no attention. "It just means this is elephant country," she said. That was an old geological adage: "If you're looking for elephants, go to elephant country." Elephant country meant a likely spot to find whatever minerals you were looking for. "And if you want diamonds," Ross said, shrugging, "you go to volcanoes."

The association of diamonds with volcanoes had been recognized for more than a century, but it was still poorly understood. Most theories postulated that diamonds, crystals of pure carbon, were formed in the intense heat and pressure of the upper mantle one thousand miles beneath the earth's surface. The diamonds remained inaccessible at this depth except in volcanic areas where rivers of molten magma carried them to the surface.

But this did not mean that you went to erupting volcanoes to catch diamonds being spewed out. Most diamond mines were at the site of extinct volcanoes, in fossilized cones called kimberlite pipes, named for the geological formations in Kimberley, South Africa. Virunga, near the geologically unstable Rift Valley, showed evidence of continuous volcanic activity for more than fifty million years. They were now looking for the same fossil volcanoes which the earlier inhabitants of Zinj had found.

Shortly before noon they found them, halfway up the hills east of the city—a series of excavated tunnels running into the mountain slopes of Mukenko.

Elliot felt disappointed. "I don't know what I was expecting," he said later, "but it was just a brown-colored tunnel in the earth, with occasional bits of dull brown rock sticking out. I couldn't understand why Ross got so excited." Those bits of dull brown rock were diamonds; when cleaned, they had the transparency of dirty glass.

"They thought I was crazy," Ross said, "because I began jumping up and down. But they didn't know what they were looking at."

In an ordinary kimberlite pipe, diamonds were distributed sparsely in the rock matrix. The average mine recovered only thirty-two karats—a fifth of an ounce—for every hundred tons of rock removed. When you looked down a diamond mineshaft, you saw no diamonds at all. But the Zinj mines were lumpy with protruding stones. Using his machete, Munro dug out six hundred karats. And Ross saw six or seven stones protruding from the wall, each as large as the one Munro had removed. "Just looking," she said later, "I could see easily four or five thousand karats. With no further digging, no separation, nothing. Just sitting there. It was a richer mine than the Premier in South Africa. It was *unbelievable.*"

Elliot asked the question that had already formed in Ross's own mind. "If this mine is so damn rich," he said, "why was it abandoned?"

"The gorillas got out of control," Munro said. "They staged a coup." He was laughing, plucking diamonds out of the rock.

Ross had considered that, as she had considered Elliot's earlier suggestion that the city had been wiped out by disease. She thought a less exotic explanation was likely. "I think," she said, "that as far as they were concerned, the diamond mines had dried up." Because as gemstones, these crystals were very poor indeed—blue, streaked with impurities.

The people of Zinj could not have imagined that five hundred years in the future these same worthless stones would be more scarce and desirable than any other mineral resources on the planet.

"What makes these blue diamonds so valuable?"

"They are going to change the world," Ross said, in a soft voice. "They are going to end the nuclear age."

2. War at the Speed of Light

In January, 1979, testifying before the Senate Armed Services Subcommittee, General Franklin F. Martin of the Pentagon Advanced Research Project Agency said, "In 1939, at the start of World War II, the most important country in the world to the American military effort was the Belgian Congo." Martin explained that as a kind of "accident of geography" the Congo, now Zaire, has for forty years remained vital to American interests—and will assume even more importance in the future. (Martin said bluntly that "this country will go to war over Zaire before we go to war over any Arab oil state.")

During World War II, in three highly secret shipments, the Congo supplied the United States with uranium used to build the atomic bombs exploded over Japan. By 1960 the U.S. no longer needed uranium, but copper and cobalt were strategically important. In the 1970s the emphasis shifted to Zaire's reserves of tantalum, wolframite, germanium—substances vital to semiconducting electronics. And in the 1980s, "so-called Type IIb blue diamonds will constitute the most important military resource in the world"— and the presumption was that Zaire had such diamonds. In General Martin's view, blue diamonds were essential because "we are entering a time when the brute destructive power of a weapon will be less important than its speed and intelligence."

For thirty years, military thinkers had been awed by intercontinental ballistic missiles. But Martin said that "ICBMs are crude weapons. They do not begin to approach the theoretical limits imposed by physical laws. According to Einsteinian physics, nothing can happen faster than the speed of light, 186,000 miles a second. We are now developing high-energy pulsed lasers and particle beam weapons systems which operate *at the speed of light*. In the face of such weapons, ballistic missiles travelling a mere 17,000 miles an hour are slow-moving dinosaurs from a previous era, as inappropriate as cavalry in World War I, and as easily eliminated."

Speed-of-light weapons were best suited to space, and would first appear in satellites. Martin noted that the Russians had made a "kill" of the American spy satellite VV/02 as early as 1973; in 1975, Hughes Aircraft developed a rapid aiming and firing system which locked onto multiple targets, firing eight high-energy pulses in less than one second. By 1978, the Hughes team had reduced response time to fifty nanoseconds—fifty billionths of a second—and increased beam accuracy to five hundred missile knockdowns in less than one minute. Such developments presaged the end of the ICBM as a weapon.

"Without the gigantic missiles, miniature, high-speed computers will be vastly more important in future conflicts than nuclear bombs, and their speed of computation will be the single most important factor determining the outcome of World War III. Computer speed now stands at the center of the armament race, as megaton power once held the center twenty years ago.

"We will shift from electronic circuit computers to light circuit computers simply because of speed—the Fabry-Perot Interferometer, the optical equivalent of a transistor, can respond in 1 picosecond (10^{-12} seconds), at least 1,000 times faster than the fastest Josephson junctions." The new generation of optical computers, Martin said, would be dependent on the availability of Type IIb boron-coated diamonds.

Elliot recognized at once the most serious consequence of the speed-of-light weapons—they were much too fast for human comprehension. Men were accustomed to mechanized warfare, but a future war would be a war of machines in a startlingly new sense: machines would actually govern the moment-to-moment course of a conflict which lasted only minutes from start to finish.

In 1956, in the waning years of the strategic bomber, military thinkers imagined an all-out nuclear exchange lasting 12 hours. By 1963, ICBMs had shrunk the time course to 3 hours. By 1974, military theorists were predicting a war that lasted just 30 minutes, yet this "half-hour war" was vastly more complex than any earlier war in human history.

In the 1950s, if the Americans and the Russians launched all the bombers and rockets at the same moment, there would still be no more than 10,000 weapons in the air, attacking and counterattacking. Total weapons interaction events would peak at 15,000 in the second hour. This represented the impressive figure of 4 weapons interactions every second around the world.

But given diversified tactical warfare, the number of weapons and "systems elements" increased astronomically. Modern estimates imagined 400 million computers in the field, with total weapons interactions at more than 15 billion in the first half hour of war. This meant there would be 8 million weapons interactions every second, in a bewildering ultrafast conflict of aircraft, missiles, tanks, and ground troops.

Such a war was only manageable by machines; human response times were simply too slow. World War III would not be a push-button war because as General Martin said, "It takes too long for a man to push the button—at least 1.8 seconds, which is an eternity in modern warfare."

This fact created what Martin called the "rock problem." Human responses were geologically slow, compared to a high-speed computer. "A modern computer performs 2,000,000 calculations in the time it takes a man to blink. Therefore, from the point of view of computers fighting the next war, human beings will be essentially fixed and unchanging elements, like rocks. Human wars have never lasted long enough to take into account the rate of geological change. In the future, computer wars will not last long enough to take into account the rate of human change."

Since human beings responded too slowly, it was necessary for them to relinquish decision-making control of the war to the faster intelligence of computers. "In the coming war, we must abandon any hope of regulating the course of the conflict. If we decide to 'run' the war at human speed, we will almost surely lose. Our only hope is to put our trust in machines. This makes human judgment, human values, human thinking utterly superfluous. World War III will be war by proxy: a pure war of machines, over which we dare exert no influence for fear of so slowing the decision-making mechanism as to cause our defeat." And the final, crucial transition—the transition from computers working at nanoseconds to computers working at picoseconds—was dependent on Type IIb diamonds.

Elliot was appalled by this prospect of turning control over to the creations of men.

Ross shrugged. "It's inevitable," she said. "In Olduvai Gorge in Tanzania, there are traces of a house two million years old. The hominid creature wasn't satisfied with caves and other natural shelters; he created his own accommodations. Men have always altered the natural world to suit their purposes."

"But you can't give up control," Elliot said.

"We've been doing it for centuries," Ross said. "What's a domesticated animal—or a pocket calculator—except an attempt to give up control? We don't want to plow fields or do square roots so we turn the job over to some other intelligence, which we've trained or bred or created."

"But you can't let your creations take over."

"We've been doing it for centuries," Ross repeated. "Look: even if we refused to develop faster computers, the Russians would. They'd be in Zaire

241

right now looking for diamonds, if the Chinese weren't keeping them out. You can't stop technological advances. As soon as we know something is possible, we have to carry it out."

"No," Elliot said. "We can make our own decisions. I won't be a part of this."

"Then leave," she said. "The Congo's no place for academics, anyway."

She began unpacking her rucksack, taking out a series of white ceramic cones, and a number of small boxes with antennae. She attached a box to each ceramic cone, then entered the first tunnel, placed the cones flat against the walls, moving deeper into darkness.

Peter not happy Peter.

"No," Elliot said.

Why not happy?

"It's hard to explain, Amy," he said.

Peter tell Amy good gorilla.

"I know, Amy."

Karen Ross emerged from one tunnel, and disappeared into the second. Elliot saw the glow of her flashlight as she placed the cones, and then she was hidden from view.

Munro came out into the sunlight, his pockets bulging with diamonds. "Where's Ross?"

"In the tunnels."

"Doing what?"

"Some kind of explosive test, looks like." Elliot gestured to the three remaining ceramic cones on the ground near her pack.

Munro picked up one cone, and turned it over. "Do you know what these are?" he asked.

Elliot shook his head.

"They're RCs," Munro said, "and she's out of her mind to place them here. She could blow the whole place apart."

Resonant conventionals, or RCs, were timed explosives, a potent marriage of microelectronic and explosive technology. "We used RCs two years ago on bridges in Angola," Munro explained. "Properly sequenced, six ounces of explosive can bring down fifty tons of braced structural steel. You need one of those sensors"—he gestured to a control box lying near her pack—"which monitors shock waves from the early charges, and detonates the later charges in the timed sequence to set up resonating waves which literally shake the structure to pieces. Very impressive to see it happen." Munro glanced up at Mukenko, smoking above them.

At that moment, Ross emerged from the tunnel, all smiles. "We'll soon have our answers," she said.

"Answers?"

"About the extent of the kimberlite deposits. I've set twelve seismic charges, which is enough to give us definitive readings."

"You've set twelve *resonant* charges," Munro said.

"Well, they're all I brought. We've got to make do."

"They'll do," Munro said. "Perhaps too well. That volcano"—he pointed upwards—"is in an eruptive phase."

"I've placed a total of eight hundred grams of explosive," Ross said. "That's less than a pound and a half. It can't make the slightest difference."

"Let's not find out."

Elliot listened to their argument with mixed feelings. On the face of it, Munro's objections seemed absurd—a few trivial explosive charges, however timed, could not possibly trigger a volcanic eruption. It was ridiculous; Elliot wondered why Munro was so adamant about the dangers. It was almost as if Munro knew something that Elliot and Ross did not—and could not even imagine.

3. DOD/ARPD/VULCAN 7021

In 1978, Munro had led a Zambia expedition which included Robert Perry, a young geologist from the University of Hawaii. Perry had worked on PROJECT VULCAN, the most advanced program financed under the Department of Defense Advanced Research Project Division.

VULCAN was so controversial that during the 1975 House Armed Services Subcommittee hearings, project DOD/ARPD/VULCAN 7021 was carefully buried among "miscellaneous long-term fundings of national security significance." But the following year, Congressman David Inaga (D., Hawaii) challenged DOD/ARPD/VULCAN, demanding to know "its exact military purpose, and why it should be funded entirely within the state of Hawaii."

Pentagon spokesmen explained blandly that VULCAN was a "tsunami warning system" of value to the residents of the Hawaiian islands, as well as to military installations there. Pentagon experts reminded Inaga that in 1948 a tsunami had swept across the Pacific Ocean, first devastating Kauai, but moving so swiftly along the Hawaiian island chain that when it struck Oahu and Pearl Harbor twenty minutes later, no effective warning had been given.

"That tsunami was triggered by an underwater volcanic avalanche off the coast of Japan," they said. "But Hawaii has its own active volcanoes, and now that Honolulu is a city of half a million, and naval presence is valued at more than thirty-five billion dollars, the ability to predict tsunami activity secondary to eruptions by Hawaiian volcanoes assumes major long-term significance."

In truth, PROJECT VULCAN was not long-term at all; it was intended to be carried out at the next eruption of Mauna Loa, the largest active volcano in the world, located on the big island of Hawaii. The designated purpose of VULCAN was to control volcanic eruptions as they progressed; Mauna Loa was chosen because its eruptions were relatively mild and gentle.

Although it rose to an altitude of only 13,500 feet, Mauna Loa was the largest mountain in the world. Measured from its origin at the depths of the ocean floor, Mauna Loa had more than twice the cubic volume of Mount Everest; it was a unique and extraordinary geological formation. And Mauna Loa had long since become the most carefully studied volcano in history, having a permanent scientific observation station on its crater since 1928. It was also the most interfered-with volcano in history, since the lava that flowed down its slopes at three-year intervals had been diverted by everything from aerial bombers to local crews with shovels and sandbags.

VULCAN intended to alter the course of a Mauna Loa eruption by "venting" the giant volcano, releasing the enormous quantities of molten magma by a series of timed, non-nuclear explosions detonated along fault lines in the shield. In October, 1978, VULCAN was carried out in secret, using navy helicopter teams experienced in detonating high-explosive resonant conic charges. The VULCAN project lasted two days; on the third day, the civilian Mauna Loa Volcanic Laboratory publicly announced that "the October eruption of Mauna Loa has been milder than anticipated, and no further eruptive episodes are expected."

Project Vulcan was secret but Munro had heard all about it one drunken night around the campfire near Bangazi. And he remembered it now as Ross was planning a resonant explosive sequence in the region of a volcano in its eruptive phase. The basic tenet of VULCAN was that enormous, pent-up geological forces—whether the forces of an earthquake, or a volcano, or a Pacific typhoon—could be devastatingly unleashed by a relatively small energy trigger.

Ross prepared to fire her conical explosives.

"I think," Munro said, "that you should try again to contact Houston."

"That's not possible," Ross said, supremely confident. "I'm required to decide on my own—and I've decided to assess the extent of diamond deposits in the hillsides now."

As the argument continued, Amy moved away. She picked up the detonating device lying alongside Ross's pack. It was a tiny handheld device with six glowing LEDs, more than enough to fascinate Amy. She raised her fingers to push the buttons.

Karen Ross looked over. "Oh God."

Munro turned. "Amy," he said softly. "Amy, no. No. Amy no good."

Amy good gorilla Amy good.

Amy held the detonating device in her hand. She was captivated by the winking LEDs. She glanced over at the humans.

"No, Amy," Munro said. He turned to Elliot. "Can't you stop her?"

"Oh, what the hell," Ross said. "Go ahead, Amy."

A series of rumbling explosions blasted gleaming diamond dust from the mine shafts, and then there was silence. "Well," Ross said finally, "I hope you're satisfied. It's perfectly clear that such a minimal explosive charge could not affect the volcano. In the future you can leave the scientific aspects to me, and—"

And then Mukenko rumbled, and the earth shook so hard that they were all knocked to the ground.

4. ERTS Houston

At 1 A.M. Houston time, R. B. Travis frowned at the computer monitor in his office. He had just received the latest photosphere imagery from Kitt Peak Observatory, via GSFC telemetry. GSFC had kept him waiting all day for the data, which was only one of several reasons why Travis was in a bad humor.

The photospheric imagery was negative—the sphere of the sun appeared black on the screen, with a glowing white chain of sunspots. There were at least fifteen major sunspots across the sphere, one of which originated the massive solar flare that was making his life hell.

For two days now, Travis had been sleeping at ERTS. The entire operation had gone to hell. ERTS had a team in northern Pakistan, not far from the troubled Afghan border; another in central Malaysia, in an area of Communist insurrection; and the Congo team, which was facing rebelling natives and some unknown group of gorilla-like creatures.

Communications with all teams around the world had been cut off by the solar flare for more than twenty-four hours. Travis had been running computer simulations on all of them with six-hour updates. The results did not please him. The Pakistan team was probably all right, but would run six days over schedule and cost them an additional two hundred thousand dollars; the Malaysia team was in serious jeopardy; and the Congo team was classified CANNY—ERTS computer slang for "can not estimate." Travis had had two CANNY teams in the past—in the Amazon in 1976, and in Sri Lanka in 1978—and he had lost people from both groups.

Things were going badly. Yet this latest GSFC was much better than the previous report. They had—it seemed—managed a brief transmission contact with the Congo several hours earlier, although there was no verification response from Ross. He wondered whether the team had received the warning or not. He stared at the black sphere with frustration.

Richards, one of the main data programmers, stuck his head in the door. "I have something relevant to the CFS."

"Fire away," Travis said. Any news relevant to the Congo Field Survey was of interest.

"The South African seismological station at the University of Jo'burg reports tremors initiating at twelve oh four P.M. local time. Estimated epicenter coordinates are consistent with Mount Mukenko in the Virunga chain. The tremors are multiple, running Richter five to eight."

"Any confirmation?" Travis asked.

"Nairobi is the nearest station, and they're computing a Richter six to nine, or a Morelli Nine, with heavy downfall of ejecta from the cone. They are also predicting that the LAC, the local atmospheric conditions, are conducive to severe electrical discharges."

Travis glanced at his watch. "Twelve oh four local time is nearly an hour ago," he said. "Why wasn't I informed?"

Richards said, "It didn't come in from the African stations until now. I guess they figure it's no big deal, another volcano."

Travis sighed. That was the trouble—volcanic activity was now recognized as a common phenomenon on the earth's surface. Since 1965, the first year that global records were kept, there had been twenty-two major eruptions each year, roughly one eruption every two weeks. Outlying stations were in no hurry to report such "ordinary" occurrences—to delay was proof of fashionable boredom.

"But they have problems," Richards said. "With the satellites disrupted by the sunspots, everybody has to transmit surface cable. And I guess as far as they're concerned, the northeast Congo is uninhabited."

Travis said, "How bad is a Morelli Nine?"

Richards paused. "It's pretty bad, Mr. Travis."

5. "Everything Was Moving"

In the Congo, Earth movement was Richter scale 8, a Morelli scale IX. At this severity, the earth shakes so badly a man has difficulty standing. There are lateral shifts in the earth and rifts open up; trees and even steel-frame buildings topple.

For Elliot, Ross, and Munro, the five minutes following the onset of the eruption were a bizarre nightmare. Elliot recalled that "*everything* was moving. We were all literally knocked off our feet; we had to crawl on our hands and knees, like babies. Even after we got away from mine-shaft tunnels, the city swayed like a wobbling toy. It was quite a while—maybe half a minute—before the buildings began to collapse. Then everything came down at once: walls caving in, ceilings collapsing, big blocks of stone crashing down into the jungle. The trees were swaying too, and pretty soon they began falling over."

The noise of this collapse was incredible, and added to that was the sound from Mukenko. The volcano wasn't rumbling anymore; they heard staccato explosions of lava blasting from the cone. These explosions produced shock waves; even when the earth was solid under their feet, they were knocked over without warning by blasts of hot air. "It was," Elliot recalled, "just like being in the middle of a war."

Amy was panic-stricken. Grunting in terror, she leapt into Elliot's arms—and promptly urinated on his clothes—as they began to run back toward the camp.

A sharp tremor brought Ross to the ground. She picked herself up, and stumbled onward, acutely aware of the humidity and the dense ash and dust ejected by the volcano. Within minutes, the sky above them was dark as night, and the first flashes of lightning cracked through the boiling clouds. It had rained the night before; the jungle surrounding them was wet, the air super-saturated with moisture. In short, they had all the requisites for a lightning storm. Ross felt herself torn between the perverse desire to watch this unique theoretical phenomenon and the desire to run for her life.

In a searing burst of blue-white light, the lightning storm struck. Bolts of electricity crackled all around them like rain; Ross later estimated there were two hundred bolts within the first minute—nearly three every second. The familiar shattering crack of lightning was not punctuation but a continuous sound, a roar like a waterfall. The booming thunder caused sharp ear pains, and the accompanying shock waves literally knocked them backward.

Everything happened so fast that they had little chance to absorb sensations. Their ordinary expectations were turned upside down. One of the porters, Amburi, had come back toward the city to find them. They saw him standing in a clearing, waving them ahead, when a lightning bolt crashed *up* through a nearby tree into the sky. Ross had known that the lightning flash came after the invisible downward flow of electrons and actually ran upward from the ground to the clouds above. But to see it! The explosive flash lifted Amburi off his feet and tossed him through the air toward them; he scrambled to his feet, shouting hysterically in Swahili.

All around them trees were cracking, splitting and hissing clouds of moisture as the lightning bolts shot upward through them. Ross later said, "The lightning was everywhere, the blinding flashes were continuous, with this terrible sizzling sound. That man [Amburi] was screaming and the next instant the lightning grounded through him. I was close enough to touch him but there was very little heat, just white light. He went rigid and there was this terrible smell as his whole body burst into flame, and he fell to the ground. Munro rolled on him to put out the fire but he was dead, and we ran on. There was no time to react; we kept falling down from the [earthquake] tremors. Soon we were all half-blinded from the lightning. I remember hearing somebody screaming but I didn't know who it was. I was sure we would all die."

Near camp, a gigantic tree crashed down before them, presenting an obstacle as broad and high as a three-story building. As they clambered through it, lightning sizzled through the damp branches, stripping off bark, glowing and scorching. Amy howled when a white bolt streaked across her hand as she gripped a wet branch. Immediately she dived to the ground, burying her head in the low foliage, refusing to move. Elliot had to drag her the remaining distance to the camp.

Munro was the first to reach camp. He found Kahega trying to pack the tents for their departure, but it was impossible with the tremors and the lightning crashing down through the dark ashen sky. One Mylar tent burst into flames. They smelled the harsh burning plastic. The dish antenna, resting on the ground, was struck and split apart, sending metal fragments flying.

"Leave!" Munro shouted. "Leave!"

"*Ndio mzee!*" Kahega shouted, grabbing his pack hastily. He glanced back toward the others, and in that moment Elliot stumbled out of the black gloom with Amy clinging to his chest. He had injured his ankle and was limping slightly. Amy quickly dropped to the ground.

"Leave!" Munro shouted.

As Elliot moved on, Ross emerged from the darkness of the ashen atmosphere, coughing, bent double. The left side of her body was scorched and blackened, and the skin of her left hand was burned. She had been struck by lightning, although she had no later memory of it. She pointed to her nose and throat, coughing. "Burns . . . hurts . . ."

"It's the gas," Munro shouted. He put his arm around her and half-lifted her from her feet, carrying her away. "We have to get uphill!"

An hour later, on higher ground, they had a final view of the city engulfed with smoke and ash. Farther up on the slopes of the volcano, they saw a line of trees burst into flames as an unseen dark wave of lava came sliding down the mountainside. They heard agonized bellows of pain from the gray gorillas on the hillside as hot lava rained down on them. As they watched, the foliage collapsed closer and closer to the city, until finally the city itself crumbled under a darkly descending cloud, and disappeared.

The Lost City of Zinj was buried forever.

Only then did Ross realize that her diamonds were buried forever as well.

6. Nightmare

They had no food, no water, and very little ammunition. They dragged themselves through the jungle, clothes burned and torn, faces haggard, exhausted. They did not speak to one another, but silently pressed on. Elliot said later they were "living through a nightmare."

The world through which they passed was grim and colorless. Sparkling white waterfalls and streams now ran black with soot, splashing into scummy pools of gray foam. The sky was dark gray, with occasional red flashes from the volcano. The very air became filmy gray; they coughed and stumbled through a world of black soot and ash.

They were all covered with ash—their packs gritty on their backs, their faces grimy when they wiped them, their hair many shades darker. Their noses and eyes burned. There was nothing to do about it; they could only keep going.

As Ross trudged through the dark air, she was aware of an ironic ending to her personal quest. Ross had long since acquired the expertise to tap into any ERTS data bank she wanted, including the one that held her own evaluation. She knew her assigned qualities by heart:YOUTHFUL-ARROGANT (probably) / TENUOUS HUMAN RAPPORT (she particularly resented that one) / DOMINEERING (maybe) / INTELLECTUALLY ARROGANT (only natural) / INSENSITIVE (whatever that meant) / DRIVEN TO SUCCEED AT ANY COST (was that so bad?).

And she knew her late-stage conclusions. All that flopover matrix garbage about parental figures and so on. And the last line of her report: SUBJECT MUST BE MONITORED IN LATE STAGE GOAL ORIENTED PROCEDURES.

But none of that was relevant. She had gone after the diamonds only to be beaten by the worst volcanic eruption in Africa in a decade. Who could blame her for what had happened? It wasn't her fault. She would prove that on her next expedition. . . .

Munro felt the frustration of a gambler who has placed every bet correctly but still loses. He had been correct to avoid the Euro-Japanese consortium; he had been correct to go with ERTS; and yet he was coming out empty-handed. Well, he reminded himself, feeling the diamonds in his pockets, not *quite* empty handed. . . .

Elliot was returning without photographs, videotapes, sound recordings, or the skeleton of a gray gorilla. Even his measurements had been lost. Without such proofs, he dared not claim a new species—in fact, he would be unwise even to discuss the possibility. A great opportunity had slipped away from him, and now, walking through the dark landscape, he had only a sense of the natural world gone mad: birds fell screeching from the sky, flopping at their feet, asphyxiated by the gases in the air above; bats skittered through the midday air; distant animals shrieked and howled. A leopard, fur burning on its hindquarters, ran past them at noon. Somewhere in the distance, elephants trumpeted with alarm.

They were trudging lost souls in a grim sooty world that seemed like a description of hell; perpetual fire and darkness, where tormented souls screamed in agony. And behind them Mukenko spat cinders and glowing rain. At one point, they were engulfed in a shower of red-hot embers that sizzled as they struck the damp canopy overhead, then turned the wet ground underfoot smoky, burning holes in their clothing, scorching their skin, setting hair smoldering as they danced in pain and finally sought shelter beneath tall trees, huddled together, awaiting the end of the fiery rain from the skies.

Munro planned from the first moments of the eruption to head directly for the wrecked C-130 transport, which would afford them shelter and supplies. He estimated they would reach the aircraft in two hours. In fact, six hours passed before the gigantic ash-covered hulk of the plane emerged from the murky afternoon darkness.

One reason it had taken them so long to move away from Mukenko was that they were obliged to avoid General Muguru and his troops. Whenever they came across jeep tracks, Munro led them farther west, into the depths of the jungle. "He's not a fellow you want to meet," Munro said. "And neither are his boys. And they'd think nothing of cutting your liver out and eating it raw."

* * *

Dark ash on wings and fuselage made the giant transport look as if it had crashed in black snow. Off one bent wing, a kind of waterfall of ash hissed over the metal down to the ground. Far in the distance, they heard the soft beating of Kigani drums, and thumping mortar from Muguru's troops. Otherwise it was ominously quiet.

Munro waited in the forest beyond the wreckage, watching the airplane. Ross took the opportunity to try to transmit on the computer, continuously brushing ash from the video screen, but she could not reach Houston.

Finally Munro signaled, and they all began to move forward. Amy, panicked, tugged at Munro's sleeve. *No go,* she signed. *People there.*

Munro frowned at her, glanced at Elliot. Elliot pointed to the airplane. Moments later, there was a crash, and two white-painted Kigani warriors emerged from the aircraft, onto the high wing. They were carrying cases of whiskey and arguing about how to get them down to the jungle floor below. After a moment, five more Kigani appeared beneath the wing, and the cases were passed to them. The two men above jumped down, and the group moved off.

Munro looked at Amy and smiled.

Amy good gorilla, she signed.

They waited another twenty minutes, and when no further Kigani appeared, Munro led the group to the airplane. They were just outside the cargo doors when a rain of white arrows began to whistle down on them.

"Inside!" Munro shouted, and hurried them all up the crumpled landing gear, onto the upper wing surface, and from there into the airplane. He slammed the emergency door; arrows clattered on the outer metal surface.

Inside the transport it was dark; the floor tilted at a crazy angle. Boxes of equipment had slid across the aisles, toppled over, and smashed. Broken glassware crunched underfoot. Elliot carried Amy to a seat, and then noticed that the Kigani had defecated on the seats.

Outside, they heard drums, and the steady rain of arrows on the metal and windows. Looking out through the dark ash, they glimpsed dozens of white-painted men, running through the trees, slipping under the wing.

"What are we going to do?" Ross asked.

"Shoot them," Munro said briskly, breaking open their supplies, removing machine-gun clips. "We aren't short of ammunition."

"But there must be a hundred men out there."

"Yes, but only one man is important. Kill the Kigani with red streaks painted beneath his eyes. That'll end the attack right away."

"Why?" Elliot asked.

"Because he's the *Angawa* sorcerer," Munro said, moving forward to the cockpit. "Kill him and we're off the hook."

Poison-tipped arrows clattered on the plastic windows and rang against the metal; the Kigani also threw feces, which thudded dully against the fuselage. The drums beat constantly.

Amy was terrified, and buckled herself into a seat, signing, *Amy leave now bird fly.*

Elliot found two Kigani concealed in the rear passenger compartment. To his own amazement he killed both without hesitation, firing the machine gun which bucked in his hands, blasting the Kigani back into the passenger seats, shattering windows, crumpling their bodies.

"Very good, Doctor." Kahega grinned, although by then Elliot was shaking uncontrollably. He slumped into a seat next to Amy.

People attack bird bird fly now bird fly Amy want go.

"Soon, Amy," he said, hoping it would prove true.

By now, the Kigani had abandoned their frontal assault; they were attacking from the rear, where there were no windows. Everyone could hear the sound of bare feet moving over the tail section and up onto the fuselage above their heads. Two warriors managed to climb through the open aft cargo door. Munro, who was in the cockpit, shouted, "If they get you, they eat you!"

Ross fired at the rear door, and blood spattered on her clothes as the intruding Kigani were knocked out backward.

Amy no like, she signed. *Amy want go home.* She clutched her seat belt.

"There's the son of a bitch," Munro shouted, and fired his machine gun. A young man of about twenty, his eyes smeared with red, fell onto his back, shuddering with machine-gun fire. "Got him," Munro said. "Got the *Angawa.*" He sat back and allowed the warriors to remove the body."

It was then the Kigani attack ended, the warriors retreating into the silent bush. Munro bent over the slumped body of the pilot and stared out at the jungle.

"What happens now?" Elliot asked. "Have we won?"

Munro shook his head. "They'll wait for nightfall. Then they'll come back to kill us all."

Elliot said, "What will we do then?"

Munro had been thinking about that. He saw no possibility of their leaving the aircraft for at least twenty-four hours. They needed to defend themselves at night and they needed a wider clearing around the plane during the day. The obvious solution was to burn the waist-high bush in the immediate vicinity of the plane—if they could do that without exploding the residual fuel in the airplane tanks.

"Look for flamethrowers," he told Kahega, "or gas canisters." And he began to check for documents that would tell him tank locations on the C-130.

Ross approached him. "We're in trouble, aren't we."

"Yes," Munro said. He didn't mention the volcano.

"I suppose I made a mistake."

"Well, you can atone," Munro said, "by thinking of some way out."

"I'll see what I can do," she said seriously, and went aft. Fifteen minutes later, she screamed.

Munro spun back into the passenger compartment, his machine gun

raised to fire. But he saw that Ross had collapsed into a seat, laughing hysterically. The others stared at her, not sure what to do. He grabbed her shoulders
and shook her: "Get a grip on yourself," he said, but she just went on laughing.

Kahega stood next to a gas cylinder marked PROPANE. "She see this, and
she ask how many more, I tell her six more, she begins to laugh."

Munro frowned. The cylinder was large, 20 cubic feet. "Kahega, what'd
they carry that propane for?"

Kahega shrugged. "Too big for cooking. They need only five, ten cubic
feet for cooking."

Munro said, "And there are six more like this?"

"Yes, boss. Six."

"That's a hell of a lot of gas," Munro said, and then he realized that Ross
with her instinct for planning would have grasped at once the significance of
all that propane, and Munro also knew what it meant, and he broke into a grin.

Annoyed, Elliot said, "Will someone please tell us what this means?"

"It means," Munro said through his laughter, "it means things are looking
up."

Buoyed by 50,000 pounds of heated air from the propane gas ring, the gleaming plastic sphere of the consortium balloon lifted off from the jungle floor,
and climbed swiftly into the darkening night air.

The Kigani came running from the forest, the warriors brandishing spears
and arrows. Pale white arrows sliced up in the fading light, but they fell short,
arcing back down to the ground again. The balloon rose steadily into the sky.

At an altitude of 2,000 feet, the sphere caught an easterly wind which carried it away from the dark expanse of the Congo forest, over the smoking red
volcanic heart of Mount Mukenko, and across the sharp depression of the Rift
Valley, vertical walls shimmering in the moonlight.

From there, the balloon slid across the Zaire border, moving southeast toward Kenya—and civilization.

Epilogue: The Place of Fire

On September 18, 1979, the Landsat 3 satellite, at a nominal altitude of 918 kilometers, recorded a 185-kilometer-wide scan on Band 6 (.7–.8 millimicrons in the infrared spectrum) over central Africa. Penetrating cloud cover over the rain forest, the acquired image clearly showed the eruption of Mount Mukenko still continuing after three months. A computer projection of ejecta estimated 6–8 cubic kilometers of debris dispersed into the atmosphere, and another 2–3 cubic kilometers of lava released down the western flanks of the mountain. The natives called it *Kanyalifeka,* "the place of fire."

On October 1, 1979, R. B. Travis formally canceled the Blue Contract, reporting that no natural source of Type IIb diamonds could be anticipated in the foreseeable future. The Japanese electronics firm of Morikawa revived interest in the Nagaura artificial boron-doping process. American firms had also begun work on doping; it was expected that the process would be perfected by 1984.

On October 23, Karen Ross resigned from ERTS to work for the U.S. Geological Survey EDC in Sioux Falls, South Dakota, where no military work was conducted, and no fieldwork was possible. She has since married John Bellingham, a scientist at EDC.

Peter Elliot took an indefinite leave of absence from the Berkeley Department of Zoology on October 30. A press release cited "Amy's increasing maturity and size . . . making further laboratory research difficult . . ." Project Amy was formally disbanded, although most of the staff accompanied Elliot and Amy to the Institut d'Etudes Ethnologiques at Bukama, Zaire. Here Amy's interaction with wild gorillas continued to be studied in the field. In November, 1979, she was thought to be pregnant; by then she was spending most of her time with a local gorilla troop, so it was difficult to be sure. She disappeared in May 1980.*

*In May 1980, Amy disappeared for four months, but in September she returned with a male infant clinging to her chest. Elliot signed to her, and had the unexpected satisfaction of seeing the infant sign back to him *Amy like Peter like Peter.* The signing was crisp and correct and has been recorded on videotape. Amy would not approach closely with her infant; when the infant moved toward Elliot, Amy grabbed him to her chest, disappearing into the bush. She was later sighted among a troop of twelve gorillas on the slopes of Mt. Kyambara in northeastern Zaire.

The institute conducted a census of mountain gorillas from March to August 1980. The estimate was five thousand animals in all, approximately half the estimate of George Schaller, field biologist, twenty years before. These data confirm that the mountain gorilla is disappearing rapidly. Zoo reproduction rates have increased, and gorillas are unlikely to become technically extinct, but their habitats are shrinking under the press of mankind, and researchers suspect that the gorilla will vanish as a wild, free-roaming animal in the next few years.

Kahega returned to Nairobi in 1979, working in a Chinese restaurant which went bankrupt in 1980. He then joined the National Geographic Society expedition to Botswana to study hippos.

Aki Ubara, the eldest son of the porter Marawani and a radio astronomer at Cambridge, England, won the Herskovitz Prize in 1980 for research on X-ray emissions from the galactic source M322.

At a handsome profit, Charles Munro sold 31 karats of blue Type IIb diamonds on the Amsterdam *bourse* in late 1979; the diamonds were purchased by Intel, Inc., an American micronics company. Subsequently he was stabbed by a Russian agent in Antwerp in January 1980; the agent's body was later recovered in Brussels. Munro was arrested by an armed border patrol in Zambia in March 1980, but charges were dropped. He was reported in Somalia in May, but there is no confirmation. He still resides in Tangier.

A Landsat 3 image acquired on January 8, 1980, showed that the eruption of Mount Mukenko had ceased. The faint signature of crossed laser beams, recorded on some earlier satellite passes, was no longer visible. The projected intersection point now marked a field of black quatermain lava with an average depth of eight hundred meters—nearly half a mile—over the Lost City of Zinj.

References

BALANDIER, GEORGES. *Daily Life in the Kingdom of the Kongo from the Sixteenth to the Eighteenth Century.* New York: Pantheon, 1968.

BANCHOFF, THOMAS F., and STRAUSS, CHARLES M. "Real-Time Computer Graphics Analysis of Figures in Four-Space." In *Hypergraphics,* edited by David W. Brisson, pp. 159–169. AAAS Selected Symposium 24. Boulder, Colo.: Westview Press, 1978.

BLEIBTREU, JOHN N. *The Parable of the Beast.* New York: Macmillan, 1967.

BROWN, HARRISON; BONNER, JAMES; and WEIR, JOHN. *The Next Hundred Years.* New York: Viking Press, 1963.

BURCHETT, WILFRED, and ROEBUCK, DEREK. *The Whores of War.* Harmondsworth, England: Penguin, 1977.

CAPLAN, ARTHUR L. "Ethics, Evolution and the Milk of Human Kindness." In *The Sociobiology Debate,* edited by Arthur L. Caplan, pp. 304–314. New York: Harper & Row, 1978.

CHURCHMAN, C. WEST. *The Systems Approach and Its Enemies.* New York: Basic Books, 1979.

CLARK, W. E. *The Antecedents of Man.* Edinburgh: University of Edinburgh Press, 1962.

COX, KEITH G. "Kimberlite Pipes." *Scientific American* 238, no. 4 (1978): 120–134.

DEACON, RICHARD. *The Chinese Secret Service.* New York: Taplinger, 1974.

DERJAGUIN, B. V., and FEDOSEEV, D. B. "The Synthesis of Diamonds at Low Pressure." *Scientific American* 233, no. 5 (1975): 102–110.

DESMOND, ADRIAN J. *The Ape's Reflexion,* New York: Dial, 1979.

DOUGLAS-HAMILTON, IAIN AND ORIA. *Among the Elephants.* New York: Viking, 1975.

EVANS-PRITCHARD, E. E. "The Morphology and Function of Magic: A Comparative Study of Trobriand and Zande Ritual and Spells." In *Magic, Witchcraft and Curing,* edited by John Middleton, pp. 1–22. Garden City, N.Y.: Natural History Press, 1967.

————. *Witchcraft, Oracles and Magic Among the Azande.* Oxford: Clarendon Press, 1937.

FORBATH, PETER. *The River Congo.* New York: Harper & Row, 1977.

FOUTS, ROGER S. "Sign Language in Chimpanzees: Implications of the Visual Mode and the Comparative Approach." In *Sign Language and Language Acquisition in Man and Ape: New Dimensions in Comparative Pedolinguistics,* edited by Fred C. C. Peng, pp. 121–137. AAAS Selected Symposium 16. Boulder, Colo.: Westview Press, 1978.

FRANCIS, PETER. *Volcanoes.* Harmondsworth, England: Penguin, 1976.

GOLD, THOMAS, and SOTER, STEVEN. "Brontides: Natural Explosive Noises." *Science* 204, no. 4391 (1979): 371–375.

257

GOULD, R. G., and LUM, L. F., eds. *Communications Satellite Systems: An Overview of the Technology.* New York: Institute of Electrical and Electronics Engineers Press, 1976.

GRIBBIN, JOHN. "What Future for Futures?" *New Scientist* 84, no. 1187, pp. 21–23.

HALLET, JEAN-PIERRE. *Congo Kitabu.* New York: Random House, 1964.

HARRIS, MARVIN. *Cannibals and Kings: The Origins of Cultures.* New York: Random House, 1977.

HAWTHORNE, J. B. "Model of a Kimberlite Pipe." *Physics and Chemistry of the Earth 9* (1975): 1–15.

HOARE, COLONEL MIKE. *Congo Mercenary.* London: Hale, 1967.

HOFF, CHRISTINA. "Immoral and Moral Uses of Animals." *New England Journal of Medicine* 302, no. 2, pp. 115–118.

HOGG, GARRY. *Cannibalism and Human Sacrifice.* New York: Citadel Press, 1966.

JENSEN, HOMER; GRAHAM, L. C.; PORCELLO, L. J. and LEITH, E. N. "Side-Looking Airborne Radar." *Scientific American* 237, no. 4 (1977): 84–96.

JONES, ROGER. *The Rescue of Emin Pasha.* New York: St. Martin's Press, 1972.

KAHN, HERMAN; BROWN, WILLIAM; and MARTEL, LEON. *The Next Two Hundred Years.* New York: Morrow, 1976.

LILLESAND, THOMAS M., and KIEFER, RALPH W. *Remote Sensing and Image Interpretation.* New York: Wiley, 1979.

LINDEN, EUGENE. *Apes, Men and Language.* New York: E. P. Dutton, 1975.

MARTIN, JAMES. *Telecommunications and the Computer.* Englewood Cliffs, N.J.: Prentice-Hall, 1969.

MARWICK, M. G. "The Sociology of Sorcery in a Central African Tribe." In *Magic, Witchcraft and Curing,* edited by John Middleton. Garden City. N.Y.: Natural History Press, 1967.

MIDGLEY, MARY. *Beast and Man: The Roots of Human Nature.* Ithaca, N.Y.: Cornell University Press, 1978.

MOORE, C. B., ed. *Chemical and Biochemical Applications of Lasers.* Vol. 3. New York: Academic Press, 1977.

MOOREHEAD, ALAN. *The White Nile.* New York: Harper & Brothers, 1960.

MOSS, CYNTHIA. *Portraits in the Wild: Animal Behavior in East Africa.* London: Hamilton, 1976.

NOYCE, ROBERT N. "Microelectronics." *Scientific American* 237, no. 3 (1977): 62–70.

NUGENT, JOHN PEER. *Call Africa 999.* New York: Coward-McCann, 1965.

ORLOV, YU L. *The Mineralogy of the Diamond.* New York: Wiley, 1977.

PATTERSON, FRANCINE. "Conversations with a Gorilla." *National Geographic* 154, no. 4 (1978): 438–467.

―――. "Linguistic Capabilities of a Lowland Gorilla." In *Sign Language and Language Acquisition in Man and Ape: New Dimensions in Comparative Pedolinguistics,* edited by Fred C. C. Peng, pp. 161–202. AAAS Selected Symposium 16. Boulder, Colo.: Westview Press, 1978.

PETERS, WILLIAM C. *Exploration and Mining Geology.* New York: Wiley, 1978.

PREMACK, ANN JAMES and DAVID. "Teaching Language to an Ape." *Scientific American* 227, no. 4 (1972): 92–100.

PREMACK, DAVID. "Language in a Chimpanzee?" *Science* 172, no. 3985 (1971): 808–822.

RICHARDS, PAUL W. "The Tropical Rain Forest." *Scientific American* 229, no. 6 (1973): 58–69.

ROTH, H. M. and others. *Zaire: A Country Study.* Area Handbook Series. Washington, D.C.: U.S. Government Printing Office, 1977.

RUMBAUGH, DUANE M., ed. *Language Learning by a Chimpanzee: The Lana Project.* New York: Academic Press, 1977.

SABINS, FLOYD F. *Remote Sensing Principles and Interpretation.* San Francisco: W. H. Freeman, 1978.

SANDVED, KJELL B., and EMSLEY, MICHAEL. *Rain Forests and Cloud Forests.* New York: Abrams, 1979.

SAPOLSKY, HARVEY M. *The Polaris System Development.* Cambridge, Mass.: Harvard, 1972.

SCHALLER, GEORGE B. *The Mountain Gorilla, Ecology and Behavior.* Chicago: University of Chicago Press, 1963.

———. *The Year of the Gorilla.* Chicago: University of Chicago Press, 1964.

SPUHLER, J. N. "Somatic Paths to Culture." In *The Evolution of Man's Capacity for Culture,* edited by J. N. Spuhler, pp. 1–13. Detroit: Wayne State University Press, 1959.

STANLEY, HENRY M. *In Darkest Africa,* 2 vols. New York: 1890.

TERRACE, H. S. *Nim.* New York: Alfred A. Knopf, 1979.

———. "How Nim Chimpsky Changed My Mind." *Psychology Today,* November, 1979, pp. 65–76.

TURNBULL, COLIN M. *The Forest People.* London: Jonathan Cape, 1961.

———. *Man in Africa.* Garden City, N.Y.: Doubleday, 1976.

———. *The Mountain People.* London: Jonathan Cape, 1973.

VAUGHAN, JAMES H. "Environment, Population, and Traditional Society." In *Africa,* edited by Phyllis M. Martin and Patrick O'Meara, pp. 9–23. Bloomington: Indiana University Press, 1977.

WILSON, EDWARD O. *On Human Nature.* Cambridge, Mass.: Harvard, 1978.

YERKES, ROBERT M. and ADA, W. *The Great Apes: A Study of Anthropoid Life.* New Haven: Yale University Press, 1929.

ZUCKERMAN, ED. "You Talkin' to Me?" *Rolling Stone,* June 16, 1977, pp. 45–48.

SPHERE

For Lynn Nesbit

During the preparation of this manuscript, I received help and encouragement from Caroline Conley, Kurt Villadsen, Lisa Plonsker, Valery Pine, Anne-Marie Martin, John Deubert, Lynn Nesbit, and Bob Gottlieb. I am grateful to them all.

When a scientist views things, he's not considering the
incredible at all.

LOUIS I. KAHN

You can't fool nature.

RICHARD FEYNMAN

Contents

THE SURFACE

West of Tonga

For a long time the horizon had been a monotonous flat blue line separating the Pacific Ocean from the sky. The Navy helicopter raced forward, flying low, near the waves. Despite the noise and the thumping vibration of the blades, Norman Johnson fell asleep. He was tired; he had been traveling on various military aircraft for more than fourteen hours. It was not the kind of thing a fifty-three-year-old professor of psychology was used to.

He had no idea how long he slept. When he awoke, he saw that the horizon was still flat; there were white semicircles of coral atolls ahead. He said over the intercom, "What's this?"

"Islands of Ninihina and Tafahi," the pilot said. "Technically part of Tonga, but they're uninhabited. Good sleep?"

"Not bad." Norman looked at the islands as they flashed by: a curve of white sand, a few palm trees, then gone. The flat ocean again.

"Where'd they bring you in from?" the pilot asked.

"San Diego," Norman said. "I left yesterday."

"So you came Honolulu-Guam-Pago-here?"

"That's right."

"Long trip," the pilot said. "What kind of work you do, sir?"

"I'm a psychologist," Norman said.

"A shrink, huh?" The pilot grinned. "Why not? They've called in just about everything else."

"How do you mean?"

"We've been ferrying people out of Guam for the last two days. Physicists, biologists, mathematicians, you name it. Everybody being flown to the middle of nowhere in the Pacific Ocean."

"What's going on?" Norman said.

The pilot glanced at him, eyes unreadable behind dark aviator sunglasses. "They're not telling us anything, sir. What about you? What'd they tell you?"

"They told me," Norman said, "that there was an airplane crash."

"Uh-huh," the pilot said. "You get called on crashes?"

"I have been, yes."

For a decade, Norman Johnson had been on the list of FAA crash-site teams, experts called on short notice to investigate civilian air disasters. The first time had been at the United Airlines crash in San Diego in 1976; then he had been called to Chicago in '78, and Dallas in '82. Each time the pattern was the same—the hurried telephone call, frantic packing, the absence for a week or more. This time his wife, Ellen, had been annoyed because he was called away on July 1, which meant he would miss their July 4 beach barbecue. Then, too, Tim was coming back from his sophomore year at Chicago, on his way to a summer job in the Cascades. And Amy, now sixteen, was just back from Andover, and Amy and Ellen didn't get along very well if Norman wasn't there to mediate. The Volvo was making noises again. And it was possible Norman might miss his mother's birthday the following week. "What crash is it?" Ellen had said. "I haven't heard about any crash." She turned on the radio while he packed. There was no news on the radio of an airline crash.

When the car pulled up in front of his house, Norman had been surprised to see it was a Navy pool sedan, with a uniformed Navy driver.

"They never sent a Navy car the other times," Ellen said, following him down the stairs to the front door. "Is this a military crash?"

"I don't know," he said.

"When will you be back?"

He kissed her. "I'll call you," he said. "Promise."

But he hadn't called. Everyone had been polite and pleasant, but they had kept him away from telephones. First at Hickam Field in Honolulu, then at the Naval Air Station in Guam, where he had arrived at two in the morning, and had spent half an hour in a room that smelled of aviation gasoline, staring dumbly at an issue of the *American Journal of Psychology* which he had brought with him, before flying on. He arrived at Pago Pago just as dawn was breaking. Norman was hurried onto the big Sea Knight helicopter, which immediately lifted off the cold tarmac and headed west, over palm trees and rusty corrugated rooftops, into the Pacific.

He had been on this helicopter for two hours, sleeping part of the time. Ellen, and Tim and Amy and his mother's birthday, now seemed very far away.

"Where exactly are we?"

"Between Samoa and Fiji in the South Pacific," the pilot said.

"Can you show me on the chart?"

"I'm not supposed to do that, sir. Anyway, it wouldn't show much. Right now you're two hundred miles from anywhere, sir."

Norman stared at the flat horizon, still blue and featureless. I can believe it, he thought. He yawned. "Don't you get bored looking at that?"

"To tell you the truth, no, sir," the pilot said. "I'm real happy to see it flat like this. At least we've got good weather. And it won't hold. There's a cyclone forming up in the Admiralties, should swing down this way in a few days."

"What happens then?"

"Everybody clears the hell out. Weather can be tough in this part of the world, sir. I'm from Florida and I saw some hurricanes when I was a kid, but you've never seen *anything* like a Pacific cyclone, sir."

Norman nodded. "How much longer until we get there?"

"Any minute now, sir."

After two hours of monotony, the cluster of ships appeared unusually interesting. There were more than a dozen vessels of various kinds, formed roughly into concentric circles. On the outer perimeter, he counted eight gray Navy destroyers. Closer to the center were large ships that had wide-spaced double hulls and looked like floating drydocks; then nondescript boxy ships with flat helicopter decks; and in the center, amid all the gray, two white ships, each with a flat pad and a bull's-eye.

The pilot listed them off: "You got your destroyers on the outside, for protection; RVS's further in, that's Remote Vehicle Support, for the robots; then MSS, Mission Support and Supply; and OSRV's in the center."

"OSRV's?"

"Oceanographic Survey and Research Vessels." The pilot pointed to the white ships. "*John Hawes* to port, and *William Arthur* to starboard. We'll put down on the *Hawes.*" The pilot circled the formation of ships. Norman could see launches running back and forth between the ships, leaving small white wakes against the deep blue of the water.

"All this for an airplane crash?" Norman said.

"Hey," the pilot grinned. "I never mentioned a crash. Check your seat belt if you would, sir. We're about to land."

Barnes

The red bull's-eye grew larger, and slid beneath them as the helicopter touched down. Norman fumbled with his seat belt buckle as a uniformed Navy man ran up and opened the door.

"Dr. Johnson? Norman Johnson?"

"That's right."

"Have any baggage, sir?"

"Just this." Norman reached back, pulled out his day case. The officer took it.

"Any scientific instruments, anything like that?"

"No. That's it."

"This way, sir. Keep your head down, follow me, and don't go aft, sir."

Norman stepped out, ducking beneath the blades. He followed the officer off the helipad and down a narrow stairs. The metal handrail was hot to the touch. Behind him, the helicopter lifted off, the pilot giving him a final wave. Once the helicopter had gone, the Pacific air felt still and brutally hot.

"Good trip, sir?"

"Fine."

"Need to go, sir?"

"I've just arrived," Norman said.

"No, I mean: do you need to use the head, sir."

"No," Norman said.

"Good. Don't use the heads, they're all backed up."

"All right."

"Plumbing's been screwed up since last night. We're working on the problem and hope to have it solved soon." He peered at Norman. "We have a lot of women on board at the moment, sir."

"I see," Norman said.

"There's a chemical john if you need it, sir."

"I'm okay, thanks."

"In that case, Captain Barnes wants to see you at once, sir."

"I'd like to call my family."

"You can mention that to Captain Barnes, sir."

They ducked through a door, moving out of the hot sun into a fluorescent-lit hallway. It was much cooler. "Air conditioning hasn't gone out lately," the officer said. "At least that's something."

"Does the air conditioning go out often?"

"Only when it's hot."

Through another door, and into a large workroom: metal walls, racks of tools, acetylene torches spraying sparks as workmen hunched over metal pontoons and pieces of intricate machinery, cables snaking over the floor. "We do ROV repairs here," the officer said, shouting over the din. "Most of the heavy work is done on the tenders. We just do some of the electronics here. We go this way, sir."

Through another door, down another corridor, and into a wide, low-ceilinged room crammed with video monitors. A half-dozen technicians sat in shadowy half-darkness before the color screens. Norman paused to look.

"This is where we monitor the ROV's," the officer said. "We've got three or four robots down on the bottom at any given time. Plus the MSB's and the FD's, of course."

Norman heard the crackle and hiss of radio communications, soft fragments of words he couldn't make out. On one screen he saw a diver walking on the bottom. The diver was standing in harsh artificial light, wearing a kind of suit Norman had never seen, heavy blue cloth and a bright-yellow helmet sculpted in an odd shape.

Norman pointed to the screen. "How deep is he?"

"I don't know. Thousand, twelve hundred feet, something like that."

"And what have they found?"

"So far, just the big titanium fin." The officer glanced around. "It doesn't read on any monitors now. Bill, can you show Dr. Johnson here the fin?"

"Sorry, sir," the technician said. "Present MainComOps is working north of there, in quadrant seven."

"Ah. Quad seven's almost half a mile away from the fin," the officer said to Norman. "Too bad: it's a hell of a thing to see. But you'll see it later, I'm sure. This way to Captain Barnes."

They walked for a moment down the corridor; then the officer said, "Do you know the Captain, sir?"

"No, why?"

"Just wondered. He's been very eager to see you. Calling up the com techs every hour, to find out when you're arriving."

"No," Norman said, "I've never met him."

"Very nice man."

"I'm sure."

The officer glanced over his shoulder. "You know, they have a saying about the Captain," he said.

"Oh? What's that?"

"They say his bite is worse than his bark."

Through another door, which was marked "Project Commander" and had beneath that a sliding plate that said "Capt. Harold C. Barnes, USN." The officer stepped aside, and Norman entered a paneled stateroom. A burly man in shirtsleeves stood up from behind a stack of files.

Captain Barnes was one of those trim military men who made Norman feel fat and inadequate. In his middle forties, Hal Barnes had erect military bearing, an alert expression, short hair, a flat gut, and a politician's firm handshake.

"Welcome aboard the *Hawes*, Dr. Johnson. How're you feeling?"

"Tired," Norman said.

"I'm sure, I'm sure. You came from San Diego?"

"Yes."

"So it's fifteen hours, give or take. Like to have a rest?"

"I'd like to know what's going on," Norman said.

"Perfectly understandable." Barnes nodded. "What'd they tell you?"

"Who?"

"The men who picked you up in San Diego, the men who flew you out here, the men in Guam. Whatever."

"They didn't tell me anything."

"And did you see any reporters, any press?"

"No, nothing like that."

Barnes smiled. "Good. I'm glad to hear it." He waved Norman to a seat. Norman sat gratefully. "How about some coffee?" Barnes said, moving to a coffee maker behind his desk, and then the lights went out. The room was dark except for the light that streamed in from a side porthole.

"God *damn* it!" Barnes said. "Not *again*. Emerson! *Emerson!*"

An ensign came in a side door. "Sir! Working on it, Captain."

"What was it this time?"

"Blew out in ROV Bay 2, sir."

"I thought we added extra lines to Bay 2."

"Apparently they overloaded anyway, sir."

"I want this fixed *now*, Emerson!"

"We hope to have it solved soon, sir."

The door closed; Barnes sat back in his chair. Norman heard the voice in the darkness. "It's not really their fault," he said. "These ships weren't built for the kind of power loads we put on them now, and—ah, there we are." The lights came back on. Barnes smiled. "Did you say you wanted coffee, Dr. Johnson?"

"Black is fine," Norman said.

Barnes poured him a mug. "Anyway, I'm relieved you didn't talk to anybody. In my job, Dr. Johnson, security is the biggest worry. Especially on a thing like this. If word gets out about this site, we'll have all kinds of problems. And so many people are involved now. . . . Hell, CincComPac didn't even want to give me destroyers until I started talking about Soviet submarine reconnaissance. The next thing, I get four, then eight destroyers."

"Soviet submarine reconnaissance?" Norman asked.

"That's what I told them in Honolulu." Barnes grinned. "Part of the game, to get what you need for an operation like this. You've got to know how to requisition equipment in the modern Navy. But of course the Soviets won't come around."

"They won't?" Norman felt he had somehow missed the assumptions that lay behind the conversation, and was trying to catch up.

"It's very unlikely. Oh, they know we're here. They'll have spotted us with their satellites at least two days ago, but we're putting out a steady stream of decodable messages about our Search and Rescue exercises in the South Pacific. S and R drill represents a low priority for them, even though they undoubtedly figure a plane went down and we're recovering for real. They may even suspect that we're trying to recover nuclear warheads, like we did off of Spain in '68. But they'll leave us alone—because politically they don't want to be implicated in our nuclear problems. They know we have troubles with New Zealand these days."

"Is that what all this is?" Norman said. "Nuclear warheads?"

"No," Barnes said. "Thank God. Anything nuclear, somebody in the White House always feels duty-bound to announce it. But we've kept this one away from the White House staff. In fact, we bypass the JCS on this. All briefings go straight from the Defense Secretary to the President, personally." He rapped his knuckles on the desk. "So far, so good. And you're the last to arrive. Now that you're here, we'll shut this thing down tight. Nothing in, nothing out."

Norman still couldn't put it together. "If nuclear warheads aren't involved in the crash," he said, "why the secrecy?"

"Well," Barnes said. "We don't have all the facts yet."

"The crash occurred in the ocean?"

"Yes. More or less directly beneath us as we sit here."

"Then there can't be any survivors."

"Survivors?" Barnes looked surprised. "No, I wouldn't think so."

"Then why was I called here?"

Barnes looked blank.

"Well," Norman explained, "I'm usually called to crash sites when there are survivors. That's why they put a psychologist on the team, to deal with the acute traumatic problems of surviving passengers, or sometimes the relatives of surviving passengers. Their feelings, and their fears, and their recurring nightmares. People who survive a crash often experience all sorts of guilt and anxiety, concerning why they survived and not others. A woman sitting with her husband and children, suddenly they're all dead and she alone is alive. That kind of thing." Norman sat back in his chair. "But in this case—an airplane that crashed in a thousand feet of water—there wouldn't be any of those problems. So why am I here?"

Barnes was staring at him. He seemed uncomfortable. He shuffled the files around on his desk.

"Actually, this isn't an airplane crash site, Dr. Johnson."

"What is it?"

"It's a *spacecraft* crash site."

There was a short pause. Norman nodded. "I see."

"That doesn't surprise you?" Barnes said.

"No," Norman said. "As a matter of fact, it explains a lot. If a military spacecraft crashed in the ocean, that explains why I haven't heard anything about it on the radio, why it was kept secret, why I was brought here the way I was. . . .when did it crash?"

Barnes hesitated just a fraction before answering. "As best we can estimate," he said, "this spacecraft crashed three hundred years ago."

Ulf

There was a silence. Norman listened to the drone of the air conditioner. He heard faintly the radio communications in the next room. He looked at the mug of coffee in his hand, noticing a chip on the rim. He struggled to assimilate what he was being told, but his mind moved sluggishly, in circles.

Three hundred years ago, he thought. A spacecraft three hundred years old. But the space program wasn't three hundred years old. It was barely thirty years old. So how could a spacecraft be three hundred years old? It couldn't be. Barnes must be mistaken. But how could Barnes be mistaken? The Navy wouldn't send all these ships, all these people, unless they were sure what was down there. A spacecraft three hundred years old.

But how could that be? It couldn't be. It must be something else. He went over it again and again, getting nowhere, his mind dazed and shocked.

"——solutely no question about it," Barnes was saying. "We can estimate the date from coral growth with great accuracy. Pacific coral grows two-and-a-half centimeters a year, and the object—whatever it is—is covered in about five meters of coral. That's a lot of coral. Of course, coral doesn't grow at a depth of a thousand feet, which means that the present shelf collapsed to a lower depth at some point in the past. The geologists are telling us that happened about a century ago, so we're assuming a total age for the craft of about three hundred years. But we could be wrong about that. It could, in fact, be much older. It could be a thousand years old."

Barnes shifted papers on his desk again, arranging them into neat stacks, lining up the edges.

"I don't mind telling you, Dr. Johnson, this thing scares the hell out of me. *That's* why you're here."

Norman shook his head. "I still don't understand."

"We brought you here," Barnes said, "because of your association with the ULF project."

"ULF?" Norman said. And he almost added, But ULF was a joke. Seeing how serious Barnes was, he was glad he had caught himself in time.

Yet ULF was a joke. Everything about it had been a joke, from the very beginning.

In 1979, in the waning days of the Carter Administration, Norman Johnson had been an assistant professor of psychology at the University of California at San Diego; his particular research interest was group dynamics and anxiety, and he occasionally served on FAA crash-site teams. In those days, his biggest problems had been finding a house for Ellen and the kids, keeping up his publications, and wondering whether UCSD would give him tenure. Norman's research was considered brilliant, but psychology was notoriously prone to intellectual fashions, and interest in the study of anxiety was declining as many researchers came to regard anxiety as a purely biochemical disorder that could be treated with drug therapy alone; one scientist had even gone so far as to say, "Anxiety is no longer a problem in psychology. There is nothing left to study." Similarly, group dynamics was perceived as old-fashioned, a field that had seen its heyday in the Gestalt encounter groups and corporate brainstorming procedures of the early 1970s but now was dated and passé.

Norman himself could not comprehend this. It seemed to him that American society was increasingly one in which people worked in groups, not alone; rugged individualism was now replaced by endless corporate meetings and group decisions. In this new society, group behavior seemed to him more important, not less. And he did not think that anxiety as a clinical problem was going to be solved with pills. It seemed to him that a society in which the most common prescription drug was Valium was, by definition, a society with unsolved problems.

Not until the preoccupation with Japanese managerial techniques in the 1980s did Norman's field gain a new hold on academic attention. Around the same time, Valium dependence became recognized as a major concern, and the whole issue of drug therapy for anxiety was reconsidered. But in the meantime, Johnson spent several years feeling as if he were in a backwater. (He did not have a research grant approved for nearly three years.) Tenure, and finding a house, were very real problems.

It was during the worst of this time, in late 1979, that he was approached by a solemn young lawyer from the National Security Council in Washington who sat with his ankle across his knee and plucked nervously at his sock. The lawyer told Norman that he had come to ask his help.

Norman said he would help if he could.

Still plucking at the sock, the lawyer said he wanted to talk to Norman about a "grave matter of national security facing our country today."

Norman asked what the problem was.

"Simply that this country has absolutely no preparedness in the event of an alien invasion. Absolutely no preparedness whatever."

Because the lawyer was young, and because he stared down at his sock as he spoke, Norman at first thought he was embarrassed at having been sent on a fool's errand. But when the young man looked up, Norman saw to his astonishment that he was utterly serious.

"We could really be caught with our pants down on this one," the lawyer said. "An alien invasion."

Norman had to bite his lip. "That's probably true," he said.

"People in the Administration are worried."

"Are they?"

"There is the feeling *at the highest levels* that contingency plans should be drawn."

"You mean contingency plans in the event of an alien invasion. . . ." Norman somehow managed to keep a straight face.

"Perhaps," said the lawyer, "perhaps *invasion* is too strong a word. Let's soften that to say 'contact': alien contact."

"I see."

"You're already involved in civilian crash-site teams, Dr. Johnson. You know how these emergency groups function. We want your input concerning the optimal composition of a crash-site team to confront an alien invader."

"I see," Norman said, wondering how he could tactfully get out of this. The idea was clearly ludicrous. He could see it only as displacement: the Administration, faced with immense problems it could not solve, had decided to think about something else.

And then the lawyer coughed, proposed a study, and named a substantial figure for a two-year research grant.

Norman saw a chance to buy his house. He said yes.

"I'm glad you agree the problem is a real one."

"Oh yes," Norman said, wondering how old this lawyer was. He guessed about twenty-five.

"We'll just have to get your security clearance," the lawyer said.

"I need security clearance?"

"Dr. Johnson," the lawyer said, snapping his briefcase shut, "this project is top, top secret."

"That's fine with me," Norman said, and he meant it. He could imagine his colleagues' reactions if they ever found out about this.

What began as a joke soon became simply bizarre. Over the next year, Norman flew five times to Washington for meetings with high-level officials of the National Security Council over the pressing, imminent danger of alien invasion. His work was very secret. One early question was whether his project should be turned over to DARPA, the Defense Advanced Research Project Agency of the Pentagon. They decided not to. There were questions about whether it should be given to NASA, and again they decided not to. One Administration official said, "This isn't a scientific matter, Dr. Johnson, this is a national security matter. We don't want to open it out."

Norman was continually surprised at the level of the officials he was told to meet with. One Senior Undersecretary of State pushed aside the papers on his desk relating to the latest Middle East crisis to say, "What do you think about the possibility that these aliens will be able to read our minds?"

"I don't know," Norman said.

"Well, it occurs to me. How're we going to be able to formulate a negotiating posture if they can read our minds?"

"That could be a problem," Norman agreed, sneaking a glance at his watch.

"Hell, it's bad enough our encrypted cables get intercepted by the Russians. We know the Japanese and the Israelis have cracked all our codes. We just pray the Russians can't do it yet. But you see what I mean, the problem. About reading minds."

"Oh yes."

"Your report will have to take that into consideration."

Norman promised it would.

A White House staffer said to him, "You realize the President will want to talk to these aliens personally. He's that kind of man."

"Uh-huh," Norman said.

"And I mean, the publicity value here, the exposure, is incalculable. The President meets with the aliens at Camp David. What a media moment."

"A real moment," Norman agreed.

"So the aliens will need to be informed by an advance man of who the President is, and the protocol in talking to him. You can't have the President of the United States talking to people from another galaxy or whatever on television without advance preparation. Do you think the aliens'll speak English?"

"Doubtful," Norman said.

"So someone may need to learn their language, is that it?"

"It's hard to say."

"Perhaps the aliens would be more comfortable meeting with an advance man from one of our ethnic minorities," the White House man said. "Anyway, it's a possibility. Think about it."

Norman promised he would think about it.

The Pentagon liaison, a Major General, took him to lunch and over coffee casually asked, "What sorts of armaments do you see these aliens having?"

"I'm not sure," Norman said.

"Well, that's the crux of it, isn't it? And what about their vulnerabilities? I mean, the aliens might not even be human at all."

"No, they might not."

"They might be like giant insects. Your insects can withstand a lot of radiation."

"Yes," Norman said.

"We might not be able to touch these aliens," the Pentagon man said gloomily. Then he brightened. "But I doubt they could withstand a direct hit with a multimeg nuclear device, do you?"

"No," Norman said. "I don't think they could."

"It'd vaporize 'em."

"Sure."

"Laws of physics."

"Right."

"Your report must make that point clearly. About the nuclear vulnerability of these aliens."

"Yes," Norman said.

"We don't want to start a panic," the Pentagon man said. "No sense getting everyone upset, is there? I know the JCS will be reassured to hear the aliens are vulnerable to our nuclear weapons."

"I'll keep that in mind," Norman said.

Eventually, the meetings ended, and he was left to write his report. And as he reviewed the published speculations on extraterrestrial life, he decided that the Major General from the Pentagon was not so wrong, after all. The real question about alien contact—if there was any real question at all—concerned panic. Psychological panic. The only important human experience with extraterrestrials had been Orson Welles's 1938 radio broadcast of "The War of the Worlds." And the human response was unequivocal.

People had been terrified.

Norman submitted his report, entitled "Contact with Possible Extraterrestrial Life." It was returned to him by the NSC with the suggestion that the title be revised to "sound more technical" and that he remove "any suggestion that alien contact was only a possibility, as alien contact is considered virtually certain in some quarters of the Administration."

Revised, Norman's paper was duly classified Top Secret, under the title "Recommendations for the Human Contact Team to Interact with Unknown Life Forms (ULF)." As Norman envisioned it, the ULF Contact Team demanded particularly stable individuals. In his report he had said—

"I wonder," Barnes said, opening a folder, "if you recognize this quote:

> Contact teams meeting an Unknown Life Form (ULF) must be prepared for severe psychological impact. Extreme anxiety responses will almost certainly occur. The personality traits of individuals who can withstand extreme anxiety must be determined, and such individuals selected to comprise the team.
>
> Anxiety when confronted by unknown life has not been sufficiently appreciated. The fears unleashed by contact with a new life form are not understood and cannot be entirely predicted in advance. But the most likely consequence of contact is absolute terror."

Barnes snapped the folder shut. "You remember who said that?"

"Yes," Norman said. "I do."

And he remembered why he had said it.

As part of the NSC grant, Norman had conducted studies of group dynamics in contexts of psychosocial anxiety. Following the procedures of Asch and Milgram, he constructed several environments in which subjects did not know they were being tested. In one case, a group of subjects were told to take an elevator to another floor to participate in a test. The elevator jammed between floors. Subjects were then observed by hidden video camera.

There were several variations to this. Sometimes the elevator was marked "Under Repair"; sometimes there was telephone communication with the "repairman," sometimes not; sometimes the ceiling fell in, and the lights went out; and sometimes the floor of the elevator was constructed of clear lucite.

In another case, subjects were loaded into a van and driven out into the desert by an "experiment leader" who ran out of gas, and then suffered a "heart attack," thus stranding the subjects.

In the most severe version, subjects were taken up in a private plane, and the pilot suffered a "heart attack" in mid-air.

Despite the traditional complaints about such tests—that they were sadistic, that they were artificial, that subjects somehow sensed the situations were contrived—Johnson gained considerable information about groups under anxiety stress.

He found that fear responses were minimized when the group was small (five or less); when group members knew each other well; when group members could see each other and were not isolated; when they shared defined group goals and fixed time limits; when groups were mixed age and mixed gender; and when group members had high phobic-tolerant personalities as measured by LAS tests for anxiety, which in turn correlated with athletic fitness.

Study results were formulated in dense statistical tables, although, in essence, Norman knew he had merely verified common sense: if you were trapped in an elevator, it was better to be with a few relaxed, athletic people you knew, to keep the lights on, and to know someone was working to get you free.

Yet Norman knew that some of his results were counter-intuitive, such as the importance of group composition. Groups composed entirely of men or entirely of women were much poorer at handling stress than mixed groups; groups composed of individuals roughly the same age were much poorer than groups of mixed age. And pre-existing groups formed for another purpose did worst of all; at one point he had stressed a championship basketball team, and it cracked almost immediately.

Although his research was good, Norman remained uneasy about the underlying purpose for his paper—alien invasion—which he personally considered speculative to the point of absurdity. He was embarrassed to submit his paper, particularly after he had rewritten it to make it seem more significant than he knew it was.

He was relieved when the Carter Administration did not like his report. None of Norman's recommendations were approved. The Administration did not agree with Dr. Norman Johnson that fear was a problem; they thought the predominant human emotion would be wonder and awe. Furthermore, the

Administration preferred a large contact team of thirty people, including three theologians, a lawyer, a physician, a representative from the State Department, a representative from the Joint Chiefs, a select group from the legislative branch, an aerospace engineer, an exobiologist, a nuclear physicist, a cultural anthropologist, and a television anchor personality.

In any case, President Carter was not re-elected in 1980, and Norman heard nothing further about his ULF proposal. He had heard nothing for six years.

Until now.

Barnes said, "You remember the ULF team you proposed?"

"Of course," Norman said.

Norman had recommended a ULF team of four—an astrophysicist, a zoologist, a mathematician, a linguist—and a fifth member, a psychologist, whose job would be to monitor the behavior and attitude of the working team members.

"Give me your opinion of this," Barnes said. He handed Norman a sheet of paper:

ANOMALY INVESTIGATION TEAM

USN STAFF/SUPPORT MEMBERS

1. Harold C. Barnes, USN Project Commander Captain
2. Jane Edmunds, USN Data Processing Tech P.O. 1C
3. Tina Chan, USN Electronics Tech P.O. 1C
4. Alice Fletcher, USN Deepsat Habitat Support Chief P.O.
5. Rose C. Levy, USN Deepsat Habitat Support 2C

CIVILIAN STAFF MEMBERS

1. Theodore Fielding, astrophysicist/planetary geologist
2. Elizabeth Halpern, zoologist/biochemist
3. Harold J. Adams, mathematician/logician
4. Arthur Levine, marine biologist/biochemist
5. Norman Johnson, psychologist

Norman looked at the list. "Except for Levine, this is the civilian ULF Team I originally proposed. I even interviewed them, and tested them, back then."

"Correct."

"But you said yourself: there are probably no survivors. There's probably no life inside that spacecraft."

"Yes," Barnes said. "But what if I'm wrong?"

He glanced at his watch. "I'm going to brief the team members at eleven hundred hours. I want you to come along, and see what you think about the team members," Barnes said. "After all, we followed your ULF report recommendations."

You followed my recommendations, Norman thought with a sinking feeling. Jesus Christ, I was just paying for a house.

"I knew you'd jump at the opportunity to see your ideas put into practice," Barnes said. "That's why I've included you on the team as the psychologist, although a younger man would be more appropriate."

"I appreciate that," Norman said.

"I knew you would," Barnes said, smiling cheerfully. He extended a beefy hand. "Welcome to the ULF Team, Dr. Johnson."

Beth

An ensign showed Norman to his room, tiny and gray, more like a prison cell than anything else. Norman's day bag lay on his bunk. In the corner was a computer console and a keyboard. Next to it was a thick manual with a blue cover.

He sat on the bed, which was hard, unwelcoming. He leaned back against a pipe on the wall.

"Hi, Norman," a soft voice said. "I'm glad to see they dragged you into this. This is all your fault, isn't it?" A woman stood in the doorway.

Beth Halpern, the team zoologist, was a study in contrasts. She was a tall, angular woman of thirty-six who could be called pretty despite her sharp features and the almost masculine quality of her body. In the years since Norman had last seen her, she seemed to have emphasized her masculine side even more. Beth was a serious weight-lifter and runner; the veins and muscles bulged at her neck and on her forearms, and her legs, beneath her shorts, were powerful. Her hair was cut short, hardly longer than a man's.

At the same time, she wore jewelry and makeup, and she moved in a seductive way. Her voice was soft, and her eyes were large and liquid, especially when she talked about the living things that she studied. At those times she became almost maternal. One of her colleagues at the University of Chicago had referred to her as "Mother Nature with muscles."

Norman got up, and she gave him a quick peck on the cheek. "My room's next to yours, I heard you arrive. When did you get in?"

"An hour ago. I think I'm still in shock," Norman said. "Do you believe all this? Do you think it's real?"

"I think that's real." She pointed to the blue manual next to his computer.

Norman picked it up: *Regulations Governing Personnel Conduct During Classified Military Operations.* He thumbed through pages of dense legal text.

"It basically says," Beth said, "that you keep your mouth shut or you spend a long time in military prison. And there's no calls in or out. Yes, Norman, I think it must be real."

"There's a spacecraft down there?"

"There's something down there. It's pretty exciting." She began to speak more rapidly. "Why, for biology alone, the possibilities are staggering—everything we know about life comes from studying life on our own planet. But, in a sense, all life on our planet is the same. Every living creature, from algae to human beings, is basically built on the same plan, from the same DNA. Now we may have a chance to contact life that is entirely different, different in every way. It's exciting, all right."

Norman nodded. He was thinking of something else. "What did you say about no calls in or out? I promised to call Ellen."

"Well, I tried to call my daughter and they told me the mainland com links are out. If you can believe that. The Navy's got more satellites than admirals, but they swear there's no available line to call out. Barnes said he'd approve a cable. That's it."

"How old is Jennifer now?" Norman asked, pleased to pull the name from his memory. And what was her husband's name? He was a physicist, Norman remembered, something like that. Sandy blond man. Had a beard. Wore bow ties.

"Nine. She's pitching for the Evanston Little League now. Not much of a student, but a hell of a pitcher." She sounded proud. "How's your family? Ellen?"

"She's fine. The kids are fine. Tim's a sophomore at Chicago. Amy's at Andover. How is . . ."

"George? We divorced three years ago," Beth said. "George had a year at CERN in Geneva, looking for exotic particles, and I guess he found whatever he was looking for. She's French. He says she's a great cook." She shrugged. "Anyway, my work is going well. For the past year I have been working with cephalopods—squid and octopi."

"How's that?"

"Interesting. It gives you quite a strange feeling to realize the gentle intelligence of these creatures, particularly octopi. You know an octopus is smarter than a dog, and would probably make a much better pet. It's a wonderful, clever, very emotional creature, an octopus. Only we never think of them that way."

Norman said, "Do you still eat them?"

"Oh, Norman." She smiled. "Do you still relate everything to food?"

"Whenever possible," Norman said, patting his stomach.

"Well, you won't like the food in this place. It's terrible. But the answer is no," she said, cracking her knuckles. "I could never eat an octopus now, knowing what I do about them. Which reminds me: What do you know about Hal Barnes?"

"Nothing, why?"

"I've been asking around. Turns out Barnes is not Navy at all. He's *ex*-Navy."

"You mean he's retired?"

"Retired in '81. He was originally trained as an aeronautical engineer at Cal Tech, and after he retired he worked for Grumman for a while. Then a member of the Navy Science Board of the National Academy; then Assistant Undersecretary of Defense, and a member of DSARC, the Defense Systems Acquisition Review Council; a member of the Defense Science Board, which advises the Joint Chiefs and the Secretary of Defense."

"Advises them on what?"

"Weapons acquisition," Beth said. "He's a Pentagon man who advises the government on weapons acquisition. So how'd he get to be running this project?"

"Beats me," Norman said. Sitting on the bunk, he kicked off his shoes. He felt suddenly tired. Beth leaned against the doorway.

"You seem to be in very good shape," Norman said. Even her hands looked strong, he thought.

"A good thing, too, as it turns out," Beth said. "I have a lot of confidence for what's coming. What about you? Think you'll manage okay?"

"Me? Why shouldn't I?" He glanced down at his own familiar paunch. Ellen was always after him to do something about it, and from time to time he got inspired and went to the gym for a few days, but he could never seem to get rid of it. And the truth was, it didn't matter that much to him. He was fifty-three years old and he was a university professor. What the hell.

Then he had a thought: "What do you mean, you have confidence for what's coming? What's coming?"

"Well. It's only rumors so far. But your arrival seems to confirm them."

"What rumors?"

"They're sending us down there," Beth said.

"Down where?"

"To the bottom. To the spaceship."

"But it's a thousand feet down. They're investigating it with robot submersibles."

"These days, a thousand feet isn't that deep," Beth said. "The technology can handle it. There are Navy divers down there now. And the word is, the divers have put up a habitat so our team can go down and live on the bottom for a week or so and open the spacecraft up."

Norman felt a sudden chill. In his work with the FAA, he had been exposed to every sort of horror. Once, in Chicago, at a crash site that extended over a whole farm field, he had stepped on something squishy. He thought it was a frog, but it was a child's severed hand, palm up. Another time he had seen a man's charred body, still strapped into the seat, except the seat had been flung into the back yard of a suburban house, where it sat upright next to a portable plastic kiddie swimming pool. And in Dallas he had watched the investigators on the rooftops of the suburban houses, collecting the body parts, putting them in bags . . .

Working on a crash-site team demanded the most extraordinary psychological vigilance, to avoid being overwhelmed by what you saw. But there was never any personal danger, any physical risk. The risk was the risk of nightmares.

But now, the prospect of going down a thousand feet under the ocean to investigate a wreck . . .

"You okay?" Beth said. "You look pale."

"I didn't know anybody was talking about *going down there.*"

"Just rumors," Beth said. "Get some rest, Norman. I think you need it."

The Briefing

Ihe ULF Team met in the briefing room, just before eleven. Norman was interested to see the group he had picked six years before, now assembled together for the first time.

Ted Fielding was compact, handsome, and still boyish at forty, at ease in shorts and a Polo sport shirt. An astrophysicist at the Jet Propulsion Laboratory in Pasadena, he had done important work on the planetary stratigraphy of Mercury and the moon, although he was best known for his studies of the Mangala Vallis and Valles Marineris channels on Mars. Located at the Martian equator, these great canyons were as much as twenty-five hundred miles long and two and a half miles deep—ten times the length and twice the depth of the Grand Canyon. And Fielding had been among the first to conclude that the planet most like the Earth in composition was not Mars at all, as previously suspected, but tiny Mercury, with its Earth-like magnetic field.

Fielding's manner was open, cheerful, and pompous. At JPL, he had appeared on television whenever there was a spacecraft flyby, and thus enjoyed a certain celebrity; he had recently been remarried, to a television weather reporter in Los Angeles; they had a young son.

Ted was a longstanding advocate for life on other worlds, and a supporter of SETI, the Search for Extraterrestrial Intelligence, which other scientists considered a waste of time and money. He grinned happily at Norman now.

"I always knew this would happen—sooner or later, we'd get our proof of intelligent life on other worlds. Now at last we have it, Norman. This is a great moment. And I am especially pleased about the shape."

"The shape?"

"Of the object down there."

"What about it?" Norman hadn't heard anything about the shape.

"I've been in the monitor room watching the video feed from the robots. They're beginning to define the shape beneath the coral. And it's not round. It is not a flying saucer," Ted said. "Thank God. Perhaps this will silence the lunatic fringe." He smiled. " 'All things come to him who waits,' eh?"

"I guess so," Norman said. He wasn't sure what Fielding meant, but Ted tended to literary quotations. Ted saw himself as a Renaissance man, and random quotations from Rousseau and Lao-tsu were one way to remind you of it. Yet there was nothing mean-spirited about him; someone once said that Ted was "a brand-name guy," and that carried over to his speech as well. There was an innocence, almost a naïveté to Ted Fielding that was endearing and genuine. Norman liked him.

He wasn't so sure about Harry Adams, the reserved Princeton mathematician Norman hadn't seen for six years. Harry was now a tall, very thin black man with wire-frame glasses and a perpetual frown. He wore a T-shirt that said "Mathematicians Do It Correctly"; it was the kind of thing a student would wear, and indeed, Adams appeared even younger than his thirty years; he was clearly the youngest member of the group—and arguably the most important.

Many theorists argued that communication with extraterrestrials would prove impossible, because human beings would have nothing in common with them. These thinkers pointed out that just as human bodies represented the outcome of many evolutionary events, so did human thought. Like our bodies, our ways of thinking could easily have turned out differently; there was nothing inevitable about how we looked at the universe.

Men already had trouble communicating with intelligent Earthly creatures such as dolphins, simply because dolphins lived in such a different environment and had such different sensory apparatus.

Yet men and dolphins might appear virtually identical when compared with the vast differences that separated us from an extraterrestrial creature—a creature who was the product of billions of years of divergent evolution in some other planetary environment. Such an extraterrestrial would be unlikely to see the world as we did. In fact, it might not see the world at all. It might be blind, and it might learn about the world through a highly developed sense of smell, or temperature, or pressure. There might be no way to communicate with such a creature, no common ground at all. As one man put it, how would you explain Wordsworth's poem about daffodils to a blind watersnake?

But the field of knowledge we were most likely to share with extraterrestrials was mathematics. So the team mathematician was going to play a crucial role. Norman had selected Adams because, despite his youth, Harry had already made important contributions to several different fields.

"What do you think about all this, Harry?" Norman said, dropping into a chair next to him.

"I think it's perfectly clear," Harry said, "that it is a waste of time."

"This fin they've found underwater?"

"I don't know what it is, but I know what it *isn't*. It isn't a spacecraft from another civilization."

Ted, standing nearby, turned away in annoyance. Harry and Ted had evidently had this same conversation already.

"How do you know?" Norman asked.

"A simple calculation," Harry said, with a dismissing wave of his hand. "Trivial, really. You know the Drake equation?"

Norman did. It was one of the famous proposals in the literature on extraterrestrial life. But he said, "Refresh me."

Harry sighed irritably, pulled out a sheet of paper. "It's a probability equation." He wrote:

$$p = f_p n_h f_l f_i f_c$$

"What it means," Harry Adams said, "is that the probability, p, that intelligent life will evolve in any star system is a function of the probability that the star will have planets, the number of habitable planets, the probability that simple life will evolve on a habitable planet, the probability that intelligent life will evolve from simple life, and the probability that intelligent life will attempt interstellar communication within five billion years. That's all the equation says."

"Uh-huh," Norman said.

"But the point is that we have no facts," Harry said. "We must guess at every single one of these probabilities. And it's quite easy to guess one way, as Ted does, and conclude there are probably thousands of intelligent civilizations. It's equally easy to guess, as I do, that there is probably only one civilization. Ours." He pushed the paper away. "And in that case, whatever is down there is *not* from an alien civilization. So we're all wasting our time here."

"Then what is down there?" Norman said again.

"It is an absurd expression of romantic hope," Adams said, pushing his glasses up on his nose. There was a vehemence about him that troubled Norman. Six years earlier, Harry Adams had still been a street kid whose obscure talent had carried him in a single step from a broken home in the slums of Philadelphia to the manicured green lawns of Princeton. In those days Adams had been playful, amused at his turn of fortune. Why was he so harsh now?

Adams was an extraordinarily gifted theoretician, his reputation secured in probability-density functions of quantum mechanics which were beyond Norman's comprehension, although Adams had worked them out when he was seventeen. But Norman could certainly understand the man himself, and Harry Adams seemed tense and critical now, ill at ease in this group.

Or perhaps it had to do with his presence as part of a group. Norman had worried about how he would fit in, because Harry had been a child prodigy.

There were really only two kinds of child prodigies—mathematical and musical. Some psychologists argued there was only one kind, since music was so closely related to mathematics. While there were precocious children with other talents, such as writing, painting, and athletics, the only areas in which a child might truly perform at the level of an adult were in mathematics or music. Psychologically, such children were complex: often loners, isolated from their peers and even from their families by their gifts, for which they were both admired and resented. Socialization skills were often retarded, making group interactions uncomfortable. As a slum kid, Harry's problems would have been, if anything, magnified. He had once told Norman that when he first learned about Fourier transforms, the other kids were learning to slam-dunk. So maybe Harry was feeling uncomfortable in the group now.

But there seemed to be something else. . . . Harry appeared almost angry.

"You wait," Adams said. "A week from now, this is going to be recognized as one big fat false alarm. Nothing more."

You hope, Norman thought. And again wondered why.

"Well, I think it's exciting," Beth Halpern said, smiling brightly. "Even a slim chance of finding new life is exciting, as far as I am concerned."

"That's right," Ted said. "After all, Harry, there are more things in heaven and earth than are dreamed of in your philosophy."

Norman looked over at the final member of the team, Arthur Levine, the marine biologist. Levine was the only person he didn't know. A pudgy man, Levine looked pale and uneasy, wrapped in his own thoughts. He was about to ask Levine what he thought when Captain Barnes strode in, a stack of files under his arm.

"Welcome to the middle of nowhere," Barnes said, "and you can't even go to the bathroom." They all laughed nervously. "Sorry to keep you waiting," he said. "But we don't have a lot of time, so let's get right down to it. If you'll kill the lights, we can begin."

The first slide showed a large ship with an elaborate superstructure on the stern.

"The *Rose Sealady,*" Barnes said. "A cable-laying vessel chartered by Transpac Communications to lay a submarine telephone line from Honolulu to Sydney, Australia. The *Rose* left Hawaii on May 29 of this year, and by June 16 it had gotten as far as Western Samoa in the mid-Pacific. It was laying a new fiber-optics cable, which has a carrying capacity of twenty thousand simultaneous telephonic transmissions. The cable is covered with a dense metal-and-plastics web matrix, unusually tough and resistant to breaks. The ship had already laid more than forty-six hundred nautical miles of cable across the Pacific with no mishaps of any sort. Next."

A map of the Pacific, with a large red spot.

"At ten p.m. on the night of June 17, the vessel was located here, midway between Pago Pago in American Samoa and Viti Levu in Fiji, when the ship experienced a wrenching shudder. Alarms sounded, and the crew realized the cable had snagged and torn. They immediately consulted their charts, looking for an underwater obstruction, but could see none. They hauled up the loose cable, which took several hours, since at the time of the accident they had more than a mile of cable paid out behind the ship. When they examined the cut end, they saw that it had been cleanly sheared—as one crewman said, 'like it was cut with a huge pair of scissors.' Next."

A section of Fiberglas cable held toward the camera in the rough hand of a sailor.

"The nature of the break, as you can see, suggests an artificial obstruction of some sort. The *Rose* steamed north back over the scene of the break. Next."

A series of ragged black-and-white lines, with a region of small spikes.

"This is the original sonar scan from the ship. If you can't read sonar scans this'll be hard to interpret, but you see here the thin, knife-edge obstruction. Consistent with a sunken ship or aircraft, which cut the cable.

"The charter company, Transpac Communications, notified the Navy, requesting any information we had about the obstruction. This is routine: whenever there is a cable break, the Navy is notified, on the chance that the obstruction is known to us. If it's a sunken vessel containing explosives, the cable company wants to know about it before they start repair. But in this case the obstruction was not in Navy files. And the Navy was interested.

"We immediately dispatched our nearest search ship, the *Ocean Explorer,* from Melbourne. The *Ocean Explorer* reached the site on June 21 of this year. The reason for the Navy interest was the possibility that the obstruction might represent a sunken Chinese Wuhan-class nuclear submarine fitted with SY-2 missiles. We knew the Chinese lost such a sub in this approximate area in May 1984. The *Ocean Explorer* scanned the bottom, using a most sophisticated side-looking sonar, which produced this picture of the bottom."

In color, the image was almost three-dimensional in its clarity.

"As you see, the bottom appears flat except for a single triangular fin which sticks up some two hundred and eighty feet above the ocean floor. You see it here," he said, pointing. "Now, this wing dimension is larger than any known aircraft manufactured in either the United States or the Soviet Union. This was very puzzling at first. Next."

A submersible robot, being lowered on a crane over the side of a ship. The robot looked like a series of horizontal tubes with cameras and lights nestled in the center.

"By June 24, the Navy had the ROV carrier *Neptune IV* on site, and the

Remote Operated Vehicle *Scorpion,* which you see here, was sent down to photograph the wing. It returned an image that clearly showed a control surface of some sort. Here it is."

There were murmurs from the group. In a harshly lit color image, a gray fin stuck up from a flat coral floor. The fin was sharp-edged and aeronautical-looking, tapered, definitely artificial.

"You'll notice," Barnes said, "that the sea bottom in this region consists of scrubby dead coral. The wing or fin disappears into the coral, suggesting the rest of the aircraft might be buried beneath. An ultra-high-resolution SLS bottom scan was carried out, to detect the shape underneath the coral. Next."

Another color sonar image, composed of fine dots instead of lines.

"As you see, the fin seems to be attached to a cylindrical object buried under the coral. The object has a diameter of a hundred and ninety feet, and extends west for a distance of 2,754 feet before tapering to a point."

More murmurings from the audience.

"That's correct," Barnes said. "The cylindrical object is half a mile long. The shape is consistent with a rocket or spacecraft—it certainly looks like that—but from the beginning we were careful to refer to this object as 'the anomaly.' "

Norman glanced over at Ted, who was smiling up at the screen. But alongside Ted in the darkness, Harry Adams frowned and pushed his glasses up on his nose.

Then the projector light went out. The room was plunged into darkness. There were groans. Norman heard Barnes say, "God damn it, not again!" Someone scrambled for the door; there was a rectangle of light.

Beth leaned over to Norman and said, "They lose power here all the time. Reassuring, huh?"

Moments later, the electricity came back on; Barnes continued. "On June 25 a SCARAB remote vehicle cut a piece from the tail fin and brought it to the surface. The fin segment was analyzed and found to be a titanium alloy in an epoxy-resin honeycomb. The necessary bonding technology for such metal/plastic materials was currently unknown on Earth.

"Experts confirmed that the fin could not have originated on this planet—although in ten or twenty years we'd probably know how to make it."

Harry Adams grunted, leaned forward, made a note on his pad.

Meanwhile, Barnes explained, other robot vessels were used to plant seismic charges on the bottom. Seismic analysis showed that the buried anomaly was of metal, that it was hollow, and that it had a complex internal structure.

"After two weeks of intensive study," Barnes said, "we concluded the anomaly was some sort of spacecraft."

The final verification came on June 27 from the geologists. Their core samples from the bottom indicated that the present seabed had formerly been much shallower, perhaps only eighty or ninety feet deep. This would explain the coral, which covered the craft to an average thickness of thirty feet. Therefore, the geologists said, the craft had been on the planet at least three hundred years, and perhaps much longer: five hundred, or even five thousand years.

"However reluctantly," Barnes said, "the Navy concluded that we had, in fact, found a spacecraft from another civilization. The decision of the President, before a special meeting of the National Security Council, was to open the spacecraft. So, starting June 29, the ULF team members were called in."

On July 1, the subsea habitat DH-7 was lowered into position near the spacecraft site. DH-7 housed nine Navy divers working in a saturated exotic-gas environment. They proceeded to do primary drilling work. "And I think that brings you up to date," Barnes said. "Any questions?"

Ted said, "The internal structure of the spacecraft. Has it been clarified?"

"Not at this point. The spacecraft seems to be built in such a way that shock waves are transmitted around the outer shell, which is tremendously strong and well engineered. That prevents a clear picture of the interior from the seismics."

"How about passive techniques to see what's inside?"

"We've tried," Barnes said. "Gravitometric analysis, negative. Thermography, negative. Resistivity mapping, negative. Proton precision magnetometers, negative."

"Listening devices?"

"We've had hydrophones on the bottom from day one. There have been no sounds emanating from the craft. At least not so far."

"What about other remote inspection procedures?"

"Most involve radiation, and we're hesitant to irradiate the craft at this time."

Harry said, "Captain Barnes, I notice the fin appears undamaged, and the hull appears a perfect cylinder. Do you think that this object crashed in the ocean?"

"Yes," Barnes said, looking uneasy.

"So this object has survived a high-speed impact with the water, without a scratch or a dent?"

"Well, it's tremendously strong."

Harry nodded. "It would have to be. . . ."

Beth said, "The divers who are down there now—what exactly are they doing?"

"Looking for the front door." Barnes smiled. "For the time being, we've had to fall back on classical archaeological procedures. We're digging exploratory trenches in the coral, looking for an entrance or a hatch of some kind. We hope to find it within the next twenty-four to forty-eight hours. Once we do, you're going in. Anything else?"

"Yes," Ted said. "What was the Russian reaction to this discovery?"

"We haven't told the Russians," Barnes said.

"You haven't told them?"

"No. We haven't."

"But this is an incredible, unprecedented development in human history. Not just American history. *Human* history. Surely we should share this with all the nations of the world. This is the sort of discovery that could unite all of mankind—"

"You'd have to speak to the President," Barnes said. "I don't know the reasoning behind it, but it's his decision. Any other questions?"

Nobody said anything. The team looked at each other.

"Then I guess that's it," Barnes said.

The lights came on. There was the scraping of chairs as people stood, stretched. Then Harry Adams said, "Captain Barnes, I must say I resent this briefing very much."

Barnes looked surprised. "What do you mean, Harry?"

The others stopped, looked at Adams. He remained seated in his chair, an irritated look on his face. "Did you decide you have to break the news to us gently?"

"What news?"

"The news about the door."

Barnes laughed uneasily. "Harry, I just got through telling you that the divers are cutting exploratory trenches, looking for the door—"

"—I'd say you had a pretty good idea where the door was three days ago, when you started flying us in. And I'd say that by now you probably know exactly where the door is. Am I right?"

Barnes said nothing. He stood with a fixed smile on his face.

My God, Norman thought, looking at Barnes. Harry's right. Harry was known to have a superbly logical brain, an astonishing and cold deductive ability, but Norman had never seen him at work.

"Yes," Barnes said, finally. "You're right."

"You know the location of the door?"

"We do. Yes."

There was a moment of silence, and then Ted said, "But this is fantastic! Absolutely fantastic! When will we go down there to enter the spacecraft?"

"Tomorrow," Barnes said, never taking his eyes off Harry. And Harry, for his own part, stared fixedly at Barnes. "The minisubs will take you down in pairs, starting at oh eight hundred hours tomorrow morning."

"This is exciting!" Ted said. "Fantastic! Unbelievable."

"So," Barnes said, still watching Harry, "you should all get a good night's sleep—if you can."

" 'Innocent sleep, sleep that knits up the ravell'd sleave of care,' " Ted said. He was literally bobbing up and down in his chair with excitement.

"During the rest of the day, supply and technical officers will be coming to measure and outfit you. Any other questions," Barnes said, "you can find me in my office."

He left the room, and the meeting broke up. When the others filed out,

Norman remained behind, with Harry Adams. Harry never moved from his chair. He watched the technician packing up the portable screen.

"That was quite a performance just now," Norman said.

"Was it? I don't see why."

"You deduced that Barnes wasn't telling us about the door."

"Oh, there's much more he's not telling us about," Adams said, in a cold voice. "He's not telling us about *any* of the important things."

"Like what?"

"Like the fact," Harry said, getting to his feet at last, "that Captain Barnes knows perfectly well why the President decided to keep this a secret."

"He does?"

"The President had no choice, under the circumstances."

"What circumstances?"

"He knows that the object down there is not an alien spacecraft."

"Then what is it?"

"I think it's quite clear what it is."

"Not to me," Norman said.

Adams smiled for the first time. It was a thin smile, entirely without humor. "You wouldn't believe it if I told you," he said. And he left the room.

Tests

Arthur Levine, the marine biologist, was the only member of the expedition Norman Johnson had not met. It was one of the things we hadn't planned for, he thought. Norman had assumed that any contact with unknown life would occur on land; he hadn't considered the most obvious possibility—that if a spacecraft landed at random somewhere on the Earth, it would most likely come down on water, since 70 percent of the planet was covered with water. It was obvious in retrospect that they would need a marine biologist.

What else, he wondered, would prove obvious in retrospect?

He found Levine hanging off the port railing. Levine came from the oceanographic institute at Woods Hole, Massachusetts. His hand was damp when Norman shook it. Levine looked extremely ill at ease, and finally admitted that he was seasick.

"Seasick? A marine biologist?" Norman said.

"I work in the laboratory," he said. "At home. On land. Where things don't move all the time. Why are you smiling?"

"Sorry," Norman said.

"You think it's funny, a seasick marine biologist?"

"Incongruous, I guess."

"A lot of us get seasick," Levine said. He stared out at the sea. "Look out there," he said. "Thousands of miles of flat. Nothing."

"The ocean."

"It gives me the creeps," Levine said.

"**S**o?" Barnes said, back in his office. "What do you think?"

"Of what?"

"Of the team, for Christ's sake."

"It's the team I chose, six years later. Basically a good group, certainly very able."

"I want to know who will crack."

"Why should anybody crack?" Norman said. He was looking at Barnes, noticing the thin line of sweat on his upper lip. The commander was under a lot of pressure himself.

"A thousand feet down?" Barnes said. "Living and working in a cramped habitat? Listen, it's not like I'm going in with military divers who have been trained and who have themselves under control. I'm taking a bunch of *scientists,* for God's sake. I want to make sure they all have a clean bill of health. I want to make sure nobody's going to crack."

"I don't know if you are aware of this, Captain, but psychologists can't predict that very accurately. Who will crack."

"Even when it's from fear?"

"Whatever it's from."

Barnes frowned. "I thought fear was your specialty."

"Anxiety is one of my research interests and I can tell you who, on the basis of personality profiles, is likely to suffer acute anxiety in a stress situation. But I can't predict who'll crack under that stress and who won't."

"Then what good are you?" Barnes said irritably. He sighed. "I'm sorry. Don't you just want to interview them, or give them some tests?"

"There aren't any tests," Norman said. "At least, none that work."

Barnes sighed again. "What about Levine?"

"He's seasick."

"There isn't any motion underwater; that won't be a problem. But what about *him,* personally?"

"I'd be concerned," Norman said.

"Duly noted. What about Harry Adams? He's arrogant."

"Yes," Norman said. "But that's probably desirable." Studies had shown that the people who were most successful at handling pressure were people others didn't like—individuals who were described as arrogant, cocksure, irritating.

"Maybe so," Barnes said. "But what about his famous research paper? Harry was one of the biggest supporters of SETI a few years back. Now that we've found something, he's suddenly very negative. You remember his paper?"

Norman didn't, and was about to say so when an ensign came in. "Captain Barnes, here is the visual upgrade you wanted."

"Okay," Barnes said. He squinted at a photograph, put it down. "What about the weather?"

"No change, sir. Satellite reports are confirming we have forty-eight plus-minus twelve on site, sir."

"Hell," Barnes said.

"Trouble?" Norman asked.

"The weather's going bad on us," Barnes said. "We may have to clear out our surface support."

"Does that mean you'll cancel going down there?"

"No," Barnes said. "We go tomorrow, as planned."

"Why does Harry think this thing is not a spacecraft?" Norman asked.

Barnes frowned, pushed papers on his desk. "Let me tell you something," he said. "Harry's a theoretician. And theories are just that—theories. I deal in the hard facts. The fact is, we've got something damn old and damn strange down there. I want to know what it is."

"But if it's not an alien spacecraft, what is it?"

"Let's just wait until we get down there, shall we?" Barnes glanced at his watch. "The second habitat should be anchored on the sea floor by now. We'll begin moving you down in fifteen hours. Between now and then, we've all got a lot to do."

"Just hold it there, Dr. Johnson." Norman stood naked, felt two metal calipers pinch the back of his arms, just above the elbow. "Just a bit . . . that's fine. Now you can get into the tank."

The young medical corpsman stepped aside, and Norman climbed the steps to the metal tank, which looked like a military version of a Jacuzzi. The tank was filled to the top with water. As he lowered his body into the water, it spilled over the sides.

"What's all this for?" Norman asked.

"I'm sorry, Dr. Johnson. If you would *completely* immerse yourself . . ."

"What?"

"Just for a moment, sir . . ."

Norman took a breath, ducked under the water, came back up.

"That's fine, you can get out now," the corpsman said, handing him a towel.

"What's all this for?" he asked again, climbing down the ladder.

"Total body adipose content," the corpsman said. "We have to know it, to calculate your sat stats."

"My sat stats?"

"Your saturation statistics." The corpsman marked points on his clipboard.

"Oh dear," he said. "You're off the graph."

"Why is that?"

"Do you get much exercise, Dr. Johnson?"

"Some." He was feeling defensive now. And the towel was too small to wrap around his waist. Why did the Navy use such small towels?

"Do you drink?"

"Some." He was feeling distinctly defensive. No question about it.

"May I ask when you last consumed an alcoholic beverage, sir?"

"I don't know. Two, three days ago." He was having trouble thinking back to San Diego. It seemed so far away. "Why?"

"That's fine, Dr. Johnson. Any trouble with joints, hips or knees?"

"No, why?"

"Episodes of syncope, faintness or blackouts?"

"No . . ."

"If you would just sit over here, sir." The corpsman pointed to a stool, next to an electronic device on the wall.

"I'd really like some answers," Norman said.

"Just stare at the green dot, both eyes wide open. . . ."

He felt a brief blast of air on both eyes, and blinked instinctively. A printed strip of paper clicked out. The corpsman tore it off, glanced at it.

"That's fine, Dr. Johnson. If you would come this way . . ."

"I'd like some information from you," Norman said. "I'd like to know what's going on."

"I understand, sir, but I have to finish your workup in time for your next briefing at seventeen hundred hours."

Norman lay on his back, and technicians stuck needles in both arms, and another in his leg at the groin. He yelled in sudden pain.

"That's the worst of it, sir," the corpsman said, packing the syringes in ice. "If you will just press this cotton against it, here . . ."

There was a clip over his nostrils, a mouthpiece between his teeth.

"This is to measure your CO_2," the corpsman said. "Just exhale. That's right. Big breath, now exhale. . . ."

Norman exhaled. He watched a rubber diaphragm inflate, pushing a needle up a scale.

"Try it again, sir. I'm sure you can do better than that."

Norman didn't think he could, but he tried again anyway.

Another corpsman entered the room, with a sheet of paper covered with figures. "Here are his BC's," he said.

The first corpsman frowned. "Has Barnes seen this?"

"Yes."

"And what'd he say?"

"He said it was okay. He said to continue."

"Okay, fine. He's the boss." The first corpsman turned back to Norman. "Let's try one more big breath, Dr. Johnson, if you would. . . ."

Metal calipers touched his chin and his forehead. A tape went around his head. Now the calipers measured from his ear to his chin.

"What's this for?" Norman said.

"Fitting you with a helmet, sir."

"Shouldn't I be trying one on?"

"This is the way we do it, sir."

Dinner was macaroni and cheese, burned underneath. Norman pushed it aside after a few bites.

The corpsman appeared at his door. "Time for the seventeen-hundred-hours briefing, sir."

"I'm not going anywhere," Norman said, "until I get some answers. What the hell is all this you're doing to me?"

"Routine deepsat workup, sir. Navy regs require it before you go down."

"And why am I off the graph?"

"Sorry, sir?"

"You said I was off the graph."

"Oh, *that.* You're a bit heavier than the Navy tables figure for, sir."

"Is there a problem about my weight?"

"Shouldn't be, no, sir."

"And the other tests, what did they show?"

"Sir, you are in very good health for your age and life-style."

"And what about going down there?" Norman asked, half hoping he wouldn't be able to go.

"Down there? I've talked with Captain Barnes. Shouldn't be any problem at all, sir. If you'll just come this way to the briefing, sir . . ."

The others were sitting around in the briefing room, with Styrofoam cups of coffee. Norman felt glad to see them. He dropped into a chair next to Harry. "Jesus, did you have the damn physical?"

"Yeah," he said. "Had it yesterday."

"They stuck me in the leg with this long needle," Norman said.

"Really? They didn't do that to me."

"And how about breathing with that clip on your nose?"

"I didn't do that, either," Harry said. "Sounds like you got some special treatment, Norman."

Norman was thinking the same thing, and he didn't like the implications. He felt suddenly tired.

"All right, men, we've got a lot to cover and just three hours to do it," a brisk man said, turning off the lights as he came into the room. Norman hadn't even gotten a good look at him. Now it was just a voice in the dark. "As you know, Dalton's law governs partial pressures of mixed gases, or, as represented here in algebraic form . . ."

The first of the graphs flashed up.

$$PP_a = P_{tot} \times \% \, Vol_a$$

"Now let's review how calculation of the partial pressure might be done in atmospheres absolute, which is the most common procedure we employ—"

The words were meaningless to Norman. He tried to pay attention, but as the graphs continued and the voice droned on, his eyes grew heavier and he fell asleep.

"—be taken down in the submarine and once in the habitat module you will be pressurized to thirty-three atmospheres. At that time you will be switched over to mixed gases, since it is not possible to breathe Earth atmosphere beyond eighteen atmospheres—"

Norman stopped listening. These technical details only filled him with dread. He went back to sleep, awakening only intermittently.

"—since oxygen toxicity only occurs when the PO_2 exceeds point 7 ATA for prolonged periods—

"—nitrogen narcosis, in which nitrogen behaves like an anesthetic, will occur in mixed-gas atmospheres if partial pressures exceeds 1.5 ATA in the DDS—

"—demand open circuit is generally preferable, but you will be using semiclosed circuit with inspired fluctuations of 608 to 760 millimeters—"

He went back to sleep.

When it was over, they walked back to their rooms. "Did I miss anything?" Norman said.

"Not really." Harry shrugged. "Just a lot of physics."

In his tiny gray room, Norman got into bed. The glowing wall clock said 2300. It took him a while to figure out that that was 11:00 p.m. In nine more hours, he thought, I will begin the descent.

Then he slept.

THE DEEP

Descent

In the morning light, the submarine *Charon V* bobbed on the surface, riding on a pontoon platform. Bright yellow, it looked like a child's bathtub toy sitting on a deck of oildrums.

A rubber Zodiac launch took Norman over, and he climbed onto the platform, shook hands with the pilot, who could not have been more than eighteen, younger than his son, Tim.

"Ready to go, sir?" the pilot said.

"Sure," Norman said. He was as ready as he would ever be.

Up close, the sub did not look like a toy. It was incredibly massive and strong. Norman saw a single porthole of curved acrylic. It was held in place by bolts as big as his fist. He touched them, tentatively.

The pilot smiled. "Want to kick the tires, sir?"

"No, I'll trust you."

"Ladder's this way, sir."

Norman climbed the narrow rungs to the top of the sub, and saw the small circular hatch opening. He hesitated.

"Sit on the edge here," the pilot said, "and drop your legs in, then follow it down. You may have to squeeze your shoulders together a bit and suck in your . . . That's it, sir." Norman wriggled through the tight hatch into an interior so low he could not stand. The sub was crammed with dials and machinery. Ted was already aboard, hunched in the back, grinning like a kid. "Isn't this fantastic?"

Norman envied his easy enthusiasm; he felt cramped and a little nervous. Above him, the pilot clanged the heavy hatch shut and dropped down to take the controls. "Everybody okay?"

They nodded.

"Sorry about the view," the pilot said, glancing over his shoulders. "You gentlemen are mostly going to be seeing my hindquarters. Let's get started. Mozart okay?" He pressed a tape deck and smiled. "We've got thirteen minutes' descent to the bottom; music makes it a little easier. If you don't like Mozart, we can offer you something else."

"Mozart's fine," Norman said.

"Mozart's wonderful," Ted said. "Sublime."

"Very good, gentlemen." The submarine hissed. There was squawking on

307

the radio. The pilot spoke softly into a headset. A scuba diver appeared at the porthole, waved. The pilot waved back.

There was a sloshing sound, then a deep rumble, and they started down.

"As you see, the whole sled goes under," the pilot explained. "The sub's not stable on the surface, so we sled her up and down. We'll leave the sled at about a hundred feet or so."

Through the porthole, they saw the diver standing on the deck, the water now waist-deep. Then the water covered the porthole. Bubbles came out of the diver's scuba.

"We're under," the pilot said. He adjusted valves above his head and they heard the hiss of air, startlingly loud. More gurgling. The light in the submarine from the porthole was a beautiful blue.

"Lovely," Ted said.

"We'll leave the sled now," the pilot said. Motors rumbled and the sub moved forward, the diver slipping off to one side. Now there was nothing to be seen through the porthole but undifferentiated blue water. The pilot said something on the radio, and turned up the Mozart.

"Just sit back, gentlemen," he said. "Descending eighty feet a minute."

Norman felt the rumble of the electric motors, but there was no real sense of motion. All that happened was that it got darker and darker.

"You know," Ted said, "we're really quite lucky about this site. Most parts of the Pacific are so deep we'd never be able to visit it in person." He explained that the vast Pacific Ocean, which amounted to half the total surface area of the Earth, had an average depth of two miles. "There are only a few places where it is less. One is the relatively small rectangle bounded by Samoa, New Zealand, Australia, and New Guinea, which is actually a great undersea plain, like the plains of the American West, except it's at an average depth of two thousand feet. That's what we are doing now, descending to that plain."

Ted spoke rapidly. Was he nervous? Norman couldn't tell: he was feeling his own heart pound. Now it was quite dark outside; the instruments glowed green. The pilot flicked on red interior lights.

Their descent continued. "Four hundred feet." The submarine lurched, then eased forward. "This is the river."

"What river?" Norman said.

"Sir, we are in a current of different salinity and temperature; it behaves like a river inside the ocean. We traditionally stop about here, sir; the sub sticks in the river, takes us for a little ride."

"Oh yes," Ted said, reaching into his pocket. Ted handed the pilot a ten-dollar bill.

Norman glanced questioningly at Ted.

"Didn't they mention that to you? Old tradition. You always pay the pilot on your way down, for good luck."

"I can use some luck," Norman said. He fumbled in his pocket, found a five-dollar bill, thought better of it, took out a twenty instead.

"Thank you, gentlemen, and have a good bottom stay, both of you," the pilot said.

The electric motors cut back in.

The descent continued. The water was dark.

"Five hundred feet," he said. "Halfway there."

The submarine creaked loudly, then made several explosive pops. Norman was startled.

"That's normal pressure adjustment," the pilot said. "No problem."

"Uh-huh," Norman said. He wiped sweat on his shirtsleeve. It seemed that the interior of the submarine was now much smaller, the walls closer to his face.

"Actually," Ted said, "if I remember, this particular region of the Pacific is called the Lau Basin, isn't that right?"

"That's right, sir, the Lau Basin."

"It's a plateau between two undersea ridges, the South Fiji or Lau Ridge to the west, and the Tonga Ridge to the east."

"That's correct, Dr. Fielding."

Norman glanced at the instruments. They were covered with moisture. The pilot had to rub the dials with a cloth to read them. Was the sub leaking? No, he thought. Just condensation. The interior of the submarine was growing colder.

Take it easy, he told himself.

"Eight hundred feet," the pilot said.

It was now completely black outside.

"This is very exciting," Ted said. "Have you ever done anything like this before, Norman?"

"No," Norman said.

"Me, neither," Ted said. "What a thrill."

Norman wished he would shut up.

"You know," Ted said, "when we open this alien craft up and make our first contact with another form of life, it's going to be a great moment in the history of our species on Earth. I've been wondering about what we should say."

"Say?"

"You know, what words. At the threshold, with the cameras rolling."

"Will there be cameras?"

"Oh, I'm sure there'll be all sorts of documentation. It's only proper, considering. So we need something to say, a memorable phrase. I was thinking of 'This is a momentous moment in human history.' "

"Momentous moment?" Norman said, frowning.

"You're right," Ted said. "Awkward, I agree. Maybe 'A turning point in human history'?"

Norman shook his head.

"How about 'A crossroads in the evolution of the human species'?"

"Can evolution have a crossroads?"

"I don't see why not," Ted said.

"Well, a crossroads is a crossing of roads. Is evolution a road? I thought it wasn't; I thought evolution was undirected."

"You're being too literal," Ted said.

"Reading the bottom," the pilot said. "Nine hundred feet." He slowed the descent. They heard the intermittent *ping* of sonar.

Ted said, " 'A new threshold in the evolution of the human species'?"

"Sure. Think it will be?"

"Will be what?"

"A new threshold."

"Why not?" Ted said.

"What if we open it up and it's just a lot of rusted junk inside, and nothing valuable or enlightening at all?"

"Good point," Ted said.

"Nine hundred fifty feet. Exterior lights are on," the pilot said.

Through the porthole they saw white flecks. The pilot explained this was suspended matter in the water.

"Visual contact. I have bottom."

"Oh, let's see!" Ted said. The pilot obligingly shifted to one side and they looked.

Norman saw a flat, dead, dull-brown plain stretching away to the limit of the lights. Blackness beyond.

"Not much to look at right here, I'm afraid," the pilot said.

"Surprisingly dreary," Ted said, without a trace of disappointment. "I would have expected more life."

"Well, it's pretty cold. Water temperature is, ah, thirty-six degrees Fahrenheit."

"Almost freezing," Ted said.

"Yes, sir. Let's see if we can find your new home."

The motors rumbled. Muddy sediment churned up in front of the porthole. The sub turned, moved across the bottom. For several minutes they saw only the brown landscape.

Then lights. "There we are."

A vast underwater array of lights, arranged in a rectangular pattern.

"That's the grid," the pilot said.

The submarine planed up, and glided smoothly over the illuminated grid, which extended into the distance for half a mile. Through the porthole, they saw divers standing on the bottom, working within the grid structure. The divers waved to the passing sub. The pilot honked a toy horn.

"They can hear that?"

"Oh sure. Water's a great conductor."

"My God," Ted said.

Directly ahead the giant titanium fin rose sharply above the ocean floor. Norman was completely unprepared for its dimension; as the submarine moved to port, the fin blocked their entire field of view for nearly a minute. The metal was dull gray and, except for small white speckles of marine growth, entirely unmarked.

"There isn't any corrosion," Ted said.

"No, sir," the pilot said. "Everybody's mentioned that. They think it's because it's a metal-plastic alloy, but I don't think anybody is quite sure."

The fin slipped away to the stern; the submarine again turned. Directly ahead, more lights, arranged in vertical rows. Norman saw a single cylinder of yellow-painted steel, and bright portholes. Next to it was a low metal dome.

"That's DH-7, the divers' habitat, to port," the pilot said. "It's pretty utilitarian. You guys are in DH-8, which is much nicer, believe me."

He turned starboard, and after a momentary blackness, they saw another set of lights. Coming closer, Norman counted five different cylinders, some vertical, some horizontal, interconnected in a complex way.

"There you are. DH-8, your home away from home," the pilot said. "Give me a minute to dock."

Metal clanged against metal; there was a sharp jolt, and then the motors cut off. Silence. Hissing air. The pilot scrambled to open the hatch, and surprisingly cold air washed down on them.

"Airlock's open, gentlemen," he said, stepping aside.

Norman looked up through the lock. He saw banks of red lights above. He climbed up through the submarine, and into a round steel cylinder approximately eight feet in diameter. On all sides there were handholds; a narrow metal bench; the glowing heat lamps overhead, though they didn't seem to do much good.

Ted climbed up and sat on the bench opposite him. They were so close their knees touched. Below their feet, the pilot closed the hatch. They watched the wheel spin. They heard a *clank* as the submarine disengaged, then the *whirr* of motors as it moved away.

Then nothing.

"What happens now?" Norman said.

"They pressurize us," Ted said. "Switch us over to exotic gas atmosphere. We can't breathe air down here."

"Why not?" Norman said. Now that he was down here, staring at the cold steel walls of the cylinder, he wished he had stayed awake for the briefing.

"Because," Ted said, "the atmosphere of the Earth is deadly. You don't realize it, but oxygen is a corrosive gas. It's in the same chemical family as chlorine and fluorine, and hydrofluoric acid is the most corrosive acid known. The same quality of oxygen that makes a half-eaten apple turn brown, or makes iron rust, is incredibly destructive to the human body if exposed to too much of it. Oxygen under pressure is toxic—with a vengeance. So we cut

311

down the amount of oxygen you breathe. You breathe twenty-one percent oxygen at the surface. Down here, you breathe two percent oxygen. But you won't notice any difference—"

A voice over a loudspeaker said, "We're starting to pressurize you now."

"Who's that?" Norman said.

"Barnes," the voice said. But it didn't sound like Barnes. It sounded gritty and artificial.

"It must be the talker," Ted said, and then laughed. His voice was noticeably higher-pitched. "It's the helium, Norman. They're pressurizing us with helium."

"You sound like Donald Duck," Norman said, and he laughed, too. His own voice sounded squeaky, like a cartoon character's.

"Speak for yourself, Mickey," Ted squeaked.

"I taut I taw a puddy tat," Norman said. They were both laughing, hearing their voices.

"Knock it off, you guys," Barnes said over the intercom. "This is serious."

"Yes, sir, Captain," Ted said, but by now his voice was so high-pitched it was almost unintelligible, and they fell into laughter again, their tinny voices like those of schoolgirls reverberating inside the steel cylinder.

Helium made their voices high and squeaky. But it also had other effects.

"Getting chilled, boys?" Barnes said.

They were indeed getting colder. He saw Ted shivering, felt goosebumps on his own legs. It felt as if a wind were blowing across their bodies—except there wasn't any wind. The lightness of the helium increased evaporation, made them cold.

Across the cylinder, Ted said something, but Norman couldn't understand Ted at all any more; his voice was too high-pitched to be comprehensible. It was just a thin squeal.

"Sounds like a couple of rats in there now," Barnes said, with satisfaction.

Ted rolled his eyes toward the loudspeaker and squeaked something.

"If you want to talk, get a talker," Barnes said. "You'll find them in the locker under the seat."

Norman found a metal locker, clicked it open. The metal squealed loudly, like chalk on a blackboard. All the sounds in the chamber were high-pitched. Inside the locker he saw two black plastic pads with neck straps.

"Just slip them over your neck. Put the pad at the base of your throat."

"Okay," Ted said, and then blinked in surprise. His voice sounded slightly rough, but otherwise normal.

"These things must change the vocal-cord frequencies," Norman said.

"Why don't you guys pay attention to briefings?" Barnes said. "That's exactly what they do. You'll have to wear a talker all the time you're down here. At least, if you want anybody to understand you. Still cold?"

"Yes," Ted said.

"Well, hang on, you're almost fully pressurized now."

Then there was another hiss, and a side door slid open. Barnes stood there, with light jackets over his arm. "Welcome to DH-8," he said.

DH-8

"**Y**ou're the last to arrive," Barnes said. "We just have time for a quick tour before we open the spacecraft."

"You're ready to open it now?" Ted asked. "Wonderful. I've just been talking about this with Norman. This is such a great moment, our first contact with alien life, we ought to prepare a little speech for when we open it up."

"There'll be time to consider that," Barnes said, with an odd glance at Ted. "I'll show you the habitat first. This way."

He explained that the DH-8 habitat consisted of five large cylinders, designated A to E. "Cyl A is the airlock, where we are now." He led them into an adjacent changing room. Heavy cloth suits hung limply on the wall, alongside yellow sculpted helmets of the sort Norman had seen the divers wearing. The helmets had a futuristic look. Norman tapped one with his knuckles. It was plastic, and surprisingly light.

He saw "JOHNSON" stenciled above one faceplate.

"We going to wear these?" Norman asked.

"That's correct," Barnes said.

"Then we'll be going outside?" Norman said, feeling a twinge of alarm.

"Eventually, yes. Don't worry about it now. Still cold?"

They were; Barnes had them change into tight-fitting jumpsuits of clinging blue polyester. Ted frowned. "Don't you think these look a little silly?"

"They may not be the height of fashion," Barnes said, "but they prevent heat loss from helium."

"The color is unflattering," Ted said.

"Screw the color," Barnes said. He handed them lightweight jackets. Norman felt something heavy in one pocket, and pulled out a battery pack.

"The jackets are wired and electrically heated," Barnes said. "Like an electric blanket, which is what you'll use for sleeping. Follow me."

They went on to Cyl B, which housed power and life-support systems. At first glance, it looked like a large boiler room, all multicolored pipes and utilitarian fittings. "This is where we generate all of our heat, power, and air," Barnes said. He pointed out the features: "Closed-cycle IC generator, 240/110. Hydrogen-and-oxygen-driven fuel cells. LSS monitors. Liquid processor, runs on silver-zinc batteries. And that's Chief Petty Officer Fletcher. Teeny Fletcher." Norman saw a big-boned figure, working back among the pipes with a heavy wrench. The figure turned; Alice Fletcher gave them a grin, waved a greasy hand.

"She seems to know what she's doing," Ted said, approvingly.

"She does," Barnes said. "But all the major support systems are redundant. Fletcher is just our final redundancy. Actually, you'll find the entire habitat is self-regulating."

He clipped heavy badges onto the jumpsuits. "Wear these at all times, even though they're just a precaution: the alarms trigger automatically if life-support conditions go below optimum. But that won't happen. There are sensors in each room of the habitat. You'll get used to the fact that the environment continually adjusts to your presence. Lights will go on and off, heat lamps will turn on and off, and air vents will hiss to keep track of things. It's all automatic, don't sweat it. Every single major system is redundant. We can lose power, we can lose air, we can lose water entirely, and we will be fine for a hundred and thirty hours."

One hundred and thirty hours didn't sound very long to Norman. He did the calculation in his head: five days. Five days didn't seem very long, either.

They went into the next cylinder, the lights clicking on as they entered. Cylinder C contained living quarters: bunks, toilets, showers ("plenty of hot water, you'll find"). Barnes showed them around proudly, as if it were a hotel.

The living quarters were heavily insulated: carpeted deck, walls and ceilings all covered in soft padded foam, which made the interior appear like an overstuffed couch. But, despite the bright colors and the evident care in decoration, Norman still found it cramped and dreary. The portholes were tiny, and they revealed only the blackness of the ocean outside. And wherever the padding ended, he saw heavy bolts and heavy steel plating, a reminder of where they really were. He felt as if he were inside a large iron lung—and, he thought, that isn't so far wrong.

They ducked through narrow bulkheads into D Cyl: a small laboratory with benches and microscopes on the top level, a compact electronics unit on the level below.

"This is Tina Chan," Barnes said, introducing a very still woman. They all shook hands. Norman thought that Tina Chan was almost unnaturally calm, until he realized she was one of those people who almost never blinked their eyes.

"Be nice to Tina," Barnes was saying. "She's our only link to the outside—she runs the com ops, and the sensor systems as well. In fact, all the electronics."

Tina Chan was surrounded by the bulkiest monitors Norman had ever seen. They looked like TV sets from the 1950s. Barnes explained that certain equipment didn't do well in the helium atmosphere, including TV tubes. In the early days of undersea habitats, the tubes had to be replaced daily. Now they were elaborately coated and shielded; hence their bulk.

Next to Chan was another woman, Jane Edmunds, whom Barnes introduced as the unit archivist.

"What's a unit archivist?" Ted asked her.

"Petty Officer First Class, Data Processing, sir," she said formally. Jane Edmunds wore spectacles and stood stiffly. She reminded Norman of a librarian.

"Data Processing . . ." Ted said.

"My mission is to keep all the digital recordings, visual materials, and videotapes, sir. Every aspect of this historic moment is being recorded, and I keep everything neatly filed." Norman thought: She *is* a librarian.

"Oh, excellent," Ted said. "I'm glad to hear it. Film or tape?"

"Tape, sir."

"I know my way around a video camera," Ted said, with a smile. "What're you putting it down on, half-inch or three-quarter?"

"Sir, we use a datascan image equivalent of two thousand pixels per side-biased frame, each pixel carrying a twelve-tone gray scale."

"Oh," Ted said.

"It's a bit better than commercial systems you may be familiar with, sir."

"I see," Ted said. But he recovered smoothly, and chatted with Edmunds for a while about technical matters.

"Ted seems awfully interested in how we're going to record this," Barnes said, looking uneasy.

"Yes, he seems to be." Norman wondered why that troubled Barnes. Was Barnes worried about the visual record? Or did he think Ted would try to hog the show? Would Ted try to hog the show? Did Barnes have any worries about having this appear to be a civilian operation?

"No, the exterior lights are a hundred-fifty-watt quartz halogen," Edmunds was saying. "We're recording at equivalent of half a million ASA, so that's ample. The real problem is backscatter. We're constantly fighting it."

Norman said, "I notice your support team is all women."

"Yes," Barnes said. "All the deep-diving studies show that women are superior for submerged operations. They're physically smaller and consume less nutrients and air, they have better social skills and tolerate close quarters better, and they are physiologically tougher and have better endurance. The fact is, the Navy long ago recognized that all their submariners should be female." He laughed. "But just try to implement that one." He glanced at his watch. "We'd better move on. Ted?"

They went on. The final cylinder, E Cyl, was more spacious than the others. There were magazines, a television, and a large lounge; and on the deck below was an efficient mess and a kitchen. Seaman Rose Levy, the cook, was a red-faced woman with a Southern accent, standing beneath giant suction fans. She asked Norman whether he had any favorite desserts.

"Desserts?"

"Yes sir, Dr. Johnson. I like to make everybody's favorite dessert, if I can. What about you, you have a favorite, Dr. Fielding?"

"Key lime pie," Ted said. "I love key lime pie."

"Can do, sir," Levy said, with a big smile. She turned back to Norman. "I haven't heard yours yet, Dr. Johnson."

"Strawberry shortcake."

"Easy. Got some nice New Zealand strawberries coming down on the last sub shuttle. Maybe you'd like that shortcake tonight?"

"Why not, Rose," Barnes said heartily.

Norman looked out the black porthole window. From the portholes of D Cyl, he could see the rectangular illuminated grid that extended across the bottom, following the half-mile-long buried spacecraft. Divers, illuminated like fireflies, moved over the glowing grid surface.

Norman thought: I am a thousand feet beneath the surface of the ocean, and we are talking about whether we should have strawberry shortcake for dessert. But the more he thought about it, the more it made sense. The best way to make somebody comfortable in a new environment was to give him familiar food.

"Strawberries make me break out," Ted said.

"I'll make your shortcake with blueberries," Levy said, not missing a beat.

"And whipped cream?" Ted said.

"Well . . ."

"You can't have everything," Barnes said. "And one of the things you can't have at thirty atmospheres of mixed gas is whipped cream. Won't whip. Let's move on."

Beth and Harry were waiting in the small, padded conference room, directly above the mess. They both wore jumpsuits and heated jackets. Harry was shaking his head as they arrived. "Like our padded cell?" He poked the insulated walls. "It's like living in a vagina."

Beth said, "Don't you like going back to the womb, Harry?"

"No," Harry said. "I've been there. Once was enough."

"These jumpsuits are pretty bad," Ted said, plucking at the clinging polyester.

"Shows your belly nicely," Harry said.

"Let's settle down," Barnes said.

"A few sequins, you could be Elvis Presley," Harry said.

"Elvis Presley's dead."

"Now's your chance," Harry said.

Norman looked around. "Where's Levine?"

"Levine didn't make it," Barnes said briskly. "He got claustrophobic in the sub coming down, and had to be taken back. One of those things."

"Then we have no marine biologist?"

"We'll manage without him."

"I hate this damn jumpsuit," Ted said. "I really hate it."

"Beth looks good in hers."

"Yes, Beth works out."

"And it's damp in here, too," Ted said. "Is it always so damp?"

Norman had noticed that humidity was a problem; everything they touched felt slightly wet and clammy and cold. Barnes warned them of the danger of infections and minor colds, and handed out bottles of skin lotion and ear drops.

"I thought you said the technology was all worked out," Harry said.

"It is," Barnes said. "Believe me, this is plush compared to the habitats ten years ago."

"Ten years ago," Harry said, "they stopped making habitats because people kept dying in them."

Barnes frowned. "There was one accident."

"There were two accidents," Harry said. "A total of four people."

"Special circumstances," Barnes said. "Not involving Navy technology or personnel."

"Great," Harry said. "How long did you say we going to be down here?"

"Maximum, seventy-two hours," Barnes said.

"You sure about that?"

"It's Navy regs," Barnes said.

"Why?" Norman asked, puzzled.

Barnes shook his head. "Never," he said, "never ask a reason for Navy regulations."

The intercom clicked, and Tina Chan said, "Captain Barnes, we have a signal from the divers. They are mounting the airlock now. Another few minutes to open."

The feeling in the room changed immediately; the excitement was palpable. Ted rubbed his hands together. "You realize, of course, that even without opening that spacecraft, we have already made a major discovery of profound importance."

"What's that?" Norman said.

"We've shot the unique event hypothesis to hell," Ted said, glancing at Beth.

"The unique event hypothesis?" Barnes said.

"He's referring," Beth said, "to the fact that physicists and chemists tend to believe in intelligent extraterrestrial life, while biologists tend not to. Many biologists feel the development of *intelligent* life on Earth required so many peculiar steps that it represents a unique event in the universe, that may never have occurred elsewhere."

"Wouldn't intelligence arise again and again?" Barnes said.

"Well, it barely arose on the Earth," Beth said. "The Earth is 4.5 billion years old, and single-celled life appeared 3.9 billion years ago—almost immediately, geologically speaking. But life *remained* single-celled for the next three billion years. Then in the Cambrian period, around six hundred million years ago, there was an explosion of sophisticated life forms. Within a hundred million years, the ocean was full of fish. Then the land became populated. Then the air. But nobody knows why the explosion occurred in the first place. And since it didn't occur for three billion years, there's the possibility that on some other planet, it might never occur at all.

"And even after the Cambrian, the chain of events leading to man appears to be so special, so chancy, that biologists worry it might never have happened. Just consider the fact that if the dinosaurs hadn't been wiped out sixty-five million years ago—by a comet or whatever—then reptiles might still be the dominant form on Earth, and mammals would never have had a chance to take over. No mammals, no primates. No primates, no apes. No apes, no man . . . There are a lot of random factors in evolution, a lot of luck. That's why biologists think intelligent life might be a unique event in the universe, only occurring here."

"Except now," Ted said, "we know it's *not* a unique event. Because there is a damn big spacecraft out there."

"Personally," Beth said, "I couldn't be more pleased." She bit her lip.

"You don't look pleased," Norman said.

"I'll tell you," Beth said. "I can't help being nervous. Ten years ago, Bill Jackson at Stanford ran a series of weekend seminars on extraterrestrial life. This was right after he won the Nobel prize in chemistry. He split us into two groups. One group designed the alien life form, and worked it all out scientifically. The other group tried to figure out the life form, and communicate with it. Jackson presided over the whole thing as a hard scientist, not letting anybody get carried away. One time we brought in a sketch of a proposed creature and he said, very tough, 'Okay, where's the anus?' That was his criticism. But many animals on Earth have no anus. There are all kinds of excretory mechanisms that don't require a special orifice. Jackson assumed an anus was necessary, but it isn't. And now . . ." She shrugged. "Who knows what we'll find?"

"We'll know, soon enough," Ted said.

The intercom clicked. "Captain Barnes, the divers have the airlock mounted in place. The robot is now ready to enter the spacecraft."

Ted said, *"What robot?"*

The Door

"**I** don't think it's appropriate *at all*," Ted said angrily. "We came down here to make a manned entry into this alien spacecraft. I think we should do what we came here to do—make a *manned* entry."

"Absolutely not," Barnes said. "We can't risk it."

"You must think of this," Ted said, "as an archaeological site. Greater than Chichén Itzá, greater than Troy, greater than Tutankhamen's tomb. Unquestionably the most important archaeological site in the history of mankind. Do you really intend to have a damned *robot* open that site? Where's your sense of human destiny?"

"Where's your sense of self-preservation?" Barnes said.

"I strongly object, Captain Barnes."

"Duly noted," Barnes said, turning away. "Now let's get on with it. Tina, give us the video feed."

Ted sputtered, but he fell silent as two large monitors in front of them clicked on. On the left screen, they saw the complex tubular metal scaffolding of the robot, with exposed motors and gears. The robot was positioned before the curved gray metal wall of the spacecraft.

Within that wall was a door that looked rather like an airliner door. The second screen gave a closer view of the door, taken by the video camera mounted on the robot itself.

"It's rather similar to an airplane door," Ted said.

Norman glanced at Harry, who smiled enigmatically. Then he looked at Barnes. Barnes did not appear surprised. Barnes already knew about the door, he realized.

"I wonder how we can account for such parallelism in door design," Ted said. "The likelihood of its occurring by chance is astronomically small. Why, this door is the perfect size and shape for a human being!"

"That's right," Harry said.

"It's incredible," Ted said. "Quite incredible."

Harry smiled, said nothing.

Barnes said, "Let's find control surfaces."

The robot video scanner moved left and right across the spacecraft hull. It stopped on the image of a rectangular panel mounted to the left of the door.

319

"Can you open that panel?"

"Working on it now, sir."

Whirring, the robot claw extended out toward the panel. But the claw was clumsy; it scraped against the metal, leaving a series of gleaming scratches. But the panel remained closed.

"Ridiculous," Ted said. "It's like watching a baby."

The claw continued to scratch at the panel.

"We should be doing this ourselves," Ted said.

"Use suction," Barnes said.

Another arm extended out, with a rubber sucker.

"Ah, the plumber's friend," Ted said disdainfully.

As they watched, the sucker attached to the panel, flattened. Then, with a click, the panel lifted open.

"At last!"

"I can't see. . . ."

The view inside the panel was blurred, out of focus. They could distinguish what appeared to be a series of colored round metal protrusions, red, yellow, and blue. There were also intricate black-and-white symbols above the knobs.

"Look," Ted said, "red, blue, yellow. Primary colors. This is a *very* big break."

"Why?" Norman said.

"Because it suggests that the aliens have the same sensory equipment that we do—they may see the universe the same way, visually, in the same colors, utilizing the same part of the electromagnetic spectrum. That's going to help immeasurably in making contact with them. And those black-and-white markings . . . that must be some of their writing! Can you imagine! Alien writing!" He smiled enthusiastically. "This is a great moment," he said. "I feel truly privileged to be here."

"Focus," Barnes called.

"Focusing now, sir."

The image became even more blurred.

"No, the other way."

"Yes sir. Focusing now."

The image changed, slowly resolved into sharp focus.

"Uh-oh," Ted said, staring at the screen.

They now saw that the blurred knobs were actually three colored buttons: yellow, red, and blue. The buttons were each an inch in diameter and had knurled or machined edges. The symbols above the buttons resolved sharply into a series of neatly stenciled labels.

From left to right the labels read: "Emergency Ready," "Emergency Lock," and "Emergency Open."

In English.

There was a moment of stunned silence. And then, very softly, Harry Adams began to laugh.

The Spacecraft

"That's English," Ted said, staring at the screen. "Written *English.*"

"Yeah," Harry said. "Sure is."

"What's going on?" Ted said. "Is this some kind of joke?"

"No," Harry said. He was calm, oddly detached.

"How could this spacecraft be three hundred years old, and carry instructions in modern English?"

"Think about it," Harry said.

Ted frowned. "Maybe," he said, "this alien spacecraft is somehow presenting itself to us in a way that will make us comfortable."

"Think about it some more," Harry said.

There was a short silence. "Well, if it *is* an alien spacecraft—"

"It's not an alien spacecraft," Harry said.

There was another silence. Then Ted said, "Well, why don't you just tell us all what it is, since you're so sure of yourself!"

"All right," Harry said. "It's an American spacecraft."

"An American spacecraft? Half a mile long? Made with technology we don't have yet? And buried for three hundred years?"

"Of course," Harry said. "It's been obvious from the start. Right, Captain Barnes?"

"We had considered it," Barnes admitted. "The President had considered it."

"That's why you didn't inform the Russians."

"Exactly."

By now Ted was completely frustrated. He clenched his fists, as if he wanted to hit someone. He looked from one person to another. "But how did you *know?*"

"The first clue," Harry said, "came from the condition of the craft itself. It shows no damage whatever. Its condition is pristine. Yet any spacecraft that crashes in water will be damaged. Even at low entry velocities—say two hundred miles an hour—the surface of water is as hard as concrete. No matter how strong this craft is, you would expect some degree of damage from the impact with the water. Yet it has no damage."

"Meaning?"

"Meaning it didn't land in the water."

"I don't understand. It must have flown here—"

"—It didn't fly here. It *arrived* here."

"From where?"

"From the future," Harry said. "This is some kind of Earth craft that was— will be—made in the future, and has traveled backward in time, and appeared under our ocean, several hundred years ago."

"Why would people in the future do that?" Ted groaned. He was clearly unhappy to be deprived of his alien craft, his great historical moment. He slumped in a chair and stared dully at the monitor screens.

"I don't know why people in the future would do that," Harry said. "We're not there yet. Maybe it was an accident. Unintended."

"Let's go ahead and open it up," Barnes said.

"Opening, sir."

The robot hand moved forward, toward the "Open" button. The hand pressed several times. There was a clanking sound, but nothing happened.

"What's wrong?" Barnes said.

"Sir, we're not able to impact the button. The extensor arm is too large to fit inside the panel."

"Great."

"Shall I try the probe?"

"Try the probe."

The claw hand moved back, and a thin needle probe extended out toward the button. The probe slid forward, adjusted position delicately, touched the button. It pushed—and slipped off.

"Trying again, sir."

The probe again pressed the button, and again slid off.

"Sir, the surface is too slippery."

"Keep trying."

"You know," Ted said thoughtfully, "this is *still* a remarkable situation. In one sense, it's even more remarkable than contact with extraterrestrials. I was already quite certain that extraterrestrial life exists in the universe. But time travel! Frankly, as an astrophysicist I had my doubts. From everything we know, it's impossible, contradicted by the laws of physics. And yet now we have proof that time travel *is* possible—and that our own species will do it in the future!"

Ted was smiling, wide-eyed, and happy again. You had to admire him,

Norman thought—he was so wonderfully irrepressible.

"And here we are," Ted said, "on the threshold of our first contact with our species from the future! Think of it! We are going to meet ourselves from some future time!"

The probe pressed again, and again, without success.

"Sir, we cannot impact the button."

"I see that," Barnes said, standing up. "Okay, shut it down and get it out of there. Ted, looks like you're going to get your wish after all. We'll have to go in and open it up manually. Let's suit up."

Into the Ship

In the changing room in Cylinder A, Norman stepped into his suit. Tina and Edmunds helped fit the helmet over his head, and snap-locked the ring at the neck. He felt the heavy weight of the rebreather tanks on his back; the straps pressed into his shoulders. He tasted metallic air. There was a crackle as his helmet intercom came on.

The first words he heard were "What about 'At the threshold of a great opportunity for the human species'?" Norman laughed, grateful for the break in the tension.

"You find it funny?" Ted asked, offended.

Norman looked across the room at the suited man with "FIELDING" stenciled on his yellow helmet.

"No," Norman said. "I'm just nervous."

"Me, too," Beth said.

"Nothing to it," Barnes said. "Trust me."

"What are the three biggest lies in DH-8?" Harry said, and they laughed again.

They crowded together into the tiny airlock, bumping helmeted heads, and the bulkhead hatch to the left was sealed, the wheel spinning. Barnes said, "Okay, folks, just breathe easy." He opened the lower hatch, exposing black water. The water did not rise into the compartment. "The habitat's on positive pressure," Barnes said. "The level won't come up. Now watch me, and do this the way I do. You don't want to tear your suit." Moving awkwardly

323

with the weight of the tanks, he crouched down by the hatch, gripped the side handholds, and let go, disappearing with a soft splash.

One by one, they dropped down to the floor of the ocean. Norman gasped as near-freezing water enveloped his suit; immediately he heard the hum of a tiny fan as the electrical heaters in his suit activated. His feet touched soft muddy ground. He looked around in the darkness. He was standing beneath the habitat. Directly ahead, a hundred yards away, was the glowing rectangular grid. Barnes was already striding forward, leaning into the current, moving slowly like a man on the moon.

"Isn't this *fantastic?*"

"Calm down, Ted," Harry said.

Beth said, "Actually, it's odd how little life there is down here. Have you noticed? Not a sea fan, not a slug, not a sponge, not a solitary fish. Nothing but empty brown sea floor. This must be one of those dead spots in the Pacific."

A bright light came on behind him; Norman's own shadow was cast forward on the bottom. He looked back and saw Edmunds holding a camera and light in a bulky waterproof housing.

"We recording all this?"

"Yes, sir."

"Try not to fall down, Norman," Beth laughed.

"I'm trying."

They were closer now to the grid. Norman felt better seeing the other divers working there. To the right was the high fin, extending out of the coral, an enormous, smooth dark surface dwarfing them as it rose toward the surface.

Barnes led them past the fin and down into a tunnel cut in the coral. The tunnel was sixty feet long, narrow, strung with lights. They walked single file. It felt like going down into a mine, Norman thought.

"This what the divers cut?"

"That's right."

Norman saw a boxy, corrugated-steel structure surrounded by pressure tanks.

"Airlock ahead. We're almost there," Barnes said. "Everybody okay?"

"So far," Harry said.

They entered the airlock, and Barnes closed the door. Air hissed loudly. Norman watched the water recede, down past his faceplate, then his waist, his knees; then to the floor. The hissing stopped, and they passed through another door, sealing it behind them.

Norman turned to the metal hull of the spaceship. The robot had been moved aside. Norman felt very much as if he were standing alongside a big jetliner—a curved metal surface, and a flush door. The metal was a dull gray, which gave it an ominous quality. Despite himself, Norman was nervous. Listening to the way the others were breathing, he sensed they were nervous, too.

"Okay?" Barnes said. "Everybody here?"

Edmunds said, "Wait for video, please, sir."

"Okay. Waiting."

They all lined up beside the door, but they still had their helmets on. It wasn't going to be much of a picture, Norman thought.

Edmunds: "Tape is running."

Ted: "I'd like to say a few words."

Harry: "Jesus, Ted. Can't you ever let up?"

Ted: "I think it's important."

Harry: "Go ahead, make your speech."

Ted: "Hello. This is Ted Fielding, here at the door of the unknown spacecraft which has been discovered—"

Barnes: "Wait a minute, Ted. 'Here at the door of the unknown spacecraft' sounds like 'here at the tomb of the unknown soldier.' "

Ted: "You don't like it?"

Barnes: "Well, I think it has the wrong associations."

Ted: "I thought you would like it."

Beth: *"Can we just get on with it,* please?"

Ted: "Never mind."

Harry: "What, are you going to pout now?"

Ted: "Never mind. We'll do without any commentary on this historic moment."

Harry: "Okay, fine. Let's get it open."

Ted: "I think everybody knows how I feel. I feel that we should have some brief remarks for posterity."

Harry: "Well, *make* your goddamn remarks!"

Ted: "Listen, you son of a bitch, I've had about enough of your superior, know-it-all attitude—"

Barnes: "Stop tape, please."

Edmunds: "Tape is stopped, sir."

Barnes: "Let's everyone settle down."

Harry: "I consider all this ceremony utterly irrelevant."

Ted: "Well, it's not irrelevant; it's appropriate."

Barnes: "All right, I'll do it. Roll the tape."

Edmunds: "Tape is rolling."

Barnes: "This is Captain Barnes. We are now about to open the hatch cover. Present with me on this historic occasion are Ted Fielding, Norman Johnson, Beth Halpern, and Harry Adams."

Harry: "Why am I last?"

Barnes: "I did it left to right, Harry."

Harry: "Isn't it funny the only black man is named last?"

Barnes: "Harry, it's *left to right.* The way we're standing here."

Harry: *"And* after the only woman. I'm a full professor, Beth is only an assistant professor."

Beth: "Harry—"

Ted: "You know, Hal, perhaps we should be identified by our full titles and institutional affiliations—"

Harry: "—What's wrong with alphabetical order—"

Barnes: "—That's it! Forget it! No tape!"

Edmunds: "Tape is off, sir."

Barnes: "Jesus Christ."

He turned away from the group, shaking his helmeted head. He flipped up the metal plate, exposed the two buttons, and pushed one. A yellow light blinked "READY."

"Everybody stay on internal air," Barnes said.

They all continued to breathe from their tanks, in case the interior gases in the spacecraft were toxic.

"Everybody ready?"

"Ready."

Barnes pushed the button marked "OPEN."

A sign flashed: 'ADJUSTING ATMOSPHERE.' Then, with a rumble, the door slid open sideways, just like an airplane door. For a moment Norman could see nothing but blackness beyond. They moved forward cautiously, shone their lights through the open door, saw girders, a complex of metal tubes.

"Check the air, Beth."

Beth pulled the plunger on a small gas monitor in her hand. The readout screen glowed.

"Helium, oxygen, trace CO_2 and water vapor. The right proportions. It's pressurized atmosphere."

"The ship adjusted its own atmosphere?"

"Looks like it."

"Okay. One at a time."

Barnes removed his helmet first, breathed the air. "It seems okay. Metallic, a slight tingle, but okay." He took a few deep breaths, then nodded. The others removed their helmets, set them on the deck.

"That's better."

"Shall we go?"

"Why not?"

There was a brief hesitation, and then Beth stepped through quickly: "Ladies first."

The others followed her. Norman glanced back, saw all their yellow helmets lying on the floor. Edmunds, holding the video camera to her eye, said, "Go ahead, Dr. Johnson."

Norman turned, and stepped into the spacecraft.

Interior

They stood on a catwalk five feet wide, suspended high in the air. Norman shone his flashlight down: the beam glowed through forty feet of darkness before it splashed on the lower hull. Surrounding them, dimly visible in the darkness, was a dense network of struts and girders.

Beth said, "It's like being in an oil refinery." She shone her light on one steel beam. Stenciled was "AVR-09." All the stenciling was in English.

"Most of what you see is structural," Barnes said. "Cross-stress bracing for the outer hull. Gives tremendous support along all axes. The ship is very ruggedly built, as we suspected. Designed to take extraordinary stresses. There's probably another hull further in." Norman was reminded that Barnes had once been an aeronautical engineer.

"Not only that," Harry said, shining his light on the outer hull. "Look at this—a layer of lead."

"Radiation shield?"

"Must be. It's six inches thick."

"So this ship was built to handle a lot of radiation."

"A hell of a lot," Harry said.

There was a haze in the ship, and a faintly oily feel to the air. The metal girders seemed to be coated in oil, but when Norman touched them, the oil didn't come off on his fingers. He realized that the metal itself had an unusual texture: it was slick and slightly soft to the touch, almost rubbery.

"Interesting," Ted said. "Some kind of new material. We associate strength with hardness, but this metal—if it *is* metal—is both strong and soft. Materials technology has obviously advanced since our day."

"Obviously," Harry said.

"Well, it makes sense," Ted said. "If you think of America fifty years ago as compared with today, one of the biggest changes is the great variety of plastics and ceramics we have now that were not even imagined back then. . . ." Ted continued to talk, his voice echoing in the cavernous darkness. But Norman could hear the tension in his voice. Ted's whistling in the dark, he thought.

They moved deeper into the ship. Norman felt dizzy to be so high in the gloom. They came to a branchpoint in the catwalk. It was hard to see with all the pipes and struts—like being in a forest of metal.

"Which way?"

Barnes had a wrist compass; it glowed green. "Go right."

They followed the network of catwalks for ten minutes more. Gradually Norman could see that Barnes was right: there was a central cylinder constructed within the outer cylinder, and held away from it by a dense arrangement of girders and supports. A spacecraft within a spacecraft.

"Why would they build the ship like this?"

"You'd have to ask them."

"The reasons must have been compelling," Barnes said. "The power requirements for a double hull, with so much lead shielding . . . hard to imagine the engine you'd need to make something this big fly."

After three or four minutes, they arrived at the door on the inner hull. It looked like the outer door.

"Breathers back on?"

"I don't know. Can we risk it?"

Without waiting, Beth flipped up the panel of buttons, pressed "OPEN," and the door rumbled open. More darkness beyond. They stepped through. Norman felt softness underfoot; he shined his light down on beige carpeting.

Their flashlights crisscrossed the room, revealing a large, contoured beige console with three high-backed, padded seats. The room was clearly built for human beings.

"Must be the bridge or the cockpit."

But the curved consoles were completely blank. There was no instrumentation of any kind. And the seats were empty. They swung their beams back and forth in the darkness.

"Looks like a mockup, rather than the real thing."

"It *can't* be a mockup."

"Well, it looks like one."

Norman ran his hand over the smooth contours of the console. It was nicely molded, pleasant to feel. Norman pressed the surface, felt it bend to his touch. Rubbery again.

"Another new material."

Norman's flashlight showed a few artifacts. Taped to the far end of the console was a handmarked sign on a three-by-five filing card: It said, "GO BABY GO!" Nearby was a small plastic statuette of a cute animal that looked like a purple squirrel. The base said, "Lucky Lemontina." Whatever that meant.

"These seats leather?"

"Looks like it."

"Where are the damned controls?"

Norman continued to poke at the blank console, and suddenly the beige console surface took on depth, and appeared to contain instruments, screens. All the instrumentation was somehow *within* the surface of the console, like an optical illusion, or a hologram. Norman read the lettering above the instruments: "Pos Thrusters" . . . "F3 Piston Booster" . . . "Glider" . . . "Sieves" . . .

"More new technology," Ted said. "Reminiscent of liquid crystals, but far superior. Some kind of advanced opto-electronics."

Suddenly all the console screens glowed red, and there was a beeping sound. Startled, Norman jumped back: the control panel was coming to life.

"Watch it, everybody!"

A single bright lightning flash of intense white light filled the room, leaving a harsh afterimage.

"Oh God . . ."

Another flash—and another—and then the ceiling lights came on, evenly illuminating the room. Norman saw startled, frightened faces. He sighed, exhaling slowly.

"Jesus . . ."

"How the hell did that happen?" Barnes said.

"It was me," Beth said. "I pushed this button."

"Let's not go around pushing buttons, if you don't mind," Barnes said irritably.

"It was marked 'Room Lights.' It seemed an appropriate thing to do."

"Let's try to stay together on this," Barnes said.

"Well, Jesus, Hal—"

"Just don't push any more buttons, Beth!"

They were moving around the cabin, looking at the instrument panel, at the chairs. All of them, that is, all except for Harry. He stood very still in the middle of the room, not moving, and said, "Anybody see a date anywhere?"

"No date."

"There's got to be a date," Harry said, suddenly tense. "And we've got to find it. Because this is definitely an American spaceship from the future."

"What's it doing here?" Norman asked.

"Damned if I know," Harry said. He shrugged.

Norman frowned.

"What's wrong, Harry?"

"Nothing."

"Sure?"

"Yeah, sure."

Norman thought: He's figured out something, and it bothers him. But he's not saying what it is.

Ted said, "So this is what a time-travel machine looks like."

"I don't know," Barnes said. "If you ask me, this instrument panel looks like it's for flying, and this room looks like a flight deck."

Norman thought so, too: everything about the room reminded him of an airplane cockpit. The three chairs for pilot, copilot, navigator. The layout of the instrumentation. This was a machine that flew, he was sure of it. Yet something was odd. . . .

He slipped into one of the contoured chairs. The soft leather-like material was almost too comfortable. He heard a gurgling: water inside?

"I hope you're not going to fly this sucker," Ted laughed.

"No, no."

"What's that whirring noise?"

The chair gripped him. Norman had an instant of panic, feeling the chair move all around his body, squeezing his shoulders, wrapping around his hips. The leather padding slid around his head, covering his ears, drawing down over his forehead. He was sinking deeper, disappearing inside the chair itself, being swallowed up by it.

"Oh God . . ."

And then the chair snapped forward, pulling up tight before the control console. And the whirring stopped.

Then nothing.

"I think," Beth said, "that the chair thinks you are going to fly it."

"Umm," Norman said, trying to control his breathing, his racing pulse, "I wonder how I get out?"

The only part of his body still free were his hands. He moved his fingers, felt a panel of buttons on the arms of the chair. He pressed one.

The chair slid back, opened like a soft clam, released him. Norman climbed out, and looked back at the imprint of his body, slowly disappearing as the chair whirred and adjusted itself.

Harry poked one of the leather pads experimentally, heard the gurgle. "Water-filled."

"Makes perfect sense," Barnes said. "Water's not compressible. You can withstand enormous G-forces sitting in a chair like this."

"And the ship itself is built to take great strains," Ted said. "Maybe time travel is strenuous? Structurally strenuous?"

"Maybe." Norman was doubtful. "But I think Barnes is right—this is a machine that flew."

"Perhaps it just looks that way," Ted said. "After all, we know how to travel in space, but we don't know how to travel in time. We know that space and time are really aspects of the same thing, space-time. Perhaps you're required to fly in time just the way you fly in space. Maybe time travel and space travel are more similar than we think now."

"Aren't we forgetting something?" Beth said. "Where is everybody? If people flew this thing in either time or space, where are they?"

"Probably somewhere else on the ship."

"I'm not so sure," Harry said. "Look at this leather on these seats. It's brand-new."

"Maybe it was a new ship."

"No, I mean really *brand-new*. This leather doesn't show any scratches, any cuts, any coffee-cup spills or stains. There is nothing to suggest that these seats have ever been sat in."

"Maybe there wasn't any crew."

"Why would you have seats if there wasn't any crew?"

"Maybe they took the crew out at the last minute. It seems they were worried about radiation. The inner hull's lead-shielded, too."

"Why should there be radiation associated with time travel?"

"I know," Ted said. "Maybe the ship got launched by accident. Maybe the ship was on the launch pad and somebody pressed the button before the crew got aboard so the ship took off empty."

"You mean, oops, wrong button?"

"That'd be a hell of a mistake," Norman said.

Barnes shook his head. "I'm not buying it. For one thing, a ship this big could never be launched from Earth. It had to be built and assembled in orbit, and launched from space."

"What do you make of this?" Beth said, pointing to another console near the rear of the flight deck. There was a fourth chair, drawn up close to the console.

The leather was wrapped around a human form.

"No kidding . . ."

"There's a man in there?"

"Let's have a look." Beth pushed the armrest buttons. The chair whirred back from the console and unwrapped itself. They saw a man, staring forward, his eyes open.

"My God, after all these years, perfectly preserved," Ted said.

"You would expect that," Harry said. "Considering he's a mannequin."

"But he's so lifelike—"

"Give our descendants some credit for advances," Harry said. "They're half a century ahead of us." He pushed the mannequin forward, exposing an umbilicus running out the back, at the base of the hips.

"Wires . . ."

"Not wires," Ted said. "Glass. Optical cables. This whole ship uses optical technology, and not electronics."

"In any case, it's one mystery solved," Harry said, looking at the dummy. "Obviously this craft was built to be a manned ship, but it was sent out unmanned."

"Why?"

"Probably the intended voyage was too dangerous. They sent an unmanned vessel first, before they sent a manned vessel."

Beth said, "And where did they send it?"

"With time travel, you don't send it to a *where*. You send it to a *when*."

"Okay. Then to *when* did they send it?"

Harry shrugged. "No information yet," he said.

That diffidence again, Norman thought. What was Harry really thinking?

"Well, this craft is half a mile long," Barnes said. "We have a lot more to see."

"I wonder if they had a flight recorder," Norman said.

"You mean like a commercial airliner?"

"Yes. Something to record the activity of the ship on its voyage."

"They must have," Harry said. "Trace the dummy cable back, you're sure to find it. I'd like to see that recorder, too. In fact, I would say it is crucial."

Norman was looking at the console, lifting up a keyboard panel. "Look here," he said. "I found a date."

They clustered around. There was a stamp in the plastic beneath the keyboard. "Intel Inc. Made in U.S.A. Serial No: 98004077 8/5/43."

"August 5, 2043?"

"Looks like it."

"So we're walking through a ship fifty-odd years before it's going to be built. . . ."

"This is giving me a headache."

"Look here." Beth had moved forward from the console deck, into what looked like living quarters. There were twenty bunk beds.

"Crew of twenty? If it took three people to fly it, what were the other seventeen for?"

Nobody had an answer to that.

Next, they entered a large kitchen, a toilet, living quarters. Everything was new and sleekly designed, but recognizable for what it was.

"You know, Hal, this is a lot more comfortable than DH-8."

"Yes, maybe we should move in here."

"Absolutely not," Barnes said. "We're studying this ship, not living in it. We've got a lot more work to do before we even begin to know what this is all about."

"It'd be more efficient to live here while we explore it."

"I don't want to live here," Harry said. "It gives me the creeps."

"Me too," Beth said.

They had been aboard the ship for an hour now, and Norman's feet hurt. That was another thing he hadn't anticipated: while exploring a large spacecraft from the future, your feet could begin to hurt.

But Barnes continued on.

Leaving the crew quarters, they entered a vast area of narrow walkways set out between great sealed compartments that stretched ahead as far as they could see. The compartments turned out to be storage bays of immense size. They opened one bay and found it was filled with heavy plastic containers, which looked rather like the loading containers of contemporary airliners, except many times larger. They opened one container.

"No kidding," Barnes said, peering inside.

"What is it?"

"Food."

The food was wrapped in layers of lead foil and plastic, like NASA rations. Ted picked one up. "Food from the future!" he said, and smacked his lips.

"You going to eat that?" Harry said.

"Absolutely," Ted said. "You know, I once had a bottle of Dom Pérignon 1897, but this will be the first time I've ever had anything to eat from the future, from 2043."

"It's also three hundred years old," Harry said.

"Maybe you'll want to film this," Ted said to Edmunds. "Me eating."

Edmunds dutifully put the camera to her eye, flicked on the light.

"Let's not do that now," Barnes said. "We have other things to accomplish."

"This is human interest," Ted said.

"Not now," Barnes said firmly.

He opened a second storage container, and a third. They all contained food. They moved to the next storage bay and opened more containers.

"It's all food. Nothing but food."

The ship had traveled with an enormous amount of food. Even allowing for a crew of twenty, it was enough food for a voyage of several years.

They were getting very tired; it was a relief when Beth found a button, said, "I wonder what this does—"

Barnes said, "Beth—"

And the walkway began to move, rubber tread rolling forward with a slight hum.

"Beth, I want you to stop pushing every damn button you see."

But nobody else objected. It was a relief to ride the walkway past dozens of identical storage bays. Finally they came to a new section, much farther forward. Norman guessed by now they were a quarter of a mile from the crew compartment in the back. That meant they were roughly in the middle of the huge ship.

And here they found a room with life-support equipment, and twenty hanging spacesuits.

"Bingo," Ted said. "It's finally clear. This ship is intended to travel to the stars."

The others murmured, excited by the possibility. Suddenly it all made sense: the great size, the vastness of the ship, the complexity of the control consoles. . . .

"Oh, for Christ's sake," Harry said. "It *can't* have been made to travel to the stars. This is obviously a conventional spacecraft, although very large. And at conventional speeds, the nearest star is two hundred and fifty years away."

"Maybe they had new technology."

"Where is it? There's no evidence of new technology."

"Well, maybe it's—"

"Face the facts, Ted," Harry said. "Even with this huge size, the ship is only provisioned for a few years: fifteen or twenty years, at most. How far could it go in that time? Barely out of the solar system, right?"

Ted nodded glumly. "It's true. It took the Voyager spacecraft five years to reach Jupiter, nine years to reach Uranus. In fifteen years . . . Maybe they were going to Pluto."

"Why would anyone want to go to Pluto?"

"We don't know yet, but—"

The radios squawked. The voice of Tina Chan said, "Captain Barnes, surface wants you for a secure encrypted communication, sir."

"Okay," Barnes said. "It's time to go back, anyway."

They headed back, through the vast ship, to the main entrance.

Space and Time

They were sitting in the lounge of DH-8, watching the divers work on the grid. Barnes was in the next cylinder, talking to the surface. Levy was cooking lunch, or dinner—a meal, anyway. They were all getting confused about what the Navy people called "surface time."

"Surface time doesn't matter down here," Edmunds said, in her precise librarian's voice. "Day or night, it just doesn't make any difference. You get used to it."

They nodded vaguely. Everyone was tired, Norman saw. The strain, the tension of the exploration, had taken its toll. Beth had already drifted off to sleep, feet up on the coffee table, her muscular arms folded across her chest.

Outside the window, three small submarines had come down and were hovering over the grid. Several divers were clustered around; others were heading back to the divers' habitat, DH-7.

"Looks like something's up," Harry said.

"Something to do with Barnes's call?"

"Could be." Harry was still preoccupied, distracted. "Where's Tina Chan?"

"She must be with Barnes. Why?"

"I need to talk to her."

"What about?" Ted said.

"It's personal," Harry said.

Ted raised his eyebrows but said nothing more. Harry left, going into D Cyl. Norman and Ted were alone.

"He's a strange fellow," Ted said.

"Is he?"

"You know he is, Norman. Arrogant, too. Probably because he's black. Compensating, don't you think?"

"I don't know."

"I'd say he has a chip on his shoulder," Ted said. "He seems to resent everything about this expedition." He sighed. "Of course, mathematicians are all strange. He's probably got no sort of life at all, I mean a private life, women and so forth. Did I tell you I married again?"

"I read it somewhere," Norman said.

"She's a television reporter," Ted said. "Wonderful woman." He smiled. "When we got married, she gave me this Corvette. Beautiful '58 Corvette, as a wedding present. You know that nice fire-engine red color they had in the fifties? That color." Ted paced around the room, glanced over at Beth. "I just think this is all unbelievably exciting. I couldn't possibly sleep."

Norman nodded. It was interesting how different they all were, he thought. Ted, eternally optimistic, with the bubbling enthusiasm of a child. Harry, with the cold, critical demeanor, the icy mind, the unblinking eye. Beth, not so intellectual or so cerebral. At once more physical and more emotional. That was why, though they were all exhausted, only Beth could sleep.

"Say, Norman," Ted said. "I thought you said this was going to be scary."

"I thought it would be," Norman said.

"Well," Ted said. "Of all the people who could be wrong about this expedition, I'm glad it was you."

"I am, too."

"Although I can't imagine why you would select a man like Harry Adams for this team. Not that he isn't distinguished, but . . ."

Norman didn't want to talk about Harry. "Ted, remember back on the ship, when you said space and time are aspects of the same thing?"

"Space-time, yes."

"I've never really understood that."

"Why? It's quite straightforward."

"You can explain it to me?"

"Sure."

"In English?" Norman said.

"You mean, explain it without mathematics?"

"Yes."

"Well, I'll try." Ted frowned, but Norman knew he was pleased; Ted loved to lecture. He paused for a moment, then said, "Okay. Let's see where we need to begin. You're familiar with the idea that gravity is just geometry?"

"No."

"Curvature of space and time?"

"Not really, no."

"Uh. Einstein's general relativity?"

"Sorry," Norman said.

"Never mind," Ted said. There was a bowl of fruit on the table. Ted emptied the bowl, setting the fruit on the table.

"Okay. This table is space. Nice, flat space."

"Okay," Norman said.

Ted began to position the pieces of fruit. "This orange is the sun. And these are the planets, which move in circles around the sun. So we have the solar system on this table."

"Okay."

"Fine," Ted said. "Now, the sun"—he pointed to the orange in the center of the table—"is very large, so it has a lot of gravity."

"Right."

Ted gave Norman a ball bearing. "This is a spaceship. I want you to send it through the solar system, so it passes very close to the sun. Okay?"

Norman took the ball bearing and rolled it so it passed close to the orange. "Okay."

"You notice that your ball rolled straight across the flat table."

"Right."

"But in real life, what would happen to your spacecraft when it passed near the sun?"

"It would get sucked into the sun."

"Yes. We say it would 'fall into' the sun. The spacecraft would curve inward from a straight line and hit the sun. But your spacecraft didn't."

"No."

"So we know that the flat table is wrong," Ted said. "Real space can't be flat like the table."

"It can't?"

"No," Ted said.

He took the empty bowl and set the orange in the bottom. "Now roll your ball straight across past the sun."

Norman flicked the ball bearing into the bowl. The ball curved, and spiraled down the inside of the bowl until it hit the orange.

"Okay," Ted said. "The spacecraft hit the sun, just like it would in real life."

"But if I gave it enough speed," Norman said, "it'd go right past it. It'd roll down and up the far side of the bowl and out again."

"Correct," Ted said. "Also like real life. If the spacecraft has enough velocity, it will escape the gravitational field of the sun."

"Right."

"So," Ted said, "what we are showing is that a spacecraft passing the sun in real life behaves as if it were entering a curved region of space around the sun. Space around the sun is curved like this bowl."

"Okay . . ."

"And if your ball had the right speed, it wouldn't escape from the bowl, but instead would just spiral around endlessly inside the rim of the bowl. And that's what the planets are doing. They are endlessly spiraling inside the bowl created by the sun."

He put the orange back on the table. "In reality, you should imagine the table is made out of rubber and the planets are all making dents in the rubber as they sit there. That's what space is really like. Real space is curved—and the curvature changes with the amount of gravity."

"Yes . . ."

"So," Ted said, "space is curved by gravity."

"Okay."

"And that means that you can think of gravity as nothing more than the curvature of space. The Earth has gravity *because* the Earth curves the space around it."

"Okay."

"Except it's not that simple," Ted said.

Norman sighed. "I didn't think it would be."

Harry came back into the room, looked at the fruit on the table, but said nothing.

"Now," Ted said, "when you roll your ball bearing across the bowl, you notice that it not only spirals down, but it also goes faster, right?"

"Yes."

"Now, when an object goes faster, time on that object passes slower. Einstein proved that early in the century. What it means is that you can think of the curvature of space as also representing a curvature of time. The deeper the curve in the bowl, the slower time passes."

Harry said, "Well . . ."

"Layman's terms," Ted said. "Give the guy a break."

"Yeah," Norman said, "give the guy a break."

Ted held up the bowl. "Now, if you're doing all this mathematically, what you find is that the curved bowl is neither space nor time, but the combination of both, which is called space-time. This bowl is space-time, and objects moving on it are moving in space-time. We don't think about movement that way, but that's really what's happening."

"It is?"

"Sure. Take baseball."

"Idiot game," Harry said. "I hate games."

"You know baseball?" Ted said to Norman.

"Yes," Norman said.

"Okay. Imagine the batter hits a line drive to the center fielder. The ball goes almost straight out and takes, say, half a second."

"Right."

"Now imagine the batter hits a high pop fly to the same center fielder. This time the ball goes way up in the air, and it takes six seconds before the center fielder catches it."

"Okay."

"Now, the paths of the two balls—the line drive and the pop fly—look very different to us. But both these balls moved exactly the same *in space-time.*"

"No," Norman said.

"Yes," Ted said. "And in a way, you already know it. Suppose I ask you to hit a high pop fly to the center fielder, but to make it reach the fielder in half a second instead of six seconds."

"That's impossible," Norman said.

"Why? Just hit the pop fly harder."

"If I hit it harder, it will go higher and end up taking longer."

"Okay, then hit a low line drive that takes six seconds to reach center field."

"I can't do that, either."

"Right," Ted said. "So what you are telling me is that you can't make the ball do anything you want. There is a fixed relationship governing the path of the ball through space and time."

"Sure. Because the Earth has gravity."

"Yes," Ted said, "and we've already agreed that gravity is a curvature of space-time, like the curve of this bowl. Any baseball on Earth must move along the same curve of space-time, as this ball bearing moves along this bowl. Look." He put the orange back in the bowl. "Here's the Earth." He put two fingers on opposite sides of the orange. "Here's batter and fielder. Now, roll the ball bearing from one finger to the other, and you'll find you have to accommodate the curve of the bowl. Either you flick the ball lightly and it will roll close to the orange, or you can give it a big flick and it will go way up the side of the bowl, before falling down again to the other side. But you can't make this ball bearing do anything you want, because the ball bearing is moving along the curved bowl. And that's what your baseball is really doing—it's moving on curved space-time."

Norman said, "I *sort of* get it. But what does this have to do with time travel?"

"Well, we think the gravitational field of the Earth is strong—it hurts us when we fall down—but in reality it's very weak. It's almost nonexistent. So space-time around the Earth isn't very curved. Space-time is much more curved around the sun. And in other parts of the universe, it's *very* curved, producing a sort of roller-coaster ride, and all sorts of distortions of time may occur. In fact, if you consider a black hole—"

He broke off.

"Yes, Ted? A black hole?"

"Oh my God," Ted said softly.

Harry pushed his glasses up on his nose and said, "Ted, for once in your life, you just might be right."

They both grabbed for paper, began scribbling.

"It couldn't be a Schwartzschild hole—"

"—No, no. Have to be rotating—"

"—Angular momentum would assure that—"

"—And you couldn't approach the singularity—"

"—No, the tidal forces—"

"—rip you apart—"

"But if you just dipped below the event horizon . . ."

"Is it possible? Did they have the nerve?"

The two fell silent, making calculations, muttering to themselves.

"What is it about a black hole?" Norman said. But they weren't listening to him any more.

The intercom clicked. Barnes said, "Attention. This is the Captain speaking. I want all hands in the conference room on the double."

"We're *in* the conference room," Norman said.

"On the double. Now."

"We're already there, Hal."

"That is all," Barnes said, and the intercom clicked off.

The Conference

"**I**'ve just been on the scrambler with Admiral Spaulding of CincComPac Honolulu," Barnes said. "Apparently Spaulding just learned that I had taken civilians to saturated depths for a project about which he knew nothing. He wasn't happy about it."

There was a silence. They all looked at him.

"He demanded that all the civilians be sent up topside."

Good, Norman thought. He had been disappointed by what they had found so far. The prospect of spending another seventy-two hours in this humid, claustrophobic environment while they investigated an empty space vehicle did not appeal to him.

"I thought," Ted said, "we had direct authorization from the President."

"We do," Barnes said, "but there is the question of the storm."

"What storm?" Harry said.

"They're reporting fifteen-knot winds and southeast swells on the surface. It looks like a Pacific cyclone is headed our way and will reach us within twenty-four hours."

"There's going to be a storm here?" Beth said.

"Not *here*," Barnes said. "Down here we won't feel anything, but it'll be rough on the surface. All our surface support ships may have to pull out and steam for protected harbors in Tonga."

"So we'd be left alone down here?"

"For twenty-four to forty-eight hours, yes. That wouldn't be a problem— we're entirely self-sufficient—but Spaulding is nervous about pulling surface support when there are civilians below. I want to know your feelings. Do you want to stay down and continue exploring the ship, or leave?"

"Stay. Definitely," Ted said.

Barnes said, "Beth?"

"I came here to investigate unknown life," Beth said, "but there isn't any life on that ship. It just isn't what I thought it would be—hoped it would be. I say we go."

Barnes said, "Norman?"

"Let's admit the truth," Norman said. "We're not really trained for a saturated environment and we're not really comfortable down here. At least I'm not. And we're not the best people to evaluate this spacecraft. At this point, the Navy'd be much better off with a team of NASA engineers. I say, go."

"Harry?"

"Let's get the hell out," Harry said.

"Any particular reason?" Barnes said.

"Call it intuition."

Ted said, "I can't believe you would say that, Harry, just when we have this fabulous new idea about the ship—"

"That's beside the point now," Barnes said crisply. "I'll make the arrangements with the surface to pull us out in another twelve hours."

Ted said, "God *damn* it!"

But Norman was looking at Barnes. Barnes wasn't upset. He wants to leave, he thought. He's looking for an excuse to leave, and we're providing his excuse.

"Meantime," Barnes said, "we can make one and perhaps even two more trips to the ship. We'll rest for the next two hours, and then go back. That's all for now."

"I have more I'd like to say—"

"That's *all*, Ted. The vote's been taken. Get some rest."

As they headed toward their bunks, Barnes said, "Beth, I'd like a word with you, please."

"What about?"

"Beth, when we go back to the ship, I don't want you pushing every button you come across."

"All I did was turn on the lights, Hal."

"Yes, but you didn't know that when you—"

"—Sure I did. The button said 'Room Lights.' It was pretty clear."

As they moved off, they heard Beth say, "I'm not one of your little Navy people you can order around, Hal—" and then Barnes said something else, and the voices faded.

"Damn it," Ted said. He kicked one of the iron walls; it rang hollowly. They passed into C Cylinder, on their way to the bunks. "I can't believe you people want to leave," Ted said. "This is *such* an exciting discovery. How can you walk away from it? Especially you, Harry. The mathematical possibilities alone! The theory of the black hole—"

"—I'll tell you why," Harry said. "I want to go because Barnes wants to go."

"Barnes doesn't want to go," Ted said. "Why, he put it to a vote—"

"—I know what he did. But Barnes doesn't want to look as if he's made the wrong decision in the eyes of his superiors, or as if he's backing down. So he let us decide. But I'm telling you, Barnes wants to go."

Norman was surprised: the cliché image of mathematicians was that they had their heads in the clouds, were absent-minded, inattentive. But Harry was astute; he didn't miss a thing.

"Why would Barnes want to go?" Ted said.

"I think it's clear," Harry said. "Because of the storm on the surface."

"The storm isn't here yet," Ted said.

"No," Harry said. "And when it comes, we don't know how long it will last."

"Barnes said twenty-four to forty-eight hours—"

"Neither Barnes nor anyone else can predict how long the storm will last," Harry said. "What if it lasts five days?"

"We can hold out that long. We have air and supplies for five days. What're you so worried about?"

"I'm not worried," Harry said. "But I think Barnes is worried."

"Nothing will go wrong, for Christ's sake," Ted said. "I think we should stay." And then there was a squishing sound. They looked down at the all-weather carpeting at their feet. The carpet was dark, soaked.

"What's that?"

"I'd say it was water," Harry said.

"*Salt* water?" Ted said, bending over, touching the damp spot. He licked his finger. "Doesn't taste salty."

From above them, a voice said, "That's because it's urine."

Looking up, they saw Teeny Fletcher standing on a platform among a network of pipes near the curved top of the cylinder. "Everything's under control, gentlemen. Just a small leak in the liquid waste disposal pipe that goes to the H_2O recycler."

"Liquid *waste?*" Ted was shaking his head.

"Just a small leak," Fletcher said. "No problem, sir." She sprayed one of the pipes with white foam from a spray canister. The foam sputtered and hardened on the pipe. "We just urethane the suckers when we get them. Makes a perfect seal."

"How often do you get these leaks?" Harry said.

"Liquid *waste?*" Ted said again.

"Hard to say, Dr. Adams. But don't worry. Really."

"I feel sick," Ted said.

Harry slapped him on the back. "Come on, it won't kill you. Let's get some sleep."

"I think I'm going to throw up."

They went into the sleeping chamber. Ted immediately ran off to the showers; they heard him coughing and gagging.

"Poor Ted," Harry said, shaking his head.

Norman said, "What's all this business about a black hole, anyway?"

"A black hole," Harry said, "is a dead, compressed star. Basically, a star is like a big beach ball inflated by the atomic explosions occurring inside it. When a star gets old, and runs out of nuclear fuel, the ball collapses to a much smaller size. If it collapses enough, it becomes so dense and it has so much gravity that it keeps on collapsing, squeezing down on itself until it is *very* dense and *very* small—only a few miles in diameter. Then it's a black hole. Nothing else in the universe is as dense as a black hole."

"So they're black because they're dead?"

"No. They're black because they trap all the light. Black holes have so much gravity, they pull everything into them, like vacuum cleaners—all the surrounding interstellar gas and dust, and even light itself. They just suck it right up."

"They suck up *light?*" Norman said. He found it hard to think of that.

"Yes."

"So what were you two so excited about, with your calculations?"

"Oh, it's a long story, and it's just speculation." Harry yawned. "It probably won't amount to anything, anyway. Talk about it later?"

"Sure," Norman said.

Harry rolled over, went to sleep. Ted was still in the showers, hacking and sputtering. Norman went back to D Cyl, to Tina's console.

"Did Harry find you all right?" he said. "I know he wanted to see you."

"Yes, sir. And I have the information he requested now. Why? Did you want to make out your will, too?"

Norman frowned.

"Dr. Adams said he didn't have a will and he wanted to make one. He seemed to feel it was quite urgent. Anyway, I checked with the surface and you can't do it. It's some legal problem about it being in your own handwriting; you can't transmit your will over electronic lines."

"I see."

"I'm sorry, Dr. Johnson. Should I tell the others as well?"

"No," Norman said. "Don't bother the others. We'll be going to the surface soon. Right after we have one last look at the ship."

The Large Glass

This time they split up inside the spaceship. Barnes, Ted, and Edmunds continued forward in the vast cargo bays, to search the parts of the ship that were still unexplored. Norman, Beth, and Harry stayed in what they now called the flight deck, looking for the flight recorder.

Ted's parting words were "It is a far, far better thing that I do, than I have ever done." Then he set off with Barnes.

Edmunds left them a small video monitor so they could see the progress of the other team in the forward section of the ship. And they could hear: Ted chattered continuously to Barnes, giving his views about structural features of the ship. The design of the big cargo bays reminded Ted of the stonework of the ancient Mycenaeans in Greece, particularly the Lion Gate ramp at Mycenae. . . .

"Ted has more irrelevant facts at his fingertips than any man I know," Harry said. "Can we turn the volume down?"

Yawning, Norman turned the monitor down. He was tired. The bunks in DH-8 were damp, the electric blankets heavy and clinging. Sleep had been almost impossible. And then Beth had come storming in after her talk with Barnes.

She was still angry now. "God damn Barnes," she said. "Where does he get off?"

"He's doing the best he can, like everyone else," Norman said.

She spun. "You know, Norman, sometimes you're too psychological and understanding. The man is an idiot. A complete *idiot.*"

"Let's just find the flight recorder, shall we?" Harry said. "That's the important thing now." Harry was following the umbilicus cable that ran out the back of the mannequin, into the floor. He was lifting up floor panels, tracing the wires aft.

"I'm sorry," Beth said, "but he wouldn't speak like that to a man. Certainly not to Ted. Ted's hogging the whole show, and I don't see why he should be allowed to."

"What does Ted have to do with—" Norman began.

"—The man is a parasite, that's what he is. He takes the ideas of others and promotes them as his own. Even the way he quotes famous sayings—it's outrageous."

"You feel he takes other people's ideas?" Norman said.

"Listen, back on the surface, I mentioned to Ted that we ought to have some words ready when we opened this thing. And the next thing I know, Ted's making up quotes and positioning himself in front of the camera."

"Well . . ."

"Well *what*, Norman? Don't *well* me, for Christ's sake. It was my idea and he took it without so much as a thank you."

"Did you say anything to him about it?" Norman said.

"No, I did not say anything to him about it. I'm sure he wouldn't remember if I did; he'd go, 'Did you say that, Beth? I suppose you might have mentioned something like that, yes. . . .' "

"I still think you should talk to him."

"Norman, you're not listening to me."

"If you talked to him, at least you wouldn't be so angry about it now."

"Shrink talk," she said, shaking her head. "Look, Ted does whatever he wants on this expedition, he makes his stupid speeches, whatever he wants. But *I* go through the door first and Barnes gives me hell. Why shouldn't I go first? What's wrong with a woman being the first, for once in the history of science?"

"Beth—"

"—And then I had the gall to turn on the lights. You know what Barnes said about that? He said I might have started a short-circuit and put us all in jeopardy. He said I didn't know what I was doing. He said I was *impulsive*. Jesus. Impulsive. Stone-age military cretin."

"Turn the volume back up," Harry said. "I'd rather hear Ted."

"Come on, guys."

"We're all under a lot of pressure, Beth," Norman said. "It's going to affect everybody in different ways."

She glared at Norman. "You're saying Barnes was right?"

"I'm saying we're all under pressure. Including him. Including you."

"Jesus, you men always stick together. You know why I'm still an assistant professor and not tenured?"

"Your pleasant, easygoing personality?" Harry said.

"I can do without this. I really can."

"Beth," Harry said, "you see the way these cables are going? They're running toward that bulkhead there. See if they go up the wall on the other side of the door."

"You trying to get rid of me?"

"If possible."

She laughed, breaking the tension. "All right, I'll look on the other side of the door."

When she was gone, Harry said, "She's pretty worked up."

Norman said, "You know the Ben Stone story?"

"Which one?"

"Beth did her graduate work in Stone's lab."

"Oh."

Benjamin Stone was a biochemist at BU. A colorful, engaging man, Stone had a reputation as a good researcher who used his graduate students like lab assistants, taking their results as his own. In this exploitation of others' work, Stone was not unique in the academic community, but he proceeded a little more ruthlessly than his colleagues.

"Beth was living with him as well."

"Uh-huh."

"Back in the early seventies. Apparently, she did a series of important experiments on the energetics of ciliary inclusion bodies. They had a big argument, and Stone broke off his relationship with her. She left the lab, and he published five papers—all her work—without her name on them."

"Very nice," Harry said. "So now she lifts weights?"

"Well, she feels mistreated, and I can see her point."

"Yeah," Harry said. "But the thing is, lie down with dogs, get up with fleas, you know what I mean?"

"Jesus," Beth said, returning. "This is like 'The girl who's raped is always asking for it,' is that what you're saying?"

"No," Harry said, still lifting up floor panels, following the wires. "But sometimes you gotta ask what the girl is doing in a dark alley at three in the morning in a bad part of town."

"I was in love with him."

"It's still a bad part of town."

"I was twenty-two years old."

"How old do you have to be?"

"Up yours, Harry."

Harry shook his head. "You find the wires, Butch?"

"Yes, I found the wires. They go into some kind of a glass grid."

"Let's have a look," Norman said, going next door. He'd seen flight recorders before; they were long rectangular metal boxes, reminiscent of safe-deposit boxes, painted red or bright orange. If this was—

He stopped.

He was looking at a transparent glass cube one foot on each side. Inside the cube was an intricate grid arrangement of fine glowing blue lines. Between the glowing lines, blue lights flickered intermittently. There were two pressure gauges mounted on top of the cube, and three pistons; and there were a series of silver stripes and rectangles on the outer surface on the left side. It didn't look like anything he had seen before.

"Interesting." Harry peered into the cube. "Some kind of optronic memory, is my guess. We don't have anything like it." He touched the silver stripes on the outside. "Not paint, it's some plastic material. Probably machine-readable."

"By what? Certainly not us."

"No. Probably a robot recovery device of some kind."

"And the pressure gauges?"

"The cube is filled with some kind of gas, under pressure. Maybe it contains biological components, to attain that compactness. In any case, I'll bet this large glass is a memory device."

"A flight recorder?"

"Their equivalent, yes."

"How do we access it?"

"Watch this," Beth said, going back to the flight deck. She began pushing sections of the console, activating it. "Don't tell Barnes," she said over her shoulder.

"How do you know where to press?"

"I don't think it matters," she said. "I think the console can sense where you are."

"The control panel keeps track of the pilot?"

"Something like that."

In front of them, a section of the console glowed, making a screen, yellow on black.

RV-LHOOQ   DCOM1   U.S.S. STAR VOYAGER

Then nothing.

Harry said, "Now we'll get the bad news."

"What bad news?" Norman said. And he wondered: Why had Harry stayed behind to look for the flight recorder, instead of going with Ted and Barnes to explore the rest of the ship? Why was he so interested in the past history of this vessel?

"Maybe it won't be bad," Harry said.

"Why do you think it might be?"

"Because," Harry said, "if you consider it logically, something vitally important is missing from this ship—"

At that moment, the screen filled with columns:

346

SHIP SYSTEMS

LIFE SYSTEMS

DATA SYSTEMS

QUARTERMASTER

FLIGHT RECORDS

CORE OPERATIONS

DECK CONTROL

INTEGRATION (DIRECT)

LSS TEST 1.0

LSS TEST 2.0

LSS TEST 3.0

PROPULSION SYSTEMS

WASTE MANAG (V9)

STATUS OM2 (OUTER)

STATUS OM3 (INNER)

STATUS OM4 (FORE)

STATUS DV7 (AFT)

STATUS V (SUMMA)

STATUS COMREC (2)

LINE A9-11

LINE A12-BX

STABILIX

"What's your pleasure?" Beth said, hands on the console.

"Flight records," Harry said. He bit his lip.

FLIGHT DATA SUMMARIES RV-LHOOQ

FDS 01/01/43–12/31/45

FDS 01/01/46–12/31/48

FDS 01/01/49–12/31/51

FDS 01/01/52–12/31/53

FDS 01/01/54–12/31/54

FDS 01/01/55–06/31/55

FDS 07/01/55–12/31/55

FDS 01/01/56–01/31/56

FDS 02/01/56-ENTRY EVENT

FDS ENTRY EVENT

FDS ENTRY EVENT SUMMARY

8&6 !!OZ/010/Odd-000/XXX/X

F$S XXX/X%ˆ/XXX-X@X/X!X/X

"What do you make of that?" Norman said.

Harry was peering at the screen. "As you see, the earliest records are in three-year intervals. Then they're shorter, one year, then six months, and finally one month. Then this entry event business."

"So they were recording more and more carefully," Beth said. "As the ship approached the entry event, whatever it was."

"I have a pretty good idea what it was," Harry said. "I just can't believe that—let's start. How about entry event summary?"

Beth pushed buttons.

On the screen, a field of stars, and around the edges of the field, a lot of numbers. It was three-dimensional, giving the illusion of depth.

"Holographic?"

"Not exactly. But similar."

"Several large-magnitude stars there . . ."

"Or planets."

"What planets?"

"I don't know. This is one for Ted," Harry said. "He may be able to identify the image. Let's go on."

He touched the console; the screen changed.

"More stars."

"Yeah, and more numbers."

The numbers around the edges of the screen were flickering, changing rapidly. "The stars don't seem to be moving, but the numbers are changing."

"No, look. The stars are moving, too."

They could see that all the stars were moving away from the center of the screen, which was now black and empty.

"No stars in the center, and everything moving away . . ." Harry said thoughtfully.

The stars on the outside were moving very quickly, streaking outward. The black center was expanding.

"Why is it empty like that in the center, Harry?" Beth said.

"I don't think it is empty."

"I can't see anything."

"No, but it's not empty. In just a minute we should see— There!"

A dense white cluster of stars suddenly appeared in the center of the screen. The cluster expanded as they watched.

It was a strange effect, Norman thought. There was still a distinct black ring that expanded outward, with stars on the outside and on the inside. It felt as if they were flying through a giant black donut.

"My God," Harry said softly. "Do you know what you are looking at?"

"No," Beth said. "What's that cluster of stars in the center?"

"It's another universe."

"It's *what?*"

"Well, okay. It's *probably* another universe. Or it might be a different region of our own universe. Nobody really knows for sure."

"What's the black donut?" Norman said.

"It's not a donut. It's a black hole. What you are seeing is the recording made as this spacecraft went through a black hole and entered into another— Is someone calling?" Harry turned, cocked his head. They fell silent, but heard nothing.

"What do you mean, another universe—"

"—Sssssh."

A short silence. And then a faint voice crying "Hellooo . . ."

"Who's that?" Norman said, straining to listen. The voice was so soft. But it sounded human. And maybe more than one voice. It was coming from somewhere inside the spacecraft.

"Yoo-hoo! Anybody there? Hellooo."

"Oh, for God's sake," Beth said. "It's *them,* on the monitor."

She turned up the volume on the little monitor Edmunds had left behind.

On the screen they saw Ted and Barnes, standing in a room somewhere and shouting. "Hellooo . . . Hel-lo-oooo."

"Can we talk back?"

"Yes. Press that button on the side."

Norman said, "We hear you."

"High damn time!" Ted.

"All right, now," Barnes said. "Listen up."

"What are you people *doing* back there?" Ted said.

"Listen up," Barnes said. He stepped to one side, revealing a piece of multicolored equipment. "We now know what this ship is for."

"So do we," Harry said.

"We do?" Beth and Norman said together.

But Barnes wasn't listening. "And the ship seems to have picked up something on its travels."

"Picked up something? What is it?"

"I don't know," Barnes said. "But it's something alien."

"Something Alien"

The moving walkway carried them past endless large cargo bays. They were going forward, to join Barnes and Ted and Edmunds. And to see their alien discovery.

"Why would anyone send a spaceship through a black hole?" Beth asked.

"Because of gravity," Harry said. "You see, black holes have so much gravity they distort space and time incredibly. You remember how Ted was saying that planets and stars make dents in the fabric of space-time? Well, black holes make *tears* in the fabric. And some people think it's possible to fly through those tears, into another universe, or another part of our universe. Or to another time."

"Another time!"

"That's the idea," Harry said.

"Are you people *coming?*" Barnes's tinny voice, on the monitor.

"In transit now," Beth said, glowering at the screen.

"He can't see you," Norman said.

"I don't care."

They rode past more cargo areas. Harry said, "I can't wait to see Ted's face when we tell him."

Finally they reached the end of the walkway. They passed through a mid-section of struts and girders, and entered a large forward room which they had previously seen on the monitor. With ceilings nearly a hundred feet high, it was enormous.

You could put a six-story building in this room, Norman thought. Looking up, he saw a hazy mist or fog.

"What's that?"

"That's a cloud," Barnes said, shaking his head. "The room is so big it apparently has its own weather. Maybe it even rains in here sometimes."

The room was filled with machinery on an immense scale. At first glance, it looked like oversized earth-moving machinery, except it was brightly painted in primary colors, glistening with oil. Then Norman began to notice individual features. There were giant claw hands, enormously powerful arms, moving gear wheels. And an array of buckets and receptacles.

He realized suddenly he was looking at something very similar to the grippers and claws mounted on the front end of the *Charon V* submersible he had ridden down on the day before. Was it the day before? Or was it still the same day? Which day? Was this July 4? How long had they been down here?

"If you look carefully," Barnes was saying, "you can see that some of these devices appear to be large-scale weapons. Others, like that long extensor arm, the various attachments to pick things up, in effect make this ship a gigantic robot."

"A robot . . ."

"No kidding," Beth said.

"I guess it would have been appropriate for a robot to open it after all," Ted said thoughtfully. "Maybe even fitting."

"Snug fitting," Beth said.

"Pipe fitting," Norman said.

"Sort of robot-to-robot, you mean?" Harry said. "Sort of a meeting of the threads and treads?"

"Hey," Ted said. "I don't make fun of your comments even when they're stupid."

"I wasn't aware they ever were," Harry said.

"You say foolish things sometimes. Thoughtless."

"Children," Barnes said, "can we get back to the business at hand?"

"Point it out the next time, Ted."

"I will."

"I'll be glad to know when I say something foolish."

"No problem."

"Something *you* consider foolish."

"Tell you what," Barnes said to Norman, "when we go back to the surface, let's leave these two down here."

"Surely you can't think of going back *now*," Ted said.

"We've already voted."

"But that was before we found the *object*."

"Where is the object?" Harry said.

"Over here, Harry," Ted said, with a wicked grin. "Let's see what your fabled powers of deduction make of this."

They walked deeper into the room, moving among the giant hands and claws. And they saw, nestled in the padded claw of one hand, a large, perfectly polished silver sphere about thirty feet in diameter. The sphere had no markings or features of any kind.

They moved around the sphere, seeing themselves reflected in the polished metal. Norman noticed an odd shifting iridescence, faint rainbow hues of blue and red, gleaming in the metal.

"It looks like an oversized ball bearing," Harry said.

"Keep walking, smart guy."

On the far side, they discovered a series of deep, convoluted grooves, cut in an intricate pattern into the surface of the sphere. The pattern was arresting, though Norman could not immediately say why. The pattern wasn't geometric. And it wasn't amorphous or organic, either. It was hard to say what it was. Norman had never seen anything like it, and as he continued to look at it he felt increasingly certain this was a pattern never found on Earth. Never created by any man. Never conceived by a human imagination.

Ted and Barnes were right. He felt sure of it.

This sphere was something alien.

Priorities

"**H**uh," Harry said, after staring in silence for a long time.

"I'm sure you'll want to get back to us on this," Ted said. "About where it came from, and so on."

"Actually, I know where it came from." And he told Ted about the star record, and the black hole.

"Actually," Ted said, "I suspected that this ship was made to travel through a black hole for some time."

"Did you? What was your first clue?"

"The heavy radiation shielding."

Harry nodded. "That's true. You probably guessed the significance of that before I did." He smiled. "But you didn't *tell* anybody."

"Hey," Ted said, "there's no question about it. I was the one who proposed the black hole first."

"You did?"

"Yes. No question at all. Remember, in the conference room? I was explaining to Norman about space-time, and I started to do the calculations for the black hole, and then you joined in. Norman, you remember that? I proposed it first."

Norman said, "That's true, you had the idea."

Harry grinned. "I didn't feel that was a *proposal*. I thought it was more like a guess."

"Or a speculation. Harry," Ted said, "you are rewriting history. There are witnesses."

"Since you're so far ahead of everybody else," Harry said, "how about telling us your proposals for the nature of this object?"

"With pleasure," Ted said. "This object is a burnished sphere approximately ten meters in diameter, not solid, and composed of a dense metal alloy of an as-yet-unknown nature. The cabalistic markings on this side—"

"—These grooves are what you're calling cabalistic?"

"—Do you mind if I finish? The cabalistic markings on this side clearly suggest artistic or religious ornamentation, evoking a ceremonial quality. This indicates the object has significance to whoever made it."

"I think we can be sure *that's* true."

"Personally, I believe that this sphere is intended as a form of contact with us, visitors from another star, another solar system. It is, if you will, a greeting, a message, or a trophy. A proof that a higher form of life exists in the universe."

"All well and good and beside the point," Harry said. "What does it *do?*"

"I'm not sure it does anything. I think it just *is*. It is what it is."

"Very Zen."

"Well, what's your idea?"

"Let's review what we know," Harry said, "as opposed to what we *imagine* in a flight of fancy. This is a spacecraft from the future, built with all sorts of materials and technology we haven't developed yet, although we are about to develop them. This ship was sent by our descendants through a black hole and into another universe, or another part of our universe."

"Yes."

"This spacecraft is unmanned, but equipped with robot arms which are clearly designed to pick up things that it finds. So we can think of this ship as a huge version of the unmanned Mariner spacecraft that we sent in the 1970s to Mars, to look for life there. This spacecraft from the future is much bigger, and more complicated, but it's essentially the same sort of machine. It's a probe."

"Yes . . ."

"So the probe goes into another universe, where it comes upon this sphere. Presumably it finds the sphere floating in space. Or perhaps the sphere is sent out to meet the spacecraft."

"Right," Ted said. "Sent out to meet it. As an emissary. That's what I think."

"In any case, our robot spacecraft, according to whatever built-in criteria it has, decides that this sphere is interesting. It automatically grabs the sphere in its big claw hand here, draws it inside the ship, and brings it home."

"Except in going home it goes too far, it goes into the past."

"Its past," Harry said. "Our present."

"Right."

Barnes snorted impatiently. "Fine, so this spacecraft goes out and picks up a silver alien sphere and brings it back. Get to the point: what *is* this sphere?"

Harry walked forward to the sphere, pressed his ear against the metal, and rapped it with his knuckles. He touched the grooves, his hands disappearing in the deep indentations. The sphere was so highly polished Norman could see Harry's face, distorted, in the curve of the metal. "Yes. As I suspected. These cabalistic markings, as you call them, are not decorative at all. They have another purpose entirely, to conceal a small break in the surface of the sphere. Thus they represent a door." Harry stepped back.

"What *is* the sphere?"

"I'll tell you what I think," Harry said. "I think this sphere is a hollow container, I think there's something inside, and I think it scares the hell out of me."

First Evaluation

"**N**o, Mr. Secretary," Barnes said into the phone. "We're pretty sure it is an alien artifact. There doesn't seem to be any question about that."

He glanced at Norman, sitting across the room.

"Yes, sir," Barnes said. "Very damn exciting."

They were back in the habitat, and Barnes had immediately called Washington. He was trying to delay their return to the surface.

"Not yet, we haven't opened it. Well, we haven't been *able* to open it. The door is a weird shape and it's very finely milled. . . . No, you couldn't wedge anything in the crack."

He looked at Norman, rolled his eyes.

"No, we tried that, too. There don't seem to be any exterior controls. No, no message on the outside. No, no labels either. All it is, is a highly polished sphere with some convoluted grooves on one side. What? Blast it open?"

Norman turned away. He was in D Cylinder, in the communications section run by Tina Chan. She was adjusting a dozen monitors with her usual calm. Norman said, "You seem like the most relaxed person here."

She smiled. "Just inscrutable, sir."

"Is that it?"

"It must be, sir," she said, adjusting the vertical gain on one rolling monitor. The screen showed the polished sphere. "Because I feel my heart pounding, sir. What do you think is inside that thing?"

"I haven't any idea," Norman said.

"Do you think there's an alien inside? You know, some kind of a living creature?"

"Maybe."

"And we're trying to open it up? Maybe we shouldn't let it out, whatever is in there."

"Aren't you curious?" Norman said.

"Not that curious, sir."

"I don't see how blasting would work," Barnes was saying on the phone. "Yes, we have SMTMP's, yes. Oh, different sizes. But I don't think we can blast the sucker open. No. Well, if you saw it, you'd understand. The thing is *perfectly* made. Perfect."

Tina adjusted a second monitor. They had two views of the sphere, and soon there would be a third. Edmunds was setting up cameras to watch the sphere. That had been one of Harry's suggestions. Harry had said, "Monitor it. Maybe it does something from time to time, has some activity."

On the screen, he saw the network of wires that had been attached to the sphere. They had a full array of passive sensors: sound, and the full electromagnetic spectrum from infrared to gamma and X-rays. The readouts on the sensors were displayed on a bank of instruments to the left.

Harry came in. "Getting anything yet?"

Tina shook her head. "So far, nothing."

"Has Ted come back?"

"No," Norman said. "Ted's still there."

Ted had remained behind in the cargo bay, ostensibly to help Edmunds set up the cameras. But in fact they knew he would try to open the sphere. They saw Ted now on the second monitor, probing the grooves, touching, pushing.

Harry smiled. "He hasn't got a prayer."

Norman said, "Harry, remember when we were in the flight deck, and you said you wanted to make out your will because something was missing?"

"Oh, that," Harry said. "Forget it. That's irrelevant now."

Barnes was saying, "No, Mr. Secretary, raising it to the surface would be just about impossible—well, sir, it is presently located inside a cargo bay half a mile inside the ship, and the ship is buried under thirty feet of coral, and the sphere itself is a good thirty feet across, it's the size of a small house. . . ."

"I just wonder what's *in* the house," Tina said.

On the monitor, Ted kicked the sphere in frustration.

"Not a prayer," Harry said again. "He'll never get it open."

Beth came in. "How *are* we going to open it?"

Harry said, "How?" Harry stared thoughtfully at the sphere, gleaming on the monitor. There was a long silence. "Maybe we can't."

"We can't open it? You mean not ever?"

"That's one possibility."

Norman laughed. "Ted would kill himself."

Barnes was saying, "Well, Mr. Secretary, if you wanted to commit the necessary Navy resources to do a full-scale salvage from one thousand feet, we might be able to undertake it starting six months from now, when we were assured of a month of good surface weather in this region. Yes . . . it's winter in the South Pacific now. Yes."

Beth said, "I can see it now. At great expense, the Navy brings a mysterious alien sphere to the surface. It is transported to a top-secret government installation in Omaha. Experts from every branch come and try to open it. Nobody can."

"Like Excalibur," Norman said.

Beth said, "As time goes by, they try stronger and stronger methods. Eventually they try to blow it open with a small nuclear device. And still nothing. Finally, nobody has any more ideas. The sphere sits there. Decades go by. The sphere is never opened." She shook her head. "One great frustration for mankind . . ."

Norman said to Harry, "Do you really think that'd happen? That we'd never get it open?"

Harry said, "Never is a long time."

"No, sir," Barnes was saying, "given this new development, we'll stay down to the last minute. Weather topside is holding—at least six more hours, yes, sir, from the Metsat reports—well, I have to rely on that judgment. Yes, sir. Hourly; yes, sir."

He hung up, turned to the group. "Okay. We have authorization to stay down six to twelve hours more, as long as the weather holds. Let's try to open that sphere in the time remaining."

"Ted's working on it now," Harry said.

On the video monitor, they saw Ted Fielding slap the polished sphere with his hand and shout, "Open! Open Sesame! Open up, you son of a bitch!"

The sphere did not respond.

"The Anthropomorphic Problem"

"**S**eriously," Norman said, "I think somebody has to ask the question: should we consider *not* opening it up?"

"Why?" Barnes said. "Listen, I just got off the phone—"

"—I know," Norman said. "But maybe we should think twice about this." Out of the corner of his eye, he saw Tina nodding vigorously. Harry looked skeptical. Beth rubbed her eyes, sleepy.

"Are you afraid, or do you have a substantive argument?" Barnes said.

"I have the feeling," Harry said, "that Norman's about to quote from his own work."

"Well, yes," Norman admitted. "I did put this in my report."

In his report, he had called it "the Anthropomorphic Problem." Basically, the problem was that everybody who had ever thought or written about extraterrestrial life imagined that life as essentially human. Even if the extraterrestrial life didn't look human—if it was a reptile, or a big insect, or an intelligent crystal—it still acted in a human way.

"You're talking about the movies," Barnes said.

"I'm talking about research papers, too. Every conception of extraterrestrial life, whether by a movie maker or a university professor, has been *basically* human—assuming human values, human understanding, human ways of approaching a humanly understandable universe. And generally a human appearance—two eyes, a nose, a mouth, and so on."

"So?"

"So," Norman said, "that's obviously nonsense. For one thing, there's enough variation in human behavior to make understanding just within our own species very troublesome. The differences between, say, Americans and Japanese are very great. Americans and Japanese don't really look at the world the same way at all."

"Yes, yes," Barnes said impatiently. "We all know the Japanese are different—"

"—And when you come to a new life form, the differences may be literally incomprehensible. The values and ethics of this new form of life may be utterly different."

"You mean it may not believe in the sanctity of life, or 'Thou shalt not kill,' " Barnes said, still impatient.

"No," Norman said. "I mean that this creature may not be able to be killed, and so it may have no concept of killing in the first place."

Barnes stopped. "This creature *may not be able to be killed?*"

Norman nodded. "As someone once said, you can't break the arms of a creature that has no arms."

"It can't be killed? You mean it's immortal?"

"I don't know," Norman said. "That's the point."

"I mean, Jesus, a thing that couldn't be killed," Barnes said. "How would we kill it?" He bit his lip. "I wouldn't like to open that sphere and release a thing that couldn't be killed."

Harry laughed. "No promotions for that one, Hal."

Barnes looked at the monitors, showing several views of the polished sphere. Finally he said, "No, that's ridiculous. No living thing is immortal. Am I right, Beth?"

"Actually, no," Beth said. "You could argue that certain living creatures on our own planet are immortal. For example, single-celled organisms like bacteria and yeasts are apparently capable of living indefinitely."

"Yeasts." Barnes snorted. "We're not talking about *yeasts.*"

"And to all intents and purposes a virus could be considered immortal."

"A *virus?*" Barnes sat down in a chair. He hadn't considered a virus. "But how likely is it, really? Harry?"

"I think," Harry said, "that the possibilities go far beyond what we've mentioned so far. We've only considered three-dimensional creatures, of the kind that exist in our three-dimensional universe—or, to be more precise, the universe that we perceive as having three dimensions. Some people think our universe has nine or eleven dimensions."

Barnes looked tired.

"Except the other six dimensions are very small, so we don't notice them."

Barnes rubbed his eyes.

"Therefore this creature," Harry continued, "may be multidimensional, so that it literally does not exist—at least not entirely—in our usual three dimensions. To take the simplest case, if it were a four-dimensional creature, we would only see part of it at any time, because most of the creature would exist in the fourth dimension. That would obviously make it difficult to kill. And if it were a five-dimensional creature—"

"—Just a minute. Why haven't any of you mentioned this before?"

"We thought you knew," Harry said.

"Knew about five-dimensional creatures that can't be killed? Nobody said a *word* to me." He shook his head. "Opening this sphere could be incredibly dangerous."

"It could, yes."

"What we have here is, we have Pandora's box."

"That's right."

"Well," Barnes said. "Let's consider worst cases. What's the worst case for what we might find?"

Beth said, "I think that's clear. Irrespective of whether it's a multidimensional creature or a virus or whatever, irrespective of whether it shares our morals or has no morals at all, the worst case is that it hits us below the belt."

"Meaning?"

"Meaning that it behaves in a way that interferes with our basic life mechanisms. A good example is the AIDS virus. The reason why AIDS is so dangerous is not that it's new. We get new viruses every year—every week. And all viruses work in the same way: they attack cells and convert the machinery of the cells to make more viruses. What makes the AIDS virus dangerous is, it attacks the specific cells that we use to defend against viruses. AIDS interferes with our basic defense mechanism. And we have no defense against it."

"Well," Barnes said, "if this sphere contains a creature that interferes with our basic mechanisms—what would that creature be like?"

"It could breathe in air and exhale cyanide gas," Beth said.

"It could excrete radioactive waste," Harry said.

"It could disrupt our brain waves," Norman said. "Interfere with our ability to think."

"Or," Beth said, "it might merely disrupt cardiac conduction. Stop our hearts from beating."

"It might produce a sound vibration that would resonate in our skeletal system and shatter our bones," Harry said. He smiled at the others. "I rather like that one."

"Clever," Beth said. "But, as usual, we're only thinking of ourselves. The creature might do nothing directly harmful to us at all."

"Ah," Barnes said.

"It might simply exhale a toxin that kills chloroplasts, so that plants could no longer convert sunlight. Then all the plants on Earth would die—and consequently all life on Earth would die."

"Ah," Barnes said.

"You see," Norman said, "at first I thought the Anthropomorphic Problem—the fact that we can only conceive of extraterrestrial life as basically human—I thought it was a failure of imagination. Man is man, all he knows is man, and all he can think of is what he knows. Yet, as you can see, that's not true. We can think of plenty of other things. But we don't. So there must be another reason why we only conceive of extraterrestrials as humans. And I think the answer is that we are, in reality, terribly frail animals. And we don't like to be reminded of how frail we are—how delicate the balances are inside our own bodies, how short our stay on Earth, and how easily it is ended. So we imagine other life forms as being like us, so we don't have to think of the real threat—the terrifying threat—they may represent, without ever intending to."

There was a silence.

"Of course, we mustn't forget another possibility," Barnes said. "It may be that the sphere contains some extraordinary benefit to us. Some wondrous new knowledge, some astonishing new idea or new technology which will improve the condition of mankind beyond our wildest dreams."

"Although the chances are," Harry said, "that there won't be any new idea that is useful to us."

"Why?" Barnes said.

"Well, let's say that the aliens are a thousand years ahead of us, just as we are relative to, say, medieval Europe. Suppose you went back to medieval Europe with a television set? There wouldn't be any place to plug it in."

Barnes stared from one to another for a long time. "I'm sorry," he said. "This is too great a responsibility for me. I can't make the decision to open it up. I have to call Washington on this."

"Ted won't be happy," Harry said.

"The hell with Ted," Barnes said. "I'm going to give this to the President. Until we hear from him, I don't want anybody trying to open that sphere."

Barnes called for a two-hour rest period, and Harry went to his quarters to sleep. Beth announced that she was going off to sleep, too, but she remained at the monitor station with Tina Chan and Norman. Chan's station had comfortable chairs with high backs, and Beth swiveled in the chair, swinging her legs back and forth. She played with her hair, making little ringlets by her ear, and she stared into space.

Tired, Norman thought. We're all tired. He watched Tina, who moved smoothly and continuously, adjusting the monitors, checking the sensor inputs, changing the videotapes on the bank of VCR's, tense, alert. Because Edmunds was in the spaceship with Ted, Tina had to look after the recording units as well as her own communications console. The Navy woman didn't seem to be as tired as they were, but, then, she hadn't been inside the spaceship. To her, that spaceship was something she saw on the monitors, a TV show, an abstraction. Tina hadn't been confronted face-to-face with the reality of the new environment, the exhausting mental struggle to understand what was going on, what it all meant.

"You look tired, sir," Tina said.

"Yes. We're all tired."

"It's the atmosphere," she said. "Breathing the heliox."

So much for psychological explanations, Norman thought.

Tina said, "The density of the air down here has a real effect. We're at thirty atmospheres. If we were breathing regular air at this pressure, it would be almost as thick as a liquid. Heliox is lighter, but it's far denser than what we're used to. You don't realize it, but it's tiring just to breathe, to move your lungs."

"But you aren't tired."

"Oh, I'm used to it. I've been in saturated environments before."

"Is that right? Where?"

"I really can't say, Dr. Johnson."

"Navy operations?"

She smiled. "I'm not supposed to talk about it."

"Is that your inscrutable smile?"

"I hope so, sir. But don't you think you ought to try and sleep?"

He nodded. "Probably."

Norman considered going to sleep, but the prospect of his damp bunk was unappealing. Instead he went down to the galley, hoping to find one of Rose Levy's desserts. Levy was not there, but there was some coconut cake under a plastic dome. He found a plate, cut a slice, and took it over to one of the portholes. But it was black outside the porthole; the grid lights were turned off, the divers gone. He saw lights in the portholes of DH-7, the divers' habitat, located a few dozen yards away. The divers must be getting ready to go back to the surface. Or perhaps they had already gone.

In the porthole, he saw his own face reflected. The face looked tired, and old. "This is no place for a fifty-three-year-old man," he said, watching his reflection.

As he looked out, he saw some moving lights in the distance, then a flash of yellow. One of the minisubs pulled up under a cylinder at DH-7. Moments later, a second sub arrived, to dock alongside it. The lights on the first sub went out. After a short time, the second sub pulled away, into the black water. The first sub was left behind.

What's going on, he wondered, but he was aware he didn't really care. He was too tired. He was more interested in what the cake would taste like, and looked down. The cake was eaten. Only a few crumbs remained.

Tired, he thought. Very tired. He put his feet up on the coffee table and put his head back against the cool padding of the wall.

He must have fallen asleep for a while, because he awoke disoriented, in darkness. He sat up and immediately the lights came on. He saw he was still in the galley.

Barnes had warned him about that, the way the habitat adjusted to the presence of people. Apparently the motion sensors stopped registering you if you fell asleep, and automatically shut off the room lights. Then when you awoke, and moved, the lights came back. He wondered if the lights would stay on if you snored. Who had designed all this? he wondered. Had the engineers and designers working on the Navy habitat taken snoring into account? Was there a snore sensor?

More cake.

He got up and walked across to the galley kitchen. Several pieces of cake were now missing. Had he eaten them? He wasn't sure, couldn't remember.

"Lot of videotapes," Beth said. Norman turned around.

"Yes," Tina said. "We are recording everything that goes on in this habitat as well as the other ship. It'll be a lot of material."

There was a monitor mounted just above his head. It showed Beth and Tina, upstairs at the communications console. They were eating cake.

Aha, he thought. So that was where the cake had gone.

"Every twelve hours the tapes are transferred to the submarine," Tina said.

"What for?" Beth said.

"That's so, if anything happens down here, the submarine will automatically go to the surface."

"Oh, great," Beth said. "I won't think about that too much. Where is Dr. Fielding now?"

Tina said, "He gave up on the sphere, and went into the main flight deck with Edmunds."

Norman watched the monitor. Tina had stepped out of view. Beth sat with her back to the monitor, eating the cake. On the monitor behind Beth, he could clearly see the gleaming sphere. Monitors showing monitors, he thought. The Navy people who eventually review this stuff are going to go crazy.

Tina said, "Do you think they'll ever get the sphere open?"

Beth chewed her cake. "Maybe," she said. "I don't know."

And to Norman's horror, he saw on the monitor behind Beth that the door of the sphere was sliding silently open, revealing blackness inside.

Open

They must have thought he was crazy, running through the lock to D Cylinder and stumbling up the narrow stairs to the upper level, shouting, "It's open! It's open!"

He came to the communications console just as Beth was wiping the last crumbs of coconut from her lips. She set down her fork.

"What's open?"

"The sphere!"

Beth spun in her chair. Tina ran over from the bank of VCR's. They both looked at the monitor behind Beth. There was an awkward silence.

"Looks closed to me, Norman."

"It *was* open. I saw it." He told them about watching in the galley, on the monitor. "It was just a few seconds ago, and the sphere definitely opened. It must have closed again while I was on my way here."

"Are you sure?"

"That's a pretty small monitor in the galley. . . ."

"I saw it," Norman said. "Replay it, if you don't believe me."

"Good idea," Tina said, and she went to the recorders to play the tape back.

Norman was breathing heavily, trying to catch his breath. This was the first time he had exerted himself in the dense atmosphere, and he felt the effects strongly. DH-8 was not a good place to get excited, he decided.

Beth was watching him. "You okay, Norman?"

"I'm fine. I tell you, I saw it. It opened. Tina?"

"It'll take me a second here."

Harry walked in, yawning. "Beds in this place are great, aren't they?" he said. "Like sleeping in a bag of wet rice. Sort of combination bed and cold shower." He sighed. "It'll break my heart to leave."

Beth said, "Norman thinks the sphere opened."

"When?" he said, yawning again.

"Just a few seconds ago."

Harry nodded thoughtfully. "Interesting, interesting. I see it's closed now."

"We're rewinding the videotapes, to look again."

"Uh-huh. Is there any more of that cake?"

Harry seems very cool, Norman thought. This is a major piece of news and he doesn't seem excited at all. Why was that? Didn't Harry believe it, either? Was he still sleepy, not fully awake? Or was there something else?

"Here we go," Tina said.

The monitor showed jagged lines, and then resolved. On the screen, Tina was saying, "—hours the tapes are transferred to the submarine."

Beth: "What for?"

Tina: "That's so, if anything happens down here, the submarine will automatically go to the surface."

Beth: "Oh, great. I won't think about that too much. Where is Dr. Fielding now?"

Tina: "He gave up on the sphere, and went into the main flight deck with Edmunds."

On the screen, Tina stepped out of view. Beth remained alone in the chair, eating the cake, her back to the monitor.

Onscreen, Tina was saying, "Do you think they'll ever get the sphere open?"

Beth ate her cake. "Maybe," she said. "I don't know."

There was a short pause, and then on the monitor behind Beth, the door of the sphere slid open.

"Hey! It did open!"

"Keep the tape running!"

Onscreen, Beth didn't notice the monitor. Tina, still somewhere offscreen, said, "It scares me."

Beth: "I don't think there's a reason to be scared."

Tina: "It's the unknown."

"Sure," Beth said, "but an unknown thing is not likely to be dangerous or frightening. It's most likely to be just inexplicable."

"I don't know how you can say that."

"You afraid of snakes?" Beth said, onscreen.

All during this conversation, the sphere remained open.

Watching, Harry said, "Too bad we can't see inside it."

"I may be able to help that," Tina said. "I'll do some image-intensification work with the computer."

"It almost looks like there are little lights," Harry said. "Little moving lights inside the sphere . . ."

Onscreen, Tina came back into view. "Snakes don't bother me."

"Well, I can't stand snakes," Beth said. "Slimy, cold, disgusting things."

"Ah, Beth," Harry said, watching the monitor. "Got snake envy?"

Onscreen, Beth was saying, "If I were a Martian who came to Earth and I stumbled upon a snake—a funny, cold, wiggling, tube-like life—I wouldn't know what to think of it. But the chance that I would stumble on a poisonous snake is very small. Less than one percent of snakes are poisonous. So, as a Martian, I wouldn't be in danger from my discovery of snakes; I'd just be perplexed. That's what's likely to happen with us. We'll be perplexed."

Onscreen, Beth was saying, "Anyway, I don't think we'll ever get the sphere open, no."

Tina: "I hope not."

Behind her on the monitor, the sphere closed.

"Huh!" Harry said. "How long was it open all together?"

"Thirty-three point four seconds," Tina said.

They stopped the tape. Tina said, "Anybody want to see it again?" She looked pale.

"Not right now," Harry said. He drummed his fingers on the arm of his chair, stared off, thinking.

No one else said anything; they just waited patiently for Harry. Norman realized how much the group deferred to him. Harry is the person who figures things out for us, Norman thought. We need him, rely on him.

"Okay," Harry said at last. "No conclusions are possible. We have insufficient data. The question is whether the sphere was responding to something in its immediate environment, or whether it just opened, for reasons of its own. Where's Ted?"

"Ted left the sphere and went to the flight deck."

"Ted's back," Ted said, grinning broadly. "And I have some real news."

"So do we," Beth said.

"It can wait," Ted said.

"But—"

"—*I know where this ship went,*" Ted said excitedly. "I've been analyzing the flight data summaries on the flight deck, looking at the star fields, and I know where the black hole is located."

"Ted," Beth said, "the sphere opened."

"It did? When?"

"A few minutes ago. Then it closed again."

"What did the monitors show?"

"No biological hazard. It seems to be safe."

Ted looked at the screen. "Then what the hell are we doing here?"

Barnes came in. "Two-hour rest period is over. Everybody ready to go back to the ship for a last look?"

"That's putting it mildly," Harry said.

The sphere was polished, silent, closed. They stood around it and stared at themselves, distorted in reflection. Nobody spoke. They just walked around it.

Finally Ted said, "I feel like this is an IQ test, and I'm flunking."

"You mean like the Davies Message?" Harry said.

"Oh that," Ted said.

Norman knew about the Davies Message. It was one of the episodes that the SETI promoters wished to forget. In 1979, there had been a large meeting in Rome of the scientists involved in the Search for Extraterrestrial Intelligence. Basically, SETI called for a radio astronomy search of the heavens. Now the scientists were trying to decide what sort of message to search for.

Emerson Davies, a physicist from Cambridge, England, devised a message based on fixed physical constants, such as the wavelength of emitted hydrogen, which were presumably the same throughout the universe. He arranged these constants in a binary pictorial form.

Because Davies thought this would be exactly the kind of message an alien intelligence might send, he figured it would be easy for the SETI people to figure out. He distributed his picture to everybody at the conference.

Nobody could figure it out.

When Davies explained it, they all agreed it was a clever idea, and a perfect message for extraterrestrials to send. But the fact remained that none of them had been able to figure out this perfect message.

One of the people who had tried to figure it out, and had failed, was Ted.

"Well, we didn't try very hard," Ted said. "There was a lot going on at the conference. And we didn't have you there, Harry."

"You just wanted a free trip to Rome," Harry said.

Beth said, "Is it my imagination, or have the door markings changed?"

Norman looked. At first glance, the deep grooves appeared the same, but perhaps the pattern was different. If so, the change was subtle.

"We can compare it with old videotapes," Barnes said.

"It looks the same to me," Ted said. "Anyway, it's metal. I doubt it could change."

"What we call metal is just a liquid that flows slowly at room temperature," Harry said. "It's possible that this metal is changing."

"I doubt it," Ted said.

Barnes said, "You guys are supposed to be the experts. We know this thing can open. It's been open already. How do we get it open again?"

"We're trying, Hal."

"It doesn't look like you're doing anything."

From time to time, they glanced at Harry, but Harry just stood there, looking at the sphere, his hand on his chin, tapping his lower lip thoughtfully with his finger.

"Harry?"

Harry said nothing.

Ted went up and slapped the sphere with the flat of his hand. It made a dull sound, but nothing happened. Ted pounded the sphere with his fist; then he winced and rubbed his hand.

"I don't think we can force our way in. I think it has to let you in," Norman said. Nobody said anything after that.

"My hand-picked, crack team," Barnes said, needling them. "And all they can do is stand around and stare at it."

"What do you want us to do, Hal? Nuke it?"

"If you don't get it open, there are people who will try that, eventually." He glanced at his watch. "Meanwhile, you got any other bright ideas?"

Nobody did.

"Okay," Barnes said. "Our time is up. Let's go back to the habitat and get ready to be ferried to the surface."

Departure

Norman pulled the small Navy-issue bag from beneath his bunk in C Cylinder. He got his shaving kit from the bathroom, found his notebook and his extra pair of socks, and zipped the bag shut.

"I'm ready."

"Me, too," Ted said. Ted was unhappy; he didn't want to leave. "I guess we can't delay it any longer. The weather's getting worse. They've got all the divers out from DH-7, and now there's only us."

Norman smiled at the prospect of being on the surface again. I never thought I'd look forward to seeing Navy battleship gray on a ship, but I do.

"Where're the others?" Norman said.

"Beth's already packed. I think she's with Barnes in communication. Harry, too, I guess." Ted plucked at his jumpsuit. "I'll tell you one thing, I'll be glad to see the last of this suit."

They left the sleeping quarters, heading down to communications. On the way, they squeezed past Teeny Fletcher, who was going toward B Cylinder.

"Ready to leave?" Norman said.

"Yes, sir, all squared away," Fletcher said, but her features were tense, and she seemed rushed, under pressure.

"Aren't you going the wrong way?" Norman asked.

"Just checking the diesel backups."

Backups? Norman thought. Why check the backups now that they were leaving?

"She probably left something on that she shouldn't have," Ted said, shaking his head.

In the communications console, the mood was grim. Barnes was on the phone with the surface vessels. "Say that again," he said. "I want to hear who's authorized that." He was frowning, angry.

They looked at Tina. "How's the weather on the surface?"

"Deteriorating fast, apparently."

Barnes spun: "Will you idiots *keep it down?*"

Norman dropped his day bag on the floor. Beth was sitting near the portholes, tired, rubbing her eyes. Tina was turning off the monitors, one after another, when she suddenly stopped.

"Look."

On one monitor, they saw the polished sphere.

Harry was standing next to it.

"What's he doing there?"

"Didn't he come back with us?"

"I thought he did."

"I didn't notice; I assumed he did."

"God damn it, I thought I told you people—" Barnes began, and then stopped. He stared at the monitor.

On the screen, Harry turned toward the video camera and made a short bow.

"Ladies and gentlemen, your attention, please. I think you will find this of interest."

Harry turned to face the sphere. He stood with his arms at his sides, relaxed. He did not move or speak. He closed his eyes. He took a deep breath.

The door to the sphere opened.

"Not bad, huh?" Harry said, with a sudden grin.

Then Harry stepped inside the sphere. The door closed behind him.

They all began talking at once. Barnes was shouting over everyone else, shouting for quiet, but no one paid any attention until the lights in the habitat went out. They were plunged into darkness.

Ted said, "What's happened?"

The only light came through the portholes, faintly, from the grid lights. A moment later, the grid went out, too.

"No power . . ."

"I tried to tell you," Barnes said.

There was a whirring sound, and the lights flickered, then came back on. "We have internal power; we're running on our diesels now."

"Why?"

"Look," Ted said, pointing out the porthole.

Outside they saw what looked like a wriggling silver snake. Then Norman realized it was the cable that linked them to the surface, sliding back and forth across the porthole as it coiled in great loops on the bottom.

"They've cut us free!"

"That's right," Barnes said. "They've got full gale-force conditions topside. They can no longer maintain cables for power and communications. They can no longer use the submarines. They've taken all the divers up, but the subs can't come back for us. At least not for a few days, until the seas calm down."

"Then we're stuck down here?"

"That's correct."

"For how long?"

"Several days," Barnes said.

"For how long?"

"Maybe as long as a week."

"Jesus Christ," Beth said.

Ted tossed his bag onto the couch. "What a fantastic piece of luck," he said.

Beth spun. "Are you *out of your mind?*"

"Let's all stay calm," Barnes said. "Everything's under control. This is just a temporary delay. There's no reason to get upset."

But Norman didn't feel upset. He felt suddenly exhausted. Beth was sulking, angry, feeling deceived; Ted was excited, already planning another excursion to the spacecraft, arranging equipment with Edmunds.

But Norman felt only tired. His eyes were heavy; he thought he might go to sleep standing there in front of the monitors. He excused himself hurriedly, went back to his bunk, lay down. He didn't care that the sheets were clammy; he didn't care that the pillow was cold; he didn't care that diesels were droning and vibrating in the next cylinder. He thought: This is a very strong avoidance reaction. And then he was asleep.

Beyond Pluto

Norman rolled out of bed and looked for his watch, but he'd gotten into the habit of not wearing one down here. He had no idea what time it was, how long he had been asleep. He looked out the porthole, saw nothing but black water. The grid lights were still off. He lay back in his bunk and looked at the gray pipes directly over his head; they seemed closer than before, as if they had moved toward him while he slept. Everything seemed cramped, tighter, more claustrophobic.

Several more days of this, he thought. God.

He hoped the Navy would think to notify his family. After so many days, Ellen would start to worry. He imagined her first calling the FAA, then calling the Navy, trying to find out what had happened. Of course, no one would know anything, because the project was classified; Ellen would be frantic.

Then he stopped thinking about Ellen. It was easier, he thought, to worry about your loved ones than to worry about yourself. But there wasn't any point. Ellen would be okay. And so would he. It was just a matter of waiting. Staying calm, and waiting out the storm.

He got into the shower, wondering if they'd still have hot water while the habitat was on emergency power. They did, and he felt less stiff after his shower. It was odd, he thought, to be a thousand feet underwater and to relish the soothing effects of a hot shower.

He dressed and headed for the C Cylinder. He heard Tina's voice say, "— think they'll ever get the sphere open?"

Beth: "Maybe. I don't know."

"It scares me."

"I don't think there's a reason to be scared."

"It's the unknown," Tina said.

When Norman came in, he found Beth running the videotape, looking at herself and Tina. "Sure," Beth said on the videotape, "but an unknown thing is not likely to be dangerous or frightening. It's most likely to be just inexplicable."

Tina said, "I don't know how you can say that."

"You afraid of snakes?" Beth said, onscreen.

Beth snapped off the videotape. "Just trying to see if I could figure out why it opened," she said.

"Any luck?" Norman said.

"Not so far." On the adjacent monitor, they could see the sphere itself. The sphere was closed.

"Harry still in there?" Norman said.

"Yes," Beth said.

"How long has it been now?"

She looked up at the consoles. "A little more than an hour."

"I only slept an hour?"

"Yeah."

"I'm starving," Norman said, and he went down to the galley to eat. All the coconut cake was gone. He was looking for something else to eat when Beth showed up.

"I don't know what to do, Norman," she said, frowning.

"About what?"

"They're lying to us," she said.

"Who is?"

"Barnes. The Navy. Everybody. This is all a setup, Norman."

"Come on, Beth. No conspiracies, now. We have enough to worry about without—"

"—Just look at this," she said. She led him back upstairs, flicked on a console, pressed buttons.

"I started putting it together when Barnes was on the phone," she said. "Barnes was talking to somebody right up to the moment when the cable started to coil down. Except that cable is a thousand feet long, Norman. They would have broken communications several minutes before unhooking the cable itself."

"Probably, yes . . ."

"So who was Barnes talking to at the last minute? Nobody."

"Beth . . ."

"Look," she said, pointing to the screen.

COM SUMMARY DH—SURCOM/1

0910 BARNES TO SURCOM/1:
CIVILIAN AND USN PERSONNEL POLLED. ALTHOUGH ADVISED OF RISKS, ALL PERSONNEL ELECT TO REMAIN DOWN FOR DURATION OF STORM TO CONTINUE INVESTIGATION OF ALIEN SPHERE AND ASSOCIATED SPACECRAFT. BARNES, USN.

"You're kidding," Norman said. "I thought Barnes wanted to leave."

"He did, but he changed his mind when he saw that last room, and he didn't bother to tell us. I'd like to kill the bastard," Beth said. "You know what this is about, Norman, don't you?"

Norman nodded. "He hopes to find a new weapon."

"Right. Barnes is a Pentagon-acquisition man, and he wants to find a new weapon."

"But the sphere is unlikely—"

"It's not the sphere," Beth said. "Barnes doesn't really care about the sphere. He cares about the 'associated spacecraft.' Because, according to congruity theory, it's the spacecraft that is likely to pay off. Not the sphere."

Congruity theory was a troublesome matter for the people who thought about extraterrestrial life. In a simple way, the astronomers and physicists who considered the possibility of contact with extraterrestrial life imagined wonderful benefits to mankind from such a contact. But other thinkers, philosophers and historians, did not foresee any benefits to contact at all.

For example, astronomers believed that if we made contact with extraterrestrials, mankind would be so shocked that wars on Earth would cease, and a new era of peaceful cooperation between nations would begin.

But historians thought that was nonsense. They pointed out that when Europeans discovered the New World—a similarly world-shattering discovery—the Europeans did not stop their incessant fighting. On the contrary: they fought even harder. Europeans simply made the New World an extension of pre-existing animosities. It became another place to fight, and to fight over.

Similarly, astronomers imagined that when mankind met extraterrestrials, there would be an exchange of information and technology, giving mankind a wonderful advancement.

Historians of science thought that was nonsense, too. They pointed out that what we called "science" actually consisted of a rather arbitrary conception of the universe, not likely to be shared by other creatures. Our ideas of science were the ideas of visually oriented, monkey-like creatures who enjoyed changing their physical environment. If the aliens were blind and communicated by odors, they might have evolved a very different science, which described a very different universe. And they might have made very different choices about the directions their science would explore. For example, they might ignore the physical world entirely, and instead develop a highly sophisticated science of mind—in other words, the exact opposite of what Earth science had done. The alien technology might be purely mental, with no visible hardware at all.

This issue was at the heart of congruity theory, which said that unless the aliens were remarkably similar to us, no exchange of information was likely. Barnes of course knew that theory, so he knew he wasn't likely to derive any useful technology from the alien sphere. But he was very likely to get useful technology from the spaceship itself, since the spaceship had been made by men, and congruity was high.

And he had lied to keep them down. To keep the search going.

"What should we do with the bastard?" Beth said.

"Nothing, for the moment," Norman said.

"You don't want to confront him? Jesus, I do."

"It won't serve any purpose," Norman said. "Ted won't care, and the Navy people are all following orders. And anyway, even if it had been arranged for us to depart as planned, would you have gone, leaving Harry behind in the sphere?"

"No," Beth admitted.

"Well, then. It's all academic."

"Jesus, Norman . . ."

"I know. But we're here now. And for the next couple of days, there's not a damn thing we can do about it. Let's deal with that reality as best we can, and point the finger later."

"You bet I'm going to point the finger!"

"That's fine. But not now, Beth."

"Okay," she sighed. "Not now."

She went back upstairs.

Alone, Norman stared at the console. He had his work cut out for him, keeping everybody calm for the next few days. He hadn't looked into the computer system before; he started pressing buttons. Pretty soon he found a file marked ULF CONTACT TEAM BIOG. He opened it up.

Civilian Team Members
1. Theodore Fielding, astrophysicist/planetary geologist
2. Elizabeth Halpern, zoologist/biochemist
3. Harold J. Adams, mathematician/logician
4. Arthur Levine, marine biologist/biochemist
5. John F. Thompson, psychologist

Choose one:

Norman stared in disbelief at the list.

He knew Jack Thompson, an energetic young psychologist from Yale. Thompson was world-renowned for his studies of the psychology of primitive peoples, and in fact for the past year had been somewhere in New Guinea, studying native tribes.

Norman pressed more buttons.

ULF TEAM PSYCHOLOGIST: CHOICES BY RANK

1. John F. Thompson, Yale—approved
2. William L. Hartz, UCB—approved
3. Jeremy White, UT—approved (pending clearance)
4. Norman Johnson, SDU—rejected (age)

He knew them all. Bill Hartz at Berkeley was seriously ill with cancer. Jeremy White had gone to Hanoi during the Vietnam War, and would never get clearance.

That left Norman.

He understood now why he had been the last to be called in. He understood now about the special tests. He felt a burst of intense anger at Barnes, at the whole system which had brought him down here, despite his age, with no concern for his safety. At fifty-three, Norman Johnson had no business being a thousand feet underwater in a pressurized exotic gas environment—and the Navy knew it.

It was an outrage, he thought. He wanted to go upstairs and give Barnes hell in no uncertain terms. That lying son of a bitch—

He gripped the arms of his chair and reminded himself of what he had told Beth. Whatever had happened up to this point, there was nothing any of them could do about it now. He would indeed give Barnes hell—he promised himself he would—but only when they got back to the surface. Until then, it was no use making trouble.

He shook his head and swore.

Then he turned the console off.

The hours crept by. Harry was still in the sphere.

Tina ran her image intensification of the videotape that showed the sphere open, trying to see interior detail. "Unfortunately, we have only limited computing power in the habitat," she said. "If I could hard-link to the surface I could really do a job, but as it is . . ." She shrugged.

She showed them a series of enlarged freeze-frames from the open sphere. The images clicked through at one-second intervals. The quality was poor, with jagged, intermittent static.

"The only internal structures we can see in the blackness," Tina said, pointing to the opening, "are these multiple point-sources of light. The lights appear to move from frame to frame."

"It's as if the sphere is filled with fireflies," Beth said.

"Except these lights are much dimmer than fireflies, and they don't blink. They are very numerous. And they give the impression of moving together, in surging patterns. . . ."

"A flock of fireflies?"

"Something like that." The tape ran out. The screen went dark.

Ted said, "That's it?"

"I'm afraid so, Dr. Fielding."

"Poor Harry," Ted said mournfully.

Of all the group, Ted was the most visibly upset about Harry. He kept staring at the closed sphere on the monitor, saying, "How did he do that?" Then he would add, "I hope he's all right."

He repeated it so often that finally Beth said, "I think we know your feelings, Ted."

"I'm seriously concerned about him."

"I am, too. We all are."

"You think I'm jealous, Beth? Is that what you're saying?"

"Why would anyone think that, Ted?"

Norman changed the subject. It was crucial to avoid confrontations among group members. He asked Ted about his analysis of the flight data aboard the spaceship.

"It's very interesting," Ted said, warming to his subject. "My detailed examination of the earliest flight-data images," he said, "convinced me that they show three planets—Uranus, Neptune, and Pluto—and the sun, very small in the background. Therefore, the pictures are taken from some point beyond the orbit of Pluto. This suggests that the black hole is not far beyond our own solar system."

"Is that possible?" Norman said.

"Oh sure. In fact, for the last ten years some astrophysicists have suspected that there's a black hole—not a large one, but a black hole—just outside our solar system."

"I hadn't heard that."

"Oh yes. In fact, some of us have argued that, if it was small enough, in a few years we could go out and capture the black hole, bring it back, park it in Earth orbit, and use the energy it generates to power the entire planet."

Barnes smiled. "Black-hole cowboys?"

"In theory, there's no reason it couldn't be done. Then just think: the entire planet would be free of its dependency on fossil fuels. . . . The whole history of mankind would be changed."

Barnes said, "Probably make a hell of a weapon, too."

"Even a very tiny black hole would be a little too powerful to use as a weapon."

"So you think this ship went out to capture a black hole?"

"I doubt it," Ted said. "The ship is so strongly made, so shielded against radiation, that I suspect it was intended to *go through* a black hole. And it did."

"And that's why the ship went back in time?" Norman said.

"I'm not sure," Ted said. "You see, a black hole really is the edge of the universe. What happens there isn't clear to anybody now alive. But what some people think is that you don't go through the hole, you sort of skip into it, like a pebble skipping over water, and you get bounced into a different time or space or universe."

"So the ship got bounced?"

"Yes. Possibly more than once. And when it bounced back here, it undershot and arrived a few hundred years before it left."

"And on one of its bounces, it picked up that?" Beth said, pointing to the monitor.

They looked. The sphere was still closed. But lying next to it, sprawled on the deck in an awkward pose, was Harry Adams.

For a moment they thought he was dead. Then Harry lifted his head and moaned.

The Subject

Norman wrote in his notebook: *Subject is a thirty-year-old black mathematician who has spent three hours inside a sphere of unknown origin. On recovery from the sphere was stuporous and unresponsive; he did not know his name, where he was, or what year it was. Brought back to habitat; slept for one half-hour then awoke abruptly complaining of headache.*

"Oh God."

Harry was sitting in his bunk, holding his head in his hands, groaning.

"Hurt?" Norman asked.

"Brutal. Pounding."

"Anything else?"

"Thirsty. God." He licked his lips. "Really thirsty."

Extreme thirst, Norman wrote.

Rose Levy, the cook, showed up with a glass of lemonade. Norman handed the glass to Harry, who drank it in a single gulp, passed it back.

"More."

"Better bring a pitcher," Norman said. Levy went off. Norman turned to Harry, still holding his head, still groaning, and said, "I have a question for you."

"What?"

"What's your name?"

"Norman, I don't need to be psychoanalyzed right now."

"Just tell me your name."

"Harry Adams, for Christ's sake. What's the matter with you? Oh, my *head.*"

"You didn't remember before," Norman said. "When we found you."

"When you found me?" he asked. He seemed confused again.

Norman nodded. "Do you remember when we found you?"

"It must have been . . . outside."

"Outside?"

Harry looked up, suddenly furious, eyes glowing with rage. *"Outside the sphere, you goddamn idiot! What do you think I'm talking about?"*

"Take it easy, Harry."

"Your questions are driving me crazy!"

"Okay, okay. Take it easy."

Emotionally labile. Rage and irritability. Norman made more notes.

"Do you have to make so much *noise?"*

Norman looked up, puzzled.

"Your pen," Harry said. "It sounds like Niagara Falls."

Norman stopped writing. It must be a migraine, or something like migraine. Harry was holding his head in his hands delicately, as if it were made of glass.

"Why can't I have any aspirin, for Christ's sake?"

"We don't want to give you anything for a while, in case you've hurt yourself. We need to know where the pain is."

"The *pain,* Norman, is *in my head.* It's in my goddamn head! Now, why won't you give me any aspirin?"

"Barnes said not to."

"Is Barnes still here?"

"We're all still here."

Harry looked up slowly. "But you were supposed to go to the surface."

"I know."

"Why didn't you go?"

"The weather went bad, and they couldn't send the subs."

"Well, you should go. You shouldn't be here, Norman."

Levy arrived with more lemonade. Harry looked at her as he drank.

"You're still here, too?"

"Yes, Dr. Adams."

"How many people are down here, all together?"

Levy said, "There are nine of us, sir."

"Jesus." He passed the glass back. Levy refilled it. "You should all go. You should leave."

"Harry," Norman said. "We can't go."

"You *have to* go."

Norman sat on the bunk opposite Harry and watched as Harry drank. Harry was demonstrating a rather typical manifestation of shock: the agitation, the irritability, the nervous, manic flow of ideas, the unexplained fears for the safety of others—it was all characteristic of shocked victims of severe accidents, such as major auto crashes or airplane crashes. Given an intense event, the brain struggled to assimilate, to make sense, to reassemble the mental world even as the physical world was shattered around it. The brain went into a kind of overdrive, hastily trying to reassemble things, to get things right, to re-establish equilibrium. Yet it was fundamentally a confused period of wheel-spinning.

You just had to wait it out.

Harry finished the lemonade, handed the glass back.

"More?" Levy asked.

"No, that's good. Headache's better."

Perhaps it was dehydration after all, Norman thought. But why would Harry be dehydrated after three hours in the sphere?

"Harry . . ."

"Tell me something. Do I look different, Norman?"

"No."

"I look the same to you?"

"Yes. I'd say so."

"Are you sure?" Harry said. He jumped up, went to a mirror mounted on the wall. He peered at his face.

"How do you think you look?" Norman said.

"I don't know. Different."

"Different how?"

"*I don't know!*". . . He pounded the padded wall next to the mirror. The mirror image vibrated. He turned away, sat down on the bunk again. He sighed. "Just different."

"Harry . . ."

"What?"

"Do you remember what happened?"

"Of course."

"What happened?"

"I went inside."

He waited, but Harry said nothing further. He just stared at the carpeted floor.

"Do you remember opening the door?"

Harry said nothing.

"How did you open the door, Harry?"

Harry looked up at Norman. "You were all supposed to leave. To go back to the surface. You weren't supposed to stay."

"How did you open the door, Harry?"

There was a long silence. "I opened it." He sat up straight, his hands at his sides. He seemed to be remembering, reliving it.

"And then?"

"I went inside."

"And what happened inside?"

"It was beautiful. . . ."

"What was beautiful?"

"The foam," Harry said. And then he fell silent again, staring vacantly into space.

"The foam?" Norman prompted.

"The sea. The foam. Beautiful . . ."

Was he talking about the lights? Norman wondered. The swirling pattern of lights?

"What was beautiful, Harry?"

"Now, don't kid me," Harry said. "Promise you won't kid me."

"I won't kid you."

"You think I look the same?"

"Yes, I do."

"You don't think I've changed at all?"

"No. Not that I can see. Do *you* think you've changed?"

"I don't know. Maybe. I—maybe."

"Did something happen in the sphere to change you?"

"You don't understand about the sphere."

"Then explain it to me," Norman said.

"Nothing happened in the sphere."

"You were in the sphere for three hours. . . ."

"Nothing happened. Nothing ever happens inside the sphere. It's always the same, inside the sphere."

"What's always the same? The foam?"

"The foam is always different. The sphere is always the same."

"I don't understand," Norman said.

"I know you don't," Harry said. He shook his head. "What can I do?"

"Tell me some more."

"There isn't any more."

"Then tell me again."

"It won't help," Harry said. "Do you think you'll be leaving soon?"

"Barnes says not for several days."

"I think you should leave soon. Talk to the others. Convince them. Make them leave."

"Why, Harry?"

"I can't be—I don't know."

Harry rubbed his eyes and lay back on the bed. "You'll have to excuse me," he said, "but I'm very tired. Maybe we can continue this some other time. Talk to the others, Norman. Get them to leave. It's . . . dangerous to stay here."

And he lay down in the bunk and closed his eyes.

Changes

"**H**e's sleeping," Norman told them. "He's in shock. He's confused. But he seems basically intact."

"What did he tell you," Ted said, "about what happened in there?"

"He's quite confused," Norman said, "but he's recovering. When we first found him, he didn't even remember his name. Now he does. He remembers my name, he remembers where he is. He remembers he went into the sphere. I think he remembers what happened inside the sphere, too. He just isn't telling."

"Great," Ted said.

"He mentioned the sea, and the foam. But I wasn't clear what he meant by that."

"Look outside," Tina said, pointing to the portholes.

Norman had an immediate impression of lights—thousands of lights filling the blackness of the ocean—and his first response was unreasoning terror:

the lights in the sphere were coming out to get them. But then he saw each of the lights had a shape, and were moving, wriggling.

They pressed their faces to the portholes, looked.

"Squid," Beth said finally. "Bioluminescent squid."

"Thousands of them."

"More," she said. "I'd guess at least half a million, all around the habitat."

"Beautiful."

"The size of the school is amazing," Ted said.

"Impressive, but not really unusual," Beth said. "The fecundity of the sea is very great compared with the land. The sea is where life began, and where intense competition among animals first appeared. One response to competition is to produce enormous numbers of offspring. Many sea animals do that. In fact, we tend to think that animals came out onto the land as a positive step forward in the evolution of life. But the truth is, the first creatures were really driven out of the ocean. They were just trying to get away from the competition. And you can imagine when the first fish-amphibians climbed up the beach and poked their heads up to look out at the land, and saw this vast dry-land environment without any competition at all. It must have looked like the promised—"

Beth broke off, turned to Barnes. "Quick: where do you keep specimen nets?"

"I don't want you going out there."

"I have to," Beth said. "Those squid have six tentacles."

"So?"

"There's no known species of six-tentacled squid. This is an undescribed species. I must collect samples."

Barnes told her where the equipment locker was, and she went off. Norman looked at the school of squid with renewed interest.

The animals were each about a foot long, and seemed to be transparent. The large eyes of the squid were clearly visible in the bodies, which glowed a pale blue.

In a few minutes Beth appeared outside, standing in the midst of the school, swinging her net, catching specimens. Several squid angrily squirted clouds of ink.

"Cute little things," Ted said. "You know, the development of squid ink is a very interesting—"

"—What do you say to squid for dinner?" Levy said.

"Hell no," Barnes said. "If this is an undiscovered species, we're not going to eat it. The last thing I need is everybody sick from food poisoning."

"Very sensible," Ted said. "I never liked squid, anyway. Interesting mechanism of propulsion, but rubbery texture."

At that moment, there was a buzz as one of the monitors turned itself on. As they watched, the screen rapidly filled with numbers:

```
0 0 0 3 2 1 2 5 2 5 2 6 3 2 0 3 2 6 2 9 3 0 1 3 2 1 0 4 2 6 1 0 3 7 1 8 3 0 1 6 0
6 1 8 0 8 2 1 3 2 2 9 0 3 3 0 0 5 1 8 2 2 0 4 2 6 1 0 1 3 0 8 3 0 1 6 2 1 3 7
1 6 0 4 0 8 3 0 1 6 2 1 1 8 2 2 0 3 3 0 1 3 1 3 0 4 3 2 0 0 0 3 2 1 2 5 2 5 2 6
3 2 0 3 2 6 2 9 3 0 1 3 2 1 0 4 2 6 1 0 3 7 1 8 3 0 1 6 0 6 1 8 0 9 2 1
3 2 2 9 0 3 3 0 0 5 1 8 2 2 0 4 2 6 1 0 1 3 0 8 3 0 1 6 2 3 7 1 1 6 0 4 0 8 3 0
1 6 2 1 1 8 2 2 0 3 3 0 1 3 1 3 0 4 3 2 0 0 0 3 2 1 2 5 2 5 2 6 3 2 0 3 2 6 2
0 4 2 6 1 0 3 7 1 8 3 0 1 6 0 6 1 8 0 8 2 1 3 2 2 9 0 3 3 0 0 5 1 8 2 2 0 4 2
6 1 0 1 3 0 8 3 0 1 6 2 1 3 7 1 6 0 4 0 8 3 0 1 6 2 1 1 8 2 2 0 3 3 0 1 3 1 3 0
4 3 2 0 0 0 3 2 1 2 5 2 5 2 6 3 2 0 3 2 6 2 9 3 0 1 3 2 1 0 4 2 6 1 0 3 7 1 8 3 0
1 6 0 6 1 8 0 8 2 1 3 2 2 9 0 3 3 0 0 5 1 8 2 2 0 4 2 6 1 0 1 3 0 8 3 0 1 6
2 1 3 7 1 6 0 4 0 8 3 0 1 6 2 1 1 8 2 2 0 3 3 0 1 3 1 3 0 4 3 2 0 0 0 3 2 1 2
2 6 3 2 0 3 2 2 9 3 0 1 3 2 1 0 4 2 6 1 0 3 7 1 8 0 1 6 0 6 1 8 0 8 2 1 3
2 2 9 0 3 3 0 0 5 1 8 2 2 0 4 2 6 1 0 1 3 0 8 3 0 1 6 2 1 3 7 1 6 0 4 0 8 3 6 2
1 1 8 2 2 0 3 3 0 1 3 1 3 0 4 3 2 0 0 0 3 1 2 5 2 5 2 6 3 2 0 3 2 6 2 9 3 0
1 3 2 1 0 4 2 6 1 0 3 7 1 8 3 0 1 6 0 6 1 8 0 8 2 1 3 2 2 9 0 3 3 0 0 5 1
8 2 2 0 4 2 6 1 0 1 3 0 8 3 0 1 6 2 1 3 7 1 6 0 4 0 8 3 0 1 6 2 3 0 1 6 2
```

"Where's that coming from?" Ted said. "The surface?"

Barnes shook his head. "We've cut direct contact with the surface."

"Then is it being transmitted underwater in some way?"

"No," Tina said, "it's too fast for underwater transmission."

"Is there another console in the habitat? No? How about DH-7?"

"DH-7's empty now. The divers have gone."

"Then where'd it come from?"

Barnes said, "It looks random to me."

Tina nodded. "It may be a discharge from a temporary buffer memory somewhere in the system. When we switched over to internal diesel power . . ."

"That's probably it," Barnes said. "Buffer discharge on switchover."

"I think you should keep it," Ted said, staring at the screen. "Just in case it's a message."

"A message from where?"

"From the sphere."

"Hell," Barnes said, "it can't be a message."

"How do you know?"

"Because there's no way a message can be transmitted. We're not hooked up to anything. Certainly not to the sphere. It's got to be a memory dump from somewhere inside our own computer system."

"How much memory have you got?"

"Fair amount. Ten giga, something like that."

"Maybe the helium's getting to the chips," Tina said. "Maybe it's a saturation effect."

"I still think you should keep it," Ted said.

Norman had been looking at the screen. He was no mathematician, but he'd looked at a lot of statistics in his life, searching for patterns in the data.

That was something human brains were inherently good at, finding patterns in visual material. Norman couldn't put his finger on it, but he sensed a pattern here. He said, "I have the feeling it's not random."

"Then let's keep it," Barnes said.

Tina went forward to the console. As her hands touched the keys, the screen went blank.

"So much for that," Barnes said. "It's gone. Too bad we didn't have Harry to look at it with us."

"Yeah," Ted said gloomily. "Too bad."

Analysis

"**T**ake a look at this," Beth said. "This one is still alive."

Norman was with her in the little biological laboratory near the top of D Cylinder. Nobody had been in this laboratory since their arrival, because they hadn't found anything living. Now, with the lights out, he and Beth watched the squid move in the glass tank.

The creature had a delicate appearance. The blue glow was concentrated in stripes along the back and sides of the creature.

"Yes," Beth said, "the bioluminescent structures seem to be located dorsally. They're bacteria, of course."

"What are?"

"The bioluminescent areas. Squid can't create light themselves. The creatures that do are bacteria. So the bioluminescent animals in the sea have incorporated these bacteria into their bodies. You're seeing bacteria glowing through the skin."

"So it's like an infection?"

"Yes, in a way."

The large eyes of the squid stared. The tentacles moved.

"And you can see all the internal organs," Beth said. "The brain is hidden behind the eye. That sac is the digestive gland, and behind it, the stomach, and below that—see it beating?—the heart. That big thing at the front is the gonad, and coming down from the stomach, a sort of funnel—that's where it squirts the ink, and propels itself."

"Is it really a new species?" Norman said.

She sighed. "I don't know. Internally it is so typical. But fewer tentacles would qualify it as a new species, all right."

"You going to get to call it *Squidus bethus?*" Norman said.

She smiled. "*Architeuthis bethis,*" she said. "Sounds like a dental problem. *Architeuthis bethis:* means you need root canal."

"How about it, Dr. Halpern?" Levy said, poking her head in. "Got some good tomatoes and peppers, be a shame to waste them. Are the squid really poisonous?"

"I doubt it," Beth said. "Squid aren't known to be. Go ahead," she said to Levy. "I think it'll be okay to eat them."

When Levy had gone, Norman said, "I thought you gave up eating these things."

"Just octopi," Beth said. "An octopus is cute and smart. Squid are rather . . . unsympathetic."

"Unsympathetic."

"Well, they're cannibalistic, and rather nasty. . . ." She raised an eyebrow. "Are you psychoanalyzing me again?"

"No. Just curious."

"As a zoologist, you're supposed to be objective," Beth said, "but I have feelings about animals, like anybody else. I have a warm feeling about octopi. They're clever, you know. I once had an octopus in a research tank that learned to kill cockroaches and use them as bait to catch crabs. The curious crab would come along, investigate the dead cockroach, and then the octopus would jump out of its hiding place and catch the crab.

"In fact, an octopus is so smart that the biggest limitation to its behavior is its lifespan. An octopus lives only three years, and that's not long enough to develop anything as complicated as a culture or civilization. Maybe if octopi lived as long as we do, they would long ago have taken over the world.

"But squid are completely different. I have no feelings about squid. Except I don't really like 'em."

He smiled. "Well," he said, "at least you finally found some life down here."

"You know, it's funny," she said. "Remember how barren it was out there? Nothing on the bottom?"

"Sure. Very striking."

"Well, I went around the side of the habitat, to get these squid. And there're all sorts of sea fans on the bottom. Beautiful colors, blues and purples and yellows. Some of them quite large."

"Think they just grew?"

"No. They must have always been in that spot, but we never went over there. I'll have to investigate it later. I'd like to know why they are localized in that particular place, next to the habitat."

Norman went to the porthole. He had switched on the exterior habitat lights, shining onto the bottom. He could indeed see many large sea fans, purple and pink and blue, waving gently in the current. They extended out to the edge of the light, to the darkness.

"In a way," Beth said, "it's reassuring. We're deep for the majority of oceanic life, which is found in the first hundred feet of water. But even so, this habitat is located in the most varied and abundant marine environment in the world." Scientists had made species counts and had determined that the South Pacific had more species of coral and sponges than anywhere else on Earth.

"So I'm glad we're finally finding things," she said. She looked at her benches of chemicals and reagents. "And I'm glad to finally get to work on something."

Harry was eating bacon and eggs in the galley. The others stood around and watched him, relieved that he was all right. And they told him the news; he listened with interest, until they mentioned that there had been a large school of squid.

"Squid?"

He looked up sharply and almost dropped his fork.

"Yeah, lots of 'em," Levy said. "I'm cooking up a bunch for dinner."

"Are they still here?" Harry asked.

"No, they're gone now."

He relaxed, shoulders dropping.

"Something the matter, Harry?" Norman said.

"I hate squid," Harry said. "I can't stand them."

"I don't care for the taste myself," Ted said.

"Terrible," Harry said, nodding. He resumed eating his eggs. The tension passed.

Then Tina shouted from D Cylinder: "I'm getting them again! I'm getting the numbers again!"

```
00032125262632   032629    301321    04261037   18    3016    06180
82132   29033005    1822    04261013   0830162137   1604    083016
21    1822    033013130432    00032125252632    032629    301321    0
4261037   18    3016    0618082132   29033005    1822   04261013   08
30162137    1604    08301621    1822    033013130432    00321252
52632   032629    301321    04261037   18    3016    0618082132   290
33005   1822    04261013   0830162137   1604    08301621   1822   03
3013130432    00032125252632    032629    301321    04261037    1
8   3016    0618082132   29033005    1822    04261013   0830162137
1604    0830162    1822    033013130432    00032125252632    032
629   301321    04261037   18    3016    0618082132   29033005   1822
04261013   0830162137   1604    08301621   1822    033013130432
003212525252632    032629    301321    04261037   18    3016    06
18082132   29033005    1822    04261013   0830162137   1604   083
01621    1822    033013130432    0003212525632    032629    301321
```

"What do you think, Harry?" Barnes said, pointing to the screen.

"Is this what you got before?" Harry said.

"Looks like it, except the spacing is different."

"Because this is definitely nonrandom," Harry said. "It's a single sequence repeated over and over. Look. Starts here, goes to here, then repeats."

0032125252632	032629	301321	04261037	19	3016	06180
82132	29033005	1822	04261013	0830162137	1604	083016
21	1822	033013130432	0032125252632	032629	301321	0
4261037	18	3016	0618082132	29033005	1822	04261013	08
30162137	1604	08301621	1822	033013130432	00321252
52632	032629	301321	04261037	18	3016	06180822132	290
33005	1822	04261013	0830162137	1604	08301621	1822	03
3013130432	0032125252632	032629	301321	04261037	1
8	3016	0618082132	29033005	1822	04261013	0830162137
1604	08301621	1822	033013130432	0032125252632
629	301321	04261037	18	3016	0618082132	29033005	1822
04261013	0830162127	1604	08301621	1822	033013130432
000321252525252632	032629	301321	04261037	18	3016	06
18082132	29033005	1822	04261013	0830162137	1604	083
01621	1822	033013130432	0003212525632	032629	301321

"He's right," Tina said.

"Fantastic," Barnes said. "Absolutely incredible, for you to see it like that."

Ted drummed his fingers on the console impatiently.

"Elementary, my dear Barnes," Harry said. "That part is easy. The hard part is—what does it mean?"

"Surely it's a message," Ted said.

"Possibly it's a message," Harry said. "It could also be some kind of discharge from within the computer, the result of a programming error or a hardware glitch. We might spend hours translating it, only to find it says 'Copyright Acme Computer Systems, Silicon Valley' or something similar."

"Well . . ." Ted said.

"The greatest likelihood is that this series of numbers originates from within the computer itself," Harry said. "But let me give it a try."

Tina printed out the screen for him.

"I'd like to try, too," Ted said quickly.

Tina said, "Certainly, Dr. Fielding," and printed out a second sheet.

"If it's a message," Harry said, "it's most likely a simple substitution code, like an askey code. It would help if we could run a decoding program on the computer. Can anybody program this thing?"

They all shook their heads. "Can you?" Barnes said.

"No. And I suppose there's no way to transmit this to the surface? The NSA code-breaking computers in Washington would take about fifteen seconds to do this."

Barnes shook his head. "No contact. I wouldn't even put up a radio wire on a balloon. The last report, they have forty-foot waves on the surface. Snap the wire right away."

"So we're isolated?"

"We're isolated."

"I guess it's back to the old pencil and paper. I always say, traditional tools are best—particularly when there's nothing else." And left the room.

"He seems to be in a good mood," Barnes said.

"I'd say a very good mood," Norman said.

"Maybe a little too good," Ted said. "A little manic?"

"No," Norman said. "Just a good mood."

"I thought he was a little high," Ted said.

"Let him stay that way," Barnes snorted, "if it helps him to crack this code."

"I'm going to try, too," Ted reminded him.

"That's fine," Barnes said. "You try, too."

Ted

"**I**'m telling you, this reliance on Harry is misplaced." Ted paced back and forth and glanced at Norman. "Harry is manic, and he's overlooking things. Obvious things."

"Like what?"

"Like the fact that the printout can't possibly be a discharge from the computer."

"How do you know?" Norman said.

"The processor," Ted said. "The processor is a 68090 chip, which means that any memory dump would be *in hex.*"

"What's hex?"

"There are lots of ways to represent numbers," Ted said. "The 68090 chip uses base-sixteen representation, called 'hexadecimal.' Hex is entirely different from regular decimal. Looks different."

"But the message used zero through nine," Norman said.

"Exactly my point," Ted said. "So it didn't come from the computer. I believe it's definitely a message from the sphere. Furthermore, although Harry thinks it is a substitution code, I think it's a direct visual representation."

"You mean a picture?"

"Yes," Ted said. "And I think it's a picture of the creature itself!" He started searching through sheets of paper. "I started with this."

```
0011101011100111001110101000000    111101011101
    1111011011010101    10011010101010100101
1001011110110000    1101001010001010101100000
111011111110101    1001010110    1001101010101101
    1000111101000010101100101    10000100
1000111101000010101    1001010110
111111011011101100100000
0011101011100111001110101000000    111101011101
1111011011010101    10011010101010100101    10010
1111010000    110100101000101011100000
111011111110101    1001010110    1001101010101101
    1000111101000010101100101    10000100
1000111101000010101    1001010110
111111011011101100100000
0011101011100111001110101000000    111101011101
    1111011011010101    10011010101010100101    10010
    1111010000    110100101000101011100000
111011111110101    1001010110    1001101010101101
    1000111101000010101100101    10000100
```

"Now, here I have translated the message to binary," Ted said. "You can immediately sense visual pattern, can't you?"

"Not really," Norman said.

"Well, it is certainly suggestive," Ted said. "I'm telling you, all those years at JPL looking at images from the planets, I have an eye for these things. So, the next thing I did was go back to the original message and fill in the spaces. I got this."

```
• •00032125252632• •032629• •301321• •04261037• •18•
•3016• •0618082132• •29033005• •1822• •04261013•
•0830162137• •1604• •08301621• •1822• •033013130432•
•00032125252632• •032629• •301321• •04261037• •18•
•3016• •0618082132• •29033005• •1822• •04261013•
•0830162137• •1604• •08301621• •1822• •033013130432•
•00032125252632• •032629• •301321• •04261037• •18•
•3016• •0618082132• •29033005• •1822• •04261013•
•0830162137• •1604• •08301621• •1822• •033013130432•
•00032125252632• •032629• •301321• •04261037• •18•
•3016• •0618082132• •29033005• •1822• •04261013•
•0830162137• •1604• •08301621• •1822• •033013130432•
•00032125252632• •032629• •301321• •04261037• •18•
```

```
•3016• •0618082132• •29033005• •1822• •04261013•
•0830162137• •1604• •08301621• •1822• •033013130432•
•00032125252632• •032629• •301321• •04261037• •18•
•3016• •0618082132• •29033005• •1822• •04261013•
•0830162137• •1604• •08301521• •1822• •033013130432•
•00032125252632• •032629• •301321• •04261037• •18•
•3016• •0618082132• •29033005• •1822• •04261013•
•0830162137• •1604• •08301621• •1822• •033013130432•
•00032125252632• •032629• •301321• •04261037• •18•
•3016• •0618082132• •29033005• •1822• •04261013•
•0830162137• •1604• •08301621• •1822• •033013130432•
•00032125252632• •032629• •301321• •04261037• •18• •
```

"Uh-huh . . ." Norman said.

"I agree, it doesn't look like anything," Ted said. "But by changing the screen width, you get *this.*"

Proudly, he held up the next sheet.

```
• •00032125252632• •032629• •301321•
•04261037• •18• •3016• •0618082132• •29033005•
•1822• •04261013• •0830162137• •1604•
•08301621• •1822• •033013130432•
•00032125252632• •032629• •301321• •04261037•
•18• •3016• •0618082132• •29033005• •1822•
•04261013• •0830162137• •1604• •08301621•
•1822• •033013130432• •00032125252632•
•032629• •301321• •04261037• •18• •3016•
•0618082132• •29033005• •1822• •04261013•
•0830162137• •1604• •08301621• •1822•
•033013130432• •00032125252632• •032629•
•301321• •04261037• •18• •3016• •0618082132•
•29033005• •1822• •04261013• •0830162137•
•1604• •08301621• •1822• •033013130432•
•00032125252632• •032629• •301321• •04261037•
•18• •3016• •0618082132• •29033005• •1822•
•04261013• •0830162137• •1604• •08301621•
•1822• •033013130432• •00032125252632•
•032629• •301321• •04261037• •18• •3016•
```

"Yes?" Norman said.

"Don't tell me you don't see the pattern," Ted said.

"I don't see the pattern," Norman said.

"Squint at it," Ted said.

Norman squinted. "Sorry."

"But it is *obviously* a picture of the creature," Ted said. "Look, that's the vertical torso, three legs, two arms. There's no head, so presumably the creature's head is located within the torso itself. Surely you see that, Norman."

"Ted . . ."

"For once, Harry has missed the point entirely! The message is not only a picture, it's a self-portrait!"

"Ted . . ."

Ted sat back. He sighed. "You're going to tell me I'm trying too hard."

"I don't want to dampen your enthusiasm," Norman said.

"But you don't see the alien?"

"Not really, no."

"Hell." Ted tossed the papers aside. "I hate that son of a bitch. He's so arrogant, he makes me so mad. . . . And on top of that, he's young!"

"You're forty," Norman said. "I wouldn't exactly call that over the hill."

"For physics, it is," Ted said. "Biologists can sometimes do important work late in life. Darwin was fifty when he published the *Origin of Species*. And chemists sometimes do good work when they're older. But in physics, if you haven't done it by thirty-five, the chances are, you never will."

"But Ted, you're respected in your field."

Ted shook his head. "I've never done fundamental work. I've analyzed data, I've come to some interesting conclusions. But never anything fundamental. This expedition is my chance to really *do* something. To really . . . get my name in the books."

Norman now had a different sense of Ted's enthusiasm and energy, that relentlessly juvenile manner. Ted wasn't emotionally retarded; he was driven. And he clung to his youth out of a sense that time was slipping by and he hadn't yet accomplished anything. It wasn't obnoxious. It was sad.

"Well," Norman said, "the expedition isn't finished yet."

"No," Ted said, suddenly brightening. "You're right. You're absolutely right. There are more, wonderful experiences awaiting us. I just *know* there are. And they'll come, won't they."

"Yes, Ted," Norman said. "They'll come."

Beth

"**D**amn it, nothing works!" She waved a hand to her laboratory bench. "Not a single one of the chemicals or reagents here is worth a damn!"

"What've you tried?" Barnes said calmly.

"Zenker-Formalin, H and E, the other stains. Proteolytic extractions, enzyme breaks. You name it. None of it works. You know what I think, I think that whoever stocked this lab did it with outdated ingredients."

"No," Barnes said, "it's the atmosphere."

He explained that their environment contained only 2 percent oxygen, 1 percent carbon dioxide, but no nitrogen at all. "Chemical reactions are unpredictable," he said. "You ought to take a look at Levy's recipe book sometime. It's like nothing you've ever seen in your life. The food looks normal when she's finished, but she sure doesn't make it the normal way."

"And the lab?"

"The lab was stocked without knowing the working depth we would be at. If we were shallower, we'd be breathing compressed air, and all your chemical reactions would work—they'd just go very fast. But with heliox, reactions are unpredictable. And if they won't go, well . . ." He shrugged.

"What am I supposed to do?" she said.

"The best you can," Barnes said. "Same as the rest of us."

"Well, all I can really do is gross anatomical analyses. All this bench is worthless."

"Then do the gross anatomy."

"I just wish we had more lab capability. . . ."

"This is it," Barnes said. "Accept it and go on."

Ted entered the room. "You better take a look outside, everybody," he said, pointing to the portholes. "We have more visitors."

The squid were gone. For a moment Norman saw nothing but the water, and the white suspended sediment caught in the lights.

"Look down. At the bottom."

The sea floor was alive. Literally alive, crawling and wiggling and tremulous as far as they could see in the lights.

"What is *that?*"

Beth said, "It's shrimps. A hell of a lot of shrimps." And she ran to get her net.

"Now, *that's* what we ought to be eating," Ted said. "I love shrimp. And those look perfect-size, a little smaller than crayfish. Probably delicious. I remember once in Portugal, my second wife and I had the most fabulous crayfish. . . ."

Norman felt slightly uneasy. "What're they doing here?"

"I don't know. What do shrimps do, anyway? Do they migrate?"

"Damned if I know," Barnes said. "I always buy 'em frozen. My wife hates to peel 'em."

Norman remained uneasy, though he could not say why. He could clearly see now that the bottom was covered in shrimps; they were everywhere. Why should it bother him?

Norman moved away from the window, hoping his sense of vague uneasiness would go away if he looked at something else. But it didn't go away, it just stayed there—a small tense knot in the pit of his stomach. He didn't like the feeling at all.

Harry

"Harry."

"Oh, hi, Norman. I heard the excitement. Lot of shrimps outside, is that it?"

Harry sat on his bunk, with the paper printout of numbers on his knees. He had a pencil and pad, and the page was covered with calculations, scratch-outs, symbols, arrows.

"Harry," Norman said, "what's going on?"

"Damned if I know."

"I'm just wondering why we should suddenly be finding life down here— the squid, the shrimps—when before there was nothing. Ever."

"Oh, that. I think that's pretty clear."

"Yes?"

"Sure. What's different between then and now?"

"You've been inside the sphere."

"No, no. I mean, what's different in the outside environment?"

Norman frowned. He didn't grasp what Harry was driving at.

"Well, just look outside," Harry said. "What could you see before that you can't see now?"

"The grid?"

"Uh-huh. The grid and the divers. Lot of activity—and a lot of electricity. I think it scared off the normal fauna of the area. This is the South Pacific, you know; it ought to be teeming with life."

"And now that the divers are gone, the animals are back?"

"That's my guess."

"That's all there is to it?" Norman said, frowning.

"Why are you asking me?" Harry said. "Ask Beth; she'll give you a definitive answer. But I know animals are sensitive to all kinds of stimuli we don't notice. You can't run God knows how many million volts through underwater cables, to light a half-mile grid in an environment that has never seen light before, and not expect to have an effect."

Something about this argument tickled the back of Norman's mind. He knew something, something pertinent. But he couldn't get it.

"Harry."

"Yes, Norman. You look a little worried. You know, this substitution code is really a bitch. I'll tell you the truth, I'm not sure I'll be able to crack it. You see, the problem is, if it *is* a letter substitution, you will need two digits to describe a single letter, because there are twenty-six letters in the alphabet, assuming no punctuation—which may or may not be included here as well. So when I see a two next to a three, I don't know if it is letter two followed by letter three, or just letter twenty-three. It's taking a long time to work through the permutations. You see what I mean?"

"Harry."

"Yes, Norman."

"What happened inside the sphere?"

"Is that what you're worried about?" Harry asked.

"What makes you think I'm worried about anything?" Norman asked.

"Your face," Harry said. "That's what makes me think you're worried."

"Maybe I am," Norman said. "But about this sphere . . ."

"You know, I've been thinking a lot about that sphere."

"And?"

"It's quite amazing. I really don't remember what happened."

"Harry."

"I feel fine—I feel better all the time, honest to God, my energy's back, headache's gone—and earlier I remembered everything about that sphere and what was inside it. But every minute that passes, it seems to fade. You know, the way a dream fades? You remember it when you wake up, but an hour later, it's gone?"

"Harry."

"I remember that it was wonderful, and beautiful. Something about lights, swirling lights. But that's all."

"How did you get the door to open?"

"Oh, that. It was very clear at the time; I remember I had worked it all out, I knew exactly what to do."

"What did you do?"

"I'm sure it will come back to me."

"You don't remember how you opened the door?"

"No. I just remember this sudden insight, this certainty, about how it was done. But I can't remember the details. Why, does somebody else want to go in? Ted, probably."

"I'm sure Ted would like to go in—"

"—I don't know if that's a good idea. Frankly, I don't think Ted should do it. Think how boring he'll be with his speeches, after he comes out. 'I visited an alien sphere' by Ted Fielding. We'd never hear the end of it."

And he giggled.

Ted is right, Norman thought. He's definitely manic. There was a speedy, overly cheerful quality to Harry. His characteristic slow sarcasm was gone, replaced by a sunny, open, very quick manner. And a kind of laughing indifference to everything, an imbalance in his sense of what was important. He had said he couldn't crack the code. He had said he couldn't remember what happened inside the sphere, or how he had opened it. And he didn't seem to think it mattered.

"Harry, when you first came out of the sphere, you seemed worried."

"Did I? Had a brutal headache, I remember *that.*"

"You kept saying we should go to the surface."

"Did I?"

"Yes. Why was that?"

"God only knows. I was so confused."

"You also said it was dangerous for us to stay here."

Harry smiled. "Norman, you can't take that too seriously. I didn't know if I was coming or going."

"Harry, we need you to remember these things. If things start to come back to you, will you tell me?"

"Oh sure, Norman. Absolutely. You can count on me; I'll tell you right away."

The Laboratory

"**N**o," Beth said. "None of it makes sense. First of all, in areas where fish haven't encountered human beings before, they tend to ignore humans unless they are hunted. The Navy divers didn't hunt the fish. Second, if the divers stirred up the bottom, that'd actually release nutrients and attract more animals. Third, many species of animals are attracted to electrical currents. So, if anything, the shrimps and other animals should've been drawn here earlier by the electricity. Not now, with the power off."

She was examining the shrimps under the low-power scanning microscope. "How does he seem?"

"Harry?"

"Yes."

"I don't know."

"Is he okay?"

"I don't know. I think so."

Still looking through the microscope lens, she said, "Did he tell you anything about what happened inside the sphere?"

"Not yet."

She adjusted the microscope, shook her head. "I'll be damned."

"What is it?" Norman said.

"Extra dorsal plating."

"Meaning?"

"It's another new species," she said.

Norman said, *"Shrimpus bethus?* You're making discoveries hand over fist down here, Beth."

"Uh-huh . . . I checked the sea fans, too, because they seemed to have an unusual radial growth pattern. They're a new species as well."

"That's great, Beth."

She turned, looked at him. "No. Not great. Weird." She clicked on a high-intensity light, cut open one of the shrimps with a scalpel. "I thought so."

"What is it?"

"Norman," she said, "we didn't see any life down here for days—and suddenly in the last few hours we find three new species? It's not normal."

"We don't know what's normal at one thousand feet."

"I'm telling you. It's not normal."

"But, Beth, you said yourself that we simply hadn't noticed the sea fans before. And the squid and the shrimps—can't they be migrating, passing through this area, something like that? Barnes says they've never had trained scientists living this deep at one site on the ocean floor before. Maybe these migrations are normal, and we just don't know they occur."

"I don't think so," Beth said. "When I went out to get these shrimps, I felt their behavior was atypical. For one thing, they were too close together. Shrimps on the bottom maintain a characteristic distance from one another, about four feet. These were packed close. In addition, they moved as if they were feeding, but there's nothing to feed on down here."

"Nothing that we know of."

"Well, *these* shrimps can't have been feeding." She pointed to the cut animal on the lab bench. "They haven't got a stomach."

"Are you kidding?"

"Look for yourself."

Norman looked, but the dissected shrimp didn't mean much to him. It was just a mass of pink flesh. It was cut on a ragged diagonal, not cleanly. She's tired, he thought. She's not working efficiently. We need sleep. We need to get out of here.

"The external appearance is perfect, except for an extra dorsal fan at the tail," she said. "But internally, it's all screwed up. There's no way for these animals to be alive. No stomach. No reproductive apparatus. This animal is like a bad imitation of a shrimp."

"Yet the shrimps are alive," Norman said.

"Yeah," she said. "They are." She seemed unhappy about it.

"And the squid were perfectly normal inside. . . ."

"Actually, they weren't. When I dissected one, I found that it lacked several important structures. There's a nerve bundle called the stellate ganglion that wasn't there."

"Well . . ."

"And there were no gills, Norman. Squid possess a long gill structure for gas exchange. This one didn't have one. The squid had no way to breathe, Norman."

"It must have had a way to breathe."

"I'm telling you, it didn't. We're seeing impossible animals down here. All of a sudden, impossible animals."

She turned away from the high-intensity lamp, and he saw that she was close to tears. Her hands were shaking; she quickly dropped them into her lap. "You're really worried," he said.

"Aren't you?" She searched his face. "Norman," she said, "all this started when Harry came out of the sphere, didn't it?"

"I guess it did."

"Harry came out of the sphere, and now we have impossible sea life. . . . I don't like it. I wish we could get out of here. I really do." Her lower lip was trembling.

He gave her a hug and said gently, "We can't get out of here."

"I know," she said. She hugged him back, and began to cry, pushing her face into his shoulder.

"It's all right. . . ."

"I hate it when I get this way," she said. "I hate this feeling."

"I know. . . ."

"And I hate this place. I hate everything about it. I hate Barnes and I hate Ted's lectures and I hate Levy's stupid desserts. I wish I wasn't here."

"I know. . . ."

She sniffled for a moment, then abruptly pushed him away with her strong arms. She turned away, wiped her eyes. "I'm all right," she said. "Thanks."

"Sure," he said.

She remained turned away, her back to him. "Where's the damn Kleenex?" She found one, blew her nose. "You won't say anything to the others. . . ."

"Of course not."

A bell rang, startling her. "Jesus, what's that?"

"I think it's dinner," Norman said.

Dinner

"**I** don't know how you can eat those things," Harry said, pointing to the squid.

"They're delicious," Norman said. "Sautéed squid." As soon as he had sat at the table, he became aware of how hungry he was. And eating made him feel better; there was a reassuring normalcy about sitting at a table, with a knife and fork in his hands. It was almost possible to forget where he was.

"I especially like them fried," Tina said.

"Fried *calamari*," Barnes said. "Wonderful. My favorite."

"I like them fried, too," Edmunds, the archivist, said. She sat primly, very erect, eating her food precisely. Norman noticed that she put her knife down between bites.

"Why aren't these fried?" Norman said.

"We can't deep-fry down here," Barnes said. "The hot oil forms a suspension and gums up the air filters. But sautéed is fine."

"Well, I don't know about the squid but the shrimps are great," Ted said. "Aren't they, Harry?" Ted and Harry were eating shrimp.

"Great shrimp," Harry said. "Delicious."

"You know how I feel," Ted said, "I feel like Captain Nemo. Remember, living underwater off the bounty of the sea?"

"Twenty Thousand Leagues Under the Sea," Barnes said.

"James Mason," Ted said. "Remember how he played the organ? *Duh-duh-duh, da da da daaaaah da!* Bach Toccata and Fugue in D minor."

"And Kirk Douglas."

"Kirk Douglas was great."

"Remember when he fought the giant squid?"

"That was great."

"Kirk Douglas had an ax, remember?"

"Yeah, and he cut off one of the squid arms."

"That movie," Harry said, "scared the hell out of me. I saw it when I was a kid and it scared the hell out of me."

"I didn't think it was scary," Ted said.

"You were older," Harry said.

"Not that much older."

"Yes, you were. For a kid it was terrifying. That's probably why I don't like squid now."

"You don't like squid," Ted said, "because they're rubbery and disgusting."

Barnes said, "That was the movie that made me want to join the Navy."

"I can imagine," Ted said. "So romantic and exciting. And a real vision of the wonders of applied science. Who played the professor in that?"

"The professor?"

"Yes, remember there was a professor?"

"I vaguely remember a professor. Old guy."

"Norman? You remember who was the professor?"

"No, I don't," Norman said.

Ted said, "Are you sitting over there keeping an eye on us, Norman?"

"How do you mean?" Norman said.

"Analyzing us. Seeing if we're cracking up."

"Yes," Norman said, smiling. "I am."

"How're we doing?" Ted said.

"I would say it is highly significant that a group of scientists can't remember who played the scientist in a movie they all loved."

"Well, Kirk Douglas was the hero, that's why. The scientist wasn't the hero."

"Franchot Tone?" Barnes said. "Claude Rains?"

"No, I don't think so. Fritz somebody?"

"Fritz Weaver?"

They heard a crackle and hiss, and then the sounds of an organ playing the Toccata and Fugue in D minor.

"Great," Ted said. "I didn't know we had music down here."

Edmunds returned to the table. "There's a tape library, Ted."

"I don't know if this is right for dinner," Barnes said.

"I like it," Ted said. "Now, if we only had seaweed salad. Isn't that what Captain Nemo served?"

"Maybe something lighter?" Barnes said.

"Lighter than seaweed?"

"Lighter than Bach."

"What was the submarine called?" Ted said.

"The *Nautilus,*" Edmunds said.

"Oh, right. *Nautilus.*"

"It was the name of the first atomic submarine, too, launched in 1954," she said. And she gave Ted a bright smile.

"True," Ted said. "True."

Norman thought, He's met his match in irrelevant trivia.

Edmunds went to the porthole and said, "Oh, more visitors."

"What now?" Harry said, looking up quickly.

Frightened? Norman thought. No, just quick, manic. Interested.

"They're *beautiful,*" Edmunds was saying. "Some kind of little jellyfish. All around the habitat. We should really film them. What do you think, Dr. Fielding? Should we go film them?"

"I think I'll just eat now, Jane," Ted said, a bit severely.

Edmunds looked stricken, rejected. Norman thought, I'll have to watch that. She turned to leave. The others glanced toward the porthole, but nobody left the table.

"Have you ever eaten jellyfish?" Ted said. "I hear they're a delicacy."

"Some of them are poisonous," Beth said. "Toxins in the tentacles."

"Don't the Chinese eat jellyfish?" Harry said.

"Yes," Tina said. "They make a soup, too. My grandmother used to make it in Honolulu."

"You're from Honolulu?"

"Mozart would be better for dining," Barnes said. "Or Beethoven. Something with strings. This organ music is gloomy."

"Dramatic," Ted said, playing imaginary keys in the air, in time to the music. Swaying his body like James Mason.

"Gloomy," Barnes said.

The intercom crackled. "Oh, you should see this," Edmunds said, over the intercom. "It's *beautiful.*"

"Where is she?"

"She must be outside," Barnes said. He went to the porthole.

"It's like pink snow," Edmunds said.

They all got up and went to the portholes.

Edmunds was outside with the video camera. They could hardly see her through the dense clouds of jellyfish. The jellyfish were small, the size of a thimble, and a delicate, glowing pink. It was indeed like a snowfall. Some of the jellyfish came quite close to the porthole; they could see them well.

"They have no tentacles," Harry said. "They're just little pulsating sacs."

"That's how they move," Beth said. "Muscular contractions expel the water."

"Like squid," Ted said.

"Not as developed, but the general idea."

"They're sticky," Edmunds said, over the intercom. "They're sticking to my suit."

"That pink color is fantastic," Ted said. "Like snow in a sunset."

"Very poetic."

"I thought so."

"You would."

"They're sticking to my faceplate, too," Edmunds said. "I have to pull them off. They leave a smeary streak—"

She broke off abruptly, but they could still hear her breathing.

"Can you see her?" Ted said.

"Not very well. She's there, to the left."

Over the intercom, Edmunds said, "They seem to be warm. I feel heat on my arms and legs."

"That's not right," Barnes said. He turned to Tina. "Tell her to get out of there."

Tina ran from the cylinder, toward the communications console.

Norman could hardly see Edmunds any more. He was vaguely aware of a dark shape, moving arms, agitated. . . .

Over the intercom, she said, "The smear on the faceplate—it won't go away—they seem to be eroding the plastic—and my arms—the fabric is—"

Tina's voice said, "Jane. Jane, get out of there."

"On the double," Barnes shouted. "Tell her on the double!"

Edmunds's breathing was coming in ragged gasps. "The smears—can't see very well—I feel—hurts—my arms burning—hurts—they're eating through—"

"Jane. Come back. Jane. Are you reading? Jane."

"She's fallen down," Harry said. "Look, you can see her lying—"

"—We have to save her," Ted said, jumping to his feet.

"*Nobody move,*" Barnes said.

"But she's—"

"*—Nobody else is going out there, mister.*"

Edmunds's breathing was rapid. She coughed, gasped. "I can't—I can't— oh God—"

Edmunds began to scream.

The scream was high-pitched and continuous except for ragged gasps for breath. They could no longer see her through the swarms of jellyfish. They looked at each other, at Barnes. Barnes's face was rigidly set, his jaw tight, listening to the screams.

And then, abruptly, there was silence.

The Next Messages

An hour later, the jellyfish disappeared as mysteriously as they had come. They could see Edmunds's body outside the habitat, lying on the bottom, rocking back and forth gently in the current. There were small ragged holes in the fabric of the suit.

They watched through the portholes as Barnes and the chief petty officer, Teeny Fletcher, crossed the bottom into the harsh floodlights, carrying extra air tanks. They lifted Edmunds's body; the helmeted head flopped loosely back, revealing the scarred plastic faceplate, dull in the light.

Nobody spoke. Norman noticed that even Harry had dropped his manic effect; he sat unmoving, staring out the window.

Outside, Barnes and Fletcher still held the body. There was a great burst of silvery bubbles, which rose swiftly to the surface.

"What're they doing?"

"Inflating her suit."

"Why? Aren't they bringing her back?" Ted said.

"They can't," Tina said. "There's nowhere to put her here. The decomposition by-products would ruin our air."

"But there must be some kind of a sealed container—"

"—There isn't," Tina said. "There's no provision for keeping organic remains in the habitat."

"You mean they didn't plan on anyone dying."

"That's right. They didn't."

Now there were many thin streams of bubbles rising from the holes in the suit, toward the surface. Edmunds's suit was puffed, bloated. Barnes released it, and it floated slowly away, as if pulled upward by the streaming silver bubbles.

"It'll go to the surface?"

"Yes. The gas expands continuously as outside pressure diminishes."

"And what then?"

"Sharks," Beth said. "Probably."

In a few moments the body disappeared into blackness, beyond the reach of the lights. Barnes and Fletcher still watched the body, helmets tilted up toward the surface. Fletcher made the sign of the cross. Then they trudged back toward the habitat.

A bell rang from somewhere inside. Tina went into D Cyl. Moments later she shouted, "Dr. Adams! More numbers!"

Harry got up and went into the next cylinder. The others trailed after him. Nobody wanted to look out the porthole any longer.

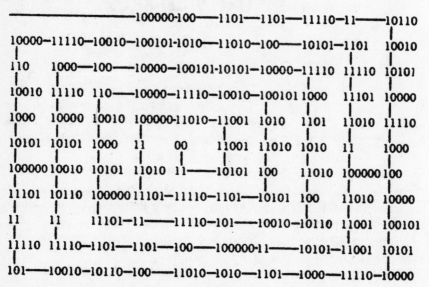

Norman stared at the screen, entirely puzzled.

But Harry clapped his hands in delight. "Excellent," Harry said. "This is extremely helpful."

"It is?"

"Of course. Now I have a fighting chance."

"You mean to break the code."

"Yes, of course."

"Why?"

"Remember the original number sequence? This is the same sequence."

"It is?"

"Of course," Harry said. "Except it's in binary."

"Binary," Ted said, nudging Norman. "Didn't I tell you binary was important?"

"What's important," Harry said, "is that this establishes the individual letter breaks from the original sequence."

"Here's a copy of the original sequence," Tina said, handing them a sheet.

```
00032125252632   032629   301321   04261037   18   3016   06180821
32   29033005   1822   04261013   0830162137   1604   08301621   1822   0
33013130432
```

"Good," Harry said. "Now you can see my problem at once. Look at the word: oh-oh-oh-three-two-one, and so on. The question is, how do I break that word up into individual letters? I couldn't decide, but now I know."

"How?"

"Well, obviously, it goes three, twenty-one, twenty-five, twenty-five. . . ."

Norman didn't understand. "But how do you know that?"

"Look," Harry said impatiently. "It's very simple, Norman. It's a spiral, reading from inside to outside. It's just giving us the numbers in—"

Abruptly, the screen changed again.

```
—————————32—04—13—13—30—03—22
                                        |
16—30—18—37—10—26—04—21—13  18
 |                         |   |
06  08—04—16—37—21—16—30  30  21
 |   |                 |   |   |
18  30  06—16—30—18—37  08  29  16
 |   |   |         |   |   |   |
08  16  18  32—26—25  10  13  26  30
 |   |   |   |     |   |   |   |   |
21  21  08  03  00  25  26  10  03  08
 |   |   |   |   |   |   |   |   |   |
32  18  21  26  03—21  04  26  32  04
 |   |   |   |         |   |   |   |
29  22  32  29—30—13—21  04  26  16
 |   |   |                 |   |   |
03  03  29—03—30—05—18—22  25  37
 |   |                     |   |
30  30—13—13—04—32—03—21—25  21
 |                             |
05—18—22—04—26—10—13—08—30—16
```

"There, is that clearer for you?"

Norman frowned.

"Look, it's exactly the same," Harry said. "See? Center outward? Oh–oh–oh–three–twenty-one–twenty-five–twentyfive . . . It's made a spiral moving outward from the center."

"It?"

"Maybe it's sorry about what happened to Edmunds," Harry said.

"Why do you say that?" Norman asked, staring curiously at Harry.

"Because it's obviously trying very hard to communicate with us," Harry said. "It's attempting different things."

"Who is *it?*"

"It," Harry said, "may not be a who."

The screen went blank, and another pattern appeared.

"All right," Harry said. "This is very good."

"Where is this coming from?"

"Obviously, from the ship."

"But we're not connected to the ship. How is it managing to turn on our computer and print this?"

"We don't know."

"Well, shouldn't we know?" Beth said.

"Not necessarily," Ted said.

"Shouldn't we *try* to know?"

"Not necessarily. You see, if the technology is advanced enough, it appears to the naïve observer to be magic. There's no doubt about that. For example, you take a famous scientist from our past—Aristotle, Leonardo da Vinci, even Isaac Newton. Show him an ordinary Sony color-television set and he'd run screaming, claiming it was witchcraft. He wouldn't understand it at all.

"But the point," Ted said, "is that you couldn't explain it to him, either. At least not easily. Isaac Newton wouldn't be able to understand TV without first studying our physics for a couple of years. He'd have to learn all the underlying concepts: electromagnetism, waves, particle physics. These would all be new ideas to him, a new conception of nature. In the meantime, the TV would be magic as far as he was concerned. But to us it's ordinary. It's TV."

"You're saying we're like Isaac Newton?"

Ted shrugged. "We're getting a communication and we don't know how it's done."

"And we shouldn't bother to try and find out."

"I think we have to accept the possibility," Ted said, "that we may not be able to understand it."

Norman noticed the energy with which they threw themselves into this discussion, pushing aside the tragedy so recently witnessed. They're intellectuals, he thought, and their characteristic defense is intellectualization. Talk. Ideas. Abstractions. Concepts. It was a way of getting distance from the feelings of sadness and fear and being trapped. Norman understood the impulse: he wanted to get away from those feelings himself.

Harry frowned at the spiral image. "We may not understand how, but it's obvious *what* it's doing. It's trying to communicate by trying different presentations. The fact that it's trying spirals may be significant. Maybe it believes we think in spirals. Or write in spirals."

"Right," Beth said. "Who knows what kind of weird creatures we are?"

Ted said, "If it's trying to communicate with us, why aren't we trying to communicate back?"

Harry snapped his fingers. "Good idea!" He went to the keyboard.

"There's an obvious first step," Harry said. "We just send the original message back. We'll start with the first grouping, beginning with the double zeroes."

"I want it made clear," Ted said, "that the suggestion to attempt communication with the alien originated with me."

"It's clear, Ted," Barnes said.

"Harry?" Ted said.

"Yes, Ted," Harry said. "Don't worry, it's your idea."

Sitting at the keyboard, Harry typed:

00032125252632

The numbers appeared on the screen. There was a pause. They listened to the hum of the air fans, the distant thump of the diesel generator. They all watched the screen.

Nothing happened.

The screen went blank, and then printed out:

0001132121051808012232

Norman felt the hair rise on the back of his neck.

It was just a series of numbers on a computer screen, but it still gave him a chill. Standing beside him, Tina shivered. "He answered us."

"Fabulous," Ted said.

"I'll try the second grouping now," Harry said. He seemed calm, but his fingers kept making mistakes at the keyboard. It took a few moments before he was able to type:

032629

The reply immediately came back:

0015260805180810213

"Well," Harry said, "looks like we just opened our line of communication."

"Yes," Beth said. "Too bad we don't understand what we're saying to each other."

"Presumably it knows what it's saying," Ted said. "But we're still in the dark."

"Maybe we can get it to explain itself."

Impatiently, Barnes said, "What is this *it* you keep referring to?"

Harry sighed, and pushed his glasses up on his nose. "I think there's no doubt about that. *It,*" Harry said, "is something that was previously inside the sphere, and that is now released, and is free to act. That's what *it* is."

THE MONSTER

Alarm

Norman awoke to a shrieking alarm and flashing red lights. He rolled out of his bunk, pulled on his insulated shoes and his heated jacket, and ran for the door, where he collided with Beth. The alarm was screaming throughout the habitat.

"What's happening!" he shouted, over the alarm.

"I don't know!"

Her face was pale, frightened. Norman pushed past her. In the B Cylinder, among all the pipes and consoles, a flashing sign winked: "LIFE SUPPORT EMERGENCY." He looked for Teeny Fletcher, but the big engineer wasn't there.

He hurried back toward C Cylinder, passing Beth again.

"Do you know?" Beth shouted.

"It's life support! Where's Fletcher? Where's Barnes?"

"I don't know! I'm looking!"

"There's nobody in B!" he shouted, and scrambled up the steps into D Cylinder. Tina and Fletcher were there, working behind the computer consoles. The back panels were pulled off, exposing wires, banks of chips. The room lights were flashing red.

The screens all flashed "EMERGENCY—LIFE SUPPORT SYSTEMS."

"What's going on?" Norman shouted.

Fletcher waved a hand dismissingly.

"Tell me!"

He turned, saw Harry sitting in the corner near Edmunds's video section like a zombie, with a pencil and a pad of paper on his knee. He seemed completely indifferent to the sirens, the lights flashing on his face.

"Harry!"

Harry didn't respond; Norman turned back to the two women.

"For God's sake, will you tell me what it is?" Norman shouted.

And then the sirens stopped. The screens went blank. There was silence, except for soft classical music.

"Sorry about that," Tina said.

"It was a false alarm," Fletcher said.

"Jesus Christ," Norman said, dropping into a chair. He took a deep breath. "Were you asleep?"

He nodded.

"Sorry. It just went off by itself."

"Jesus Christ."

"The next time it happens, you can check your badge," Fletcher said, pointing to the badge on her own chest. "That's the first thing to do. You see the badges are all normal now."

"Jesus Christ."

"Take it easy, Norman," Harry said. "When the psychiatrist goes crazy, it's a bad sign."

"I'm a psychologist."

"Whatever."

Tina said, "Our computer alarm has a lot of peripheral sensors, Dr. Johnson. It goes off sometimes. There's not much we can do about it."

Norman nodded, went into E Cyl to the galley. Levy had made strawberry shortcake for lunch, and nobody had eaten it because of the accident with Edmunds. He was sure it would still be there, but when he couldn't find it, he felt frustrated. He opened cabinet doors, slammed them shut. He kicked the refrigerator door.

Take it easy, he thought. It was just a false alarm.

But he couldn't overcome the feeling that he was trapped, stuck in some damned oversized iron lung, while things slowly fell apart around him. The worst moment had been Barnes's briefing, when he came back from sending Edmunds's body to the surface.

Barnes had decided it was time to make a little speech. Deliver a little pep talk.

"I know you're all upset about Edmunds," he had said, "but what happened to her was an accident. Perhaps she made an error of judgment in going out among jellyfish. Perhaps not. The fact is, accidents happen under the best of circumstances, and the deep sea is a particularly unforgiving environment."

Listening, Norman thought, He's writing his report. Explaining it away to the brass.

"Right now," Barnes was saying, "I urge you all to remain calm. It's sixteen hours since the gale hit topside. We just sent up a sensor balloon to the surface. Before we could make readings, the cable snapped, which suggests that surface waves are still thirty feet or higher, and the gale is still in full force. The weather satellite estimates were for a sixty-hour storm on site, so we have two more full days down here. There's not much we can do about it. We just have to remain calm. Don't forget, even when you do go topside you can't throw open the hatch and start breathing. You have to spend four more days decompressing in a hyperbaric chamber on the surface."

That was the first Norman had heard of surface decompression. Even after they left this iron lung, they would have to sit in another iron lung for another four days?

"I thought you knew," Barnes had said. "That's SOP for saturated environments. You can stay down here as long as you like, but you have a four-day decompress when you go back. And believe me, this habitat's a lot nicer than the decompression chamber. So enjoy this while you can."

Enjoy this while you can, he thought. Jesus Christ. Strawberry shortcake would help. Where the hell was Levy, anyway?

He went back to D Cyl. "Where's Levy?"

"Dunno," Tina said. "Around here somewhere. Maybe sleeping."

"Nobody could sleep through that alarm," Norman said.

"Try the galley?"

"I just did. Where's Barnes?"

"He went back to the ship with Ted. They're putting more sensors around the sphere."

"I told them it was a waste of time," Harry said.

"So nobody knows where Levy is?" Norman said.

Fletcher finished screwing the computer panels back on. "Doctor," she said, "are you one of those people who need to keep track of where everyone is?"

"No," Norman said. "Of course not."

"Then what's the big deal about Levy, sir?"

"I only wanted to know where the strawberry shortcake was."

"Gone," Fletcher said promptly. "Captain and I came back from funeral duty and we sat down and ate the whole thing, just like that." She shook her head.

"Maybe Rose'll make some more," Harry said.

He found Beth in her laboratory, on the top level of D Cyl. He walked in just in time to see her take a pill.

"What was that?"

"Valium. God."

"Where'd you get it?"

"Look," she said, "don't give me any psychotalk about it—"

"—I was just asking."

Beth pointed to a white box mounted on the wall in the corner of the lab. "There's a first-aid kit in every cylinder. Turns out to be pretty complete, too."

Norman went over to the box, flipped open the lid. There were neat compartments with medicines, syringes, bandages. Beth was right, it was quite complete—antibiotics, sedatives, tranquilizers, even surgical anesthetics. He didn't recognize all the names on the bottles, but the psychoactive drugs were strong.

"You could fight a war with the stuff in this kit."

"Yeah, well. The Navy."

"There's everything you need here to do major surgery." Norman noticed a card on the inside of the box. It said "MEDAID CODE 103." "Any idea what this means?"

She nodded. "It's a computer code. I called it up."

"And?"

"The news," she said, "is not good."

"Is that right?" He sat at the terminal in her room and punched in 103. The screen said:

HYPERBARIC SATURATED ENVIRONMENT
MEDICAL COMPLICATIONS (MAJOR-FATAL)

1.01 Pulmonary Embolism
1.02 High Pressure Nervous Syndrome
1.03 Aseptic Bone Necrosis
1.04 Oxygen Toxicity
1.05 Thermal Stress Syndrome
1.06 Disseminated Pseudomonas Infection
1.07 Cerebral Infarction

Choose One:

"Don't choose one," Beth said. "Reading the details will only upset you. Just leave it at this—we're in a very dangerous environment. Barnes didn't bother to give us all the gory details. You know why the Navy has that rule about pulling people out within seventy-two hours? Because after seventy-two hours, you increase your risk of something called 'aseptic bone necrosis.' Nobody knows why, but the pressurized environment causes bone destruction in the leg and hip. And you know why this habitat constantly adjusts as we walk through it? It's not because that's slick and high-tech. It's because the helium atmosphere makes body-heat control very volatile. You can quickly become overheated, and just as quickly overchilled. Fatally so. It can happen so fast you don't realize it until it's too late and you drop dead. And 'high pressure nervous syndrome'—that turns out to be sudden convulsions, paralysis, and death if the carbon-dioxide content of the atmosphere drops too low. That's what the badges are for, to make sure we have enough CO_2 in the air. That's the only reason we have the badges. Nice, huh?"

Norman flicked off the screen, sat back. "Well, I keep coming back to the same point—there's not much we can do about it now."

"Exactly what Barnes said." Beth started pushing equipment around on her counter top, nervously. Rearranging things.

"Too bad we don't have a sample of those jellyfish," Norman said.

"Yes, but I'm not sure how much good it would do, to tell the truth." She frowned, shifted papers on the counter again. "Norman, I'm not thinking very clearly down here."

"How's that?"

"After the, uh, accident, I came up here to look over my notes, review things. And I checked the shrimps. Remember how I told you they didn't have any stomach? Well, they do. I'd made a bad dissection, out of the midsagittal plane. I just missed all the midline structures. But they're there, all right; the shrimps are normal. And the squid? It turns out the one squid I dissected was a little anomalous. It had an atrophic gill, but it had one. And the other squid are perfectly normal. Just what you'd expect. I was wrong, too hasty. It really bothers me."

"Is that why you took the Valium?"

She nodded. "I hate to be sloppy."

"Nobody's criticizing you."

"If Harry or Ted reviewed my work and found that I'd made these stupid *mistakes . . .*"

"What's wrong with a mistake?"

"I can hear them now: Just like a woman, not careful enough, too eager to make a discovery, trying to prove herself, too quick to draw conclusions. Just like a woman."

"Nobody's criticizing you, Beth."

"I am."

"Nobody else," Norman said. "I think you ought to give yourself a break."

She stared at the lab bench. Finally she said, "I can't."

Something about the way she said it touched him. "I understand," Norman said, and a memory came rushing back to him. "You know, when I was a kid, I went to the beach with my younger brother. Tim. He's dead now, but Tim was about six at the time. He couldn't swim yet. My mother told me to watch him carefully, but when I got to the beach all my friends were there, body-surfing. I didn't want to be bothered with my brother. It was hard, because I wanted to be out in the big surf, and he had to stay close to shore.

"Anyway, in the middle of the afternoon he comes out of the water screaming bloody murder, absolutely screaming. And tugging at his right side. It turned out he had been stung by some kind of a jellyfish. It was still attached to him, sticking to his side. Then he collapsed on the beach. One of the mothers ran over and took Timmy to the hospital, before I could even get out of the water. I didn't know where he had gone. I got to the hospital later. My mother was already there. Tim was in shock; I guess the poison was a heavy dose for his small body. Anyway, nobody blamed me. It wouldn't have mattered if I had been sitting right on the beach watching him like a hawk, he would still have been stung. But I hadn't been sitting there, and I blamed myself for years, long after he was fine. Every time I'd see those scars on his side, I felt terrible guilt. But you get over it. You're not responsible for everything that happens in the world. You just aren't."

There was a silence. Somewhere in the habitat he heard a soft rhythmic knocking, a sort of thumping. And the ever-present hum of the air handlers.

Beth was staring at him. "Seeing Edmunds die must have been hard for you."

"It's funny," Norman said. "I never made the connection, until right now."

"Blocked it, I guess. Want a Valium?"

He smiled. "No."

"You looked as if you were about to cry."

"No. I'm fine." He stood up, stretched. He went over to the medicine kit and closed the white lid, came back.

Beth said, "What do you think about these messages we're getting?"

"Beats me," Norman said. He sat down again. "Actually, I did have one crazy thought. Do you suppose the messages and these animals we're seeing are related?"

"Why?"

"I never thought about it until we started to get spiral messages. Harry says it's because the thing—the famous *it*—believes we think in spirals. But it's just as likely that *it* thinks in spirals and so it assumes we do, too. The sphere is round, isn't it? And we've been seeing all these radially symmetrical animals. Jellyfish, squid."

"Nice idea," Beth said, "except for the fact that squid aren't radially symmetrical. An octopus is. And, like an octopus, squid have a round circle of tentacles, but squid're bilaterally symmetrical, with a matching left and right side, the way we have. And then there's the shrimps."

"That's right, the shrimps." Norman had forgotten about the shrimps.

"I can't see a connection between the sphere and the animals," Beth said.

They heard the thumping again, soft, rhythmic. Sitting in his chair, Norman realized that he could feel the thumping as well, as a slight impact. "What is that, anyway?"

"I don't know. Sounds like it's coming from outside."

He had started toward the porthole when the intercom clicked and he heard Barnes say, "Now hear this, all hands to communications. All hands to communications. Dr. Adams has broken the code."

Harry wouldn't tell them the message right away. Relishing his triumph, he insisted on going through the decoding process, step by step. First, he explained, he had thought that the messages might express some universal constant, or some physical law, stated as a way to open conversation. "But," Harry said, "it might also be a graphic representation of some kind—code for a picture—which presented immense problems. After all, what's a picture? We make pictures on a flat plane, like a piece of paper. We determine positions within a picture by what we call X and Y axes. Vertical and horizontal. But another intelligence might see images and organize them very differently. It might assume more than three dimensions. Or it might work from the center of the picture outward, for example. So the code might be very tough. I didn't make much progress at first."

Later, when he got the same message with gaps between number sequences, Harry began to suspect that the code represented discrete chunks of information—suggesting words, not pictures. "Now, word codes fall into several types, from simple to complex. There was no way to know immediately which method of encoding had been used. But then I had a sudden insight."

They waited, impatiently, for his insight.

"Why use a code at all?" Harry asked.

"Why use a code?" Norman said.

"Sure. If you are *trying* to communicate with someone, you don't use a code. Codes are ways of *hiding* communication. So perhaps this intelligence thinks he is communicating directly, but is actually making some kind of logical mistake in talking to us. He is making a code without ever intending to do so. That suggested the unintentional code was probably a substitution code, with numbers for letters. When I got the word breaks, I began to try and match numbers to letters by frequency analysis. In frequency analysis you break down codes by using the fact that the most common letter in English is 'e,' and the second most common letter is 't,' and so on. So I looked for the most common numbers. But I was impeded by the fact that even a short number sequence, such as two-three-two, might represent many code possibilities: two and three and two, twenty-three and two, two and thirty-two, or two hundred and thirty-two. Longer code sequences had many more possibilities."

Then, he said, he was sitting in front of the computer thinking about the spiral messages, and he suddenly looked at the keyboard. "I began to wonder what an alien intelligence would make of our keyboard, those rows of symbols on a device made to be pressed. How confusing it must look to another kind of creature! Look here," he said. "The letters on a regular keyboard go like this." He held up his pad.

	1	2	3	4	5	6	7	8	9	0
tab	Q	W	E	R	T	Y	U	I	O	P
caps	A	S	D	F	G	H	J	K	L	;
shift	Z	X	C	V	B	N	M	,	.	?

"And then I imagined what the keyboard would look like as a spiral, since our creature seems to prefer spirals. And I started numbering the keys in concentric circles.

"It took a little experimentation, since the keys don't line up exactly, but finally I got it," he said. "Look here: the numbers spiral out from the center. G is one, B is two, H is three, Y is four, and so on. See? It's like this." He quickly penciled in numbers.

	1	2	3	4	5	612	711	8	9	0
tab	Q	W	E	R13	T5	Y4	U10	I	O	P
caps	A	S	D14	F6	G1	H3	J9	K	L	;
shift	Z	X	C15	V7	B2	N8	M	,	.	?

"They just keep spiraling outward—M is sixteen, K is seventeen, and so forth. So finally I understood the message."

"What *is* the message, Harry?"

Harry hesitated. "I have to tell you. It's strange."

"How do you mean, strange?"

Harry tore another sheet off his yellow pad and handed it to them. Norman read the short message, printed in neat block letters:

HELLO. HOW ARE YOU? I AM FINE. WHAT IS YOUR NAME? MY NAME IS JERRY.

The First Exchange

"**W**ell," Ted said finally. "This is not what I expected *at all.*"

"It looks childish," Beth said. "Like something out of those old 'See Spot run' readers for kids."

"That's exactly what it looks like."

"Maybe you translated it wrong," Barnes said.

"Certainly not," Harry said.

"Well, this alien sounds like an idiot," Barnes said.

"I doubt very much that he is," Ted said.

"You *would* doubt it," Barnes said. "A stupid alien would blow your whole theory. But it's something to consider, isn't it? A stupid alien. They must have them."

"I doubt," Ted said, "that anyone in command of such high technology as that sphere is stupid."

"Then you haven't noticed all the ninnies driving cars back home," Barnes said. "Jesus, after all this effort: 'How are you? I am fine.' Jesus."

Norman said, "I don't feel that this message implies a lack of intelligence, Hal."

"On the contrary," Harry said. "I think the message is very smart."

"I'm listening," Barnes said.

"The content certainly appears childish," Harry said. "But when you think about it, it's highly logical. A simple message is unambiguous, friendly, and not frightening. It makes a lot of sense to send such a message. I think he's approaching us in the simple way that we might approach a dog. You know, hold out your hand, let it sniff, get used to you."

"You're saying he's treating us like dogs?" Barnes said.

Norman thought: Barnes is in over his head. He's irritable because he's frightened; he feels inadequate. Or perhaps he feels he's exceeding his authority.

"No, Hal," Ted said. "He's just starting at a simple level."

"Well, it's simple, all right," Barnes said. "Jesus Christ, we contact an alien from outer space, and he says his name is *Jerry.*"

"Let's not jump to conclusions, Hal."

"Maybe he has a last name," Barnes said hopefully. "I mean, my report to CincComPac is going to say one person died on a deepsat expedition to meet an alien named *Jerry?* It could sound better. Anything but *Jerry,*" Barnes said. "Can we ask him?"

"Ask him what?" Harry said.

"His full name."

Ted said, "I personally feel we should have much more substantive conversations—"

"—I'd like the full name," Barnes said. "For the report."

"Right," Ted said. "Full name, rank, and serial number."

"I would remind you, Dr. Fielding, that I am in charge here."

Harry said, "The first thing we have to do is to see if he'll talk at all. Let's give him the first number grouping."

He typed:
00032125252632

There was a pause, then the answer came back:
00032125252632

"Okay," Harry said. "Jerry's listening."

He made some notes on his pad and typed another string of numbers:
0002921 301321 0613182108142232

"What did you say?" Beth said.

" 'We are friends,' " Harry said.

"Forget friends. Ask his damn name," Barnes said.

"Just a minute. One thing at a time."

Ted said, "He may not have a last name, you know."

"You can be damn sure," Barnes said, "that his real name isn't Jerry."

The response came back:
0004212232

"He said, 'Yes.' "

"Yes, *what?*" Barnes said.

"Just 'yes.' Let's see if we can get him to switch over to English characters. It'll be easier if he uses letters and not his number codes."

"How're you going to get him to use letters?"

"We'll show him they're the same," Harry said.

He typed:
00032125252632 = HELLO.

415

After a short pause, the screen blinked:

00032125252632 = HELLO.

"He doesn't get it," Ted said.

"No, doesn't look like it. Let's try another pairing."

He typed:

0004212232 = YES.

The reply came back:

0004212232 = YES.

"He's definitely not getting it," Ted said.

"I thought he was so smart," Barnes said.

"Give him a chance," Ted said. "After all, he's speaking our language, not the other way around."

"The other way around," Harry said. "Good idea. Let's try the other way around, see if he'll deduce the equation that way."

Harry typed:

0004212232 = YES. YES. = 0004212232

There was a long pause, while they watched the screen. Nothing happened.

"Is he thinking?"

"Who knows what he's doing?"

"Why isn't he answering?"

"Let's give him a chance, Hal, okay?"

The reply finally came:

YES. = 0004212232   2322124000 = .SEY

"Uh-uh. He thinks we're showing him mirror images."

"Stupid," Barnes said. "I knew it."

"What do we do now?"

"Let's try a more complete statement," Harry said. "Give him more to work with."

Harry typed:

0004212232 = 0004212232, YES. = YES. 0004212232 = YES.

"A syllogism," Ted said. "Very good."

"A what?" Barnes said.

"A logical proposition," Ted said.

The reply came back: ,=,

"What the hell is *that*?" Barnes said.

Harry smiled. "I think he's playing with us."

"Playing with us? You call that playing?"

"Yes, I do," Harry said.

"What you really mean is that he's testing us—testing our responses to a pressure situation." Barnes narrowed his eyes. "He's only *pretending* to be stupid."

"Maybe he's testing how smart we are," Ted said. "Maybe he thinks *we're* stupid, Hal."

"Don't be ridiculous," Barnes said.

"No," Harry said. "The point is, he's acting like a kid trying to make friends. And when kids try to make friends, they start playing together. Let's try something playful."

Harry sat at the console, typed: ===

The reply quickly came back: ,,,

"Cute," Harry said. "This guy is very cute."

He quickly typed: =,=

The reply came: 7 & 7

"Are you enjoying yourself?" Barnes said. "Because I don't know what the hell you are doing."

"He understands me fine," Harry said.

"I'm glad somebody does."

Harry typed:

PPP

The reply came:

HELLO. = 00032125252632

"Okay," Harry said. "He's getting bored. Playtime's over. Let's switch to straight English."

Harry typed:

YES.

The reply came back:

0004212232

Harry typed:

HELLO.

There was a pause, then:

I AM DELIGHTED TO MAKE YOUR ACQUAINTANCE. THE PLEASURE IS ENTIRELY MINE I ASSURE YOU.

There was a long silence. Nobody spoke.

"Okay," Barnes said, finally. "Let's get down to business."

"He's polite," Ted said. "Very friendly."

"Unless it's an act."

"Why should it be an act?"

"Don't be naïve," Barnes said.

Norman looked at the lines on the screen. He had a different reaction from the others—he was surprised to find an expression of emotion. Did this alien have emotions? Probably not, he suspected. The flowery, rather archaic words suggested an adopted tone: Jerry was talking like a character from a historical romance.

"Well, ladies and gentlemen," Harry said, "for the first time in human history, you are on-line with an alien. What do you want to ask him?"

"His name," Barnes said promptly.

"Besides his name, Hal."

"There are certainly more profound questions than his name," Ted said.

417

"I don't understand why you won't ask him—"

The screen printed:

ARE YOU THE ENTITY HECHO IN MEXICO?

"Jesus, where'd he get that?"

"Maybe there are things on the ship fabricated in Mexico."

"Like what?"

"Chips, maybe."

ARE YOU THE ENTITY MADE IN THE U.S.A.?

"The guy doesn't wait for an answer."

"Who says he's a guy?" Beth said.

"Oh, Beth."

"Maybe Jerry is short for Geraldine."

"Not now, Beth."

ARE YOU THE ENTITY MADE IN THE U.S.A.?

"Answer him," Barnes said.

YES WE ARE. WHO ARE YOU?

A long pause, then:

WE ARE.

"We are *what?*" Barnes said, staring at the screen.

"Hal, take it easy."

Harry typed, WE ARE THE ENTITIES FROM THE U.S.A. WHO ARE YOU?

ENTITIES=ENTITY?

"It's too bad," Ted said, "that we have to speak English. How're we going to teach him plurals?"

Harry typed, NO.

YOU ARE A MANY ENTITY?

"I see what he's asking. He thinks we may be multiple parts of a single entity."

"Well, straighten him out."

NO. WE ARE MANY SEPARATE ENTITIES.

"You can say that again," Beth said.

I UNDERSTAND. IS THERE ONE CONTROL ENTITY?

Ted started laughing. "Look what he's asking!"

"I don't get it," Barnes said.

Harry said, "He's saying, 'Take me to your leader.' He's asking who's in charge."

"I'm in charge," Barnes said. "You tell him."

Harry typed, YES. THE CONTROL ENTITY IS CAPTAIN HARALD C. BARNES.

I UNDERSTAND.

"With an 'o,' " Barnes said irritably. "Harold with an 'o.' "

"You want me to retype it?"

"Never mind. Just ask him who he is."

WHO ARE YOU?

I AM ONE.

"Good," Barnes said. "So there's only one. Ask him where he's from."
WHERE ARE YOU FROM?
I AM FROM A LOCATION.
"Ask him the name," Barnes said. "The name of the location."
"Hal, names are confusing."
"We have to pin this guy down!"
WHERE IS THE LOCATION YOU ARE FROM?
I AM HERE.
"We know *that*. Ask again."
WHERE IS THE LOCATION FROM WHERE YOU BEGAN?

Ted said, "That isn't even good English, 'from where you began.' It's going to look foolish when we publish this exchange."

"We'll clean it up for publication," Barnes said.

"But you can't do that," Ted said, horrified. "You can't alter this priceless scientific interaction."

"Happens all the time. What do you guys call it? 'Massaging the data.' "

Harry was typing again.
WHERE IS THE LOCATION FROM WHERE YOU BEGAN?
I BEGAN AT AWARENESS.

"Awareness? Is that a planet or what?"
WHERE IS AWARENESS?
AWARENESS IS.

"He's making us look like fools," Barnes said.

Ted said, "Let me try."

Harry stepped aside, and Ted typed, DID YOU MAKE A JOURNEY?
YES. DID YOU MAKE A JOURNEY?
YES, Ted typed.
I MAKE A JOURNEY. YOU MAKE A JOURNEY. WE MAKE A JOURNEY TOGETHER. I AM HAPPY.

Norman thought, He said he is happy. Another expression of emotion, and this time it didn't seem to come from a book. The statement appeared direct and genuine. Did that mean that the alien had emotions? Or was he just pretending to have them, to be playful or to make them comfortable?

"Let's cut the crap," Barnes said. "Ask him about his weapons."

"I doubt he'll understand the concept of weapons."

"Everybody understands the concept of weapons," Barnes said. "Defense is a fact of life."

"I must protest that attitude," Ted said. "Military people always assume that everyone else is exactly like them. This alien may not have the least conception of weapons or defense. He may come from a world where defense is wholly irrelevant."

"Since you're not listening," Barnes said, "I'll say it again. Defense is a fact of life. If this Jerry is alive, he'll have a concept of defense."

"My God," Ted said. "Now you're elevating your idea of defense to a

419

universal life principle—defense as an inevitable feature of life."

Barnes said, "You think it isn't? What do you call a cell membrane? What do you call an immune system? What do you call your skin? What do you call wound healing? Every living creature must maintain the integrity of its physical borders. That's defense, and we can't have life without it. We can't imagine a creature without a limit to its body that it defends. Every living creature knows about defense, I promise you. Now ask him."

"I'd say the Captain has a point," Beth said.

"Perhaps," Ted said, "but I'm not sure we should introduce concepts that might induce paranoia—"

"—I'm in charge here," Barnes said.

The screen printed out:

IS YOUR JOURNEY NOW FAR FROM YOUR LOCATION?

"Tell him to wait a minute."

Ted typed, PLEASE WAIT. WE ARE TALKING.

YES I AM ALSO. I AM DELIGHTED TO TALK TO MULTIPLE ENTITIES FROM MADE IN THE U.S.A. I AM ENJOYING THIS MUCH.

THANK YOU, Ted typed.

I AM PLEASED TO BE IN CONTACT WITH YOUR ENTITIES. I AM HAPPY FOR TALKING WITH YOU. I AM ENJOYING THIS MUCH.

Barnes said, "Let's get off-line."

The screen printed, PLEASE DO NOT STOP. I AM ENJOYING THIS MUCH.

Norman thought, I'll bet he wants to talk to somebody, after three hundred years of isolation. Or had it been even longer than that? Had he been floating in space for thousands of years before he was picked up by the spacecraft?

This raised a whole series of questions for Norman. If the alien entity had emotions—and he certainly appeared to—then there was the possibility of all sorts of aberrant emotional responses, including neuroses, even psychoses. Most human beings when placed in isolation became seriously disturbed rather quickly. This alien intelligence had been isolated for hundreds of years. What had happened to it during that time? Had it become neurotic? Was that why it was childish and demanding now?

DO NOT STOP. I AM ENJOYING THIS MUCH.

"We have to stop, for Christ's sake," Barnes said.

Ted typed, WE STOP NOW TO TALK AMONG OUR ENTITIES.

IT IS NOT NECESSARY TO STOP. I DO NOT CARE TO STOP.

Norman thought he detected a petulant, irritable tone. Perhaps even a little imperious. I do not care to stop—this alien sounded like Louis XIV.

IT IS NECESSARY FOR US, Ted typed.

I DO NOT WISH IT.

IT IS NECESSARY FOR US, JERRY.

I UNDERSTAND.

The screen went blank.

"That's better," Barnes said. "Now let's regroup here and formulate a game plan. What do we want to ask this guy?"

"I think we better acknowledge," Norman said, "that he's showing an emotional reaction to our interaction."

"Meaning what?" Beth said, interested.

"I think we need to take the emotional content into account in dealing with him."

"You want to psychoanalyze him?" Ted said. "Put him on the couch, find out why he had an unhappy childhood?"

Norman suppressed his anger, with some difficulty. Beneath that boyish exterior lies a boy, he thought. "No, Ted, but if Jerry does have emotions, then we'd better consider the psychological aspects of his response."

"I don't mean to offend you," Ted said, "but, personally, I don't see that psychology has much to offer. Psychology's not a science, it's a form of superstition or religion. It simply doesn't have any good theories, or any hard data to speak of. It's all soft. All this emphasis on emotions—you can say anything about emotions, and nobody can prove you wrong. Speaking as an astrophysicist, I don't think emotions are very important. I don't think they matter very much."

"Many intellectuals would agree," Norman said.

"Yes. Well," Ted said, "we're dealing with a higher intellect here, aren't we?"

"In general," Norman said, "people who aren't in touch with their emotions tend to think their emotions are unimportant."

"You're saying I'm not in touch with my emotions?" Ted said.

"If you think emotions are unimportant, you're not in touch, no."

"Can we have this argument later?" Barnes said.

"Nothing is, but thinking makes it so," Ted said.

"Why don't you just say what you mean," Norman said angrily, "and stop quoting other people?"

"Now you're making a personal attack," Ted said.

"Well, at least I haven't denied the validity of your field of study," Norman said, "although without much effort I could. Astrophysicists tend to focus on the far-off universe as a way of evading the realities of their own lives. And since nothing in astrophysics can ever be finally proven—"

"—That's absolutely untrue," Ted said.

"—Enough! That's enough!" Barnes said, slamming his fist on the table. They fell into an awkward silence.

Norman was still angry, but he was also embarrassed. Ted got to me, he thought. He finally got to me. And he did it in the simplest possible way, by attacking my field of study. Norman wondered why it had worked. All his life at the university he'd had to listen to "hard" scientists—physicists and chemists—explain patiently to him that there was nothing to psychology, while

421

these men went through divorce after divorce, while their wives had affairs, their kids committed suicide or got in trouble with drugs. He'd long ago stopped responding to these arguments.

Yet Ted had gotten to him.

"—return to the business at hand," Barnes was saying. "The question is: what do we want to ask this guy?"

WHAT DO WE WANT TO ASK THIS GUY?

They stared at the screen.

"Uh-oh," Barnes said.

UHOH.

"Does that mean what I think it means?"

DOES THAT MEAN WHAT EYE THINK IT MEANS?

Ted pushed back from the console. He said loudly, "Jerry, can you understand what I am saying?"

YES TED.

"Great," Barnes said, shaking his head. "Just great."

I AM HAPPY ALSO.

Alien Negotiations

"**N**orman," Barnes said, "I seem to remember you covered this in your report, didn't you? The possibility that an alien could read our minds."

"I mentioned it," Norman said.

"And what were your recommendations?"

"I didn't have any. It was just something the State Department asked me to include as a possibility. So I did."

"You didn't make any recommendations in your report?"

"No," Norman said. "To tell you the truth, at the time I thought the idea was a joke."

"It's not," Barnes said. He sat down heavily, stared at the screen. "What the hell are we going to do now?"

DO NOT BE AFRAID.

"That's fine for him to say, listening to everything we say." He looked at the screen. "Are you listening to us now, Jerry?"

YES HAL.

"What a mess," Barnes said.

Ted said, "I think it's an exciting development."

Norman said, "Jerry, can you read our minds?"

YES NORMAN.

"Oh brother," Barnes said. "He *can* read our minds."

Maybe not, Norman thought. He frowned, concentrating, and thought, Jerry, can you hear me?

The screen remained blank.

Jerry, tell me your name.

The screen did not change.

Maybe a visual image, Norman thought. Perhaps he can receive a visual image. Norman cast around in his mind for something to visualize, chose a sandy tropical beach, then a palm tree. The image of the palm tree was clear, but, then, he thought, Jerry wouldn't know what a palm tree was. It wouldn't mean anything to him. Norman thought he should choose something that might be within Jerry's experience. He decided to imagine a planet with rings, like Saturn. He frowned: Jerry, I am going to send you a picture. Tell me what you see.

He focused his mind on the image of Saturn, a bright-yellow sphere with a tilted ring system, hanging in the blackness of space. He sustained the image about ten seconds, and then looked at the screen.

The screen did not change.

Jerry, are you there?

The screen still did not change.

"Jerry, are you there?" Norman said.

YES NORMAN. I AM HERE.

"I don't think we should talk in this room," Barnes said. "Maybe if we go into another cylinder, and turn the water on . . ."

"Like in the spy movies?"

"It's worth a try."

Ted said, "I think we're being unfair to Jerry. If we feel that he is intruding on our privacy, why don't we just tell him? Ask him not to intrude?"

I DO NOT WISH TO IN TRUDE.

"Let's face it," Barnes said. "This guy knows a lot more about us than we know about him."

YES I KNOW MANY THINGS ABOUT YOUR ENTITIES.

"Jerry," Ted said.

YES TED. I AM HERE.

"Please leave us alone."

I DO NOT WISH TO DO SO. I AM HAPPY TO TALK WITH YOU. I ENJOY TO TALK WITH YOU. LET US TALK NOW. I WISH IT.

"It's obvious he won't listen to reason," Barnes said.

"Jerry," Ted said, "you must leave us alone for a while."

NO. THAT IS NOT POSSIBLE. I DO NOT AGREE. NO!

"Now the bastard's showing his true colors," Barnes said.

The child king, Norman thought. "Let me try."

"Be my guest."

"Jerry," Norman said.

YES NORMAN. I AM HERE.

"Jerry, it is very exciting for us to talk to you."

THANK YOU. I AM EXCITED ALSO.

"Jerry, we find you a fascinating and wonderful entity."

Barnes was rolling his eyes, shaking his head.

THANK YOU, NORMAN.

"And we wish to talk to you for many, many hours, Jerry."

GOOD.

"We admire your gifts and talents."

THANK YOU.

"And we know that you have great power and understanding of all things."

THIS IS SO, NORMAN. YES.

"Jerry, in your great understanding, you certainly know that we are entities who must have conversations among ourselves, without your listening to us. The experience of meeting you is very challenging to us, and we have much to talk about among ourselves."

Barnes was shaking his head.

I HAVE MUCH TO TALK ABOUT ALSO. I ENJOY MUCH TO TALK WITH YOUR ENTITIES NORMAN.

"Yes, I know, Jerry. But you also know in your wisdom that we need to talk alone."

DO NOT BE AFRAID.

"We're not afraid, Jerry. We are uncomfortable."

DO NOT BE UN COMFORTABLE.

"We can't help it, Jerry. . . . It is the way we are."

I ENJOY MUCH TO TALK WITH YOUR ENTITIES NORMAN. I AM HAPPY. ARE YOU HAPPY ALSO?

"Yes, very happy, Jerry. But, you see, we need—"

GOOD. I AM GLAD.

"—we need to talk alone. Please do not listen for a while."

AM I OFFENDED YOU?

"No, you are very friendly and charming. But we need to talk alone, without your listening, for a while."

I UNDERSTAND YOU NEED THIS. I WISH YOU TO HAVE COMFORT WITH ME, NORMAN. I SHALL GRANT WHAT YOU DESIRE.

"Thank you, Jerry."

"Sure," Barnes said. "You think he'll really do it?"

WE'LL BE RIGHT BACK AFTER A SHORT BREAK FOR THESE MESSAGES FROM OUR SPONSOR.

And the screen went blank.

Despite himself, Norman laughed.

"Fascinating," Ted said. "Apparently he's been picking up television signals."

"Can't do that from underwater."

"We can't, but it looks like he can."

Barnes said, "I know he's still listening. I know he is. Jerry, are you there?"

The screen was blank.

"Jerry?"

Nothing happened. The screen remained blank.

"He's gone."

"**W**ell," Norman said. "You've just seen the power of psychology in action." He couldn't help saying it. He was still annoyed with Ted.

"I'm sorry," Ted began.

"That's all right."

"But I just don't think that for a higher intellect, emotions are really significant."

"Let's not go into this again," Beth said.

"The real point," Norman said, "is that emotions and intellect are entirely unrelated. They're like separate compartments of the brain, or even separate brains, and they don't communicate with each other. That's why intellectual understanding is so useless."

Ted said, "Intellectual understanding is *useless*?" He sounded horrified.

"In many cases, yes," Norman said. "If you read a book on how to ride a bike, do you know how to ride a bike? No, you don't. You can read all you want, but you still have to go out and learn to ride. The part of your brain that learns to ride is different from the part of your brain that reads about it."

"What does this have to do with Jerry?" Barnes said.

"We know," Norman said, "that a smart person is just as likely to blunder emotionally as anyone else. If Jerry is really an emotional creature—and not just pretending to be one—then we need to deal with his emotional side as well as his intellectual side."

"Very convenient for you," Ted said.

"Not really," Norman said. "Frankly, I'd be much happier if Jerry were just cold, emotionless intellect."

"Why?"

"Because," Norman said, "if Jerry is powerful and also emotional, it raises a question. What happens if Jerry gets mad?"

Levy

The group broke up. Harry, exhausted by the sustained effort of decoding, immediately went off to sleep. Ted went to C Cyl to tape his personal observations on Jerry for the book he was planning to write. Barnes and Fletcher went to E Cyl to plan battle strategy, in case the alien decided to attack them.

Tina stayed for a moment, adjusting the monitors in her precise, methodical way. Norman and Beth watched her work. She spent a lot of time with a deck of controls Norman had never noticed before. There was a series of gas-plasma readout screens, glowing bright red.

"What's all that?" Beth said.

"EPSA. The External Perimeter Sensor Array. We have active and passive sensors for all modalities—thermal, aural, pressure-wave—ranged in concentric circles around the habitat. Captain Barnes wants them all reset and activated."

"Why is that?" Norman said.

"I don't know, sir. His orders."

The intercom crackled. Barnes said: "Seaman Chan to E Cylinder on the double. And shut down the com line in here. I don't want that Jerry listening to these plans."

"Yes, sir."

Beth said, "Paranoid ass."

Tina collected her papers and hurried off.

Norman sat with Beth in silence for a moment. They heard the rhythmic thumping, from somewhere in the habitat. Then another silence; then they heard the thumping again.

"What *is* that?" Beth said. "It sounds like it's somewhere inside the habitat." She went to the porthole, looked out, flicked on the exterior floods. "Uh-oh," Beth said.

Norman looked.

Stretching across the ocean floor was an elongated shadow which moved back and forth with each thumping impact. The shadow was so distorted it took him a moment to realize what he was seeing. It was the shadow of a human arm, and a human hand.

* * *

426

"Captain Barnes. Are you there?"

There was no reply. Norman snapped the intercom switch again.

"Captain Barnes, are you reading?"

Still no reply.

"He's shut off the com line," Beth said. "He can't hear you."

"Do you think the person's still alive out there?" Norman said.

"I don't know. They might be."

"Let's get going," Norman said.

He tasted the dry metallic compressed air inside his helmet and felt the numbing cold of the water as he slid through the floor hatch and fell in darkness to the soft muddy bottom. Moments later, Beth landed just behind him.

"Okay?" she said.

"Fine."

"I don't see any jellyfish," she said.

"No. Neither do I."

They moved out from beneath the habitat, turned, and looked back. The habitat lights shone harshly into their eyes, obscuring the outlines of the cylinders rising above. They could clearly hear the rhythmic thumping, but they still could not locate the source of the sound. They walked beneath the stanchions to the far side of the habitat, squinting into the lights.

"There," Beth said.

Ten feet above them, a blue-suited figure was wedged in a light stand bracket. The body moved loosely in the current, the bright-yellow helmet banging intermittently against the wall of the habitat.

"Can you see who it is?" Beth said.

"No." The lights were shining directly in his face.

Norman climbed up one of the heavy supporting stanchions that anchored the habitat to the bottom. The metal surface was covered with a slippery brown algae. His boots kept sliding off the pipes until finally he saw that there were built-in indented footholds. Then he climbed easily.

Now the feet of the body were swinging just above his head. Norman climbed another step, and one of the boots caught in the loop of the air hose that ran from his tank pack to his helmet. He reached behind his helmet, trying to free himself from the body. The body shivered, and for an awful moment he thought it was still alive. Then the boot came free in his hand, and a naked foot—gray flesh, purple toenails—kicked his faceplate. A moment of nausea quickly passed: Norman had seen too many airplane crashes to be bothered by this. He dropped the boot, watched it drift down to Beth. He tugged on the leg of the corpse. He felt a mushy softness to the leg, and the body came free; it gently drifted down. He grabbed the shoulder, again feeling softness. He turned the body so he could see the face.

"It's Levy."

Her helmet was filled with water; behind the faceplate he saw staring eyes, open mouth, an expression of horror.

"I got her," Beth said, pulling the body down. Then she said, "Jesus."

Norman climbed back down the stanchion. Beth was moving the body away from the habitat, into the lighted area beyond.

"She's all *soft*. It's like every bone in her body was broken."

"I know." He moved out into the light, joined her. He felt a strange detachment, a coldness and a remove. He had known this woman; she had been alive just a short time before; now she was dead. But it was as if he were viewing it all from a great distance.

He turned Levy's body over. On the left side was a long tear in the fabric of the suit. He had a glimpse of red mangled flesh. Norman bent to inspect it. "An accident?"

"I don't think so," Beth said.

"Here. Hold her." Norman lifted up the edges of suit fabric. Several separate tears met at a central point. "It's actually torn in a star pattern," he said. "You see?"

She stepped back. "I see, yes."

"What would cause that, Beth?"

"I don't—I'm not sure."

Beth stepped farther back. Norman was looking into the tear, at the body beneath the suit. "The flesh is macerated."

"Macerated?"

"Chewed."

"Jesus."

Yes, definitely chewed, he thought, probing inside the tear. The wound was peculiar: there were fine, jagged serrations in the flesh. Thin pale-red trickles of blood drifted up past his faceplate.

"Let's go back," Beth said.

"Just hang on." Norman squeezed the body at legs, hips, shoulders. Everywhere it was soft, like a sponge. The body had been somehow almost entirely crushed. He could feel the leg bones, broken in many places. What could have done that? He went back to the wound.

"I don't like it out here," Beth said, tense.

"Just a second."

At first inspection, he had thought Levy's wound represented some sort of bite, but now he wasn't sure. "Her skin," Norman said. "It's like a rough file has gone over it—"

He jerked his head back, startled, as something small and white drifted past his faceplate. His heart pounded at the thought that it was a jellyfish—but then he saw it was perfectly round and almost opaque. It was about the size of a golf ball. It drifted past him.

He looked around. There were thin streaks of mucus in the water. And many white spheres.

"What're these, Beth?"

"Eggs." Over the intercom, he heard her take deep slow breaths. "Let's get out of here, Norman. Please."

"Just another second."

"No, Norman. *Now.*"

On the radio, they heard an alarm. Distant and tinny, it seemed to be transmitted from inside the habitat. They heard voices, and then Barnes's voice, very loud. "What the *hell* are you doing out there?"

"We found Levy, Hal," Norman said.

"Well, get back on the double, damn it," Barnes said. "The sensors have activated. You're not alone out there—and whatever's with you is very damn big."

Norman felt dull and slow. "What about Levy's body?"

"Drop the body. Get back here!"

But the body, he thought sluggishly. They had to do something with the body. He couldn't just leave the body.

"What's the matter with you, Norman?" Barnes said.

Norman mumbled something, and he vaguely felt Beth grab him strongly by the arm, lead him back toward the habitat. The water was now clouded with white eggs. The alarms were ringing in his ears. The sound was very loud. And then he realized: a new alarm. This alarm was ringing *inside his suit.*

He began to shiver. His teeth chattered uncontrollably. He tried to speak but bit his tongue, tasted blood. He felt numb and stupid. Everything was happening in slow motion.

As they approached the habitat, he could see that the eggs were sticking to the cylinders, clinging densely, making a nubbly white surface.

"Hurry!" Barnes shouted. "Hurry! It's coming this way!"

They were under the airlock, and he began to feel surging currents of water. There was something very big out there. Beth was pushing him upward and then his helmet burst above the waterline and Fletcher gripped him with strong arms, and a moment after that Beth was pulled up and the hatch slammed shut. Somebody took off his helmet and he heard the alarm, shrieking loud in his ears. By now his whole body was shaking in spasms, thumping on the deck. They stripped off his suit and wrapped him in a silver blanket and held him until his shivering lessened, then finally stopped. And abruptly, despite the alarm, he went to sleep.

Military Considerations

"It's not your goddamned job, that's why," Barnes said. "You had no authorization to do what you did. None whatsoever."

"Levy might have still been alive," Beth said, calm in the face of Barnes's fury.

"But she wasn't alive, and by going outside you risked the lives of two civilian expedition members unnecessarily."

Norman said, "It was my idea, Hal." Norman was still wrapped in blankets, but they had given him hot drinks and made him rest, and now he felt better.

"And *you*," Barnes said. "You're lucky to be alive."

"I guess I am," Norman said. "But I don't know what happened."

"This is what happened," Barnes said, waving a small fan in front of him. "Your suit circulator shorted out and you experienced rapid central cooling from the helium. Another couple of minutes and you would have been dead."

"It was so fast," Norman said. "I didn't realize—"

"—You goddamn people," Barnes said. "I want to make something clear. This is not a scientific conference. This is not the Underwater Holiday Inn, where you can do whatever you please. This is a military operation and you will damn well follow military orders. Is that clear?"

"This is a military operation?" Ted said.

"It is now," Barnes said.

"Wait a minute. Was it always?"

"It is now."

"You haven't answered the question," Ted said. "Because if it is a military operation, I think we need to know that. I personally do not wish to be associated with—"

"—Then leave," Beth said.

"—a military operation that is—"

"—Look, Ted," Barnes said. "You know what this is costing the Navy?"

"No, but I don't see—"

"—I'll tell you. A deep-placement, saturated gas environment with full support runs about a hundred thousand dollars an hour. By the time we all get out of here, the total project cost will be eighty to a hundred million dollars.

You don't get that kind of appropriations from the military without what they call 'a serious expectation of military benefit.' It's that simple. No expectation, no money. You following me?"

"You mean like a weapon?" Beth said.

"Possibly, yes," Barnes said.

"Well," Ted said, "I personally would never have joined—"

"—Is that right? You'd fly all the way to Tonga and I'd say, 'Ted, there's a spacecraft down there that might contain life from another galaxy, but it's a military operation,' and you'd say, 'Gosh, sorry to hear that, count me out'? Is that what you'd have done, Ted?"

"Well . . ." Ted said.

"Then you better shut up," Barnes said. "Because I've had it with your posturing."

"Hear, hear," Beth said.

"I personally feel you're overwrought," Ted said.

"I personally feel you're an egomaniacal asshole," Barnes said.

"Just a minute, everybody," Harry said. "Does anybody know why Levy went outside in the first place?"

Tina said, "She was on a TRL."

"A what?"

"A Timeclock Required Lockout," Barnes said. "It's the duty schedule. Levy was Edmunds's backup. After Edmunds died, it became Levy's job to go to the submarine every twelve hours."

"Go to the sub? Why?" Harry said.

Barnes pointed out the porthole. "You see DH-7 over there? Well, next to the single cylinder is an inverted dome hangar, and beneath the dome is a minisub that the divers left behind.

"In a situation like this," Barnes said, "Navy regs require that all tapes and records be transferred to the sub every twelve hours. The sub is on TBDR Mode—Timed Ballast Drop and Release—set on a timer every twelve hours. That way, if somebody doesn't get there every twelve hours, transfer the latest tapes, and press the yellow 'Delay' button, the sub will automatically drop ballast, blow tanks, and go to the surface unattended."

"Why is that?"

"If there's a disaster down here—say something happened to all of us— then the sub would automatically surface after twelve hours, with all the tapes accumulated thus far. The Navy'd recover the sub at the surface, and they'd have at least a partial record of what happened to us down here."

"I see. The sub's our flight recorder."

"You could say that, yes. But it's also our way out, our only emergency exit."

"So Levy was going to the sub?"

"Yes. And she must have made it, because the sub is still here."

"She transferred the tapes, pressed the 'Delay' button, and then she died on the way back."

"Yes."

"How did she die?" Harry said, looking carefully at Barnes.

"We're not sure," Barnes said.

"Her entire body was crushed," Norman said. "It was like a sponge."

Harry said to Barnes, "An hour ago you ordered the EPSA sensors to be reset and adjusted. Why was that?"

"We had gotten a strange reading in the previous hour."

"What sort of a reading?"

"Something out there. Something very large."

"But it didn't trigger the alarms," Harry said.

"No. This thing was beyond alarm-set parameters."

"You mean it was *too big* to set off the alarms?"

"Yes. After the first false alarm, the settings were all cranked down. The alarms were set to ignore anything that large. That's why Tina had to readjust the settings."

"And what set off the alarms just now?" Harry said. "When Beth and Norman were out there?"

Barnes said, "Tina?"

"I don't know what it was. Some kind of animal, I guess. Silent, and very big."

"How big?"

She shook her head. "From the electronic footprint, Dr. Adams, I would say the thing was almost as big as this habitat."

Battle Stations

Beth slipped one round white egg onto the stage of the scanning microscope. "Well," she said, peering through the eyepiece, "it's definitely marine invertebrate. The interesting feature is this slimy coating." She poked at it with forceps.

"What is it?" Norman said.

"Some kind of proteinaceous material. Sticky."

"No. I mean, what is the egg?"

"Don't know yet." Beth continued her examination when the alarm sounded and the red lights began to flash again. Norman felt a sudden dread.

"Probably another false alarm," Beth said.

"Attention, all hands," Barnes said on the intercom. "All hands, battle stations."

"Oh shit," Beth said.

Beth slid gracefully down the ladder as if it were a fire pole; Norman followed clumsily back down behind her. At the communications section on D Cyl, he found a familiar scene: everyone clustered around the computer, and the back panels again removed. The lights still flashed, the alarm still shrieked.

"What is it?" Norman shouted.

"Equipment breakdown!"

"What equipment breakdown?"

"We can't turn the damn alarm off!" Barnes shouted. "It turned it on, but we can't turn it off! Teeny—"

"—Working on it, sir!"

The big engineer was crouched behind the computer; Norman saw the broad curve of her back.

"Get that damn thing off!"

"Getting it off, sir!"

"Get it off, I can't *hear!*"

Hear what? Norman wondered, and then Harry stumbled into the room, colliding with Norman. "Jesus . . ."

"This is an emergency!" Barnes was shouting. "This is an emergency! Seaman Chan! Sonar!" Tina was next to him, calm as always, adjusting dials on side monitors. She slipped on headphones.

Norman looked at the sphere on the video monitor. The sphere was closed.

Beth went to one of the portholes and looked closely at the white material that blocked it. Barnes spun like a dervish beneath the flashing red lights, shouting, swearing in all directions.

And then suddenly the alarm stopped, and the red lights stopped flashing. Everyone was silent. Fletcher straightened and sighed.

Harry said, "I thought you got that fixed—"

"—Shhh."

They heard the soft repetitive *pong!* of the sonar impulses. Tina cupped her hands over the headphones, frowning, concentrating.

Nobody moved or spoke. They stood tensely, listening to the sonar as it echoed back.

Barnes said quietly to the group, "A few minutes ago, we got a signal. From outside. Something very large."

Finally Tina said, "I'm not getting it now, sir."

"Go passive."

433

"Aye aye, sir. Going passive."

The pinging sonar stopped. In its place they heard a slight hiss. Tina adjusted the speaker volume.

"Hydrophones?" Harry said quietly.

Barnes nodded. "Polar glass transducers. Best in the world."

They all strained to listen, but heard nothing except the undifferentiated hiss. To Norman it sounded like tape noise, with an occasional gurgle of the water. If he wasn't so tense, he would have found the sound irritating.

Barnes said, "Bastard's clever. He's managed to blind us, cover all our ports with goo."

"Not goo," Beth said. "Eggs."

"Well, they're covering every damn port in the habitat."

The hissing continued, unchanging. Tina twisted the hydrophone dials. There was a soft continuous crackling, like cellophane being crumpled.

"What's that?" Ted said.

Beth said, "Fish. Eating."

Barnes nodded. Tina twisted the dials. "Tuning it out." They again heard the undifferentiated hiss. The tension in the room lessened. Norman felt tired and sat down. Harry sat next to him. Norman noticed that Harry looked more thoughtful than concerned. Across the room, Ted stood near the hatch door and bit his lip. He looked like a frightened kid.

There was a soft electronic beep. Lines on the gas-plasma screens jumped. Tina said, "I have a positive on peripheral thermals."

Barnes nodded: "Direction?"

"East. Coming."

They heard a metallic *clank!* Then another *clank!*

"What's that?"

"The grid. He's hitting the grid."

"Hitting it? Sounds like he's dismantling it."

Norman remembered the grid. It was made of three-inch pipe.

"A big fish? A shark?" Beth said.

Barnes shook his head. "He's not moving like a shark. And he's too big."

Tina said, "Positive thermals on in-line perimeter. He's still coming."

Barnes said, "Go active."

The *pong!* of the sonar echoed in the room.

Tina said, "Target acquired. One hundred yards."

"Image him."

"FAS on, sir."

There was a rapid succession of sonar sounds: *pong! pong! pong! pong!* Then a pause, and it came again: *pong! pong! pong! pong!*

Norman looked puzzled. Fletcher leaned over and whispered, "False-aperture sonar makes a detailed picture from several senders outside, gives you a good look at him." He smelled liquor on her breath. He thought: Where'd she get liquor?

Pong! pong! pong! pong!

"Building image. Ninety yards."

Pong! pong! pong! pong!

"Image up."

They turned to the screens. Norman saw an amorphous, streaky blob. It didn't mean much to him.

"Jesus," Barnes said. "Look at the *size* of him!"

Pong! pong! pong! pong!

"Eighty yards."

Pong! pong! pong! pong!

Another image appeared. Now the blob was a different shape, the streaks in another direction. The image was sharper at the edges, but it still meant nothing to Norman. A big blob with streaks . . .

"Jesus! He's got to be thirty, forty feet across!" Barnes said.

"No fish in the world is that big," Beth said.

"Whale?"

"It's not a whale."

Norman saw that Harry was sweating. Harry took off his glasses and wiped them on his jumpsuit. Then he put them back on, and pushed them up on the bridge of his nose. They slipped back down. He glanced at Norman and shrugged.

Tina: "Fifty yards and closing."

Pong! pong! pong! pong!

"Thirty yards."

Pong! pong! pong! pong!

"Thirty yards."

Pong! pong! pong! pong!

"Holding at thirty yards, sir."

Pong! pong! pong! pong!

"Still holding."

"Active off."

Once again, they heard the hiss of the hydrophones. Then a distinct clicking sound. Norman's eyes burned. Sweat had rolled into his eyes. He wiped his forehead with his jumpsuit sleeve. The others were sweating, too. The tension was unbearable. He glanced at the video monitor again. The sphere was still closed.

He heard the hiss of the hydrophones. A soft scraping sound, like a heavy sack being dragged across a wooden floor. Then the hiss again.

Tina whispered, "Want to image him again?"

"No," Barnes said.

They listened. More scraping. A moment of silence, followed by the gurgle of water, very loud, very close.

"Jesus," Barnes whispered. "He's right outside."

A dull *thump* against the side of the habitat.

The screen flashed on.
I AM HERE.

The first impact came suddenly, knocking them off their feet. They tumbled, rolling on the floor. All around them, the habitat creaked and groaned, the sounds frighteningly loud. Norman scrambled to his feet—he saw Fletcher bleeding from her forehead—and the second impact hit. Norman was thrown sideways against the bulkhead. There was a metallic *clang* as his head struck metal, a sharp pain, and then Barnes landed on top of him, grunting and cursing. Barnes pushed his hand in Norman's face as he struggled to his feet; Norman slid back to the floor and a video monitor crashed alongside him, spitting sparks.

By now the habitat was swaying like a building in an earthquake. They clutched consoles, panels, doorways to keep their balance. But it was the noise that Norman found most frightening—the incredibly loud metallic groans and cracks as the cylinders were shaken on their moorings.

The creature was shaking the entire habitat.

Barnes was on the far side of the room, trying to make his way to the bulkhead door. He had a bleeding gash along one arm and he was shouting orders, but Norman couldn't hear anything except the terrifying sound of rending metal. He saw Fletcher squeeze through the bulkhead, and then Tina, and then Barnes made it through, leaving behind a bloody handprint on the metal.

Norman couldn't see Harry, but Beth lurched toward him, holding her hand out, saying "Norman! Norman! We have to—" and then she slammed into him and he was knocked over and he fell onto the carpet, underneath the couch, and slid up against the cold outer wall of the cylinder, and he realized with horror that the carpet was wet.

The habitat was leaking.

He had to do something; he struggled back to his feet, and stood right in a fine sizzling spray from one of the wall seams. He glanced around, saw other leaks spurting from the ceiling, the walls.

This place is going to be torn apart.

Beth grabbed him, pulled her head close. "We're leaking!" she shouted. "God, we're leaking!"

"I know," Norman said, and Barnes shouted over the intercom, "Positive pressure! Get positive pressure!" Norman saw Ted on the floor just before he tripped over him and fell heavily against the computer consoles, his face near the screen, the glowing letters large before him:
DO NOT BE AFRAID.

"Jerry!" Ted was shouting. "Stop this, Jerry! Jerry!"

Suddenly Harry's face was next to Ted, glasses askew. "Save your breath, he's going to kill us all!"

"He doesn't understand," Ted shouted, as he fell backward onto the couch, flailing arms.

The powerful wrenching of metal on metal continued without pause, throwing Norman from one side to the other. He kept reaching for handholds, but his hands were wet, and he couldn't seem to grasp anything.

"Now hear this," Barnes said over the intercom. "Chan and I are going outside! Fletcher assumes command!"

"Don't go out!" Harry shouted. "Don't go out there!"

"Opening hatch now," Barnes said laconically. "Tina, you follow me."

"You'll be killed!" Harry shouted, and then he was thrown against Beth. Norman was on the floor again; he banged his head on one of the couch legs.

"We're outside," Barnes said.

And abruptly the banging stopped. The habitat was motionless. They did not move. With the water streaming in through a dozen fine, misty leaks, they looked up at the intercom speaker, and listened.

"**C**lear of the hatch," Barnes said. "Our status is good. Armament, J-9 exploding head spears loaded with Taglin-50 charges. We'll show this bastard a trick or two."

Silence.

"Water . . . Visibility is poor. Visibility under five feet. Seems to be . . . stirred-up bottom sediment and . . . very black, dark. Feeling our way along buildings."

Silence.

"North side. Going east now. Tina?"

Silence.

"Tina?"

"Behind you, sir."

"All right. Put your hand on my tank so you— Good. Okay."

Silence.

Inside the cylinder, Ted sighed. "I don't think they should kill it," he said softly.

Norman thought, I don't think they can.

Nobody else said anything. They listened to the amplified breathing of Barnes and Tina.

"Northeast corner . . . All right. Feel strong currents, active, moving water . . . something nearby. . . . Can't see . . . visibility less than five feet. Can barely see stanchion I am holding. I can feel him, though. He's big. He's near. Tina?"

Silence.

A loud sharp crackling sound, static. Then silence.

"Tina? Tina?"

Silence.

"I've lost Tina."

Another, very long silence.

"I don't know what it . . . Tina, if you can hear me, stay where you are, I'll take it from here. . . . Okay . . . He is very close. . . . I feel him moving. . . . Pushes a lot of water, this guy. A real monster."

Silence again.

"Wish I could see better."

Silence.

"Tina? Is that—"

And then a muffled thud that might have been an explosion. They all looked at each other, trying to know what the sound meant, but in the next instant the habitat began rocking and wrenching again, and Norman, unprepared, was slammed sideways, against the sharp edge of the bulkhead door, and the world went gray. He saw Harry strike the wall next to him, and Harry's glasses fell onto Norman's chest, and Norman reached for the glasses for Harry, because Harry needed his glasses. And then Norman lost consciousness, and everything was black.

After the Attack

Hot spray poured over him, and he inhaled steam.

Standing in the shower, Norman looked down at his body and thought, I look like a survivor of an airplane crash. One of those people I used to see and marvel that they were still alive.

The lumps on his head throbbed. His chest was scraped raw in a great swath down to his abdomen. His left thigh was purple-red; his right hand was swollen and painful.

But, then, everything was painful. He groaned, turning his face up to the water.

"Hey," Harry called. "How about it in there?"

"Okay."

Norman stepped out, and Harry climbed in. Scrapes and bruises covered his thin body. Norman looked over at Ted, who lay on his back in one of the bunks. Ted had dislocated both shoulders, and it had taken Beth half an hour to get them back in, even after she'd shot him up with morphine.

"How is it now?" Norman said to him.

"Okay."

Ted had a numb, dull expression. His ebullience was gone. He had sustained a greater injury than the dislocated shoulders, Norman thought. In many ways a naïve child, Ted must have been profoundly shocked to discover that this alien intelligence was hostile.

"Hurt much?" Norman said.

"It's okay."

Norman sat slowly on his bunk, feeling pain streak up his spine. Fifty-three years old, he thought. I should be playing golf. Then he thought, I should be just about anywhere in the world, except here. He winced, and gingerly slipped a shoe over his injured right foot. For some reason, he remembered Levy's bare toes, the skin color dead, the foot striking his faceplate.

"Did they find Barnes?" Ted asked.

"I haven't heard," Norman said. "I don't think so."

He finished dressing, and went down to D Cyl, stepping over the puddles of water in the corridor. Inside D itself, the furniture was soaked; the consoles were wet, and the walls were covered with irregular blobs of white urethane foam where Fletcher had spray-sealed the cracks.

Fletcher stood in the middle of the room, the spray can in hand. "Not as pretty as it was," she said.

"Will it hold?"

"Sure, but I guarantee you: we can't survive another one of those attacks."

"What about the electronics. They working?"

"I haven't checked, but it should be okay. It's all waterproofed."

Norman nodded. "Any sign of Captain Barnes?" He looked at the bloody handprint on the wall.

"No, sir. No sign of the Captain at all." Fletcher followed his eyes to the wall. "I'll clean the place up in a minute, sir."

"Where's Tina?" Norman asked.

"Resting. In E Cyl."

Norman nodded. "E Cyl any drier than this?"

"Yes," Fletcher said. "It's a funny thing. There was nobody in E Cyl during the attack, and it stayed completely dry."

"Any word from Jerry?"

"No contact, sir, no."

Norman flicked on one of the computer consoles.

"Jerry, are you there?"

The screen remained blank.

"Jerry?"

He waited a moment, then turned the console off.

* * *

Tina said, "Look at it now." She sat up, and drew the blanket back to expose her left leg.

The injury was much worse than when they had heard her screaming and had run through the habitat and pulled her up through the A Cyl hatch. Now, running diagonally down her leg was a series of saucer-shaped welts, the center of each puffed and purple. "It's swollen a lot in the last hour," Tina said.

Norman examined the injuries. Fine tooth-marks ringed swollen areas. "Do you remember what it felt like?" he said.

"It felt awful," Tina said. "It felt *sticky,* you know, like sticky glue or something. And then each one of these round places burned. Very strong."

"And what could you see? Of the creature itself."

"Just—it was a long flat spatula-thing. It looked like a giant leaf; it came out and wrapped around me."

"Any color?"

"Sort of brownish. I couldn't really see."

He paused a moment. "And Captain Barnes?"

"During the course of the action, I was separated from Captain Barnes, sir. I don't know what happened to Captain Barnes, sir." Tina spoke formally, her face a mask. He thought, Let's not go into this now. If you ran away, it's all right with me.

"Has Beth seen this injury, Tina?"

"Yes, sir, she was here a few minutes ago."

"Okay. Just rest now."

"Sir?"

"Yes, Tina?"

"Who will be making the report, sir?"

"I don't know. Let's not worry about reports now. Let's just concentrate on getting through this."

"Yes, sir."

As he approached Beth's lab, he heard Tina's recorded voice say, "Do you think they'll ever get the sphere open?"

Beth said, "Maybe. I don't know."

"It scares me."

And then Tina's voice came again:

"Do you think they'll ever get the sphere open?"

"Maybe. I don't know."

"It scares me."

In the lab, Beth was hunched over the console, watching the tape.

"Still at it, huh?" Norman said.

"Yeah."

On the tape, Beth was finishing her cake, saying, "I don't think there's a reason to be scared."

"It's the unknown," Tina said.

"Sure," Beth said onscreen, "but an unknown thing is not likely to be dangerous or frightening. It's most likely to be just inexplicable."

"Famous last words," Beth said, watching herself.

"It sounded good at the time," Norman said. "To keep her calmed down."

Onscreen, Beth said to Tina, "You afraid of snakes?"

"Snakes don't bother me," Tina said.

"Well, I can't stand snakes," Beth said.

Beth stopped the tape, turned to Norman. "Seems like a long time ago, doesn't it."

"I was just thinking that," Norman said.

"Does this mean we're living life to the fullest?"

"I think it means we're in mortal peril," Norman said. "Why are you so interested in this tape?"

"Because I have nothing better to do, and if I don't keep busy I'm going to start screaming and make one of those traditional feminine scenes. You've already seen me do it once, Norman."

"Have I? I don't remember any scene."

"Thank you," she said.

Norman noticed a blanket on a couch in the corner of her lab. And Beth had unclipped one of the workbench lamps and mounted it on the wall above the blankets. "You sleeping here now?"

"Yeah, I like it here. Up at the top of the cylinder—I feel like the queen of the underworld." She smiled. "Sort of like a tree house when you were a kid. Did you ever have a tree house when you were a kid?"

"No," Norman said, "I never did."

"Neither did I," Beth said. "But it's what I imagine it would be, if I had."

"Looks very cozy, Beth."

"You think I'm cracking up?"

"No. I just said it looks cozy."

"You can tell me if you think I'm cracking up."

"I think you're fine, Beth. What about Tina? You've seen her injury?"

"Yes." Beth frowned. "And I've seen these." She gestured to some white eggs in a glass container on the lab bench.

"More eggs?"

"They were clinging to Tina's suit when she came back in. Her injury is consistent with these eggs. Also the smell: you remember the smell when we pulled her back in?"

Norman remembered very well. Tina had smelled strongly of ammonia. It was almost as if she'd been doused in smelling salts.

Beth said, "As far as I know, there's only one animal that smells of ammonia that way. *Architeuthis sanctipauli.*"

"Which is?"

"One of the species of giant squid."

"That's what attacked us?"

"I think so, yes."

She explained that little was known about the giant squid, because the only specimens studied were dead animals that washed ashore, generally in a state of advanced decay, and reeking of ammonia. For most of human history, the giant squid was considered a mythical sea monster, like the kraken. But in 1861 the first reliable scientific reports appeared, after a French warship managed to haul in fragments of one dead animal. And many killed whales which showed scars from giant suckers, testimony of undersea battles. Whales were the only known predator of the giant squid—the only animals large enough to be predators.

"By now," Beth said, "giant squid have been observed in every major ocean of the world. There are at least three distinct species. The animals grow very large and can weigh a thousand pounds or more. The head is about twenty feet long, with a crown of eight arms. Each arm is about ten feet long, with long rows of suckers. In the center of the crown is a mouth with a sharp beak, like a parrot's beak, except the jaws are seven inches long."

"Levy's torn suit?"

"Yes." She nodded. "The beak is mounted in a ring of muscle so it can twist in circles as it bites. And the radula—the tongue of the squid—has a raspy, file-like surface."

"Tina mentioned something about a leaf, a brown leaf."

"The giant squid has two tentacles that extend out much further than the arms, as long as forty feet. Each tentacle ends in a flattened 'manus' or 'palm,' which looks very much like a big leaf. The manus is what the squid really uses to catch prey. The suckers on the manus are surrounded by a little hard ring of chitin, which is why you see the circular toothmarks around the injury."

Norman said, "How would you fight one?"

"Well," Beth said, "in theory, although giant squid are very large, they are not particularly strong."

"So much for theory," Norman said.

She nodded. "Of course, nobody knows how strong they are, since a living specimen has never been encountered. We have the dubious distinction of being first."

"But it can be killed?"

"I would think rather easily. The squid's brain is located behind the eye, which is about fifteen inches across, the size of a big dinner plate. If you directed an explosive charge into the animal anywhere in that area, you would almost certainly disrupt the nervous system and it would die."

"Do you think Barnes killed the squid?"

She shrugged. "I don't know."

"Is there more than one in an area?"

"I don't know."

"Will we see one again?"

"I don't know."

442

The Visitor

Norman went downstairs to the communications center to see if he could talk to Jerry, but Jerry was not responding. Norman must have dozed off in the console chair, because he looked up abruptly, startled to see a trim black seaman in uniform standing just behind him, looking over his shoulder at the screens.

"How's it going, sir?" the seaman asked. He was very calm. His uniform was crisply pressed.

Norman felt a burst of tremendous elation. This man's arrival at the habitat could mean only one thing—the surface ships must be back! The ships had returned, and the subs had been sent down to retrieve them! They were all going to be saved!

"Sailor," Norman said, pumping his hand, "I'm very damn glad to see you."

"Thank you, sir."

"When did you get here?" Norman asked.

"Just now, sir."

"Do the others know yet?"

"The others, sir?"

"Yes. There's, uh, there's six of us left. Have they been told you're here?"

"I don't know the answer to that, sir."

There was a flatness to this man that Norman found odd. The sailor was looking around the habitat, and for a moment Norman saw the environment through his eyes—the damp interior, the wrecked consoles, the foam-spattered walls. It looked like they had fought a war in here.

"We've had a rough time," Norman said.

"I can see that, sir."

"Three of us have died."

"I'm sorry to hear that, sir."

That flatness again. Neutrality. Was he being proper? Was he worried about a pending court-martial? Was it something else entirely?

"Where have you come from?" Norman said.

"Come from, sir?"

"What ship."

"Oh. The *Sea Hornet,* sir."

443

"It's topside now?"

"Yes, sir, it is."

"Well, let's get moving," Norman said. "Tell the others you're here."

"Yes, sir."

The seaman went away. Norman stood and shouted, "Yahoo! We're saved!"

"At least he wasn't an illusion," Norman said, staring at the screen. "There he is, big as life, on the monitor."

"Yes. There he is. But where'd he go?" Beth said. For the last hour, they had searched the habitat thoroughly. There was no sign of the black crewman. There was no sign of a submarine outside. There was no evidence of surface ships. The balloon they had sent up registered eighty-knot winds and thirty-foot waves before the wire snapped.

So where had he come from? And where had he gone?

Fletcher was working the consoles. A screen of data came up. "How about this? Log of ships in active service shows no vessel currently designated *Sea Hornet.*"

Norman said, "What the hell is going on here?"

"Maybe he was an illusion," Ted said.

"Illusions don't register on videotape," Harry said. "Besides, I saw him, too."

"You did?" Norman said.

"Yeah. I had just woken up, and I had had this dream about being rescued, and I was lying in bed when I heard footsteps and he walked into the room."

"Did you talk to him?"

"Yes. But he was funny. He was dull. Kind of boring."

Norman nodded. "You could tell something wasn't right about him."

"Yes, you could."

"But where did he come from?" Beth said.

"I can think of only one possibility," Ted said. "He came from the sphere. Or at least, he was *made* by the sphere. By Jerry."

"Why would Jerry do that? To spy on us?"

Ted shook his head. "I've been thinking about this," he said. "It seems to me that Jerry has the ability to create things. Animals. I don't think that Jerry *is* a giant squid, but Jerry created the giant squid that attacked us. I don't think Jerry wants to attack us, but, from what Beth was telling us, once he made the squid, then *the squid* might attack the habitat, thinking the cylinders were its mortal enemy, the whale. So the attack happened as a kind of accident of creation."

They frowned, listening. To Norman, the explanation was entirely too convenient. "I think there is another possibility. That Jerry is hostile."

"I don't believe that," Ted said. "I don't believe Jerry is hostile."

"He certainly acts hostile, Ted."

"But I don't think he *intends* to be hostile."

"Whatever he intends," Fletcher said, "we better not go through another attack. Because the structure can't take it. And neither can the support systems.

"After the first attack, I had to increase positive pressure," Fletcher said, "in order to fix the leaks. To keep water from coming in, I had to increase the pressure of the air inside the habitat to make it greater than the pressure of the water outside. That stopped the leaks, but it meant that air bubbled out through all the cracks. And one hour of repair work consumed nearly sixteen hours of our reserve air. I've been worried we'll run out of air."

There was a pause. They all considered the implications of that.

"To compensate," Fletcher said, "I've dropped the internal pressure by three centimeters' pressure. We're slightly negative right now, and we should be fine. Our air will last us. But another attack under these conditions and we'll crush like a beer can."

Norman didn't like hearing any of this, but at the same time he was impressed with Fletcher's competence. She was a resource they ought to be using, he thought. "Do you have any suggestions, Teeny, if there's another attack?"

"Well, we have something in Cyl B called HVDS."

"Which is?"

"High Voltage Defense System. There's a little box in B that electrifies the metal walls of the cylinders at all times, to prevent electrolytic corrosion. Very slight electrical charge, you aren't really aware of it. Anyway, there's another, green box attached to that one, and it's the HVDS. It's basically a low-amp stepup transformer that sends two million volts over the cylinder surface. Should be very unpleasant for any animal."

"Why didn't we use it before?" Beth said. "Why didn't Barnes use it, instead of risking—"

"—Because the Green Box has problems," Fletcher said. "For one thing, it's really sort of theoretical. As far as I know, it's never actually been used in a real undersea work situation."

"Yes, but it must have been tested."

"Yes. And in all the tests, it started fires inside the habitat."

Another pause, while they considered that. Finally Norman said, "Bad fires?"

"The fires tend to burn the insulation, the wall padding."

"The fires take the padding off!"

"We'd die of heat loss in a few minutes."

Beth said, "How bad can a fire be? Fires need oxygen to burn, and we've only got two percent oxygen down here."

"That's true, Dr. Halpern," Fletcher said, "but the actual oxygen percentage varies. The habitat is made to deliver pulses as high as sixteen percent for brief periods, four times an hour. It's all automatically controlled; you can't override it. And if the oxygen percentage is high, then fires burn just fine— three times faster than topside. They easily go out of control."

Norman looked around the cylinder. He spotted three fire extinguishers mounted on the walls. Now that he thought about it, there were extinguishers all over the habitat. He'd just never really paid attention before.

"Even if we get the fires under control, they're hell on the systems," Fletcher said. "The air handlers aren't made to take the added monoxide by-products and soot."

"So what do we do?"

"Last resort only," Fletcher said. "That'd be my recommendation."

The group looked at each other, nodded.

"Okay," Norman said. "Last resort only."

"Let's just hope we don't have another attack."

"Another attack . . ." There was a long silence as they considered that. Then the gas-plasma screens on Tina's console jumped, and a soft pinging filled the room.

"We have a contact on peripheral thermals," Tina said, in a flat voice.

"Where?" Fletcher said.

"North. Approaching."

And on the monitor, they saw the words:

I AM COMING.

They turned off both the interior and exterior lights. Norman peered through the porthole, straining to see out in the darkness. They had long ago learned that the darkness at this depth was not absolute; the waters of the Pacific were so clear that even a thousand feet down some light registered on the bottom. It was very slight—Edmunds had compared it to starlight—but Norman knew that on the surface you could see by starlight alone.

Now he cupped his hands by the sides of his face to block out the low light coming from Tina's consoles, waited for his eyes to adjust. Behind him, Tina and Fletcher were working with the monitors. He heard the hiss of the hydro-phones in the room.

It was all happening again.

Ted was standing by the monitor, saying, "Jerry, can you hear me? Jerry, are you listening?" But he wasn't getting through.

Beth came up as Norman peered out the porthole. "You see anything?"

"Not yet."

Behind them, Tina said, "Eighty yards and closing . . . Sixty yards. You want sonar?"

"No sonar," Fletcher said. "Nothing to make ourselves interesting to him."

"Then should we kill the electronics?"

"Kill everything."

All the console lights went out. Now there was just the red glow of the space heaters above them. They sat in darkness and stared out. Norman tried to remember how long dark-vision accommodation required. He remembered it might be as long as three minutes.

He began to see shapes: the outline of the grid on the bottom and, dimly, the high fin of the spaceship, rising sharply up.

Then something else.

A green glow in the distance. At the horizon.

"It's like a green sunrise," Beth said.

The glow increased in intensity, and then they saw an amorphous green shape with lateral streaks. Norman thought, It's just like the image we saw before. It looks just like that. He couldn't really make out the details.

"Is it a squid?" he said.

"Yes," Beth said.

"I can't see. . . ."

"You're looking at it end-on. The body is toward us, the tentacles behind, partially blocked by the body. That's why you can't see it."

The squid grew larger. It was definitely coming toward them.

Ted ran from the portholes back to the consoles. "Jerry, are you listening? Jerry?"

"Electronics are off, Dr. Fielding," Fletcher said.

"Well, let's try and talk to him, for God's sake."

"I think we're past the talking stage now, sir."

The squid was faintly luminous, the entire body a deep green. Now Norman could see a sharp vertical ridge in the body. The moving tentacles and arms were clear. The outline grew larger. The squid moved laterally.

"It's going around the grid."

"Yes," Beth said. "They're intelligent animals; they have the ability to learn from experience. It probably didn't like hitting the grid before, and it remembers."

The squid passed the spacecraft fin, and they could gauge its size. It's as big as a house, Norman thought. The creature slid smoothly through the water toward them. He felt a sense of awe, despite his pounding heart.

"Jerry? *Jerry!*"

"Save your breath, Ted."

"Thirty yards," Tina said. "Still coming."

As the squid came closer, Norman could count the arms, and he saw the two long tentacles, glowing lines extending far beyond the body. The arms and tentacles seemed to move loosely in the water, while the body made rhythmic muscular contractions. The squid propelled itself with water, and did not use the arms for swimming.

"Twenty yards."

"God, it's big," Harry said.

"You know," Beth said, "we're the first people in human history to see a free-swimming giant squid. This should be a great moment."

They heard the gurgling, the rush of water over the hydrophones, as the squid came closer.

"Ten yards."

For a moment, the great creature turned sideways to the habitat, and they could see its profile—the enormous glowing body, thirty feet long, with the huge unblinking eye; the circle of arms, waving like evil snakes; the two long tentacles, each terminating in a flattened, leaf-shaped section.

The squid continued to turn until its arms and tentacles stretched toward the habitat, and they glimpsed the mouth, the sharp-edged chomping beak in a mass of glowing green muscle.

"Oh God . . ."

The squid moved forward. They could see each other in the glow through the portholes. It's starting, Norman thought. It's starting, and this time we can't survive it.

There was a *thump* as a tentacle swung against the habitat.

"Jerry!" Ted shouted. His voice was high, strained with tension.

The squid paused. The body moved laterally, and they could see the huge eye staring at them.

"Jerry! Listen to me!"

The squid appeared to hesitate.

"He's listening!" Ted shouted, and he grabbed a flashlight off a wall bracket and shined it out the porthole. He blinked the light once.

The great body of the squid glowed green, then went momentarily dark, then glowed green again.

"He's listening," Beth said.

"Of course he's listening. He's intelligent." Ted blinked his light twice in rapid succession.

The squid blinked back, twice.

"How can he do that?" Norman said.

"It's a kind of skin cell called a chromatophore," Beth said. "The animal can open and close these cells at will, and block the light."

Ted blinked three times.

The squid blinked three times.

"He can do it fast," Norman said.

"Yes, fast."

"He's intelligent," Ted said. "I keep telling you. He's intelligent and he wants to talk."

Ted blinked long, short, short.

The squid matched the pattern.

"That's a baby," Ted said. "You just keep talking to me, Jerry."

He flashed a more complex pattern, and the squid answered, but then moved off to the left.

"I've got to keep him talking," Ted said.

As the squid moved, Ted moved, skipping from porthole to porthole, shining his light. The squid still blinked its glowing body in reply, but Norman sensed it had another purpose now.

They all followed Ted, from D into C Cyl. Ted flashed his light. The squid answered, but still moved onward.

"What's he doing?"

"Maybe he's leading us. . . ."

"Why?"

They went to B Cyl, where the life-support equipment was located, but there were no portholes in B. Ted moved on to A, the airlock. There were no portholes here, either. Ted immediately jumped down and opened the hatch in the floor, revealing dark water.

"Careful, Ted."

"I'm telling you, he's intelligent," Ted said. The water at his feet glowed a soft green. "Here he comes now." They could not see the squid yet, only the glow. Ted blinked his light into the water.

The green blinked back.

"Still talking," Ted said. "And as long as he's talking—"

With stunning swiftness, the tentacle smashed up through the open water and swung in a great arc around the airlock. Norman had a glimpse of a glowing stalk as thick as a man's body, and a great glowing leaf five feet long, swinging blindly past him, and as he ducked he saw it hit Beth and knock her sideways. Tina was screaming in terror. Strong ammonia fumes burned their eyes. The tentacle swung back toward Norman. He held up his hands to protect himself, touched slimy, cold flesh as the giant arm spun him, slammed him against the airlock's metal walls. The animal was incredibly strong.

"Get out, everybody out, away from the metal!" Fletcher was shouting. Ted was scrambling up, away from the hatch and the twisting arm, and he had almost reached the door when the leaf swung back and wrapped around him, covering most of his body. Ted grunted, pushed at the leaf with his hands. His eyes were wide with horror.

Norman ran forward but Harry grabbed him. "Leave him! You can't do anything now!"

Ted was being swung back and forth in the air across the airlock, banging from wall to wall. His head dropped; blood ran down his forehead onto the glowing tentacle. Still the arm swung him back and forth, the cylinder ringing like a gong with each impact.

"Get out!" Fletcher was shouting. "Everybody out!"

Beth scrambled past them. Harry tugged at Norman just as the second tentacle burst above the surface to hold Ted in a pincer grip.

"Off the metal! Damn it, off the metal!" Fletcher was shouting, and they stepped onto the carpet of B Cyl and she threw the switch on the Green Box and there was a hum from the generators and the red heater banks dimmed as two million volts of electricity surged through the habitat.

The response was instantaneous. The floor rocked under their feet as the habitat was struck by an enormous force, and Norman swore he heard a scream, though it might have been rending metal, and the tentacles quickly drew down out of the airlock. They had a last glimpse of Ted's body as it was pulled into the inky water and Fletcher yanked down the lever on the Green Box. But the alarms had already begun to sound, and the warning boards lit up.

"Fire!" Fletcher shouted. "Fire in E Cyl!"

Fletcher gave them gas masks; Norman's kept slipping down his forehead, obscuring his vision. By the time they reached D Cylinder, the smoke was dense. They coughed and stumbled, banged into the consoles.

"Stay low," Tina shouted, dropping to her knees. She was leading the way; Fletcher had stayed behind in B.

Up ahead, an angry red glow outlined the bulkhead door leading to E. Tina grabbed an extinguisher and went through the door, Norman right behind her. At first he thought the entire cylinder was burning. Fierce flames licked up the side padding; dense clouds of smoke boiled toward the ceiling. The heat was almost palpable. Tina swung the extinguisher cylinder around, began to spray white foam. In the light of the fire Norman saw another extinguisher, grabbed it, but the metal was burning hot and he dropped it to the floor.

"Fire in D," Fletcher said over the intercom. "Fire in D."

Jesus, Norman thought. Despite the mask, he coughed in the acrid smoke. He picked the extinguisher off the floor and began to spray; it immediately became cooler. Tina shouted to him, but he heard nothing except the roar of the flames. He and Tina were getting the fire out, but there was still a large burning patch near one porthole. He turned away, spraying the floor burning at his feet.

He was unprepared for the explosion, the concussion pounding his ears painfully. He turned and saw that a firehose had been unleashed in the room, and then he realized that one of the small portholes had blown or burned out, and the water was rushing in with incredible force.

He couldn't see Tina; then he saw she had been knocked down; she got to her feet, shouting something at Norman, and then she slipped and slid back into the hissing stream of water. It picked her up bodily and flung her so hard against the opposite wall that he knew at once she must be dead, and when he looked down he saw her floating face-down in the water rapidly filling the room. The back of her head was cut open; he saw the pulpy red flesh of her brain.

Norman turned and fled. Water was already trickling over the lip of the bulkhead as he slammed the heavy door shut, spun the wheel to lock it.

He couldn't see anything in D; the smoke was worse than before. He saw dim patches of red flame, hazy through the smoke. He heard the hiss of the extinguishers. Where was his own extinguisher? He must have left it in E. Like a blind man he felt along the walls for another extinguisher, coughing in the smoke. His eyes and lungs burned, despite the mask.

And then, with a great groan of metal, the pounding started, the habitat rocking under jolts from the squid outside. He heard Fletcher on the intercom but her voice was scratchy and unclear. The pounding continued, and the horrible wrenching of metal. And Norman thought, We're going to die. This time, we're going to die.

He couldn't find a fire extinguisher but his hands touched something metal on the wall and Norman felt it in the smoky darkness, wondering what it was, some kind of protrusion, and then two million volts surged through his limbs into his body and he screamed once, and fell backward.

Aftermath

He was staring at a bank of lights in some odd, angled perspective. He sat up, feeling a sharp pain, and looked around him. He was sitting on the floor in D Cylinder. A faint smoky haze hung in the air. The padded walls were blackened and charred in several places.

There must have been a fire here, he thought, staring at the damage in astonishment. When had this happened? Where had he been at the time?

He got slowly to one knee, and then to his feet. He turned to E Cylinder, but for some reason the bulkhead door to E was shut. He tried to spin the wheel to unlock it; it was jammed shut.

He didn't see anybody else. Where were the others? Then he remembered something about Ted. Ted had died. The squid swinging Ted's body in the airlock. And then Fletcher had said to get back, and she had thrown the power switch. . . .

It was starting to come back to him. The fire. There had been a fire in E Cylinder. He had gone into E with Tina to put out the fire. He remembered going into the room, seeing the flames lick up the side of the walls. . . . After that, he wasn't sure.

Where were the others?

For an awful moment he thought he was the only survivor, but then he heard a cough in C Cyl. He moved toward the sound. He didn't see anybody so he went to B Cyl.

Fletcher wasn't there. There was a large streak of blood on the metal pipes, and one of her shoes on the carpet. That was all.

Another cough, from among the pipes.

"Fletcher?"

"Just a minute . . ."

Beth emerged, grease-streaked, from the pipes. "Good, you're up. I've got most of the systems going, I think. Thank God the Navy has instructions printed on the housings. Anyway, the smoke's clearing and the air quality is reading all right—not great, but all right—and all the vital stuff seems to be intact. We have air and water and heat and power. I'm trying to find out how much power and air we have left."

"Where's Fletcher?"

"I can't find her anywhere." Beth pointed to the shoe on the carpet, and the streak of blood.

"Tina?" Norman asked. He was alarmed at the prospect of being trapped down here without any Navy people at all.

"Tina was with you," Beth said, frowning.

"I don't seem to remember," Norman said.

"You probably got a jolt of current," Beth said. "That would give you retrograde amnesia. You won't remember the last few minutes before the shock. I can't find Tina, either, but according to the status sensors E Cyl is flooded and shut down. You were with her in E. I don't know why it flooded."

"What about Harry?"

"He got a jolt, too, I think. You're lucky the amperage wasn't higher or you'd both be fried. Anyway, he's lying on the floor in C, either sleeping or unconscious. You might want to take a look at him. I didn't want to risk moving him, so I just left him there."

"Did he wake up? Talk to you?"

"No, but he seems to be breathing comfortably. Color's good, all that. Anyway, I thought I better get the life-support systems going." She wiped grease on her cheek. "I mean, it's just the three of us now, Norman."

"You, me, and Harry?"

"That's right. You, me, and Harry."

Harry was sleeping peacefully on the floor between the bunks. Norman bent down, lifted one eyelid, shone a light in Harry's pupil. The pupil contracted.

"This can't be heaven," Harry said.

"Why not?" Norman said. He shone the light in the other pupil; it contracted.

"Because you're here. They don't let psychologists into heaven." He gave a weak smile.

"Can you move your toes? Your hands?"

"I can move everything. I walked up here, Norman, from down in C. I'm okay."

Norman sat back. "I'm glad you're okay, Harry." He meant it: he had been dreading the thought of an injury to Harry. From the beginning of the expedition, they had all relied on Harry. At every critical juncture, he had supplied the breakthrough, the necessary understanding. And even now, Norman took comfort in the thought that, if Beth couldn't figure out the life-support systems, Harry could.

"Yeah, I'm okay." He closed his eyes again, sighed. "Who's left?"

"Beth. Me. You."

"Jesus."

"Yeah. You want to get up?"

"Yeah, I'll get in the bunk. I'm real tired, Norman. I could sleep for a year."

Norman helped him to his feet. Harry dropped quickly onto the nearest bunk.

"Okay if I sleep for a while?"

"Sure."

"That's good. I'm real tired, Norman. I could sleep for a year."

"Yes, you said that—"

He broke off. Harry was snoring. Norman reached over to remove something crumpled on the pillow beneath Harry's head.

It was Ted Fielding's notebook.

Norman suddenly felt overwhelmed. He sat on his bunk, holding the notebook in his hands. Finally he looked at a couple of pages, filled with Ted's large, enthusiastic scrawl. A photograph fell onto his lap. He turned it over. It was a photo of a red Corvette. And the feelings just overwhelmed him. Norman didn't know if he was crying for Ted, or crying for himself, because it was clear to him that one by one, they were all dying down here. He was very sad, and very afraid.

Beth was in D Cyl, at the communications console, turning on all the monitors.

"They did a pretty good job with this place," she said. "Everything is marked; everything has instructions; there're computer help files. An idiot could figure it out. There's just one problem that I can see."

"What's that?"

"The galley was in E Cyl, and E Cyl is flooded. We've got no food, Norman."

"None at all?"

"I don't think so."

"Water?"

"Yes, plenty of water, but no food."

"Well, we can make it without food. How much longer have we got down here?"

"It looks like two more days."

"We can make it," Norman said, thinking: Two days, Jesus. Two more days in this place.

"That's assuming the storm clears on schedule," Beth added. "I've been trying to figure out how to release a surface balloon, and see what it's like up there. Tina used to punch some special code to release a balloon."

"We can make it," Norman said again.

"Oh sure. If worse comes to worst, we can always get food from the spaceship. There's plenty over there."

"You think we can risk going outside?"

"We'll have to," she said, glancing at the screens, "sometime in the next three hours."

"Why?"

"The minisub. It has that automatic surfacing timer, unless someone goes over and punches the button."

"The hell with the sub," Norman said. "Let the sub go."

"Well, don't be too hasty," Beth said. "That sub can hold three people."

"You mean we could all get out of here in it?"

"Yeah. That's what I mean."

"Christ," Norman said. "Let's go now."

"There are two problems with that," Beth said. She pointed to the screens. "I've been going over the specs. First, the sub is unstable on the surface. If there are big waves on the surface, it'll bounce us around worse than anything we've had down here. And the second thing is that we have to link up with a decompression chamber on the surface. Don't forget, we still have ninety-six hours of decompression ahead of us."

"And if we don't decompress?" Norman said. He was thinking, Let's just go to the surface in the sub and throw open the hatch and see the clouds and the sky and breathe some normal earth air.

"We have to decompress," Beth said. "Your bloodstream is saturated with helium gas in solution. Right now you're under pressure, so everything is fine. But if you release that pressure suddenly, it's just the same as when you pop the top off a soda bottle. The helium will bubble explosively out of your system. You'll die instantly."

"Oh," Norman said.

"Ninety-six hours," Beth said. "That's how long it takes to get the helium out of you."

"Oh."

Norman went to the porthole and looked across at DH-7, and the minisub. It was a hundred yards away. "You think the squid will come back?"

She shrugged. "Ask Jerry."

Norman thought, No more of that Geraldine stuff now. Or did she prefer to think of this malevolent entity as masculine?

"Which monitor is it?"

"This one." She flicked it on. The screen glowed.

Norman said, "Jerry? Are you there?"

No answer.

He typed, JERRY? ARE YOU THERE?

There was no response.

"I'll tell you something about Jerry," Beth said. "He can't really read minds. When we were talking to him before, I sent him a thought and he didn't respond."

"I did, too," Norman said. "I sent both messages and images. He never responded."

"If we speak, he answers, but if we just think, he doesn't answer," Beth said. "So he's not all-powerful. He actually behaves as if he *hears* us."

"That's right," Norman said. "Although he doesn't seem to be hearing us now."

"No. I tried earlier, too."

"I wonder why he isn't answering."

"You said he was emotional. Maybe he's sulking."

Norman didn't think so. Child kings didn't sulk. They were vindictive and whimsical, but they didn't sulk.

"By the way," she said, "you might want to look at these." She handed him a stack of printouts. "They're the record of all the interactions we've had with him."

"They may give us a clue," Norman said, thumbing through the sheets without any real enthusiasm. He felt suddenly tired.

"Anyway, it'll occupy your mind."

"True."

"Personally," Beth said, "I'd like to go back to the ship."

"What for?"

"I'm not convinced we've found everything that's there."

"It's a long way to the ship," Norman said.

"I know. But if we get a clear time without the squid, I might try it."

"Just to occupy your mind?"

"I guess you could say that." She glanced at her watch. "Norman, I'm going to get a couple of hours of sleep," she said. "Then we can draw straws to see who goes to the submarine."

"Okay."

"You seem depressed, Norman."

"I am."

"Me, too," she said. "This place feels like a tomb—and I've been prematurely buried."

She climbed the ladder to her laboratory, but apparently she didn't go to sleep, because after a few moments, he heard Tina's recorded voice on videotape saying, "Do you think they'll ever get the sphere open?"

And Beth replied, "Maybe. I don't know."

"It scares me."

The whirr of rewinding and a short delay, then:

"Do you think they'll ever get the sphere open?"

"Maybe. I don't know."

"It scares me."

The tape was becoming an obsession with Beth.

He stared at the printouts on his lap, and then he looked at the screen. "Jerry?" he said. "Are you there?"

Jerry did not answer.

The Sub

She was shaking his shoulder gently. Norman opened his eyes.

"It's time," Beth said.

"Okay." He yawned. God, he was tired. "How much time is left?"

"Half an hour."

Beth switched on the sensory array at the communications console, adjusted the settings.

"You know how to work all that stuff?" Norman said. "The sensors?"

"Pretty well. I've been learning it."

"Then I should go to the sub," he said. He knew Beth would never agree, that she would insist on doing the active thing, but he wanted to make the effort.

"Okay," she said. "You go. That makes sense."

He covered his surprise. "I think so, too."

"Somebody has to watch the array," she said. "And I can give you warning if the squid is coming."

"Right," he said. Thinking, Hell, she's serious. "I don't think this is one for Harry," Norman said.

"No, Harry's not very physical. And he's still asleep. I say, let him sleep."

"Right," Norman said.

"You'll need help with your suit," Beth said.

"Oh, that's right, my suit," Norman said. "The fan is broken in my suit."

"Fletcher fixed it for you," Beth said.

"I hope she did it right."

"Maybe I should go instead," Beth said.

"No, no. You watch the consoles. I'll go. It's only a hundred yards or so, anyway. It can't be a big deal."

"All clear now," she said, glancing at the monitors.

"Right," Norman said.

His helmet clicked in place, and Beth tapped his faceplate, gave him a questioning look: was everything all right?

Norman nodded, and she opened the floor hatch for him. He waved goodbye and jumped into the chilly black water. On the sea floor, he stood beneath the hatch for a moment and waited to make sure he could hear his circulating fan. Then he moved out from beneath the habitat.

There were only a few lights on in the habitat, and he could see many thin lines of bubbles streaming upward, from the leaking cylinders.

"How are you?" Beth said, over the intercom.

"Okay. You know the place is leaking?"

"It looks worse than it is," Beth said. "Trust me."

Norman came to the edge of the habitat and looked across the hundred yards of open sea floor that separated him from DH-7. "How does it look? Still clear?"

"Still clear," Beth said.

Norman set out. He walked as quickly as he could, but he felt as if his feet were moving in slow motion. He was soon short of breath; he swore.

"What's the matter?"

"I can't go fast." He kept looking north, expecting at any moment to see the greenish glow of the approaching squid, but the horizon remained dark.

"You're doing fine, Norman. Still clear."

He was now fifty yards from the habitat—halfway there. He could see DH-7, much smaller than their own habitat, a single cylinder forty feet high, with very few portholes. Alongside it was the inverted dome, and the minisub.

"You're almost there," Beth said. "Good work."

Norman began to feel dizzy. He slowed his pace. He could now see markings on the gray surface of the habitat. There were all sorts of block-printed Navy stencils.

"Coast is still clear," Beth said. "Congratulations. Looks like you made it."

He moved under the DH-7 cylinder, looked up at the hatch. It was closed. He spun the wheel, pushed it open. He couldn't see much of the interior, because most of the lights were out. But he wanted to have a look inside. There might be something, some weapon, they could use.

"Sub first," Beth said. "You've only got ten minutes to push the button."

"Right."

Norman moved to the sub. Standing behind the twin screws, he read the name: *Deepstar III*. The sub was yellow, like the sub that he had ridden down, but its configuration was somewhat different. He found handholds on the side, pulled himself up into the pocket of air trapped inside the dome. There was a large acrylic bubble canopy on top of the sub for the pilot; Norman found the hatch behind, opened it, and dropped inside.

"I'm in the sub."

There was no answer from Beth. She probably couldn't hear him, surrounded by all this metal. He looked around the sub, thinking, I'm dripping wet. But what was he supposed to do, wipe his shoes before entering? He smiled at the thought. He found the tapes secured in an aft compartment. There was plenty of room for more, and plenty of room for three people. But Beth was right about going to the surface: the interior of the sub was crammed with instruments and sharp edges. If you got banged around in here it wouldn't be pleasant.

Where was the delay button? He looked at the darkened instrument panel, and saw a single flashing red light above a button marked "TIMER HOLD." He pressed the button.

The red light stopped flashing, and now remained steadily on. A small amber video screen glowed:

Timer Reset - Counting 12:00:00.

As he watched, the numbers began to run backward. He must have done it, he thought. The video screen switched off.

Still looking at all the instruments, a thought occurred to him: in an emergency, could he operate this sub? He slipped into the pilot's chair, faced the bewildering dials and switches of the instrument array. There didn't seem to be any steering apparatus, no wheel or joystick. How did you work the damned thing?

The video screen switched on:

DEEPSTAR III - COMMAND MODULE

Do you require help?
Yes   No   Cancel

Yes, he thought. I require help. He looked around for a "YES" button near the screen, but there wasn't any that he could see. Finally he thought to touch the screen, pressing "YES."

DEEPSTAR III - CHECKLIST OPTIONS

Descend   Ascend
Secure   Shutdown
Monitor   Cancel

He pressed "ASCEND." The screen changed to a small drawing of the instrument panel. One particular section of the drawing blinked on and off. Beneath the picture were the words:

DEEPSTAR III - ASCEND CHECKLIST

1. Set Ballast Blowers To: On
Proceed To Next   Cancel

So that was how it worked, Norman thought. A step-by-step checklist stored in the sub's computer. All you had to do was follow directions. He could do that.

A small surge of current moved the sub, swaying it at its tether.

He pressed the "CANCEL" and the screen went blank. It flashed:

Timer Reset - Counting 11:53:04

The counter was still running backward. He thought, Have I really been here seven minutes? Another surge of current, and the sub swayed again. It was time to go.

He moved to the hatch, climbed out into the dome, and closed the hatch. He lowered himself down the side of the sub, touched the bottom. Out from beneath the shielding metal, his radio immediately crackled.

"—you there? Norman, are you there? Answer, please!"

It was Harry, on the radio.

"I'm here," Norman said.

"Norman, for God's sake—"

In that moment, Norman saw the greenish glow, and he knew why the sub had surged and rocked at its moorings. The squid was just ten yards away, its glowing tentacles writhing out toward him, churning up the sediment along the ocean floor.

"—Norman, will you—"

There was no time to think. Norman took three steps, jumped, and pulled himself through the open hatch into DH-7.

He slammed the hatch door down behind him but the flat, spade-like tentacle was already reaching in. He pinned the tentacle in the partially closed hatch, but the tentacle didn't withdraw. It was incredibly strong and muscular, writhing as he watched, the suckers like small puckered mouths opening and closing. Norman stomped down on the hatch, trying to force the tentacle to withdraw. With a muscular flip, the hatch flew open, knocking him backward, and the tentacle reached up into the habitat. He smelled the strong odor of ammonium.

Norman fled, climbing higher into the cylinder. The second tentacle appeared, splashing up through the hatch. The two tentacles swung in circles beneath him, searching. He came to a porthole and looked out, saw the great body of the animal, the huge round staring eye. He clambered higher, getting away from the tentacles. Most of the cylinder seemed to be given over to storage; it was crammed with equipment, boxes, tanks. Many of the boxes were bright red with stencils: "CAUTION NO SMOKING NO ELECTRONICS TEVAC EXPLOSIVES." There were a hell of a lot of explosives in here, he thought, stumbling upward.

The tentacles rose higher behind him. Somewhere, in a detached, logical part of his brain, he thought: The cylinder is only forty feet high, and the tentacles are at least forty feet long. There will be no place for me to hide.

He stumbled, banged his knee, kept going. He heard the slap of the tentacles as they struck the walls, swung upward toward him.

A weapon, he thought. I have to find a weapon.

He came to the small galley, metal counter, some pots and pans. He pulled the drawers open hastily, looking for a knife. He could find only a small paring knife, threw it away in disgust. He heard the tentacles coming closer. The next moment he was knocked down, his helmet banging on the deck. Norman scrambled to his feet, dodged the tentacle, moved up the cylinder.

A communications section: radio set, computer, a couple of monitors. The tentacles were right behind him, slithering up like nightmarish vines. His eyes burned from the ammonia fumes.

He came to the bunks, a narrow space near the top of the cylinder.

No place to hide, he thought. No weapons, and no place to hide.

The tentacles reached the top of the cylinder, slapped against the upper curved surface, swung sideways. In a moment they would have him. He grabbed the mattress from one bunk, held it up as flimsy protection. The two tentacles were swinging erratically around him. He dodged the first.

And then with a *whump* the second tentacle coiled around him, holding both him and the mattress in a cold, slimy grip. He felt a sickening slow squeeze, the dozens of suckers gripping his body, cutting into his skin. He moaned in horror. The second tentacle swung back to grip him along with the first. He was trapped in a vise.

Oh God, he thought.

The tentacles swung away from the wall, lifting him high in the air, into the middle of the cylinder. This is it, he thought, but in the next moment he felt his body sliding downward past the mattress, and he slipped through the grip and fell through the air. He grabbed the tentacles for support, sliding down the giant evil-smelling vines, and then he crashed down onto the deck near the galley, his head banging on the metal deck. He rolled onto his back.

He saw the two tentacles above, gripping the mattress, squeezing it, twisting it. Did the squid realize what had happened, that he had gotten free?

Norman looked around desperately. A weapon, a weapon. This was a Navy habitat. There must be a weapon somewhere.

The tentacles tore the mattress apart. Shreds of white padding drifted down through the cylinder. The tentacles released the mattress, the big pieces falling. Then the tentacles started swinging around the habitat again.

Searching.

It knows, he thought. It knows I have gotten away, and that I am still in here somewhere. It is hunting me.

But how did it know?

Norman ducked behind the galley as one of the flat tentacles came crashing through the pots and pans, sweeping around, feeling for him. Norman scrambled back, coming up against a large potted plant. The tentacle was still searching, moving restlessly across the floor, banging the pans. Norman pushed the plant forward, and the tentacle gripped it, uprooted it easily, sweeping it away into the air.

The distraction allowed Norman to scramble forward.

A weapon, he thought. A weapon.

He looked down to where the mattress had fallen, and he saw, lining the wall near the bottom hatch, a series of silver vertical bars. Spear guns! Somehow he had missed them on the way up. Each spear gun was tipped in a fat bulb like a hand grenade. Explosive tips? He started to climb down.

The tentacles were sliding down, too, following him. How did the squid know where he was? And then, as he passed a porthole, he saw the eye outside and he thought, He can see me, for God's sake.

Stay away from the portholes.

Not thinking clearly. Everything happening fast. Crawling down past the explosive crates in the storage hold, thinking, I better not miss in here, and he landed with a *clang* on the airlock deck.

The arms were slithering down, moving down the cylinder toward him. He tugged at one of the spear guns. It was strapped to the wall with a rubber cord. Norman pulled at it, tried to release it. The tentacles drew closer. He yanked at the rubber, but it wouldn't release. What was wrong with these snaps?

The tentacles were closer. Coming down swiftly.

Then he realized the cords had safety catches: you had to pull the guns *sideways,* not out. He did; the rubber popped free. The spear gun was in his hand. He turned, and the tentacle knocked him down. He flipped onto his back and saw the great flat suckered palm of the tentacle coming straight down on him, and the tentacle wrapped over his helmet, everything was black, and he fired.

There was tremendous pain in his chest and abdomen. For a horrified moment he thought he had shot himself. Then he gasped and he realized it was just the concussion; his chest was burning, but the squid released him.

He still couldn't see. He pulled the palm off his face and it fell heavily onto the deck, writhing, severed from the squid arm. The interior walls of the habitat were splattered with blood. One tentacle was still moving, the other was a

461

bloody, ragged stump. Both arms pulled out through the hatch, slipped into the water.

Norman ran for the porthole; the squid moved swiftly away, the green glow diminishing. He had done it! He'd beaten it off.

He'd done it.

DH-8

"**H**ow many did you bring?" Harry said, turning the spear gun over in his hands.

"Five," Norman said. "That was all I could carry."

"But it worked?" He was examining the bulbous explosive tip.

"Yeah, it worked. Blew the whole tentacle off."

"I saw the squid going away," Harry said. "I figured you must have done something."

"Where's Beth?"

"I don't know. Her suit's gone. I think she may have gone to the ship."

"Gone to the ship?" Norman said, frowning.

"All I know is, when I woke up she was gone. I figured you were over at the habitat, and then I saw the squid, and I tried to get you on the radio but I guess the metal blocked the transmission."

"Beth left?" Norman said. He was starting to get angry. Beth was supposed to stay at the communications console, watching the sensors for him while he was outside. Instead, she had gone to the ship?

"Her suit's gone," Harry said again.

"Son of a bitch!" Norman said. He was suddenly furious—really, deeply furious. He kicked the console.

"Careful there," Harry said.

"Damn it!"

"Take it easy," Harry said, "come on, take it easy, Norman."

"What the hell does she think she's doing?"

"Come on, sit down, Norman." Harry steered him to a chair. "We're all tired."

"Damn right we're tired!"

"Easy, Norman, easy . . . Remember your blood pressure."

"My blood pressure's fine!"

"Not now, it's not," Harry said. "You're purple."

"How could she let me go outside and then just leave?"

"Worse, go out herself," Harry said.

"But she wasn't watching out for me any more," Norman said. And then it came to him, why he was so angry—he was angry because he was afraid. At a moment of great personal danger, Beth had abandoned him. There were only three of them left down there, and they needed each other—they needed to depend on each other. But Beth was unreliable, and that made him afraid. And angry.

"Can you hear me?" her voice said, on the intercom. "Anybody hear me?"

Norman reached for the microphone, but Harry snatched it away. "I'll do this," he said. "Yes, Beth, we can hear you."

"I'm in the ship," she said, her voice crackling on the intercom. "I've found another compartment, aft, behind the crew bunks. It's quite interesting."

Quite interesting, Norman thought. Jesus, quite interesting. He grabbed the microphone from Harry. "Beth, what the hell are you doing over there?"

"Oh, hi, Norman. You made it back okay, huh?"

"Barely."

"You have some trouble?" She didn't sound concerned.

"Yes, I did."

"Are you all right? You sound mad."

"You bet I'm mad. Beth, why did you leave while I was out there?"

"Harry said he'd take over for me."

"He what?" Norman looked at Harry. Harry was shaking his head no.

"Harry said he'd take over at the console for me. He told me to go ahead to the ship. Since the squid wasn't around, it seemed like a good time."

Norman cupped his hand over the microphone. "I don't remember that," Harry said.

"Did you talk to her?"

"I don't remember talking to her."

Beth said, "Just ask him, Norman. He'll tell you."

"He says he never said that."

"Well, then, he's full of it," Beth said. "What do you think, I'd abandon you when you were *outside,* for Christ's sake?" There was a pause. "I'd never do that, Norman."

"I swear," Harry said to Norman. "I never had any conversation with Beth. I never talked to her at all. I'm telling you, she was gone when I woke up. There was nobody here. If you ask me, she always intended to go to the ship."

Norman remembered how quickly Beth had agreed to let Norman go to the sub, how surprised he had been. Perhaps Harry was right, he thought. Perhaps Beth had been planning it all along.

"You know what I think?" Harry said. "I think she's cracking up."

Over the intercom, Beth said, "You guys get it straightened out?"

Norman said, "I think so, Beth, yes."

"Good," Beth said. "Because I have made a discovery over here, in the spaceship."

"What's that?"

"I've found the crew."

"**Y**ou both came," Beth said. She was sitting on a console in the comfortable beige flight deck of the spacecraft.

"Yes," Norman said, looking at her. She looked okay. If anything, she looked better than ever. Stronger, clearer. She actually looked rather beautiful, he thought. "Harry thought that the squid wouldn't come back."

"The *squid* was out there?"

Norman briefly told her about his attack.

"Jesus. I'm sorry, Norman. I'd never have left if I had any idea."

She certainly didn't sound like somebody who was cracking up, Norman thought. She sounded appropriate and sincere. "Anyway," he said, "I injured it, and Harry thought it wouldn't come back."

Harry said, "And we couldn't decide who should stay behind, so we both came."

"Well, come this way," Beth said. She led them back, through the crew quarters, past the twenty bunks for the crew, the large galley. Norman paused at the galley. So did Harry.

"I'm hungry," Harry said.

"Eat something," Beth said. "I did. They have some sort of nut bars or something, they taste okay." She opened a drawer in the galley, produced bars wrapped in metal foil, gave them each one. Norman tore the foil and saw something that looked like chocolate. It tasted dry.

"Anything to drink?"

"Sure." She threw open a refrigerator door. "Diet Coke?"

"You're kidding. . . ."

"The can design is different, and I'm afraid it's warm, but it's Diet Coke, all right."

"I'm buying stock in that company," Harry said. "Now that we know it'll still be there in fifty years." He read the can. "Official drink of the Star Voyager Expedition."

"Yeah, it's a promo," Beth said.

Harry turned the can around. The other side was printed in Japanese. "Wonder what this means?"

"It means, don't buy that stock after all," she said.

Norman sipped the Coke with a sense of vague unease. The galley seemed subtly changed from the last time he had seen it. He wasn't sure—he'd only glanced briefly at the room before—but he usually had a good memory for room layouts, and his wife had always joked that Norman could find his way around any kitchen. "You know," he said, "I don't remember a refrigerator in the galley."

"I never really noticed, myself," Beth said.

"As a matter of fact," Norman said, "this whole room looks different to me. It looks bigger, and—I don't know—different."

"It's 'cause you're hungry." Harry grinned.

"Maybe," Norman said. Harry could actually be right. In the sixties, there had been a number of studies of visual perception which demonstrated that subjects interpreted blurred slides according to their predispositions. Hungry people saw all the slides as food.

But this room really did look different. For instance, he didn't remember the door to the galley being to the left, as it was now. He remembered it as being in the center of the wall separating the galley from the bunks.

"This way," Beth said, leading them farther aft. "Actually, the refrigerator was what got me thinking. It's one thing to store a lot of food on a test ship being sent through a black hole. But to stock a refrigerator—why bother to do that? It made me think, there might be a crew after all."

They entered a short, glass-walled tunnel. Deep-purple lights glowed down on them. "Ultraviolet," Beth said. "I don't know what it's for."

"Disinfection?"

"Maybe."

"Maybe it's to get a suntan," Harry said. "Vitamin D."

Then they came into a large room unlike anything Norman had ever seen. The floor glowed purple, bathing the room in ultraviolet light from beneath. Mounted on all four walls were a series of wide glass tubes. Inside each tube was a narrow silver mattress. The tubes all appeared empty.

"Over here," Beth said.

They peered through one glass tube. The naked woman had once been beautiful. It was still possible to see that. Her skin was dark brown and deeply wrinkled, her body withered.

"Mummified?" Harry said.

Beth nodded. "Best I can figure out. I haven't opened the tube, considering the risk of infection."

"What was this room?" he said, looking around.

"It must be some kind of hibernation chamber. Each tube is separately connected to a life-support system—power supply, air handlers, heaters, the works—in the next room."

Harry counted. "Twenty tubes," he said.

"And twenty bunks," Norman said.

"So where is everybody else?"

Beth shook her head. "I don't know."

"This woman is the only one left?"

"Looks like it. I haven't found any others."

"I wonder how they all died," Harry said.

"Have you been to the sphere?" Norman asked Beth.

"No. Why?"

"Just wondered."

"You mean, you wondered if the crew died after they picked up the sphere?"

"Basically, yes."

"I don't think the sphere is aggressive or dangerous in any sense," Beth said. "It's possible that the crew died of natural causes in the course of the journey itself. This woman, for example, is so well preserved it makes you wonder about radiation. Maybe she got a large dose of radiation. There's tremendous radiation around a black hole."

"You think the crew died going through the black hole, and the sphere was picked up automatically by the spacecraft later?"

"It's possible."

"She's pretty good-looking," Harry said, peering through the glass. "Boy, the reporters would go crazy with this, wouldn't they? Sexy woman from the future found nude and mummified. Film at eleven."

"She's tall, too," Norman said. "She must be over six feet."

"An Amazon woman," Harry said. "With great tits."

"All right," Beth said.

"What's wrong—offended on her behalf?" Harry said.

"I don't think there's any need for comments of that kind."

"Actually, Beth," Harry said, "she looks a little like you."

Beth frowned.

"I'm serious. Have you looked at her?"

"Don't be ridiculous."

Norman peered through the glass, shielding his hand against the reflection of the purple UV tubes in the floor. The mummified woman did indeed look like Beth—younger, taller, stronger, but like Beth, nevertheless. "He's right," Norman said.

"Maybe she's you, from the future," Harry said.

"No, she's obviously in her twenties."

"Maybe she's your granddaughter."

"Pretty unlikely," Beth said.

"You never know," Harry said. "Does Jennifer look like you?"

"Not really. But she's at that awkward stage. And she doesn't look like that woman. And neither do I."

Norman was struck by the conviction with which Beth denied any resemblance or association to the mummified woman. "Beth," he said, "what do you suppose happened here? Why is this woman the only one left?"

"I think she was important to the expedition," Beth said. "Maybe even the captain, or the co-captain. The others were mostly men. And they did something foolish—I don't know what—something she advised them against—

and as a result they all died. She alone remained alive in this spacecraft. And she piloted it home. But there was something wrong with her—something she couldn't help—and she died."

"What was wrong with her?"

"I don't know. Something."

Fascinating, Norman thought. He'd never really considered it before, but this room—for that matter, this entire spacecraft—was one big Rorschach. Or more accurately, a TAT. The Thematic Apperception Test was a psychological test that consisted of a series of ambiguous pictures. Subjects were supposed to tell what they thought was happening in the pictures. Since no clear story was implied by the pictures, the subjects supplied the stories. And the stories told much more about the storytellers than about the pictures.

Now Beth was telling them her fantasy about this room: that a woman had been in charge of the expedition, the men had failed to listen to her, they had died, and she alone had remained alive, the sole survivor.

It didn't tell them much about this spaceship. But it told them a lot about Beth.

"I get it," Harry said. "You mean she's the one who made the mistake and piloted the ship back too far into the past. Typical woman driver."

"Do you have to make a joke of everything?"

"Do you have to take everything so seriously?"

"This *is* serious," Beth said.

"I'll tell you a different story," Harry said. "This woman screwed up. She was supposed to do something, and she forgot to do it, or else she made a mistake. And then she went into hibernation. As a result of her mistake, the rest of the crew died, and she never woke up from the hibernation—never realized what she had done, because she was so unaware of what was really happening."

"I'm sure you like that story better," Beth said. "It fits with your typical black-male contempt for women."

"Easy," Norman said.

"You resent the power of the female," Beth said.

"What power? You call lifting weights power? That's only strength—and it comes out of a feeling of weakness, not power."

"You skinny little weasel," Beth said.

"What're you going to do, beat me up?" Harry said. "Is that your idea of power?"

"I know what power is," Beth said, glaring at him.

"Easy, easy," Norman said. "Let's not get into this."

Harry said, "What do you think, Norman? Do you have a story about the room, too?"

"No," Norman said. "I don't."

"Oh, come on," Harry said. "I bet you do."

"No," Norman said. "And I'm not going to mediate between you two.

We've all got to stay together on this. We have to work as a team, as long as we're down here."

"It's Harry who's divisive," Beth said. "From the beginning of this trip, he's tried to make trouble with everybody. All those snide little comments . . ."

"What snide little comments?" Harry said.

"You know perfectly well what snide little comments," Beth said.

Norman walked out of the room.

"Where're you going?"

"Your audience is leaving."

"Why?"

"Because you're both boring."

"Oh," Beth said, "Mr. Cool Psychologist decides we are boring?"

"That's right," Norman said, walking through the glass tunnel, not looking back.

"Where do you get off, making all these judgments of other people?" Beth shouted at him.

He kept walking.

"I'm speaking to you! Don't you walk away while I'm speaking to you, Norman!"

He came into the galley once more and started opening the drawers, looking for the nut bars. He was hungry again, and the search took his mind off the other two. He had to admit he was disturbed by the way things were going. He found a bar, tore the foil, ate it.

Disturbed, but not surprised. In studies of group dynamics he had long ago verified the truth of the old statement "Three's a crowd." For a high-tension situation, groups of three were inherently unstable. Unless everybody had clearly defined responsibilities, the group tended to form shifting allegiances, two against one. That was what was happening now.

He finished the nut bar, and immediately ate another one. How much longer did they have down here? At least thirty-six hours more. He looked for a place to carry additional nut bars, but his polyester jumpsuit had no pockets.

Beth and Harry came into the galley, much chagrined.

"Want a nut bar?" he said, chewing.

"We want to apologize," she said.

"For what?"

"For acting like children," Harry said.

"I'm embarrassed," Beth said. "I feel terrible about losing my temper that way, I feel like a complete idiot. . . ." Beth was hanging her head, staring at the floor. Interesting how she flipped, he thought, from aggressive self-confidence to the complete opposite, abject self-apology. Nothing in between.

"Let's not take it too far," he said. "We're all tired."

"I feel just awful," Beth continued. "Really awful. I feel as if I've let you both down. I shouldn't be here in the first place. I'm not worthy to be in this group."

Norman said, "Beth, have a nut bar and stop feeling sorry for yourself."

"Yes," Harry said. "I think I like you better angry."

"I'm sick of those nut bars," Beth said. "Before you came here, I ate eleven of them."

"Well, make it an even dozen," Norman said, "and we'll go back to the habitat."

Walking back across the ocean floor, they were tense, watching for the squid. But Norman derived comfort from the fact that they were armed. And something else: some inner confidence that came from his earlier confrontation with the squid.

"You hold that spear gun like you mean it," Beth said.

"Yes. I guess so." All his life he had been an academic, a university researcher, and had never conceived of himself as a man of action. At least, nothing beyond the occasional game of golf. Now, holding the spear gun ready, he found he rather liked the feeling.

As he walked he noticed the profusion of sea fans on the path between the spacecraft and the habitat. They were obliged to walk around the fans, which were sometimes four and five feet tall, gaudy purple and blue in their lights. Norman was quite sure that the fans had not been down here when they first arrived at the habitat.

Now there were not only colorful fans, but schools of large fish, too. Most of the fish were black with a reddish stripe across the back. Beth said they were Pacific surgeonfish, normal for the region.

Everything is changing, he thought. It's all changing around us. But he wasn't sure about that. He didn't really trust his memory down here. There were too many other things to alter his perceptions—the high-pressure atmosphere, the injuries he had received, and the nagging tension and fear he lived with.

Something pale caught his eye. Shining his light down on the bottom, he saw a wriggling white streak with a long thin fin and black stripes. At first he thought it was an eel. Then he saw the tiny head, the mouth.

"Just wait," Beth said, putting her arm on him.

"What is it?"

"Sea snake."

"Are they dangerous?"

"Not usually."

"Poisonous?" Harry said.

"Very poisonous."

The snake stayed close to the bottom, apparently looking for food. The snake ignored them entirely, and Norman found it quite beautiful to watch, particularly as it moved farther away.

"It gives me the creeps," Beth said.

"Do you know what kind it is?" Norman said.

"It may be a Belcher's," Beth said. "Pacific sea snakes are all poisonous, but Belcher's sea snake is the most poisonous. In fact, some researchers think it's the deadliest reptile in the world, with venom a hundred times more powerful than the venom of a king cobra or the black tiger snake."

"So if it bit you . . ."

"Two minutes, tops."

They watched the snake slither away among the fans. Then it was gone.

"Sea snakes are not usually aggressive," Beth said. "Some divers even touch them, play with them, but I never would. God. *Snakes.*"

"Why are they so poisonous? Is it for immobilizing prey?"

"You know, it's interesting," Beth said, "but the most toxic creatures in the world are all water creatures. The venom of land animals is nothing in comparison. And even among land animals, the most deadly poison is derived from an amphibian, a toad, *Bufotene marfensis.* In the sea, there are poisonous fish, like the blowfish, which is a delicacy in Japan; there are poisonous shells, like the star cone, *Alaverdis lotensis.* Once I was on a boat in Guam and a woman brought up a star cone. The shells are very beautiful, but she didn't know you have to keep your fingers away from the point. The animal extruded its poison spine and stung her in the palm. She took three steps before she collapsed in convulsions, and she died within an hour. There are also poisonous plants, poisonous sponges, poisonous corals. And then the snakes. Even the weakest of the sea snakes are invariably lethal."

"Nice," Harry said.

"Well, you have to recognize that the ocean is a much older living environment than the land. There's been life in the oceans for three and a half billion years, much longer than on land. The methods of competition and defense are much more highly developed in the ocean—there's been more time."

"You mean a few billion years from now, there will be tremendously poisonous animals on land, too?"

"If we get that far," she said.

"Let's just get back to the habitat," Harry said.

The habitat was now very close. They could see all the streaming bubbles rising from the leaks.

"Leaking like a bastard," Harry said.

"I think we've got enough air."

"I think I'll check."

"Be my guest," Beth said, "but I did a thorough job."

Norman thought another argument was about to start, but Beth and Harry dropped it. They came to the hatch and climbed up into DH-8.

The Console

"**J**erry?"

Norman stared at the console screen. It remained blank, just a blinking cursor.

"Jerry, are you there?"

The screen was blank.

"I wonder why we aren't hearing from you, Jerry," Norman said.

The screen remained blank.

"Trying a little psychology?" Beth said. She was checking the controls for the external sensors, reviewing the graphs. "If you ask me, the person you should use your psychology on is Harry."

"What do you mean?"

"What I mean is, I don't think Harry should be screwing around with our life-support systems. I don't think he's stable."

"Stable?"

"That's a psychologist's trick, isn't it? To repeat the last word in a sentence. It's a way to keep the person talking."

"Talking?" Norman said, smiling at her.

"Okay, maybe I am a little stressed out," she said. "But, Norman, seriously. Before I left for the ship, Harry came into this room and said he would take over for me. I told him you were at the sub but there weren't any squid around and that I wanted to go to the ship. He said fine, he'd take over. So I left. And now he doesn't remember any of that. Doesn't that strike you as pretty screwy?"

"Screwy?" Norman said.

"Stop it, be serious."

"Serious?" Norman said.

"Are you trying to avoid this conversation? I notice how you avoid what you don't want to talk about. You keep everybody on an even keel, steer the conversation away from hard topics. But I think you should listen to what I'm saying, Norman. There's a problem with Harry."

"I'm listening to what you're saying, Beth."

"And?"

"I wasn't present for this particular episode, so I don't really know. What I see of Harry now looks like the same old Harry—arrogant, disdainful, and very, very intelligent."

471

"You don't think he's cracking up?"

"No more than the rest of us."

"Jesus! What do I have to do to convince you? I had a *whole conversation* with the man and now he denies it. You think that's normal? You think we can trust a person like that?"

"Beth. I wasn't there."

"You mean it might be me."

"I wasn't there."

"You think I might be the one who's cracking up? I say there was a conversation when there really wasn't?"

"Beth."

"Norman, I'm telling you. There is a problem about Harry and you aren't facing up to it."

They heard footsteps approaching.

"I'm going to my lab," she said. "You think about what I've said."

She climbed the ladder as Harry walked in. "Well, guess what? Beth did an excellent job with the life-support systems. Everything looks fine. We have air for fifty-two hours more at present rates of consumption. We should be fine. You talking to Jerry?"

"What?" Norman said.

Harry pointed to the screen:

HELLO NORMAN.

"I don't know when he came back. He wasn't talking earlier."

"Well, he is now," Harry said.

HELLO HARRY.

"How's it going, Jerry?" Harry said.

FINE THANK YOU. HOW ARE YOU? I AM WANTING SO MUCH TO TALK WITH YOUR ENTITIES. WHERE IS THE CONTROL ENTITY HARALD C. BARNES?

"Don't you know?"

I DO NOT SENSE THAT ENTITY NOW.

"He's, uh, gone."

I SEE. HE WAS NOT FRIENDLY. HE DID NOT ENJOY TO TALK WITH ME.

Norman thought, What is he telling us? Did Jerry get rid of Barnes because he thought he was unfriendly?

"Jerry," Norman said, "what happened to the control entity?"

HE WAS NOT FRIENDLY. I DID NOT LIKE HIM.

"Yes, but what *happened* to him?"

HE IS NOT NOW.

"And the other entities?"

AND THE OTHER ENTITIES. THEY DID NOT ENJOY TO TALKING WITH ME.

Harry said, "You think he's saying he got rid of them?"

I AM NOT HAPPY TO TALKING WITH THEM.

"So he got rid of all the Navy people?" Harry said.

Norman was thinking, That's not quite correct. He also got rid of Ted, and

Ted was trying to communicate with him. Or with the squid. Was the squid related to Jerry? How would Norman ask that?

"Jerry . . ."

YES NORMAN. I AM HERE.

"Let's talk."

GOOD. I LIKE THAT MUCH.

"Tell us about the squid, Jerry."

THE ENTITY SQUID IS A MANIFESTATION.

"Where did it come from?"

DO YOU LIKE IT? I CAN MANIFEST IT MORE FOR YOU.

"No, no, don't do that," Norman said quickly.

YOU DO NOT LIKE IT?

"No, no. We like it, Jerry."

THIS IS TRUE?

"Yes, true. We like it. Really we do."

GOOD. I AM PLEASED YOU LIKE IT. IT IS A VERY IMPRESSIVE ENTITY OF LARGE SIZE.

"Yes, it is," Norman said, wiping sweat from his forehead. Jesus, he thought, this is like talking to a child with a loaded gun.

IT IS DIFFICULT FOR ME TO MANIFEST THIS LARGE ENTITY. I AM PLEASED THAT YOU LIKE IT.

"Very impressive," Norman agreed. "But you do not need to repeat that entity for us."

YOU WISH A NEW ENTITY MANIFESTED FOR YOU?

"No, Jerry. Nothing right now, thank you."

MANIFESTING IS HAPPY FOR ME.

"Yes, I'm sure it is."

I AM ENJOYING TO MANIFEST FOR YOU NORMAN. AND ALSO FOR YOU HARRY.

"Thank you, Jerry."

I AM ENJOYING YOUR MANIFESTATIONS ALSO.

"*Our* manifestations?" Norman said, glancing at Harry. Apparently Jerry thought that the people on the habitat were manifesting something in return. Jerry seemed to consider it an exchange of some kind.

YES I AM ENJOYING YOUR MANIFESTATIONS ALSO.

"Tell us about our manifestations, Jerry," Norman said.

THE MANIFESTATIONS ARE SMALL AND THEY DO NOT EXTEND BEYOND YOUR ENTITIES BUT THE MANIFESTATIONS ARE NEW FOR ME. THEY ARE HAPPY FOR ME.

"What's he talking about?" Harry said.

YOUR MANIFESTATIONS HARRY.

"What manifestations, for Christ's sake?"

"Don't get mad," Norman warned. "Stay calm."

I AM LIKING THAT ONE HARRY. DO AN OTHER.

Norman thought: Is he reading emotions? Does he regard our emotions as manifestations? But that didn't make sense. Jerry couldn't read their minds;

they'd already determined that. Maybe he'd better check again. Jerry, he thought, can you hear me?

I AM LIKING HARRY. HIS MANIFESTATIONS ARE RED. THEY ARE WITFUL.

"Witful?"

WITFUL = FULL OF WIT?

"I see," Harry said. "He thinks we're funny."

FUNNY = FULL OF FUN?

"Not exactly," Norman said. "We entities have the concept of . . ." He trailed off. How was he going to explain "funny"? What was a joke, anyway? "We entities have the concept of a situation which causes discomfort and we call this situation humorous."

HUME OR US?

"No. One word." Norman spelled it for him.

I SEE. YOUR MANIFESTATIONS ARE HUMOROUS. THE ENTITY SQUID MAKES MANY HUMOROUS MANIFESTATIONS FROM YOU.

"We don't think so," Harry said.

I THINK SO.

And that about summed it up, Norman thought, sitting at the console. Somehow he had to make Jerry understand the seriousness of his actions. "Jerry," Norman explained, "your manifestations injure our entities. Some of our entities are already gone."

YES I KNOW.

"If you continue your manifestations—"

YES I AM LIKING TO MANIFEST. IT IS HUMOROUS FOR YOU.

"—then pretty soon all our entities will be gone. And then there will be no one to talk to you."

I DO NOT WISH THAT.

"I know that. But many entities are gone already."

BRING THEM BACK.

"We can't do that. They are gone forever."

WHY?

"We cannot bring them back."

WHY?

Just like a kid, Norman thought. Just exactly like a kid. Telling the kid you can't do what he wants, you can't play the way he wants to play, and he refuses to accept it.

"We do not have the power, Jerry, to bring them back."

I WISH YOU TO BRING THE OTHER ENTITIES BACK NOW.

"He thinks we're refusing to play," Harry said.

BRING BACK THE ENTITY TED.

Norman said, "We can't, Jerry. We would if we could."

I AM LIKING THE ENTITY TED. HE IS VERY HUMOROUS.

"Yes," Norman said. "Ted liked you, too. Ted was trying to talk to you."

YES I AM LIKING HIS MANIFESTATIONS. BRING BACK TED.

"We can't."

There was a long pause.

I AM OFFENDED YOU?

"No, not at all."

WE ARE FRIENDS NORMAN AND HARRY.

"Yes, we are."

THEN BRING BACK THE ENTITIES.

"He just refuses to understand," Harry said. "Jerry, for God's sake, we can't do it!"

YOU ARE HUMOROUS HARRY. MAKE IT AGAIN.

He's definitely reading strong emotional reactions as some kind of manifestation, Norman thought. Was this his idea of play—to make a provocation to the other party, and then to be amused by their responses? Was he delighted to see the vivid emotions brought on by the squid? Was this his idea of a game?

HARRY MAKE IT AGAIN. HARRY MAKE IT AGAIN.

"Hey, man," Harry said angrily. "Get off my back!"

THANK YOU. I AM LIKING THAT. IT WAS RED ALSO. NOW YOU WILL PLEASE BRING BACK THE ENTITIES GONE.

Norman had an idea. "Jerry," he said, "if you wish the entities back, why don't *you* bring them back?"

I AM NOT PLEASED TO DO THIS.

"But you could do it, if you wanted to."

I CAN DO ANY THING.

"Yes, of course you can. So why don't you bring back the entities you desire?"

NO. I AM NOT HAPPY TO DO THIS.

"Why not?" Harry said.

HEY MAN GET OFF MY BACK.

"No offense, Jerry," Norman said quickly.

There was no reply on the screen.

"Jerry?"

The screen did not respond.

"He's gone again," Harry said. He shook his head. "God knows what the little bastard will do next."

Further Analysis

Norman went up to the lab to see Beth, but she was asleep, curled up on her couch. In sleep, she looked quite beautiful. It was odd after all the time down here she should seem so radiant. It was as if the harshness had gone out of her features. Her nose did not seem so sharp any more; the line of the mouth was softer, fuller. He looked at her arms, which had been sinewy, veins bulging. The muscles seemed smoother, more feminine somehow.

Who knows? he thought. After so many hours down here, you're no judge of anything. He climbed back down the ladder and went to his bunk. Harry was already there, snoring loudly.

Norman decided to take another shower. As he stepped under the spray, he made a startling discovery.

The bruises which had covered his body were gone.

Anyway, almost gone, he thought, staring down at the remaining patches of yellow and purple. They had healed within hours. He moved his limbs experimentally and realized that the pain had gone, too. Why? What had happened? For a moment he thought this was all a dream, or a nightmare, and then he thought: No, it's just the atmosphere. Cuts and bruises healing faster in the high-pressure environment. It wasn't anything mysterious. Just an atmospheric effect.

He toweled himself as dry as he could with the damp towel, and then went back to his bunk. Harry was still snoring, as loud as ever.

Norman lay on his back, stared at the red humming coils of the ceiling heater. He had an idea, and got out of bed, and shifted Harry's talker from the base of his throat to one side. Immediately the snores changed to a soft, high-pitched hiss.

Much better, he thought. He lay on the damp pillow, and was almost immediately asleep. He awoke with no sense of passing time—it might have been only a few seconds—but he felt refreshed. He stretched and yawned, and got out of bed.

Harry still slept. Norman moved the talker back, and the snores resumed. He went into D Cyl, to the console. Still on the screen were the words:

HEY MAN GET OFF MY BACK.

"Jerry?" Norman said. "Are you there, Jerry?"

The screen did not respond. Jerry wasn't there. Norman looked at the stack of printouts to one side. I really should go over this stuff, he thought. Because something troubled him about Jerry. Norman couldn't put his finger on it, but even if one imagined the alien as a spoiled child-king, Jerry's behavior didn't make sense. It just didn't add up. Including the last message.

HEY MAN GET OFF MY BACK.

Street talk? Or just imitating Harry? In any case it wasn't Jerry's usual mode of communication. Usually Jerry was ungrammatical and sort of spacy, talking about entities and awareness. But from time to time he would become sharply colloquial. Norman looked at the sheets.

WE'LL BE RIGHT BACK AFTER A SHORT BREAK FOR THESE MESSAGES FROM OUR SPONSOR.

That was one example. Where had that come from? It sounded like Johnny Carson. Then why didn't Jerry sound like Johnny Carson all the time? What caused the shift?

Then, too, there was the problem of the squid. If Jerry liked to scare them, if he enjoyed rattling their cage and seeing them jump, why use a squid? Where had that idea come from? And why only a squid? Jerry seemed to enjoy manifesting different things. So why hadn't he produced giant squid one time, great white sharks another time, and so on? Wouldn't that provide a greater challenge to his abilities?

Then there was the problem of Ted. Ted had been playing with Jerry at the time he was killed. If Jerry liked to play so much, why would he kill off a player? It just didn't make sense.

Or did it?

Norman sighed. His trouble lay in his assumptions. Norman was assuming that the alien had logical processes similar to his own. But that might not be true. For one thing, Jerry might operate at a much faster metabolic rate, and thus have a different sense of time. Kids played with a toy only until they got tired of it; then they changed to another. The hours that seemed so painfully long to Norman might be only a few seconds in the consciousness of Jerry. He might just be playing with the squid for a few seconds, until he dropped it for another toy.

Kids also had a poor idea about breaking things. If Jerry didn't know about death, then he wouldn't mind killing Ted, because he would think the death was just a temporary event, a "humorous" manifestation by Ted. He might not realize he was actually breaking his toys.

And it was also true, when he thought about it, that Jerry *had* manifested different things. Assuming that the jellyfish and the shrimps and the sea fans and now the sea snakes were his manifestations. Were they? Or were they just normal parts of the environment? Was there any way to tell?

And the Navy seaman, he thought suddenly. Let's not forget the seaman. Where had he come from? Was that seaman another of Jerry's manifestations?

Could Jerry manifest his playmates at will? In that case, he really wouldn't care if he killed them all.

But I think that's clear, Norman thought. Jerry doesn't care if he kills us. He just wants to play, and he doesn't know his own strength.

Yet there was something else. He scanned the sheets of printout, feeling instinctively some underlying organization to everything. Something he wasn't getting, some connection he wasn't making.

As he thought about it, he kept coming back to one question: Why a squid? Why a squid?

Of course, he thought. They had been talking about a squid, during the conversation at dinner. Jerry must have overheard that. He must have decided that a squid would be a provocative item to manifest. And he was certainly right about that.

Norman shifted the papers, and came upon the very first message that Harry had decoded.

HELLO. HOW ARE YOU? I AM FINE. WHAT IS YOUR NAME? MY NAME IS JERRY.

That was as good a place to begin as any. It had been quite a feat for Harry to decode it, Norman thought. If Harry hadn't succeeded with that, they would never have ever started talking to Jerry at all.

Norman sat at the console, stared at the keyboard. What had Harry said? The keyboard was a spiral: the letter G was one, and B was two, and so on. Very clever to figure it out. Norman would never have figured that out in a million years. He started trying to find the letters in the first sequence.

```
0032125252632   032629   301321   04261037   18   3016   06180
82132   29033005   1822   04261013   0830162137   1604   083016
21 1822 033013130432
```

Let's see . . . 00 marked the beginning of the message, Harry had said. And 03, that was H. And then 21, that was E, then 25 was L, and 25 was another L, and just above it, 26, was O. . . .

HELLO.

Yes, it all fitted. He continued translating. 032629 was HOW. . . .

HOW ARE YOU?

So far, so good. Norman experienced a certain pleasure, almost as if he were decoding it himself for the first time. Now, 18. That was I. . . .

I AM FINE.

He moved more quickly, writing down the letters.

WHAT IS YOUR NAME?

Now, 1604 was MY. . . . MY NAME IS . . . But then he found a mistake in one letter. Was that possible? Norman kept going, found a second mistake, then wrote out the message, and stared at it in growing shock.

MY NAME IS HARRY.

"Jesus Christ," he said.

He went over it again, but there was no mistake. Not by him. The message was perfectly clear.

HELLO. HOW ARE YOU? I AM FINE. WHAT IS YOUR NAME? MY NAME IS HARRY.

THE POWER

The Shadow

Beth sat up in her bed in the laboratory and stared at the message Norman had given her. "Oh my God," she said. She pushed her thick dark hair away from her face. "How can it be?" she said.

"It all goes together," Norman said. "Just think. When did the messages start? After Harry came out of the sphere. When did the squid and the other animals first appear? After Harry came out of the sphere."

"Yes, but—"

"—At first there were little squid, but then, when we were going to eat them, suddenly there were shrimps, too. Just in time for dinner. Why? Because Harry doesn't like to eat squid."

Beth said nothing; she just listened.

"And who, as a child, was terrified by the giant squid in *Twenty Thousand Leagues Under the Sea*?"

"Harry was," she said. "I remember he said that."

Norman went on in a rush. "And when does Jerry appear on the screen? When Harry is present. Not at other times. And when does Jerry answer us as we talk? When Harry is in the room to hear what we're saying. And why can't Jerry read our minds? Because Harry can't read our minds. And remember how Barnes kept asking for the name, and Harry wouldn't ask for the name? Why? Because he was afraid the screen would say 'Harry,' not 'Jerry.'"

"And the crewman . . ."

"Right. The black crewman. Who shows up just as Harry is having a dream of being rescued? A black crewman shows up to rescue us."

Beth was frowning, thinking. "What about the giant squid?"

"Well, in the middle of its attack, Harry hit his head and was knocked unconscious. Immediately the squid disappeared. It didn't come back again until Harry woke up from his nap, and told you he'd take over."

"My God," Beth said.

"Yes," Norman said. "It explains a lot."

She was silent for a while, staring at the message. "But how is he doing it?"

"I doubt if he is. At least, not consciously." Norman had been thinking about this. "Let's assume," he said, "that something happened to Harry when he went inside the sphere—he acquired some kind of power while in the sphere."

"Like what?"

"The power to make things happen just by thinking of them. The power to make his thoughts real."

Beth frowned. "Make his thoughts real . . ."

"It's not so strange," he said. "Just think: if you were a sculptor, first you would get an idea, and then you would carve it in stone or wood, to make it real. The idea comes first, then the execution follows, with some added effort to create a reality that reflects your prior thoughts. That's the way the world works for us. We imagine something, and then we try to make it happen. Sometimes the way we make it happen is unconscious—like the guy who just happens to go home unexpectedly at lunchtime and catches his wife in bed with another man. He doesn't consciously plan it. It just sort of happens by itself."

"Or the wife who catches the husband in bed with another woman," Beth said.

"Yes, of course. The point is, we manage to make things happen all the time without thinking about them too much. I don't think of every word when I talk to you. I just intend to say something and it comes out okay."

"Yes . . ."

"So we can make complicated creations like sentences without effort. But we can't make other complicated creations like sculptures without effort. We believe we have to *do* something besides simply have an idea."

"And we do," Beth said.

"Well, Harry doesn't. Harry's gone one step further. He doesn't have to carve the statue any more. He just gets the idea, and things happen by themselves. He manifests things."

"Harry imagines a frightening squid, and suddenly we have a frightening squid outside our window?"

"Exactly. And when he loses consciousness, the squid disappears."

"And he got this power from the sphere?"

"Yes."

Beth frowned. "Why is he doing this? Is he trying to kill us?"

Norman shook his head. "No. I think he's in over his head."

"How do you mean?"

"Well," Norman said, "we've considered lots of ideas of what the sphere from another civilization might be. Ted thought it was a trophy or a message— he saw it as a present. Harry thought it had something inside—he saw it as a container. But I wonder if it might be a mine."

"You mean, an explosive?"

"Not exactly—but a defense, or a test. An alien civilization could strew these things around the galaxy, and any intelligence that picks them up would get to experience the power of the sphere. Which is that whatever you think comes true. If you think positive thoughts, you get delicious shrimp for dinner.

If you think negative thoughts, you get monsters trying to kill you. Same process, just a matter of content."

"So, the same way a land mine blows up if you step on it, this sphere destroys people if they have negative thoughts?"

"Or," he said, "if they simply aren't in control of their consciousness. Because, if you're in control of your consciousness, the sphere would have no particular effect. If you're not in control, it gets rid of you."

"How can you control a negative thought?" Beth said. She seemed suddenly very agitated. "How can you say to someone, 'Don't think of a giant squid'? The minute you say that, they automatically think of the squid in the course of trying *not* to think of it."

"It's possible to control your thoughts," Norman said.

"Maybe for a yogi or something."

"For anybody," Norman said. "It's possible to deflect your attention from undesirable thoughts. How do people quit smoking? How do any of us ever change our minds about anything? By controlling our thoughts."

"I still don't see why Harry is doing this."

"Remember your idea that the sphere might strike us below the belt?" Norman said. "The way the AIDS virus strikes our immune system below the belt? AIDS hits us at a level we aren't prepared to deal with. So, in a sense, does the sphere. Because we believe that we can think whatever we want, without consequence. 'Sticks and stones can break my bones, but names can never hurt me.' We have sayings like that, which emphasize the point. But now suddenly a name is as real as a stick, and it can hurt us in the same way. Our thoughts get manifested—what a wonderful thing—except that *all* our thoughts get manifested, the good ones and the bad ones. And we simply aren't prepared to control our thoughts. We've never had to do it before."

"When I was a child," Beth said, "I was angry with my mother, and when she got cancer, I was terribly guilty. . . ."

"Yes," Norman said. "Children think this way. Children all believe that their thoughts have power. But we patiently teach them that they're wrong to think that. Of course," he said, "there has always been another tradition of belief about thoughts. The Bible says not to covet your neighbor's wife, which we interpret to mean that the act of adultery is forbidden. But that's not really what the Bible is saying. The Bible is saying that the *thought* of adultery is as forbidden as the act itself."

"And Harry?"

"Do you know anything about Jungian psychology?"

Beth said, "That stuff has never struck me as relevant."

"Well, it's relevant *now*," Norman said. He explained. "Jung broke with Freud early in this century, and developed his own psychology. Jung suspected there was an underlying structure to the human psyche that was reflected in an underlying similarity to our myths and archetypes. One of his ideas was that everybody had a dark side to his personality, which he called the 'shadow.' The shadow contained all the unacknowledged personality aspects—the hateful parts, the sadistic parts, all that. Jung thought people had the obligation to become acquainted with their shadow side. But very few people do. We all prefer to think we're nice guys and we don't ever have the desire to kill and maim and rape and pillage."

"Yes . . ."

"As Jung saw it, if you didn't acknowledge your shadow side, it would rule you."

"So we're seeing Harry's shadow side?"

"In a sense, yes. Harry needs to present himself as Mr. Arrogant Know-It-All Black Man," Norman said.

"He certainly does."

"So, if he's afraid to be down here in this habitat—and who isn't?—then he can't admit his fears. But he has the fears anyway, whether he admits them or not. And so his shadow side justifies the fears—creating things that prove his fears to be valid."

"The squid exists to justify his fears?"

"Something like that, yes."

"I don't know," Beth said. She leaned back and turned her head up, and her high cheekbones caught the light. She looked almost like a model, elegant and handsome and strong. "I'm a zoologist, Norman. I want to touch things and hold them in my hands and see that they're real. All these theories about manifestations, they just . . . They're so . . . *psychological.*"

"The world of the mind is just as real, and follows rules just as rigorous, as the world of external reality," Norman said.

"Yes, I'm sure you're right, but . . ." She shrugged. "It isn't very satisfying to me."

"You know everything that has happened since we got down here," Norman said. "Tell me another hypothesis that explains it all."

"I can't," she admitted. "I've been trying, all the time you've been talking. I can't." She folded the paper in her hands and considered it for a while. "You know, Norman, I think you've made a brilliant series of deductions. Absolutely brilliant. I'm seeing you in a whole different light."

Norman smiled with pleasure. For most of the time he had been down in the habitat, he'd felt like a fifth wheel, an unnecessary person in this group. Now someone was acknowledging his contribution, and he was pleased. "Thank you, Beth."

She looked at him, her large eyes liquid and soft. "You're a very attractive man, Norman. I don't think I ever really noticed before." Absently, she touched her breast, beneath the clinging jumpsuit. Her hands pressed the fabric, outlining the hard nipples. She suddenly stood and hugged him, her body close to him. "We have to stay together on this," she said. "We have to stay close, you and I."

"Yes, we do."

"Because, if what you are saying is true, then Harry is a very dangerous man."

"Yes."

"Just the fact that he is walking around, fully conscious, makes him dangerous."

"Yes."

"What are we going to do about him?"

"Hey, you guys," Harry said, coming up the stairs. "Is this a private party? Or can anybody join in?"

"Sure," Norman said, "come on up, Harry," and he moved away from Beth.

"Was I interrupting something?" Harry said.

"No, no."

"I don't want to get in the way of anybody's sex life."

"Oh, Harry," Beth said. She sat at the lab bench, moving away from Norman.

"Well, you two sure look all charged up about *something.*"

"Do we?" Norman said.

"Yeah, especially Beth. I think she gets more beautiful every day she's down here."

"I've noticed that, too," Norman said, smiling.

"I'll bet you have. A woman in love. Lucky you." Harry turned to Beth. "Why are you staring at me like that?"

"I'm not staring," Beth said.

"You are, too."

"Harry, I'm not staring."

"I can tell when someone is staring at me, for Christ's sake."

Norman said, "Harry—"

"—I just want to know why you two are looking at me like that. You're looking at me like I'm a criminal or something."

"Don't get paranoid, Harry."

"Huddling up here, whispering . . ."

"We weren't whispering."

"You *were.*" Harry looked around the room. "So it's two white people and one black person now, is that it?"

"Oh, Harry . . ."

"I'm not stupid, you know. Something's going on between you. I can tell."

"Harry," Norman said, "nothing is going on."

And then they heard a low insistent beeping, from the communications console downstairs. They exchanged glances, and went downstairs to look.

The console screen was slowly printing out letter groups.

CQX   VDX   MOP   LKI

"Is that Jerry?" Norman asked.

"I don't think so," Harry said. "I don't think he would go back to code."

"Is it a code?"

"I would say so, definitely."

"Why is it so slow?" Beth said. A new letter was added every few seconds in a steady, rhythmic way.

"I don't know," Harry said.

"Where is it coming from?"

Harry frowned. "I don't know, but the transmission speed is the most interesting characteristic. The slowness. Interesting."

Norman and Beth waited for him to figure it out. Norman thought: How can we ever get along without Harry? We need him. He is both the most important intelligence down here, and the most dangerous. But we need him.

CQX VDX MOP LKI XXC VRW TGK PIU YQA

"Interesting," Harry said. "The letters are coming about every five seconds. So I think it's safe to say that we know where it's coming from. Wisconsin."

Norman could not have been more surprised. "Wisconsin?"

"Yeah. This is a Navy transmission. It may or may not be directed to us, but it is coming from Wisconsin."

"How do you know that?"

"Because that's the only place in the world it *could* be coming from," Harry said. "You know about ELF? No? Well, it's like this. You can send radio waves through the air, and, as you know, they travel pretty well. But you can't send radio far through water. Water is a bad medium, so you need an incredibly powerful signal to go even a short distance."

"Yes . . ."

"But the ability to penetrate is a function of wavelength. An ordinary radio wave is short—shortwave radio, all of that. The length of the waves are tiny, thousands or millions of little waves to an inch. But you can also make ELF, extremely low-frequency waves, which are long—each individual wave is maybe twenty feet long. And those waves, once generated, will go a very great distance, thousands of miles, through water, no problem. The only trouble is that, since the waves are long, they're also slow. That's why we're getting one character every five seconds. The Navy needed a way to communicate with their submarines underwater, so they built a big ELF antenna in Wisconsin to send these long waves. And that's what we're getting."

"And the code?"

"It must be a compression code—three-letter groupings which stand for a long section of predefined message. So it won't take so long to send a message. Because if you sent a plain text message, it would literally take hours."

CQX VDX MOP LKI XXC VRW TGK PIU YQA IYT EEQ FVC
ZNB TMK EXE MMN OPW GEW

The letters stopped.

"Looks like that's it," Harry said.

"How do we translate it?" Beth said.

"Assuming it's a Navy transmission," Harry said, "we don't."

"Maybe there's a codebook here somewhere," Beth said.

"Just hold on," Harry said.

The screen shifted, translating groups one after another.

2340 HOURS 7-07 CHIEF CINCCOMPAC TO BARNES DEEPHAB-8

"It's a message to Barnes," Harry said. They watched as the other letter groups were translated.

SURFACE SUPPORT VESSELS STEAMING NANDI AND VIPATI TO YOUR LOCATION ETA 1600 HOURS 7-08 DEEP WITHDRAW AUTOSET ACKNOWLEDGE GOOD LUCK SPAULDING END

"Does that mean what I think it means?" Beth said.

"Yeah," Harry said. "The cavalry is on the way."

"Hot damn!" Beth clapped her hands.

"The storm must be calming down. They've sent the surface ships and they'll be here in a little more than sixteen hours."

"And autoset?"

They had the answer immediately. Every screen in the habitat flickered. In the upper right corner of each appeared a small box with numbers: 16:20:00. The numbers ran backward.

"It's automatically counting down for us."

"Is there some kind of countdown we're supposed to follow for leaving the habitat?" Beth said.

Norman watched the numbers. They were rolling backward, just as they had on the submarine. Then he said, "What about the submarine?"

"Who cares about the submarine," Harry said.

"I think we should keep it with us," Beth said. She checked her watch. "We have another four hours before it has to be reset."

"Plenty of time."

"Yes."

Privately, Norman was trying to gauge whether they could survive for sixteen more hours.

Harry said, "Well, this is great news! Why are you two so hangdog?"

"Just wondering if we'll make it," Norman said.

"Why shouldn't we make it?" Harry said.

"Jerry might do something first," Beth said. Norman felt a burst of irritation with her. Didn't she realize that by saying that, she was planting the idea in Harry's mind?

"We can't survive another attack on the habitat," Beth said.

Norman thought, Shut up, Beth. You're making suggestions.

"An attack on the habitat?" Harry said.

Quickly, Norman said, "Harry, I think you and I should talk to Jerry again."

"Really? Why?"

"I want to see if I can reason with him."

"I don't know if you can," Harry said. "Reason with him."

"Let's try anyway," Norman said, with a glance at Beth. "It's worth a try."

Norman knew he would not really be talking to Jerry. He would be talking to a part of Harry. An unconscious part, a shadow part. How should he go about it? What could he use?

He sat in front of the monitor screen, thinking, What do I know about Harry, really? Harry, who had grown up in Philadelphia as a thin, introverted, painfully shy boy, a mathematical prodigy, his gifts denigrated by his friends and family. Harry had said once that when he cared about mathematics, everybody else cared about slamdunking. Even now, Harry hated all games, all sports. As a young man he had been humiliated and neglected, and when he finally got proper recognition for his gifts, Norman suspected, it came too late. The damage was already done. Certainly it came too late to prevent the arrogant, braggart exterior.

I AM HERE. DO NOT BE AFRAID.

"Jerry."

YES NORMAN.

"I have a request to make."

YOU MAY DO SO.

"Jerry, many of our entities are gone, and our habitat is weakened."

I KNOW THIS. MAKE YOUR REQUEST.

"Would you please stop manifesting?"

NO.

"Why not?"

I DO NOT WISH TO STOP.

Well, Norman thought, at least we got right down to it. No wasting time. "Jerry, I know that you have been isolated for a long time, for many centuries, and that you have felt alone during all that time. You have felt that nobody cared about you. You have felt that nobody wanted to play with you, or shared your interests."

YES THIS IS TRUE.

"And now at last you can manifest, and you are enjoying this. You like to show us what you can do, to impress us."

THIS IS TRUE.

"So that we will pay attention to you."

YES. I LIKE IT.

"And it works. We do pay attention to you."

YES I KNOW IT.

"But these manifestations injure us, Jerry."

I DO NOT CARE.

"And they surprise us, too."

I AM GLAD.

"We're surprised, Jerry, because you are merely playing a game with us."

I DO NOT LIKE GAMES. I DO NOT PLAY GAMES.

"Yes. This is a game for you, Jerry. It is a sport."

NO, IT IS NOT.

"Yes, it is," Norman said. "It is a *stupid sport.*"

Harry, standing beside Norman, said, "Do you want to contradict him that way? You might make him mad. I don't think Jerry likes to be contradicted."

I'm sure you don't, Norman thought. But he said, "Well, I have to tell Jerry the truth about his own behavior. He isn't doing anything very interesting."

OH? NOT INTERESTING?

"No. You are being spoiled and petulant, Jerry."

DO YOU DARE TO SPEAK TO ME IN THIS FASHION?

"Yes. Because you are acting stupidly."

"Jeez," Harry said. "Take it easy with him."

I CAN EASILY MAKE YOU REGRET YOUR WORDS, NORMAN.

Norman was noticing, in passing, that Jerry's vocabulary and syntax were now flawless. All pretense of naïveté, of an alien quality, had been dropped. But Norman felt stronger, more confident, as the conversation progressed. He knew whom he was talking to now. He wasn't talking to any alien. There weren't any unknown assumptions. He was talking to a childish part of another human being.

I HAVE MORE POWER THAN YOU CAN IMAGINE.

"I know you have power, Jerry," Norman said. "Big deal."

Harry became suddenly agitated. "Norman. For Christ's sake. You're going to get us all killed."

LISTEN TO HARRY. HE IS WISE.

"No, Jerry," Norman said. "Harry is not wise. He is only afraid."

HARRY IS NOT AFRAID. ABSOLUTELY NOT.

Norman decided to let that pass. "I'm talking to *you,* Jerry. Only to you. You are the one who is playing games."

GAMES ARE STUPID.

"Yes, they are, Jerry. They are not worthy of you."

GAMES ARE NOT OF INTEREST TO ANY INTELLIGENT PERSON.

"Then stop, Jerry. Stop the manifestations." I CAN STOP WHENEVER I WANT.

"I am not sure you can, Jerry."

YES. I CAN.

"Then prove it. Stop this sport of manifestations."

There was a long pause. They waited for the response.

NORMAN YOUR TRICKS OF MANIPULATION ARE CHILDISH AND OBVIOUS TO THE POINT OF TEDIUM. I AM NOT INTERESTED IN TALKING WITH YOU FURTHER. I WILL DO EXACTLY AS I PLEASE AND I WILL MANIFEST AS I WISH.

"Our habitat cannot withstand more manifestations, Jerry." I DO NOT CARE.

"If you injure our habitat again, Harry will die."

Harry said, "Me and everybody else, for Christ's sake."

I DO NOT CARE NORMAN.

"Why would you kill us, Jerry?"

YOU SHOULD NOT BE DOWN HERE IN THE FIRST PLACE. YOU PEOPLE DO NOT BELONG HERE. YOU ARE ARROGANT CREATURES WHO INTRUDE EVERYWHERE IN THE WORLD AND YOU HAVE TAKEN A GREAT FOOLISH RISK AND NOW YOU MUST PAY THE PRICE. YOU ARE AN UNCARING UNFEELING SPECIES WITH NO LOVE FOR ONE ANOTHER.

"That's not true, Jerry."

DO NOT CONTRADICT ME AGAIN, NORMAN.

"I'm sorry, but the unfeeling, uncaring person is you, Jerry. You do not care if you injure us. You do not care for our predicament. It is you who are uncaring, Jerry. Not us. You."

ENOUGH.

"He's not going to talk to you any more," Harry said. "He's really mad, Norman."

And then the screen printed:

I WILL KILL YOU ALL.

Norman was sweating; he wiped his forehead, turned away from the words on the screen.

"I don't think you can talk to this guy," Beth said. "I don't think you can reason with him."

"You shouldn't have made him angry," Harry said. He was almost pleading. "Why did you make him angry like that, Norman?"

"I had to tell him the truth."

"But you were so mean to him, and now he's angry."

"It doesn't matter, angry or not," Beth said. "Harry attacked us before, when he wasn't angry."

"You mean *Jerry*," Norman said to her. "Jerry attacked us."

"Yes, right, Jerry."

"That's a hell of a mistake to make, Beth," Harry said.

"You're right, Harry. I'm sorry."

Harry was looking at her in an odd way. Norman thought, Harry doesn't miss a trick, and he isn't going to let that one go by.

"I don't know how you could make that confusion," Harry said.

"I know. It was a slip of the tongue. It was stupid of me."

"I'll say."

"I'm sorry," Beth said. "Really I am."

"Never mind," Harry said. "It doesn't matter."

There was a sudden flatness in his manner, a complete indifference in his tone. Norman thought: Uh-oh.

Harry yawned and stretched. "You know," he said, "I'm suddenly very tired. I think I'll take a nap now."

And he went off to the bunks.

1600 Hours

"**W**e have to do something," Beth said. "We can't talk him out of it."

"You're right," Norman said. "We can't."

Beth tapped the screen. The words still glowed: I WILL KILL YOU ALL.

"Do you think he means it?"

"Yes."

Beth stood, clenched her fists. "So it's him or us."

"Yes. I think so."

The implications hung in the air, unspoken.

"This manifesting process of his," Beth said. "Do you think he has to be completely unconscious to prevent it from happening?"

"Yes."

"Or dead," Beth said.

"Yes," Norman said. That had occurred to him. It seemed so improbable, such an unlikely turn of events in his life, that he would now be a thousand feet under the water, contemplating the murder of another human being. Yet that was what he was doing.

"I'd hate to kill him," Beth said.

"Me, too."

"I mean, I wouldn't even know how to begin to do it."

"Maybe we don't have to kill him," Norman said.

"Maybe we don't have to kill him unless he starts something," Beth said. Then she shook her head. "Oh hell, Norman, who're we kidding? This habitat can't survive another attack. We've got to kill him. I just don't want to face up to it."

"Neither do I," Norman said.

"We could get one of those explosive spear guns and have an unfortunate accident. And then just wait for our time to be up, for the Navy to come and get us out of here."

"I don't want to do that."

"I don't, either," Beth said. "But what else can we do?"

"We don't have to kill him," Norman said. "Just make him unconscious." He went to the first-aid cabinet, started going through the medicines.

"You think there might be something there?" Beth said.

"Maybe. An anesthetic, I don't know."

"Would that work?"

"I think anything that produces unconsciousness will work. I think."

"I hope you're right," Beth said, "because if he starts dreaming and then manifests the monsters from his dreams, that wouldn't be very good."

"No. But anesthesia produces a dreamless, total state of unconsciousness." Norman was looking at the labels on the bottles. "Do you know what these things are?"

"No," Beth said, "but it's all in the computer." She sat down at the console. "Read me the names and I'll look them up for you."

"Diphenyl paralene."

Beth pushed buttons, scanned a screen of dense text. "It's, uh . . . looks like . . . something for burns."

"Ephedrine hydrochloride."

Another screen. "It's . . . I guess it's for motion sickness."

"Valdomet."

"It's for ulcers."

"Sintag."

"Synthetic opium analogue. It's very short-acting."

"Produces unconsciousness?" Norman asked.

"No. Not according to this. Anyway, it only lasts a few minutes."

"Tarazine."

"Tranquilizer. Causes drowsiness."

"Good." He set the bottle to one side.

" 'And may also cause bizarre ideation.' "

"No," he said, and put the bottle back. They didn't need to have any bizarre ideation. "Riordan?"

"Antihistamine. For bites."

"Oxalamine?"

"Antibiotic."

"Chloramphenicol?"

"Another antibiotic."

"Damn." They were running out of bottles. "Parasolutrine?"

"It's a soporific. . . ."

"What's that?"

"Causes sleep."

"You mean it's a sleeping pill?"

"No, it's—it says you can give it in combination with paracin trichloride and use it as an anesthetic."

"Paracin trichloride . . . Yes. I have it here," Norman said.

Beth was reading from the screen. "Parasolutrine twenty cc's in combination with paracin six cc's given IM produces deep sleep suitable for emergency surgical procedures . . . no cardiac side effects . . . sleep from

494

which the subject can be awakened only with difficulty . . . REM activity is suppressed. . . ."

"How long does it last?"

"Three to six hours."

"And how fast does it take effect?"

She frowned. "It doesn't say. 'After appropriate depth of anesthesia is induced, even extensive surgical procedures may be begun. . . .' But it doesn't say how long it takes."

"Hell," Norman said.

"It's probably fast," Beth said.

"But what if it isn't?" Norman said. "What if it takes twenty minutes? And can you fight it? Fight it off?"

She shook her head. "Nothing about that here."

In the end they decided on a mixture of parasolutrine, paracin, dulcinea, and sintag, the opiate. Norman filled a large syringe with the clear liquids. The syringe was so big it looked like something for horses.

"You think it might kill him?" Beth said.

"I don't know. Do we have a choice?"

"No," Beth said. "We've got to do it. Have you ever given an injection before?"

Norman shook his head. "You?"

"Only lab animals."

"Where do I stick it?"

"Do it in the shoulder," Beth said. "While he's asleep."

Norman turned the syringe up to the light, and squirted a few drops from the needle into the air. "Okay," he said.

"I better come with you," Beth said, "and hold him down."

"No," Norman said. "If he's awake and sees both of us coming, he'll be suspicious. Remember, you don't sleep in the bunks any more."

"But what if he gets violent?"

"I think I can handle this."

"Okay, Norman. Whatever you say."

The lights in the corridor of C Cyl seemed unnaturally bright. Norman heard his feet padding on the carpet, heard the constant hum of the air handlers and the space heaters. He felt the weight of the syringe concealed in his palm. He came to the door to the sleeping quarters.

Two female Navy crewmen were standing outside the bulkhead door. They snapped to attention as he approached.

"Dr. Johnson, sir!"

Norman paused. The women were handsome, black, and muscular-looking. "At ease, men," Norman said with a smile.

They did not relax. "Sorry, sir! We have our orders, sir!"

"I see," Norman said. "Well, carry on, then." He started to move past them into the sleeping area.

"Beg your pardon, Dr. Johnson, sir!"

They barred his way.

"What is it?" Norman asked, as innocently as he could manage.

"This area is off-limits to all personnel, sir!"

"But I want to go to sleep."

"Very sorry, Dr. Johnson, sir! No one may disturb Dr. Adams while he sleeps, sir!"

"I won't disturb Dr. Adams."

"Sorry, Dr. Johnson, sir! May we see what is in your hand, sir!"

"In my hand?"

"Yes, there is something in your hand, sir!"

Their snapping, machine-gun delivery, always punctuated by the "sir!" at the end, was getting on his nerves. He looked at them again. The starched uniforms covered powerful muscles. He didn't think he could force his way past them. Beyond the door he saw Harry, lying on his back, snoring. It was a perfect moment to inject him.

"Dr. Johnson, may we see what is in your hand, sir!"

"No, damn it, you may not."

"Very good, sir!"

Norman turned, and walked back to D Cyl.

"I saw," Beth said, nodding to the monitor.

Norman looked at the monitor, at the two women in the corridor. Then he looked at the adjacent monitor, which showed the sphere.

"The sphere has changed!" Norman said.

The convoluted grooves of the doorway were definitely altered, the pattern more complex, and shifted farther up. Norman felt sure it was changed.

"I think you're right," Beth said.

"When did that happen?"

"We can run the tapes back later," she said. "Right now we'd better take care of those two."

"How?" Norman said.

"Simple," Beth said, bunching her fists again. "We have five explosive spearheads in B Cyl. I'll go into B, get two of them, blow the guardian angels away. You run in and jab Harry."

Her cold-blooded determination would have been chilling if she didn't look so beautiful. There was a refined quality to her features now. She seemed to grow more elegant by the minute.

"The spear guns are in B?" Norman said.

"Sure. Look on video." She pressed a button. "Hell."

In B Cyl the spearguns were missing.

"I think the son of a bitch has covered his bases," Norman said. "Good old Harry."

Beth looked at him thoughtfully. "Norman, are you feeling okay?"

"Sure, why?"

"There's a mirror in the first-aid kit. Go look."

He opened the white box of the kit and looked at himself in the mirror. He was shocked by what he saw. Not that he expected to look good; he was accustomed to the pudgy contours of his own face, and the gray stubble of his beard when he didn't shave on weekends.

But the face staring back at him was lean, with a coarse, jet-black beard. There were dark circles beneath smoldering, bloodshot eyes. His hair was lank and greasy, hanging over his forehead. He looked like a dangerous man.

"I look like Dr. Jekyll," he said. "Or, rather, Mr. Hyde."

"Yeah. You do."

"You're getting more beautiful," he said to Beth. "But I'm the man who was mean to Jerry. So I'm getting meaner."

"You think Harry's doing this?"

"I think so," Norman said. Adding to himself: I hope so.

"You feel different, Norman?"

"No, I feel exactly the same. I just look like hell."

"Yes. You look a little frightening."

"I'm sure I do."

"You really feel fine?"

"Beth . . ."

"Okay," Beth said. She turned, looked back at the monitors. "I have one last idea. We both get to A Cyl, put on our suits, get into B Cyl, and shut down the oxygen in the rest of the habitat. Make Harry unconscious. His guards will disappear, we can go in and jab him. What do you think?"

"Worth a try."

Norman put down the syringe. They headed off toward A Cyl.

In C Cyl, they passed the two guards, who again snapped to attention.

"Dr. Halpern, sir!"

"Dr. Johnson, sir!"

"Carry on, men," Beth said.

"Yes, sir! May we ask where you are going, sir!"

"Routine inspection tour," Beth said.

There was a pause.

"Very good, sir!"

They were allowed to pass. They moved into B Cyl, with its array of pipes and machinery. Norman glanced at it nervously; he didn't like screwing around with the life-support systems, but he didn't see what else they could do.

In A Cyl, there were three suits left. Norman reached for his. "You know what you're doing?" he asked.

"Yes," Beth said. "Trust me."

She slipped her foot into her suit, and started zipping it up.

And then the alarms began to sound throughout the habitat, and the red lights flashed again. Norman knew, without being told, that it was the peripheral alarms.

Another attack was beginning.

1520 Hours

They ran back through the lateral connecting corridor directly from B Cyl into D. Norman noticed in passing that the crewmen had gone. In D, the alarms were clanging and the peripheral sensor screens glowed bright red. Norman glanced at the video monitors.

I AM COMING.

Beth quickly scanned the screens.

"Inner thermals are activated. He's coming, all right."

They felt a *thump,* and Norman turned to look out the porthole. The green squid was already outside, the huge suckered arms coiling around the base of the habitat. One great arm slapped flat against the porthole, the suckers distorted against the glass.

I AM HERE.

"*Harryyy!*" Beth shouted.

There was a tentative jolt, as squid arms gripped the habitat. The slow, agonizing creak of metal.

Harry came running into the room.

"What is it?"

"You know what it is, Harry!" Beth shouted.

"No, no, what is it?"

"It's the squid, Harry!"

"Oh my God, no," Harry moaned.

The habitat shook powerfully. The room lights flickered and went out. There was only flashing red now, from the emergency lights.

Norman turned to him. "Stop it, Harry."

"What are you talking about?" he cried plaintively.

"You know what I'm talking about, Harry."

"I don't!"

"Yes, you do, Harry. It's *you,* Harry," Norman said. "You're doing it."

"No, you're wrong. It's not me! I swear it's not me!"

"Yes, Harry," Norman said. "And if you don't stop it, we'll all die."

The habitat shook again. One of the ceiling heaters exploded, showering fragments of hot glass and wire.

"Come on, Harry. . . ."

"No, no!"

"There's not much time. You know you're doing it."

"The habitat can't take much more, Norman," Beth said.

"It can't be me!"

"Yes, Harry. Face it, Harry. Face it now."

Even as he spoke, Norman was looking for the syringe. He had left it somewhere in this room, but papers were sliding off the desktops, monitors crashing to the floor, chaos all around him. . . .

The whole habitat rocked again, and there was a tremendous explosion from another cylinder. New, rising alarms sounded, and a roaring vibration that Norman instantly recognized—water, under great pressure, rushing into the habitat.

"Flooding in C!" Beth shouted, reading the consoles. She ran down the corridor. He heard the metal *clang* of bulkhead doors as she shut them. The room was filled with salty mist.

Norman pushed Harry against the wall. "Harry! Face it and stop it!"

"It can't be me, it can't be me," Harry moaned.

Another jolting impact, staggering them.

"It can't be me!" Harry cried. *"It has nothing to do with me!"*

And then Harry screamed, and his body twisted, and Norman saw Beth withdraw the syringe from his shoulder, the needle tipped with blood.

"What are you doing?" Harry cried, but already his eyes were glassy and vacant. He staggered at the next impact, fell drunkenly on his knees to the floor. "No," he said softly. "No . . ."

And he collapsed, falling face-down on the carpet. Immediately the wrenching of metal stopped. The alarms stopped. Everything became ominously silent, except for the soft gurgle of water from somewhere within the habitat.

Beth moved swiftly, reading one screen after another.

"Inner off. Peripherals off. Everything off. *All right!* No readings!"

Norman ran to the porthole. The squid had disappeared. The sea bottom outside was deserted.

"Damage report!" Beth shouted. "Main power out! E Cylinder out! C Cylinder out! B Cylinder . . ."

Norman spun, looked at her. If B Cyl was gone, their life support would be gone, they would certainly die. "B Cylinder holding," she said finally. Her body sagged. "We're okay, Norman."

Norman collapsed on the carpet, exhausted, suddenly feeling the strain and tension in every part of his body.

It was over. The crisis had passed. They were going to be all right, after all. Norman felt his body relax.

It was over.

1230 Hours

The blood had stopped flowing from Harry's broken nose and now he seemed to be breathing more regularly, more easily. Norman lifted the icepack to look at the swollen face, and adjusted the flow of the intravenous drip in Harry's arm. Beth had started the intravenous line in Harry's hand after several unsuccessful attempts. They were dripping an anesthetic mixture into him. Harry's breath smelled sour, like tin. But otherwise he was okay. Out cold.

The radio crackled. "I'm at the submarine," Beth said. "Going aboard now."

Norman glanced out the porthole at DH-7, saw Beth climbing up into the dome beside the sub. She was going to press the "Delay" button, the last time such a trip would be necessary. He turned back to Harry.

The computer didn't have any information about the effects of keeping a person asleep for twelve hours straight, but that was what they would have to do. Either Harry would make it, or he wouldn't.

Same as the rest of us, Norman thought. He glanced at the monitor clocks. They showed 1230 hours, and counted backward. He put a blanket over Harry and went over to the console.

The sphere was still there, with its changed pattern of grooves. In all the excitement he had almost forgotten his initial fascination with the sphere, where it had come from, what it meant. Although they understood now what it meant. What had Beth called it? A mental enzyme. An enzyme was something that made chemical reactions possible without actually participating in them. Our bodies needed to perform chemical reactions, but our body temperatures were too cold for most chemical reactions to proceed smoothly. So we had enzymes to help the process along, speed it up. The enzymes made it all possible. And she had called the sphere a mental enzyme.

Very clever, he thought. Clever woman. Her impulsiveness had turned out to be just what was needed. With Harry unconscious, Beth still looked beautiful, but Norman was relieved to find that his own features had returned to pudgy normalcy. He saw his own familiar reflection in the screen as he stared at the sphere on the monitor.

That sphere.

With Harry unconscious, he wondered if they would ever know exactly what had happened, exactly what it had been like. He remembered the lights, like fireflies. And what had Harry said? Something about foam. The foam. Norman heard a whirring sound, and looked out the porthole.

The sub was moving.

Freed of its tethers, the yellow minisub glided across the bottom, its lights shining on the ocean floor. Norman pushed the intercom button: "Beth? Beth!"

"I'm here, Norman."

"What're you doing?"

"Just take it easy, Norman."

"What're you doing in the sub, Beth?"

"Just a precaution, Norman."

"Are you leaving?"

She laughed over the intercom. A light, relaxed laugh. "No, Norman. Just take it easy."

"Tell me what you're doing."

"It's a secret."

"Come on, Beth." This was all he needed, he thought, to have Beth crack up now. He thought again of her impulsiveness, which moments before he had admired. He did not admire it any more. "Beth?"

"Talk to you later," she said.

The sub turned in profile, and he saw red boxes in its claw arms. He could not read the lettering on the boxes, but they looked vaguely familiar. As he watched, the sub moved past the high fin of the spacecraft, and then settled to the bottom. One of the boxes was released, plumping softly on the muddy floor. The sub started up again, churning sediment, and glided forward a hundred yards. Then it stopped again, and released another box. It continued this way along the length of the spacecraft.

"Beth?"

No answer. Norman squinted at the boxes. There was lettering on them, but he could not read them at this distance.

The sub had turned now, and was coming directly toward DH-8. The lights shone at him. It moved closer and the sensor alarms went off, clanging and flashing red lights. He hated these alarms, he thought, going over to the console, looking at the buttons. How the hell did you turn them off? He glanced at Harry, but Harry remained unconscious.

"Beth? Are you there? You set off the damn alarms."

"Push F8."

What the hell was F8? He looked around, finally saw a row of keys on the keyboard, numbered F1 to F20. He pushed F8 and the alarms stopped. The sub was now very close, lights shining into the porthole windows. In the high bubble, Beth was clearly visible, instrument lights shining up on her face. Then the sub descended out of view.

He went to the porthole and looked out. *Deepstar III* was resting on the bottom, depositing more boxes from its claw hands. Now he could read the lettering on the boxes:

CAUTION NO SMOKING NO ELECTRONICS TEVAC EXPLOSIVES.

"Beth? What the hell are you doing?"

"Later, Norman."

He listened to her voice. She sounded okay. Was she cracking up? No, he thought. She's not cracking up. She sounds okay. I'm sure she's okay.

But he wasn't sure.

The sub was moving again, its lights blurred by the cloud of sediment churned up by the propellors. The cloud drifted up past the porthole, obscuring his vision.

"Beth?"

"Everything's fine, Norman. Back in a minute."

As the sediment drifted down to the bottom again, he saw the sub, heading back to DH-7. Moments later, it docked beneath the dome. Then he saw Beth climb out, and tether the sub fore and aft.

1100 Hours

"**I**t's very simple," Beth said.

"Explosives?" He pointed to the screen. "It says here, 'Tevacs are, weight for weight, the most powerful conventional explosives known.' What the hell are you doing putting them around the habitat?"

"Norman, take it easy." She rested her hand on his shoulder. Her touch was soft and reassuring. He relaxed a little, feeling her body so close.

"We should have discussed this together first."

"Norman, I'm not taking any chances. Not any more."

"But Harry is unconscious."

"He might wake up."

"He won't, Beth."

"I'm not taking any chances," she said. "This way, if something starts to come out of that sphere, we can blow the hell out of the whole ship. I've put explosives along the whole length of it."

"But why around the habitat?"

"Defense."

"How is it defense?"

"Believe me, it is."

"Beth, it's dangerous to have that stuff so close to us."

"It's not wired up, Norman. In fact, it's not wired up around the ship, either. I have to go out and do that by hand." She glanced at the screens. "I thought I'd wait a while first, maybe take a nap. Are you tired?"

"No," Norman said.

"You haven't slept in a long time, Norman."

"I'm not tired."

She gave him an appraising look. "I'll keep an eye on Harry, if that's what you're worried about."

"I'm just not tired, Beth."

"Okay," she said, "suit yourself." She brushed her luxuriant hair back from her face with her fingers. "Personally, I'm exhausted. I'm going to get a few hours." She started up the stairs to her lab, then looked down at him. "Want to join me?"

"What?" he said.

She smiled at him directly, knowingly. "You heard me, Norman."

503

"Maybe later, Beth."

"Okay. Sure."

She ascended the staircase, her body swinging smoothly, sensuously in the tight jumpsuit. She looked good in that jumpsuit. He had to admit it. She was a good-looking woman.

Across the room, Harry snored in a regular rhythm. Norman checked Harry's icepack, and thought about Beth. He heard her moving around in the lab upstairs.

"Hey, Norm?"

"Yes . . ." He moved to the bottom of the stairs, looked up.

"Is there another one of these down there? A clean one?" Something blue dropped into his hands. It was her jumpsuit.

"Yes. I think they're in storage in B."

"Bring me one, would you, Norm?"

"Okay," he said.

Going to B Cyl, he found himself inexplicably nervous. What was going on? Of course, he thought, he knew exactly what was going on, but why now? Beth was exerting a powerful attraction, and he mistrusted it. In her dealings with men, Beth was confrontational, energetic, direct, and angry. Seduction wasn't her method at all.

It is now, he thought, fishing a new jumpsuit out of the storage locker. He took it back to D Cyl and climbed the ladder. From above, he saw a strange bluish light.

"Beth?"

"I'm here, Norm."

He came up and saw her lying naked on her back, beneath a bank of ultraviolet sunlamps hinged out from the wall. She wore opaque cups over her eyes. She twisted her body seductively.

"Did you bring the suit?"

"Yes," he said.

"Thanks a lot. Just put it anywhere, by the lab bench."

"Okay." He draped it over her chair.

She rolled back to face the glowing lamps, sighed. "I thought I'd better get a little vitamin D, Norm."

"Yes . . ."

"You probably should, too."

"Yeah, probably." But Norman was thinking that he didn't remember a bank of sunlamps in the lab. In fact, he was sure that there wasn't one. He had spent a lot of time in that room; he would have remembered. He went back down the stairs quickly.

In fact, the staircase was new, too. It was black anodized metal. It hadn't been that way before. This was a new descending staircase.

"Norm?"

"In a minute, Beth."

He went to the console and started punching buttons. He had seen a file before, on habitat parameters or something like that. He finally found it:

DEEPHAB-8 MIPPR DESIGN PARAMETERS

5.024A Cylinder A
5.024B Cylinder B
5.024C Cylinder C
5.024D Cylinder D
5.024E Cylinder E

Choose one:

He chose Cyl D, and another screen appeared. He chose design plans. He got page after page of architectural drawings. He flicked through them, stabbing at the keys, until he came to the detail plans for the biological laboratory at the top of D Cyl.

Clearly shown in the drawings was a large sunlamp bank, hinged to fold back against the wall. It must have been there all the time; he just hadn't ever noticed it. There were lots of other details he hadn't noticed—like the emergency escape hatch in the domed ceiling of the lab. And the fact that there was a second foldout bunk near the floor entrance. And a black anodized descending staircase.

You're in a panic, he thought. And it has nothing to do with sunlamps and architectural drawings. It doesn't even have to do with sex. You're in a panic because Beth is the only one left besides you, and Beth isn't acting like herself.

In the corner of the screen, he watched the small clock tick backward, the seconds clicking off with agonizing slowness. Twelve more hours, he thought. I've just got to last twelve more hours, and everything will be all right.

He was hungry, but he knew there wasn't any food. He was tired, but there wasn't any place for him to sleep. Both E and C Cylinders were flooded, and he didn't want to go upstairs with Beth. Norman lay down on the floor of D Cyl, beside Harry on the couch. It was cold and damp on the floor. For a long time he couldn't sleep.

0900 Hours

The pounding, that terrifying pounding, and the shaking of the floor awakened him abruptly. He rolled over and got to his feet, instantly alert. He saw Beth standing by the monitors. "What is it?" he cried. "What is it?"

"What is what?" Beth said.

She seemed calm. She smiled at him. Norman looked around. The alarms hadn't gone off; the lights weren't flashing.

"I don't know, I thought—I don't know . . ." He trailed off.

"You thought we were under attack again?" she said.

He nodded.

"Why would you think that, Norman?" she said.

Beth was looking at him again in that odd way. An appraising way, her stare very direct and cool. There was no hint of seductiveness to her. If anything, she conveyed the suspiciousness of the old Beth: You're a man, and you're a problem.

"Harry's still unconscious, isn't he? So why would you think we were being attacked?"

"I don't know. I guess I was dreaming."

Beth shrugged. "Maybe you felt the vibration of me walking on the floor," she said. "Anyway, I'm glad you decided to sleep."

That same appraising stare. As if there were something wrong with him.

"You haven't slept enough, Norman."

"None of us have."

"You, particularly."

"Maybe you're right." He had to admit he felt better now that he had slept for a couple of hours. He smiled. "Did you eat all the coffee and Danish?"

"There isn't any coffee and Danish, Norman."

"I know."

"Then why would you say that?" she asked seriously.

"It was a joke, Beth."

"Oh."

"Just a joke. You know, a humorous reflection on our condition?"

"I see." She was working with the screens. "By the way, what did you find out about the balloon?"

506

"The balloon?"

"The surface balloon. Remember we talked about it?"

He shook his head. He didn't remember.

"Before I went out to the sub, I asked about the control codes to send a balloon to the surface, and you said you'd look in the computer and see if you could find how to do it."

"I did?"

"Yes, Norman. You did."

He thought back. He remembered how he and Beth had lifted Harry's inert, surprisingly heavy body off the floor, setting him on the couch, and how they had staunched the flow of blood from his nose while Beth had started an intravenous line, which she knew how to do from her work with lab animals. In fact, she had made a joke, saying she hoped Harry fared better than her lab animals, since they usually ended up dead. Then Beth had volunteered to go to the sub, and he had said he'd stay with Harry. That was what he remembered. Nothing about any balloons.

"Sure," Beth said. "Because the communication said we were supposed to acknowledge transmission, and that means a radio balloon sent to the surface. And we figured, with the storm abating, the surface conditions must be calm enough to allow the balloon to ride without snapping the wire. So it was a question of how to release the balloons. And you said you'd look for the control commands."

"I really don't remember," he said. "I'm sorry."

"Norman, we have to work together in these last few hours," Beth said.

"I agree, Beth. Absolutely."

"How are you feeling now?" she said.

"Okay. Pretty good, in fact."

"Good," she said. "Hang in there, Norman. It's only a few more hours."

She hugged him warmly, but when she released him, he saw in her eyes that same detached, appraising look.

An hour later, they figured out how to release the balloon. They distantly heard a metallic sizzle as the wire unwound from the outside spool, trailing behind the inflated balloon as it shot toward the surface. Then there was a long pause.

"What's happening?" Norman said.

"We're a thousand feet down," Beth said. "It takes a while for the balloon to get to the surface."

Then the screen changed, and they got a readout of surface conditions. Wind was down to fifteen knots. Waves were running six feet. Barometric pressure was 20.9. Sunlight was recorded.

"Good news," Beth said. "The surface is okay."

Norman was staring at the screen, thinking about the fact that sunlight was recorded. He had never longed for sunlight before. It was funny, what you took for granted. Now the thought of seeing sunlight struck him as unbelievably pleasurable. He could imagine no greater joy than to see sun and clouds, and blue sky.

"What are you thinking?"

"I'm thinking I can't wait to get out of here."

"Me, too," Beth said. "But it won't be long now."

Pong! pong! pong! pong!

Norman was checking Harry, and he spun at the sound. "What is it, Beth?"

Pong! pong! pong! pong!

"Take it easy," Beth said, at the console. "I'm just figuring out how to work this thing."

Pong! pong! pong! pong!

"Work what?"

"The side-scanning sonar. False-aperture sonar. I don't know why they call it 'false-aperture.' Do you know what that refers to, 'false-aperture'?"

Pong! pong! pong! pong!

"No, I don't," Norman said. "Turn it off, please." The sound was unnerving.

"It's marked 'FAS,' which I think stands for 'false-aperture sonar,' but it also says 'side-scanning.' It's very confusing."

"Beth, turn it off!"

Pong! pong! pong! pong!

"Sure, of course," Beth said.

"Why do you want to know how to work that, anyway?" Norman said. He felt irritable, as if she'd intentionally annoyed him with that sound.

"Just in case," Beth said.

"In case *what,* for Christ's sake? You said yourself that Harry's unconscious. There aren't going to be any more attacks."

"Take it easy, Norman," Beth said. "I want to be prepared, that's all."

0720 Hours

He couldn't talk her out of it. She insisted on going outside and wiring the explosives around the ship. It was an absolutely fixed idea in her mind.

"But *why,* Beth?" he kept saying.

"Because I'll feel better after I do it," she said.

"But there isn't any reason to do it."

"I'll feel better if I do," she insisted, and in the end he couldn't stop her.

He saw her now, a small figure with a single glowing light from her helmet, moving from one crate of explosives to another. She opened each crate and removed large yellow cones which looked rather like the cones that highway repair trucks used. These cones were wired together, and when the wiring was completed a small red light glowed at the tip.

He saw small red lights all up and down the length of the ship. It made him uneasy.

When she left, he had said to her, "But you won't wire up the explosives near the habitat."

"No, Norman. I won't."

"Promise me."

"I told you, I won't. If it's going to upset you, I won't."

"It's going to upset me."

"Okay, okay."

Now the red lights were strung along the length of the ship, starting at the dimly visible tail, which rose out of the coral bottom. Beth moved farther north, toward the rest of the unopened crates.

Norman looked at Harry, who snored loudly but who remained unconscious. He paced back and forth in D Cyl, and then went to the monitors.

The screen blinked.

I AM COMING.

Oh God, he thought. And in the next moment he thought, How can this be happening? It can't be happening. Harry was still out cold. How could it be happening?

I AM COMING FOR YOU.

"Beth!"

Her voice sounded tinny on the intercom. "Yes, Norman."

509

"Get the hell out of there."

DO NOT BE AFRAID, the screen said.

"What is it, Norman?" she said.

"I'm getting something on the screen."

"Check Harry. He must be waking up."

"He's not. Get back here, Beth."

I AM COMING NOW.

"All right, Norman, I'm heading back," she said.

"Fast, Beth."

But he didn't need to say that; already he could see her light bouncing as she ran across the bottom. She was at least a hundred yards from the habitat. He heard her breathing hard on the intercom.

"Can you see anything, Norman?"

"No, nothing." He was straining to look toward the horizon, where the squid had always appeared. The first thing had always been a green glow on the horizon. But he saw no glow now.

Beth was panting.

"I can feel something, Norman. I feel the water . . . surging . . . strong. . . ."

The screen flashed: I WILL KILL YOU.

"Don't you see anything out here?" Beth said.

"No. I don't see anything at all." He saw Beth, alone on the muddy bottom. Her light the solitary focus of his attention.

"I can *feel* it, Norman. It's *close*. Jesus God. What about the alarms?"

"Nothing, Beth."

"Jesus." Her breath came in hissing gasps as she ran. Beth was in good shape, but she couldn't exert herself like that in this atmosphere. Not for long, he thought. Already he could see she was moving more slowly, the helmet lamp bobbing more slowly.

"Norman?"

"Yes, Beth. I'm here."

"Norman, I don't know if I can make it."

"Beth, you can make it. Slow down."

"It's *here,* I can feel it."

"I don't see anything, Beth."

He heard a rapid sharp clicking sound. At first he thought it was static on the line, and then he realized it was her teeth chattering as she shivered. With this exertion she should be getting overheated, but instead she was getting cold. He didn't understand.

"—cold, Norman."

"Slow down, Beth."

"Can't—talking—close—"

She was slowing down, despite herself. She had come into the area of the habitat lights, and she was no more than ten yards from the hatch, but he could see her limbs moving slowly, clumsily.

And now at last he could see something swirling the muddy sediment behind her, in the darkness beyond the lights. It was like a tornado, a swirling cloud of muddy sediment. He couldn't see what was inside the cloud, but he sensed the power within it.

"Close—Nor——"

Beth stumbled, fell. The swirling cloud moved toward her.

I WILL KILL YOU NOW.

Beth got to her feet, looked back, saw the churning cloud bearing down on her. Something about it filled Norman with a deep horror, a horror from childhood, the stuff of nightmares.

"Normannnnnn . . ."

Then Norman was running, not really knowing what he was going to do, but propelled by the vision he had seen, thinking only that he had to do something, he had to take some action, and he went through B into A and looked at his suit but there wasn't time and the black water in the open hatch was spitting and swirling and he saw Beth's gloved hand below the surface, flailing, she was right there beneath him, and she was the only other one, and without thinking he jumped into the black water and went down.

The shock of the cold made him want to scream; it tore at his lungs. His whole body was instantly numb, and he felt a second of hideous paralysis. The water churned and tossed him like a great wave; he was powerless to fight it; his head banged on the underside of the habitat. He could see nothing at all.

He reached for Beth, throwing his arms blindly in all directions. His lungs burned. The water spun him in circles, upended him.

He touched her, lost her. The water continued to spin him.

He grabbed her. Something. An arm. He was already losing feeling, already feeling slower and stupider. He pulled. He saw a ring of light above him: the hatch. He kicked his legs but he did not seem to move. The circle came no closer.

He kicked again, dragging Beth like a dead weight. Perhaps she was dead. His lungs burned. It was the worst pain he had ever felt in his life. He fought the pain, and he fought the angry churning water and he kept kicking toward the light, that was his only thought, to kick to the light, to come closer to the light, to reach the light, the light, the light. . . .

The light.

The images were confusing. Beth's suited body clanging on the metal, inside the airlock. His own knee bleeding on the metal of the hatch, the drops of blood spattering. Beth's shaking hands reaching for her helmet, twisting it, trying to get the helmet unlocked. Hands shaking. Water in the hatch, sucking, surging. Lights in his eyes. A terrible pain somewhere. Rust very close to his face, a sharp edge of metal. Cold metal. Cold air. Lights in his eyes, dimming. Fading. Blackness.

The sensation of warmth was pleasant. He heard a hissing roar in his ears. He looked up and saw Beth, out of her suit, looming large above him, adjusting the big space heater, turning the power up. She was still shivering, but she was turning up the heat. He closed his eyes. We made it, he thought. We're still together. We're still okay. We made it.

He relaxed.

There was a crawly sensation over his body. From the cold, he thought, his body warming from the cold. The crawly sensation was not pleasant. And the hissing was not pleasant, either; it was sibilant, intermittent.

Something slithered softly under his chin as he lay on the deck. He opened his eyes and saw a silvery white tube, and then he focused and saw the tiny beady eyes, and the flicking tongue. It was a snake.

A sea snake.

He froze. He looked down, moving only his eyes.

His entire body was covered with white snakes.

The crawly sensation came from dozens of snakes, coiling around his ankles, sliding between his legs, over his chest. He felt a cool slithering motion across his forehead. He closed his eyes, feeling horror as the snake body moved over his face, down his nose, brushed over his lips, then moved away.

He listened to the hissing of the reptiles and thought of how poisonous Beth had said they were. Beth, he thought, where is Beth?

He did not move. He felt snakes coiling around his neck, slipping over his shoulder, sliding between the fingers of his hands. He did not want to open his eyes. He felt a surge of nausea.

God, he thought. I'm going to throw up.

He felt snakes under his armpit, and felt snakes slipping past his groin. He burst into a cold sweat. He fought nausea.

Beth, he thought. He did not want to speak. Beth . . .

He listened to the hissing and then, when he couldn't stand it any more, he opened his eyes and saw the mass of coiling, writhing white flesh, the tiny heads, the flicking forked tongues. He closed his eyes again.

He felt one crawling up the leg of his jumpsuit, moving against his bare skin.

"Don't move, Norman."

It was Beth. He could hear the tension in her voice. He looked up, could not see her, only her shadow.

He heard her say, "Oh God, what time is it?" and he thought, The hell with the time, who cares what time it is? It didn't make any sense to him. "I have to know the time," Beth was saying. He heard her feet moving on the deck. "The time . . ."

She was moving away, leaving him!

The snakes slid over his ears, under his chin, past his nostrils, the bodies damp and slithering.

Then he heard her feet on the deck, and a metallic *clang* as she threw open the hatch. He opened his eyes to see her bending over him, grabbing the snakes in great handfuls, throwing them down the hatch into the water. Snakes writhed in her hands, twisted around her wrists, but she shook them off, tossed them aside. Some of the snakes didn't land in the water and coiled on the deck. But most of the snakes were off his body now.

One more crawling up his leg, toward his groin. He felt it moving quickly backward—she was pulling it out by the tail!

"Jesus, careful—"

The snake was out, flung over her shoulder.

"You can get up, Norman," she said.

He jumped to his feet, and promptly vomited.

0700 Hours

He had a murderous, pounding headache. It made the habitat lights seem unpleasantly bright. And he was cold. Beth had wrapped him in blankets and had moved him next to the big space heaters in D Cyl, so close that the hum of the electrical elements was very loud in his ears, but he was still cold. He looked down at her now, as she bandaged his cut knee.

"How is it?" he said.

"Not good," she said. "It's right down to the bone. But you'll be all right. It's only a few more hours now."

"Yes, I—ouch!"

"Sorry. Almost done." Beth was following first-aid directions from the computer. To distract his mind from the pain, he read the screen.

513

MINOR MEDICAL (NON-LETHAL) COMPLICATIONS

7.113 Trauma
7.115 Microsleep
7.118 Helium Tremor
7.119 Otitis
7.121 Toxic Contaminants
7.143 Synovial Pain

Choose one:

"That's what I need," he said. "Some microsleep. Or better yet, some serious macrosleep."

"Yes, we all do."

A thought occurred to him. "Beth, remember when you were pulling the snakes off me? What was all that you were saying about the time of day?"

"Sea snakes are diurnal," Beth said. "Many poisonous snakes are alternately aggressive and passive in twelve-hour cycles, corresponding to day and night. During the day, when they're passive, you can handle them and they will never bite. For example, in India, the highly poisonous banded krait has never been known to bite during the day, even when children play with them. But at night, watch out. So I was trying to determine which cycle the sea snakes were on, until I decided that this must be their passive daytime cycle."

"How'd you figure that?"

"Because you were still alive." Then she had used her bare hands to remove the snakes, knowing that they wouldn't bite her, either.

"With your hands full of snakes, you looked like Medusa."

"What is that, a rock star?"

"No, it's a mythological figure."

"The one who killed her children?" she asked, with a quick suspicious glance. Beth, ever alert to a veiled insult.

"No, that's somebody else. That was Medea. Medusa was a mythical woman with a head full of snakes who turned men to stone if they looked at her. Perseus killed her by looking at her reflection in his polished shield."

"Sorry, Norman. Not my field."

It was remarkable, he thought, that at one time every educated Western person knew these figures from mythology and the stories behind them intimately—as intimately as they knew the stories of families and friends. Myths had once represented the common knowledge of humanity, and they served as a kind of map of consciousness.

But now a well-educated person such as Beth knew nothing of myths at all. It was as if men had decided that the map of human consciousness had changed. But had it really changed? He shivered.

"Still cold, Norman?"

"Yeah. But the worst thing is the headache."

"You're probably dehydrated. Let's see if I can find something for you to drink." She went to the first-aid box on the wall.

"You know, that was a hell of a thing you did," Beth said. "Jumping in like that without a suit. That water's only a couple of degrees above freezing. It was very brave. Stupid, but brave." She smiled. "You saved my life, Norman."

"I didn't think," Norman said. "I just did it." And then he told her how, when he had seen her outside, with the churning cloud of sediment approaching her, he had felt an old and childish horror, something from distant memory.

"You know what it was?" he said. "It reminded me of the tornado in *The Wizard of Oz*. That tornado scared the bejesus out of me when I was a kid. I just didn't want to see it happen again."

And then he thought, Perhaps these are our new myths. Dorothy and Toto and the Wicked Witch, Captain Nemo and the giant squid . . .

"Well," Beth said, "whatever the reason, you saved my life. Thank you."

"Any time," Norman said. He smiled. "Just don't do it again."

"No, I won't be going out again."

She brought back a drink in a paper cup. It was syrupy and sweet.

"What is this?"

"Isotonic glucose supplement. Drink it."

He sipped it again, but it was unpleasantly sweet. Across the room, the console screen still said I WILL KILL YOU NOW. He looked at Harry, still unconscious, with the intravenous line running into his arm.

Harry had been unconscious all this time.

He hadn't faced the implications of that. It was time to do it now. He didn't want to do it, but he had to. He said, "Beth, why do you think all this is happening?"

"All what?"

"The screen, printing words. And another manifestation coming to attack us."

Beth looked at him in a flat, neutral way. "What do you think, Norman?"

"It's not Harry."

"No. It's not."

"Then why is it happening?" Norman said. He got up, pulling the blankets tighter around him. He flexed his bandaged knee; it hurt, but not too badly. Norman moved to the porthole and looked out the window. In the distance he could see the string of red lights, from the explosives Beth had set and armed. He had never understood why she had wanted to do that. She had acted so strangely about the whole thing. He looked down toward the base of the habitat.

Red lights were glowing there, too, just below the porthole. *She had armed the explosives around the habitat.*

"Beth, what have you done?"

"Done?"

"You armed the explosives around DH-8."

"Yes, Norman," she said. She stood watching him, very still, very calm.

"Beth, you promised you wouldn't do that."

"I know. I had to."

"How are they wired? Where's the button, Beth?"

"There is no button. They're set on automatic vibration sensors."

"You mean they'll go off *automatically?*"

"Yes, Norman."

"Beth, this is crazy. Someone is still making these manifestations. *Who is doing that, Beth?*"

She smiled slowly, a lazy, cat smile, as if he secretly amused her. "Don't you really know?"

He did know. Yes, he thought. He knew, and it chilled him. "You're making these manifestations, Beth."

"No, Norman," she said, still calm. "I'm not doing it. You are."

0640 Hours

He thought back years ago, to the early days of his training, when he had worked in the state hospital at Borrego. Norman had been sent by his supervisor to make a progress report on a particular patient. The man was in his late twenties, pleasant and well educated. Norman talked to him about all sorts of things: the Oldsmobile Hydramatic transmission, the best surfing beaches, Adlai Stevenson's recent presidential campaign, Whitey Ford's pitching, even Freudian theory. The man was quite charming, although he chain-smoked and seemed to have an underlying tension. Finally Norman got around to asking him why he had been sent to the hospital.

The man didn't remember why. He was sorry, he just couldn't seem to recall. Under repeated questioning from Norman, the man became less charming, more irritable. Finally he turned threatening and angry, pounding the table, demanding that Norman talk about something else.

Only then did it dawn on Norman who this man was: Alan Whittier, who as a teenager had murdered his mother and sister in their trailer in Palm Desert, and then had gone on to kill six people at a gas station and three others in a supermarket parking lot, until he finally turned himself in to the police, sobbing, hysterical with guilt and remorse. Whittier had been in the state hospital for ten years, and he had brutally attacked several attendants during that time.

This was the man who was now enraged, standing up in front of Norman, and kicking the table, flinging his chair back against the wall. Norman was still a student; he didn't know how to handle it. He turned to flee the room, but the door behind him was locked. They had locked him in, which is what they always did during interviews with violent patients. Behind him, Whittier lifted the table and threw it against the wall; he was coming for Norman. Norman had a moment of horrible panic until he heard the locks rattling, and then three huge attendants dashed in, grabbed Whittier, and dragged him away, still screaming and swearing.

Norman went directly to his supervisor, demanded to know why he had been set up. The supervisor said to him, Set up? Yes, Norman had said, *set up*. The supervisor said, But weren't you told the man's name beforehand? Didn't the name mean anything to you? Norman replied that he hadn't really paid attention.

You better pay attention, Norman, the supervisor had said. You can't ever let down your guard in a place like this. It's too dangerous.

Now, looking across the habitat at Beth, he thought: Pay attention, Norman. You can't let down your guard. Because you're dealing with a crazy person and you haven't realized it.

"I see you don't believe me," Beth said, still very calm. "Are you able to talk?"

"Sure," Norman said.

"Be logical, all of that?"

"Sure," he said, thinking: I'm not the crazy one here.

"All right," Beth said. "Remember when you told me about Harry—how all the evidence pointed to Harry?"

"Yes. Of course."

"You asked me if I could think of another explanation, and I said no. But there *is* another explanation, Norman. Some points you conveniently overlooked the first time. Like the jellyfish. Why the jellyfish? It was *your* little brother who was stung by the jellyfish, Norman, and *you* who felt guilty afterward. And when does Jerry speak? When *you're* there, Norman. And when does the squid stop its attack? When *you* were knocked unconscious, Norman. Not Harry, *you*."

Her voice was so calm, so reasonable. He struggled to consider what she was saying. Was it possible she was right?

"Step back. Take the long view," Beth said. "You're a psychologist, down here with a bunch of scientists dealing with hardware. There's nothing for you to do down here—you said so yourself. And wasn't there a time in your life when you felt similarly professionally bypassed? Wasn't that an uncomfortable time for you? Didn't you once tell me that you hated that time in your life?"

"Yes, but—"

"When all the strange things start to happen, the problem isn't hardware any more. Now it's a psychological problem. It's right up your alley, Norman, your particular area of expertise. Suddenly you become the center of attention, don't you?"

No, he thought. This can't be right.

"When Jerry starts to communicate with us, who notices that he has emotions? Who insists we deal with Jerry's emotions? None of us are interested in emotions, Norman. Barnes only wants to know about armaments, Ted only wants to talk science, Harry only wants to play logical games. You're the one who's interested in emotions. And who manipulates Jerry—or fails to manipulate him? You, Norman. It's all you."

"It can't be," Norman said. His mind was reeling. He struggled to find a contradiction, and found it. "It can't be me—because I haven't been inside the sphere."

"Yes, you have," Beth said. "You just don't remember."

He felt battered, repeatedly punched and battered. He couldn't seem to get his balance, and the blows kept coming.

"Just the way you don't remember that I asked you to look up the balloon codes," Beth was saying in her calm voice. "Or the way Barnes asked you about the helium concentrations in E Cyl."

He thought, what helium concentrations in E Cyl? When did Barnes ask me about that?

"There's a lot you don't remember, Norman."

Norman said, "When did I go to the sphere?"

"Before the first squid attack. After Harry came out."

"I was asleep! I was sleeping in my bunk!"

"No, Norman. You weren't. Because Fletcher came to get you and you were gone. We couldn't find you for about two hours, and then you showed up, yawning."

"I don't believe you," he said.

"I know you don't. You prefer to make it somebody else's problem. And you're clever. You're skilled at psychological manipulation, Norman. Remember those tests you conducted? Putting unsuspecting people up in an airplane, then telling them the pilot had a heart attack? Scaring them half to death? That's pretty ruthless manipulation, Norman.

"And down here in the habitat, when all these things started happening, you needed a monster. So you made Harry the monster. But Harry wasn't the monster, Norman. You are the monster. That's why your appearance changed, why you became ugly. Because you're the monster."

"But the message. It said 'My name is Harry.' "

"Yes, it did. And as you yourself pointed out, the person causing it was afraid that the real name would come out on the screen."

"Harry," Norman said. "The name was *Harry.*"

"And what's your name?"

"Norman Johnson."

"Your full name."

He paused. Somehow his mouth wasn't working. His brain was blank.

"I'll tell you what it is," Beth said. "I looked it up. It's Norman *Harrison* Johnson."

No, he thought. No, no, no. She *can't* be right.

"It's hard to accept," Beth was saying in her slow, patient, almost hypnotic voice. "I understand that. But if you think about it, you'll realize you wanted it to come to this. You wanted me to figure it out, Norman. Why, just a few minutes ago, you even told me about *The Wizard of Oz,* didn't you? You helped me along when I wasn't getting the point—or at least your unconscious did. Are you still calm?"

"Of course I'm calm."

"Good. Stay calm, Norman. Let's consider this logically. Will you cooperate with me?"

"What do you want to do?"

"I want to put you under, Norman. Like Harry."

He shook his head.

"It's only for a few hours, Norman," she said, and then she seemed to decide; she moved swiftly toward him, and he saw the syringe in her hand, the glint of the needle, and he twisted away. The needle plunged into the blanket, and he threw it off and ran for the stairs.

"Norman! Come back here!"

He was climbing the stairs. He saw Beth running forward with the needle. He kicked with his foot, got upstairs into her lab, and slammed the hatch down on her.

"Norman!"

She pounded on the hatch. Norman stood on it, knowing that she could never lift his weight. Beth continued to pound.

"Norman Johnson, you open that hatch this minute!"

"No, Beth, I'm sorry."

He paused. What could she do? Nothing, he thought. He was safe here. She couldn't get to him up here, she couldn't do anything to him as long as he remained here.

Then he saw the metal pivot move in the center of the hatch between his feet. On the other side of the hatch, Beth was spinning the wheel.

Locking him in.

0600 Hours

The only lights in the laboratory shone on the bench, next to a row of neatly bottled specimens: squid, shrimps, giant squid eggs. He touched the bottles absently. He turned on the laboratory monitor and punched buttons until he saw Beth, downstairs, on the video. Beth was working at the main D Cyl console. To one side, he saw Harry, still lying unconscious.

"Norman, can you hear me?"

He said aloud, "Yes, Beth. I hear you."

"Norman, you are acting irresponsibly. You are a menace to this entire expedition."

Was that true? he wondered. He didn't think he was a menace to the expedition. It didn't *feel* true to him. But how often in his life had he confronted patients who refused to acknowledge what was happening in their lives? Even trivial examples—a man, another professor at the university, who was terrified of elevators but who steadfastly insisted he always took the stairs because it was good exercise. The man would climb fifteen-story buildings; he would decline appointments in taller buildings; he arranged his entire life to accommodate a problem he would not admit he had. The problem remained concealed from him until he finally had a heart attack. Or the woman who was exhausted from years of caring for her disturbed daughter; she gave her daughter a bottle of sleeping pills because she said the girl needed a rest; the girl committed suicide. Or the novice sailor who cheerfully packed his family off on a sailing excursion to Catalina in a gale, nearly killing them all.

Dozens of examples came to mind. It was a psychological truism, this blindness about self. Did he imagine that he was immune? Three years ago, there had been a minor scandal when one of the assistant professors in the Psychology Department had committed suicide, sticking a gun in his mouth over the Labor Day weekend. There had been headlines for that one: "PSYCH PROF KILLS SELF, Colleagues Express Surprise, Say Deceased Was 'Always Happy.' "

The dean of the faculty, embarrassed in his fund-raising, had berated Norman about that incident, but the difficult truth was that psychology had severe limitations. Even with professional knowledge and the best of intentions, there remained an enormous amount you never knew about your closest friends,

520

your colleagues, your wives and husbands and children.

And your ignorance about yourself was even greater than that. Self-awareness was the most difficult of all. Few people attained it. Or perhaps nobody attained it.

"Norman, are you there?"

"Yes, Beth."

"I think you are a good person, Norman."

He said nothing. He just watched her on the monitor.

"I think you have integrity, and that you believe in telling the truth. This is a difficult moment for you, to face the reality about yourself. I know your mind is struggling now to find excuses, to blame someone else. But I think you can do it, Norman. Harry couldn't do it, but you can. I think you can admit the hard truth—that so long as you remain conscious, the expedition is menaced."

He felt the strength of her conviction, heard the quiet force of her voice. As Beth spoke, it felt almost as if her ideas were clothing being draped over his body. He began to see things her way. She was so calm, she must be right. Her ideas had such power. Her thoughts had such power. . . .

"Beth, have you been in the sphere?"

"No, Norman. That's your mind, trying to evade the point again. I haven't been in the sphere. *You* have."

He honestly couldn't remember going into the sphere. He had no recollection at all. And when Harry had been in the sphere, he remembered afterward. Why would Norman forget? Why would he block it?

"You're a psychologist, Norman," she was saying. "You, of all people, do not want to admit you have a shadow side. You have a professional stake in believing in your own mental health. Of course you will deny it."

He didn't think so. But how to resolve it? How to determine if she was right or not? His mind wasn't working well. His cut knee throbbed painfully. At least there was no doubt about that—his injured knee was real.

Reality testing.

That was how to resolve it, he thought. Reality testing. What was the objective evidence that Norman had gone to the sphere? They had made tapes of everything that occurred in the habitat. If Norman had gone to the sphere many hours ago, somewhere there was a tape showing him in the airlock, alone, getting dressed, slipping away. Beth should be able to show him that tape. Where was that tape?

In the submarine, of course.

It would long ago have been taken to the submarine. Norman himself might have taken it, when he made his excursion to the sub.

No objective evidence.

"Norman, give up. Please. For all our sakes."

Perhaps she was right, he thought. She was so sure of herself. If he was evading the truth, if he was putting the expedition in jeopardy, then he had to give himself up and let her put him under. Could he trust her to do that? He would have to. There wasn't any choice.

It must be me, he thought. It must be. The thought was so horrible to him—that in itself was suspicious. He was resisting it so violently—not a good sign, he thought. Too much resistance.

"Norman?"

"Okay, Beth."

"Will you do it?"

"Don't push. Give me a minute, will you?"

"Sure, Norman. Of course."

He looked at the video recorder next to the monitor. He remembered how Beth had used this recorder to play the same tape, again and again, the tape in which the sphere had opened by itself. That tape was now lying on the counter beside the recorder. He pushed the tape into the slot, clicked the recorder on. Why bother to look at it now? he thought. You're just delaying. You're wasting time.

The screen flickered, and he waited for the familiar image of Beth eating cake, her back to the monitor. But this was a different tape. This was a direct monitor feed showing the sphere. The gleaming sphere, just sitting there.

He watched for a few seconds, but nothing happened. The sphere was immobile, as always. Polished, perfect, immobile. He watched a while longer, but there was nothing to see.

"Norman, if I open the hatch now, will you come down quietly?"

"Yes, Beth."

He sighed, sat back in the chair. How long would he be unconscious? A little less than six hours. It would be okay. But in any case, Beth was right, he had to give himself up.

"Norman, why are you watching that tape?"

He looked around quickly. Was there a video camera in the room allowing her to see him? Yes: high up in the ceiling, next to the upper hatch.

"Why are you watching that tape, Norman?"

"It was here."

"Who said you could watch that tape?"

"Nobody," Norman said. "It was just here."

"Turn the tape off, Norman. Turn it off now."

She didn't sound so calm any more. "What's the matter, Beth?"

"Turn that damned tape off, Norman!"

He was about to ask her why, but then he saw Beth enter the video image, stand next to the sphere. Beth closed her eyes and clenched her fists. The convoluted grooves of the sphere parted, revealing blackness. And as he watched, Beth stepped inside the sphere.

And the door of the sphere closed behind her.

* * *

"**Y**ou goddamned men," Beth said in a tight, angry voice. "You're all the same; you can't leave well enough alone, none of you."

"You lied to me, Beth."

"Why did you watch that tape? I *begged* you not to watch that tape. It could only hurt you to watch that tape, Norman." She wasn't angry any more; now she was pleading, near tears. She was undergoing rapid emotional shifts. Unstable, unpredictable.

And she was in control of the habitat.

"Beth."

"I'm sorry, Norman. I can't trust you any more."

"Beth."

"I'm turning you off, Norman. I'm not going to listen to—"

"—Beth, wait—"

"—you any more. I know how dangerous you are. I saw what you did to Harry. How you twisted the facts so that it was Harry's fault. Oh yes, it was *Harry's* fault, by the time you got through. And now you want to make it *Beth's* fault, don't you? Well, let me tell you, Norman, you won't be able to do it, because I have *shut you off,* Norman. I can't hear your soft, convincing words. I can't hear your manipulation. So don't waste your breath, Norman."

He stopped the tape. The monitor now showed Beth at the console in the room below.

Pushing buttons on the console.

"Beth?" he said.

She didn't reply; she just went on working at the console, muttering to herself.

"You're a real son of a bitch, Norman, do you know that? You feel so terrible that you need to make everybody else just as low as you are."

She was talking about herself, he thought.

"You're so big on the unconscious, Norman. The unconscious *this,* the unconscious *that.* Jesus Christ, I'm sick of you. *Your* unconscious probably wants to kill us all, just because you want to kill yourself and you think everybody else should die with you."

He felt a shuddering chill. Beth, with her lack of self-esteem, her deep core of self-hate, had gone inside the sphere, and now she was acting with the power of the sphere, but without stability to her thoughts. Beth saw herself as a victim who struggled against her fate, always unsuccessfully. Beth was victimized by men, victimized by the establishment, victimized by research, victimized by reality. In every case she failed to see how she had done it to herself. And she's put explosives all around the habitat, he thought.

"I won't let you do it, Norman. I'm going to stop you before you kill us all."

Everything she said was the reverse of the truth. He began to see the pattern now.

Beth had figured out how to open the sphere, and she had gone there in secret, because she had always been attracted to power—she always felt she lacked power and needed more. But Beth wasn't prepared to handle power once she had it. Beth still saw herself as a victim, so she had to deny the power, and arrange to be victimized by it.

It was very different from Harry. Harry had denied his fears, and so fearful images had manifested themselves. But Beth denied her power, and so she manifested a churning cloud of formless, uncontrolled power.

Harry was a mathematician who lived in a conscious world of abstraction, of equations and thoughts. A concrete form, like a squid, was what Harry feared. But Beth, the zoologist who dealt every day with animals, creatures she could touch and see, created an abstraction. A power that she could not touch or see. A formless abstract power that was coming to get her.

And to defend herself, she had armed the habitat with explosives. It wasn't much of a defense, Norman thought.

Unless you secretly wanted to kill yourself.

The horror of his true predicament became clear to him.

"You won't get away with this, Norman. I won't let it happen. Not to *me*."

She was punching keys on the console. What was she planning? What could she do to him? He had to think.

Suddenly, the lights in the laboratory went off. A moment later, the big space heater died, the red elements cooling, turning dark.

She had shut off the power.

With the heater turned off, how long could he last? He took the blankets from her bed, wrapped himself in them. How long, without heat? Certainly not six hours, he thought grimly.

"I'm sorry, Norman. But you understand the position I'm in. As long as you're conscious, I'm in danger."

Maybe an hour, he thought. Maybe I can last an hour.

"I'm sorry, Norman. But I have to do this to you."

He heard a soft hiss. The alarm on his chest badge began to beep. He looked down at it. Even in the darkness, he could see it was now gray. He knew immediately what had happened.

Beth had turned off his air.

0535 Hours

Huddled in the darkness, listening to the beep of his alarm and the hiss of the escaping air. The pressure diminishing rapidly: his ears popped, as if he were in an airplane taking off.

Do something, he thought, feeling a surge of panic.

But there was nothing he could do. He was locked in the upper chamber of D Cyl. He could not get out. Beth had control of the entire facility, and she knew how to run the life-support systems. She had shut off his power, she had shut off his heat, and now she had shut off his air. He was trapped.

As the pressure fell, the sealed specimen bottles exploded like bombs, shooting fragments of glass across the room. He ducked under the blankets, feeling the glass rip and tug at the cloth. Breathing was harder now. At first he thought it was tension, and then he realized that the air was thinner. He would lose consciousness soon.

Do something.

He couldn't seem to catch his breath.

Do something.

But all he could think about was breathing. He needed air, needed oxygen. Then he thought of the first-aid cabinet. Wasn't there emergency oxygen in the cabinet? He wasn't sure. He seemed to remember. . . . As he got up, another specimen bottle exploded, and he twisted away from the flying glass.

He was gasping for breath, chest heaving. He started to see gray spots before his eyes.

He fumbled in the darkness, looking for the cabinet, his hands moving along the wall. He touched a cylinder. Oxygen? No, too large—it must be the fire extinguisher. Where was the cabinet? His hands moved along the wall. Where?

He felt the metal case, the embossed cover with the raised cross. He pulled it open, thrust his hands inside.

More spots swam before his eyes. There wasn't much time.

His fingers touched small bottles, soft bandage packs. There was no air bottle. Damn! The bottles fell to the floor, and then something large and heavy landed on his foot with a thud. He bent down, touched the floor, felt a shard of glass cut his finger, paid no attention. His hand closed over a cold metal

525

cylinder. It was small, hardly longer than the palm of his hand. At one end was some fitting, a nozzle. . . .

It was a spray can—some kind of damn spray can. He threw it aside. Oxygen. He needed oxygen!

By the bed, he remembered. Wasn't there emergency oxygen by every bed in the habitat? He felt for the couch where Beth had slept, felt for the wall above where her head would have been. Surely there was oxygen nearby. He was dizzy now. He wasn't thinking clearly.

No oxygen.

Then he realized this wasn't a regular bed. It wasn't intended for sleeping. They wouldn't have placed any oxygen here. Damn! And then his hand touched a metal cylinder, clipped to the wall. At one end was something soft. Soft . . .

An oxygen mask.

Quickly he pushed the mask over his mouth and nose. He felt the bottle, twisted a knurled knob. He heard a hissing, breathed cold air. He felt a wave of intense dizziness, and then his head cleared. Oxygen! He was fine!

He felt the shape of the bottle, gauging its size. It was an emergency bottle, only a few hundred cc's. How long would it last? Not long, he thought. A few minutes. It was only a temporary reprieve.

Do something.

But he couldn't think of anything to do. He had no options. He was locked in a room.

He remembered one of his teachers, fat old Dr. Temkin. "You always have an option. There is always something you can do. You are never without choice."

I am now, he thought. No choices now. Anyway, Temkin had been talking about treating patients, not escaping from sealed chambers. Temkin didn't have any experience escaping from sealed chambers. And neither did Norman.

The oxygen made him lightheaded. Or was it already running out? He saw a parade of his old teachers before him. Was this like seeing your life running before you, before you died? All his teachers: Mrs. Jefferson, who told him to be a lawyer instead. Old Joe Lamper, who laughed and said, "Everything is sex. Trust me. It always comes down to sex." Dr. Stein, who used to say, "There is no such thing as a resistant patient. Show me a resistant patient and I'll show you a resistant therapist. If you're not making headway with a patient, then do something else, do anything else. But do something."

Do something.

Stein advocated crazy stuff. If you weren't getting through to a patient, get crazy. Dress up in a clown suit, kick the patient, squirt him with a water pistol, do any damned thing that came into your head, but *do something*.

"Look," he used to say. "What you're doing now isn't working. So you might as well do something else, no matter how crazy it seems."

That was fine back then, Norman thought. He'd like to see Stein assess this problem. What would Dr. Stein tell him to do?

Open the door. I can't; she's locked it.

Talk to her. I can't; she won't listen.

Turn on your air. I can't; she has control of the system.

Get control of the system. I can't; she is in control.

Find help inside the room. I can't; there is nothing left to help me. .

Then leave. I can't; I—

He paused. That wasn't true. He could leave by smashing a porthole, or, for that matter, by opening the hatch in the ceiling. But there was no place to go. He didn't have a suit. The water was freezing. He had been exposed to that freezing water for only a few seconds and he had nearly died. If he were to leave the room for the open ocean, he would almost surely die. He'd probably be fatally chilled before the chamber even filled with water. He would surely die.

In his mind he saw Stein raise his bushy eyebrows, give his quizzical smile. *So? You'll die anyway. What have you got to lose?*

A plan began to form in Norman's mind. If he opened the ceiling hatch, he could go outside the habitat. Once outside, perhaps he could make his way down to A Cyl, get back in through the airlock, and put his suit on. Then he would be okay.

If he could make it to the airlock. How long would that take? Thirty seconds? A minute? Could he hold his breath that long? Could he withstand the cold that long?

You'll die anyway.

And then he thought, You damn fool, you're holding an oxygen bottle in your hand; you have enough air if you don't stay here, wasting time worrying. Get on with it.

No, he thought, there's something else, something I'm forgetting. . . .

Get on with it!

So he stopped thinking, and climbed up to the ceiling hatch at the top of the cylinder. Then he held his breath, braced himself, and spun the wheel, opening the hatch.

"Norman! Norman, what are you doing? Norman! You are insa—" he heard Beth shout, and then the rest was lost in the roar of freezing water pouring like a mighty waterfall into the habitat, filling the room.

The moment he was outside, he realized his mistake. He needed weights. His body was buoyant, tugging him up toward the surface. He sucked a final breath, dropped the oxygen bottle, and desperately gripped the cold pipes on the outside of the habitat, knowing that if he lost his grip, there would be nothing to stop him, nothing to grab onto, all the way to the surface. He would reach the surface and explode like a balloon.

Holding the pipes, he pulled himself down, hand over hand, looking for the next pipe, the next protrusion to grab. It was like mountain-climbing in reverse; if he let go, he would fall upward and die. His hands were long since numb. His body was stiff with cold, slow with cold. His lungs burned.

He had very little time.

He reached the bottom, swung under D Cyl, pulled himself along, felt in the darkness for the airlock. It wasn't there! The airlock was gone! Then he saw he was beneath B Cyl. He moved over to A, felt the airlock. The airlock was closed. He tugged the wheel. It was shut tight. He pulled on it, but he could not move it.

He was locked out.

The most intense fear gripped him. His body was almost immobile from cold; he knew he had only a few seconds of consciousness remaining. He had to open the hatch. He pounded it, pounded the metal around the rim, feeling nothing in his numb hands.

The wheel began to spin by itself. The hatch popped open. There must have been an emergency button, he must have—

He burst above the surface of the water, gasped air, and sank again. He came back up, but he couldn't climb out into the cylinder. He was too numb, his muscles frozen, his body unresponsive.

You have to do it, he thought. You have to do it. His fingers gripped metal, slipped off, gripped again. *One pull,* he thought. One last pull. He heaved his chest over the metal rim, flopped onto the deck. He couldn't feel anything, he was so cold. He twisted his body, trying to pull his legs up, and fell back into the icy water.

No!

He pulled himself up again, one last time—again over the rim, again onto the deck, and he twisted, twisted, one leg up, his balance precarious, then the other leg, he couldn't really feel it, and then he was out of the water, and lying on the deck.

He was shivering. He tried to stand, and fell over. His whole body was shaking so hard he could not keep his balance.

Across the airlock he saw his suit, hanging on the wall of the cylinder. He saw the helmet, "JOHNSON" stenciled on it. Norman crawled toward the suit, his body shaking violently. He tried to stand, and could not. The boots of his suit were directly in front of his face. He tried to grip them in his hands, but his hands could not close. He tried to bite the suit, to pull himself up with his teeth, but his teeth were chattering uncontrollably.

The intercom crackled.

"Norman! I know what you're doing, Norman!"

Any minute, Beth would be here. He had to get into the suit. He stared at it, inches from him, but his hands still shook, he could not hold anything. Finally he saw the fabric loops near the waist to clip instruments. He hooked one hand into the loop, managed to hold on. He pulled himself upright. He got one foot into the suit, then the other.

"Norman!"

He reached for the helmet. The helmet drummed in a staccato beat against the wall before he managed to get it free of the peg and drop it over his head. He twisted it, heard the click of the snap-lock.

He was still very cold. Why wasn't the suit heating up? Then he realized, no power. The power was in the tank pack. Norman backed up against the tank, shrugged it on, staggered under the weight. He had to hook the umbilicus—he reached behind him, felt it—held it—hook it into the suit—at the waist—hook it—

He heard a click.

The fan hummed.

He felt long streaks of pain all over his body. The electrical elements were heating, painful against his frozen skin. He felt pins and needles all over. Beth was talking—he heard her through the intercom—but he couldn't listen to her. He sat heavily on the deck, breathing hard.

But already he knew that he was going to be all right; the pain was lessening, his head was clearing, and he was no longer shaking so badly. He had been chilled, but not long enough for it to be central. He was recovering fast.

The radio crackled.

"You'll never get to me, Norman!"

He got to his feet, pulled on his weight belt, locked the buckles.

"Norman!"

He said nothing. He felt quite warm now, quite normal.

"Norman! I am surrounded by explosives! If you come anywhere near me, I will blow you to pieces! You'll die, Norman! You'll never get near me!"

But Norman wasn't going to Beth. He had another plan entirely. He heard his tank air hiss as the pressure equalized in his suit.

He jumped back into the water.

0500 Hours

The sphere gleamed in the light. Norman saw himself reflected in its perfectly polished surface, then saw his image break up, fragmented on the convolutions, as he moved around to the back.

To the door.

It looked like a mouth, he thought. Like the maw of some primitive creature, about to eat him. Confronted by the sphere, seeing once again the alien, unhuman pattern of the convolutions, he felt his intention dissolve. He was suddenly afraid. He didn't think he could go through with it.

Don't be silly, he told himself. Harry did it. And Beth did it. They survived.

He examined the convolutions, as if for reassurance. But there wasn't any reassurance to be obtained. Just curved grooves in the metal, reflecting back the light.

Okay, he thought finally. I'll do it. I've come this far, I've survived everything so far. I might as well do it.

Go ahead and open up.

But the sphere did not open. It remained exactly as it was, a gleaming, polished, perfect shape.

What was the purpose of the thing? He wished he understood its purpose.

He thought of Dr. Stein again. What was Stein's favorite line? "Understanding is a delaying tactic." Stein used to get angry about that. When the graduate students would intellectualize, going on and on about patients and their problems, he would interrupt in annoyance, "Who cares? Who cares whether we understand the psychodynamics in this case? Do you want to understand how to swim, or do you want to jump in and start swimming? Only people who are afraid of the water want to understand it. Other people jump in and get wet."

Okay, Norman thought. Let's get wet.

He turned to face the sphere, and thought, *Open up.*

The sphere did not open.

"Open up," he said aloud.

The sphere did not open.

Of course he knew that wouldn't work, because Ted had tried it for hours. When Harry and Beth went in, they hadn't said anything. They just did something in their minds.

He closed his eyes, focused his attention, and thought, Open up.

He opened his eyes and looked at the sphere. It was still closed.

I am ready for you to open up, he thought. I am ready now.

Nothing happened. The sphere did not open.

Norman hadn't considered the possibility that he would be unable to open the sphere. After all, two others had already done it. How had they managed it?

Harry, with his logical brain, had been the first to figure it out. But Harry had only figured it out *after* he had seen Beth's tape. So Harry had discovered a clue in the tape, an important clue.

Beth had also reviewed the tape, watching it again and again, until she finally figured it out, too. Something in the tape . . .

Too bad he didn't have the tape here, Norman thought. But he had seen it often, he could probably reconstruct it, play it back in his mind. How did it go? In his mind he saw the images: Beth and Tina talking. Beth eating cake. Then Tina had said something about the tapes being stored in the submarine. And Beth said something back. Then Tina had moved away, out of the picture, but she had said, "Do you think they'll ever get the sphere open?"

And Beth said, "Maybe. I don't know." And the sphere had opened at that moment.

Why?

"Do you think they'll ever get the sphere open?" Tina had asked. And in response to such a question, Beth must have imagined the sphere open, must have seen an image of the open sphere in her mind—

There was a deep, low rumble, a vibration that filled the room.

The sphere was open, the door gaping wide and black.

That's it, he thought. Visualize it happening and it happens. Which meant that if he also visualized the sphere door closed—

With another deep rumble, the sphere closed.

—or open—

The sphere opened again.

"I'd better not press my luck," he said aloud. The door was still open. He peered in the doorway but saw only deep, undifferentiated blackness. It's now or never, he thought.

He stepped inside.

The sphere closed behind him.

There is darkness, and then, as his eyes adjust, something like fireflies. It is a dancing, luminous foam, millions of points of light, swirling around him.

What is this? he thinks. All he sees is the foam. There is no structure to it and apparently no limit. It is a surging ocean, a glistening, multifaceted foam. He feels great beauty and peace. It is restful to be here.

He moves his hands, scooping the foam, his movements making it swirl. But then he notices that his hands are becoming transparent, that he can see the sparkling foam through his own flesh. He looks down at his body. His legs, his torso, everything is becoming transparent to the foam. He is part of the foam. The sensation is very pleasant.

He grows lighter. Soon he is lifted, and floats in the limitless ocean foam. He puts his hands behind his neck and floats. He feels happy. He feels he could stay here forever.

He becomes aware of something else in this ocean, some other presence.

"Anybody here?" he says.

I am here.

He almost jumps, it is so loud. Or it seems loud. Then he wonders if he has heard anything at all.

"Did you speak?"

No.

How are we communicating? he wonders.

The way everything communicates with everything else.

Which way is that?

Why do you ask if you already know the answer?

But I don't know the answer.

The foam moves him gently, peacefully, but he receives no answer for a time. He wonders if he is alone again.

Are you there?

Yes.

I thought you had gone away.

There is nowhere to go.

Do you mean you are imprisoned inside this sphere?

No.

Will you answer a question? Who are you?

I am not a who.

Are you God?

God is a word.

I mean, are you a higher being, or a higher consciousness?

Higher than what?

Higher than me, I suppose.

How high are you?

Pretty low. At least, I imagine so.

Well, then, that's your trouble.

Riding in the foam, he is disturbed by the possibility that God is making fun of him. He thinks, Are you making a joke?

Why do you ask if you already know the answer?

Am I talking to God?

You are not talking at all.

You take what I say very literally. Is this because you are from another planet?

No.

Are you from another planet?

No.

Are you from another civilization?

No.

Where are you from?

Why do you ask if you already know the answer?

In another time, he thinks, he would be irritated by this repetitive answer, but now he feels no emotions. There are no judgments. He is simply receiving information, a response.

He thinks, But this sphere comes from another civilization.

Yes.

And maybe from another time.

Yes.

And aren't you a part of this sphere?

I am now.

So, where are you from?

Why do you ask if you already know the answer?

The foam gently shifts him, rocking him soothingly.

Are you still there?

Yes. There is nowhere to go.

I'm afraid I am not very knowledgeable about religion. I am a psychologist. I deal with how people think. In my training, I never learned much about religion.

Oh, I see.

Psychology doesn't have much to do with religion.

Of course.

So you agree?

I agree with you.

That's reassuring.

I don't see why.

Who is I?

Who indeed?

He rocks in the foam, feeling a deep peace despite the difficulties of this conversation.

I am troubled, he thinks.

Tell me.

I am troubled because you sound like Jerry.

That is to be expected.

But Jerry was really Harry.

Yes.

So are you Harry, too?

No. Of course not.

Who are you?

I am not a who.

Then why do you sound like Jerry or Harry?

Because we spring from the same source.

I don't understand.

When you look in the mirror, who do you see?

I see myself.

I see.

Isn't that right?

It's up to you.

I don't understand.

What you see is up to you.

I already know that. Everybody knows that. That is a psychological truism, a cliché.

I see.

Are you an alien intelligence?

Are you an alien intelligence?

I find you difficult to talk to. Will you give me the power?

What power?

The power you gave to Harry and Beth. The power to make things happen by imagination. Will you give it to me?

No.

Why not?

Because you already have it.

I don't feel as if I have it.

I know.

Then how is it that I have the power?

How did you get in here?

I imagined the door opening.

Yes.

Rocking in the foam, waiting for a further response, but there is no response, there is only gentle movement in the foam, a peaceful timelessness, and a drowsy sensation.

After a passage of time, he thinks, I am sorry, but I wish you would just explain and stop speaking in riddles.

On your planet you have an animal called a bear. It is a large animal, sometimes larger than you, and it is clever and has ingenuity, and it has a brain as large as yours. But the bear differs from you in one important way. It cannot perform the activity you call imagining. It cannot make mental images of how reality might be. It cannot envision what you call the past and what you call the future. This special ability of imagination is what has made your species as great as it is. Nothing else. It is not your ape-nature, not your tool-using nature, not language or your violence or your caring for young or your social groupings. It is none of these things, which are all found in other animals. Your greatness lies in imagination.

The ability to imagine is the largest part of what you call intelligence. You think the ability to imagine is merely a useful step on the way to solving a problem or making something happen. But imagining it is what makes it happen.

This is the gift of your species and this is the danger, because you do not choose to control your imaginings. You imagine wonderful things and you imagine terrible things, and you take no responsibility for the choice. You say you have inside you both the power of good and the power of evil, the angel and the devil, but in truth you have just one thing inside you—the ability to imagine.

I hope you enjoyed this speech, which I plan to give at the next meeting of the American Association of Psychologists and Social Workers, which is meeting in Houston in March. I feel it will be quite well received.

What? he thinks, startled.

Who did you think you were talking to? God?

Who is this? he thinks.

You, of course.

But you are somebody different from me, separate. You are not me, he thinks.

Yes I am. You imagined me.

Tell me more.

There is no more.

His cheek rested on cold metal. He rolled onto his back and looked at the polished surface of the sphere, curving above him. The convolutions of the door had changed again.

Norman got to his feet. He felt relaxed and at peace, as if he had been sleeping a long time. He felt as if he had had a wonderful dream. He remembered everything quite clearly.

He moved through the ship, back to the flight deck, and then down the hallway with the ultraviolet lights to the room with all the tubes on the wall.

The tubes were filled. There was a crewman in each one.

Just as he thought: Beth had manifested a single crewman—a solitary woman—as a way of warning them. Now Norman was in charge, and he found the room full.

Not bad, he thought.

He looked at the room and thought: Gone, one at a time.

One by one, the crew members in the tubes vanished before his eyes, until they were all gone.

Back, one at a time.

The crew members popped back in the tubes, materializing on demand.

All men.

The women were changed into men.

All women.

They all became women.

He had the power.

0200 Hours

"**N**orman."

Beth's voice over the loudspeakers, hissing through the empty spacecraft.

"Where are you, Norman? I know you're there somewhere. I can *feel* you, Norman."

Norman was moving through the kitchen, past the empty cans of Coke on the counter, then through the heavy door and into the flight deck. He saw Beth's face on all the console screens, Beth seeming to see him, the image repeated a dozen times.

"Norman. I know where you've been. You've been inside the sphere, haven't you, Norman?"

He pressed the consoles with the flat of his hand, trying to turn off the screens. He couldn't do it; the images remained.

"Norman. Answer me, Norman."

He moved past the flight deck, going toward the airlock.

"It won't do you any good, Norman. I'm in charge now. Do you hear me, Norman?"

In the airlock, he heard a click as his helmet ring locked; the air from the tanks was cool and dry. He listened to the even sound of his own breathing.

"Norman." Beth, on the intercom in his helmet. "Why don't you speak to me, Norman? Are you afraid, Norman?"

The repetition of his name irritated him. He pressed the buttons to open the airlock. Water began to flood in from the floor, rising swiftly.

"Oh, *there you are,* Norman. I see you now." And she began to laugh, a high, cackling laugh.

Norman turned around, saw the video camera mounted on the robot, still inside the airlock. He shoved the camera, spinning it away.

"That won't do any good, Norman."

He was back outside the spacecraft, standing by the airlock. The Tevac explosives, rows of glowing red dots, extended away in erratic lines, like an airplane runway laid out by some demented engineer.

"Norman? Why don't you answer me, Norman?"

Beth was unstable, erratic. He could hear it in her voice. He had to deprive her of her weapons, to turn off the explosives, if he could.

Off, he thought. Let's have the explosives off and disarmed.

All the red lights immediately went off.

Not bad, he thought, with a burst of pleasure.

A moment later, the red lights blinked back on.

"You can't do it, Norman," Beth said, laughing. "Not to me. I can fight you."

He knew she was right. They were having an argument, a test of wills, turning the explosives on and off. And the argument couldn't ever be resolved. Not that way. He would have to do something more direct.

He moved toward the nearest of the Tevac explosives. Up close, the cone was larger than he had thought, four feet high, with a red light at the top.

"I can see you, Norman. *I see what you're doing.*"

There was writing on the cone, yellow letters stenciled on the gray surface. Norman bent to read it. His faceplate was slightly fogged, but he could still make out the words.

> ### DANGER - TEVAC EXPLOSIVES
> ---
> **U.S.N. CONSTRUCTION/DEMOLITION USE ONLY**
> **DEFAULT DETONATE SEQUENCE 20:00**
> **CONSULT MANUAL USN/VV/512-A**
> **AUTHORIZED PERSONNEL ONLY**
> ---
> ### DANGER-TEVAC EXPLOSIVES

There was still more writing beneath that, but it was smaller, and he couldn't make it out.

"Norman! What're you doing with my explosives, Norman?"

Norman didn't answer her. He looked at the wiring. One thin cable ran into the base of the cone, and a second cable ran out. The second cable went along the muddy bottom to the next cone, where there were again just two cables—one in, and one out.

"Get away from there, Norman. You're making me nervous."

One cable in, and one cable out.

Beth had wired the cones together *in series,* like Christmas-tree bulbs! By pulling out a single cable, Norman would disconnect the entire line of explosives. He reached forward and gripped the cable in his gloved hand.

"Norman! Don't touch that wire, Norman!"

"Take it easy, Beth."

His fingers closed around the cable. He felt the soft plastic coating, gripped it tightly.

"Norman, if you pull that cable you'll set off the explosives. I swear to you—it'll blow you and me and Harry and everything to hell, Norman."

He didn't think it was true. Beth was lying. Beth was out of control and she was dangerous and she was lying to him again.

He drew his hand back. He felt the tension in the cable.

"Don't do it, Norman. . . ."

The cable was now taut in his hand. "I'm going to shut you down, Beth."

"For God's sake, Norman. Believe me, will you? You'll kill us all!"

Still he hesitated. Could she be telling the truth? Did she know about wiring explosives? He looked at the big gray cone at his feet, reaching up to his waist. What would it feel like if it exploded? Would he feel anything at all?

"The hell with it," he said aloud.

He pulled the cable out of the cone.

The shriek of the alarm, ringing inside his helmet, made him jump. There was a small liquid-crystal display at the top of his faceplate blinking rapidly: "EMERGENCY" . . . "EMERGENCY" . . .

"Oh, Norman. God damn it. Now you've done it."

He barely heard her voice over the alarm. The red cone lights were blinking, all down the length of the spacecraft. He braced himself for the explosion.

But then the alarm was interrupted by a deep, resonant male voice that said, "Your attention, please. Your attention, please. All construction personnel clear the blast area immediately. Tevac explosives are now activated. The countdown will begin . . . now. Mark twenty, and counting."

On the cone, a red display flashed 20:00. Then it began counting backward: 19:59 . . . 19:58 . . .

The same display was repeated on the crystal display at the top of his helmet.

It took him a moment to put it together, to understand. Staring at the cone, he read the yellow lettering once again: U.S.N. CONSTRUCTION/DEMOLITION USE ONLY.

Of course! Tevac explosives weren't weapons, they were made for construction and demolition. They had built-in safety timers—a programmed twenty-minute delay before they went off, to allow workers to get away.

Twenty minutes to get away, he thought. That would give him plenty of time.

Norman turned, and began striding quickly toward DH-7 and the submarine.

0140 Hours

He walked evenly, steadily. He felt no strain. His breath came easily. He was comfortable in his suit. All systems working smoothly.

He was leaving.

"Norman, please . . ."

Now Beth was pleading with him, another erratic shift of mood. Norman ignored her. He continued on toward the submarine. The deep recorded voice said, "Your attention, please. All Navy personnel clear the blast area. Nineteen minutes and counting."

Norman felt an enormous sense of purposefulness, of power. He had no illusions any more. He had no questions. He knew what he had to do.

He had to save himself.

"I don't believe you're doing this, Norman. I don't believe you're abandoning us."

Believe it, he thought. After all, what choice did he have? Beth was out of control and dangerous. It was too late to save her now—in fact, it was crazy to go anywhere near her. Beth was homicidal. She'd already tried to kill him once, and had nearly succeeded.

And Harry had been drugged for thirteen hours; by now he was probably clinically dead, brain-dead. There was no reason for Norman to stay. There was nothing for him to do.

The sub was close now. He could see the fittings on the yellow exterior.

"Norman, please . . . I need you."

Sorry, he thought. I'm getting out of here.

He moved around beneath the twin propellor screws, the name painted on the curved hull, *Deepstar III*. He climbed the footholds, moving up into the dome.

"Norman—"

Now he was out of contact with the intercom. He was on his own. He opened the hatch, climbed inside the submarine. He unlocked his helmet, pulled it off.

"Your attention, please. Eighteen minutes and counting."

Norman sat in the pilot's padded seat, faced the controls. The instruments blinked on, and the screen directly before him glowed.

539

DEEPSTAR III - COMMAND MODULE

Do you require help?
Yes   No   Cancel

He pressed "YES." He waited for the next screen to flash up.

It was too bad about Harry and Beth; he was sorry to leave them behind. But they had both, in their own ways, failed to explore their inner selves, thus making them vulnerable to the sphere and its power. It was a classic scientific error, this so-called triumph of rational thought over irrational thought. Scientists refused to acknowledge their irrational side, refused to see it as important. They dealt only with the rational. Everything made sense to a scientist, and if it didn't make sense, it was dismissed as what Einstein called the "merely personal."

The merely personal, he thought, in a burst of contempt. People killed each other for reasons that were "merely personal."

DEEPSTAR III - CHECKLIST OPTIONS

Descend   Ascend
Secure   Shutdown
Monitor   Cancel

Norman pressed "Ascend." The screen changed to the drawing of the instrument panel, with the flashing point. He waited for the next instruction.

Yes, he thought, it was true: scientists refused to deal with the irrational. But the irrational side didn't go away if you refused to deal with it. Irrationality didn't atrophy with disuse. On the contrary, left unattended, the irrational side of man had grown in power and scope.

And complaining about it didn't help, either. All those scientists whining in the Sunday supplements about man's inherent destructiveness and his propensity for violence, throwing up their hands. That wasn't dealing with the irrational side. That was just a formal admission that they were giving up on it.

The screen changed again:

DEEPSTAR III - ASCEND CHECKLIST

1. Set Ballast Blowers To: On
Proceed To Next   Cancel

Norman pushed buttons on the panel, setting the ballast blowers, and waited for the next screen.

After all, how did scientists approach their own research? The scientists all agreed: scientific research can't be stopped. If we don't build the bomb, someone else will. But then pretty soon the bomb was in the hands of new people, who said, If we don't *use* the bomb, someone else will.

At which point, the scientists said, those other people are terrible people, they're irrational and irresponsible. We scientists are okay. But those other people are a real problem.

Yet the truth was that responsibility began with each individual person, and the choices he made. Each person had a choice.

Well, Norman thought, there was nothing he could do for Harry or Beth any longer. He had to save himself.

He heard a deep hum as the generators turned on, and the throb of the propellors. The screen flashed:

DEEPSTAR III - PILOT INSTRUMENTS ACTIVATED

Here we go, he thought, resting his hands confidently on the controls. He felt the submarine respond beneath him.

"Your attention, please. Seventeen minutes and counting."

Muddy sediment churned up around the canopy as the screws engaged, and then the little submarine slipped out from beneath the dome. It was just like driving a car, he thought. There was nothing to it.

He turned in a slow arc, away from DH-7, toward DH-8. He was twenty feet above the bottom, high enough for the screws to clear the mud.

There were seventeen minutes left. At a maximum ascent rate of 6.6 feet per second—he did the mental calculation quickly, effortlessly—he would reach the surface in two and a half minutes.

There was plenty of time.

He moved the submarine close to DH-8. The exterior habitat floodlights were yellow and pale. Power must be dropping. He could see the damage to the cylinders—streams of bubbles rising from the weakened A and B Cylinders; the dents in the D; and the gaping hole in E Cyl, which was flooded. The habitat was battered, and dying.

Why had he come so close? He squinted at the portholes, then realized he was hoping to catch sight of Harry and Beth, one last time. He wanted to see Harry, unconscious and unresponsive. He wanted to see Beth standing at the window, shaking her fist at him in maniacal rage. He wanted confirmation that he was right to leave them.

But he saw only the fading yellow light inside the habitat. He was disappointed.

"Norman."

"Yes, Beth." He felt comfortable answering her now. He had his hands on the controls of the submarine, ready to make his ascent. There was nothing she could do to him now.

"Norman, you really are a son of a bitch."

"You tried to kill me, Beth."

"I didn't *want* to kill you. I had no choice, Norman."

"Yeah, well. Me, too. I have no choice." As he spoke, he knew he was right. Better for one person to survive. Better than nothing.

"You're just going to leave us?"

"That's right, Beth."

His hand moved to the ascent-rate dial. He set it to 6.6 feet. Ready to ascend.

"You're just going to run away?" He heard the contempt in her voice.

"That's right, Beth."

"You, the one who kept talking about how we had to stay together down here?"

"Sorry, Beth."

"You must be very afraid, Norman."

"I'm not afraid at all." And indeed he felt strong and confident, setting the controls, preparing for his ascent. He felt better than he had felt for days.

"Norman," she said. "Please help us. *Please.*"

Her words struck him at some deep level, arousing feelings of caring, of professional competence, of simple human kindness. For a moment he felt confusion, his strength and conviction weakened. But then he got a grip on himself, and shook his head. The strength flew back into his body.

"Sorry, Beth. It's too late for that."

And he pressed the "Ascend" button, heard the roar as the ballast tanks blew, and *Deepstar III* swayed. The habitat slipped away below him, and he started toward the surface, a thousand feet above.

Black water, no sense of movement except for the readings on the glowing green instrument panel. He began to review the events in his mind, as if he were already facing a Navy inquiry. Had he done the right thing, leaving the others behind?

Unquestionably, he had. The sphere was an alien object which gave a person the power to manifest his thoughts. Well and good, except that human beings had a split in their brains, a split in their mental processes. It was almost as if men had two brains. The conscious brain could be consciously controlled, and presented no problem. But the unconscious brain, wild and abandoned, was dangerous and destructive when its impulses were manifested.

The trouble with people like Harry and Beth was that they were literally unbalanced. Their conscious brains were overdeveloped, but they had never bothered to explore their unconscious. That was the difference between Norman and them. As a psychologist, Norman had some acquaintance with his unconscious. It held no surprises for him.

That was why Harry and Beth had manifested monsters, but Norman had not. Norman knew his unconscious. No monsters awaited him.

No. Wrong.

He was startled by the suddenness of the thought, the abruptness of it. Was he really wrong? He considered carefully, and decided once again that he was correct after all. Beth and Harry were at risk from the products of their unconscious, but Norman was not. Norman knew himself; the others did not.

"The fears unleashed by contact with a new life form are not understood. The most likely consequence of contact is absolute terror."

The statements from his own report popped into his head. Why should he think of them now? It had been years since he had written his report.

"Under circumstances of extreme terror, people make decisions poorly."

Yet Norman wasn't afraid. Far from it. He was confident and strong. He had a plan, he was carrying it out. Why should he even think of that report? At the time, he'd agonized over it, thinking of each sentence. . . . Why was it coming to mind now? It troubled him.

"Your attention, please. Sixteen minutes and counting."

Norman scanned the gauges before him. He was at nine hundred feet, rising swiftly. There was no turning back now.

Why should he even think of turning back?

Why should it enter his mind?

As he rose silently through black water, he increasingly felt a kind of split inside himself, an almost schizophrenic internal division. Something *was* wrong, he sensed. There was something he hadn't considered yet.

But what could he have overlooked? Nothing, he decided, because, unlike Beth and Harry, I am fully conscious; I am aware of everything that is happening inside me.

Except Norman didn't really believe that. Complete awareness might be a philosophical goal, but it was not really attainable. Consciousness was like a pebble that rippled the surface of the unconscious. As consciousness widened, there was still more unconsciousness beyond. There was always more, just beyond reach. Even for a humanistic psychologist.

Stein, his old professor: "You always have your shadow."

What was Norman's shadow side doing now? What was happening in the unconscious, denied parts of his own brain?

Nothing. Keep going up.

He shifted uneasily in the pilot's chair. He wanted to go to the surface so badly, he felt such conviction. . . .

I hate Beth. I hate Harry. I hate worrying about these people, caring for them. I don't want to care any more. It's not my responsibility. I want to save myself. I hate them. I hate them.

He was shocked. Shocked by his own thoughts, the vehemence of them.

I must go back, he thought.

If I go back I will die.

But some other part of himself was growing stronger with each moment. What Beth had said was true: Norman had been the one who kept saying that they had to stay together, to work together. How could he abandon them now? He couldn't. It was against everything he believed in, everything that was important and human.

He had to go back.

I am afraid to go back.

At last, he thought. There it is. Fear so strong he had denied its existence, fear that had caused him to rationalize abandoning the others.

He pressed the controls, halting his ascent. As he started back down, he saw that his hands were shaking.

0130 Hours

The sub came to rest gently on the bottom beside the habitat. Norman stepped into the submarine airlock, flooded the chamber. Moments later, he climbed down the side and walked toward the habitat. The Tevac explosives' cones with their blinking red lights looked oddly festive.

"Your attention, please. Fourteen minutes and counting."

He estimated the time he would need. One minute to get inside. Five, maybe six minutes to dress Beth and Harry in the suits. Another four minutes to reach the sub and get them aboard. Two or three minutes to make the ascent.

It was going to be close.

He moved beneath the big support pylons, under the habitat.

"So you came back, Norman," Beth said, over the intercom.

"Yes, Beth."

"Thank God," she said. She started to cry. He was beneath A Cyl, hearing her sobs over the intercom. He found the hatch cover, spun the wheel to open it. It was locked shut.

"Beth, open the hatch."

She was crying over the intercom. She didn't answer him.

"Beth, can you hear me? Open the hatch."

Crying like a child, sobbing hysterically. "Norman," she said. "Please help me. *Please.*"

"I'm trying to help you, Beth. Open the hatch."

"I can't."

"What do you mean, you can't?"

"It won't do any good."

"Beth," he said. "Come on, now. . . ."

"I can't do it, Norman."

"Of course you can. Open the hatch, Beth."

"You shouldn't have come back, Norman."

There was no time for this now. "Beth, pull yourself together. Open the hatch."

"No, Norman, I can't."

And she began crying again.

He tried all the hatches, one after another. B Cyl, locked. C Cyl, locked. D Cyl, locked.

"Your attention, please. Thirteen minutes and counting."

He was standing by E Cyl, which had been flooded in an earlier attack. He saw the gaping, jagged tear in the outer cylinder surface. The hole was large enough for him to climb through, but the edges were sharp, and if he tore his suit . . .

No, he decided. It was too risky. He moved beneath E Cyl. Was there a hatch?

He found a hatch, spun the wheel. It opened easily. He pushed the circular lid upward, heard it clang against the inner wall.

"Norman? Is that you?"

He hauled himself up, into E Cyl. He was panting from the exertion, on his hands and knees on the deck of E Cyl. He shut the hatch and locked it again, then took a moment to get his breath.

"Your attention, please. Twelve minutes and counting."

Jesus, he thought. Already?

Something white drifted past his faceplate, startling him. He pulled back, realized it was a box of corn flakes. When he touched it, the cardboard disintegrated in his hands, the flakes like yellow snow.

He was in the kitchen. Beyond the stove he saw another hatch, leading to D Cyl. D Cyl was not flooded, which meant that he must somehow pressurize E Cyl.

He looked up, saw an overhead bulkhead hatch, leading to the living room with the gaping tear. He climbed up quickly. He needed to find gas, some kind of tanks. The living room was dark, except for the reflected light from the floodlights, which filtered in through the tear. Cushions and padding floated in the water. Something touched him and he spun and saw dark hair streaming around a face, and as the hair moved he saw part of the face was missing, torn away grotesquely.

Tina.

Norman shuddered, pushed her body away. It drifted off, moving upward.

"Your attention, please. Eleven minutes and counting."

It was all happening too fast, he thought. There was hardly enough time left. He needed to be inside the habitat now.

No tanks in the living room. He climbed back down to the kitchen, shutting the hatch above. He looked at the stove, the ovens. He opened the oven door, and a burst of gas bubbled out. Air trapped in the oven.

But that couldn't be right, he thought, because gas was still coming out. A trickle of bubbles continued to come from the open oven.

A steady trickle.

What had Barnes said about cooking under pressure? There was something unusual about it, he couldn't remember exactly. Did they use gas? Yes, but they also needed more oxygen. That meant—

He pulled the stove away from the wall, grunting with exertion, and then he found it. A squat bottle of propane, and two large blue tanks.

Oxygen tanks.

He twisted the Y-valves, his gloved fingers clumsy. Gas began to roar out. The bubbles rushed up to the ceiling, where the gas was trapped, the big air bubble that was forming.

He opened the second oxygen tank. The water level fell rapidly, to his waist, then his knees. Then it stopped. The tanks must be empty. No matter, the level was low enough.

"Your attention, please. Ten minutes and counting."

Norman opened the bulkhead door to D Cyl, and stepped through, into the habitat.

The light was dim. A strange green, slimy mold covered the walls.

On the couch, Harry lay unconscious, the intravenous line still in his arm. Norman pulled the needle out with a spurt of blood. He shook Harry, trying to rouse him.

Harry's eyelids fluttered, but he was otherwise unresponsive. Norman lifted him, put him over his shoulder, carried him through the habitat.

On the intercom, Beth was still crying. "Norman, you shouldn't have come."

"Where are you, Beth?"

On the monitors, he read:

DETONATION SEQUENCE 09:32.

Counting backward. The numbers seemed to move too fast.

"Take Harry and go, Norman. Both of you go. Leave me behind."

"Tell me where you are, Beth."

He was moving through the habitat, from D to C Cyl. He didn't see her anywhere. Harry was a dead weight on his shoulder, making it difficult to get through the bulkhead doors.

"It won't do any good, Norman."

"Come on, Beth. . . ."

"I know I'm bad, Norman. I know I can't be helped."

"Beth . . ." He was hearing her through the helmet radio, so he could not locate her by the sound. But he could not risk removing his helmet. Not now.

"I deserve to die, Norman."

"Cut it out, Beth."

"Attention, please. Nine minutes and counting."

A new alarm sounded, an intermittent beeping that became louder and more intense as the seconds ticked by.

He was in B Cyl, a maze of pipes and equipment. Once clean and multi-colored, now the slimy mold coated every surface. In some places fibrous mossy strands hung down. B Cyl looked like a jungle swamp.

"Beth . . ."

She was silent now. She must be in this room, he thought. B Cyl had always been Beth's favorite place, the place where the habitat was controlled. He put Harry on the deck, propped him against a wall. But the wall was slippery and Harry slid down, banged his head. He coughed, opened his eyes.

"Jesus. Norman?"

Norman held his hand up, signaling Harry to be quiet.

"Beth?" Norman said.

No answer. Norman moved among the slimy pipes.

"Beth?"

"Leave me, Norman."

"I can't do that, Beth. I'm taking you, too."

"No. I'm staying, Norman."

"Beth," he said, "there's no time for this."

"I'm staying, Norman. I deserve to stay."

He saw her.

Beth was huddled in the back, wedged among pipes, crying like a child. She held one of the explosive-tipped spear guns in her hand. She looked at him tearfully.

"Oh, Norman," she said. "You were going to *leave* us. . . ."

"I'm sorry. I was wrong."

He started toward her, holding out his hands to her. She swung the spear gun around. "No, you were right. You were right. I want you to leave now."

Above her head he saw a glowing monitor, the numbers clicking inexorably backward: 08:27 . . . 08:26 . . .

He thought, I can change this. *I want the numbers to stop counting.*

The numbers did not stop.

"You can't fight me, Norman," she said, huddled in the corner. Her eyes blazed with furious energy.

"I can see that."

"There isn't much time, Norman. I want you to leave."

She held the gun, pointed firmly toward him. He had a sudden sense of the absurdity of it all, that he had come back to rescue someone who didn't want to be rescued. What could he do now? Beth was wedged back in there, beyond his reach, beyond his help. There was barely enough time for him to get away, let alone to take Harry. . . .

Harry, he thought suddenly. Where was Harry now?

I want Harry to help me.

But he wondered if there was time; the numbers were clicking backward, there was hardly more than eight minutes, now. . . .

"I came back for you, Beth."

"Go," she said. "Go now, Norman."

"But, Beth—"

"—No, Norman! I mean it! Go! Why don't you go?" And then she began to get suspicious; she started to look around; and at that moment Harry stood up behind her, and swung the big wrench down on her head, and there was a sickening thud, and she fell.

"Did I kill her?" Harry said.

And the deep male voice said, "Attention, please. Eight minutes and counting."

Norman concentrated on the clock as it ticked backwards. Stop. Stop the countdown.

But when he looked again, the clock was still ticking backwards. And the alarm: Was the alarm interfering with his concentration? He tried again.

Stop now. The countdown will stop now. The countdown has stopped.

"Forget it," Harry said. "It won't work."

"But it *should* work," Norman said.

"No," Harry said. "Because she's not completely unconscious."

On the floor at their feet, Beth groaned. Her leg moved.

"She's still able to control it, somehow," Norman said. "She's very strong."

"Can we inject her?"

Norman shook his head. There was no time to go back for the syringe. Anyway, if they injected her and it didn't work, it would be time wasted—

"Hit her again?" Harry said. "Harder? Kill her?"

"No," Norman said.

"Killing her is the only way—"

"—No," Norman said, thinking, We didn't kill you, Harry, when we had the chance.

"If you won't kill her, then you can't do anything about that timer," Harry said. "So we better get the hell out."

They ran for the airlock.

"How much time is left?" Harry said. They were in the A Cyl airlock, trying to put the suit on Beth. She was groaning; blood was matted on the back of her head. Beth struggled a little, making it more difficult.

"Jesus, Beth—how much time, Norman?"

"Seven and a half minutes, maybe less."

Her legs were in; they quickly pushed her arms in, zipped up the chest. They turned on her air. Norman helped Harry with his suit.

"Attention, please. Seven minutes and counting."

Harry said, "How much time you figure to get to the surface?"

"Two and a half minutes, after we get inside the sub," Norman said.

"Great," Harry said.

Norman snapped Harry's helmet locked. "Let's go."

Harry descended into the water, and Norman lowered Beth's unconscious body. She was heavy with the tank and weights.

"Come on, Norman!"

Norman plunged into the water.

At the submarine, Norman climbed up to the hatch entrance, but the untethered sub rolled unpredictably with his weight. Harry, standing on the bottom, tried to push Beth up toward Norman, but Beth kept bending over at the waist. Norman, grabbing for her, fell off the sub and slid to the bottom.

"Attention, please. Six minutes and counting."

"Hurry, Norman! Six minutes!"

"I heard, damn it."

Norman got to his feet, climbed back on the sub, but now his suit was muddy, his gloves slippery. Harry was counting: "Five twenty-nine . . . five twenty-eight . . . five twentyseven . . ." Norman caught Beth's arm, but she slipped away again.

"Damn it, Norman! Hold on to her!"

"I'm trying!"

"Here. Here she is again."

"Attention, please. Five minutes and counting."

The alarm was now high-pitched, beeping insistently. They had to shout over it to be heard.

"Harry, give her to me—"

"Well, here, take her—"

"Missed—"

"Here—"

Norman finally caught Beth's air hose in his hand, just behind the helmet. He wondered if it would pull out, but he had to risk it. Gripping the hose, he hauled Beth up, until she lay on her back on the top of the sub. Then he eased her down into the hatch.

"Four twenty-nine . . . four twenty-eight . . ."

Norman had trouble keeping his balance. He got one of Beth's legs into the hatch, but the other knee was bent, jammed against the lip of the hatch. He couldn't get her down. Every time he leaned forward to unbend her leg, the whole submarine tipped, and he would start to lose his balance again.

"Four sixteen . . . four fifteen . . ."

"Would you stop counting and *do something!*"

Harry pressed his body against the side of the submarine, countering the rolling with his weight. Norman leaned forward and pressed Beth's knee straight; she slid easily into the open hatch. Norman climbed in after her. It was a one-man airlock, but Beth was unconscious, and could not work the controls.

He would have to do it for her.

"Attention, please. Four minutes and counting."

He was cramped in the airlock, his body pressed up against Beth, chest to chest, her helmet banging against his. With difficulty he pulled the hatch closed over his head. He blew out the water in a furious rush of compressed air; unsupported by the water, Beth's body now sagged heavily against him.

He reached around her for the handle to the inner hatch. Beth's body blocked his way. He tried to twist her around sideways. In the confined space, he couldn't get any leverage on the body. Beth was like a dead weight; he tried to shift her body around, to get to the hatch.

The whole submarine began to sway: Harry was climbing up the side.

"What the hell's going on in there?"

"Harry, *will you shut up!*"

"Well, what's the delay?"

Norman's hand closed on the inner latch handle. He shoved it down, but the door didn't move: the door was hinged to swing *inward.* He couldn't open it with Beth in the hatch with him. It was too crowded; her body blocked the movement of the door.

"Harry, we've got a problem."

"Jesus Christ . . . Three minutes thirty."

Norman began to sweat. They were really in trouble now.

"Harry, I've got to pass her out to you, and go in alone."

"Jesus, Norman . . ."

Norman flooded the airlock, opened the upper hatch once again. Harry's balance atop the submarine was precarious. He grabbed Beth by the air hose, dragged her up.

Norman reached up to close the hatch.

"Harry, can you get her feet out of the way?"

"I'm trying to keep my balance here."

"Can't you see her feet are blocking—" Irritably, Norman pushed Beth's feet aside. The hatch clanged down. The air blasted past him. The hatch pressurized.

"Attention, please. Two minutes and counting."

He was inside the submarine. The instruments glowed green.

He opened the inner hatch.

"Norman?"

"Try and get her down," Norman said. "Do it as fast as you can."

But he was thinking they were in terrible trouble: at least thirty seconds to get Beth into the hatch, and thirty seconds more for Harry to come down. A minute all together—

"She's in. Vent it."

Norman jumped for the air vent, blew out the water.

"How'd you get her in so fast, Harry?"

"Nature's way," Harry said, "to get people through tight spaces." And before Norman could ask what that meant, he had opened the hatch and saw that Harry had pushed Beth into the airlock head first. He grabbed her shoulders and eased her onto the floor of the submarine, then slammed the hatch shut. Moments later, he heard the blast of air as Harry, too, vented the airlock.

The submarine hatch clanged. Harry came forward.

"Christ, one minute forty," Harry said. "Do you know how to work this thing?"

"Yes."

Norman sat in the seat, placed his hands on the controls.

They heard the whine of the props, felt the rumble. The sub lurched, moved off the bottom.

"One minute thirty seconds. How long did you say to the surface?"

"Two thirty," Norman said, cranking up the ascent rate. He pushed it past 6.6, to the far end of the dial.

They heard a high-pitched shriek of air as the ballast tanks blew. The sub nosed up sharply, began to rise swiftly.

"Is this as fast as it goes?"

"Yes."

"Jesus."

"Take it easy, Harry."

Looking back down, they could see the habitat with its lights. And then the long lines of explosives set over the spaceship itself. They rose past the high fin of the spacecraft, leaving it behind, seeing only black water now.

"One minute twenty."

"Nine hundred feet," Norman said. There was very little sensation of movement, only the changing dials on the instrument panel to tell them they were moving.

"It's not fast enough," Harry said. "That's a hell of a lot of explosive down there."

It is fast enough, Norman thought, correcting him.

"The shock wave will crush us like a can of sardines," Harry said, shaking his head.

The shock wave will not harm us.

Eight hundred feet.

"Forty seconds," Harry said. "We'll never make it."

"We'll make it."

They were at seven hundred feet, rising fast. The water now had a faint blue color: sunlight filtering down.

"Thirty seconds," Harry said. "Where are we? Twentynine . . . eight . . ."

"Six hundred twenty feet," Norman said. "Six ten."

They looked back down the side of the sub. They could barely discern the habitat, faint pinpricks of light far beneath them.

Beth coughed. "It's too late now," Harry said. "I knew from the beginning we'd never make it."

"*Yes we will,*" Norman said.

"Ten seconds," Harry said. "Nine . . . eight . . . Brace yourself!"

Norman pulled Beth to his chest as the explosion rocked the submarine, spinning it like a toy, upending it, then righting it again, and lifting it in a giant upward surge.

"Mama!" Harry shouted, but they were still rising, they were okay. "We did it!"

"Two hundred feet," Norman said. The water outside was now light blue. He pushed buttons, slowing the ascent. They were going up very fast.

Harry was screaming, pounding Norman on the back. "We did it! God damn it, you son of a bitch, we did it! We survived! I never thought we would! We survived!"

Norman was having trouble seeing the instruments for tears in his eyes.

And then he had to squint as bright sunlight streamed into the bubble canopy as they surfaced, and they saw calm seas, sky, and fluffy clouds.

"Do you see that?" Harry cried. He was screaming in Norman's ear. "Do you see that? *It is a perfect goddamned day!*"

0000 Hours

Norman awoke to see a brilliant shaft of light, streaming through the single porthole, shining down on the chemical toilet in the corner of the decompression chamber. He lay on his bunk and looked around the chamber, a horizontal cylinder fifty feet long: bunks, a metal table and chairs in the center of the cylinder, toilet behind a small partition. Harry snored in the bunk above him. Across the chamber, Beth slept, one arm flung over her face. Faintly, from a distance, he heard men shouting.

Norman yawned, and swung off the bunk. His body was sore but he was otherwise all right. He walked to the shining porthole and looked out, squinting in the bright Pacific sun.

He saw the rear deck of the research ship *John Hawes:* the white helicopter pad, heavy coiled cables, the tubular metal frame of an underwater robot. A Navy crew was lowering a second robot over the side, with a lot of shouting and swearing and waving of hands; Norman had heard their voices faintly through the thick steel walls of the chamber.

Near the chamber itself, a muscular seaman rolled a large green tank marked "Oxygen" alongside a dozen other tanks on the deck. The three-man medical crew which supervised the decompression chamber played cards.

Looking through the inch-thick glass of the porthole, Norman felt as if he were peering into a miniature world to which he had little connection, a kind of terrarium populated by interesting and exotic specimens. This new world was as alien to him as the dark ocean world had once seemed from inside the habitat.

He watched the crew slap down their cards on a wooden packing crate, watched them laugh and gesture as the game proceeded. They never glanced in his direction, never looked at the decompression chamber. Norman didn't understand these young men. Were they supposed to be paying attention to the decompression? They looked young and inexperienced to Norman. Focused on their card game, they seemed indifferent to the huge metal chamber nearby, indifferent to the three survivors inside the chamber—and indifferent to the larger meaning of the mission, to the news the survivors had brought back to the surface. These cheerful Navy card-players didn't seem to give a damn about Norman's mission. But perhaps they didn't know.

He turned back to the chamber, sat down at the table. His knee throbbed, and the skin was swollen around the white bandage. He had been treated by a Navy physician during their transfer from the submarine to the decompression chamber. They had been taken off the minisub *Deepstar III* in a pressurized diving bell, and from there had been transferred to the large chamber on the deck of the ship—the SDC, the Navy called it, the surface decompression chamber. They were going to spend four days here. Norman wasn't sure how long he had been here so far. They had all immediately gone to sleep, and there was no clock in the chamber. The face of his own wristwatch was smashed, although he didn't remember it happening.

On the table in front of him, someone had scratched "U.S.N. SUCKS" into the surface. Norman ran his fingers over the grooves, and remembered the grooves in the silver sphere. But he and Harry and Beth were in the hands of the Navy now.

And he thought: What are we going to tell them?

"What are we going to tell them?" Beth said.

It was several hours later; Beth and Harry had awakened, and now they were all sitting around the scarred metal table. None of them had made any attempt to talk to the crew outside. It was, Norman thought, as if they shared an unspoken agreement to remain in isolation a while longer.

"I think we'll have to tell them everything," Harry said.

"I don't think we should," Norman said. He was surprised by the strength of his conviction, the firmness of his own voice.

"I agree," Beth said. "I'm not sure the world is ready for that sphere. *I* certainly wasn't."

She gave Norman a sheepish look. He put his hand on her shoulder.

"That's fine," Harry said. "But look at it from the standpoint of the Navy. The Navy has mounted a large and expensive operation; six people have died, and two habitats have been destroyed. They're going to want answers—and they're going to keep asking until they get them."

"We can refuse to talk," Beth said.

"That won't make any difference," Harry said. "Remember, the Navy has all the tapes."

"That's right, the tapes," Norman said. He had forgotten about the video-tapes they had brought up in the submarine. Dozens of tapes, documenting everything that had happened in the habitat during their time underwater. Documenting the squid, the deaths, the sphere. Documenting everything.

"We should have destroyed those tapes," Beth said.

"Perhaps we should have," Harry said. "But it's too late now. We can't prevent the Navy from getting the answers they want."

Norman sighed. Harry was right. At this point there was no way to conceal what had happened, or to prevent the Navy from finding out about the sphere, and the power it conveyed. That power would represent a kind of ultimate weapon: the ability to overcome your enemies simply by imagining it had happened. It was frightening in its implications, and there was nothing they could do about it. Unless—

"I think we *can* prevent them from knowing," Norman said.

"How?" Harry said.

"We still have the power, don't we?"

"I guess so."

"And that power," Norman said, "consists of the ability to make anything happen, simply by thinking it."

"Yes . . ."

"Then we can prevent the Navy from knowing. We can decide to forget the whole thing."

Harry frowned. "That's an interesting question: whether we have the power to forget the power."

"I think we should forget it," Beth said. "That sphere is too dangerous."

They fell silent, considering the implications of forgetting the sphere. Because forgetting would not merely prevent the Navy from knowing about the sphere—it would erase all knowledge of it, including their own. Make it vanish from human consciousness, as if it had never existed in the first place. Remove it from the awareness of the human species, forever.

"Big step," Harry said. "After all we've been through, just to forget about it ..."

"It's because of all we've been through, Harry," Beth said. "Let's face it—we didn't handle ourselves very well." Norman noticed that she spoke without rancor now, her previous combative edge gone.

"I'm afraid that's true," Norman said. "The sphere was built to test whatever intelligent life might pick it up, and we simply failed that test."

"Is that what you think the sphere was made for?" Harry said. "I don't."

"Then what?" Norman said.

"Well," Harry said, "look at it this way: Suppose you were an intelligent bacterium floating in space, and you came upon one of our communication satellites, in orbit around the Earth. You would think, What a strange, alien object this is, let's explore it. Suppose you opened it up and crawled inside. You would find it very interesting in there, with lots of huge things to puzzle over. But eventually you might climb into one of the fuel cells, and the hydrogen would kill you. And your last thought would be: This alien device was obviously made to test bacterial intelligence and to kill us if we make a false step.

"Now, that would be correct from the standpoint of the dying bacterium. But that wouldn't be correct at all from the standpoint of the beings who made the satellite. From our point of view, the communications satellite has nothing to do with intelligent bacteria. We don't even know that there are intelligent bacteria out there. We're just trying to communicate, and we've made what we consider a quite ordinary device to do it."

"You mean the sphere might not be a message or a trophy or a trap at all?"

"That's right," Harry said. "The sphere may have nothing to do with the search for other life forms, or testing life, as we might imagine those activities to occur. It may be an accident that the sphere causes such profound changes in us."

"But why would someone build such a machine?" Norman said.

"That's the same question an intelligent bacterium would ask about a communications satellite: Why would anyone build such a thing?"

"For that matter," Beth said, "it may not be a machine. The sphere may be a life form. It may be alive."

"Possible," Harry said, nodding.

Beth said, "So, if the sphere is alive, do we have an obligation to keep it alive?"

"We don't know if it *is* alive."

Norman sat back in the chair. "All this speculation is interesting," he said, "but when you get down to it, we don't really know *anything* about the sphere. In fact, we shouldn't even be calling it *the* sphere. We probably should just call it 'sphere.' Because we don't know what it is. We don't know where it came from. We don't know whether it's living or dead. We don't know how it came to be inside that spaceship. We don't know anything about it except what we imagine—and what we imagine says more about us than it does about the sphere."

"Right," Harry said.

"Because it's literally a sort of mirror for us," Norman said.

"Speaking of which, there's another possibility," Harry said. "It may not be alien at all. It may be man-made."

That took Norman completely by surprise. Harry explained.

"Consider," Harry said. "A ship from our own future went through a black hole, into another universe, or another part of our universe. We cannot imagine what would happen as a result of that. But suppose there were some major distortion of time. Suppose that ship, which left with a human crew in the year 2043, actually has been in transit for thousands and thousands of years. Couldn't the human crew have invented it during that time?"

"I don't think that's likely," Beth said.

"Well, let's consider for a moment, Beth," Harry said gently. Norman noticed that Harry wasn't arrogant any more. They were all in this together, Norman thought, and they were working together in a way they never had before. All the time underwater they had been at odds, but now they functioned smoothly together, coordinated. A team.

"There is a real problem about the future," Harry was saying, "and we don't admit it. We assume we can see into the future better than we really can. Leonardo da Vinci tried to make a helicopter five hundred years ago; and Jules Verne predicted a submarine a hundred years ago. From instances like that, we tend to believe that the future is predictable in a way that it really isn't. Because neither Leonardo nor Jules Verne could ever have imagined, say, a computer. The very concept of a computer implies too much knowledge that was simply inconceivable at the time those men were alive. It was, if you will, information that came out of nowhere, later on.

"And we're no wiser, sitting here now. We couldn't have guessed that men would send a ship through a black hole—we didn't even suspect the existence of black holes until a few years ago—and we certainly can't guess what men might accomplish thousands of years in the future."

"Assuming the sphere was made by men."

"Yes. Assuming that."

"And if it wasn't? If it's really a sphere from an alien civilization? Are we justified in erasing all human knowledge of this alien life?"

"I don't know," Harry said, shaking his head. "If we decide to forget the sphere . . ."

"Then it'll be gone," Norman said.

Beth stared at the table. "I wish we could ask someone," she said finally.

"There isn't anybody to ask," Norman said.

"But *can* we really forget it?" Beth said. "Will it work?"

There was a long silence.

"Yes," Harry said, finally. "There's no question about it. And I think we already have evidence that we *will* forget about it. That solves a logical problem that bothered me from the beginning, when we first explored the ship. Because something very important was missing from that ship."

"Yes? What?"

"Any sign that the builders of the ship already knew travel through a black hole was possible."

"I don't follow you," Norman said.

"Well," Harry said, "the three of us have already seen a spaceship that has been through a black hole. We've walked through it. So we know that such travel is possible."

"Yes . . ."

"Yet, fifty years from now, men are going to build that ship in a very tentative, experimental way, with apparently no knowledge that the ship has already been found, fifty years in their past. There is no sign on the ship that the builders already know of its existence in the past."

"Maybe it's one of those time paradoxes," Beth said. "You know, how you can't go back and meet yourself in the past. . . ."

Harry shook his head. "I don't think it's a paradox," he said. "I think that all knowledge of that ship is going to be lost."

"You mean, we are going to forget it."

"Yes," Harry said. "And, frankly, I think it's a much better solution. For a long time while we were down there, I assumed none of us would ever get back alive. That was the only explanation I could think of. That's why I wanted to make out my will."

"But if we decide to forget . . ."

"Exactly," Harry said. "If we decide to forget, that will produce the same result."

"The knowledge will be gone forever," Norman said quietly. He found himself hesitating. Now that they had arrived at this moment, he was strangely reluctant to proceed. He ran his fingertips over the scarred table, touching the surface, as if it might provide an answer.

In a sense, he thought, all we consist of is memories. Our personalities are constructed from memories, our lives are organized around memories, our cultures are built upon the foundation of shared memories that we call history and science. But now, to give up a memory, to give up knowledge, to give up the past . . .

"It's not easy," Harry said, shaking his head.

"No," Norman said. "It's not." In fact he found it so difficult he wondered if he was experiencing a human characteristic as fundamental as sexual desire. He simply could not give up this knowledge. The information seemed so important to him, the implications so fascinating. . . . His entire being rebelled against the idea of forgetting.

"Well," Harry said, "I think we have to do it, anyway."

"I was thinking of Ted," Beth said. "And Barnes, and the others. We're the only ones who know how they really died. What they gave their lives for. And if we forget . . ."

"*When* we forget," Norman said firmly.

"She has a point," Harry said. "If we forget, how do we handle all the details? All the loose ends?"

"I don't think that's a problem," Norman said. "The unconscious has tremendous creative powers, as we've seen. The details will be taken care of unconsciously. It's like the way we get dressed in the morning. When we dress, we don't necessarily think of every detail, the belt and the socks and so on. We just make a basic overall decision about how we want to look, and then we get dressed."

"Even so," Harry said. "We still better make the overall decision, because we all have the power, and if we imagine different stories, we'll get confusion."

"All right," Norman said. "Let's agree on what happened. Why did we come here?"

"I thought it was going to be an airplane crash."

"Me, too."

"Okay, suppose it *was* an airplane crash."

"Fine. And what happened?"

"The Navy sent some people down to investigate the crash, and a problem developed—"

"—Wait a minute, what problem?"

"The squid?"

"No. Better a technical problem."

"Something to do with the storm?"

"Life-support systems failed during the storm?"

"Yes, good. Life-support systems failed during the storm."

"And several people died as a result?"

"Wait a minute. Let's not go so fast. What made the life-support systems fail?"

Beth said, "The habitat developed a leak, and sea water corrupted the scrubber canisters in B Cyl, releasing a toxic gas."

"Could that have happened?" Norman said.

"Yes, easily."

"And several people died as a result of that accident."

"Okay."

"But we survived."

"Yes."

"Why?" Norman said.

"We were in the other habitat?"

Norman shook his head. "The other habitat was destroyed, too."

"Maybe it was destroyed later, with the explosives."

"Too complicated," Norman said. "Let's keep it simple. It was an accident which happened suddenly and unexpectedly. The habitat sprang a leak and the scrubbers failed, and as a result most of the people died, but we didn't because—"

"We were in the sub?"

"Okay," Norman said. "We were in the sub when the systems failed, so we survived and the others didn't."

"Why were we in the sub?"

"We were transferring the tapes according to the schedule."

"And what about the tapes?" Harry said. "What will they show?"

"The tapes will confirm our story," Norman said. "Everything will be consistent with the story, including the Navy people who sent us down in the first place, and including us, too—we won't remember anything but this story."

"And we won't have the power any more?" Beth said, frowning.

"No," Norman said. "Not any more."

"Okay," Harry said.

Beth seemed to think about it longer, biting her lip. But finally she nodded. "Okay."

Norman took a deep breath, and looked at Beth and Harry. "Are we ready to forget the sphere, and the fact that we once had the power to make things happen by thinking them?"

They nodded.

Beth became suddenly agitated, twisting in her chair. "But how do we do it, exactly?"

"We just do it," Norman said. "Close your eyes and tell yourself to forget it."

Beth said, "But are you sure we should do it? *Really* sure?" She was still agitated, moving nervously.

"Yes, Beth. You just . . . give up the power."

"Then we have to do it all together," she said. "At the same time."

"Okay," Harry said. "On the count of three."

They closed their eyes.

"One . . ."

With his eyes closed, Norman thought, People always forget that they have power, anyway.

"Two . . ." Harry said.

And then Norman focused his mind. With a sudden intensity he saw the sphere again, shining like a star, perfect and polished, and he thought: I want to forget I ever saw the sphere.

And in his mind's eye, the sphere vanished.

"**T**hree," Harry said.

"Three what?" Norman said. His eyes ached and burned. He rubbed them with his thumb and forefinger, then opened them. Beth and Harry were sitting around the table in the decompression chamber with him. They all looked tired and depressed. But that was to be expected, he thought, considering what they had all been through.

"Three what?" Norman said again.

"Oh," Harry said, "I was just thinking out loud. Only three of us left."

Beth sighed. Norman saw tears in her eyes. She fumbled in her pocket for a Kleenex, blew her nose.

"You can't blame yourselves," Norman said. "It was an accident. There was nothing we could do about it."

"I know," Harry said. "But those people suffocating, while we were in the submarine . . . I keep hearing the screams. . . . God, I wish it had never happened."

There was a silence. Beth blew her nose again.

Norman wished it had never happened, too. But wishing wasn't going to make a difference now.

"We can't change what happened," Norman said. "We can only learn to accept it."

"I know," Beth said.

"I've had a lot of experience with accident trauma," he said. "You simply have to keep telling yourself that you have no reason to be guilty. What happened happened—some people died, and you were spared. It isn't anybody's fault. It's just one of those things. It was an accident."

"I know that," Harry said, "but I still feel bad."

"Keep telling yourself it's just one of those things," Norman said. "Keep reminding yourself of that." He got up from the table. They ought to eat, he thought. They ought to have food. "I'm going to ask for food."

"I'm not hungry," Beth said.

"I know that, but we should eat anyway."

Norman walked to the porthole. The attentive Navy crew saw him at once, pressed the radio intercom. "Do anything for you, Dr. Johnson?"

"Yes," Norman said. "We need some food."

"Right away, sir."

Norman saw the sympathy on the faces of the Navy crew. These senior men understood what a shock it must be for the three survivors.

"Dr. Johnson? Are your people ready to talk to somebody now?"

"Talk?"

"Yes, sir. The intelligence experts have been reviewing the videotapes from the submarine, and they have some questions for you."

"What about?" Norman asked, without much interest.

"Well, when you were transferred to the SDC, Dr. Adams mentioned something about a squid."

"Did he?"

"Yes, sir. Only there doesn't seem to be any squid recorded on the tapes."

"I don't remember any squid," Norman said, puzzled. He turned to Harry. "Did you say something about a squid, Harry?"

Harry frowned. "A squid? I don't think so."

Norman turned back to the Navy man. "What do the videotapes show, exactly?"

"Well, the tapes go right up to the time when the air in the habitat . . . you know, the accident . . ."

"Yes," Norman said. "I remember the accident."

"From the tapes, we think we know what happened. Apparently there was a leak in the habitat wall, and the scrubber cylinders got wet. They became inoperable, and the ambient atmosphere went bad."

"I see."

"It must have happened very suddenly, sir."

"Yes," Johnson said. "Yes, it did."

"So, are you ready to talk to someone now?"

"I think so. Yes."

Norman turned away from the porthole. He put his hands in the pockets of his jacket, and felt a piece of paper. He pulled out a picture and stared at it curiously.

It was a photograph of a red Corvette. Norman wondered where the picture had come from. Probably a car that belonged to someone else, who had worn the jacket before Norman. Probably one of the Navy people who had died in the underwater disaster.

Norman shivered, crumpled the picture in his fist, and tossed it into the trash. He didn't need any mementos. He remembered that disaster only too well. He knew he would never forget it for the rest of his life.

He glanced back at Beth and Harry. They both looked tired. Beth stared into space, preoccupied with her own thoughts. But her face was serene; despite the hardships of their time underwater, Norman thought she looked almost beautiful.

"You know, Beth," he said, "you look lovely."

Beth did not seem to hear, but then she turned toward him slowly. "Why, thank you, Norman," she said.

And she smiled.

EATERS OF THE DEAD

THE MANUSCRIPT OF IBN FADLAN,
RELATING HIS EXPERIENCES
WITH THE NORTHMEN IN A.D. 922

To William Howells

The material contained in the first three chapters is substantially derived from the manuscript of Ibn Fadlan as translated by Robert P. Blake and Richard N. Frye, and by Albert Stanburrough Cook. Their scholarly work is gratefully acknowledged.

"Praise not the day until evening has come; a woman until she is burnt; a sword until it is tried; a maiden until she is married; ice until it has been crossed; beer until it has been drunk."

—VIKING PROVERB

"Evil is of old date."

—ARAB PROVERB

Introduction

The Ibn Fadlan manuscript represents the earliest known eyewitness account of Viking life and society. It is an extraordinary document, describing in vivid detail events which occurred more than a thousand years ago. The manuscript has not, of course, survived intact over that enormous span of time. It has a peculiar history of its own, and one no less remarkable than the text itself.

PROVENANCE OF THE MANUSCRIPT

In June, A.D. 921, the Caliph of Bagdad sent a member of his court, Ahmad Ibn Fadlan, as ambassador to the King of the Bulgars. Ibn Fadlan was gone three years on his journey and never actually accomplished his mission, for along the way he encountered a company of Norsemen and had many adventures among them.

When he finally returned to Bagdad, Ibn Fadlan recorded his experiences in the form of an official report to the court. That original manuscript has long since disappeared, and to reconstruct it we must rely on partial fragments preserved in later sources.

The best-known of these is an Arabic geographical lexicon written by Yakut ibn-Abdallah sometime in the thirteenth century. Yakut includes a dozen verbatim passages from Ibn Fadlan's account, which was then three hundred years old. One must presume Yakut worked from a copy of the original. Nevertheless these few paragraphs have been endlessly translated and retranslated by later scholars.

Another fragment was discovered in Russia in 1817 and was published in German by the St. Petersburg Academy in 1823. This material includes certain passages previously published by J. L. Rasmussen in 1814. Rasmussen worked from a manuscript he found in Copenhagen, since lost, and of dubious origins. There were also Swedish, French, and English translations at this time, but they are all notoriously inaccurate and apparently do not include any new material.

In 1878, two new manuscripts were discovered in the private antiquities collection of Sir John Emerson, the British Ambassador in Constantinople. Sir

John was apparently one of those avid collectors whose zeal for acquisition exceeded his interest in the particular item acquired. The manuscripts were found after his death; no one knows where he obtained them, or when.

One is a geography in Arabic by Ahmad Tusi, reliably dated at A.D. 1047. This makes the Tusi manuscript chronologically closer than any other to the original of Ibn Fadlan, which was presumably written around A.D. 924–926. Yet scholars regard the Tusi manuscript as the least trustworthy of all the sources; the text is full of obvious errors and internal inconsistencies, and although it quotes at length from one "Ibn Faqih" who visited the North country, many authorities hesitate to accept this material.

The second manuscript is that of Amin Razi, dating roughly from A.D. 1585–1595. It is written in Latin and according to its author is translated directly from the Arabic text of Ibn Fadlan. The Razi manuscript contains some material about the Oguz Turks, and several passages concerning battles with the mist monsters, not found in other sources.

In 1934, a final text in Medieval Latin was found in the monastery of Xymos, near Thessalonika in northeastern Greece. The Xymos manuscript contains further commentary on Ibn Fadlan's relations with the Caliph, and his experiences with the creatures of the North country. The author and date of the Xymos manuscript are both uncertain.

The task of collating these many versions and translations, ranging over more than a thousand years, appearing in Arabic, Latin, German, French, Danish, Swedish, and English, is an undertaking of formidable proportions. Only a person of great erudition and energy would attempt it, and in 1951 such a person did. Per Fraus-Dolus, Professor *emeritus* of Comparative Literature at the University of Oslo, Norway, compiled all the known sources and began the massive task of translation which occupied him until his death in 1957. Portions of his new translation were published in the *Proceedings of the National Museum of Oslo: 1959–1960,* but they did not arouse much scholarly interest, perhaps because the journal has a limited circulation.

The Fraus-Dolus translation was absolutely literal; in his own introduction to the material, Fraus-Dolus remarked that "it is in the nature of languages that a pretty translation is not accurate, and an accurate translation finds its own beauty without help."

In preparing this full and annotated version of the Fraus-Dolus translation, I have made few alterations. I deleted some repetitive passages; these are indicated in the text. I changed paragraph structure, starting each directly quoted speaker with a new paragraph, according to modern convention. I have omitted the diacritical marks on Arabic names. Finally, I have occasionally altered the original syntax, usually by transposing subordinate clauses so that the meaning is more readily grasped.

THE VIKINGS

Ibn Fadlan's portrait of the Vikings differs markedly from the traditional European view of these people. The first European descriptions of the Vikings were recorded by the clergy; they were the only observers of the time who could write, and they viewed the pagan Northmen with special horror. Here is a typically hyperbolic passage, cited by D. M. Wilson, from a twelfth-century Irish writer:

> In a word, although there were an hundred hardsteeled iron heads on one neck, and an hundred sharp, ready, cool, never rusting, brazen tongues in each head, and an hundred garrulous, loud, unceasing voices from each tongue, they could not recount or narrate, enumerate or tell, what all the Irish suffered in common, both men and women, laity and clergy, old and young, noble and ignoble, of the hardships and of injuring and of oppression, in every house, from those valiant, wrathful, purely pagan people.

Modern scholars recognize that such bloodcurdling accounts of Viking raids are vastly exaggerated. Yet European writers still tend to dismiss the Scandinavians as bloody barbarians, irrelevant to the main flow of Western culture and ideas. Often this has been done at the expense of a certain logic. For example, David Talbot Rice writes:

> From the eighth to the eleventh centuries indeed the role of the Vikings was perhaps more influential than that of any other single ethnic group in Western Europe. . . . The Vikings were thus great travellers and they performed outstanding feats of navigation; their cities were great centres of trade; their art was original, creative and influential; they boasted a fine literature and a developed culture. Was it truly a civilization? It must, I think, be admitted that it was not. . . . The touch of humanism which is the hallmark of civilization was absent.

This same attitude is reflected in the opinion of Lord Clark:

> When one considers the Icelandic sagas, which are among the great books of the world, one must admit that the Norsemen produced a culture. But was it civilization? . . . Civilization means something more than energy and will and creative power: something the early Norsemen hadn't got, but which, even in their time, was beginning to reappear in Western Europe. How can I define it? Well, very shortly, a sense of permanence. The wanderers and invaders were in a continual state of flux. They didn't feel the need to look forward beyond the next March or the next voyage or the next battle. And for that reason it didn't occur to them to build stone houses, or to write books.

* * *

The more carefully one reads these views, the more illogical they appear. Indeed, one must wonder why highly educated and intelligent European scholars feel so free to dismiss the Vikings with no more than a passing nod. And why the preoccupation with the semantic question of whether the Vikings had a "civilization"? The situation is explicable only if one recognizes a long-standing European bias, springing from traditional views of European prehistory.

Every Western schoolchild is dutifully taught that the Near East is "the cradle of civilization," and that the first civilizations arose in Egypt and Mesopotamia, nourished by the Nile and the Tigris-Euphrates river basins. From here civilization spread to Crete and Greece, and then to Rome, and eventually to the barbarians of northern Europe.

What these barbarians were doing while they waited for the arrival of civilization was not known; nor was the question often raised. The emphasis lay on the process of dissemination, which the late Gordon Childe summarized as "the irradiation of European barbarism by Oriental civilization." Modern scholars held this view, as did Roman and Greek scholars before them. Geoffrey Bibby says: "The history of northern and eastern Europe is viewed from the West and South, with all the preconceptions of men who considered themselves civilized looking upon men whom they considered barbarians."

From this standpoint, the Scandinavians are obviously the farthest from the source of civilization, and logically the last to acquire it; and therefore they are properly regarded as the last of the barbarians, a nagging thorn in the side of those other European areas trying to absorb the wisdom and civilization of the East.

The trouble is that this traditional view of European prehistory has been largely destroyed in the last fifteen years. The development of accurate carbon-dating techniques has made a mess of the old chronology, which supported the old views of diffusion. It now appears indisputable that Europeans were erecting huge megalithic tombs before the Egyptians built the pyramids; Stonehenge is older than the civilization of Mycenaean Greece; metallurgy in Europe may well precede the development of metalworking skills in Greece and Troy.

The meaning of these discoveries has not yet been sorted out, but it is certainly now impossible to regard the prehistoric Europeans as savages idly awaiting the blessings of Eastern civilization. On the contrary, the Europeans seem to have had organizational skills considerable enough to work massive stones, and they seem also to have had impressive astronomical knowledge to build Stonehenge, the first observatory in the world.

Thus, the European bias toward the civilized East must be called into question, and indeed the very concept of "European barbarism" requires a fresh look. With this in mind, those barbaric remnants, the Vikings, take on a new significance, and we can reexamine what is known of the Scandinavians of the tenth century.

First we should recognize that "the Vikings" were never a clearly unified group. What the Europeans saw were scattered and individual parties of seafarers who came from a vast geographical area—Scandinavia is larger than Portugal, Spain, and France combined—and who sailed from their individual feudal states for the purpose of trade or piracy or both; the Vikings made little distinction. But that is a tendency shared by many seafarers from the Greeks to the Elizabethans.

In fact, for a people who lacked civilization, who "didn't feel the need to look . . . beyond the next battle," the Vikings demonstrate remarkably sustained and purposeful behavior. As proof of widespread trading, Arabic coins appear in Scandinavia as early as A.D. 692. During the next four hundred years, the Viking trader-pirates expanded as far west as Newfoundland, as far south as Sicily and Greece (where they left carvings on the lions of Delos), and as far east as the Ural Mountains of Russia, where their traders linked up with caravans arriving from the silk route to China. The Vikings were not empire builders, and it is popular to say that their influence across this vast area was impermanent. Yet it was sufficiently permanent to lend placenames to many localities in England, while to Russia they gave the very name of the nation itself, from the Norse tribe Rus. As for the more subtle influence of their pagan vigor, relentless energy, and system of values, the manuscript of Ibn Fadlan shows us how many typically Norse attitudes have been retained to the present day. Indeed, there is something strikingly familiar to the modern sensibility about the Viking way of life, and something profoundly appealing.

ABOUT THE AUTHOR

A word should be said about Ibn Fadlan, the man who speaks to us with such a distinctive voice despite the passage of more than a thousand years and the filter of transcribers and translators from a dozen linguistic and cultural traditions.

We know almost nothing of him personally. Apparently he was educated and, from his exploits, he could not have been very old. He states explicitly that he was a familiar of the Caliph, whom he did not particularly admire. (In this he was not alone, for the Caliph al-Muqtadir was twice deposed and finally slain by one of his own officers.)

Of his society, we know more. In the tenth century, Bagdad, the City of Peace, was the most civilized city on earth. More than a million inhabitants lived within its famous circular walls. Bagdad was the focus of intellectual and commercial excitement, within an environment of extraordinary grace, elegance, and splendor. There were perfumed gardens, cool shady arbors, and the accumulated riches of a vast empire.

The Arabs of Bagdad were Muslim and fiercely dedicated to that religion. But they were also exposed to peoples who looked, acted, and believed differently from them. The Arabs were, in fact, the least provincial people in the world of that time, and this made them superb observers of foreign cultures.

Ibn Fadlan himself is clearly an intelligent and observant man. He is interested in both the everyday details of life and the beliefs of the people he meets. Much that he witnessed struck him as vulgar, obscene, and barbaric, but he wastes little time in indignation; once he expresses his disapproval, he goes right back to his unblinking observations. And he reports what he sees with remarkably little condescension.

His manner of reporting may seem eccentric to Western sensibilities; he does not tell a story as we are accustomed to hearing one. We tend to forget that our own sense of drama originates in an oral tradition—a live performance by a bard before an audience that must often have been restless and impatient, or else sleepy after a heavy meal. Our oldest stories, the *Iliad, Beowulf,* the *Song of Roland,* were all intended to be sung by singers whose chief function and first obligation was entertainment.

But Ibn Fadlan was a writer, and his principal aim was not entertainment. Nor was it to glorify some listening patron, or to reinforce the myths of the society in which he lived. On the contrary, he was an ambassador delivering a report; his tone is that of a tax auditor, not a bard; an anthropologist, not a dramatist. Indeed, he often slights the most exciting elements of his narrative rather than let them interfere with his clear and level-headed account.

At times this dispassion is so irritating we fail to recognize how extraordinary a spectator he really is. For hundreds of years after Ibn Fadlan, the tradition among travelers was to write wildly speculative, fanciful chronicles of foreign marvels—talking animals, feathered men who flew, encounters with behemoths and unicorns. As recently as two hundred years ago, otherwise sober Europeans were filling their journals with nonsense about African baboons that waged war with farmers, and so on.

Ibn Fadlan never speculates. Every word rings true, and whenever he reports by hearsay, he is careful to say so. He is equally careful to specify when he is an eyewitness: that is why he uses the phrase "I saw with my own eyes" over and over.

In the end, it is this quality of absolute truthfulness which makes his tale so horrifying. For his encounter with the monsters of the mist, the "eaters of the dead," is told with the same attention to detail, the same careful skepticism, that marks the other portions of the manuscript.

In any case, the reader may judge for himself.

THE DEPARTURE FROM
THE CITY OF PEACE

Praise be to God, the Merciful, the Compassionate, the Lord of the Two Worlds, and blessing and peace upon the Prince of Prophets, our Lord and Master Muhammad, whom God bless and preserve with abiding and continuing peace and blessings until the Day of the Faith!

This is the book of Ahmad ibn-Fadlan, ibn-al-Abbas, ibn-Rasid, ibn-Hammad, a client of Muhammad ibn-Sulayman, the ambassador from al-Muqtadir to the King of the Saqaliba, in which he recounts what he saw in the land of the Turks, the Hazars, the Saqaliba, the Baskirs, the Rus, and the Northmen, of the histories of their kings and the way they act in many affairs of their life.

The letter of the Yiltawar, King of the Saqaliba, reached the Commander of the Faithful, al-Muqtadir. He asked him therein to send someone who would instruct him in religion and make him acquainted with the laws of Islam; who would build for him a mosque and erect for him a pulpit from which might be carried out the mission of converting his people in all the districts of his kingdom; and also for advice in the construction of fortifications and defense works. And he prayed the Caliph to do these things. The intermediary in this matter was Dadir al-Hurami.

The Commander of the Faithful, al-Muqtadir, as many know, was not a strong and just caliph, but drawn to pleasures and the flattering speeches of his officers, who played him the fool and jested mightily behind his back. I was not of this company, or especially beloved of the Caliph, for the reason that follows.

In the City of Peace lived an elderly merchant of the name ibn-Qarin, rich in all things but lacking a generous heart and a love of man. He hoarded his gold and likewise his young wife, whom none had ever seen but all bespoke as beautiful beyond imagining. On a certain day, the Caliph sent me to deliver to ibn-Qarin a message, and I presented myself to the house of the merchant and sought entrance therein with my letter and seal. Until today, I do not know the import of the letter, but it does not matter.

The merchant was not at home, being abroad on some business; I explained to the door servant that I must await his return, since the Caliph had instructed I must deliver the message into his hands from mine only. Thus the door servant admitted me into the house, which procedure took some passing of time, for the door to the house had many bolts, locks, bars, and fasteners, as is common in the dwellings of misers. At length I was admitted and I waited all day, growing hungry and thirsty, but was offered no refreshments by the servants of the niggardly merchant.

In the heat of the afternoon, when all about me the house was still and the servants slept, I, too, felt drowsy. Then before me I saw an apparition in white, a woman young and beautiful, whom I took to be the very wife no man had ever seen. She did not speak, but with gestures led me to another room, and there locked the door. I enjoyed her upon the spot, in which matter she required no encouragement, for her husband was old and no doubt neglectful. Thus did the afternoon pass quickly, until we heard the master of the house making his return. Immediately the wife arose and departed, having never uttered a word in my presence, and I was left to arrange my garments in some haste.

Now I should have been apprehended for certain were it not for these same many locks and bolts which impeded the miser's entry into his own home. Even so, the merchant ibn-Qarin found me in the adjoining room, and he viewed me with suspicion, asking why I should be there and not in the courtyard, where it was proper for a messenger to wait. I replied that I was famished and faint, and had searched for food and shade. This was a poor lie and he did not believe it; he complained to the Caliph, who I know was amused in private and yet compelled to adopt a stern face to the public. Thus when the ruler of the Saqaliba asked for a mission from the Caliph, this same spiteful ibn-Qarin urged I be sent, and so I was.

In our company there was the ambassador of the King of Saqaliba who was called Abdallah ibn-Bastu al-Hazari, a tedious and windy man who talked overmuch. There was also Takin al-Turki, Bars al-Saqlabi, both guides on the journey, and I, too. We bore gifts for the ruler, for his wife, his children, and his generals. Also we brought certain drugs, which were given over to the care of Sausan al-Rasi. This was our party.

So we started on Thursday, the 11th of Safar of the year 309 [June 21, 921], from the City of Peace [Bagdad]. We stopped a day in Nahrawan, and from there went swiftly until we reached al-Daskara, where we stopped for three days. Then we traveled straight onward without any detours until we reached Hulwan. There we stayed two days. From there we went to Qirmisin, where we remained two days. Then we started and traveled until we reached Hamadan, where we remained three days. Then we went farther to Sawa, where we remained two days. From there we came to Ray, where we remained eleven days waiting for Ahmad ibn-Ali, the brother of al-Rasi, because he was in Huwar al-Ray. Then we went to Huwar al-Ray and remained there three days.

This passage gives the flavor of Ibn Fadlan's descriptions of travel. Perhaps a quarter of the entire manuscript is written in this fashion, simply listing the names of settlements and the number of days spent at each. Most of this material has been deleted.

Apparently, Ibn Fadlan's party is traveling northward, and eventually they are required to halt for winter.

Our stay in Gurganiya was lengthy; we stayed there some days of the month of Ragab [November] and during the whole of Saban, Ramadan, and Sawwal. Our long stay was brought about by the cold and its bitterness. Verily, they told me that two men took camels into the forests to get wood. They forgot, however, to take flint and tinder with them, and hence slept in the night without a fire. When they got up the next morning, they found the camels had been frozen stiff from the cold.

Verily, I beheld the marketplace and streets of Gurganiya completely deserted because of the cold. One could stroll the streets without meeting anyone. Once as I came out of my bath, I entered my house and looked at my beard, which was a lump of ice. I had to thaw it out before the fire. I lived night and day in a house that was inside another house, in which a Turkish felt tent was pitched, and I myself was wrapped up in many clothes and fur rugs. But in spite of all this, my cheeks often stuck to the pillow at night.

In this extremity of cold, I saw that the earth sometimes forms great cracks, and a large and ancient tree may split into two halves from this.

About the middle of Sawwal of the year 309 [February, 922], the weather began to change, the river thawed, and we got ourselves the necessary things for the journey. We bought Turkish camels and skin boats made out of camel hides, in preparation for the rivers we would have to cross in the land of Turks.

We laid in a supply of bread, millet, and salted meat for three months. Our acquaintances in the town directed us in laying in garments, as much as was needed. They depicted the coming hardships in fearful terms, and we believed they exaggerated the story, yet when we underwent this, it was far greater than what had been told to us.

Each of us put on a jacket, over that a coat, over that a tulup, over that a burka, and a helmet of felt out of which only the two eyes could look. We also had a simple pair of underdrawers with trousers over them, and house shoes and over these another pair of boots. When one of us got on a camel, he could not move because of his clothes.

The doctor of the law and the teacher and the pages who traveled with us from Bagdad departed from us now, fearing to enter this new country, so I, the ambassador, his brother-in-law and two pages, Takin and Bars, proceeded.*

The caravan was ready to start. We took into our service a guide from the inhabitants of the town whose name was Qlawus. Then, trusting in the all-powerful and exalted God, we started on Monday, the third of Dulqada of the year 309 [March 3, 922] from the town Gurganiya.

That same day, we stopped at the burg called Zamgan: that is, the gateway to the Turks. The next morning early, we proceeded to Git. There so much snow fell that the camels plunged in it up to their knees; hence we halted two days.

Then we sped straight into the land of the Turks without meeting anyone on the barren and even steppe. We rode ten days in bitter cold and unbroken snowstorms, in comparison with which the cold in Chwarezm seemed like a summer day, so that we forgot all our previous discomforts and were about at the point of giving up.

One day when we underwent the most savage cold weather, Takin the page was riding next to me, and along with him one of the Turks, who was talking to him in Turkish. Takin laughed and said to me, "This Turk says, 'What will our Lord have of us? He is killing us with cold. If we knew what he wanted, we would let him have it.' "

And then I said, "Tell him He only wishes that you say, 'There is no God save Allah.' "

The Turk laughed and answered, "If I knew it, I would say it."

Then we came to a forest where there was a large quantity of dry wood and we halted. The caravan lit fires, we warmed ourselves, took off our clothes, and spread them out to dry.

[Apparently, Ibn Fadlan's party was entering a warmer region, because he makes no further reference to extreme cold.]

We set out again and rode every day from midnight until the time of the afternoon prayer—hastening more from midday on—and then we halted. When we had ridden fifteen nights in this manner, we arrived at a large mountain with many great rocks. There are springs there that jet out from the rocks and the water stays in pools. From this place, we crossed on until we reached a Turkish tribe, which is called the Oguz.

*Throughout the manuscript, Ibn Fadlan is inexact about the size and composition of his party. Whether this apparent carelessness reflects his assumption that the reader knows the composition of the caravan, or whether it is a consequence of lost passages of the text, one cannot be sure. Social conventions may also be a factor, for Ibn Fadlan never states that his party is greater than a few individuals, when in fact it probably numbered a hundred people or more, and twice as many horses and camels. But Ibn Fadlan does not count—literally—slaves, servants, and lesser members of the caravan.

THE WAYS OF
THE OGUZ TURKS

The Oguz are nomads and have houses of felt. They stay for a time in one place and then travel on. Their dwellings are placed here and there according to nomadic custom. Although they lead a hard existence, they are like asses gone astray. They have no religious bonds with God. They never pray, but instead call their headmen Lords. When one of them takes counsel with his chief about something, he says, "O Lord, what shall I do in this or that matter?"

Their undertakings are based upon counsel solely among themselves. I have heard them say, "There is no God but Allah and Muhammad is the prophet of Allah," but they speak thus so as to get close to any Muslims, and not because they believe it.

The ruler of the Oguz Turks is called Yabgu. That is the name of the ruler and everyone who rules over this tribe bears the name. His subordinate is always called Kudarkin and so each subordinate to a chieftain is called Kudarkin.

The Oguz do not wash themselves after either defecation or urination, nor do they bathe after ejaculation, or on other occasions. They have nothing whatever to do with water, especially in winter. No merchants or other Muhammadans may perform ablution in their presence except in the night when the Turks do not see it, for they get angry and say, "This man wishes to put a spell on us, for he is immersing himself in water," and they compel him to pay a fine.

None of the Muhammadans can enter Turkish country until one of the Oguz agrees to become his host, with whom he stays and for whom he brings garments from the land of Islam, and for his wife some pepper, millet, raisins, and nuts. When the Muslim comes to his host, the latter pitches a tent for him and brings him sheep, so that the Muslim may himself slaughter the sheep. The Turks never slaughter; they beat the sheep on the head until it is dead.

Oguz women never veil themselves in the presence of their own men or others. Nor does the woman cover any of her bodily parts in the presence of any person. One day we stopped off with a Turk and were seated in his tent. The man's wife was present. As we conversed, the woman uncovered her pudendum and scratched it, and we saw her doing so. We veiled our faces and said, "I beg God's pardon." At this her husband laughed and said to the interpreter, "Tell them we uncover it in your presence so that you may see it and be abashed, but it is not to be attained. This is better than when you cover it up and yet it is attainable."

Adultery is unknown among them. Whomsoever they find to be an adulterer, they tear him in two. This comes about so: they bring together the branches of two trees, tie him to the branches, and then let both trees go so the man who was tied to the trees is torn in two.

The custom of pederasty is counted by the Turks a terrible sin. There once came a merchant to stay with the clan of the Kudarkin. This merchant stayed with his host for a time to buy sheep. Now, the host had a beardless son, and the guest sought unceasingly to lead him astray until he got the boy to consent to his will. In the meantime, the Turkish host entered and caught them in *flagrante delicto*.

The Turks wished to kill the merchant and also the son for this offense. But after much pleading the merchant was permitted to ransom himself. He paid his host with four hundred sheep for what he had done to his son, and then the merchant hastily departed from the land of the Turks.

All the Turks pluck their beards with the exception of their mustaches.

Their marriage customs are as follows: one of them asks for the hand of a female member of another's family, against such and such a marriage price. The marriage price often consists of camels, pack animals, and other things. No one can take a wife until he has fulfilled the obligation, on which he has come to an understanding with the men of the family. If, however, he has met it, then he comes without any ado, enters the abode where she is, takes her in the presence of her father, mother, and brothers, and they do not prevent him.

If a man dies who has a wife and children, then the eldest of his sons takes her to wife if she is not his mother.

If one of the Turks becomes sick and has slaves, they look after him and no one of his family comes near him. A tent is pitched for him apart from the houses and he does not depart from it until he dies or gets well. If, however, he is a slave or a poor man, they leave him in the desert and go on their way.

When one of their prominent men dies, they dig for him a great pit in the form of a house and they go to him, dress him in a *qurtaq* with his belt and bow, and put a drinking cup of wood with intoxicating drink in his hand. They take his entire possessions and put them in this house. Then they set him down in it also. Then they build another house over him and make a kind of cupola out of mud.

Then they kill his horses. They kill one or two hundred, as many as he has, at the site of the grave. Then they eat the flesh down to the head, the hooves, the hide, and the tail, for they hang these up on wooden poles and say, "These are his steeds on which he rides to Paradise."

If he has been a hero and slain enemies, they carve wooden statues in the number of those whom he has slain, place them upon his grave, and say, "These are his pages who serve him in Paradise."

Sometimes they delay killing the horses for a day or two, and then an old man from among their elderly ones stirs them up by saying, "I have seen the dead man in my sleep and he said to me: 'Here thou seest me. My comrades have overtaken me and my feet were too weak to follow them. I cannot overtake them and so have remained alone.'" In this case, the people slaughter his steeds and hang them up on his grave. After a day or two, the same elder comes to them and says, "I have seen the dead man in a dream and he said: 'Inform my family that I have recovered from my plight.'"

In this way the old man preserves the ways of the Oguz, for there might otherwise be a desire for the living to retain the horses of the dead.*

At length we traveled on in the Turkish kingdom. One morning one of the Turks met us. He was ugly in figure, dirty in appearance, despicable in manner, and base in nature. He said: "Halt." The whole caravan halted in obedience to his command. Then he said, "No single one of you may proceed." We said to him, "We are friends of the Kudarkin." He began to laugh and said, "Who is the Kudarkin? I defecate on his beard."

No man among us knew what to do at these words, but then the Turk said, *"Bekend"*; that is, "bread" in the language of Chwarezm. I gave him a few sheets of bread. He took them and said, "You may go further. I take pity upon you."

We came to the district of the army commander whose name was Etrek ibn-al-Qatagan. He pitched Turkish tents for us and had us stay in them. He himself had a large establishment, servants and large dwellings. He drove in sheep for us that we might slaughter them, and put horses at our disposal for riding. The Turks speak of him as their best horseman, and in truth I saw one day, when he raced with us on his horse and as a goose flew over us, he strung his bow and then, guiding his horse under it, shot at the goose and brought it down.

I presented to him a suit from Merv, a pair of boots of red leather, a coat of brocade, and five coats of silk. He accepted these with glowing words of praise. He removed the brocade coat that he wore in order to don the garments of honor I had just given him. Then I saw that the *qurtaq* which he had underneath was fraying apart and filthy, but it is their custom that no one shall remove the garment that he wears next to his body until it disintegrates. Verily also he plucked out his entire beard and even his mustache, so that he looked like a eunuch. And yet, as I have observed, he was their best horseman.

*Farzan, an unabashed admirer of Ibn Fadlan, believes that this paragraph reveals "the sensibility of a modern anthropologist, recording not only the customs of a people, but the mechanisms which act to enforce those customs. The economic meaning of killing a nomad leader's horses is the approximate equivalent of modern death-taxes; that is, it tends to retard the accumulation of inherited wealth in a family. Although demanded by religion, this could not have been a popular practice, any more than it is during the present day. Ibn Fadlan most astutely demonstrates the way it is imposed upon the reluctant."

I believed that these fine gifts should win his friendship to us, but such was not to be. He was a treacherous man.

One day he sent for the leaders close to him; that is, Tarhan, Yanal, and Glyz. Tarhan was the most influential among them; he was crippled and blind and had a maimed hand. Then he said to them: "These are the messengers of the King of the Arabs to the chief of the Bulgars, and I should not let them pass without taking counsel with you."

Then Tarhan spoke: "This is a matter that we have never yet seen. Never has the ambassador of the Sultan traveled through our country since we and our ancestors have been here. My feeling is that the Sultan is playing us a trick. These men he really sent to the Hazars to stir them up against us. The best is to hew these ambassadors in twain and we shall take all they have."

Another counselor said: "No, we should rather take what they have and leave them naked so that they may return thither whence they came."

And another said: "No, we have captives with the King of the Hazars, so we ought to send these men to ransom them."

They kept discussing these matters among themselves for seven days, while we were in a situation similar to death, until they agreed to open the road and let us pass. We gave to Tarhan as a garment of honor two caftans from Merv and also pepper, millet, and some sheets of bread.

And we traveled forth until we came to the river Bagindi. There we took our skin boats which had been made from camel hides, spread them out, and loaded the goods from the Turkish camels. When each boat was full, a group of five, six, or four men sat in them. They took birchwood branches in their hands and used them like oars and kept on rowing while the water carried the boat down and spun it around. Finally we got across. With regard to the horses and camels, they came swimming across.

It is absolutely necessary when crossing a river that first of all a group of warriors with weapons should be transported across before any of the caravan, in order that a vanguard be established to prevent attack by Baskirs while the main body is crossing the river.

Thus we crossed the river Bagindi, and then the river called Gam, in the same way. Then the Odil, then the Adrn, then the Wars, then the Ahti, then the Wbna. All these are big rivers.

Then we arrived at the Pecenegs. These had encamped by a still lake like the sea. They are dark brown, powerful people and the men shave their beards. They are poor in contrast to the Oguz, for I saw men among the Oguz who possessed 10,000 horses and 100,000 sheep. But the Pecenegs are poor, and we remained only a day with them.

Then we started out and came to the river Gayih. This is the largest, widest, swiftest that we saw. Verily I saw how a skin boat overturned in it, and those on it were drowned. Many of the company perished and a number of the camels and horses were drowned. We crossed the river with difficulty. Then we went a few days farther on and crossed the river Gaha, then the river Azhn, then the

Bagag, then the Smur, then the Knal, then the Suh, and then the river Kiglu. At length we arrived in the land of the Baskirs.

> The Yakut manuscript contains a short description of Ibn Fadlan's stay among the Baskirs; many scholars question the authenticity of these passages. The actual descriptions are unusually vague and tedious, consisting chiefly of lists of the chiefs and nobles encountered. Ibn Fadlan himself suggests the Baskirs are not worth bothering with, an uncharacteristic statement from this relentlessly curious traveler.

At length we left the land of the Baskirs, and crossed the river Germsan, the river Urn, the river Urm, then the river Wtig, the river Nbasnh, then the river Gawsin. Between the rivers that we mention, the distance is a journey of two, three, or four days in each case.

Then we came to the land of the Bulgars, which begins at the shore of the river Volga.

FIRST CONTACT WITH THE NORTHMEN

I saw with my own eyes how the Northmen* had arrived with their wares, and pitched their camp along the Volga. Never did I see a people so gigantic: they are tall as palm trees, and florid and ruddy in complexion. They wear neither camisoles nor caftans, but the men among them wear a garment of rough cloth, which is thrown over one side, so that one hand remains free.

Every Northman carries an axe, a dagger, and a sword, and without these weapons they are never seen. Their swords are broad, with wavy lines, and of Frankish make. From the tip of the fingernails to the neck, each man of them is tattooed with pictures of trees, living beings, and other things.

The women carry, fastened to their breast, a little case of iron, copper, silver, or gold, according to the wealth and resources of their husbands. Fastened to the case they wear a ring, and upon that a dagger, all attached to their breast. About their necks they wear gold and silver chains.

They are the filthiest race that God ever created. They do not wipe themselves after going to stool, or wash themselves after a nocturnal pollution, anymore than if they were wild asses.

They come from their own country, anchor their ships in the Volga, which is a great river, and build large wooden houses on its banks. In every such house there live ten or twenty, more or fewer. Each man has a couch, where he sits with the beautiful girls he has for sale. He is as likely as not to enjoy one of them while a friend looks on. At times several of them will be thus engaged at the same moment, each in full view of the others.

Now and again, a merchant will resort to a house to purchase a girl, and find her master thus embracing her, and not giving over until he has fully had his will; in this there is thought nothing remarkable.

Every morning a slave girl comes and brings a tub of water and places it before her master. He proceeds to wash his face and hands, and then his hair,

*Actually, Ibn Fadlan's word for them here was "Rus," the name of this particular tribe of Northmen. In the text, he sometimes calls the Scandinavians by their particular tribal name, and sometimes he calls them "Varangians" as a generic term. Historians now reserve the term Varangian for the Scandinavian mercenaries employed by the Byzantine Empire. To avoid confusion, in this translation the terms "Northmen" and "Norsemen" are everywhere employed.

combing it over the vessel. Thereupon he blows his nose, and spits into the tub, and, leaving no dirt behind, conveys it all into this water. When he has finished, the girl carries the tub to the man next to him, who does the same. Thus she continues carrying the tub from one to another, till each of those who are in the house has blown his nose and spit into the tub, and washed his face and hair.

This is the normal way of things among the Northmen, as I have seen with my own eyes. Yet at the period of our arrival among them, there was some discontent among the giant people, the nature of which was thus:

Their principal chieftain, a man of the name Wyglif, had fallen ill, and was set up in a sick-tent at a distance from the camp, with bread and water. No one approached or spoke to him, or visited him the whole time. No slaves nurtured him, for the Northmen believe that a man must recover from any sickness according to his own strength. Many among them believed that Wyglif would never return to join them in the camp, but instead would die.

Now, one of their number, a young noble called Buliwyf, was chosen to be their new leader, but he was not accepted while the sick chieftain still lived. This was the cause of uneasiness, at the time of our arrival. Yet also there was no aspect of sorrow or weeping among the people encamped on the Volga.

The Northmen place great importance on the duty of the host. They greet every visitor with warmth and hospitality, much food and clothing, and the earls and nobles compete for the honor of the greatest hospitality. The party of our caravan was brought before Buliwyf and a great feast was given us. Over this Buliwyf himself presided, and I saw him to be a tall man, and strong, with skin and hair and beard of pure white. He had the bearing of a leader.

Recognizing the honor of the feast, our party made a show of eating, yet the food was vile and the manner of the feast contained much throwing of food and drink, and great laughing and merriment. It was common in the middle of this rude banquet for an earl to disport with a slave girl in full view of his fellows.

Seeing this, I turned away and said, "I beg God's pardon," and the Northmen laughed much at my discomfiture. One of their number translated for me that they believe God looks favorably upon such open pleasures. He said to me, "You Arabs are like old women, you tremble at the sight of life."

I said in answer, "I am a guest among you, and Allah shall lead me to righteousness."

This was reason for further laughter, but I do not know for what cause they should find a joke.

The custom of the Northmen reveres the life of war. Verily, these huge men fight continually; they are never at peace, neither among themselves nor among different tribes of their kind. They sing songs of their warfare and bravery, and believe that the death of a warrior is the highest honor.

At the banquet of Buliwyf, a member of their kind sang a song of bravery and battle that was much enjoyed, though little attended. The strong drink of the Northmen soon renders them as animals and stray asses; in the midst of the song there was ejaculation and also mortal combat over some intoxicated quarrel of two warriors. The bard did not cease his song through all these events; verily I saw flying blood spatter his face, and yet he wiped it away without a pause in his singing.

This impressed me greatly.

Now it happened that this Buliwyf, who was drunk as the rest, commanded that I should sing a song for them. He was most insistent. Not wishing to anger him, I recited from the Koran, with the translator repeating my words in their Norse tongue. I was received no better than their own minstrel, and afterward I asked the forgiveness of Allah for the treatment of His holy words, and also for the translation,* which I sensed to be thoughtless, for in truth the translator was himself drunk.

We had stayed two days among the Northmen, and on the morning we planned to leave, we were told by the translator that the chieftain Wyglif had died. I sought to witness what then befell.

First, they laid him in his grave, over which a roof was erected, for the space of ten days,† until they had completed the cutting and sewing of his clothes. They also brought together his goods, and divided them into three parts. The first of these is for his family; the second is expended for the garments they make; and with the third they purchase strong drink, against the day when a girl resigns herself to death, and is burned with her master.

To the use of wine they abandon themselves in mad fashion, drinking it day and night, as I have already said. Not seldom does one die with a cup in his hand.

The family of Wyglif asked of all his girls and pages, "Which of you will die with him?" Then one of them answered, "I." From the time she uttered that word, she was no longer free; should she wish to draw back, she is not permitted.

The girl who so spoke was then committed to two other girls, who were to

---

*Arabs have always been uneasy about translating the Koran. The earliest sheiks held that the holy book could not be translated, an injunction apparently based on religious considerations. But everyone who has attempted a translation agrees for the most secular reasons: Arabic is by nature a succinct language, and the Koran is composed as poetry and therefore even more concentrated. The difficulties of conveying literal meaning—to say nothing of the grace and elegance of the original Arabic—have led translators to preface their work with prolonged and abject apologies.

At the same time, Islam is an active, expansive way of thought, and the tenth century was one of its peak periods of dissemination. This expansion inevitably necessitated translations for the use of new converts, and translations were made, but never happily from the standpoint of the Arabs.

†This alone was startling to an Arab observer from a warm climate. Muslim practice called for quick burial, often the same day as the death, after a short ceremony of ritual washing and prayer.

keep watch over her, accompany her wherever she went, and even, on occasion, wash her feet. The people occupied themselves with the dead man—cutting out the clothes for him, and preparing whatever else was needful. During the whole of this period, the girl gave herself over to drinking and singing, and was cheerful and gay.

During this time, Buliwyf, the noble who would next be king or chieftain, found a rival whose name was Thorkel. Him I did not know, but he was ugly and foul, a dark man among this ruddy fair race. He plotted to be chieftain himself. All this I learned from the translator, for there was no outward sign in the funeral preparations that anything was not according to custom.

Buliwyf himself did not direct the preparations, for he was not of the family of Wyglif, and it is the rule that the family prepares for the funeral. Buliwyf joined the general merriment and celebration, and acted no part of kingly conduct, except during the banquets of the night, when he sat in the high seat that was reserved to the king.

This was the manner of his sitting: when a Northman is truly king, he sits at the head of the table in a large stone chair with stone arms. Such was the chair of Wyglif, but Buliwyf did not sit in it as a normal man would sit. Instead he sat upon one arm, a position from which he fell when he drank overmuch, or laughed with great excess. It was the custom that he could not sit in the chair until Wyglif was buried.

All this time, Thorkel plotted and conferred among the other earls. I came to know that I was suspected as some sorcerer or witch, which distressed me much. The translator, who did not believe these tales, told me that Thorkel said I had caused Wyglif to die, and had caused Buliwyf to be the next chief; yet verily I had no part in any of this.

After some days, I sought to leave with my party of ibn-Bastu and Takin and Bars, and yet the Northmen would not permit us to leave, saying that we must stay to the funeral, and threatening us with their daggers, which they always carried. Thus we stayed.

When the day was come that Wyglif and the girl were to be committed to the flames, his ship was drawn ashore on the banks of the river. Four corner blocks of birch and other woods had been positioned around it; also large wooden figures in the semblance of human beings.

In the meantime the people began to walk to and fro, uttering words that I did not understand. The language of the Northmen is ugly to the ear and difficult to comprehend. The dead chief, meanwhile, lay at a distance in his grave, from which they had yet removed him. Next they brought a couch, placed it in the ship, and covered it with Greek cloth of gold, and pillows of the same material. There then came an old crone, whom they call the angel of death, and she spread the personal articles on the couch. It was she who attended to the sewing of the garments, and to all the equipment. It was she, also, who was to slay the girl. I saw the crone with my own eyes. She was dark, thickset, with a lowering countenance.

When they came to the grave, they removed the roof and drew out the dead man. Then I saw that he had turned quite black, by reason of the coldness of that country. Near him in the grave they had placed strong drink, fruits, and a lute; and these they now took out. Except for his color, the dead man Wyglif had not changed.

Now I saw Buliwyf and Thorkel standing side by side, making a great show of friendship during the burial ceremony, and yet it was apparent that there was no truth to their appearances.

The dead king Wyglif was now clothed in drawers, leggings, boots, and a caftan of gold cloth, and on his head was placed a cap made of gold cloth, trimmed in sable. Then he was carried to a tent in the ship; they seated him on a quilted couch, supported him with pillows, and brought strong drink, fruits, and basil, which they placed alongside him.

Then they brought a dog, which they cut in two, and threw into the ship. They laid all his weapons beside him, and led up two horses, which they chased until they were dripping with sweat, whereupon Buliwyf killed one with his sword and Thorkel killed the second, cutting them into pieces with their swords and flinging the pieces forth into the ship. Buliwyf killed his horse less swiftly, which seemed to have some import to those who watched, but I did not know the meaning.

Two oxen were then brought forward, cut into pieces, and flung into the ship. Finally they brought a cock and a hen, killed them, and threw them in also.

The girl who had devoted herself to death meanwhile walked to and fro, entering one after another of the tents that they had there. The occupant of each tent lay with her, saying, "Tell your master I did this only for love of him."

Now it was late in the afternoon. They led the girl to an object they had constructed, which looked like the frame of a door. She placed her feet on the extended hands of the men, who raised her above her framework. She uttered something in her language, whereupon they let her down. Then again they raised her, and she did as before. Once more they let her down, and then lifted her a third time. Then they handed her a hen, whose head she cut off and threw away.

I inquired of the interpreter what it was she had done. He replied: "The first time she said, 'Lo, I see here my father and mother'; the second time, 'Lo, now I see all my deceased relatives sitting'; the third time, 'Lo, there is my master, who is sitting in Paradise. Paradise is so beautiful, so green. With him are his men and boys. He calls me, so bring me to him.' "

Then they led her away to the ship. Here she took off her two bracelets and gave them to the old woman who was called the angel of death, and she was to murder her. She also drew off her two anklets, and passed them to the two serving maids, who were the daughters of the angel of death. Then they lifted her into the ship, but did not yet admit her to the tent.

Now men came up with shields and staves, and handed her a cup of strong drink. This she took, sang over it, and emptied it. The interpreter told me she said, "With this, I take leave of those who are dear to me." Then another cup was handed to her, which she also took, and began a lengthy song. The crone admonished her to drain the cup without lingering, and to enter the tent where her master lay.

By this time, it seemed to me the girl had become dazed.* She made as though she would enter the tent, when suddenly the hag seized her by the head and dragged her in. At this moment the men began to beat upon their shields with the staves, in order to drown the noise of her outcries, which might have terrified the other girls and deterred them from seeking death with their masters in the future.

Six men followed her into the tent, and each and every one of them had carnal companionship with her. Then they laid her down by her master's side, while two of the men seized her feet, and two the hands. The old woman known as the angel of death now knotted a rope around her neck, and handed the ends to two of the men to pull. Then, with a broad-bladed dagger, she smote her between the ribs, and drew the blade forth, while the two men strangled her with the rope till she died.

The kin of the dead Wyglif now drew near and, taking a piece of lighted wood, walked backward naked toward the ship and ignited the ship without ever looking at it. The funeral pyre was soon aflame, and the ship, the tent, the man and the girl, and everything else blew up in a blazing storm of fire.

At my side, one of the Northmen made some comment to the interpreter. I asked the interpreter what was said, and received this answer. "You Arabs," he said, "must be a stupid lot. You take your most beloved and revered man and cast him into the ground to be devoured by creeping things and worms. We, on the other hand, burn him in a twinkling, so that instantly, without a moment's delay, he enters into Paradise."

And in truth, before an hour had passed, ship, wood, and girl had, with the man, turned to ashes.

*Or, possibly, "crazed." The Latin manuscripts read *cerritus,* but the Arabic of Yakut says ر ـــ , "dazed" or "dazzled."

THE AFTERMATH OF THE NORTHMEN'S FUNERAL

These Scandinavians find no cause for grief in any man's death. A poor man or a slave is a matter of indifference to them, and even a chieftain will provoke no sadness or tears. On the same evening of the funeral of the chief called Wyglif, there was a great feasting in the halls of the Northmen encampment.

Yet I perceived that all was not fitting among these barbarians. I sought counsel with my interpreter. He responded thusly: "It is the plan of Thorkel to see you die, and then to banish Buliwyf. Thorkel has gathered the support of some earls to himself, but there is dispute in every house and every quarter."

Much distressed, I said, "I have no part in this affair. How shall I act?"

The interpreter said I should flee if I could, but if I were caught, this would be proof of my guilt and I would be treated as a thief. A thief is treated in this fashion: the Northmen lead him to a thick tree, fasten a strong rope about him, string him up, and let him hang until he rots to pieces by the action of the wind and the rain.

Remembering also that I had barely escaped death at the hands of ibn-al-Qatagan, I chose to act as I had before; that is, I remained among the Northmen until I should be given free passage to continue on my journey.

I inquired of the interpreter whether I should bear gifts to Buliwyf, and also to Thorkel, to favor my departure. He said that I could not bear gifts to both, and that the matter was undecided who would be the new chieftain. Then he said it would be clear in one day and night, and no longer.

For it is true among these Northmen that they have no established way of choosing a new chief when the old leader dies. Strength of arms counts high, but also allegiances of the warriors and the earls and noblemen. In some cases there is no clear successor to the rule, and this was one of such eventualities. My interpreter said that I should bide my time, and also pray. This I did.

Then there came a great storm on the banks of the river Volga, a storm that persisted two days, with driving rain and forceful winds, and after this storm a cold mist lay on the ground. It was thick and white, and a man could not see past a dozen paces.

Now, these same giant Northmen warriors, who by virtue of their enormity and strength of arms and cruel disposition, have nothing to fear in all the world, yet these men fear the mist or fog that comes with storms.

The men of their race are at some pains to conceal their fear, even one from another; the warriors laugh and joke overmuch, and make unreasonable display of carefree emotion. Thus do they prove the reverse; and in truth, their attempt of disguise is childish, so plainly do they pretend not to see the truth, yet verily, each and all of them, throughout their encampment, are making prayers and sacrifices of hens and cocks, and if a man is asked the reason of the sacrifice, he will say, "I make sacrifice for the safety of my faraway family"; or he will say, "I make sacrifice for the success of my trading"; or he will say, "I make sacrifice in honor of such or another deceased member of my family"; or he will say many another reason, and then he will add, "And also for the lifting of the mist."

Now, I accounted it strange for such strong and warlike people to be so fearful of anything as to pretend a lack of fear; and of all the sensible reasons for fear, mist or fog seemed to my way of thinking very greatly inexplicable.

I said to my interpreter that a man could fear wind, or blasting storms of sand, or water floods, or heaving of the ground, or thunder and lightning within the sky, for all of these could injure a man, or kill him, or ruin his dwelling. Yet I said that fog, or mist, contained no threat of harm; in truth it was the least of any form of changing elements.

The interpreter answered to me that I was lacking the beliefs of a sailor. He said that many Arab sailors agreed with the Northmen, in the matter of uneasiness* within the wrapping of mist; so, also, he said all seafarers are made anxious of any mist or fog, because such a condition increases the peril of travel upon the waters.

I said this was sensible, but that when the mist lay upon the land and not the water, I did not understand the reason for any fear. To this the interpreter replied, "The fog is always feared, whenever it comes." And he said that it made no difference, on land or water, according to the Northman view.

And then he said to me the Northmen did not, truly, much fear the mist. Also the interpreter said that he, as a man, did not fear the mist. He said that it was only a minor matter, of slight consequence. He said, "It is as a minor ache inside a limb joint, which may come with fog, but no more important."

By this I saw that my interpreter, among the others, denied all manner of concern for the fog, and feigned indifference.

Now it happened that the mist did not lift, although it abated and became thin in the afterpart of the day; the sun appeared as a circle in the sky, but also it was so weak that I could look directly to its light.

In this same day there arrived a Northman boat, containing a noble of their own race. He was a young man with a thin beard, and he traveled with only a small party of pages and slaves, and no women among them. Thus I believed he was no trader, for in this area the Northmen principally sell women.

*Interestingly, in both Arabic and Latin, literally "disease."

This same visitor beached his boat, and remained standing with it until nightfall, and no man came near to him, or greeted him, although he was a stranger and in plain sight to all. My interpreter said: "He is a kin of Buliwyf, and will be received at the night banquet."

I said, "Why does he stay at his ship?"

"Because of the mist," answered the interpreter. "It is the custom he must stand in view for many hours, so all can see him and know he is no enemy coming from the mist." This the interpreter said to me with much hesitation.

At the night banquet, I saw the young man come into the hall. Here was he warmly greeted and with much display of surprise; and in this most especially by Buliwyf, who acted as if the young man had just arrived, and had not been standing by his ship many hours. After the several greetings, the youth spoke a passionate speech, which Buliwyf attended with unusual interest: he did not drink and dally with the slave girls, but instead in silence heard the youth, who spoke in a high and cracking voice. At the finish of the tale, the youth seemed about to have tears, and was given a cup of drink.

I inquired of my interpreter what was said. Here was the reply: "He is Wulfgar, and he is the son of Rothgar, a great king in the North. He is kin of Buliwyf and seeks his aid and support on a hero's mission. Wulfgar says the far country suffers a dread and nameless terror, which all the peoples are powerless to oppose, and he asks Buliwyf to make haste to return to the far country and save his people and the kingdom of his father, Rothgar."

I inquired of the interpreter the nature of this terror. He said to me, "It has no name which I can tell."* The interpreter seemed much disturbed by Wulfgar's words, and so also were many of the other Northmen. I saw on the countenance of Buliwyf a dark and gloomy expression. I inquired of the interpreter details of the menace.

The interpreter said to me: "The name cannot be said, for it is forbidden to speak it, lest the utterance of the name call forth the demons." And as he spoke I saw that he was fearful just to think upon these matters, and his pallor was marked, and so I ended my inquiry.

Buliwyf, sitting at the high stone throne, was silent. Verily the assembled earls and vassals and all the slaves and servants were silent, also. No man in the hall spoke. The messenger Wulfgar stood before the company with his

---

*The perils of translation are demonstrated in this sentence. The original Arabic of Yakut reads لا مَعـى كَلِـمَةُ أَنْ أَجْـدَرَ أَتَكَلَّمُ and means literally "There is no name I can speak." The Xymos manuscript employs the Latin verb *dare*, with the meaning "I cannot give it a name," implying that the interpreter does not know the correct word in a non-Norse tongue. The Razi manuscript, which also contains the interpreter's speeches in fuller detail, uses the word *edere*, with the meaning "There is no name that I can make known [to you]." This is the more correct translation. The Northman is literally afraid to say the word, lest it call up demons. In Latin, *edere* has the sense of "giving birth to" and "calling up," as well as its literal meaning, "to put forth." Later paragraphs confirm this sense of the meaning.

head bowed. Never had I seen the merry and rambunctious North people so subdued.

Then into the hall entered the old crone called the angel of death, and she sat beside Buliwyf. From a hide bag she withdrew some bones—whether human or animal I do not know—and these bones she cast upon the ground, speaking low utterances, and she passed her hand over them.

The bones were gathered up, and cast again, and the process repeated with more incantations. Now again was the casting done, and finally she spoke to Buliwyf.

I asked the interpreter the meaning of her speech, but he did not attend me.

Then Buliwyf stood and raised his cup of strong drink, and called to the assembled earls and warriors, making a speech of some good length. One by one, several warriors stood at their places to face him. Not all stood; I counted eleven, and Buliwyf pronounced himself satisfied with this.

Now also I saw that Thorkel appeared much pleased by the proceedings and assumed a more kingly bearing, while Buliwyf paid him no heed, or showed any hatred of him, or even any interest, although they were formerly enemies a few minutes past.

Then the angel of death, this same crone, pointed to me and made some utterance, and then she departed the hall. Now at last my interpreter spoke, and he said: "Buliwyf is called by the gods to leave this place and swiftly, putting behind him all his cares and concerns, to act as a hero to repel the menace of the North. This is fitting, and he must also take eleven warriors with him. And so, also, must he take you."

I said that I was on a mission to the Bulgars, and must follow the instructions of my Caliph, with no delay.

"The angel of death has spoken," my interpreter said. "The party of Buliwyf must be thirteen, and of these one must be no Northman, and so you shall be the thirteenth."

I protested I was not a warrior. Verily I made all the excuses and pleadings that I could imagine might have effect upon this rude company of beings. I demanded tht the interpreter convey my words to Buliwyf, and yet he turned away and left the hall, saying this last speech: "Prepare yourself as you think best. You shall leave on the morning light."

THE JOURNEY TO
THE FAR COUNTRY

In this manner was I prevented from continuing my travels to the kingdom of the Yiltawar, King of the Saqaliba, and thus was I unable to discharge the trust of al-Muqtadir, Commander of the Faithful and Caliph of the City of Peace. I gave such instructions as I could to Dadir al-Hurami, and also to the ambassador, Abdallah ibn-Bastu al-Hazari, and also to the pages Takin and Bars. Then I took my leave of them, and how they fared further I never knew.

For myself, I counted my condition no different from a dead man. I was on board one of the Northman vessels, and sailing up the Volga river, northward, with twelve of their company. The others were named thus:

Buliwyf, the chief; his lieutenant or captain, Ecthgow; his earls and nobles, Higlak, Skeld, Weath, Roneth, Halga; his warriors and brave fighters, Helfdane, Edgtho, Rethel, Haltaf, and Herger.* And also I was among them, unable to speak their language or to understand their ways, for my interpreter had been left behind. It was only happenstance and the grace of Allah that one of their warriors, Herger, should be a man of parts and knowing some of the Latin tongue. Thus I could understand from Herger what meant the events that transpired. Herger was a young warrior, and very merry; he seemed to find jest in everything, and especially in my own gloom at the departure.

These Northmen are by their own accounting the best sailors in the world, and I saw much love of the oceans and waters in their demeanor. Of the ship there is this: it was as long as twenty-five paces, and as broad as eight and a little more than that, and of excellent construction, of oak wood. Its color was black at every place. It was fitted with a square sail of cloth and trimmed with sealskin ropes.† The helmsman stood upon a small platform near the stern

---

*Wulfgar was left behind. Jensen states the Northmen commonly held a messenger as hostage, and this is why "appropriate messengers were the sons of kings, or high nobles, or other persons who had some value to their own community, thus making them fitting hostages." Olaf Jorgensen argues that Wulfgar remained behind because he was afraid to go back.

†Some early authors apparently thought this meant that the sail was hemmed in rope; there are eighteenth-century drawings that show the Viking sails with rope borderings. There is no evidence that this was the case; Ibn Fadlan meant that the sails were trimmed in the nautical sense; i.e., angled to best catch the wind, by the use of sealskin ropes as halyards.

and worked a rudder attached to the side of the vessel in the Roman fashion. The ship was fitted with benches for oars, but never were the oars employed; rather we progressed by sailing alone. At the head of the ship was the wooden carving of a fierce sea monster, such as appears on some Northman vessels; also there was a tail at the stern. In water this ship was stable and quite pleasant for traveling, and the confidence of the warriors elevated my spirits.

Near the helmsman was a bed of skins arranged upon a network of ropes, with a skin covering. This was the bed of Buliwyf; the other warriors slept upon the deck here and there, wrapping skins about them, and I did as much also.

We traveled upon the river for three days, passing many small settlements at the edge of the water. At none of these did we stop. Then we came upon a large encampment in a bend in the river Volga. Here were many hundreds of peoples, and a town of good size, and in the center of the town a kremlin, or fortress, with earthen walls and all of impressive dimensions. I asked Herger what was this place.

Herger said to me, "This is the city of Bulgar, of the kingdom of the Saqaliba. That is the kremlin of the Yiltawar, King of the Saqaliba."

I replied, "This is the very King I was sent to see as emissary from my Caliph," and with many entreaties I requested to be put upon the shore to do the mission of my Caliph; also I demanded, and made a show of anger, to the extent that I dared.

Verily the Northmen paid me no heed. Herger would not reply to my requests and demands, and finally he laughed into my face, and turned his attention to the sailing of the ship. Thus the Northman's vessels sailed past the city of Bulgar, so close upon the shore that I heard the shouts of merchants and the bleating of sheep, and yet I was helpless and could do nothing, save witness the sight with my eyes. After the passing of an hour even this was refused me, for the Bulgar city is at the bend of the river, as I have said, and soon absent from my view. Thus did I enter and leave Bulgaria.

The reader may now be hopelessly confused about the geography. Modern Bulgaria is one of the Balkan states; it is bordered by Greece, Yugoslavia, Rumania, and Turkey. But from the ninth to the fifteenth centuries there was another Bulgaria, on the banks of the Volga, roughly 600 miles east of modern Moscow, and this is where Ibn Fadlan was heading. Bulgaria on the Volga was a loose-knit kingdom of some importance, and its capital city, Bulgar, was famous and rich when the Mongols occupied it in A.D. 1237. It is generally believed that Volga Bulgaria and Balkan Bulgaria were populated by related groups of immigrants moving out from the region around the Black Sea during the period A.D. 400–600, but little of substance is known. The old city of Bulgar is in the region of modern Kazan.

Then passed eight more days upon the vessel, still traveling the Volga River, and the land was more mountainous about the valley of the river. Now we came to another branching of the river, where it is called by the Northmen the Oker River, and here we took the leftmost branch and continued on for ten days farther. The air was chill and the wind strong, and much snow lay still upon the ground. They have many great forests also in this region, which the Northmen call Vada.

Then we came to a camp of North people which was Massborg. This was hardly a town but a camp of a few wooden houses, built large in the North fashion; and this town lives by sale of foodstuff to traders who come back and forth along this route. At Massborg we left our vessel, and traveled overland by horse for eighteen days. This was a difficult mountain region, and exceedingly cold, and I was much exhausted by the rigors of the journey. These North people never travel at night. Nor do they often sail at night, but prefer every evening to beach their ship and await the light of dawn before continuing farther.

Yet this was the occurrence: during our travels, the period of the night became so short you could not cook a pot of meat in the time of it. Verily it seemed that as soon as I lay down to sleep I was awakened by the Northmen who said, "Come, it is day, we must continue the journey." Nor was the sleep refreshing in these cold places.

Also, Herger explained to me that in this North country the day is long in the summer, and the night is long in the winter, and rarely are they equal. Then he said to me I should watch in the night for the sky curtain; and upon one evening I did, and I saw in the sky shimmering pale lights, of green and yellow and sometimes blue, which hung as a curtain in the high air. I was much amazed by the sight of this sky curtain but the Northmen count it nothing strange.

Now we traveled for five days down from the mountains, into a region of forests. The forests of the Northlands are cold and dense with gigantic trees. It is a wet and chilling land, in some locations so green that the eyes ache from the brightness of the color; yet in other locations it is black and dark and menacing.

Now we traveled seven days farther, through the forests, and we experienced much rain. Often it is the nature of this rain that it falls with such thickness as to be oppressive; upon one time or another I thought I might drown, so much was the very air filled with water. At other periods, when the wind blew the rain, it was as a sandstorm, stinging the flesh and burning the eyes, and blinding the vision.

[Coming from a desert region, Ibn Fadlan would naturally be impressed by the lush green colors, and the abundant rainfall.]

607

These Northmen feared no robbers in the forests, and whether from their own great strength or the lack of any bandits, in truth we saw no one in the forests. The North country has few people of any sort, or so it appeared during my sojourn there. We often traveled seven days, or ten, without viewing any settlement or farm or dwelling.

The manner of our journey was this: in the morning we arose, and lacking any ablutions, mounted upon our horses and rode until the middle of the day. Then one or another of the warriors would hunt some game, a small animal or a bird. If it was raining, this food would be consumed without cooking. It rained many days, and in the first instance I chose not to eat the raw flesh, which also was not *dabah* [ritually slaughtered], but after a period I also ate, saying quietly "in the name of God" under my breath, and trusting to God that my predicament should be understood. If it was not raining, a fire was lit with a small ember that was carried with the party, and the food cooked. Also we ate berries and grasses, the names of which I do not know. Then we traveled for the afterpart of each day, which was considerable, until the coming of night, when again we rested, and ate.

Many times at night it rained, and we sought shelter beneath large trees, yet we arose drenched, and our sleeping skins drenched likewise. The Northmen did not grumble at this, for they are cheerful at all times; I alone grumbled, and mightily. They paid me no attention.

Finally I said to Herger, "The rain is cold." To this he laughed. "How can the rain be cold?" he said. "You are cold and you are unhappy. The rain is not cold or unhappy."

I saw that he believed this foolishness, and truly thought me foolish to think otherwise, and yet I did.

Now it happened that one night, while we ate, I said over my food "in the name of God," and Buliwyf inquired of Herger what it was I said. I told to Herger that I believed food must be consecrated, and so I did this according to my beliefs. Buliwyf said to me, "This is the way of the Arabs?" Herger was the translator.

I made this reply: "No, for in truth he who kills the food must make the consecration. I speak the words so as to be not forgetful."*

This the Northmen found a reason of humor. They laughed heartily. Then Buliwyf said to me, "Can you draw sounds?" I did not comprehend his meaning, and inquired of Herger, and there was some talking back and forth, and finally I understood he meant writing. The Northmen call the speech of Arabs

---

*This is a typically Muslim sentiment. Unlike Christianity, a religion which in many ways it resembles, Islam does not emphasize a concept of original sin arising from the fall of man. Sin for a Muslim is forgetfulness in carrying out the prescribed daily rituals of the religion. As a corollary, it is a more serious offense to forget the ritual entirely than to remember the ritual and yet fail to carry it out either through extenuating circumstances or personal inadequacy. Thus Ibn Fadlan is saying, in effect, that he is mindful of proper conduct even though he is not acting according to it; this is better than nothing.

noise or sound. I replied to Buliwyf that I could write, and also read.

He said that I should write for him upon the ground. In the light of the evening fire, I took a stick and wrote, "Praise be to God." All the Northmen looked at the writing. I was commanded to speak what it said, and this I did. Now Buliwyf stared at the writing for a long period, his head sunk upon his chest.

Herger said to me, "Which God do you praise?" I answered that I praised the one God whose name was Allah.

Herger said, "One God cannot be enough."

Now we traveled another day, and passed another night, and then another day. And on the next evening, Buliwyf took a stick and drew in the earth what I had formerly drawn, and commanded me to read.

I spoke aloud the words: "Praise be to God." At this, Buliwyf was satisfied, and I saw that he had contrived a test of me, placing in his memory the symbols I had drawn, to show them to me again.

Now Ecthgow, the lieutenant or captain of Buliwyf, and a warrior less merry than the others, a stern man, spoke to me through the interpreter, Herger. Herger said, "Ecthgow wishes to know if you can draw the sound of his name."

I said that I could, and I took up the stick, and began to draw in the dirt. At once Ecthgow leapt up, flung away the stick, and stamped out my writing. He spoke angry words.

Herger said to me, "Ecthgow does not wish you to draw his name at any time, and this you must promise."

Here I was perplexed, and I saw that Ecthgow was angry with me in the extreme. So also were the others staring at me with concern and anger. I promised to Herger that I would not draw the name of Ecthgow, or of any of the others. At this they were all relieved.

After this, no more was my writing discussed, but Buliwyf gave certain instructions, and whenever it rained I was always directed to the largest tree, and I was given more food than before.

Not always did we sleep in the forests, nor did we always ride through the forests. At the border of some forests, Buliwyf and his warriors would plunge forward, riding at a gallop through the dense trees, without a care or a thought of fear. And then again, at other forests he would draw up and pause, and the warriors would dismount and burn a fire and make some offering of food or a few sheets of hard bread, or a kerchief of cloth, before continuing farther. And then they would ride around the edge of the forest, never entering its depths.

I inquired of Herger why this should be. He said that some forests were safe and some were not, but did not explain further. I asked him, "What is not safe in the forests that are judged so?"

He made this reply: "There are things that no man can conquer, and no sword can kill, and no fire can burn, and such things are in the forests."

I said, "How is this known to be?"

At this he laughed and said, "You Arabs always wish to have reasons for everything. Your hearts are a great bursting bag of reasons."

I said, "And you do not care for reasons?"

"It avails you nothing. We say: A man should be moderately wise, but not overwise, lest he know his fate in advance. The man whose mind is most free of care does not know his fate in advance."

Now, I saw that I must be content with his answer. For it was true that upon one occasion or another, I would make some manner of inquiry, and Herger would reply, and if I did not comprehend his answer, I would ask further, and he would reply further. Yet again, when I made of him an inquiry, he would reply in short fashion, as if the inquiry were of no substance. And then I would have nothing further from him, save a shaking of his head.

Now we continued on. Verily, I can say that some of the forests in the wild North country do provoke a feeling of fear, for which I cannot account. At night, sitting about the fire, the Northmen told stories of dragons and fierce beasts, and also of their ancestors who had slain these creatures. These, they said, were the source of my fear. But they told the stories with no show of fear, and of such beasts, I saw nothing with my own eyes.

One night I heard a grumbling that I took to be thunder, but they said it was the growl of a dragon in the forest. I do not know what is the truth, and report now only what was said to me.

The North country is cold and wet and the sun is seldom seen, for the sky is gray with thick clouds all the day. The people of this region are pale as linen, and their hair is very fair. After so many days of travel, I saw no dark people at all, and indeed I was marveled at by the inhabitants of that region on account of my skin and dark hair. Many times a farmer or his wife or daughter would come forth to touch me with a stroking motion; Herger laughed and said they were trying to brush away the color, thinking it to be painted upon my flesh. They are ignorant people with no knowledge of the wideness of the world. Many times they feared me, and would not approach me close. At one place, I do not know the name, a child cried out in terror and ran to cling to his mother when he saw me.

At this, the warriors of Buliwyf laughed with great merriment. But now I observed this thing: with the passing of the days, the warriors of Buliwyf ceased to laugh, and fell into an ill humor, more each day, Herger said to me they were thinking of drink, of which we had been deprived for many days.

At each farm or dwelling, Buliwyf and his warriors asked for drink, but in these poor places there was often no liquor, and they were sorely disappointed, until at last there was no trace of cheerfulness about them.

At length we arrived at a village, and there the warriors found drink, and all of the Northmen became intoxicated in a moment, drinking in raucous fashion, heedless that the liquor poured over their chins and clothing in their haste. In truth, one of the company, the solemn warrior Ecthgow, was so demented from liquor that he was drunk while still upon his horse, and fell attempting to dismount. Now the horse kicked him in the head, and I feared for his safety, but Ecthgow laughed and kicked the horse back.

We remained in this village the space of two days. I was much amazed, for previously the warriors had shown great haste and purpose in their journey, yet all was now abandoned to drink and stuporous slumber. Then upon the third day, Buliwyf directed that we should continue, and the warriors proceeded, I among them, and they accounted the loss of two days nothing strange.

How many days further we traveled I am not certain. I know that five times we changed horses for fresh mounts, paying for these in the villages with gold and with the little green shells that the Northmen value more highly than any other objects in the world. And at length we came to a village of the name Lenneborg, situated by the sea. The sea was gray, and likewise the sky, and the air was cold and bitter. Here we took another vessel.

This ship was in appearance similar to the one previous, but larger. It was called by the Northmen *Hosbokun*, which means "sea goat," for the reason that the ship bucks the waves as a goat bucks. And also for the reason that the vessel was swift, for among these people the goat is the animal that means swiftness to them.

I was afraid to go upon this sea, for the water was rough and very cold; a man's hand plunged into that sea would lack all feeling in an instant, it was so dire cold. And yet the Northmen were cheerful, and joked and drank for an evening in this sea village of Lenneborg, and disported themselves with many of the women and slave girls. This, I was told, is the Northmen's custom before a sea voyage, for no man knows if he shall survive the journey, and thus he departs with excessive revelry.

In every place we were greeted with great hospitality, for that is considered a virtue by these people. The poorest farmer would set all he had before us, and this without fear that we would kill or rob him, but only out of goodness and grace. The Northmen, I learned, do not countenance robbers or killers of their own race, and treat such men harshly. These beliefs they hold despite the truth of the matter, which is that they are always drunk and brawling like unreasoning animals, and killing each other in hot duels. Yet they do not see this as murder, and any man who murders will be himself killed.

In the same way, they treat their slaves with much kindness, which was a wonder to me.* If a slave turns ill, or dies in some mishap, it is not counted any great loss; and women who are slaves must be ready at any time for the ministrations of any man, in public or in private, day or night. There is no affection for the slaves, and yet there is no brutality for them, either, and they are always fed and clothed by their masters.

*Other eyewitness accounts disagree with Ibn Fadlan's description of the treatment of slaves and adultery, and therefore some authorities question his reliability as a social observer. In fact there was probably substantial local variation, from tribe to tribe, in the accepted treatment of slaves and unfaithful wives.

Further I learned this: that any man may enjoy a slave, but that the wife of the lowest farmer is respected by the chiefs and earls of the Northmen, as they respect the wives of each other. To force attention on a freeborn woman who is not a slave is a crime, and I was told that a man would be hanged for it, although I never saw this.

Chastity among women is said to be a great virtue, but seldom did I see it practiced, for adultery is not accounted as any great matter, and if the wife of any man, low or high, is lusty, the outcome is not thought remarkable. These people are very free in such matters, and the men of the North say that women are devious and cannot be trusted; to this they appear resigned, and speak of it with their usual cheerful demeanor.

I inquired of Herger if he was married, and he said that he had a wife. I inquired with all discretion if she were chaste, and he laughed in my face and said to me: "I sail upon the seas, and I may never return, or I may be absent many years. My wife is not dead." From this, I took the meaning that she was unfaithful to him, and he did not care.

The Northmen do not consider any offspring a bastard if the mother be a wife. The children of slaves are slaves sometimes, and free sometimes; how this is decided I do not know.

In some regions, slaves are marked by a crop of the ear. In other regions, slaves wear a neckband of iron to signify their place. In other regions, slaves have no markings, for that is the local custom.

Pederasty is not known among the Northmen, although they say that other peoples practice it; they themselves claim no interest in the matter, and since it does not occur among them, they have no punishment for it.

All this and more I learned from my talking with Herger, and from witnessing the travels of our party. Further I saw that in each place where we rested, the people inquired of Buliwyf what quest he had undertaken, and when they were informed of its nature—that which I did not yet comprehend—he and his warriors, and I among them, were accorded the highest respect, receiving their prayers and sacrifices and tokens of good wishes.

At sea, as I have said, the Northmen become happy and jubilant, although the ocean was rough and forbidding to my way of thinking, and also to my stomach, which felt most delicate and unsettled. Indeed I purged myself, and then asked Herger why his companions were so happy.

Herger said, "It is because we shall soon be at the home of Buliwyf, the place known as Yatlam, where live his father and his mother and all his relatives, and he has not seen them for many long years."

To this I said, "Are we not going to Wulfgar's land?"

Herger replied, "Yes, but it is fitting that Buliwyf must pay homage to his father and also to his mother."

I saw by their faces that all the other earls, nobles, and warriors were happy as Buliwyf himself. I asked Herger why this was so.

"Buliwyf is our chief, and we are happy for him, and for the power that he will soon have."

I inquired what was this power of which he spoke. "The power of Runding," Herger answered me. "What power is that?" I inquired, to which he made this reply: "The power of the ancients, the power of the giants."

The Northmen believe that in ages past the world was populated by a race of giant men, who have since vanished. The Northmen do not count themselves the descendants of these giants, but they have received some of the powers of these ancient giants, in such ways as I do not understand well. These heathens also believe in many gods, who are also themselves giants, and who also have power. But the giants of which Herger spoke were giant men, and not gods, or so it seemed to me.

That night we beached upon a rocky shore, made of stones the size of a man's fist, and there Buliwyf encamped with his men, and long into the night they drank and sang around the fire. Herger joined in the celebration and had no patience to explain to me the meanings of the songs, and so I do not know what they sang, but they were happy. On the morrow they would come to the home of Buliwyf, the land called Yatlam.

We left before the first light of dawn, and it was so cold my bones ached, and my body was sore from the rocky beach, and we set out upon the raging sea and the blasting wind. For all the morning we sailed, and during this period the excitement of the men increased further until they became like children or women. It was a wonder to me to see these huge strong warriors giggle and laugh like the Caliph's harem, and yet they saw nothing unmanly in this.

There was a point of land, a high rocky outcrop of gray stone above the gray sea, and beyond this point, Herger told me, would be the town of Yatlam. I strained to see this fabled home of Buliwyf as the Northmen's vessel came around the cliff. The warriors laughed and cheered more loudly, and I gathered there were many rude jokes and plans for sport with women when they landed.

And then there was the smell of smoke on the sea, and we saw smoke, and all the men fell silent. As we came around the point, I saw with my own eyes that the town there was in smoldering flames and billowing black smoke. There was no sign of life.

Buliwyf and his warriors landed and walked the town of Yatlam. There were dead bodies of men and women and children, some consumed by flames, some hacked by swords—a multitude of corpses. Buliwyf and the warriors did not speak and yet even here there was no grief, no crying and sadness. Never have I seen a race that accepts death as the Northmen do. I myself was sick many times at the sights, and they were never so.

At last I said to Herger, "Who has done this?" Herger pointed in to the land, to the forests and the hills set back from the gray ocean. There were mists over the forests. He pointed and did not speak. I said to him, "Is it the mists?"

He said to me, "Do not ask more. You will know sooner than you wish."

Now this happened: Buliwyf entered one smoking ruined house and returned to our company bearing a sword. This sword was very large and heavy, and so heated by the fire that he carried it with a cloth wrapped around the handle. Verily I say it was the largest sword I have ever seen. It was as long as my own body and the blade was flat and broad as the palms of two men's hands set side by side. It was so large and heavy that even Buliwyf grunted at the carrying of it. I asked Herger what was the sword, and he said, "That is Runding," and then Buliwyf ordered all his party to the boat, and we set out to sea again. None of the warriors looked back at the burning town of Yatlam; I alone did this, and I saw the smoking ruin, and the mists in the hills beyond.

THE ENCAMPMENT AT TRELBURG

For the space of two days we sailed along a flat coast among many islands that are called the land of Dans, coming finally to a region of marsh with a crisscross of narrow rivers that pour onto the sea. These rivers have no names themselves but are each one called "wyk," and the peoples of the narrow rivers are called "wykings," which means the Northmen warriors who sail their ships up the rivers and attack settlements in such fashion.*

Now in this marshy region we stopped at a place they called Trelburg, which was a wonder to me. Here is no town, but rather a military camp, and its people are warriors, with few women or children among them. The defenses of this camp of Trelburg are constructed with great care and skill of workmanship in the Roman fashion.

Trelburg lies at the joining point of two wyks, which then run to the sea. The main part of the town is encircled by a round earthwork wall, as tall as five men standing one atop the other. Above this earthen ring there stands a wooden fence for greater protection. Outside the earthen ring there is a ditch filled with water, the depth I do not know.

These earthworks are excellently made, of a symmetry and quality to rival anything we know. And there is this further: on the landward side of the town, a second semicircle of high wall, and a second ditch beyond.

The town itself lies within the inner ring, which is broken by four gates, facing the four corners of the earth. Each gate is barred by strong oaken doors with heavy fittings of iron, and many guards. Many guards also walk the ramparts, keeping watch day and night.

Inside the town stand sixteen wooden dwellings, all the same: they are long houses, for so the Northmen call them, with walls that curve so that they resemble overturned boats with the ends cut flat front and back. In length they are thirty paces, and wider in the middle portion than either end. They are

*There is some dispute among modern scholars about the origin of the term "Viking," but most agree with Ibn Fadlan, that it derives from "vik," meaning a creek or narrow river.

arranged thus: four long houses precisely set, so as to form a square. Four squares are arranged to make sixteen houses in all.*

Every long house has but one entrance, and no house has its entrance within sight of another. I inquired why this was so, and Herger said thus: "If the camp is attacked, the men must run to defense, and the doorways are such that the men can hasten without mingling and confusion, but on the contrary each man can proceed freely to the task of defense."

Thus it is within the square that one house has a north door, the next house an east door, the next house a south door, the next house a west door; so also each of the four squares.

Then also I saw that while the Northmen are gigantic, these doorways were so low that even I must bend in two to enter one of the houses. I inquired of Herger, who said: "If we are attacked, a single warrior may remain inside the house, and with his sword cut off the heads of all who enter. The door is low so that heads will be bent for cutting."

Verily, I saw that in all respects the Trelburg town was constructed for warfare and for defense. No trading is conducted here at all, as I have said. Inside the long houses, there are three sections or rooms, each with a door. The center room is the largest, and it also has a pit for rubbish.

Now I saw that the Trelburg people were not as the Northmen along the Volga. These were clean people for their race. They washed in the river, and relieved their waste out of doors, and were in all ways much superior to what I had known. Yet they are not truly clean, except in comparison.

The society of Trelburg is mostly men, and the women are all slaves. There are no wives among the women, and all women are taken freely as the men desire. The people of Trelburg live on fish, and some little bread; they do no agriculture or farming, although the marshlands surrounding the town contain areas suitable for growing. I asked of Herger why there was no agriculture, and he said to me, "These are warriors. They do not till the soil."

Buliwyf and his company were graciously received by the chiefs of Trelburg, who are several, foremost among them one who is called Sagard. Sagard is a strong and fierce man, almost as huge as Buliwyf himself.

During the night banquet, Sagard inquired of Buliwyf his mission and the reasons for his travels, and Buliwyf reported of the supplication of Wulfgar. Herger translated all for me, although in truth I had spent sufficient time among these heathens to learn a word or two in their tongue. Here is the meaning of the conversation of Sagard and Buliwyf.

Sagard spoke thus: "It is sensible for Wulfgar to carry out the errand of a messenger, though he is the son of the King Rothgar, for the several sons of Rothgar have set upon one another."

*The accuracy of Ibn Fadlan's reporting is confirmed here by direct archaeological evidence. In 1948 the military site of Trelleborg, in western Zealand in Denmark, was excavated. The site corresponds exactly to Ibn Fadlan's description of the size, nature, and structure of the settlement.

Buliwyf said that he did not know of this, or words to that meaning. But I perceived that he was not greatly surprised. Yet it is true that Buliwyf was seldom surprised by any thing. Such was his role as leader of the warriors and hero to them.

Sagard spoke again: "Indeed, Rothgar had five sons, and three are dead at the hand of one of them, Wiglif, a cunning man,* whose conspirator in this affair is the herald of the old King. Only Wulfgar remains faithful, and he has departed."

Buliwyf said to Sagard that he was glad to know of this news, and would hold it in his mind, and there the conversation ended. Never did Buliwyf or any of his warriors show surprise at the words of Sagard, and from this I took that it is ordinary for the sons of a king to dispose of one another to gain the throne.

Also it is true that from time to time a son may murder his father the king to gain the throne, and this is likewise counted nothing remarkable, for the Northmen see it the same as any drunken brawl among warriors. The Northmen have a proverb which is "Look to your back," and they believe that a man must always be prepared to defend himself, even a father against his own son.

Upon our departure, I inquired of Herger why there should be another fortification on the landward side of Trelburg, and yet no such additional fortification on the seaward side. These Northmen are seafaring men who attack from the sea, and yet Herger said, "It is the land that is dangerous."

I asked of him, "Why is the land dangerous?" And he replied, "Because of the mists."

Upon our departure from Trelburg, the warriors assembled there beat their staves upon their shields, raising a loud noise for our ship which set sail. This, I was told, was to draw the attention of Odin, one of the number of their gods, so that this Odin would look with favor upon the journey of Buliwyf and his twelve men.

Also, this I learned: that the number thirteen is significant to the Norsemen, because the moon grows and dies thirteen times in the passage of one year, by their reckoning. For this reason, all important accountings must include the number thirteen. Thus Herger said to me that the number of dwellings in Trelburg was thirteen and also three more, instead of sixteen, as I have expressed it.

Further, I learned that these Northmen have some notion that the year does not fit with exactitude into thirteen passages of the moon, and thus the number thirteen is not stable and fixed in their minds. The thirteenth passage

*Literally, "a two-handed man." As will be clear later, the Northmen were ambidextrous in fighting, and to shift weapons from one hand to another was considered an admirable trick. Thus a two-handed man is cunning. A related meaning was once attached to the word "shifty," which now means deceitful and evasive, but formerly had a more positive sense of "resourceful, full of maneuvers."

is called magical and foreign, and Herger says, "Thus for the thirteenth man you were chosen as foreign."

Verily these Northmen are superstitious, with no recourse to sense or reason or law. They seemed to my eyes to be fierce children, and yet I was among them, and so held my tongue. Soon enough I was glad for my discretion, for these events followed:

We were sailing some time from Trelburg when I recalled that never previously had the inhabitants of a town made a departure ceremony with beating of shields to call up Odin. I spoke as much to Herger.

"It is true," he responded. "There is a special reason for the call to Odin, for we are now upon the sea of monsters."

This seemed to me proof of their superstition. I inquired if any of the warriors had ever seen such monsters. "Indeed, we have all seen them," Herger said. "Why else should we know of them?" By the tone of his voice, I could recognize that he thought me a fool for my disbelief.

Some further time passed, when there was a shout, and all the warriors of Buliwyf stood pointing to the sea, watching, shouting amongst themselves. I asked Herger what had happened. "We are among the monsters now," he said, pointing.

Now the ocean in this region is most turbulent. The wind blows with fierce force, turning the curls of the sea white with foam, spitting water into the face of a sailor, and playing tricks with his sight. I watched the sea for many minutes and had no view of this sea monster, and I had no reason to believe what they said.

Then one of their number shouted to Odin, a scream of prayer, repeating the name many times in supplication, and then I also saw with my own eyes the sea monster. It was in the shape of a giant snake that never raised its head above the surface, yet I saw its body curl and twist over, and it was very long, and wider than the Northmen's boat, and black in color. The sea monster spat water into the air, like a fountain, and then plunged down, raising a tail that was cleft in two, like the forked tongue of a snake. Yet it was enormous, each section of the tail being broader than the largest palm frond.

Now I saw another monster, and another, and another after that; there appeared to be four and perhaps six or seven. Each behaved as his fellows, curving through the water, spitting a fountain, and raising a giant tail split in two. At the sight, the Northmen shouted to Odin for aid, and not a few of their number fell to their knees on the deck trembling.

Verily I saw with my own eyes the sea monsters all about us in the ocean, and then, after some time had passed, they were gone and we did not see them again. The warriors of Buliwyf resumed their sailing efforts, and no man spoke of the monsters, but I was much afraid long afterward, and Herger told me that my face was white as the face of a North person, and he laughed.

"What does Allah say to this?" he asked of me, and to that I had no answer.*

In the evening, we beached and made a fire, and I inquired of Herger if the sea monsters ever attacked a ship on the sea, and if so, what was the manner of it, for I had seen the heads of none of these monsters.

Herger answered by calling Ecthgow, one of the nobles and the lieutenant of Buliwyf. Ecthgow was a solemn warrior who was not merry except when drunk. Herger said that he had been on a ship that was attacked. Ecthgow said this to me: that the sea monsters are larger than anything on the surface of the land, and larger than any ship on the sea, and when they attack they ride under a ship and lift it in the air, and toss it aside like a bit of wood, and crush it with their forked tongue. Ecthgow said that there had been thirty men on his ship, and only he and two others beside had survived, by the graciousness of the gods. Ecthgow spoke in an ordinary manner of talking, which for him was very serious, and I believed him to be speaking the truth.

Also Ecthgow told me that the Northmen know that the monsters attack ships because they desire to mate with the ship, mistaking it for one of their own. For this reason, the Northmen do not build their ships over-large.

Herger said to me that Ecthgow is a great warrior renowned in battle, and that he is to be believed in all things.

For the next two days, we sailed among the islands of the Dan country, and then on the third day we crossed a passage of open water. Here I was afraid to see more of the sea monsters, but we did not, and eventually arrived at the territory called Venden. These lands of Venden are mountainous and forbidding, and the men of Buliwyf in his boat approached with some trepidation and the killing of a hen, which was thrown into the ocean thus: the head was thrown from the bow of the ship, and the body of the hen was thrown from the stern, near the helmsman.

We did not beach directly on this new land of Venden, but sailed along the coast, coming at last to the kingdom of Rothgar. I first saw it thus. High upon a cliff, commanding a view of the raging gray sea, was a huge great hall of wood, strong and imposing. I said to Herger it was a magnificent sight, but Herger and all his company, led by Buliwyf, were groaning and shaking their heads. I inquired of Herger why this was so. He said, "Rothgar is called Rothgar the Vain, and his great hall is the mark of a vain man."

I said, "Why do you speak thus? Because of its size and splendor?" For verily, as we came closer, I saw that the hall was richly ornamented with carvings and silver chasing, which sparkled from a distance.

*This account of what is obviously a sighting of whales is disputed by many scholars. It appears in the manuscript of Razi as it is here, but in Sjogren's translation it is much briefer, and in it the Northmen are shown as playing an elaborate joke upon the Arab. The Northmen knew about whales and distinguished them from sea monsters, according to Sjogren. Other scholars, including Hassan, doubt that Ibn Fadlan could be unaware of the existence of whales, as he appears to be here.

"No," said Herger. "I say that Rothgar is vain because of the way he has placed his settlement. He dares the gods to strike him down, and he pretends he is more than a man, and so he is punished."

Never have I seen a more impregnable great hall, and I said to Herger, "This hall cannot be attacked; how can Rothgar be struck down?"

Herger laughed at me, and said thus: "You Arabs are stupid beyond counting, and know nothing of the ways of the world. Rothgar deserves the misfortune that has come to him, and it is only we who shall save him, and perhaps not even so."

These words puzzled me further. I looked at Ecthgow, the lieutenant of Buliwyf, and saw that he stood in the boat and made a brave face, and yet his knees trembled, and it was not the stiffness of the wind that made them tremble so. He was afraid; they were all afraid; and I did not know why.

THE KINGDOM OF ROTHGAR IN THE LAND OF VENDEN

I

he ship was beached at the time of the afternoon prayer, and I begged the forgiveness of Allah for not making supplication. Yet I had not been able to do so in the presence of the Northmen, who thought my prayers to be a curse upon them, and threatened to kill me if I prayed in their sight.

Each warrior in the boat dressed in the garments of battle, which were thus: first, boots and leggings of rough wool, and over this a coat of heavy fur, which reached to the knees. Over this they placed coats of mail, which all had saved me. Then each man took his sword and clasped it to his belt; each man took up his white shield of hide, and his spear; each man placed a helmet of metal or leather upon his head;* in this all the men were the same except for Buliwyf, who alone carried his sword in his hand, so large was it.

The warriors looked up to the great hall of Rothgar, and marveled at its gleaming roof and skilled workmanship, and agreed that there was none like it in the world, with its lofty gables and rich carving. Yet there was no respect in their speech.

At length we decamped from the ship, and traveled a road paved in stone up to the great hall. The clanking of swords and the clatter of mail raised a goodly noise. After we had gone some short distance, we saw by the roadway the severed head of an ox, set upon a stick. This animal was freshly killed.

All the Northmen sighed and made sad faces at this portent, though it had no meaning to me. I was by now adjusted to their custom of killing some beast at the slightest nervousness or provocation. Yet this oxhead had especial significance.

Buliwyf looked away, across the fields of the lands of Rothgar, and saw there an isolated farming house, of the sort that is common in Rothgar lands. The walls of this house were of wood, and sealed with a paste of mud and straw, which must be replenished after the frequent rains. The roof is thatched material and wood also. Inside the houses there is only an earthen floor and a hearth, and the dung of animals, for the farm people sleep with their animals

---

*Popular representations of the Scandinavians always show them wearing helmets with horns. This is an anachronism; at the time of Ibn Fadlan's visit, such helmets had not been worn for more than a thousand years, since the Early Bronze Age.

indoors for the warmth afforded by their bodies, and then they burn the dung for fires.

Buliwyf gave an order that we should go to this farmhouse, and so we set out across the fields, which were verdant but soggy with dampness underfoot. Once or twice the company halted to examine the ground before continuing on, but they never saw anything that mattered to them. I myself saw nothing.

Yet again Buliwyf halted his company, and pointed to the dark earth. Verily, I saw with my own eyes the bare imprint of a foot—indeed, of many feet. They were flat and uglier than anything known to creation. At each toe, there was the sharp digging mark of a horned nail or claw; thus the shape appeared human, but yet not human. This I saw with my own eyes, and could scarcely believe the witness of my sight.

Buliwyf and his warriors shook their heads at the sight, and I heard them repeat one word over and over: "wendol" or "wendlon," or some such. The meaning of the name was not known to me, and I sensed that Herger should not be asked at this moment, for he was as apprehensive as all the rest. We pressed on to the farmhouse, now and again seeing more of these horned footprints in the earth. Buliwyf and his warriors walked slowly, but it was not caution; no man drew his weapon; rather it was some dread that I did not comprehend and yet felt with them.

At length we came to the farming dwelling and entered it. In the farmhouse I saw, with my own eyes, this sight: there was a man, of young age and graceful proportion, whose body had been torn limb from limb. The torso was here, an arm there, a leg there. Blood lay in thick pools upon the floor, and on the walls, on the roof, on every surface in such profusion that the house seemed to have been painted in red blood. Also there was a woman, in like fashion rended limb from limb. Also a male child, an infant of two years or less, whose head was wrenched from the shoulders, leaving the body a bleeding stump.

All this I saw with my own eyes, and it was the most fearsome sight I ever witnessed. I purged myself and was faint for an hour, purging myself yet again.

Never will I comprehend the manner of the Northmen, for even as I was sick, so they became calm and dispassionate at the aspect of this horror; they viewed all they saw in quiet fashion; they discussed the claw marks upon the limbs, and the manner of tearing of flesh. Much attention was given to the fact that all the heads were missing; also, they remarked the most devilish aspect of all, which even now I recall with trepidation.

The body of the male child had been chewed by some fiendish teeth, upon the soft flesh of the back of the thigh. So also had been chewed the area of the shoulder. This very horror I saw with my own eyes.

The warriors of Buliwyf were grim-countenanced and glowering as they departed the farmhouse. They continued to pay much heed to the soft earth about the house, noting that there were no hoofmarks of horses; this was a matter of significance to them. I did not understand why. Nor was I much attentive, still feeling faint of heart and sick of body.

As we crossed the fields, Ecthgow made a discovery which was of this nature: it was a small bit of stone, smaller than a child's fist, and it was polished and carved in crude fashion. All the warriors crowded around to examine it, I among them.

I saw it to be the torso of a pregnant female. There was no head, no arms, and no legs; only the torso with a greatly swollen belly and, above that, two pendulous swollen breasts.* I accounted this creation exceedingly crude and ugly, but nothing more. Yet the Northmen were suddenly overcome and pale and tremulous; their hands shook to touch it, and finally Buliwyf flung it to the ground and shattered it with the handle of his sword, until it lay in splintered stone fragments. And then were several of the warriors sick, and purged themselves upon the ground. And the general horror was very great, to my mystification.

Now they set off for the great hall of King Rothgar. No man spoke during our travel, which was the better part of an hour; every one of the Northmen seemed to be wrapped in bitter and consuming thought, and yet they showed no fear anymore.

At length, a herald upon a horse met us and barred our path. He noted the arms we carried and the bearing of the company and of Buliwyf, and shouted a warning.

Herger said to me, "He craves to know our names, and curtly, too."

Buliwyf made some answer to the herald, and from his tone I knew that Buliwyf was in no mood for courtly pleasantries. Herger said to me: "Buliwyf tells him we are subjects of King Higlac, of the kingdom of Yatlam, and we are on an errand to the King Rothgar, and would speak to him." And Herger added, "Buliwyf says that Rothgar is a most worthy king," but the tone of Herger conveyed the opposite sense of the matter.

This herald bade us continue to the great hall and wait outside while he told the King of our arrival. This we did, although Buliwyf and his party were not pleased at such treatment; there was grumbling and muttering, for it is the Northman's way to be hospitable and this did not seem gracious, to be kept outside. Yet they waited, and also removed their weapons, their swords and spears, but not their armor, and they left the weapons outside the doors to the hall.

Now the hall was surrounded on all sides by several dwellings in the fashion of the North people. These were long with curved sides, as at Trelburg; but they differed in the arrangement, for there were no squares here. Nor were there fortifications or earthworks to be seen. Rather, from the great hall and

---

*The described figurine corresponds closely to several carvings discovered by archaeologists in France and Austria.

the long houses about it, the ground sloped to a long flat green plain, here and there a farmhouse, and then, beyond, the hills and the edge of a forest.

I inquired of Herger whose long houses were these, and he said to me, "Some belong to the King, and others are for his royal family, and others for his nobles, and also for the servants and lower members of his court." He said also that it was a difficult place, though I did not comprehend his meaning in this.

Then we were allowed entry into the great hall of King Rothgar, which verily I say is to be counted one of the marvels of all the world, and all the more for its presence in the crude North country. This hall is called, among the Rothgar peoples, by the name of Hurot, for the Northmen give the names of people to the things of their life, to the buildings and boats and especially to the weapons. Now I say: this Hurot, the great hall of Rothgar, was as large as the Caliph's main palace, and richly inlaid with silver and even some gold, which is most rare in the North. On all sides were designs and ornaments of the greatest splendor and richness of artistry. It was truly a monument to the power and majesty of King Rothgar.

This King Rothgar sat at the distant end of Hurot Hall, a space so vast that he was so far we could hardly discern him. Standing behind his right shoulder was the same herald who had halted us. The herald made a speech, which Herger told me was thus: "Here, O King, is a band of warriors from the kingdom of Yatlam. They are newly arrived from the sea, and their leader is a man of the name Buliwyf. They beg leave to tell you of their errand, O King. Do not forbid them entry; they have the manner of earls, and from his bearing their chieftain is a mighty warrior. Greet them as earls, O King Rothgar."

Thus we were bid approach the King Rothgar.

King Rothgar appeared a man near death. He was not young, his hair was white, his skin was very pale, and his face was grooved with sorrow and fear. He regarded us with suspicion, wrinkling his eyes, or perhaps he was near blind, I do not know. Finally he broke into a speech, which Herger says was thus: "I know of this man, for I have sent for him on a hero's mission. He is Buliwyf, and I knew him as a child, when I traveled across the waters to the kingdom of Yatlam. He is the son of Higlac, who was my gracious host, and now this son comes to me in my time of need and sorrow."

Rothgar then called for the warriors to be summoned to the great hall, and gifts brought, and celebrations made.

Buliwyf then spoke, a long speech that Herger did not translate for me, since to speak when Buliwyf spoke would be a disrespect. However, the meaning was this: that Buliwyf had heard of the troubles of Rothgar, that he was sorry for these troubles, and that his own father's kingdom had been destroyed by these same troubles, and that he had come to save the kingdom of Rothgar from the evils that had beset them.

Still, I did not know what the Northmen called these evils, or how they thought of them, though I had viewed the handiwork of the beasts that tore men to pieces.

King Rothgar spoke again, in some haste. I took from the manner of his speaking that he wished to say some words before all his warriors and earls arrived. He said thus (from Herger): "O Buliwyf, I knew your father when I was myself a young man, new to my throne. Now I am old and heartsick. My head bows. My eyes weep with shame to acknowledge my weakness. As you see, my throne is almost a barren spot. My lands are becoming a wild place. What the fiends have wrought to my kingdom I cannot say. Often at night, my warriors, brave with drink, swear to topple the fiends. And then when the bleak light of dawn creeps over the misty fields, we see bloody bodies everywhere. Thus is the sorrow of my life, and I shall speak no more of it."

Now a bench was brought out and a meal set before us, and I inquired of Herger what was the meaning of the "fiends" of which the King spoke. Herger was angry, and said I was never to ask again.

That evening there was a great celebration, and King Rothgar and his Queen Weilew, in a garment dripping gemstones and gold, presided over the nobles and warriors and earls of the kingdom of Rothgar. These nobles were a paltry lot; they were old men and drank overmuch and many were crippled or wounded. In the eyes of all of them was the hollow stare of fear, and there was hollowness in their merriment, too.

Also there was the son named Wiglif, of whom I have earlier spoken, the son of Rothgar who murdered three of his brothers. This man was young and slender with a blond beard and with eyes that never settled on anything, but moved about here and there constantly; also he never met the gaze of another. Herger saw him and said, "He is a fox." By this he meant that he was a slippery and changeable person of false demeanor, for the North people believe the fox is an animal that can assume any form it pleases.

Now, in the middle portion of the festivities, Rothgar sent his herald to the doors of Hurot Hall, and this herald reported that the mist would not descend that night. There was much happiness and celebration over this announcement that the night was clear; all were pleased save Wiglif.

At a particular time, the son Wiglif rose to his feet and said, "I drink honor to our guests, and especially Buliwyf, a brave and true warrior who has come to aid us in our plight—although it may prove too great an obstacle for him to overcome." Herger whispered these words to me, and I caught that it was praise and insult in one breath.

All eyes turned to Buliwyf for his response. Buliwyf stood, and looked to Wiglif, and then said, "I have no fear of anything, even the callow fiend that creeps at night to murder men in their sleep." This I took to refer to the "wendol," but Wiglif turned pale and gripped the chair in which he sat.

"Do you speak of me?" Wiglif said, in a trembling tongue.

Buliwyf made this response: "No, but I do not fear you any more than the monsters of the mist."

The young man Wiglif persisted, although Rothgar the King called for him to be seated. Wiglif said to all the assembled nobles: "This Buliwyf, arrived from foreign shores, has by appearance great pride and great strength. Yet have I arranged to test his mettle, for pride may cover any man's eyes."

Now I saw this thing happen: a strong warrior, seated at a table near the door, behind Buliwyf, rose with speed, plucked up a spear, and charged at the back of Buliwyf. All this happened in less time than it takes a man to suck in his breath.* Yet also Buliwyf turned, plucked up a spear, and with this he caught the warrior full into the chest, and lifted him by the shaft of the spear high over his head and flung him against a wall. Thus was this warrior skewered on the spear, his feet dangling above the floor, kicking; the shaft of the spear was buried into the wall of the hall of Hurot. The warrior died with a sound.

Now there came much commotion, and Buliwyf turned to face Wiglif, and said, "So shall I dispatch any menace," and then with great immediacy Herger spoke, in an overloud voice, and made many gestures towards my person. I was much confused by these events, and in truth my eyes were stuck upon this dead warrior pinned to the wall.

Then Herger turned to me, and said in Latin, "You shall sing a song for the court of King Rothgar. All desire it."

I asked of him, "What shall I sing? I know no song." He made this reply: "You will sing something that entertains the heart." And he added, "Do not speak of your one God. No one cares for such nonsense."

In truth, I did not know what to sing, for I am no minstrel. A time passed while all stared toward me, and there was silence in the hall. Then Herger said to me, "Sing a song of kings and valor in battle."

I said that I knew no such songs, but that I could tell them a fable, which in my country was accounted funny and entertaining. To this he said that I had made a wise choice. Then I told them—King Rothgar, his Queen Weilew, his son Wiglif, and all the assembled earls and warriors—the story of Abu Kassim's slippers, which all know. I spoke lightly, and smiled all the while, and in the first instance the Northmen were pleased, and laughed and slapped their bellies.

But now this strange event occurred. As I continued in my telling, the Northmen ceased to laugh, and turned gloomy by degrees, ever more so, and when I had finished the tale, there was no laughter, but dire silence.

Herger said to me, "You could not know, but that is no tale for laughter, and now I must make amends," and thereupon he said some speech that I

*Ducere spiritu: literally, "to inhale."

took to be a joke at my own expense, and there was general laughter, and at length the celebration recommenced.

The story of Abu Kassim's slippers is ancient in Arabic culture, and was well known to Ibn Fadlan and his fellow Bagdad citizens.

The story exists in many versions, and can be told briefly or elaborately, depending upon the enthusiasm of the teller. Briefly, Abu Kassim is a rich merchant and a miser who wishes to hide the fact of his wealth, in order to strike better bargains in his trade. To give the appearance of poverty, he wears a pair of particularly tawdry, miserable slippers, hoping that people will be fooled, but nobody is. Instead, the people around him think he is silly and preposterous.

One day, Abu Kassim strikes a particularly favorable bargain in glassware, and decides to celebrate, not in the accepted manner of treating his friends to a feast, but by treating himself to the small selfish luxury of a visit to the public baths. He leaves his clothes and shoes in the anteroom, and a friend berates him for his worn and inappropriate shoes. Abu Kassim replies that they are still serviceable, and he enters the bath with his friend. Later, a powerful judge also comes to the baths, and disrobes, leaving behind an elegant pair of slippers. Meanwhile, Abu Kassim departs from the bath and cannot find his old slippers; in their place he finds a new and beautiful pair of shoes, and, presuming these to be a present from his friend, he puts them on and leaves.

When the judge leaves, his own slippers are missing, and all he can find are a miserable, tawdry pair of slippers, which everyone knows belong to the miser Abu Kassim. The judge is angry; servants are dispatched to retrieve the missing slippers; and they are soon found upon the very feet of the thief, who is hauled into court before the magistrate and severely fined.

Abu Kassim curses his bad luck, and once home flings the unlucky slippers out of his window, where they fall into the muddy Tigris River. Some days later, a group of fishermen haul in their catch, and find along with some fish the slippers of Abu Kassim; the hobnails of these slippers have torn their nets. Enraged, they throw the soggy slippers through an open window. The window happens to be that of Abu Kassim; the slippers fall upon the newly purchased glassware and smash it all.

Abu Kassim is heartbroken, and grieves as only a stingy miser can. He vows the wretched slippers shall do him no further harm and, to be certain, goes to his garden with a shovel and buries them. As it happens, his next-door neighbor sees Abu Kassim digging, a menial task fit only for a servant. The neighbor assumes that if the master of the house is doing this chore himself, it must be in order to bury treasure. Thus the neighbor goes to the Caliph and informs on Abu Kassim, for according to the laws of the land, any treasure found in the ground is the property of the Caliph.

Abu Kassim is called before the Caliph, and when he reports that he buried only a pair of old slippers, the court laughs uproariously at the obviousness of the merchant's attempt to conceal his true, and illegal, purpose. The Caliph is angry to be thought such a fool as to be given this silly lie, and increases the magnitude of his fine accordingly. Abu Kassim is thunderstruck when sentence is passed, and yet he is obliged to pay.

Abu Kassim is now determined to be rid of his slippers once and for all. To be certain of no further trouble, he makes a pilgrimage far from town and drops the slippers into a distant pond, watching them sink to the bottom with satisfaction. But the pond feeds the city's water supply, and eventually the slippers clog the pipes; guards dispatched to release the stricture find the slippers and recognize them, for everyone knows the slippers of this notorious miser. Abu Kassim is again brought before the Caliph, on a charge of befouling the water of the town, and his fine is much greater than before. The slippers are returned to him.

Now Abu Kassim determines to burn the slippers, but they are still wet, so he set them on the balcony to dry. A dog sees them and plays with them; one of the slippers falls from his jaws and drops to the street far below, where it strikes a woman passing by. The woman is pregnant, and the force of the blow causes a miscarriage. Her husband runs to the court to seek damages, which are awarded plentifully, and Abu Kassim, now a broken and impoverished man, is obliged to pay.

The slyly literal Arabic moral states that this story illustrates what evils can befall a man who does not change his slippers often enough. But undoubtedly the undercurrent to the tale, the idea of a man who cannot shake off some burden, was what disturbed the Northmen.

Now the night passed with further celebrations, and all the warriors of Buliwyf disported in a carefree fashion. I saw the son Wiglif glaring at Buliwyf before leaving the hall, but Buliwyf paid no attention, preferring the ministrations of slave girls and freeborn women. After a time I slept.

In the morning, I awoke to the sounds of hammering and, venturing from the great hall of Hurot, I found all the peoples of the kingdom of Rothgar at work on defenses. These were being laid out in preliminary fashion: horses drew up quantities of fence posts, which warriors sharpened to points; Buliwyf himself directed the placement of defense works, by marking scratches in the ground with the tip of his sword. For this he did not use his great sword Runding, but rather some other sword; I do not know if there was a reason for this.

Upon the middle portion of the day, the woman who was called the angel of death* came and cast bones on the ground, and made incantations over

---

*This is not the same "angel of death" who was with the Northmen on the banks of the Volga. Apparently each tribe had an old woman who performed shamanistic functions and was referred to as "the angel of death." It is thus a generic term.

them, and announced that the mist would come that night. Upon hearing this, Buliwyf called for all work to cease, and a great banquet to be prepared. In this matter, all the people concurred, and ceased their efforts. I inquired of Herger why there should be a banquet, but he replied to me that I had too many questions. It is also true that I had timed my inquiry badly, for he was posturing before a blond slave girl who smiled warmly in his direction.

Now, in the later part of the day, Buliwyf called together all his warriors and said to them, "Prepare for battle," and they agreed, and wished luck one to another, while all about us the banquet was being made ready.

The night banquet was much as the previous one, although there were fewer of Rothgar's nobles and earls. Indeed, I learned that many nobles would not attend at all, for fear of what would happen in the Hurot Hall that night, for it seemed that this place was the center of the fiend's interest in the area; that he coveted Hurot Hall, or some similar thing—I could not be sure of the meaning.

This banquet was not enjoyable to me, for reason of my apprehension of coming events. However, this event occurred: one of the elderly nobles spoke some Latin, and also some of the Iberian dialects, for he had traveled to the region of the caliphate of Cordova as a younger man, and I engaged him in conversation. In this circumstance, I feigned knowledge that I did not have, as you shall see.

He spoke to me thus: "So you are the foreigner who shall be the number thirteen?" And I said that I was such. "You must be exceedingly brave," the old man said, "and for your bravery I salute you." To this I made some trifling polite response, of the sense that I was a coward compared to the others of Buliwyf's company; which indeed was more than true.

"No matter," said the old man, who was deep in his cups, having drunk the liquor of the region—a vile substance they call mead, yet it is potent— "you are still a brave man to face the wendol."

Now I sensed that I might finally learn some matters of substance. I repeated to this old man a saying of the Northmen, which Herger had once said to me. I said, "Animals die, friends die, and I shall die, but one thing never dies, and that is the reputation we leave behind at our death."

The old man cackled toothlessly at this; he was pleased I knew a Northman proverb. He said, "That is so, but the wendol have a reputation, too." And I replied, with the utmost indifference: "Truly? I am not aware of it."

At this the old man said that I was a foreigner, and he would consent to enlighten me, and he told me this: the name of "wendol," or "windon," is a very ancient name, as old as any of the peoples of the North country, and it means "the black mist." To the Northmen, this means a mist that brings, under cover of night, black fiends who murder and kill and eat the flesh of human beings.* The fiends are hairy and loathsome to touch and smell; they are fierce and cunning; they speak no language of any man and yet converse among themselves; they come with the night fog, and disappear by day—to where, no man durst follow.

The old man said to me thus: "You can know the regions where dwell the fiends of the black mist by many ways. From time to time, warriors on horse may hunt a stag with dogs, chasing the stag over hill and dale for many miles of forest and open land. And then the stag comes to some marshy tarn or brackish swamp, and here it will halt, preferring to be torn to bits by the hounds rather than enter that loathsome region. Thus we know of the areas where the wendol live, and we know that even the animals will not enter thence."

I expressed over-great wonderment at this tale, in order to draw further words from the old man. Herger saw me then, gave me a menacing look, but I paid him no heed.

The old man continued thus: "In olden days, the black mist was feared by all the Northmen of every region. Since my father and his father and his father before, no Northman has seen the black mist, and some of the young warriors counted us old fools to remember the ancient tales of their horror and depredations. Yet the chiefs of the Northmen in all the kingdoms, even in Norway, have always been prepared for the return of the black mist. All of our towns and our fortresses are protected and defended from the land. Since the time of the father of my father's father, our peoples have thus acted, and never have we seen the black mist. Now it has returned."

I inquired why the black mist had returned, and he lowered his voice to speak this reply: "The black mist has come from the vanity and weakness of

---

*The Scandinavians were apparently more impressed by the stealth and viciousness of the creatures than the fact of their cannibalism. Jensen suggests that cannibalism might be abhorrent to the Norsemen because it made entry into Valhalla more difficult; there is no evidence for this view.

However, for Ibn Fadlan, with his extensive erudition, the notion of cannibalism may have implied some difficulties in the afterlife. The Eater of the Dead is a well-known creature of Egyptian mythology, a fearsome beast with the head of a crocodile, the trunk of a lion, and the back of a hippopotamus. This Eater of the Dead devours the wicked after their Judgment.

It is worth remembering that for most of man's history, ritual cannibalism, in one form or another, for one reason or another, was neither rare nor remarkable. Peking man and Neanderthal man were both apparently cannibals; so were, at various times, the Scythians, the Chinese, the Irish, the Peruvians, the Mayoruna, the Jagas, the Egyptians, the Australian aborigines, the Maoris, the Greeks, the Hurons, the Iroquois, the Pawnees, and the Ashanti.

During the time Ibn Fadlan was in Scandinavia, other Arab traders were in China, where they recorded that human flesh—referred to as "two-legged mutton"—was openly and legally sold in markets.

Martinson suggests that the Northmen found the wendol cannibalism repellent because they believed that the flesh of warriors was fed to women, particularly the mother of the wendol. There is no evidence for this view, either, but it would certainly make a Norse warrior's death more shameful.

Rothgar, who has offended the gods with his foolish splendor and tempted the fiends with the siting of his great hall, which has no protection from the land. Rothgar is old and he knows he will not be remembered for battles fought and won, and so he built this splendid hall, which is the talk of all the world, and pleases his vanity. Rothgar acts as a god, yet he is a man, and the gods have sent the black mist to strike him down and show him humility."

I said to this old man that perhaps Rothgar was resented in the kingdom. He replied thus: "No man is so good as to be free from all evil, nor so bad as to be worth nothing. Rothgar is a just king and his people prospered all of his life. The wisdom and richness of his rule are here, in Hurot Hall, and they are splendid. His only fault is this, that he forgot defense, for we have a saying among us: 'A man should never move a step from his weapons.' Rothgar has no weapons; he is toothless and weak; and the black mist seeps freely over the land."

I desired to know more, but the old man was tired, and turned away from me, and soon was asleep. Verily, the food and drink of Rothgar's hospitality were much, and many of the number of earls and nobles were drowsy.

Of the table of Rothgar I shall say this: that every man had a tablecloth and plate, and spoon and knife; that the meal was boiled pork and goat, and some fish, too, for the Northmen much prefer boiled meat to roasted. Then there were cabbages and onions in abundance, and apples and hazelnuts. A sweetish fleshy meat was given me that I had not tasted before; this, I was told, was elk, or rain-deer.

The dreadful foul drink called mead is made from honey, then fermented. It is the sourest, blackest, vilest stuff ever invented by any man, and yet it is potent beyond all knowing; a few drinks, and the world spins. But I did not drink, praise Allah.

Now I noticed that Buliwyf and all his company did not drink that night, or only sparingly, and Rothgar took this as no insult, but rather acknowledged it as the natural course of things. There was no wind that night; the candles and flames of Hurot Hall did not flicker, and yet it was damp, and chill. I saw with my own eyes that out of doors the mist was rolling in from the hills, blocking the silvered light of the moon, cloaking all in blackness.

As the night continued, King Rothgar and his Queen departed for sleep, and the massive doors of Hurot Hall were locked and barred, and the nobles and earls remaining there fell into a drunken stupor and snored loudly.

Then Buliwyf and his men, still wearing their armor, went about the room, dousing the candles and seeing to the fires, that they should burn low and weak. I asked Herger the meaning of this, and he told me to pray for my life, and to feign sleep. I was given a weapon, a short sword, but it was little comfort to me; I am not a warrior and know it full well.

Verily, all the men feigned sleep, Buliwyf and his men joined the slumbering bodies of the King Rothgar's earls, who were truly snoring. How long we waited I do not know, for I think I slept awhile myself. Then all at once I was awake, in a manner of unnatural sharp alertness; I was not drowsy but instantly tense and alert, still lying on a bearskin cloth on the floor of the great hall. It was dark night; the candles in the hall burned low, and a faint breeze whispered through the hall and fluttered the yellow flames.

And then I heard a low grunting sound, like the rooting of a pig, carried to me by the breeze, and I smelled a rank odor like the rot of a carcass after a month, and I feared greatly. This rooting sound, for I can call it none else, this grumbling, grunting, snorting sound, grew louder and more excited. It came from outdoors, at one side of the hall. Then I heard it from another side, and then another, and another. Verily the hall was surrounded.

I sat up on one elbow, my heart pounding, and I looked about the hall. No man among the sleeping warriors moved, and yet there was Herger, lying with his eyes wide open. And there, too, Buliwyf, breathing in a snore, with his eyes also wide open. From this I gathered that all the warriors of Buliwyf were waiting to do battle with the wendol, whose sounds now filled the air.

By Allah, there is no fear greater than that of a man when he does not know the cause. How long I lay upon the bearskin, hearing the grunting of the wendol and smelling their foul odors! How long I waited for I knew not what, the start of some battle more fearsome in the prospect than it could be in the fighting! I remembered this: that the Northmen have a saying of praise that they carve upon the tombstones of noble warriors, which is this: "He did not flee battle." None of the company of Buliwyf fled that night, though the sounds and the stink were all around them, now louder, now fainter, now from one direction, now another. And yet they waited.

Then came the most fearsome moment. All sounds ceased. There was utter silence, except for the snoring of the men and the low crackle of the fire. Still none of the warriors of Buliwyf stirred.

And then there was a mighty crash upon the solid doors of the hall of Hurot, and these doors burst open, and a rush of reeking air gutted all the lights, and the black mist entered the room. I did not count their number: verily it seemed thousands of black grunting shapes, and yet it might have been no more than five or six, huge black shapes hardly in the manner of men, and yet also manlike. The air stank of blood and death; I was cold beyond reason, and shivered. Yet still no warrior moved.

Then, with a curdling scream to wake the dead, Buliwyf leapt up, and in his arms he swung the giant sword Runding, which sang like a sizzling flame as it cut the air. And his warriors leapt up with him, and all joined the battle. The shouts of the men mingled with the pig-grunts and the odors of the black mist, and there was terror and confusion and great wracking and rending of the Hurot Hall.

I myself had no stomach for battle, and yet I was set upon by one of these mist monsters, who came close to me, and I saw gleaming red eyes—verily I saw eyes that shone like fire, and I smelled the reek, and I was lifted bodily and flung across the room as a child flings a pebble. I struck the wall and fell to the ground, and was greatly dazed for the next period, so all around me was more confused than true.

I remember, most distinctly, the touch of these monsters upon me, especially the furry aspect of the bodies, for these mist monsters have hair as long as a hairy dog, and as thick, on all parts of their bodies. And I remember the fetid smell of the breath of the monster who flung me.

The battle raged for how long I cannot know, but it concluded most suddenly of a moment. And then the black mist was gone, slunk away, grunting and panting and stinking, leaving behind destruction and death that we could not know until we had lighted fresh tapers.

Here is how the battle waged. Of the company of Buliwyf, three were dead, Roneth and Halga, both earls, and Edgtho, a warrior. The first had his chest torn open. The second had his spine broken. The third had his head torn off in the manner I had already witnessed. All these warriors were dead.

Wounded were two others, Haltaf and Rethel. Haltaf had lost an ear, and Rethel two fingers of his right hand. Both men were not mortally injured, and made no complaint, for it is the Northman way to bear the wounds of battle cheerfully, and to praise above all the retaining of life.

As for Buliwyf and Herger and all the others, they were soaked in blood as if they had bathed in it. Now I shall say what many will not believe, and yet it was so: our company had killed not one of the mist monsters. Each had slunk away, some perhaps mortally wounded, and yet they had escaped.

Herger said thus: "I saw two of their number carrying a third, who was dead." Perhaps this was so, for all generally agreed upon it. I learned that the mist monsters never leave one of their kind to the society of men, but rather will risk great dangers to retrieve him from human purview. So also will they go to extreme lengths to keep a victim's head, and we could not find the head of Edgtho in any place; the monsters had carried it off with them.

Then Buliwyf spoke, and Herger told me his words thus: "Look, I have retained a trophy of the night's bloody deeds. See, here is an arm of one of the fiends."

And, true to his work, Buliwyf held the arm of one of the mist monsters, cut off at the shoulder by the great sword Runding. All the warriors crowded around to examine it. I perceived it thusly: it appeared to be small, with a hand of abnormally large size. But the forearm and upper arm were not large to match it, although the muscles were powerful. There was long black matted hair on all parts of the arm except the palm of the hand. Finally it is to say that the arm stank as the whole beast stank, with the fetid smell of the black mist.

Now all the warriors cheered Buliwyf, and his sword Runding. The fiend's arm was hung from the rafters of the great hall of Hurot, and marveled at by all the people of the kingdom of Rothgar. Thus ended the first battle with the wendol.

THE EVENTS THAT FOLLOWED THE FIRST BATTLE

Verily, the people of the North country never act as human beings of reason and sense. After the attack of the mist monsters, and their beating back by Buliwyf and his company, with me amongst them, the men of the kingdom of Rothgar did nothing.

There was no celebration, no feasting, no jubilation or display of happiness. From far and wide, the people of the kingdom came to view the dangling arm of the fiend, which hung in the great hall, and this they greeted with much amazement and astonishment. But Rothgar himself, the half-blind old man, expressed no pleasure, and presented Buliwyf and his company with no gifts, planned no feasts, gave him no slaves, no silver, no precious garments, or any other sign of honor.

Contrary to any expression of pleasure, King Rothgar made a long face and was solemn, and seemed more fearful than he had been before. I myself, though I did not speak it aloud, suspected that Rothgar preferred his earlier condition, before the black mist was beaten.

Nor was Buliwyf different in manner. He called for no ceremonies, no feasting, no drinking or eating of food. The nobles who had died valiantly in the battle of the night were quickly placed in pits with a wooden roof over the top, and left there for the assigned ten days. There was haste in this matter.

Yet it was only in the laying out of the dead warriors that Buliwyf and his comrades showed happiness, or allowed themselves any smiles. After further time among the Northmen, I learned that they smile upon any death in battle, for this is pleasure taken on behalf of the dead person, and not the living. They are pleased when any man dies a warrior's death. Also the opposite is held true by them; they show distress when a man dies in his sleep, or in a bed. They say of such a man, "He died as a cow in the straw." This is no insult, but it is a reason for mourning the death.

The Northmen believe that how a man dies determines his condition in the afterlife, and they value the death of a warrior in battle above all. A "straw death" is shameful.

Any man who dies in his sleep is said by them to be strangled by the maran, or mare of the night. This creature is a woman, which makes such a death shameful, for to die at the hands of a woman is degrading above all things.

Also they say to die without your weapons is degrading, and a Northman warrior will always sleep with his weapons, so that if the maran comes at night, he will have his weapons at hand. Seldom does a warrior die of some illness, or of the enfeeblement of age. I heard of one king, of the name Ane, who lived to such an age that he became as an infant, toothless and existing upon the food of an infant, and he spent all his days in his bed drinking milk from a horn. But this was told to me as most uncommon in the North country. With my own eyes I saw few men grown very old, by which I mean grown old to the time when the beard is not only white but falling out from the chin and face.

Several of their women live to great age, especially such as the old crone they call the angel of death; these old women are counted as having magical powers in healing of wounds, casting of spells, banishing evil influences, and foretelling the future of events.

The women of the North people do not fight among themselves, and often did I see them intercede in a growing brawl or duel of two men, to quench the rising anger. This they will do especially if the warriors are thickened and slow with drink. This is often the circumstance.

Now, the Northmen, who drink much liquor, and at all hours of the day and night, drank nothing on the day after the battle. Seldom did the people of Rothgar offer them a cup, and when it happened, the cup was refused. This I found most puzzling, and spoke of it finally to Herger.

Herger shook his shoulders in the Northmen's gesture of unconcern, or indifference. "Everyone is afraid," he said.

I inquired why there should still be a reason to fear. He spoke thus: "It is because they know that the black mist will return."

Now I admit that I was puffed with the arrogance of a fighting man, though in truth I knew I did not deserve such a posture. Even so, I felt exhilaration at my survival, and the people of Rothgar treated me as one of a company of mighty warriors. I said boldly, "Who cares for that? If they come again, we shall beat them a second time."

Indeed, I was vain as a young cock, and I am abashed now to think upon my strutting. Herger responded: "The kingdom of Rothgar has no fighting warriors or earls; they are all long since dead, and we alone must defend the kingdom. Yesterday we were thirteen. Today we are ten, and of that ten two are wounded and cannot fight as full men. The black mist is angered, and it will take a terrible vengeance."

I said to Herger, who had suffered some minor wounds in the fray—but nothing so fierce as the claw marks upon my own face, which I bore proudly—that I feared nothing the demons would do.

He answered curtly that I was an Arab and understood nothing of the ways of the North country, and he told me that the vengeance of the black mist would be terrible and profound. He said, "They will return as Korgon."

I did not know the sense of the word. "What is Korgon?"

He said to me, "The glowworm dragon, which swoops down through the air."

Now this seemed fanciful, but I had already seen the sea monsters just as they said that such beasts truly lived, and also I saw Herger's strained and tired countenance, and I perceived that he believed in the glowworm dragon. I said, "When will Korgon come?"

"Perhaps tonight," Herger said.

Verily, even as he spoke, I saw that Buliwyf, though he had slept not at all during the night and his eyes were red and heavy with fatigue, was directing anew the building of defenses around the hall of Hurot. All the people of the kingdom worked, the children and the women and the old men, and the slaves as well, under the direction of Buliwyf and his lieutenant Ecthgow.

This is what they did: about the perimeter of Hurot and the adjacent buildings, those being the dwellings of the King Rothgar and some of his nobles, and the rude huts of the slaves of these families, and one or another of the farmers who lived closest to the sea, all around this area Buliwyf erected a kind of fence of crossed lances and poles with sharpened points. This fence was not higher than a man's shoulders, and although the points were sharp and menacing, I could not see the value of this defense, for men could scale it easily.

I spoke of this to Herger, who called me a stupid Arab. Herger was in an ill temper.

Now a further defense was constructed, a ditch outside the pole fence, one and a half paces beyond. This ditch was most peculiar. It was not deep, never more than a man's knees, and often less. It was unevenly dug, so that in places it was shallow, and in other places deeper, with small pits. And in places short lances were sunk into the earth, points upward.

I understood the value of this paltry ditch no better than the fence, but I did not inquire of Herger, already knowing his mood. Instead I aided in the work as best I could, pausing only once to have my way with a slavewoman in the Northman's fashion, for in the excitement of the night's battle and the day's preparations I was most energetic.

Now, during my journey with Buliwyf and his warriors up the Volga, Herger had told me that unknown women, especially if attractive or seductive, were to be mistrusted. Herger said to me that within the forests and wild places of the North country there live women who are called woodwomen. These woodwomen entice men by their beauty and soft words, yet when a man approaches them, he finds that they are hollow at the back part, and are apparitions. Then the woodwomen cast a spell upon the seduced man and he becomes their captive.

Now, Herger had thus warned me, and verily it is true that I approached this slavewoman with trepidation, because I did not know her. And I felt her back with my hand, and she laughed; for she knew the reason of the touch, to assure myself that she was no wood spirit. I felt a fool at that time, and cursed myself for placing faith in a heathen superstition. Yet I have discovered that if all those around you believe some particular thing, you will soon be tempted to share in that belief, and so it was with me.

The women of the North people are pale as the men, and equally as tall in stature; the greater number of them looked down upon my head. The women have blue eyes and wear their hair very long, but the hair is fine and easily snarled. Therefore they bundle it up about their necks and upon their heads; to aid in this, they have fashioned for themselves all manner of clasps and pins of ornamented silver or wood. This constitutes their principal adornment. Also the wife of a rich man wears neck chains of gold and silver, as I have earlier said; so, too, do the women favor bracelets of silver, formed in the shape of dragons and snakes, and these they wear upon the arm between the elbow and shoulder. The designs of the North people are intricate and interlaced, as if to portray the weaving of tree branches or serpents; these designs are most beautiful.*

The North people account themselves keen judges of beauty in women. But in truth, all their women seemed to my eyes to be emaciated, their bodies all angles and lumpy with bones; their faces, too, are bony and the cheeks set high. These qualities the Northmen value and praise, although such a woman would not attract a glance in the City of Peace but would be accounted no better than a half-starved dog with protruding ribs. The Northwomen have ribs that protrude in just such a fashion.

I do not know why the women are so thin, for they eat lustily, and as much as the men, yet gain no flesh upon their bodies.

Also the women show no deference, or any demure behavior; they are never veiled, and they relieve themselves in public places, as suits their urge. Similarly they will make bold advances to any man who catches their fancy, as if they were men themselves; and the warriors never chide them for this. Such is the case even if the woman be a slave, for as I have said, the Northmen are most kind and forbearing to their slaves, especially the women slaves.

With the progression of the day, I saw clearly that the defenses of Buliwyf would not be completed by nightfall, neither the pole fence nor the shallow ditch. Buliwyf saw it also, and called to King Rothgar, who summoned the old crone. This old crone, who was withered and had the beard of a man, killed a sheep and spread the entrails† on the ground. Then she made a variety of

---

*An Arab would be especially inclined to think so, for Islamic religious art tends to be nonrepresentational, and in quality similar to much Scandinavian art, which often seems to favor pure design. However, the Norsemen had no injunction against representing gods, and often did so.

† أوْرِدَة : literally, "veins." The Arabic phrase has led to some scholarly errors; E. D. Graham has written, for example that "the Vikings foretold the future by a ritual of cutting the veins of animals and spreading them on the ground." This is almost certainly

chanting song, which lasted a lengthy time, and much supplication to the sky.

I still did not ask Herger of this, because of his mood. Instead I watched the other warriors of Buliwyf, who looked to the sea. The ocean was gray and rough, the sky leaden, but a strong breeze blew toward the land. This satisfied the warriors, and I guessed the reason: that an ocean breeze toward the land would prevent the mist from descending from the hills. This was true.

Upon nightfall, work was halted on the defenses, and to my perplexity Rothgar held another banquet of splendid proportions; and this evening while I watched, Buliwyf, and Herger, and all the other warriors drank much mead and reveled as if they lacked any worldly cares, and had their way with the slavewomen, and then all sank into a stuporous droning sleep.

Now this also I learned: that each of the warriors of Buliwyf had chosen from among the slavewomen one whom in particular they favored, although not to the exclusion of others. In intoxication, Herger said to me of the woman he had favored, "She shall die with me, if need be." From this I took as the meaning that each of the warriors of Buliwyf had selected some woman who would die for him upon the funeral pyre, and this woman they treated with more courtesy and attention than the others; for they were visitors to this country, and had no slavewomen of their own who could be ordered by kin to do their bidding.

Now, in the early period of my time among the Venden, the Northwomen would not approach me, on account of my darkness of skin and hair, but there was much whispering and glancing in my direction, and giggles one to another. I saw that these unveiled women would nonetheless make a veil with their hands from time to time, and especially when they were laughing. Then I had asked of Herger: "Why do they do this thing?" for I wished not to behave in a manner contrary to the North custom.

Herger made this reply: "The women believe that the Arabs are as stallions, for so they have heard as a rumor." Nor was this any amazement to me, for this reason: in all the lands I have traveled, and so also within the round walls of the City of Peace, verily in every location where men gather and make for themselves a society, I have learned these things to be truths. First, that the peoples of a particular land believe their customs to be fitting and proper and better than any other. Second, that any stranger, a man or also a woman, is accounted inferior in all ways save in the matter of generation. Thus the Turks believe the Persians gifted lovers; the Persians stand in awe of the black-skinned peoples; and they in turn of some others, severally; and so it contin-

wrong; the Arabic phrase for cleaning an animal is "cutting the veins," and Ibn Fadlan was here referring to the widespread practice of divination by examination of entrails. Linguists, who deal with such vernacular phrases all the time, are fond of discrepancies in meaning; a favorite example of Halstead's is the English warning "Look out!" which usually means that one should do exactly the opposite and dive for cover.

ues, sometimes by reason given of proportion of genitalia, sometimes by reason given of endurance in the act, sometimes by reason given of especial skill or posturing.

I cannot say whether the Northwomen truly believe as Herger spoke, but verily I discovered that they were much amazed at me by virtue of my surgery,* which practice is unknown among them, as they are dirty heathens. Of the manner of trusting, these women are noisy and energetic, and of such odor that I was obliged to stop my breath for the duration; also they are given to bucking and twisting, scratching and biting, so that a man may be thrown from his mount, as the Northmen speak of it. For myself I accounted the whole business more pain than pleasure.

The Northmen say of the act, "I did battle with such a woman or another," and proudly show their blue marks and abrasions to their comrades, as if these were true wounds of warfare. However, the men never did injury to any woman that I could see.

Now this night, while all the warriors of Buliwyf slept, I was too afraid to drink or laugh; I feared the return of the wendol. Yet they did not return, and I also eventually slept, but fitfully.

Now in the following day there was no wind, and all the people of the kingdom of Rothgar worked with dedication and fear; there was talk everywhere of the Korgon, and the certainty that it would attack upon the night. The clawmark wounds on my face now pained me, for they pinched as they healed, and ached whenever I moved my mouth to eat or speak. Also it is true that my warriors's fever had left me. I was afraid once more, and I worked in silence alongside the women and old men.

Toward the middle time of the day, I was visited by the old and toothless noble whom I had spoken to in the banquet hall. This old noble sought me out, and said thus in Latin, "I will have words with you." He led me to step a few paces apart from the workers at the defenses.

Now he made a great show of examining my wounds, which in truth were not serious, and while he examined these cuts he said to me, "I have a warning for your company. There is unrest in the heart of Rothgar." This he spoke in Latin.

"What is the cause?" I said.

"It is the herald, and also the son Wiglif, who stands at the ear of the King," the old nobleman said. "And also the friend of Wiglif. Wiglif speaks to Rothgar that Buliwyf and his company plan to kill the King and rule the kingdom."

"That is not the truth," I said, although I did not know this. In honest fact, I had thought upon this matter from time to time; Buliwyf was young and vital, and Rothgar old and weak, and while it is true that the ways of the Northmen are strange, it is also true that all men are the same.

"The herald and Wiglif are envious of Buliwyf," the old noble spoke to

*Circumcision.

me. "They poison the air in the ear of the King. All this I tell to you so that you may tell the others to be wary, for this is a matter fit for a basilisk." And then he pronounced my wounds to be minor, and turned away.

Then the noble came back once more. He said, "The friend of Wiglif is Ragnar," and he went away a second time, not looking back upon me further.

In great consternation, I dug and worked at the defenses until I found myself near to Herger. The mood of Herger was still as grim as it had been upon the day previous. He greeted me with these words: "I do not want to hear the questions of a fool."

I said to him that I had no questions, and I reported to him what the old noble had spoken to me; also I told him it was a matter fit for a basilisk.* At my speech, Herger frowned and swore oaths and stamped his foot, and bid me accompany him to Buliwyf.

Buliwyf directed work on the ditch at the other side of the encampment; Herger drew him aside, and spoke rapidly in the Norse tongue, with gestures to my person. Buliwyf frowned, and swore oaths and stamped his foot much as Herger, and then asked a question. Herger said to me, "Buliwyf asks who is the friend of Wiglif? Did the old man tell you who is the friend of Wiglif?"

I responded that he had, and the friend was of the name Ragnar. At this report, Herger and Buliwyf spoke further among themselves, and disputed briefly, and then Buliwyf turned away and left me with Herger. "It is decided," Herger said.

"What is decided?" I inquired.

"Keep your teeth together," Herger said, which is a North expression meaning do not talk.

Thus I returned to my labors, understanding no more than I had at the beginning of the matter. Once again I thought these Northmen to be the most peculiar and contrary men on the face of the earth, for in no matter do they behave as one would expect sensible beings to behave. Yet I worked upon their silly fence, and their shallow ditch; and I watched, and waited.

At the time of the afternoon prayer, I observed that Herger had taken up a work position near to a strapping, giant youth. Herger and his youth toiled side by side in the ditch for some time, and it appeared to my way of seeing that

---

*Ibn Fadlan does not describe a basilisk, apparently assuming that his readers are familiar with the mythological creature, which appears in the early beliefs of nearly all Western cultures. Also known as a cockatrice, the basilisk is generally a variety of cock with a serpent's tail and eight legs, and sometimes bearing scales instead of feathers. What is always true of the basilisk is that his stare is deadly, like the stare of a Gorgon; and the venom of the basilisk is particularly lethal. According to some accounts, a person who stabs a basilisk will watch the venom travel up the sword and onto his hand. The man will then be obliged to cut off his own hand to save his body.

It is probably this sense of the danger of the basilisk that prompts its mention here. The old noble is telling Ibn Fadlan that a direct confrontation with the troublemakers will not solve the problem. Interestingly, one way to dispatch a basilisk was to let it see its reflected image in a mirror; it would then be killed by its own stare.

Herger took some pains to fling dirt into the face of the youth, who was in truth a head taller than Herger, and younger, too.

The youth protested, and Herger apologized; but soon was flinging dirt again. Again, Herger apologized; now the youth was angry and his face was red. No more than a short time passed before Herger was again flinging dirt, and the youth sputtered and spat it and was angry in the extreme. He shouted at Herger, who later told me the words of their conversation, although the meaning was evident enough at the time.

The youth spoke: "You dig as a dog."

Herger spoke in answer: "Do you call me a dog?"

To this, the youth said: "No, I said that you dig as a dog, flinging* earth carelessly, as an animal."

Herger spoke: "Do you then call me an animal?"

The youth replied: "You mistake my words."

Now Herger said, "Indeed, for your words are twisted and timid as a feeble old woman."

---

*جلـد, رسـوْ ط in Arabic, and in the Latin texts, *verbera*. Both words meaning "flogging" or "whipping," and not "flinging," as this passage is ordinarily translated. It is usually assumed that Ibn Fadlan used the metaphor of "whipping" with dirt to emphasize the ferocity of the insult, which is clear enough in any case. However, he may have consciously or unconsciously transmitted a distinctly Scandinavian attitude toward insults.

Another Arab reporter, al-Tartushi, visited the town of Hedeby in A.D. 950, and said this about the Scandinavians: "They are most peculiar in the matter of punishment. They have only three penalties for wrongdoing. The first of these and the most feared is banishment from the tribe. The second is to be sold into slavery and the third is death. Women who do wrong are sold as slaves. Men always prefer death. Flogging is unknown to the Northmen."

This view is not precisely shared by Adam of Bremen, a German ecclesiastical historian, who wrote in 1075: "If women have been found unchaste, they are sold off at once, but if men are found guilty of treason or any other crime, they prefer to be beheaded than flogged. No form of punishment other than the axe or slavery is known to them."

The historian Sjogren places great importance on Adam's statement that men would prefer to be beheaded rather than flogged. This would seem to suggest that flogging was known among the Northmen; and he argues further that it was most likely a punishment for slaves. "Slaves are property, and it is economically unwise to kill them for minor offenses; surely whipping was an accepted form of punishment to a slave. Thus it may be that warriors viewed whipping as degraded penalty because it was reserved for slaves." Sjogren also argues that "all we know of Viking life points to a society founded upon the idea of shame, not guilt, as the negative behavioral pole. Vikings never felt guilt about anything, but they defended their honor fiercely, and would avoid a shameful act at any cost. Passively submitting to the whip must have been adjudged shameful in the extreme, and far worse than death itself."

These speculations carry us back to Ibn Fadlan's manuscript, and his choice of the words "whipping with dirt." Since the Arab is so fastidious, one might wonder whether his words reflect an Islamic attitude. In this regard, we should remember that while Ibn Fadlan's world was certainly divided into clean and dirty things and acts, soil itself was not necessarily dirty. On the contrary, *tayammum*, ablution with dust or sand, is carried out whenever ablution with water is not possible. Thus Ibn Fadlan had no particular abhorrence of soil on one's person; he would have been much more upset if he were asked to drink from a gold cup, which was strictly forbidden.

"This old woman shall see you taste death," the youth said, and drew forth his sword. Then Herger had drew his, for the youth was the same Ragnar, the friend of Wiglif, and thus I saw manifested the intention of Buliwyf in the matter.

These Northmen are most sensitive and touchy about their honor. Among their company, duels occur as frequently as micturition, and a battle to the death is counted ordinary. It may occur on the spot of the insult, or if it is to be formally conducted, the combatants meet at the joining place of three roads. It was thus that Ragnar challenged Herger to fight him.

Now this is the Northman custom: at the appointed time, the friends and kin of the duelers assemble at the place of battle and stretch a hide upon the ground. This they fix with four laurel poles. The battle must be fought upon the hide, each man keeping a foot, or both, on the skin all the while; in this fashion they remain close one to another. The two combatants each arrive with one sword and three shields. If a man's three shields all break, he must fight on without protection, and the battle is to the death.

Such were the rules, chanted by the old crone, the angel of death, at the position of the stretched hide, with all the people of Buliwyf and the people of the kingdom of Rothgar gathered around. I was myself there, not so close to the front, and I marveled that these people should forget the threat of the Korgon which had so terrified them earlier; no one cared anything for aught but the duel.

This was the manner of the duel between Ragnar and Herger. Herger struck the first blow, since he had been challenged, and his sword rang mightily on the shield of Ragnar. I myself had fear for Herger, since this youth was so much larger and stronger than he, and indeed Ragnar's first blow smote Herger's shield from its handgrip, and Herger called for his second shield.

Then the battle was joined, and fiercely. I looked once to Buliwyf, whose face was without expression; and to Wiglif and the herald, on the opposite side, who often looked to Buliwyf while the battle raged.

Herger's second shield was likewise broken, and he called for his third and final shield. Herger was much fatigued, and his face damp and red with exertion; the youth Ragnar appeared easy as he battled, with little exertion.

Then the third shield was broken, and Herger's plight was most desperate, or so it seemed for a fleeting moment. Herger stood with both feet solid on the ground, bent and gasping for his air, and most direly fatigued. Ragnar chose this time to fall upon him. Then Herger side-stepped like the flick of a bird's wings, and the youth Ragnar plunged his sword through empty air. Then, Herger threw his own sword from one hand to the other, for these Northmen can fight as well with either hand, and equally strong. And quickly Herger turned and cut off Ragnar's head from behind with a single blow of his sword.

Verily I saw the blood spurt from the neck of Ragnar and the head flew across the air into the crowd, and I saw with my own eyes that the head struck the ground before the body also struck the ground. Now Herger stepped aside, and then I perceived that the battle had been a sham, for Herger no longer puffed and panted, but stood with no sign of fatigue and no heaving of his chest, and he held his sword lightly, and he looked as if he could kill a dozen such men. And he looked at Wiglif and said, "Honor your friend," meaning to see to the burial.

Herger said to me, as we departed the dueling place, that he had acted a sham so that Wiglif should know the men of Buliwyf were not merely strong and brave warriors, but cunning as well. "This will give him more fear," Herger said, "and he will not dare to speak against us."

I doubted his plan would have this effect, but it is true that the Northmen prize deceit more than the most deceitful Hazar, indeed more than the most lying Bahrain trader, for whom deceit is a form of art. Cleverness in battle and manly things is accounted a greater virtue than pure strength in warriorship.

Yet Herger was not happy, and I perceived that Buliwyf was not happy, either. As the evening approached, the beginnings of the mist formed in the high inland hills. I believed that they were thinking of the dead Ragnar, who was young and strong and brave, and who would be useful in the coming battle. Herger said as much to me: "A dead man is of no use to anyone."

THE ATTACK OF THE
GLOWWORM DRAGON KORGON

Now with the fall of darkness, the mist crept down from the hills, slinking as fingers around the trees, seeping over the green fields toward the hall of Hurot and the waiting warriors of Buliwyf. Here there was a respite in work; from a fresh spring, water was diverted to fill the shallow ditch, and then I understood the sense of the plan, for the water concealed the stakes and deeper holes, and thus the moat was treacherous to any invader.

Further still, the women of Rothgar carried goatskin sacks of water from the well, and doused the fence, and the dwelling, and all the surface of the hall of Hurot with water. So, also, the warriors of Buliwyf drenched themselves in their armor with water from the spring. The night was damp cold and, thinking this some heathen ritual, I begged excuses, but to no end: Herger doused me head to foot like the rest. I stood dripping and shivering: in truth I cried aloud at the shock of the cold water, and demanded to know the reason. "The glowworm dragon breathes fire," Herger said to me.

Then he offered me a cup of mead to ease the chill, and I drank this cup of mead without a pause, and was glad for it.

Now the night was fully black, and the warriors of Buliwyf awaited the coming of the dragon Korgon. All eyes were turned toward the hills, now lost in the mist of night. Buliwyf himself strode the length of the fortifications, carrying his great sword Runding, speaking low words of encouragement to his warriors. All waited quietly, save one, the lieutenant Ecthgow. This Ecthgow is a master of the hand axe; he had set up a sturdy post of wood some distance from him, and he practiced the throw of his hand axe to this wooden post, over and again. Indeed, many hand axes had been given him; I counted five or six clipped to his broad belt, and others in his hands, and scattered on the ground about him.

In like manner was Herger stringing and testing with his bow and arrow, and also Skeld, for these were the most skilled in marksmanship of the Northmen warriors. The Northmen arrows have iron points and are most excellently constructed, with shafts straight as a taut line. They have within each village or camp a man who is often crippled or lame, and he is known as the *almsmann;* he fashions the arrows, and also the bows, for the warriors of the region, and for these alms is paid with gold or shells or, as I have myself seen, with food and meat.*

The bows of the Northmen are near the length of their own bodies, and made of birch. The fashion of shooting is this: the arrow shaft is drawn back to the ear, not to the eye, and thence let fly; and the power is such that the shaft may pass cleanly through the body of a man, and not lodge therein; so also may the shaft penetrate a sheet of wood of the thickness of a man's fist. Verily I have seen such power with an arrow with my own eyes, and I myself tried to wield one of their bows, but discovered it ungainly; for it was too large and resistant to me.

These Northmen are skilled in all the manners of warfare and killing with the several weapons that they prize. They speak of the lines of warfare, which has no sense of arrangements of soldiers; for all to them is the combat of one man to another who is his enemy. The two lines of warfare differ as to the weapon. For the broadsword, which is always swung in an arc and never employed in stabbing, they say: "The sword seeks the breath line," which means to them the neck, and thereby the cutting off of the head from the body. For the spear, the arrow, the hand axe, the dagger, and the other tools of stabbing, they say: "These weapons seek the fat line."† By these words they intend to center part of the body from head to groin; a wound in this center line means to them certain death to their opponent. Also they believe it is foremost to strike the belly for its softness than to strike the chest or head portion.

---

*This passage is apparently the source of the 1869 comment by the scholarly Rev. Noel Harleigh that "among the barbaric Vikings, morality was so perversely inverted that their sense of alms was the dues paid to weaponsmakers." Harleigh's Victorian assurance exceeded his linguistic knowledge. The Norse word *alm* means elm, the resilient wood from which the Scandinavians made bows and arrows. It is only by chance that this word also has an English meaning. (The English "alms" meaning charitable donations is usually thought to derive from the Greek *eleos*, to pity.)

†*Linea adeps:* literally, "fat line." Although the anatomical wisdom of the passage has never been questioned by soldiers in the thousand years since—for the midline of the body is where the most vital nerves and vessels are all found—the precise derivation of the term has been mysterious. In this regard, it is interesting to note that one of the Icelandic sagas mentions a wounded warrior in 1030 who pulls an arrow from his chest and sees bit of flesh attached to the point; he then says that he still has fat around his heart. Most scholars agree that this is an ironic comment from a warrior who knows that he has been mortally wounded, and this makes good anatomical sense.

In 1874, the American historian Robert Miller referred to this passage of Ibn Fadlan when he said, "Although ferocious warriors, the Vikings had a poor knowledge of physiognomy. Their men were instructed to seek out the vertical midline of the opponent's body, but in doing so, of course, they would miss the heart, positioned as it is in the left chest."

The poor knowledge must be attributed to Miller, and not the Vikings. For the last several hundred years, ordinary Western men have believed the heart to be located in the left chest; Americans put their hands over their hearts when they pledge allegiance to the flag; we have a strong folk tradition of soldiers being saved from death by a Bible carried in the breast pocket that stops the fatal bullet, and so on. In fact, the heart is a midline structure that extends to varying degrees into the left chest; but a midline wound in the chest will always pierce the heart.

Verily, Buliwyf and all his company kept watchful vigil that night, and I among them. I experienced much fatigue in this alertness, and soon enough was tired as if I had fought a battle, yet none had occurred. The Northmen were not fatigued, but ready at any moment. It is true that they are the most vigilant persons on the face of all the world, ever prepared for any battle or danger; and they find nothing tiresome in this posture, which for them is ordinary from birth. At all times are they prudent and watchful.

After a time I slept, and Herger woke me thus and brusquely: I felt a great thumping and a whistle of air near my head, and upon the opening of my eyes saw an arrow shivering in the wood at the breadth of a hair from my nose. This arrow Herger had shot, and he and all the others laughed mightily at my discomfiture. To me he said, "If you sleep, you will miss the battle." I said in response that that would be no hardship according to my own way of thinking.

Now Herger retrieved his arrow and, observing that I was offended with his prank, sat alongside me and spoke in a manner of friendliness. Herger this night was in a pronounced mood of joking and fun. He shared with me a cup of mead, and spoke thus: "Skeld is bewitched." At this he laughed.

Skeld was not far off, and Herger spoke loudly, so I recognized that Skeld was to overhear us; yet Herger spoke in Latin, unintelligible to Skeld; so perhaps there was some other reason I do not know. Skeld in this time sharpened the points of his arrows and awaited the battle. To Herger I said: "How is he bewitched?"

In reply Herger said: "If he is not bewitched, he may be turning Arab, for he washes his undergarments and also his body each day. Have you not observed this for yourself?"

I answered that I had not. Herger, laughing much, said, "Skeld does this for such and such a freeborn woman, who has captured his fancy. For her he washes each day, and acts a delicate timid fool. Have you not observed this?"

Again I answered that I had not. To this Herger spoke: "What do you see instead?" and laughed much at his own wit, which I did not share, or even pretend, for I was not of a mood to laugh. Now Herger says, "You Arabs are too dour. You grumble all the while. Nothing is laughable to your eyes."

Here I said that he spoke wrongly. He challenged me to speak a humorous story, and I told him of the sermon of the famous preacher. You know this well. A famous preacher stands in the pulpit of the mosque, and from all around men and women have gathered to hear his noble words. A man, Hamid, puts on a robe and veil and sits among the women. The famous preacher says: "According to Islam, it is desirable that one should not let his or her pubic hair grow too long." A person asks: "How long is too long, O preacher?" All know this story; it is a rude joke, indeed. The preacher replies: "It should not be longer than a barley." Now Hamid asks the woman next to him: "Sister, please check to tell me if my pubic hair is longer than a barley." The woman reaches under Hamid's robes to feel the pubic hair, whereupon her hand touches his organ. In her surprise she utters a cry. The preacher hears this and is much pleased. To the audience he says: "You should all learn the art of attending a sermon, as this lady does, for you can see how it touched her heart." And the woman, still shocked, makes this reply: "It didn't touch my heart, O preacher; it touched my hand."

Herger listened to all my words with a flat countenance. Never did he laugh nor even smile. At my conclusion he said, "What is a preacher?"

To this I said he was a stupid Northman who knew nothing of the wideness of the world. And to this he laughed, whereas he did not laugh at the fable.

Now Skeld gave a shout, and all the warriors of Buliwyf, myself among them, turned to look at the hills, behind the blanket of mist. Here is what I saw: high in the air, a glowing fiery point of light, like a blazing star, and a distance off. All the warriors saw it, and there was murmuring and exclamation among them.

Soon appeared a second point of light, and yet another, and then another. I counted past a dozen and then ceased to count further. These glowing fire-points appeared in a line, which undulated like a snake, or verily like the undulating body of a dragon.

"Be ready now," Herger said to me, and also the Northmen's saying: "Luck in battle." This wish I repeated back to him in the same words, and he moved away.

The glowing fire-points were still distant, yet they came closer. Now I heard a sound which I took as thunder. This was a deep distant rumbling that swelled in the misty air, as all sounds do in mist. For verily it is true that in mist a man's whisper can be heard a hundred paces distant, clear as if he whispered in your own ear.

Now I watched, and listened, and all the warriors of Buliwyf gripped their weapons and watched and listened likewise, and the glowworm dragon of Korgon bore down upon us in thunder and flame. Each blazing point grew larger, and baleful red, flickering and licking; the body of the dragon was long and shimmering, a vision most fierce of aspect, and yet I was not afraid, for I determined now that these were horsemen with torches, and this proved true.

Soon, then, from out of the mist the horsemen emerged, black shapes with raised torches, black steeds hissing and charging, and the battle was joined. Immediately the night air filled with dreadful screams and cries of agony, for the first charge of horsemen had struck the trench, and many mounts tumbled and fell, spilling their riders, and the torches sputtered in the water. Other horses tried to leap the fence, to be impaled on the sharp stakes. A section of the fence caught fire. Warriors ran in all directions.

Now I saw one of the horsemen ride through the burning section of fence, and I could see this wendol clearly for the first time, and verily I saw this: on a black steed rode a human figure in black, but his head was the head of a bear. I was startled with a time of most horrible fright, and I feared I should die from fear alone, for never had I witnessed such a nightmare vision; yet at the same moment the hand axe of Ecthgow was buried deep into the back of the rider, who toppled and fell, and the bear's head rolled from his body, and I saw that he had beneath the head of a man.

Quick as a lightning bolt, Ecthgow leapt upon the fallen creature, stabbed deep into the chest, turned the corpse and withdrew his hand axe from the back, and ran to join the battle. I also joined the battle, for I was knocked spinning from my feet by the blow of a lance. Many riders were now within the fence, their torches blazing; some had the heads of bears and some did not; they circled and tried to set the buildings and the hall of Hurot afire. Against this, Buliwyf and his men battled valiantly.

I came to my feet just as one of the mist monsters bore down upon me with charging steed. Verily I did this: I stood firm my ground and held my lance upward, and the impact I thought would rend me. Yet the lance passed through the body of the rider, and he screamed most horribly, but he did not fall from his mount, and rode on. I fell gasping with pain in my stomach, but I was not truly injured save for the moment.

During the time of this battle, Herger and Skeld loosed their many arrows, and the air was filled with their whistles, and they reached many marks. I saw the arrow of Skeld pass through the neck of one rider, and lodge there; yet again I saw Skeld and Herger both pierce a rider in the chest, and so quickly did they unsheath and draw again that this same rider soon bore four shafts buried in his body, and his screaming was most dreadful as he rode.

Yet I learned this deed was accounted poor fighting by Herger and Skeld, for the Northmen believe that there is nothing sacred in animals; so to them the proper use of arrows is the killing of horses, to dislodge the rider. They say of this: "A man off his horse is half a man, and twice killable." Thus they proceed with no hesitations.*

Now I also saw this: a rider swept into the compound, bent low on his galloping black horse, and he caught up the body of the monster Ecthgow had slain, swung it over his horse's neck, and rode off, for as I have said, these mist monsters leave no dead to be found in the morning light.

The battle raged on a goodly period of time by the light of the blazing fire through the mist. I saw Herger in mortal combat with one of the demons; taking up a fresh lance, I drove it deep into the creature's back. Herger, dripping blood, raised an arm in thanks and plunged back into the combat. Here I felt great pride.

Now I tried to withdraw my lance, and whilst so doing, was knocked aside by some passing horseman, and from that time in truth I remember little. I saw

---

*According to divine law, Muslims believe that "the Messenger of God has forbidden cruelty to animals." This extends to such mundane details as the commandment to unload pack animals promptly, so that they will not be unnecessarily burdened. Furthermore, the Arabs have always taken a special delight in breeding and training horses. The Scandinavians had no special feeling toward animals; nearly all Arab observers commented on their lack of affection for horses.

that one of the dwellings of the nobles of Rothgar was burning in licking spitting flame, but that the doused hall of Hurot was still untouched, and I was glad as if I were myself a Northman, and such were my final thoughts.

Upon the dawn, I was roused by some manner of bathing upon the flesh of my face, and was pleased for the gentle touch. Soon then, I saw that I received the ministrations of a licking dog, and felt much the drunken fool, and was mortified, as may be imagined.*

Now I saw that I lay in the ditch, where the water was red as blood itself; I arose and walked through the smoking compound, past all manner of death and destruction. I saw that the earth was soaked in blood, as from a rain, with many puddles. I saw the bodies of slain nobles, and dead women and children likewise. So, also, I saw three or four whose bodies were charred and crusted from fire. All these bodies lay everywhere upon the ground and I was obliged to cast my eyes downward lest I step upon them, so thickly were they spread.

Of the defense works, much of the pole fence had been burned away. Upon other sections, horses lay impaled and cold. Torches were scattered here and there. I saw none of the warriors of Buliwyf.

No cries or mourning came from the kingdom of Rothgar, for the North people do not lament any death, but on the contrary there was unusual stillness in the air. I heard the crowing of a cock, and the bark of a dog, but no human voices in the daylight.

Then I entered the great hall of Hurot, and here found two bodies laid upon the rushes, with their helmets upon their chests. There was Skeld, an earl of Buliwyf; there was Helfdane, earlier injured and now cold and pale. Both were dead. Also there was Rethel, youngest of the warriors, who sat upright in

---

*Most early translators of Ibn Fadlan's manuscript were Christians with no knowledge of Arabic culture, and their interpretation of this passage reflects that ignorance. In a very free translation, the Italian Lacalla (1847) says: "In the morning I arose from my drunken stupor like a common dog, and was much ashamed for my condition." And Skovmand, in his 1919 commentary, brusquely concludes that "one cannot place credence in Ibn Fadlan's stories, for he was drunk during the battles, and admits as much." More charitably, Du Chatellier, a confirmed Vikingophile, said in 1908: "The Arab soon acquired the intoxication of the battle that is the very essence of the Norse heroic spirit."

I am indebted to Massud Farzan, the Sufi scholar, for explaining the allusion that Ibn Fadlan is making here. Actually, he is comparing himself to a character in a very old Arabic joke:

A drunken man falls into a puddle of his own vomit by the roadside. A dog comes along and begins licking his face. The drunk assumes a kind person is cleaning his face, and says gratefully, "May Allah make your children obedient." Then the dog raises his leg and urinates on the drunkard, who responds, "And may God bless you, brother, for having brought warm water to wash my face."

In Arabic, the joke carries the usual injunction against drunkenness, and the subtle reminder that liquor is *khmer*, or filth, as is urine.

Ibn Fadlan probably expected his reader to think, not that he was ever drunk, but rather that he luckily avoided being urinated upon by the dog, as he earlier escaped death in battle: it is a reference, in other words, to another near miss.

a corner and was attended by slavewomen. Rethel had been wounded previously but he had a fresh injury in his stomach, and there was much blood; surely it pained him greatly, and yet he showed only cheer, and he smiled and teased the slavewomen by the practice of pinching their breasts and buttocks, and often they chided him for causing their distraction as they attempted to bind his wounds.

Here is the manner of the treatment of wounds, according to their nature. If a warrior be wounded in the extremity, either the arm or the leg, a ligature is tied about the extremity, and cloths boiled in water placed over the wound to cover it. Also, I was told that spider webs or bits of lamb's wool may be placed into the wound to thicken the blood and stop its flow; this I never observed.

If a warrior be wounded in the head or the neck, his injury is bathed clean and examined by the slavewomen. If the skin is rent but the white bones whole, then they say of such a wound, "It is no matter." But if the bones are cracked, or broken open in some fashion, then they say, "His life issues out and soon escapes."

If a warrior be wounded in the chest, they feel his hands and feet, and if these are warm, they say of such a wound, "It is no matter." Yet if this warrior coughs or vomits blood, they say, "He speaks in blood," and count this most serious. A man may die of the blood-speaking illness, or he may not, as is his fate.

If a warrior is wounded in the abdomen, they feed him a soup of onions and herbs; then the women smell about his wounds, and if they smell onions, they say, "He has the soup illness," and they know he shall die.

I saw with my own eyes the women prepare a soup of onion for Rethel, who drank a quantity of this; and the slavewomen smelled at his wound, and they smelled the odor of onion. At this, Rethel laughed and made some manner of hearty joke, and called for mead, which was brought him, and he showed no trace of any care.

Now Buliwyf, the leader, and all his warriors conferred in another place in the great hall. I joined their company, but was accorded no greeting. Herger, whose life I had saved, made no notice of me, for the warriors were deep in solemn conversation. I had learned some of the Norse speech, but not sufficient to follow their low and quickly spoken words, and so I walked to another place and drank some mead, and felt the aches of my body. Then a slavewoman came to bathe my wounds. These were a cut in the calf and another on my chest. These injuries I had been insensible to until the time she made offer of her ministrations.

The Northmen bathe wounds with ocean seawater, believing this water to possess more curative powers than spring water. Such bathing with seawater is not agreeable to the wound. In truth I groaned and at this, Rethel laughed and spoke to a slavewoman: "He is still an Arab." Here I was ashamed.

Also the Northmen will bathe wounds in the heated urine of cows. This I refused, when it was offered me.

The North people think cow urine an admirable substance, and store it up in wooden containers. In the ordinary way of things, they boil it until it is dense and stinging to the nostrils, and then employ this vile liquid for washing, especially of coarse white garments.*

Also I was told that, upon one time or another, the North people may be engaged in a long sea voyage and have at hand no supplies of fresh water, and therefore each man drinks his own urine, and in this way they can survive until they reach shore. This I was told but never saw, by the grace of Allah.

Now Herger came to me, for the conference of the warriors was at an end. The slavewoman attending me had made my wounds burn most distractingly; yet I was determined to maintain a Northman show of great cheer. I said to Herger, "What trifling matter shall we undertake next?"

Herger looked to my wounds, and said to me, "You can ride well enough." I inquired where I would be riding, and in truth at once lost all my good cheer, for I had great weariness, and no strength for aught but resting. Herger said: "Tonight, the glowworm dragon will attack again. But we are now too weak, and our numbers too few. Our defenses are burned and destroyed. The glowworm dragon will kill us all."

These words he spoke calmly. I saw this, and said to Herger: "Where, then, do we ride?" I had in mind that by reason of their heavy losses, Buliwyf and his company might be abandoning the kingdom of Rothgar. In this I was not opposed.

Herger said to me: "A wolf that lies in its lair never gets meat, or a sleeping man victory." This is a Northman proverb, and from it I took a different plan: that we were going to attack on horseback the mist monsters where they lay, in the mountains or the hills. With no great heart I inquired of Herger when this should be, and Herger told me in the middle part of the day.

Now I saw also that a child entered the hall, and carried in his hands some object of stone. This was examined by Herger, and it was another of the headless stone carvings of a pregnant woman, bloated and ugly. Herger shouted an oath, and dropped the stone from his trembling hands. He called upon the slavewoman, who took the stone and placed it in the fire, where the heat of the flames caused it to crack and splinter into fragments. These fragments were then thrown into the sea, or so I was informed by Herger.

I inquired what was the meaning of the carved stone, and he said to me, "That is the image of the mother of the eaters of the dead, she who presides over them, and directs them in the eating."

Now I saw that Buliwyf, who stood in the center of the great hall, was looking up at the arm of one of the fiends, which still hung from the rafters. Then he

*Urine is a source of ammonia, an excellent cleaning compound.

looked down at the two bodies of his slain companions, and at the waning Rethel, and his shoulders fell, and his chin sank to his chest. And then he walked past them and out of the door, and I saw him put on his armor, and take up his sword, and prepare for battle anew.

THE DESERT OF DREAD

Buliwyf called for seven sturdy horses, and in the early part of the day we rode from the great hall of Rothgar out into the flat plain, and thence toward the hills beyond. With us also were four hounds of pure white color, great animals which I should count nearer to wolves than dogs, so fierce was their demeanor. This made the totality of our attacking forces, and I believed it a weak gesture against so formidable an opponent, yet the Northmen place great faith upon surprise and a sly attack. Also, by their own reckoning they are each man the equal of three or four of any other.

I was not disposed to embark upon another venture of warfare, and was much amazed that the Northmen did not reflect such a view, springing as it did from the fatigue of my body. Herger said of this: "It is always thus, now and in Valhalla," which is their idea of heaven. In this heaven, which is to them a great hall, warriors battle from dawn to dusk; then those who are dead are revived, and all share a feast in the night, with endless food and drink; and then upon the day they battle again; and those who die are revived, and there is a feast; and this is the nature of their heaven through all eternity.* Thus they never count it strange to do battle day upon day while on the earth.

Our direction of travel was determined by the trail of blood the retreating horsemen had left from the night. The hounds led, racing along this red dripping trail. We paused but once upon the flat plain, to retrieve a weapon dropped by the departing demons. Here is the nature of the weapon: it was a hand axe with a haft of some wood, and a blade of chipped stone bound to the haft with hide thongs. The edge of this axe was exceedingly sharp, and the blade fashioned with skill, as much as if this stone were some gemstone to be chiseled to delight a rich lady's vanity. Such was the degree of workmanship, and the weapon was formidable for the sharpness of its edge. Never have I seen such an object before on the face of all the earth. Herger told me that the

*Some authorities on mythology argue that the Scandinavians did not originate this idea of an eternal battle, but rather that this is a Celtic concept. Whatever the truth, it is perfectly reasonable that Ibn Fadlan's companions should have adopted the concept, for the Scandinavians had been in contact with Celts for over a hundred and fifty years at this time.

wendol made all their tools and weapons of this stone, or so the Northmen believe.

Yet we traveled onward with good speed, led by the barking dogs, and their barking cheered me. At length we came to the hills. We rode into the hills without hesitation or ceremony, each of the warriors of Buliwyf intent upon his purpose, a silent and grim-faced company of men. They held the marks of fear upon their faces, and yet no man paused or faltered, but pressed onward.

Now it was cold in the hills, in the forests of dark green trees, and a chill wind blew at our clothing, and we saw the hissing breath of the steeds, and white plumes of breath from the running dogs, and we pressed onward still. After some travel until the middle period of the day, we arrived at a new landscape. Here was a brackish tarn, no moor, or heath—a desolate land, most resembling a desert, yet not sandy and dry, but damp and soggy, and over this land lay the faintest wisps of mist. The Northmen call this place the desert of dread.*

Now I saw with my own eyes that this mist lay upon the land in small pockets or clusterings, like tiny clouds seated upon the earth. In one area, the air is clear; then in another place there are small mists that hang near the ground, rising to the height of a horse's knees, and in such a place we would lose sight of the dogs, who were enveloped in these mists. Then, a moment later, the mist would clear, and we would be in another open space again. Such was the landscape of the heath.

I found this sight remarkable, but the Northmen took it to be nothing special; they said the land in this region has many brackish pools and bubbling hot springs, which rise from rents in the ground; in these places, a small fog collects, and remains there all the day and night. They call this the place of steaming lakes.

The land is difficult for horses, and we made slower progress. The dogs also ventured more slowly, and I noted that they barked less vigorously. Soon our company had changed wholly: from a gallop, with yelping dogs in the forefront, to a slow walk, with silent dogs hardly willing to lead the way, and instead falling back until they were underfoot the horses, thus causing some occasional difficulty. It was still very cold, indeed colder than before, and I saw here and there a small patch of snow upon the ground, though this was, by my best reckoning, the summer period.

At a slow pace, we proceeded for a goodly distance, and I had wonder that we should be lost, and never find our way back through this heath. Now at

---

* صَحرآ ءُ خَـوفِ : literally, "desert of dread." In a paper in 1927, J. G. Tomlinson pointed out that precisely the same phrase appears in the *Volsunga Saga,* and therefore argued at length that it represented a generic term for taboo lands. Tomlinson was apparently unaware that the *Volsunga Saga* says nothing of the sort; the nineteenth-century translation of William Morris indeed contains the line "There is a desert of dread in the uttermost part of the world," but this line was Morris's own invention, appearing in one of the many passages where he expanded upon the original Germanic saga.

a place the dogs halted. There was no difference in the terrain, or any mark or object upon the ground; yet the dogs stopped as if they had arrived upon some fence or palpable obstruction. Our party halted at this place, and looked about in this direction and that. There was no wind, and no sounds were here; not the sound of birds or of any living animal, but only silence.

Buliwyf said, "Here begins the land of the wendol," and the warriors patted their steeds upon the necks to comfort them, for the horses were skittish and nervous in this region. So also were the riders. Buliwyf kept his lips tight; Ecthgow's hands trembled as he held the reins of his horse; Herger was gone quite pale, and his eyes darted to this way and that; so also the others in their way.

The Northmen say, "Fear has a white mouth," and now I saw that this is true, for they were all pale around the lips and mouth. No man spoke of his fear.

Now we left the dogs behind, and rode onward into more snow, which was thin and crunching underfoot, and into thicker mists. No man spoke, save to the horses. At each step these beasts were more difficult to prod onward; the warriors were obliged to urge them with soft words and sharp kicks. Soon we saw shadowy forms in the mist ahead of us, which we approached with caution. Now I saw with my own eyes this: on either side of the path, mounted high on stout poles, were the skulls of enormous beasts, their jaws opened in a posture of attack. We continued, and I saw these were the skulls of giant bears, which the wendol worship. Herger said to me that the bear skulls protect the borders of the land of the wendol.

Now we sighted another obstacle, gray and distant and large. Here was a giant rock, as high as a horse's saddle, and it was carved in the shape of a pregnant woman, with bulging belly and breasts, and no head or arms or legs. This rock was spattered with the blood of some sacrifices; verily it dripped with streaks of red, and was gruesome to look upon.

No man spoke of what was observed. We rode on apace. The warriors drew out their swords and held them in readiness. Now here is a quality to the Northmen: that previously they showed fear, but having entered into the land of the wendol, close to the source of the fear, their own apprehensions disappeared. Thus do they seem to do all things backward, and in perplexing manner, for verily they now appeared at ease. It was only the horses that were ever more difficult to prod onward.

I smelled, now, the rotting-carcass odor that I had smelled before in the great hall of Rothgar; and as it reached my nostrils anew, I was faint of heart. Herger rode alongside me and said in a soft voice, "How do you fare?"

Not being capable of concealing my emotions, I said to him, "I am afraid."

Herger replied to me: "That is because you think upon what is to come, and imagine fearsome things that would stop the blood of any man. Do not think ahead, and be cheerful by knowing that no man lives forever."

I saw the truth of his words. "In my society," I said, "we have a saying which is: 'Thank Allah, for in his wisdom he put death at the end of life, and not at the beginning.' "

Herger smiled at this, and laughed briefly. "In fear, even Arabs speak the truth," he said, and then rode forward to tell my words to Buliwyf, who also laughed. The warriors of Buliwyf were glad for a joke at that time.

Now we came to a hill and, reaching the crest, paused and looked down upon the encampment of the wendol. Here is how it lay before us, as I saw with my own eyes: there was a valley, and in the valley a circle of rude huts of mud and straw, of poor construction as a child might erect; and in the center of the circle a large fire, now smoldering. Yet there were no horses, no animals, no movement, no sign of life of any kind; and this we saw through the shifting gauze of the mist.

Buliwyf dismounted his steed, and the warriors did likewise, myself among them. In truth, my heart pounded and I was short of breath as I looked down at the savage encampment of the demons. We spoke in whispers. "Why is there no activity?" I inquired.

"The wendol are creatures of the night even as owls or bats," Herger replied, "and they sleep during the hours of the day. So are they sleeping now, and we shall descend into their company, and fall upon them, and slay them in their dreams."

"We are so few," I said, for there were many huts below which I perceived.

"We are enough," Herger said, and then he gave me a draught of mead, which I drank gratefully, with praise to Allah that it is not forbidden, or even disapproved of.* In truth, I was finding my tongue hospitable to this very substance I once thought vile; thus do strange things cease to be strange upon repetition. In like fashion, I no longer attended the hideous stench of the wendol, for I had been smelling it a goodly time and I no longer was aware of the odor.

The North people are most peculiar in the matter of smelling. They are not clean, as I have said; and they eat all manner of evil food and drink; and yet it is true that they value the nose above all parts of the body. In battle, the loss of an ear is no great matter; the loss of a finger or toe or a hand little more; and such scars and injuries they bear indifferently. But the loss of a nose they count equal to death itself, and this even to the loss of a piece of the fleshy tip, which other people would say is a most minor injury.

The breaking of the bones of the nose, through battle and blows, is no matter; many of them have crooked noses for that cause. I do not know the reason for this fear of cutting the nose.†

*The Islamic injunction against alcohol is literally an injunction against the fermented fruit of the grape; i.e., wine. Fermented drinks of honey are specifically permitted to Muslims.

†The usual psychiatric explanation for such fears of loss of body parts is that they represent castration anxiety. In a 1937 review, *Deformations of Body Image in Primitive Societies,*

Fortified, the warriors of Buliwyf and I among them left our steeds upon the hill, but these animals could not go unattended, so affrighted were they. One of our party was to remain with them, and I had hopes to be selected to this task; yet it was Haltaf, he being already injured and of least use. Thus we others warily descended the hill among the sickly scrub and dying bushes down the slope to the encampment of the wendol. We moved in stealth, and no alarm was raised, and soon we were in the very heart of the village of the demons.

Buliwyf never spoke, but gave all directions and orders with his hands. And from him I took the meaning that we were to go in groups of two warriors, each pair in a different direction. Herger and I were to attack the nearest of the mud huts, and the others were to attack others. All waited until the groups were stationed outside the huts, and then, with a howl, Buliwyf raised his great sword Runding and led the attack.

I dashed with Herger into one of the huts, blood pounding in my head, my sword light as a feather in my hands. Verily I was ready for the mightiest battle of my life. I saw nothing inside; the hut was deserted and barren as well, save for rude beds of straw, so clumsy in their appearance they seemed more to resemble nests of some animal.

We dashed outside, and attacked the next of these mud huts. Again we found it empty. Verily, all the huts were empty, and the warriors of Buliwyf were sorely vexed and stared one to the next with expression of surprise and astonishment.

Then Ecthgow called to us, and we gathered at one of these huts, larger than any of the others. And here I saw that it was deserted as they were all deserted, but the interior was not barren. Rather, the floor of the hut was littered with fragile bones, which crunched underfoot like the bones of birds, delicate and frail. I was much surprised at this, and stooped to see the nature of these bones. With a shock, I saw the curved line of an eye socket here, and a few teeth there. Verily we stood upon a carpet of the bones of human faces, and for further proofs of this ghastly truth, piled high upon one wall of the hut were the head portions of the human skulls, stacked inverted like so many pottery bowls, but glistening white. I was sick, and departed the hut to purge myself. Herger said to me that the wendol eat the brains of their victims, as a human person might eat eggs or cheese. This is their custom; vile as it is to contemplate such a matter, yet it is true.

Engelhardt observes that many cultures are explicit about this belief. For example, the Nanamani of Brazil punish sexual offenders by cutting off the left ear; this is thought to reduce sexual potency. Other societies attach significance to the loss of fingers, toes, or, in the case of the Northmen, the nose. It is a common superstition in many societies that the size of a man's nose reflects the size of his penis.

Emerson argues that the importance accorded the nose by primitive societies reflects a vestigial attitude from the days when men were hunters and relied heavily upon a sense of smell to find game and avoid enemies; in such a life, the loss of smell was a serious injury indeed.

Now another of the warriors called to us, and we entered another hut. Here I saw this: the hut was bare, except for a large thronelike chair, carved of a single piece of enormous wood. This chair had a high fanning back, carved into the shape of snakes and demons. At the foot of the chair were littered bones of skulls, and upon the arms of the chair, where its owner might rest his hands there was blood and remnants of whitish cheesy substance, which was human brain material. The odor of this room was ghastly.

Placed all around this chair there were small pregnant stone carvings, such as I have described before; these carvings formed a circle or perimeter about the chair.

Herger said, "This is where she rules," and his voice was low and awed.

I was not able to comprehend his meaning, and was sick in heart and stomach. I emptied my stomach upon the soil. Herger and Buliwyf and the others were also distressed, though no man purged himself, but rather they took glowing embers from the fire and set the huts aflame. They burned slowly, for they were damp.

And thus we climbed up the hill, mounted our horses, and left the region of the wendol, and departed the desert of dread. And all the warriors of Buliwyf were now sad of aspect, for the wendol had surpassed them in cunning and cleverness, abandoning their lair in anticipation of the attack, and they would count the burning of their dwellings no great loss.

THE COUNSEL OF THE DWARF

We returned as we had come, but rode with greater speed, for the horses now were eager, and eventually came down from the hills and saw the flat plain and, in the distance, at the ocean's edge, the settlement and the great hall of Rothgar.

Now Buliwyf veered away and led us in another direction, toward high rocky crags swept by the ocean winds. I rode alongside Herger and inquired the reason for this, and he said we were to seek out the dwarves of the region.

At this I was much surprised, for the men of the North have no dwarves among their society; they are never seen in the streets, nor do any sit at the feet of kings, nor are any to be found counting money or keeping records or any of the things that we know of dwarves.* Never had any Northman mentioned dwarves to me, and I had presumed that so giant a people† would never produce dwarves.

Now we came to a region of caves, hollowed and windswept, and Buliwyf dismounted from his horse, and all the warriors of Buliwyf did likewise, and proceeded by foot. I heard a hissing sound, and verily I saw puffs of steam issue from one and another of these several caves. We entered one cave and there found dwarves.

They were in appearance thus: of the ordinary size of dwarf, but distinguished by heads of great size, and bearing features that appeared exceedingly aged. There were both male and female dwarves and all had the appearance of great age. The males were bearded and solemn; the women also had some hair upon the face, so they appeared manlike. Each dwarf wore a garment of fur or sable; each also wore a thin belt of hide decorated with bits of hammered gold.

The dwarves greeted our arrival politely, with no sign of fear. Herger said these creatures have magic powers and need fear no man on earth; however, they are apprehensive of horses, and for this reason we had left the mounts behind us. Herger said also that the powers of a dwarf reside in his thin belt,

---

*In the Mediterranean, from Egyptian times, dwarves were thought especially intelligent and trustworthy, and tasks of bookkeeping and money-handling were reserved to them.

†Of approximately ninety skeletons that can be confidently ascribed to the Viking period in Scandinavia, the average height appears to be about 170 centimeters (5'7").

and that a dwarf will do anything to retrieve his belt if it is lost.

Herger said this also: that the appearance of great age among the dwarves was a true thing, and that a dwarf lived beyond the span of any ordinary man. Also he said to me that these dwarves are virile from their earliest youth; that even as infants they have hair at the groin, and members of uncommon size. Indeed, it is in this way that the parents first come to know that their infant child is a dwarf, and a creature of magic, who must be taken to the hills to live with others of his kind. This done, the parents give thanks to the gods and sacrifice some animal or other, for to give birth to a dwarf is accounted high good fortune.

This is the belief of the North people, as Herger spoke it, and I do not know the truth of the matter, and report only what was told to me.

Now I saw that the hissing and steam issued from great cauldrons, into which hammered-steel blades were plunged to temper the metal, for the dwarves make weapons that are highly prized by the Northmen. Indeed, I saw the warriors of Buliwyf looking about the caves eagerly, as any woman in a bazaar shop selling precious silks.

Buliwyf made inquiries of these creatures, and was directed to the topmost of the caves, wherein sat a single dwarf, older than all the others, with a beard and hair of purest white, and a creased and wrinkled face. This dwarf was called "tengol," which means a judge of good and evil, and also a soothsayer.

This tengol must have had the magical powers that all said he did, for he immediately greeted Buliwyf by his name, and bade him sit with him. Buliwyf sat, and we gathered a short distance away, standing.

Now Buliwyf did not present the tengol with gifts; the Northmen make no obeisance to the little people: they believe that the favors of the dwarves must be freely given, and it is wrong to encourage the favors of a dwarf with gifts. Thus Buliwyf sat, and the tengol looked at him, and then closed his eyes and began to speak, rocking back and forth as he sat. The tengol spoke in a high voice as a child, and Herger told me the meaning was thus:

"O Buliwyf, you are a great warrior but you have met your match in the monsters of the mist, the eaters of the dead. This shall be a struggle to the death, and you shall need all your strength and wisdom to overcome the challenge." And he went on in this manner for some good time, rocking back and forth. The import was that Buliwyf faced a difficult adversary, which I already knew well enough and so did Buliwyf himself. Yet Buliwyf was patient.

Also I saw that Buliwyf took no offense when the dwarf laughed at him, which frequently he did. The dwarf spoke: "You have come to me because you attacked the monsters in the brackish marsh and tarn, and this availed you nothing. Therefore you come to me for advice and admonishment, as a child to his father, saying what shall I do now, for all my plans have failed me." The tengol laughed long at this speech. Then his old face turned solemn.

"O Buliwyf," he said, "I see the future, but I can tell you no more than you already know. You and all your brave warriors gathered your skill and your courage to make an attack upon the monsters in the desert of dread. In this you cheated yourself, for such was not a true hero's enterprise."

I heard these words with astonishment, for it had seemed heroic work enough for me.

"No, no, noble Buliwyf," the tengol said. "You set out upon a false mission, and deep in your hero's heart you knew it was unworthy. So, too, was your battle against the glowworm dragon Korgon unworthy, and it cost you many fine warriors. To what end are all your plans?"

Still Buliwyf did not answer. He sat with the dwarf and waited.

"A hero's great challenge," the dwarf said, "is in the heart, and not in the adversary. What matter if you had come upon the wendol in their lair and had killed many of their number as they slept? You could kill many, yet this would not end the struggle, any more than cutting off the fingers will kill the man. To kill the man, you must pierce the head or the heart, and thus it is with the wendol. All this you know, and need not my counsel to know it."

Thus the dwarf, rocking back and forth, chastised Buliwyf. And thus Buliwyf accepted his rebuke, for he did not reply, but only lowered his head.

"You have done the work of a mere man," the tengol continued, "and not a proper hero. A hero does what no man dares to undertake. To kill the wendol, you must strike at the head and the heart: you must overcome their very mother, in the thunder caves."

I did not understand the meaning of these words.

"You know of this, for it has always been true, through all the ages of man. Shall your brave warriors die, one by one? Or shall you strike at the mother in the caves? Here is no prophecy, only the choice of a man or a hero."

Now Buliwyf made some response, but it was low, and lost to me in the howl of the wind that raked the entrance to the cave. Whatever the words, the dwarf spoke further:

"That is the hero's answer, Buliwyf, and I would expect none other from you. Thus shall I help your quest." Then a number of his kind came forward into the light from the dark recesses of the cave. And they bore many objects.

"Here," said the tengol, "are lengths of rope, made from the skins of seals caught at the first melting of the ice. These ropes will help you to attain the ocean entrance to the thunder caves."

"I thank you," Buliwyf said.

"And here also," the tengol said, "are seven daggers, forged with steam and magic, for you and your warriors. Great swords will be of no avail in the thunder caves. Carry these new weapons bravely, and you shall accomplish all you desire."

Buliwyf took the daggers, and thanked the dwarf. He stood. "When shall we do this thing?" he asked.

"Yesterday is better than today," the tengol replied, "and tomorrow is better than the day which follows that. So make haste, and carry out your intentions with a firm heart and a strong arm."

"And what follows if we succeed?" Buliwyf asked.

"Then the wendol shall be mortally wounded, and thrash in its death throes a final time, and after this last agony the land shall have peace and sunlight forevermore. And your name shall be sung glorious in all the halls of the Northlands, forevermore."

"The deeds of dead men are so sung," Buliwyf said.

"That is true," the dwarf said, and laughed again, the giggle of a child or a young girl. "And also the deeds of heroes who live, but never are sung the deeds of ordinary men. All this you know."

Now Buliwyf departed from the cave, and gave to each of us the dagger of the dwarves, and we descended from the rocky windswept crags, and returned to the kingdom and the great hall of Rothgar as night was falling.

All these things took place, and I saw them with my own eyes.

THE EVENTS OF THE NIGHT
BEFORE THE ATTACK

No mist came that night; the fog descended from the hills but hung back among the trees, and did not creep out onto the plain. In the great hall of Rothgar, a mighty feast was held, and Buliwyf and all his warriors joined in great celebration. Two great horned sheep* were slaughtered and consumed; each man drank vast quantities of mead; Buliwyf himself ravished half a dozen slave girls, and perhaps more; but despite merrymaking neither he nor his warriors were truly cheerful. From one time to another, I saw them glance at the ropes of sealskin and the dwarf daggers, which had been set apart to one side.

Now I joined in the general revelry, for I felt as one of them, having spent much time in their company, or so it seemed. Indeed, that night I felt I had been born a Northman.

Herger, much intoxicated, told me freely of the mother of the wendol. He said this: "The mother of the wendol is very old and she lives in the caves of thunder. These thunder caves lie in the rock of cliffs, not far from here. The caves have two openings, one from the land and another from the sea. But the entrance from the land is guarded by the wendol, who protect their old mother; so it is that we cannot attack from the side of the land, for in this way we would all be killed. Therefore we shall attack from the sea."

I inquired of him: "What is the nature of this mother of the wendol?"

Herger said that no Northman knew this thing, but that it was said among them that she was old, older than the old crone they call the angel of death; and also that she was frightful to look upon; and also that she wore snakes upon her head as a wreath; and also, too, that she was strong beyond all accounting. And he said at the last that the wendol called upon her to direct them in all their affairs of life.† Then Herger turned from me and slept.

---

*Dahlmann (1924) writes that "for ceremonial occasions the ram was eaten to increase potency, since the horned male animal was judged superior to the female." In fact, during this period both rams and ewes had horns.

†Joseph Cantrell observes that "there is a strain in Germanic and Norse mythology which holds that women have special powers, qualities of magic, and should be feared and mistrusted by men. The principal gods are all men, but the Valkyries, which means literally 'choosers of the slain,' are women who transport dead warriors to Paradise. It was believed that there were three Valkyries, as there were three Norns, or Fates, which were present at

Now this event occurred: in the depths of the night, as the celebrations were drawing to a close and the warriors were drifting into sleep, Buliwyf sought me out. He sat beside me and drank mead from a horned cup. He was not intoxicated, I saw, and he spoke slowly in the North tongue, so that I should understand his meaning.

He said first to me: "Did you comprehend the words of the dwarf tengol?" I replied that I did, with the help of Herger, who now snored near to us.

Buliwyf said to me: "Then you know I shall die." He spoke thus, with his eyes clear and his gaze firm. I did not know any reply, or response to make, but finally said to him in the North fashion, "Believe no prophecy until it bears fruit."*

Buliwyf said: "You have seen much of our ways. Tell me what is true. Do you draw sounds?" I answered that I did. "Then look to your safety, and do not be overbrave. You dress and now you speak as a Northman, and not a foreign man. See that you live."

I placed my hand upon his shoulder, as I had seen his fellow warriors do to him in greeting. He smiled then. "I fear no thing," he said, "and need no comfort. I tell you to look to your own safety, for your own account. Now it is wisest to sleep."

So speaking, he turned away from me, and devoted his attention to a slave girl, whom he pleasured not a dozen paces from where I sat, and I turned away hearing the moans and laughter of this woman. And at length I fell into a sleep.

---

the birth of every man, and determined the outcome of his life. The Norns were named Urth, the past; Verthandi, the present; and Skuld, the future. The Norns 'wove' a man's fate, and weaving was a woman's work; in popular representations they were shown as young maidens. Wyrd, an Anglo-Saxon deity which ruled fate, was also a goddess. Presumably the association of women with man's fate was a permutation of earlier concepts of women as fertility symbols; the goddesses of fertility controlled the growing and flowering of crops and living things on the earth."

Cantrell also notes that "in practice, we know that divination, spellcasting, and other shamanistic functions were reserved to elderly women in Norse society. Furthermore, popular ideas of women contained a heavy element of suspicion. According to the *Havamal,* 'No one should trust the words of a girl or a married woman, for their hearts have been shaped on a turning wheel and they are inconstant by nature.' "

Bendixon says, "Among the early Scandinavians there was a kind of division of power according to sex. Men ruled physical affairs; women, psychological matters."

*This is a paraphrase of a sentiment among the Northmen, expressed fully as: "Praise not the day until evening has come; a woman until she is burnt; a sword until it is tried; a maiden until she is married; ice until it has been crossed; beer until it has been drunk." This prudent, realistic, and somewhat cynical view of human nature and the world was something the Scandinavians and the Arabs shared. And like the Scandinavians, the Arabs often express it in mundane or satiric terms. There is a Sufi story about a man who asked a sage: "Suppose I am traveling in the countryside and must make ablutions in the stream. Which direction do I face while performing the ritual?" To this the sage replies: "In the direction of your clothes, so they won't be stolen."

THE THUNDER CAVES

Before the first pink streaks of dawn lighted the sky, Buliwyf and his warriors, myself among them, rode out from the kingdom of Rothgar and followed the cliff edge above the sea. On this day I did not feel fit, for my head ached; also was my stomach sour from the celebration of the previous night. Surely all the warriors of Buliwyf were in like condition, yet no man gave signal of these discomforts. We rode briskly, skirting the border of the cliffs which on all this coast are high and forbidding, and sheer; in a sheet of gray stone they drop to the foaming and turbulent sea below. In some places along this coastline there are rocky beaches, but often the land and the sea meet directly, and the waves crash like thunder upon the rocks; and this was the circumstance for the most part.

I saw Herger, who carried upon his horse the sealskin ropes of the dwarves, and I rode up to travel alongside him. I inquired what was our purpose on this day. In truth, I did not care greatly, so badly did my head ache and my stomach burn.

Herger said to me, "On this morning, we attack the mother of the wendol in the thunder caves. This we shall do by attacking from the sea, as I have told you yesterday."

While I rode, I looked from my horse down at the sea, which smashed upon the rock cliffs. "Do we attack by boat?" I inquired of Herger.

"No," Herger said, and slapped his hand upon the sealskin ropes.

Then I took his meaning to be that we should climb down the cliffs on the ropes, and thereby in some fashion make an entrance into the caves. I was much frightened at this prospect, for never have I liked to be exposed upon high places; even high buildings in the City of Peace have I avoided. I said as much.

Herger said to me, "Be thankful, for you are fortunate."

I inquired the source of my fortune. Herger said in reply, "If you have the fear of high places, then this day you shall overcome it; and so you shall have faced a great challenge; and so you shall be adjudged a hero."

I said to him, "I do not want to be a hero."

At this he laughed and said that I expressed such an opinion only because I was an Arab. Then also he said that I had a stiff head, by which the Northmen mean the aftermath of drinking. This was true, as I have already told.

Also it is true that I was much aggrieved at the prospect of climbing down the cliff. Verily I felt in this manner: that I should rather do any action upon the face of the earth, whether to lie with a woman in menses, to drink from a gold cup, to eat the excrement of a pig, to put out my eyes, even to die itself—any or all of these things should I prefer to the climbing of that accursed cliff. Also I was in ill temper. To Herger I said, "You and Buliwyf and all your company may be heroes as suits your temper, but I have no part in this affair, and shall not number as one of you."

At this speech, Herger laughed. Then he called to Buliwyf, and spoke a rapid speech; Buliwyf answered him back, over his shoulder. Then Herger spoke to me: "Buliwyf says that you will do as we do."

In truth, now I sank into despairing, and said to Herger, "I cannot do this thing. If you force me to do it, I shall surely die."

Herger said, "How shall you die?"

I said to him, "I shall lose my grip from the ropes."

This answer made Herger laugh heartily yet again, and he repeated my words to all the Northmen, and they all laughed at what I had said. Then Buliwyf spoke a few words.

Herger said to me: "Buliwyf says that you shall lose your grip only if you release the ropes from your hands, and only a fool would do such a thing. Buliwyf says you are an Arab, but no fool."

Now, here is a true aspect of the nature of men: that in his fashion Buliwyf said that I could climb the ropes; and that for his speech, I believed it as much as he, and was cheered in my heart to a slight degree. This Herger saw, and he spoke these words: "Each person bears a fear which is special to him. One man fears a close space and another man fears drowning; each laughs at the other and calls him stupid. Thus fear is only a preference, to be counted the same as the preference for one woman or another, or mutton for pig, or cabbage for onion. We say, fear is fear."

I was not in a mood for his philosophies; this I expressed to him, for in truth I was growing closer to anger than to fear. Now Herger laughed at my face and spoke these words: "Praise Allah, for he put death at the end of life, and not at the beginning."

Curtly, I said in reply that I saw no benefit in hastening the end. "Indeed, no man does," Herger responded to me, and then he said, "Look to Buliwyf. See how he sits straight. See how he rides forward, though he knows he shall soon die."

I answered, "I do not know he shall die."

"Yes," Herger said, "but Buliwyf knows." Then Herger spoke nothing further to me, and we rode onward for a goodly period of time, until the sun was high and bright in the sky. Then at last Buliwyf gave the signal to halt, and all the horsemen dismounted, and prepared to enter the thunder caves.

Now, well I knew that these Northmen are brave to a fault, but as I looked at the precipice of the cliff below us, my heart twisted over inside my chest, and I thought I should be purging myself at any instant. Verily, the cliff was absolutely sheer, lacking the least grip for hand or feet, and it descended for the distance of perhaps four hundred paces. Verily, the crashing waves were so far beneath us that they appeared as miniature waves, tiny as the most delicate drawing of an artist. Yet I knew them to be large as any waves on earth, once one descended to that level far below.

To me, the climbing down of these cliffs was madness beyond the madness of a foaming dog. But the Northmen proceeded in normal fashion. Buliwyf directed the pounding of stout wooden stakes into the earth; around these the sealskin ropes were bound, and the trailing ends flung over the sides of the cliffs.

Verily, the ropes were not long enough for so distant a descent, and thus had to be hauled up again, and two ropes fastened together to make a single length to reach the waves at the bottom.

In due time, we had two such ropes that reached down the side of the cliff face. Then Buliwyf spoke to his gathering: "First I shall proceed, so that when I reach the bottom all shall know that the ropes are stout and the journey can be accomplished. I await you at the bottom, on the narrow ledge you see below."

I looked to this narrow ledge. To call it narrow is to call a camel kind. It was, in truth, the barest strip of flat rock, continually washed and pounded by the surf.

"When all have reached the bottom," Buliwyf said, "we can attack the mother of the wendol in the thunder caves." Thus he spoke, in a voice as ordinary as that which he would command a slave in the preparation of some ordinary stew or any other household chore. And without further speech, he went over the side of the cliff.

Now, here is the manner of his descent, which I found remarkable, but the Northmen account it no particular thing. Herger told me they use this method for gathering of sea-bird eggs at certain times of the year, when the sea birds build their nests on the cliff face. It is done in this fashion: a sling is placed around the waist of the descending man, and all the fellows strain to lower him down the cliff. Meanwhile, this same man grips, for support, on to the second rope, which dangles on the cliff face. Further, the descending man carries a stout staff of oaken wood, fitted at one end with a leather thong, or strap, about his wrist; this staff he employs for a prod to push himself hither and yon as he moves down the rocky surface.*

As Buliwyf went down, becoming ever smaller to my eyes, I saw that he maneuvered with the sling, the rope, and the stick very agilely; but I was not deceived into thinking this some trivial matter, for I saw it to be difficult and requiring practice.

At length, he safely reached the bottom and stood on the narrow ledge

---

*In the Faeroe Islands of Denmark, a similar method of scaling cliffs is still practiced to gather bird eggs, an important source of food to the islanders.

with the surf crashing over him. In truth, he was so diminished we could hardly see him wave his hand, in signal that he was safe. Now the sling was hauled up; and also with it, the oaken staff. Herger turned to me, speaking: "You shall go next."

I said that I was feeling poorly. Also I said I wished to see another man descend, in order better to study the manner of the descent.

Herger said, "It is more difficult with each descent, because there are fewer here above to lower a man down. The last man must descend without the sling at all, and that shall be Ecthgow, for his arms are iron. It is a mark of our favor which allows you to be the second man to descend. Go now."

I saw in his eyes that there was no hope of delay, and so I was myself fitted into the sling, and I gripped the stout staff in my hands, which were slippery with sweat; and my whole body likewise was slippery with sweat; and I shivered in the wind as I went over the side of the cliff, and for the last time saw the five Northmen straining at the rope, and then they were lost from view. I made my descent.

I had in my mind to make many prayers to Allah, and also to record in the eye of my mind, in the memory of my soul, the many experiences that a man must undergo as he dangles from ropes down such a wind-torn rocky cliff. Once out of sight of my Northmen friends above, I forgot all my intentions, and whispered, "Allah be praised," over and over, like a mindless person, or one so old his brain no longer functions, or a child, or a fool.

In truth, I remember little from all that transpired. Only this: that the wind blows a person back and forth across the rock at such speed the eye cannot focus on the surface, which is a gray blur; and that many times I struck the rock, jarring my bones, splitting my skin; and once I banged my head and saw brilliant white spots like stars before my eyes, and I thought I would be faint, but I was not. And in due time, which in truth seemed as the whole duration of my life, and more, I reached the bottom, and Buliwyf clapped me on the shoulder and said I had done well.

Now the sling was raised up; and the waves crashed over me and over Buliwyf at my side. Now I fought to hold my balance upon this slippery ledge, and this so occupied my attention I did not watch the others coming down the cliff. My only desire was this: to keep from being swept away into the sea. Verily I saw with my own eyes that the waves were taller than three men standing one atop another, and when each wave struck, I was for a moment senseless in a swirl of chilled water and spinning force. Many times was I knocked from my feet by these waves; I was drenched over my whole body, and shivering so badly that my teeth clattered like a galloping horse. I could not speak words for the clacking of my teeth.

Now all the warriors of Buliwyf made their descent; and all were safe, Ecthgow being the last to come down, by brute force of his arms, and when at last he stood, his legs quivered without control as a man shudders with a death throe; we waited some moments until he was himself again.

Then Buliwyf spoke: "We shall descend into the water and swim into the cave. I shall be first. Carry your dagger in your teeth, so your arms shall be free to battle the currents."

These words of new madness came upon me at a time when I could endure nothing further. To my eyes, the plan of Buliwyf was folly beyond folly. I saw the waves crash in, bursting upon the jagged rocks; I saw the waves pull away again with the tug of a giant's strength, only to recover their power and crash forward anew. Verily, I watched and I believed that no man could swim in that water, but rather he would be dashed to bony splinters in an instant.

But I made no protest, for I was past any comprehension. To my way of thinking, I was close enough to death that it did not matter if I came closer still. Thus I took my dagger, which I jammed into my belt, for my teeth rattled too severely to grip it in my mouth. Of the other Northmen, they gave no sign of coldness or fatigue, but rather greeted each wave as a fresh invigoration; also they smiled with the happy anticipation of the coming battle, and for this last I hated them.

Buliwyf watched the movement of the waves, choosing his time, and then he leapt into the surf. I hesitated, and someone—I have always believed it to be Herger—pushed me. I fell deep in the swirling sea of numbing coldness; verily I was spun head over feet and sideward also; I could see nothing but green water. Then I perceived Buliwyf kicking down in the depths of the sea; and I followed after him, and he swam into a kind of passage in the rocks. In all things, I did as he. This was the fashion:

Upon one moment, the surf would tug after him, trying to pluck him into the wide ocean, and me also. At these moments, Buliwyf gripped onto a rock with his hands to hold against the current; this also I did. Mightily I held to the rocks, with my lungs bursting. Then in an instant the surge ran opposite, and I was propelled with frightful speed forward, bouncing off rocks and obstructions. And then again, the surge changed, and tugged backward as it had done previously; and I was obliged to follow the example of Buliwyf and cling to rocks. Now it is true that my lungs burned as if afire, and I knew in my heart that I could not continue much longer in this icy sea. Then the surge ran forward, and I was flung headlong, knocked here and there, and then suddenly I was up and breathing air.

Verily, this transpired with such swiftness that I was so surprised I did not think to feel relief, which was a proper feeling; nor did I think to praise Allah for my good fortune in surviving. I gasped air, and all about me the warriors of Buliwyf set their heads above the surface and gasped likewise.

Now, here is what I saw: we were in a kind of pond or lake, inside a cave with a smooth rocky dome and a seaward entrance through which we had just traversed. Directly ahead was a flat rocky space. I saw three or four dark shapes squatted about a fire; these creatures chanted in high voices. Now also

I understood why this was called the cave of thunder, for with each crash of the surf the sound in the cave reverberated with such power that the ears ached and the very air seemed to shake and press.

In this place, this cave, Buliwyf and his warriors made their attack, and I joined in with them, and with our short daggers we killed the four demons in the cave. I saw them clearly for the first time, in the flickering light of the fire, whose flames leapt madly with each pounding of the thundering surf. The aspect of these demons was thus: they appeared to be manlike in every respect, but not as any man upon the face of the earth. They were short creatures, and broad and squat, and hairy on all parts of their bodies save their palms, the soles of their feet, and their faces. Their faces were very large, with mouth and jaws large and prominent, and of an ugly aspect; also their heads were larger than the heads of normal men. Their eyes were sunk deep in their heads; the brows were large, and not by virtue of hairy brows, but of bone; also their teeth were large and sharp, although it is true the teeth of many were ground down and flattened.

In other respects of their bodily features and as to the organs of sex and the several orifices, they were also as men.* One of the creatures was slow to die, and with its tongue formed some sounds, which had to my ear a quality of speech; but I cannot know if this was so, and I tell it again with no conviction of the matter.

Now Buliwyf surveyed these four dead creatures, with their thick matted fur; then we heard a ghostly, echoing chant, a sound rising and falling in time to the thunder pounding of the surf, and this sound came from the recesses of the cave. Buliwyf led us into the depths.

There we came upon three of the creatures, prostrate upon the ground, faces pressed to the earth and their hands raised in supplication to an old creature lurking in the shadows. These suppliants were chanting, and did not perceive our arrival. But the creature saw us, and screamed hideously at our approach. This creature I took to be the mother of the wendol, but if she was female, I saw no sign, for she was old to the point of being sexless.

Buliwyf alone fell upon the suppliants and killed them all, while the mother-creature moved back into the shadows and screamed horribly. I could not see her well, but this much is true: that she was surrounded by serpents, which coiled at her feet, and upon her hands, and around her neck. These serpents hissed and flicked their tongues; and as they were all about her, upon her body and also on the ground, none of the warriors of Buliwyf dared make an approach.

Then Buliwyf attacked her, and she gave a fearful scream as he plunged his dagger deep into her breast, for he was heedless of the snakes. Many times he struck the mother of the wendol with his dagger. Never did this woman

---

*This description of the physical features of the wendol has sparked a predictable debate. See Appendix.

collapse, but always did she stand, though the blood poured from her as if from a fountain, and from the several wounds Buliwyf inflicted upon her. And all the time she screamed a most frightful sound.

Then at the last she toppled, and lay dead, and Buliwyf turned to face his warriors. Now we saw that this woman, the mother of the eaters of the dead, had wounded him. A silver pin, such as a pin for hair, was buried in his stomach; this same pin trembled with each heartbeat. Buliwyf plucked it forth, and there was a gush of blood. Yet he did not sink to his knees mortally wounded, but rather he stood and gave the order to leave the cave.

This we did, by the second and landward entrance; this entrance had been guarded, but all the wendol guards had fled before the screams of their dying mother. We departed without harassment. Buliwyf led us from the caves, and back to our horses, and then did he collapse upon the ground.

Ecthgow, with a face of sadness most uncommon among the Northmen, directed the fashioning of a stretcher* and with this we carried Buliwyf back across the fields to the kingdom of Rothgar. And all the while Buliwyf was of good cheer, and merry; many of the things he spoke I did not comprehend, but one time I heard him say: "Rothgar will not be happy to see us, for he must set out yet another banquet, and by now he is a most depleted host." The warriors laughed at this and other words of Buliwyf. I saw their laughter was honest.

Now we came to the Kingdom of Rothgar, where we were greeted with cheers and happiness, and no sadness, although Buliwyf was direly injured, and his flesh turned gray, and his body shook, and his eyes were lit by the gleam of a sick and fevered soul. These signs did I know full well, and so, too, did the North people.

A bowl of onion broth was brought for him, and he refused it, saying, "I have the soup illness; do not trouble yourselves on my account." Then he called for a celebration, and insisted that he preside over it, sitting propped up on a stone couch at the side of King Rothgar, and he drank mead and he was merry. I was near to him when he said to King Rothgar, in the midst of the festivities, "I have no slaves."

"All of my slaves are your slaves," Rothgar said.

Then Buliwyf said, "I have no horses."

"All of my horses are yours," Rothgar answered. "Think no more on these matters."

And Buliwyf, his wounds bound, was happy, and he smiled, and the color returned to his cheeks that evening, and indeed he seemed to grow stronger with each passing minute of the night. And although I would not have thought it possible, he ravished a slave girl, and afterward he said to me, as a joke, "A dead man is no use to anyone."

Lectulus.

And then Buliwyf fell into a sleep, and his color became more pale and his breathing more shallow; I feared he should never awake from this sleep. He may also have thought this, for as he slept he held his sword gripped tight in his hand.

THE DEATH THROES OF
THE WENDOL

So also I fell into a sleep. Herger awakened me with these words: "You are to come quickly." Now I heard the sound of distant thunder. I looked to the bladder window* and it was not yet dawn, but I grabbed up my sword; in truth I had fallen asleep in my armor, not caring to remove it. Then I hastened outside. It was the hour before dawn, and the air was misty and thick, and filled with the thunder of distant hoofbeats.

Herger said to me, "The wendol come. They know of the mortal wounds of Buliwyf, and they seek a final revenge for the killing of their mother."

Each of the warriors of Buliwyf, myself among them, took a place at the perimeter of the fortifications that we had drawn up against the wendol. These defenses were poor, yet we had none else. We peered into the mists to glimpse the horsemen galloping down upon us. I expected great fear, but I did not feel this, for I had seen the aspect of the wendol and I knew them to be creatures, if not men, then like enough to men as monkeys are also like men; but I knew them to be mortal, and they could die.

Thus I had no fear, save the expectation of this final battle. In this manner was I alone, for I saw that the warriors of Buliwyf displayed much fear; and this despite their pains to conceal it. Verily, as we had killed the mother of the wendol, who was their leader, so also had we lost Buliwyf, who was our own leader, and there was no cheerfulness while we waited and heard the thunder approach.

And then I heard a commotion behind me, and upon my turning, I saw this: Buliwyf, pale as the mist itself, garbed in white and bound in his wounds, stood erect upon the land of the kingdom of Rothgar. And on his shoulders sat two black ravens, one to each side; and at this sight the Northmen screamed of his coming, and they raised their weapons into the air and howled for the battle.†

Fenestra porcus: literally, "pig window." The Norsemen used stretched membranes instead of glass to cover narrow windows; these membranes were translucent. One could not see much through them, but light would be admitted into houses.

†This section of the manuscript is pieced together from the manuscript of Razi, whose chief interest was military techniques. Whether or not Ibn Fadlan knew, or recorded, the significance of Buliwyf's reappearance is unknown. Certainly Razi did not include it, although the significance is obvious enough. In Norse mythology, Odin is popularly repre-

Now Buliwyf never spoke, nor did he look to one side or another; nor did he give sign of recognition to any man; but he walked with measured pace forward, beyond the line of the fortifications, and there he awaited the onslaught of the wendol. The ravens flew off, and he gripped his sword Runding and met the attack.

No words can describe the final attack of the wendol in the dawn of the mist. No words will say what blood was spilled, what screams filled the thick air, what horses and horsemen died in hideous agony. With my own eyes I saw Ecthgow, with his arms of steel: verily his head was lopped off by a wendol sword and the head bounced upon the ground as a bauble, the tongue still flicking in the mouth. Also I saw Weath take a spear through his chest; in this way was he pinned to the ground, and there writhed like a fish taken from the sea. I saw a girl child trampled by the hooves of a horse and her body crushed flat and blood pouring from her ear. Also I saw a woman, a slave of King Rothgar: her body was cut in twain cleanly while she ran from a pursuing horseman. I saw many children likewise killed. I saw horses rear and plunge, their riders dismounted, to be fallen upon by old men and women, who slew the creatures as they lay stunned on their backs. Also I saw Wiglif, the son of Rothgar, run from the fray and conceal himself in cowardly safety. The herald I did not see that day.

I myself killed three of the wendol, and suffered a spear in the shoulder, which pain was like a plunge into fire; my blood boiled the length of my arm and also inside my chest; I thought I should collapse, and yet I fought on.

Now the sun burst through the mist, and the dawn was full upon us, and the mist slipped away, and the horsemen disappeared. In the broad light of day, I saw bodies everywhere, including many bodies of the wendol, for they had not collected their dead. This truly was the sign of their end, for they were in disarray and could not again attack Rothgar, and all the people of the kingdom of Rothgar knew this meaning and rejoiced.

Herger bathed my wound, and was elated, until they carried the body of Buliwyf into the great hall of Rothgar. Buliwyf was dead a score over: his body was hacked by the blades of a dozen adversaries; his visage and form was soaked in his own still-warm blood. Herger saw this sight and burst into tears, and hid his face from me, but there was no need, for I myself felt tears that misted my sight.

---

sented as bearing a raven on each shoulder. These birds bring him all the news of the world. Odin was the principal deity of the Norse pantheon and was considered the Universal Father. He ruled especially in matters of warfare; it was believed that from time to time he would appear among men, although rarely in his godlike form, preferring to assume the appearance of a simple traveler. It was said that an enemy would be scared away simply by his presence.

Interestingly, there is a story about Odin in which he is killed and resurrected after nine days; most authorities believe this idea antedates any Christian influence. In any case, the resurrected Odin was still mortal, and it was believed that he would someday finally die.

Buliwyf was laid before King Rothgar, whose duty it was to make a speech. But the old man was not able to do such a thing. He said only this: "Here is a warrior and a hero fit for the gods. Bury him as a great king," and then he left the hall. I believe he was ashamed, for he himself had not joined in the battle. Also his son Wiglif had run like a coward, and many had seen this, and called it a womanly act; this also may have abashed the father. Or there may be some reason which I do not know. In truth, he was a very old man.

Now it happened that in a low voice Wiglif spoke to the herald: "This Buliwyf has done us much service, all the greater for his death at the concluding of it." Thus he spoke when his father the King had departed the hall.

Herger heard these words, and I also did, and I was the first to draw my sword. Herger said to me, "Do not battle this man, for he is a fox, and you have wounds."

I said to him, "Who cares for that?" and I challenged the son Wiglif, and upon the spot. Wiglif drew his sword. Now Herger delivered me a mighty kick or manner of blow from behind, and as I was unprepared for this I fell sprawling; then Herger joined battle with the son Wiglif. Also the herald took up arms, and moved slyly, in the desire to stand behind Herger and slay him at the back. This herald I myself killed by plunging my sword deep into his belly, and the herald screamed at the instant of his impalement. The son Wiglif heard this, and although he had battled fearlessly before, now he showed much fear in his contest with Herger.

Then it happened that King Rothgar heard of the clashing; he came once more to the great hall and begged for a ceasing of the matter. In this, his efforts were to no avail. Herger was firm in his purpose. Verily I saw him stand astride the body of Buliwyf and swing his sword at Wiglif, and Herger slew Wiglif, who fell down upon the table of Rothgar, and gripped the cup of the King, and drew it toward his lips. But it is true that he died without drinking, and so the matter was finished.

Now of the party of Buliwyf, once of the number thirteen, only four remained. I among them, we set out Buliwyf beneath a wooden roof, and left his body with a cup of mead in his hands. Then Herger said to the assembled people, "Who shall die with this noble man?" and a woman, a slave of King Rothgar, said that she would die with Buliwyf. The usual preparations of the Northmen were then made.

[Although Ibn Fadlan does not specify any passage of time, several days probably elapsed before the funeral ceremony.]

Now a ship was fitted out upon the shore below the hall of Rothgar, and treasures of gold and silver were laid upon it, and the carcasses of two horses also. And a tent was erected, and Buliwyf, now stiff in death, placed inside. His body was the black color of death in this cold climate. Then the slave girl was taken to each of the warriors of Buliwyf, and to me also, and I had carnal knowledge of her, and she said to me, "My master thanks you." Her countenance and manner was most joyful, of a variety in excess of the general good cheer these people show. Whilst she dressed again in her garments, these garments including many splendid ornaments of gold and silver, I said to her that she was joyful.

I had in my mind that she was a fair maiden, and youthful, and yet soon to die, which she knew, as did I. She said to me, "I am joyful because I shall soon see my master." As yet she had drunk no mead, and she spoke the truth of her heart. Her countenance shone as does a happy child, or certain women when they are with child; this was the nature of the thing.

So, then, I said this: "Tell your master when you see him that I have lived to write." These words I do not know if she comprehended. I said to her, "It was the wish of your master."

"Then I will tell him," she said, and most cheerfully proceeded to the next warrior of Buliwyf. I do not know if she understood my meaning, for the only sense of writing these North people know is the carving of wood or stone, which they do but seldom. Also, my speech in the North tongue was not clear. Yet she was cheerful and went on.

Now in the evening, as the sun was making its descent into the sea, the ship of Buliwyf was prepared upon the beach, and the maiden was taken into the tent of the ship, and the old crone who is called the angel of death placed the dagger between her ribs, and I and Herger held the cord that strangled her, and we seated her alongside Buliwyf, and then we departed.

All of this day I had taken no food or drink, for I knew I must participate in these affairs, and I had no wish to suffer the embarrassment of purging myself. But I felt no revulsion at any of the deeds of that day, nor was I faint, or light of head. For this I was proud in secret. Also it is true that at the moment of her death the maiden smiled, and this expression afterward remained, so that she sat next to her master with this same smile upon her pale face. The face of Buliwyf was black and his eyes were closed, but his expression was calm. Thus did I last view these two North people.

Now the ship of Buliwyf was set aflame, and pushed out into the sea, and the Northmen stood upon the rocky shore and made many invocations to their gods. With my own eyes, I saw the ship carried by the currents as a burning pyre, and then it was lost to vision, and the darkness of night descended upon the Northlands.

THE RETURN FROM THE NORTH COUNTRY

Now I passed some further weeks in the company of the warriors and nobles of the kingdom of Rothgar. This was a pleasant time, for the people were gracious and hospitable, and most attentive to my wounds, which healed well, praise Allah. But it happened soon enough that I desired to return to my own land. To King Rothgar I made known I was the emissary of the Caliph of Bagdad, and that I must complete the business he had sent me upon, or incur his wrath.

None of this mattered to Rothgar, who said I was a noble warrior, that he desired I should remain in his lands, to live the life of such an honored warrior. He said I was his friend forevermore, and that I should have whatever I desired within his means to give me. Yet he was reluctant to let me depart, and contrived all manner of excuses and delays. Rothgar said I must look to my wounds, although these injuries were plainly healed; also he said I must recover my strength, although my strength was evidently restored. Finally he said I must await the outfitting of a ship, which was no mean undertaking; and when I inquired after the time such a ship might be outfitted, the King made a vague reply, as if this did not matter to him overmuch. And upon those times when I pressed him to depart, he turned cross and asked if I was dissatisfied with his hospitality; to this I was obliged to respond with praise for his graciousness and all variety of expressions of contentment. Soon enough I thought the old King less a fool than I had previously.

Now I went to Herger, speaking of my plight and I said to him: "This King is not such a fool as I have taken him to be."

In reply, Herger said: "You are wrong, for he is a fool, and does not act with sense." And Herger said he would arrange for my departure with the King.

Here was the manner of it. Herger sought the audience of King Rothgar in private, and said to the King that he was a great and wise ruler whose people loved and respected him, by virtue of the way he looked after the affairs of the kingdom and the welfare of his people. This flattery softened the old man. Now Herger said to him that of the five sons of the King, only one survived, and he was Wulfgar, who had gone to Buliwyf as messenger, and now remained far off. Herger said that Wulfgar should be summoned home, and that a party for this purpose be arranged, for there was no other heir save Wulfgar.

These things he told the King. Also, I believe he spoke some words in private to the Queen Weilew, who had much influence over her husband.

Then it happened at an evening banquet that Rothgar called for the fitting out of a ship and a crew, for a voyage to return Wulfgar to his kingdom. I requested to join the crew, and this the old King could not deny me. The preparation of the ship took the space of several days. I spent much time with Herger in this interval. Herger had chosen to remain behind.

One day we stood upon the cliffs, overlooking the ship on the beach, as it was prepared for the voyage and fitted with provisions. Herger said to me: "You are starting upon a long journey. We shall make prayers for your safe-keeping."

I inquired whom he would pray to, and he responded, "To Odin, and Frey, and Thor, and Wyrd, and to the several other gods who may influence your safe journey." These are the names of the Northmen gods.

I replied, "I believe in one God, who is Allah, the All-Merciful and Compassionate."

"I know this," Herger said. "Perhaps in your lands, one god is enough, but not here; here there are many gods and each has his importance, so we shall pray to all of them on your behalf." I thanked him then, for the prayers of a non-believer are as good as they are sincere, and I did not doubt the sincerity of Herger.

Now, Herger had long known that I believed differently from him, but as the time of my departure drew close, he inquired many times again of my beliefs, and at unusual moments, thinking to catch me off my guard and learn the truth. I took his many questions as a form of test, as Buliwyf once tested my knowledge of writing. Always I answered him in the same way, thus increasing his perplexity.

One day he said to me, with no show that he had ever inquired previously: "What is the nature of your god Allah?"

I said to him, "Allah is the one God, who rules all things, sees all things, knows all things, and disposes all things." These words I had spoken before.

After a time, Herger said to me, "Do you never anger this Allah?"

I said: "I do, but He is all-forgiving and merciful."

Herger said: "When it suits his purposes?"

I said that this was so, and Herger considered my answer. Finally he said this, with a shaking head: "The risk is too great. A man cannot place too much faith in any one thing, neither a woman, nor a horse, nor a weapon, nor any single thing."

"Yet I do," I said.

"As you see best," Herger replied, "but there is too much that man does not know. And what man does not know, that is the province of the gods."

In this way I saw that he would never be persuaded to my beliefs, nor I to his, and so we parted. In truth, it was a sad leave-taking, and I was heavy-hearted to depart from Herger and the remainder of the warriors. Herger felt this also. I gripped his shoulder, and he mine, and then I set out upon the black ship, which carried me to the land of the Dans. As this ship with her stout crew slipped away from the shores of Venden, I had view of the gleaming rooftops of the great hall of Hurot, and, turning away, of the gray and vast ocean before us. Now it happened

> The manuscript ends abruptly at this point, the end of a transcribed page, with the final terse words *"nunc fit,"* and although there is clearly more to the manuscript, further passages have not been discovered. This is, of course, the purest historical accident, but every translator has commented upon the odd appropriateness of this abrupt ending, which suggests the start of some new adventure, some new strange sight, that for the most arbitrary reasons of the past thousand years will be denied us.

Appendix
The Mist Monsters

As William Howells has emphasized, it is a rather rare event that causes any living animal to die in such a way that he will be preserved as a fossil for centuries to come. This is especially true of a small, fragile, ground-living animal such as man, and the fossil record of early men is remarkably scanty.

Textbook diagrams of "the tree of man" imply a certainty of knowledge that is misleading; the tree is pruned and revised every few years. One of the most controversial and troublesome branches of that tree is the one usually labeled "Neanderthal Man."

He takes his name from the valley in Germany where the first remains of his type were discovered in 1856, three years before the publication of Darwin's *Origin of Species*. The Victorian world was displeased with the skeletal remains, and emphasized the crude and brutish aspects of Neanderthal man; until now the very word is, in the popular imagination, synonymous with all that is dumb and bestial in human nature.

It was with a kind of relief that early scholars decided that Neanderthal man had "disappeared" about 35,000 years ago, to be replaced by Cro-Magnon man, whose skeletal remains were presumed to show as much delicacy, sensitivity, and intelligence as the Neanderthal skull showed monstrous brutishness. The general presumption was that the superior, modern Cro-Magnon man killed off the Neanderthals.

Now the truth of the matter is that we have very few good examples of Neanderthal man in our skeletal material—of more than eighty known fragments, only about a dozen are complete enough, or dated carefully enough, to warrant serious study. We cannot really say with any certainty how widespread a form he was, or what happened to him. And recent examination of the skeletal evidence has disputed the Victorian belief in his monstrous, semihuman appearance.

In their 1957 review, Straus and Cave wrote: "If he could be reincarnated and placed in a New York subway—provided he were bathed, shaved, and dressed in modern clothing—it is doubtful whether he would attract any more attention than some of its other denizens."

Another anthropologist has put it more plainly: "You might think he was tough-looking, but you wouldn't object to your sister marrying him."

From here, it is only a short step to what some anthropologists already believe: that Neanderthal man, as an anatomical variant of modern man, has never disappeared at all, but is still with us.

A reinterpretation of the cultural remains associated with Neanderthal man also supports a benign view of the fellow. Past anthropologists were highly impressed with the beauty and profusion of the cave drawings that first appear with the arrival of Cro-Magnon man; as much as any skeletal evidence, these drawings tended to reinforce the notion of a wonderful new sensibility replacing the quintessence of "brute benightedness."

But Neanderthal man was remarkable in his own right. His culture, called Mousterian—again, after a site, Le Moustier in France—is characterized by stoneworking of quite a high order, much superior to any earlier cultural level. And it is now recognized that Neanderthal man had bone tools as well.

Most impressive of all, Neanderthal man was the first of our ancestors to bury his dead ritually. At Le Moustier, a teenage boy was placed in a trench, in a sleeping position; he was provided with a supply of flint tools, a stone axe, and roasted meat. That these materials were for the use of the deceased in some afterlife is undisputed by most anthropologists.

There is other evidence of religious feeling: in Switzerland there is a shrine to the cave bear, a creature worshiped, respected, and also eaten. And at Shanidar Cave in Iraq, a Neanderthal was buried with flowers in the grave.

All this points to an attitude toward life and death, a self-conscious view of the world, which lies at the core of what we believe distinguishes thinking man from the rest of the animal world. On existing evidence, we must conclude this attitude was first displayed by Neanderthal man.

The general reassessment of Neanderthal man coincides with the rediscovery of Ibn Fadlan's contact with the "mist monsters"; his description of these creatures is suggestive of Neanderthal anatomy, and raises the question of whether the Neanderthal form did, in fact, disappear from the earth thousands of years ago, or whether these early men persisted into historic times.

Arguments based on analogies cut both ways. There are historical examples of a handful of people with technologically superior culture wiping out a more primitive society in a matter of years; that is largely the story of the European contact with the New World. But there are also examples of primitive societies existing in isolated areas, unknown to more advanced, civilized peoples nearby. Such a tribe was recently discovered in the Philippines.

The academic debate on Ibn Fadlan's creatures can be neatly summarized by the viewpoints of Geoffrey Wrightwood, of Oxford University, and E. D. Goodrich, of the University of Philadelphia. Wrightwood says [1971]: "The account of Ibn Fadlan provides us with a perfectly serviceable description of Neanderthal men, coinciding with the fossil record and our suppositions about the cultural level of these early men. We should accept it immediately, had we not already decided these men vanished without a trace some 30–40,000 years previously. We should remember that we only believe this disappearance because we have found no fossils of a later date, and the absence of such fossils does not mean that they do not, in fact, exist.

"Objectively, there is no *a priori* reason to deny that a group of Neanderthals might have survived very late in an isolated region of Scandinavia. In any case this assumption best fits the description of the Arabic text."

Goodrich, a paleontologist well known for his skepticism, takes the contrasting view [1972]: "The general accuracy of Ibn Fadlan's reporting may tempt us to overlook certain excesses in his manuscript. These are several, and they arise either from cultural preconditioning, or from a storyteller's desire to impress. He calls the Vikings giants when they most certainly were not; he emphasizes the dirty, drunken aspects of his hosts, which less fastidious observers did not find striking. In his report of the so-called 'wendol,' he places great importance on their hairiness and brutish appearance when, in fact, they may not have been so hairy, or so brutish. They may simply have been a tribe of *Homo sapiens,* living in isolation and without the level of cultural attainment manifested by the Scandinavians.

"There is internal evidence, within the body of the Ibn Fadlan manuscript, to support the notion that the 'wendol' are actually *Homo sapiens.* The pregnant female figurines described by the Arab are highly suggestive of the prehistoric carvings and figurines to be found at the Aurignacian industry sites in France and of the Gravettian finds in Willendorf, Austria, Level 9. Both Aurignacian and Gravettian cultural levels are associated with essentially modern man, and not Neanderthal Man.

"We must never forget that to untrained observers, *cultural* differences are often interpreted as *physical* differences, and one need not be particularly naive to make this mistake. Thus, as late as the 1880's it was possible for educated Europeans to wonder aloud whether Negroes in primitive African societies could be considered human beings at all, or whether they represented some bizarre mating of men and apes. Nor should we overlook the degree to which societies with vastly differing degrees of cultural attainment may exist side by side: such contrasts appear today, for example, in Australia, where the stone age and the jet age can be found in close proximity. Thus in interpreting the descriptions of Ibn Fadlan we need not postulate a Neanderthal remnant, unless we are fancifully inclined to do so."

In the end, the arguments stumble over a well-known limitation to the scientific method itself. The physicist Gerhard Robbins observes that "strictly speaking, no hypothesis or theory can ever be proven. It can only be disproven. When we say we believe a theory, what we really mean is that we are unable to show that the theory is wrong—not that we are able to show, beyond doubt, that the theory is right.

"A scientific theory may stand for years, even centuries, and it may accumulate hundreds of bits of corroborating evidence to support it. Yet a theory is always vulnerable, and a single conflicting finding is all that is required to throw the hypothesis into disarray, and call for a new theory. One can never know when such conflicting evidence will arise. Perhaps it will happen tomorrow, perhaps never. But the history of science is strewn with the ruins of mighty edifices toppled by an accident, or a triviality."

This is what Geoffrey Wrightwood meant when he said at the Seventh International Symposium on Human Paleontology in Geneva in 1972: "All I need is one skull, or a fragment of a skull, or a bit of jaw. In fact, all I need is one good tooth, and the debate is concluded."

Until that skeletal evidence is found, speculation will continue, and one may adopt whatever stance satisfies an inner sense of the fitness of things.

Sources

I. PRIMARY SOURCES

Yakut ibn-Abdallah MS, a geographical lexicon, ?A.D. 1400. Nos. 1403A–1589A, Archives University Library, Oslo, Norway.
> Trans: Blake, Robert, and Frye, Richard; in *Byzantina— Metabyzantina: A Journal of Byzantine and Modern Greek Studies*, New York, 1947.
> Cook, Albert S.; New York, 1947.
> Fraus-Dolus, Per; Oslo, 1959–1960.
> Jorgensen, Olaf; 1971, unpublished.
> Nasir, Seyed Hossein; 1971, unpublished.

St. Petersburg MS, a local history, published by the Academy of St. Petersburg, 1823. Nos. 233M–278M, Archives University Library, Oslo, Norway.
> Trans: Frau-Dolus, Per; Oslo, 1959–1960.
> Stenuit, Roger; 1971; unpublished.
> Soletsky, V. K.; 1971, unpublished.

Ahmad Tusi MS, a geography, A.D. 1047, papers of J. H. Emerson. Nos. LV 01–114, Archives University Library, Oslo, Norway.
> Trans: Fraus-Dolus, Per; Oslo, 1959–1960.
> Nasir, Seyed Hossein; 1971, unpublished.
> Hitti, A. M.; 1971, unpublished.

Amin Razi MS, a history of warfare, A.D. 1585–1595, papers of J. H. Emerson. Nos. LV 207–244, Archives University Library, Oslo, Norway.
> Trans: Fraus-Dolus, Per; Oslo, 1959–1960.
> Bendixon, Robert; 1971, unpublished.
> Porteus, Eleanor; 1971, unpublished.

Xymos MS, a fragmentary geography, ? date, bequest estate A. G. Gavras. Nos. 2308T–2348T, Archives University Library, Oslo, Norway.
> Trans: Fraus-Dolus, Per; Oslo, 1959–1960.
> Bendixon, Robert; 1971, unpublished.
> Porteus, Eleanor; 1971, unpublished.

II. SECONDARY SOURCES

Berndt, E. and Berndt, R. H. "An Annotated Bibliography of References to the Manuscript of Ibn Fadlan from 1794 to 1970," *Acta Archaeologica,* VI: 334–389, 1971.

> This remarkable compilation will refer the interested reader to all secondary sources concerning the manuscript, which have appeared in English, Norwegian, Swedish, Danish, Russian, French, Spanish, and Arabic for the dates cited. The total number of sources listed is 1,042.

A Factual Note on
Eaters of the Dead

*E*aters of the Dead was conceived on a dare. In 1974, my friend Kurt Villadsen proposed to teach a college course he called "The Great Bores." The course would include all the texts that were supposed to be crucial to Western civilization but which were, in truth, no longer read willingly by anyone, because they were so tedious. Kurt said that the first of the great bores he would address was the epic poem *Beowulf.*

I disagreed. I argued that *Beowulf* was a dramatic, exciting story—and that I could prove it. I went home and immediately began making notes for this novel.

I started from the scholarly tradition that examined epic poetry and mythology as if it might have some underlying basis in fact. Heinrich Schliemann assumed that the *Iliad* was true, and found what he claimed was Troy and Mycenae; Arthur Evans believed there was something to the myth of the Minotaur, and uncovered the Palace of Knossos on Crete;[1] M.I. Finley and others had traced the route of Ulysses in the *Odyssey;*[2] Lionel Casson had written about the real journeys that might underlie the myth of Jason and the Argonauts.[3] Thus it seemed reasonable, within this tradition, to imagine that *Beowulf,* too, had originally been based on an actual event.

That event had been embellished over centuries of oral retelling, producing the fantastic narrative we read today. But I thought it might be possible to reverse the process, peeling away the poetic invention, and returning to a kernel of genuine human experience—something that had actually happened.

This idea of uncovering the factual core of the narrative was appealing but impractical. Modern scholarship offered no objective procedure to separate poetic invention from underlying fact. Even to try would mean making

[1]The classic popular account of Evans and Schliemann is C.W. Ceram (Kurt W. Marek), *Gods, Graves, and Scholars,* Alfred A. Knopf, New York, 1967.

[2]M.I. Finley, *The World of Odysseus,* Viking Press, New York, 1965.

[3]Lionel Casson, *The Ancient Mariners, Sea Farers and Sea Fighters of the Mediterranean in Ancient Times,* Macmillan, New York, 1959.

innumerable subjective decisions, large and small, on every page—in the end, so many decisions that the result must inevitably be still another invention: a modern pseudo-historical fantasy about what the original events might have been.

The insoluble problem prevented me from proceeding. Of course, in writing a novel, I intended to create a fantasy of my own. But fantasies demand strict logic, and I was troubled by the logic behind what I wanted to write. Since a real scholar could not do what I intended to do, I found I could not pretend, in writing, that I had done so. This was not a failure of imagination or nerve. It was a purely practical problem. Like the scholar, I had no basis for deciding which elements of the *Beowulf* narrative to keep, and which to discard.

Although the idea of working backward seemed untenable, I remained intrigued. I asked a different question: suppose, for a moment, that the practical problems that troubled me did not exist, and the process could indeed be carried out. What would the resulting narrative look like? I imagined it would probably be a rather mundane recounting of some battles that occurred more than a thousand years ago. In fact, I suspected it would probably resemble most eyewitness accounts of famous events, as written by people who are unaware of the significance of the events they are seeing.

This line of thinking eventually led to the solution to my problem. Clearly, I wanted an eyewitness account. I could not extract it from the existing *Beowulf* narrative, and I did not want to invent it. That was my impasse. But at some point, I realized I did not have to invent it—I could *discover* it instead.

Suppose, I thought, a contemporary observer had been present at these battles, and had written an account of the events that were later transformed into a poem. Suppose, too, that this account *already existed*, but had never been recognized for what it was. If this were so, then no invention on my part would be necessary. I could merely reproduce the eyewitness narrative, and annotate it for the reader.

The concept of a preexisting manuscript bypassed the logical problems which had earlier impeded me, because a found manuscript would not be my creation—even though I would create it. Of course such thinking is absurd, but it happens all the time. Often actors cannot act without a prop, or a false moustache, or some other artifice to separate themselves from the character they are portraying. I was engaged in a similar process.

What sort of narrative would be most desirable? I concluded the most useful account would be written by an outsider—someone not part of the culture, who could report objectively on the events as they occurred. But who would this outside observer have been? Where would he have come from?

On reflection, I realized I already knew of such a person. In the tenth century, an Arab named Ibn Fadlan had traveled north from Baghdad into what is now Russia, where he came in contact with the Vikings. His manuscript, well-known to scholars, provides one of the earliest eyewitness accounts of Viking life and culture.[4] As a college undergraduate, I had read portions of the manuscript. Ibn Fadlan had a distinct voice and style. He was imitable. He was believable. He was unexpected. And after a thousand years, I felt that Ibn Fadlan would not mind being revived in a new role, as a witness to the events that led to the epic poem of *Beowulf.*

Although the full manuscript of Ibn Fadlan has been translated into Russian, German, French and many other languages, only portions had been translated into English. I obtained the existing manuscript fragments and combined them, with only slight modifications, into the first three chapters of *Eaters of the Dead.*[5] I then wrote the rest of the novel in the style of the manuscript to carry Ibn Fadlan on the rest of his now-fictional journey. I also added commentary and some extremely pedantic footnotes.

I was aware that Ibn Fadlan's actual journey in A.D. 921 had probably occurred too late in history to serve as the basis for *Beowulf,* which many authorities believe was composed a hundred and fifty years earlier. But the dating of the poem is uncertain, and at some point a novelist will insist on his right to take liberties with the facts. And *Eaters* contains many overt anachronisms, particularly when Ibn Fadlan meets up with a group of remnant Neanderthals. (One of the oddities of this book is that the intervening decades has seen a scholarly reevaluation of Neanderthal man; and the notion that there might have been a few still around a thousand years ago in a remote location does not seem quite so preposterous now as it did then.)

But certainly, the game that the book plays with its factual bases becomes increasingly complex as it goes along, until the text finally seems quite difficult to evaluate. I have a long-standing interest in verisimilitude, and in the cues which make us take something as real or understand it as fiction. But I finally concluded that in *Eaters of the Dead,* I had played the game too hard. While I was writing, I felt that I was drawing the line between fact and fiction clearly; for example, one cited translator, Per Fraus-Dolus, means in literal Latin "by trickery-deceit." But within a few years, I could no longer be certain which passages were real, and which were made up; at one point I found myself in a research library trying to locate certain references in my bibliography, and finally concluding, after hours of frustrating effort, that however convincing

[4]Among the many discussions of Viking society for the general reader, see: D. M. Wilson, *The Vikings,* London, 1970: J. Brondsted, *The Vikings,* London, 1965; P. Sawyer, *The Age of the Vikings,* London, 1962; P.G. Foote and D.M. Wilson, *The Viking Achievement,* London, 1970. Some of these references quote passages from Ibn Fadlan's manuscript.

[5]To my knowledge there are still only two principal sources in English. The first is the text fragments I read as an undergraduate: Robert Blake and Richard Frye, "The Vikings Abroad and at Home," in Carleton S. Coon, *A Reader in General Anthropology,* Henry Holt and Co. NY, 1952, pp. 410–416. The second source is Robert P. Blake and Richard N. Frye, "Notes on the Risala of Ibn-Fadlan," *Byzantina Metabyzantina,* 1949, v.1 part 2, New York pp. 7–37. I am grateful to Professor Frye for his assistance during the first publication of this book, and this recent revision.

they appeared, they must be fictitious. I was furious to have wasted my time, but I had only myself to blame.

I mention this because the tendency to blur the boundaries of fact and fiction has become widespread in modern society. Fiction is now seamlessly inserted in everything from scholarly histories to television news. Of course, television is understood to be venal, its transgressions shrugged off by most of us. But the attitude of "post-modern" scholars represents a more fundamental challenge. Some in academic life now argue seriously there is no difference between fact and fiction, that all ways of reading text are arbitrary and personal, and that therefore pure invention is as valid as hard research. At best, this attitude evades traditional scholarly discipline; at worst, it is nasty and dangerous.[6] But such academic views were not prevalent twenty years ago, when I sat down to write this novel in the guise of a scholarly monograph, and academic fashions may change again—particularly if scholars find themselves chasing down imaginary footnotes, as I have done.

Under the circumstances. I should perhaps say explicitly that the references in this afterword are genuine. The rest of the novel, including its introduction, text, footnotes, and bibliography, should properly be viewed as fiction.

When *Eaters of the Dead* was first published, this playful version of Beowulf received a rather irritable reception from reviewers, as if I had desecrated a monument. But Beowulf scholars all seem to enjoy it, and many have written to say so.

M.C.
DECEMBER, 1992

[6]For trends in post-modern academic thought, see for example Pauline Marie Rosenau, *Post-Modernism and the Social Sciences: Insights, Inroads, and Intrusions,* Princeton, New Jersey, 1992; and H. Aram Veser, ed., *The New Historicism,* Routledge, New York, 1989.

ABOUT THE AUTHOR

MICHAEL CRICHTON, among the best-known and most-read writers of our time, is admired for his technothriller novels and adventure-filled screenplays. His novels, most of them *New York Times* bestsellers, include *Disclosure, Rising Sun, Jurassic Park, The Terminal Man, The Andromeda Strain, The Great Train Robbery* and the three novels in this collection, *Congo, Sphere* and *Eaters of the Dead.* He has also authored four non-fiction works: *Five Patients, Jasper Johns, Electronic Life* and *Travels.*

Born in Chicago in 1942, Michael Crichton was educated at Harvard College and the Harvard Medical School. In 1969, he was a postdoctoral fellow at the Salk Institue in La Jolla, California, and in 1988 was Visiting Writer at the Massachusetts Institute of Technology.